BLACKDOG

K. V. JOHANSEN

BLACKDOG

an imprint of **Prometheus Books**
Amherst, NY

Published 2011 by Pyr®, an imprint of Prometheus Books

Cover illustration © Raymond Swanland
Map by Rhys Davies

Inquiries should be addressed to
Pyr
59 John Glenn Drive
Amherst, New York 14228–2119
VOICE: 716–691–0133
FAX: 716–691–0137
WWW.PYRSF.COM

15 14 13 12 11   5 4 3 2 1

Library of Congress Cataloging-in-Publication Data

Johansen, K. V.
    Blackdog / by K. V. Johansen.
        p. cm.
    ISBN 978–1–61614–521–7 (pbk. : acid-free paper)
    ISBN 978–1–61614–522–4 (e-book)
    I. Title.

PR9199.3.J555B53 2011
813'.54—dc22

2011019202

Printed in the United States of America

In memoriam

DAD,
who gave me my first etymological dictionary
and bought me Chaucer,

and PIPPIN,
who was always at my side while I wrote this book.

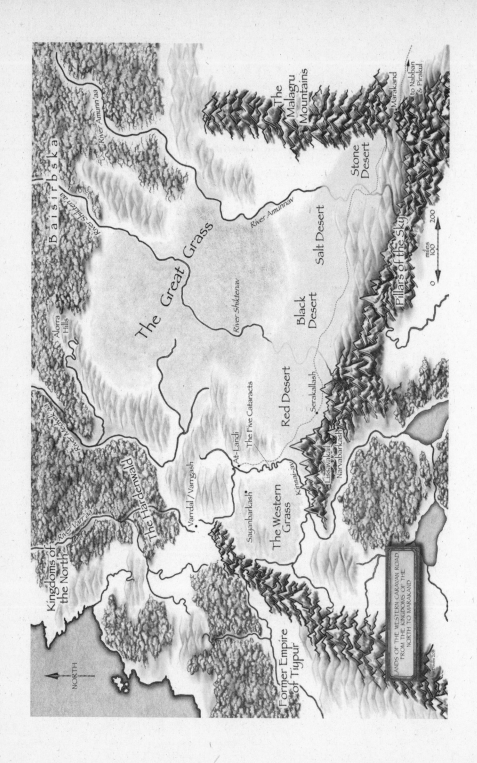

PART ONE

CHAPTER I

Evening prayers took place on the flat-topped bell-tower that rose above the gatehouse. Otokas was not a particularly devout man. Prayer had always seemed a pointless ritual.

The sun, sliding between the peaks at the western end of the lake, turned the Lissavakail's waters to molten copper, while the swallows made their last scrolling passes over the waves. The chief of the priestesses, whose title was simply "Old Lady," swayed back and forth as she chanted the prayer that was chanted every evening. Thanks for the day past, hopes for the day to come. Plentiful fish, millet in the terraced fields, fertile yaks, healthy babies, happy folk—peace and prosperity for the folk of the goddess Attalissa, the folk of Lissavakail, which was both lake and town.

The goddess met his eyes and smiled, a neat, correct figure standing against the west, patience itself in a girl's small body. Attalissa had heard the prayers as many times as he, the same words wearing the same deep grooves in the memory, until one did not hear them at all and could not remember if the ceremony were ending or had only just begun. She wore layers of stiff white silk embroidered in indigo and gold, gold rings in her ears, conical crown of gold filigree and turquoise plaques on her hair, dangling pearls over her brow. The priestesses whose turn it was to attend evening prayer fanned out before her, a flutter of indigo-blue gowns, except for the pair flanking her, who wore wide-legged blue trousers and shirts of scale armour, and carried broad-bladed spears.

Their armed presence was a formality, as so much of life on the holy islet of the temple adjoining the island town was formality; there had been no attack on the temple in generations. Still, the warrior priestesses of Lissavakail were more than ceremonial guard for the living goddess; they were sought out by the villages of distant valleys when raiders were troublesome, and they served as mercenaries, guarding wealthy travellers, gem-traders, and the chieftains of the gold-washing villages on the wild mountain tracks.

Otokas was more than ceremonial guard himself; he remembered raiders coming up from the desert, seeking control of the gold-bearing rivers of the mountains. He remembered years when the communities of the high valleys warred among themselves, with the encouragement of their gods and goddesses or in defiance of their pleas. Born forty winters before, he remembered centuries. He was the Blackdog, and the only man permitted on the temple islet.

The words of the prayer ran on. Did they make any difference, and had they ever? Would the snows refuse to melt and fill the streams, or the hot desert winds sweep up from the north to blight the sprouting grain, or the butter fail to come in the churns, if evening and dawn prayers were not said?

Attalissa met his gaze, expressionless, black eyes deep, unreadable, in her round child's face. She had caught, he realized, the shape of that private thought. A year ago she would not have. She grew, slowly, into godhead.

Prayer is for them, dog, not for you and me, she told him, in the silent speech, mind to mind, that they shared. She had seen eight summers, this incarnation of Attalissa. When Otokas first took on the burden of the Blackdog, Attalissa had been an elderly woman, older than his grandmother, older than the grandfather who had served her as Blackdog before him. When Attalissa died herself Otokas had wept as though she were his grandmother. But nine months later a newborn baby had stared up at him, cradled in his arms, and he had seen Attalissa recognize him, ancient familiarity in the infant's startled eyes.

Attalissa lived, and died, and was reborn in a girlchild conceived the day of her death. Some goddesses shaped themselves a physical body only when they so desired, remaining for the most part a spirit within the waters or appearing as a mist or a dance of light, but

Attalissa returned, mortal life after mortal life, in a human body. Thus it was said she never grew remote from the concerns and the suffering and the joys of her folk; that was part of the fervent love the people of Lissavakail professed for her.

There were only a handful of the goddess's folk gathered at the western end of the red-lacquered bridge that arched from the temple islet across the channel to the island town. A pair of old women, eyes fixed devoutly on what to them must be only a cluster of blue figures and a tiny, occasionally bobbing, gold crown. A young couple, their minds quite evidently on something other than devotions. A family in their best clothes, indigo and red, the wife wearing her bride-gift circlet of gold coins across a weather-worn brow. They were not from town, by the cut of their clothes; peasants from one of the high villages. The children were paying more attention to the young couple than to the remote figures atop the tower.

They used to pray on the town's end of the bridge, the Blackdog remembered, meeting the townsfolk there. The folk had come to sing hymns for Attalissa, and she had held their babies and blessed them, kissed the foreheads of the brides and the grooms, exchanged stories of the old days with the old folk whom she had kissed as babies.

What Otokas was . . . no tradition of the temple preserved, if it had ever been known. Old, as old as the goddess, or older, perhaps. God, demon, spirit of the wilds—even the Blackdog no longer remembered what it had been, before it became Attalissa's guardian, bound, like her, to human life.

The litany tottered to its end; the women bowed to the goddess, who bowed in return, carefully, to keep the tall headdress from falling. And then she cried out suddenly and dropped to her knees, at the same moment Otokas heard, smelt, felt—a crack like a thunderclap all about them, hot metal, a shock like an avalanche, mowing trees before it . . .

He had his arm around the girl the next moment, kneeling by her, sword drawn, though there was no one to defend her against that he could see. The armed priestesses had moved as he did, barring the stairs, the only obvious entry for threat.

"The road," Old Lady said. "Sweet Attalissa save us! Look at the road!"

Otokas passed Attalissa to the arms of Kayugh, who was Spear Lady, captain of the warriors, and joined Old Lady at the parapet.

A black, shifting swarm covered the road on the southern shore of the lake, approaching the bridge to the town.

"Sound the bells," he shouted back to the armed pair by the stairs. "Raiders!"

The dog snarled in his soul, roused by the threat, and dangerous. Nothing the Blackdog could do here to defend the goddess.

Old Lady's hands shook as she gripped his arm.

"They weren't there," she said, and her voice shook as well. "Otokas, they weren't there, even a few moments ago."

"Wizardry," whispered the plump Mistress of Novices. "Or divinity." She looked at him, making it a question.

"Wizardry," Otokas confirmed. "I smell it. And—something else. But not a god. Not a goddess."

A scent to the spirit like old ashes on stone and the hot tang of metal and fire. Not familiar and yet . . . no, that strange hot smell of ash and metal was nothing the Blackdog could ever have smelt before, but it raised the dog's hackles, roared of danger and death and the need to defend, deafening Otokas to all else for a moment.

It was not the time or the place. He forced the Blackdog quiet, calming it, calming himself.

Whatever the threat was, it could not be mere wizardry. No lone wizard, no group of wizards he had ever heard of except in the oldest tales, could hide an army, certainly not so close to a deity's holy place—if they had been hidden, and not dropped from some other location. He had felt the air shatter.

He called them raiders; that was what the mind expected. This was an army that poured down towards the island town's one bridge. They were not even coming from the east, the way around the lake and down to the Red Desert in the north, but from the narrow trail that meandered higher into the southern mountains of the Pillars of the Sky, branching and branching, connecting Lissavakail with its fields and high summer pastures, and the scatter of remote tributary villages. No way for them to have assembled there without passing Lissavakail.

Some few of the men and women were mounted on stocky Grassland horses; most were afoot. A hundred, two, three . . . more came into sight in the narrow gap where a path scrambled up to the temple's own terraced fields. Nothing beyond that, no way they could have gained that height without climbing the very path they descended. The last of the red light picked out spearheads and helmets, sword-edges and armour. The temple bells rang out, a discordant jangling settling to a clashing peal that shook the floor beneath his feet. The town's bell-tower picked it up, and the few people who had gathered for prayers at the temple bridge hurried away into the spilling confusion of the town.

"The bridge," said Kayugh, and thrust the limp goddess back at Otokas. "We have to get it down!" She snapped orders; sisters followed her, the temple rousing to arms.

The temple was Kayugh's to defend, as the goddess was his and the town was the goddess's.

The goddess was in no state to defend anyone or anything, not even herself. The humanity that was Attalissa's virtue was also her weakness. The goddess grew into her powers slowly, came into full strength and understanding of herself only with womanhood. There was little she could do as she was now. The militia, and what sisters Kayugh would spare from defence of the temple, were all Lissavakail had.

"He comes for me," the goddess said, stirring suddenly. She pushed away from Otokas to find her feet, wild-eyed. "Otokas, he's coming for me. He'll take me and swallow me like a snake, devour me, Otokas, dog, I'm scared, don't let him, the lake will die . . ." Her face was grey and her teeth chattered. As he bent to pick her up, her eyes rolled back white in her head and she collapsed again, limp as a dead rat. Old Lady stood with hands upraised, facing the lake with her back to Attalissa.

Prayer was no use now. If ever it had been.

"Down," Otokas ordered the sisters. "Arm, join your dormitories.

No, two of you, keep watch, and you—" singling out a fleet-footed young sister, his own niece "—Attavaia, you be runner for the watchers. Bring word to Kayugh and me of the raiders' advance, if we're not back here when they reach the town bridge."

Torches flared in the town, men already arming, running to bar the stone bridge that was Lissavakail's only fixed link to the shore.

Otokas swung the goddess to his shoulder, started down the stairs, the two spearwomen hurrying to keep up. The bells were deafening; the tower shook with them.

"Where to?" the younger of the pair, Meeray, asked. Old Lady left her prayers and came puffing behind them.

"The chapel," Old Lady said. "We must assemble and pray for guidance."

"The Old Chapel," Otokas countered. It was the most defensible part of the fortress-like temple; the islet was nothing more than an upheaval of rock from the lake, cracked and seamed. The widest crack had been quarried, carved into a chapel in the earliest days when the priestesses first came. The temple had grown over the hill, obscuring stone and crevices and human-made cave, consuming much of the original hill for its masonry, but enough remained at the core to make the temple a warren of dead ends and sudden stairs. A few could hold off a horde in the passages around the Old Chapel. But a few could die there, trapped and starving.

There was a second, secret way out, though none but he and the goddess could take it.

Kayugh met them again on the way. She had changed to trousers and armour, had her helmet under her arm and a dozen armed sisters behind her, two dormitories, as they called the six-woman squads which slept and trained together.

"Our bridge?" he asked.

"They're cutting the beams away at the nearest posts, and taking up the planking," she reported, falling in beside him. "I sent Lilmass and a dozen archers across first, to help hold the town bridge. They asked to go."

Fear crawled under Kayugh's voice. Sent them to die in the town, she clearly thought.

"Can Attalissa help?" Kayugh asked. "Break the town's bridge, even? That would buy time. We could send someone across the lake and down to Serakallash, beg help from their militia, even hire mercenaries from the caravan-gangs."

"No," Otokas said, more harshly than he meant to, but the dog was fighting to break free, distracting him, and there was absolutely nothing the Blackdog could do, here.

"What do we do, then—wait behind our walls, hope they get bored and go home?" Kayugh snapped. "You saw them, Oto. Those aren't raiders. It's an invasion!"

"Faith," panted Old Lady. "Have faith. We will be guided. I will go out to speak to the strangers, after I've prayed. I dreamed—the goddess told me change was coming, a time of great change, a renewal of our glory and our might, by the will of the Old Great Gods. Faith will prevail."

"Faith in what?" Kayugh demanded, but under her breath.

Old Lady talked too often of glory and power as something quite separate from the child they served. They mostly stopped listening, except to head her off, if she seemed likely to start preaching it at the novices. Time she stepped down, they both thought, but that was supposed to be Attalissa's decision, and Old Lady claimed dreams approving her that the goddess could neither confirm nor deny, merely looking a puzzled, nervous child, when asked to do so.

"Oto, if we don't send for help now, before we're besieged—"

Otokas stopped, forced himself to listen, to look Kayugh in the eyes and see her, to shut out the dog's drowning urge to fight, which deafened him to all else. "I'm sorry. I meant, no, 'Lissa can do nothing about the stone bridge. But yes, you're right, send to Serakallash. Beg help, buy it, offer whatever they ask."

Old Lady squawked in protest. "You can't sell Attalissa's treasury to foreigners."

"Neighbours, surely," Kayugh murmured. "With respect, Old Lady, the treasury is worth nothing to dead women. To a dead incarnation. To the dead of Lissavakail, and if they are not already dying in the town, they will be before long. Your kinsfolk and mine. All of our kin."

Old Lady huffed and blew out her cheeks. "The senior sisters must vote on any such decision. We can convene them tomorrow, after dawn prayers. We're safe behind our walls here and defended by the goddess's lake. As I said, I'll pray for guidance, and then meet the leader of these raiders. I dreamed . . . one would come whose service to Attalissa would raise her above all other gods. Wise words may turn enmity to fellowship. We can afford to take proper counsel and not let ourselves be panicked into rash acts. And any decision so important as spending the treasury *must* go to the senior sisters."

"The goddess can make such a decision herself," Kayugh said, with a worried look at the still unconscious girl. "And in her default, a tribunal, which is the three of us—the Old Lady, the Spear Lady, and the Blackdog. And with respect, Old Lady, you've said nothing about such a dream before. Neither has she."

"The child is but a shadow of the goddess's will," Old Lady said, with undue complacency. "A symbol."

Kayugh hissed. "Attalissa is Attalissa—"

"Offer the Serakallashi whatever you need to," Otokas said again. "*I* say so."

Old Lady squeaked and ducked away from his glare.

"Blackdog." Kayugh gave him a hasty bow, more for Old Lady's benefit than his own, he hoped. Followed it with a widening of the eyes, an almost imperceptible nod away from the women who flanked them both, waiting and worried at heated words and open discord.

He transferred Attalissa to Meeray's arms reluctantly, stroked the goddess's cool forehead. Shock, he thought. The goddess's fear was more than the child's experience could comprehend, rebounding on her.

"Take Attalissa and Old Lady to the Old Chapel and make them comfortable. Try to warm the place up. 'Lissa should be all right, she's only fainted. When she wakes, tell her I'll come to her soon, but I need to see what's happening in the town. Tell her, don't expect her to know. Remember she's only a child."

Attalissa's ability to reach his mind was still limited. She might find him, if he was out of sight, but she might not, and either way, she would still be more than half a panicked little girl, reaching for the only father she had ever known.

Old Lady began a protest about the damp Old Chapel, but fell silent at no more than a glance, took the arm Meeray's partner offered, and hobbled off. Otokas watched Attalissa out of sight and did not know his hands were clenched till Kayugh touched his fist, gently.

"A word?" she said, and to the dormitories with her, "You know your posts. Go. I'll be on the bell-tower."

Kayugh's hair coiled like the tendrils of pea-vines, and Otokas, shoving down the dog's need to follow 'Lissa, folded his arms and ignored the urge he had never once gratified, to comb it back from her face, wind fingers in it. The priestesses were sworn to celibacy, to honour their ever-maiden goddess. The Blackdog was not, but there had been no woman for him since he had realized he wanted only Kayugh.

"How long can we hold out here?" Kayugh asked bluntly. "It's at least two days to Serakallash, and they'll hardly set out the moment a messenger arrives—it'll take them a day or more just to summon their sept-chiefs. We have walls, but the town doesn't. I was thinking . . . if we can get Old Lady to agree, we can let the townsfolk in, as many as we can take."

"She won't allow it."

"Will you?"

Otokas frowned at the challenge in Kayugh's voice. "We don't have the supplies to support ourselves for long, let alone many others. But if they come, yes."

It was so engrained that no one but the vowed women set foot on the island, he doubted many townsfolk would think of it. The holy islet was a place of reverence and awe, not a refuge. And he was not sure it would be a refuge, not from this attack. The edge of the goddess's terror gnawed at him.

"They might be safer in the town."

"Safer! How?"

He shook his head. "There are wizards out there, or a wizard, more powerful than any I've ever heard of—probably just one, since Attalissa said *he*. She believes he's coming here for her. To destroy her."

"To kill the girl?" More puzzlement in Kayugh's voice than anything. It seemed too unlikely a thing to evoke anger.

"No. To destroy *Attalissa*, not just her avatar. Devour her, she said." That shocked her. "Why? *How?*"

"I don't know. The dog doesn't know. But it—I—we, if you like, we believe it. The dog . . . understands things it can't seem to express. Remembers things. You know the stories say that there were gods who died in the west in a wizards' war, long ago before ever there were kings in the north? I remember things, like . . . shadows seen out of the corner of the eye. Nothing to seize hold of, but enough to be afraid. Gods can die, and not only by their own will."

Kayugh drew a deep breath. "Well then. What do we do?"

Otokas didn't know. Run. Hide. Kill the source of the threat. The Blackdog's solutions were few, and not necessarily the best. He did not think the Blackdog could overcome unaided whatever had the power to summon an army unseen out of the temple's own millet fields. And Attalissa was not going to be able to help.

"Send out the novices and lay-sisters, and the old sisters too, not just your messengers to Serakallash. Fill whatever boats we have and get them away. Tell them to scatter to the villages in the high valleys, tell them to hide."

"Otokas—"

"Do it now, while there's time. It's dark enough the boats won't be seen."

Her hand on his again, and she had no idea how distracting that was. He hoped she didn't.

"Are you all right, Oto? Your eyes—"

He laughed. "Aside from being ready to go howling over to town to get myself killed, looking for whatever she thinks is coming for her? Oh yes."

"Go to her."

"I'm going back to the tower, now she's safe for the moment. I want to see what's out there."

"I'll send someone to tell you."

"I can see more in the dark than you could in broad daylight. I'll be all right. We've—I and all the men before me—we've been arguing down our single-minded mongrel for a very long time now. We're getting good at it."

"Then go put your armour on, first. Remind your single-minded mongrel she's a little girl and it's you she loves, not just the Blackdog."

Otokas gave Kayugh a mocking bow, fist over his heart. "As you command, Spear Lady." But she had drawn him a little away from Attalissa's panic, and that was a moment's easing of the Blackdog's own fears. "I'll join you at the tower."

The shirt of scale armour was heavy on his shoulders, a weight familiar mostly from drilling with the women, practised and easy and not at all welcome. Otokas slung his sword over his shoulder again, found his helmet, with its wavelike crest and snarling dog facemask. There were dormitories hurrying to the defence of the walls and to guard the water-gate, which was no more than a single narrow door in the eastern wall. It let onto a narrow path and a drop of smooth, curving rock so precipitous he doubted any attack in force could come that way—which was why the water-gate was in so inconvenient and even dangerous a location. Most people going to or from the landing-stage preferred to take the broader path along the water's edge, which circled to the front gates facing the red bridge in the west. The priestesses might be able to come at any besiegers that way, circle around to their rear while they attacked the front gates.

Not a tactic to use against an army, though, not if there were twice the number of sisters to send against them.

Otokas, where are you? I'm afraid. Attalissa's mind's voice, soul's voice, was faint, coloured with her fear, wavering. But she was awake, and that lessened the dog's anxiety a little more. Otokas stood where

19

he was to answer, so she did not lose the contact with him. It felt to him like two people who stand at arms' utter stretch, fingertip to fingertip, where the slightest movement might separate them. But it was not so long since the girl had to see him to find his mind.

I know you're afraid. It's all right. Be strong, 'Lissa, love.

People are dying in the town. I can feel them. It hurts, dog.

I know.

I can't help them. The waters can't hear me yet.

It's all right, love. We're here to look after you.

But them . . . dog, dog, I should be helping them. They shouldn't die for me. And it's not the town he wants, it's me, just me!

They're your people. They want to protect you. They ought to, at least. *'Lissa, who is he? Do you know him? Is he their leader? A wizard? A god?*

I don't know. I don't know what he is, dog. Something wrong. Evil. Strong. You felt it, what he did. Tearing the world like that.

I felt something, he admitted.

I want you here.

I need to see what's happening. I'll come soon.

Soon. You promise.

I promise.

Old Lady wouldn't stay with me. She went to the New Chapel to pray.

You said prayer is for them. If it helps her, let her pray, so long as she doesn't take sisters from the walls to do it.

It isn't even the lake she prays to. It's something she makes up in her own head, to fill the emptiness she won't let me into. She wants me to be more than even the Old Great Gods ever were. Attalissa fell into the child again, her thoughts growing fainter. *She doesn't really like me very much. She doesn't like children.*

Either she lost the strength to touch him, or she had said all she needed to. Either way, Otokas hoped Meeray or some of the others would find her something to do to distract her. He resumed his course through the labyrinthine interconnection of rooms and passages at a near run.

His niece Attavaia, still in her blue gown, ran into him, pelting around a corner, and bounced off into the wall.

"They're on the town bridge, Uncle," she gasped, wide-eyed, as he steadied her. "Spear Lady sent me to tell you. I heard it, when they met . . . I never thought . . . it was so loud. They just kept coming, arrows didn't even slow them down, there were so many. The militia's stopped them at the north end of the bridge but they're fighting hand to hand there, and . . . there's just so many. Rideen's in the militia. He'll be there. In that."

Rideen was her older brother.

"Everyone'll be there," Otokas said. She was shaking in his grasp. Attavaia, just out of her novitiate, had not yet served a turn as a mercenary. "Go arm yourself and join your dormitory at your post, unless Spear Lady had any other orders after you found me?"

"No."

Being with her friends would steady her, let her pull the discipline of the practice courts back.

"Where are you supposed to be?"

"We assemble in the lower east court. We're to bring arrows from the armoury to the sisters in the tower by the water-gate, and act as a reserve."

"Good." He hugged her close and kissed her forehead. "Go on, then."

She gave him a fleeting, forced smile, turned, and ran again, her bare feet flashing beneath her skirt, showing an anklet of turquoise.

"Attavaia!"

She skidded to a stop. "Uncle?"

He caught up with her, gripped her by the shoulders. "If things go badly—if the temple's lost—"

"Lost!"

"If. At the end. Go into the mountains."

She gave him a wary look. "Why?"

"She'll need you again someday."

"I'm scared, but I'm no coward! I'm not breaking my vows and running away."

"I'm not telling you to, child. But if we have to run, we will. The temple is not the goddess. Remember that, 'Vaia."

"Ah." Attavaia swallowed. "I will. Uncle . . ." She stood on tiptoe, kissed his cheek. "I'll see you later, Uncle. Blackdog."

A self-conscious salute, fist over heart, and then she was gone again, feet slapping.

He hoped he hadn't just set a panic in her dormitory, hoped she would have the sense not to repeat his unconsidered advice until the moment came. The Blackdog's fears unbalanced judgement, made it hard to understand the true shape of the threat. And she was his favourite sister's only daughter.

Night had come down on them. From the tower, Otokas watched, with the Blackdog's owl-sharp vision in the darkness, the defenders of Lissavakail's bridge fall, overwhelmed. Lilmass was dead, and her dozen with her, he thought. There were no indigo-trousered women among the townsmen who broke and bolted away, a handful, a knot unravelling into the alleys and steep twisting lanes, no order to them, every man running to his own household, to bar his own door.

The raiders poured over the bridge, their own order breaking, becoming no more than that, raiders, every man and woman pursuing their own path. The discipline they had shown taking the bridge, where they had climbed over their own dead to take their places, was forgotten. They swarmed over bodies lying like barricades on the near end of the bridge, some pausing even there to loot and rummage among the dead. Horses snorted and finicked at the uncertain, death-reeking footing. Those mounted carried torches, trailing flames and bands of foot soldiers up amid the terraced houses of the steep-sided island.

The dog stretched its awareness out, followed sound and scent of shattered spirits. The raiders stormed through the narrow alleys between the rubble-and-clay buildings of the town, hacking down doors, looting, killing those who resisted, setting fires that burned the furnishings and the beams of the flat-roofed houses. Roofs fell in and people died, trapped in their homes. Townsfolk and raiders alike ran mindless, shouting. Geese and hens screeched, goats bleated frantically, as some among the raiders butchered for the cookfires, making camp amid the madness. They settled in to enjoy themselves, quarrelling over the spoils of the town's wine shop and the household jars of thin beer, while on higher terraces townsfolk still fought, and died.

The sisters watched the fires. Some prayed.

Not a single boat from the town had fled to the holy islet for shelter. Why corner themselves? Any who had chosen to flee, or had taken warning soon enough to do so, would have headed for shore and the chance to escape deeper into the mountains.

There was order among the invaders, despite the looting. The Blackdog saw it in the concentration of torchlight, the tramp of feet not running, a snaking file that made straight along Lissavakail's main road of packed shale from the town bridge to the ruins of the temple bridge. Otokas saw with his own eyes, then, not the dog's: movement and bustle, duck and flare of torchlight, heard orders shouted in some alien tongue. These were the ones who had let the others die on the bridge to clear the way for them.

"What are they doing?" Kayugh asked softly.

"The town's overrun. It looks as though most of them have broken off to loot, but a core of them are still under control. Those are coming for us." After a moment he added, "They're bringing boats along the shore."

Madness, to fight on into the night. He might have expected them to establish themselves in the town, confident in holding the only near approach to the temple islet. He might have expected a conquering warlord to attempt to come to terms with Old Lady, to offer Attalissa some degree of service and respect, seeking her good graces once the town was taken. He did not, and would rather have been wrong, in not expecting anything but this.

"We stay here," Kayugh ordered, in response to the rising murmur among the women as Otokas's words spread. "We're too few to keep them from landing. If we get scattered out along the shore, they'll just push through us and find the walls unguarded."

Otokas watched their progress. The warriors at the bridgehead took little interest in the broken bridge, as though they in turn had expected it. They merely awaited the arrival of the town's fishing boats, rowed from the nearby landing beach. If they meant to ferry attackers across the channel, they would need more than those to land in enough force to pose a threat.

"What are they doing?" Kayugh asked, as the torchlight showed figures bending, scrambling over boats, figures milling on shore.

They were lashing the boats together, broadside on, alongside the broken spans of the temple bridge.

"Making a bridge," Otokas said.

"Why the hurry?" she muttered. "Why not wait until dawn, at least? I don't like this, Oto. You should get back to Attalissa."

"Not till I know what he wants."

"If what you believe is true," she said guardedly, "he must not want to give us time to send her away. Though where around the lake she'd be out of his reach, I don't know . . ."

He didn't know either.

Someone loosed an arrow at the warriors building the bridge. It fell harmlessly in the garden of artfully dwarfed pines and rhododendrons just breaking bud, which covered the sloping ground between the main gates and the channel. Kayugh turned on that sister, roaring.

"Save your arrows, curse you. You think we have any to spare?"

"Sorry, Spear Lady," the young woman muttered, eyes downcast. "Sorry."

Kayugh turned back to watching the channel. "Young fools."

"Nerves," Otokas said.

"They can have nerves later." Kayugh eyed him. "How are you?"

He grinned, and saw her flinch away from his eyes, the Blackdog looking out, the world a moment hazed with its fury. "Holding on."

"Do. I don't want you loose in here. You should be with her."

"Not yet."

"Spear Lady?" One of the women drew their attention back to the raiders' makeshift bridge. Seen with human eyes, it was a copper shimmer of torchlight on water, an orange flare of torches catching the glint of armour, a helm, a spearpoint, a drawn sword. Shadows that ducked and leapt and rocked across the light. "There's someone coming there, beyond, Spear Lady. Look. Their warlord?"

Some*thing*. He came in the darkness, riding, flanked close by other riders, preceded by more torches.

Otokas . . . snarled. Some of the women gave him wary looks.

"Oto?"

"The warlord's a wizard," he said hoarsely.

Wizards, even the least, carried the scent of their magic with them: earthy, cool, damp, like water on stone, spiced with the tang of fire and frost. Wizards' magic was neither good nor bad; it simply was, though it raised the dog's hackles. But this was overlain, entwined with what he had first sensed when the army appeared: the reek of burning metal, a poisonous breath in the air, ashes on stone.

"Something worse." The words were hard to shape, coherent thought suddenly very far away.

"What do you mean?" Kayugh peered into the night. "Where is he? There in the centre?"

Otokas watched that tight formation of torchlight draw closer at an unhurried and dignified walk. He swayed, dizzy, feeling eyes on him. "Kill him."

"He's out of arrowshot yet." Kayugh seized his elbow, steadied him. "Oto, what's wrong? Get back to the goddess."

"No." He forced the word out through clenched teeth.

Ah. The Blackdog. The voice that spoke in his head was amused, satisfied. It was male, and carried the accents of the man's speech, fluent in the desert tongue that was the common language of the trade road, but with a foreign overtone, syllables too precisely chopped. *And where is your maiden goddess? Bring her out to me now, and you shall continue to serve her once she is my bride.*

The wizard lied. He smelt it. The dog fought him to break free into the world. Lies, lies. The wizard hungered for Attalissa like a snow-leopard with the taste of sheep's blood on its tongue.

Fight me and I will kill you, man, and take the Blackdog spirit into myself. And it will be I who sits in the saddle, never imagine otherwise, not that poor mad animal that rides you and has forgotten all it once was.

He saw it, a moment, the shape of the wizard's hunger, a shadow the dog's fear made clear. The goddess bound in snares of flesh and blood and chains of power such as wizards only dreamed of, drawn into the soul of this . . . *thing* that sat its horse across the narrow channel.

Go. Announce me to my bride, Blackdog. Before any more of her women have to die.

Otokas snatched arrow and bow from the sister to his left, bent it near to breaking, and shot, unaimed. There was no hope of the shaft reaching the wizard. Amid the warriors building the bridge of boats, though, one shrieked and splashed, sank. There was an uneasy stir among those around the wizard, an edging back from the lakeshore.

"I said, don't waste arrows." Kayugh's voice was gentle and very, very far away. She prised the bow from his grip. "Blackdog: look at me. Stay sane, or go to Attalissa."

Otokas sighed and folded a hand around Kayugh's shaking fingers. Bad, if he was frightening even her. He forced the dog to settle and found words again. "He'll have to cross the bridge to get to her. We have to kill him then."

"We will." As though she soothed a child. Or a half-wild beast.

Kayugh freed her hand from his, still gently, but rested it on his shoulder, an anchoring touch. Or a readiness to seize him if he flung himself over the parapet.

But the other sisters edged away. From the corner of his vision he could see the dog's shadow lying over him, black form on the edge of existence, a breath from taking shape. The yellow-green peridot light of the Blackdog's eyes would be burning in his own.

There is a storyteller's cycle of tales, and they begin like this:

Long ago, in the days of the first kings in the north—who were Viga Fork-beard, and Red Geir, and Hravnmod the Wise, as all but fools should know—there were seven devils, and their names were Honeytongued Ogada, Vartu Kingsbane, Jasberek Fireborn, Twice-Betrayed Ghatai, Dotemon the Dreamshaper, Tu'usha the Restless, and Jochiz Stonebreaker. If other tellers tell you different, they are ignorant singers not worthy of their hire.

CHAPTER II

Old Lady crouched before the altar in the New Chapel. It was covered with golden plaques depicting scenes of Attalissa's former glories: processions bearing tribute, warbands of women marching, the god Narva prostrate, raising a pickaxe on extended hands, symbol of his lordship of some of the wealthiest turquoise mines of the high peaks. Slain enemies and accumulated wealth and joyously dancing human souls. The lamplight made the raised figures shimmer and move, gave them life.

In the past, Attalissa had been a true power. A glory to bring folk to their knees, a great mother to them all. When had she fallen away from that? Old Lady didn't know. Before her time, generations gone. Gods and goddesses rose, and ruled, and fell away to act as nothing more than petty wisewomen and wisemen, as though they lost their will after a few generations of life. That was what all her reading and her study, the travels she had indulged in younger years, had taught her. Gods and goddesses simply . . . lost interest, like children bored of playing house, of echoing their parents' strength.

Even the Old Great Gods had abdicated all concern for the world and retreated from it.

She had believed that abandonment to be the truth, in her youth. She knew better now. Like every sister, she had served her turn as a mercenary. From travellers, she first heard of the nameless god who had come to the west, who was spirit, nothing but spirit, and spoke through the conscience and wisdom of priests, not in the supercilious platitudes of a village grandmother. And some said that god was but a servant of the Old Great Gods, a messenger, to call the folk back to their true path. She asked permission to travel herself, and eventually,

27

though the Old Lady of that day was reluctant, received it. In the caravan towns she sought wisdom, and she found it, very occasionally, in travellers' talk and in a few rare, precious books, gleaned from the treasure trove of the abominable ferrymen on the Kinsai-av. She copied much, since that was what she had leave as their guest to do, but others, the rarest, the truest, she stole. It was unfitting that such books, the teachings of the new faith of the west, should remain in such a place, with the folk of such a defiled and corrupting goddess as Kinsai.

It was not an uncaring abandonment. The world was grown too impure for the Old Great Gods. Devils had walked among the Northron folk and on the Great Grass, had overthrown kings, defied the gods of the high places and the goddesses of the waters, and though in the end the Old Great Gods had heard the pleas of the war-torn world and bound the devils again, they had been angered by the wizards' pride and human weakness that let the devils loose. They had removed themselves and would not return until human hearts were purified. And that would not happen while humans clung to the little gods and goddesses of the earth, who taught nothing of purity but led men and women to bind themselves in worldly cares.

Like the nameless god of the west, the gods and goddesses of the earth should remember that they were mere messengers, servants; they should lead the way back to the Old Great Gods, lead their folk to make themselves pure. But they could not do so when they mired themselves in the world, hardly different from the folk they guided. People were like children; they needed to see power and authority in order to be drawn to listen, to emulate. To lead folk to cast off the world's cares, it was needful to have the strength to be respected, to be obeyed. Then, and only then, could the purblind folk be led back to the Old Great Gods.

But there was no strength, no certainty, in the divinities of the earth and waters, and by their example they kept folk fixed to the petty worries of field and trade, the squalling of babes and the pains of old age. They kept human folk from understanding that their true home was not this world, but the land of the Great Gods; they kept them weak, their minds clouded, so that all of human life was passed as one waking in the morning afraid and doubting and wondering.

Luli had been full of fear and doubt and wondering herself, until that last trip to Marakand, twenty years before, when she had been newly appointed Old Lady. It was her scholarship, her curiosity about the world, that led to that appointment, voted on by the sisters, approved by the goddess. Blind. They did not see that she had found a new truth, found *the* truth, that she knew all the temple a sham, a dead-end trail that trapped them all. The Westrons wrote that the dead, even the purest in heart, could no longer reach the land of the Old Great Gods, never know the great and overwhelming peace they had earned through their sufferings in life. They waited on the road, thousands upon thousands, for the way to open, and that could not happen till the Great Gods returned to the purified earth.

That Attalissa approved Luli's appointment showed her, beyond any doubt, that the strength of the goddess was a lie, that she knew nothing of the hearts of her folk.

That was when Luli had sinned against her vows in body as well as spirit. And again, Attalissa had never rebuked her. Perhaps had never even known. The final proof Old Lady needed: Attalissa was nothing.

He had agreed with her, in so many things. He was a wizard, a scholar, for all he looked a Great Grass barbarian with nothing more on his mind than horses and women and brawling. He was only a little younger than her, and beautiful, lean and strong and vital like a tawny cat, no dull-witted mountain farmer but a man, truly a *man* a woman could lean on. She had found herself, astonished and amazed, listening to herself while they talked of more than gods and philosophies and the blindness of human folk who trudged cattlelike through empty lives and never lifted their eyes to the sky. She had found herself on fire, willing, wanting to give him anything, to keep the teasing smile and the knowing, cool eyes hers, to keep the deep voice whispering her name, *Luli*, against her ear, hoarse with passion she could not have imagined when she chose the temple over marriage to any of the dull, demanding young men of her village.

It was wrong, of course. Not a wrong against Attalissa. A sin against herself, against the Old Great Gods they both sought, to feel this passion, to fix such value to another mortal being, to tie oneself into the world so. But oh, those few days, they had been worth a lifetime . . .

She had told him of mortal Attalissa and the stultifying empty days, of the temple, all its secrets. Of the old woman her goddess had become, surely soon to die, and the dreary years she could see ahead of herself, the years of her prime, to be wasted rearing a child, like any fat-hipped peasant mother, surrounded by the clamouring needs of the temple that was no place of contemplation, no place to refine the soul, but a training ground for soldiers to safeguard men's greed for the soulless treasures of the earth. He had said, a man's, a wizard's will, wedded to divine power, could start to change the world, could begin the reform, begin to lead the folk towards the true path they could not see for themselves, but that the time and the stars must be right.

She had never, truly, believed that he would come. A lover's idle speculation, games they played, planning an impossible future. But now, finally, he *had* come, bringing fire and sword, to tear down the old and build it all anew. And now she was old, while he, a man, aged less swiftly, and being a wizard, less swiftly still. He might yet have only the first grey in his hair.

Old Lady wept, and the sisters she had summoned to prayer eyed her sidelong at their own empty devotions. But she was not going to be weak, she could not afford to be. The body was nothing; it was the Old Great Gods, the future, she served. In times to come she would be a saint, a servant who had shown not only her folk but her goddess the way back to the Gods. And all she and Tamghat had planned, lighthearted, a lovers' game, over wine and books in his rumpled bed in a Marakander inn, lay before her. First was to stop the needless fighting. But Spear Lady and the Blackdog were narrow-minded, traditionbound, and they had turned the sullen child of this incarnation against her. No support there. Let them suffer, then. Fire would cleanse the temple, and she could build it anew, if not as Tamghat's consort (and such thoughts showed that even she must look deeper into her soul, where the desires of the world yet lingered), then as his partner in all else. Attalissa would thank her for her vision in the end, when in sharing power with the wizard she stretched beyond the limitations of place that shackled all the gods, and understood the freedom she had gained to seek her own soul's purification and to lead her folk to true knowledge of the Old Great Gods.

"Attalissa enlightens me," Old Lady said aloud, rising stiffly. Two sisters hurried to offer her support. Her knees creaked, taunted her with pain. "She will have peace with this warlord. He comes to fling open the shutters on a new dawn of glory for Lissavakail, he comes to show us the true path back to the Old Great Gods. We are wicked to resist; it is not Attalissa's will."

"Should I go to the Spear Lady . . . ?" her assistant asked, hesitantly. Sister Darshin aspired to the position of Old Lady, was all too assiduous in trying to ease the burdens of office from her, as though she were ancient, not merely arthritic and greying.

Go to Spear Lady Kayugh and the arrogant Blackdog, who thought himself so much closer to the goddess than all the women who truly served her. Go to plot against Old Lady, that's what Darshin would do, scenting a chance to weaken Old Lady's authority yet further with that pair of vow-breaking reactionaries, who would have the goddess subordinate to their will forever, having forced themselves into her malleable child's heart as parental authorities.

"No," she said. "I've already told them we should have waited and offered to negotiate, and they refused to hear the goddess's word. If they are deaf to Attalissa's will, they are damned. We will wait here till wiser counsels can prevail."

The women looked shocked.

"Bar the doors," she snapped. "Admit no one. Attalissa has been betrayed by those who fight against her will. Attalissa will have peace with this warlord and love between our peoples. We will wait, and welcome him in her name."

CHAPTER III

The air smelt heavily of blood; a priestess sat white-faced with her back against the parapet, her arm below the short sleeve of her armour tied with soaking bandages. There was more blood on the stairs where they had carried someone else down.

"We're nearly out of arrows already," Kayugh said grimly. "I said we needed to keep more in the stores, but Old Lady said the fletchers' guild was charging too much and we weren't going to send more than a few dormitories out as mercenaries this summer." She wiped the back of her hand over her mouth, as if that could settle the unsteadiness of her voice. "'Prayer is our work,' she said. 'Lissa forgive me, I should have stood up to her."

"She is Old Lady." The Blackdog was Attalissa's champion, and by tradition avoided becoming entangled in administrative debates among the priestesses. But Otokas should have backed Kayugh up in that. He'd feared to seem partial, to betray that which probably half the temple knew already.

Kayugh handed him an arrow that had come clattering down on the stones behind them. He straightened its fletching absently, found the bowman who had shot it, and sent it back. Not an accurate shot, not a straight flight, but it scratched over the man's helmet and sent the raider skipping back, to slip and fall on the algae-slimed stones of the shore, in a puddle of torchlight, and Kayugh's following shot was truer, piercing his unprotected cheek.

"Attalissa's luck was with me on that one." Kayugh took a deep breath. "The lack's past remedying, anyway. Prayer won't make arrows."

Otokas nodded, never taking his eyes off the lake. The near shore was littered with raiders dead and wounded. They had come within bowshot carrying torches to light their work, and though the first splashing rush ashore had carried large wicker shields to cover their fellows fixing the last few boats into the bridge, and raider archers had shot blindly at the lightless gate-tower roof, finding targets by mischance, Attalissa's priestesses had had the better of it.

Where the sisters shot at shadows briefly caught in torchlight or blocking the water's dark gleam, the Blackdog had clear sight. Otokas had lost himself in killing, settling the dog's fury against the invaders in the smooth action of draw and release, the selection of targets, picking off the raiders' archers, always with half his attention on the waiting, watching wizard.

The warlord—the wizard was that, Otokas had no doubt, though wizards were more wont to stand in the shadows at some leader's shoulder—seemed content to wait, and watch, as his followers died.

Or as the defenders expended their arrows. Sisters of the dormitories assigned to support those on the bell-tower roof brought no more arrows, but began to carry up weightier missiles, in case of a direct attack on the gates the tower straddled. They had already depleted the supplies meant for the water-gate's defence.

"Crows," Kayugh muttered. "Seems like there's two more for every one we kill. Hold, Sisters. Save what shafts we have left. That means you too, Oto."

He lowered the bow, flexed a hand that was starting to cramp. Kayugh gave him a worried look.

"How's Attalissa now?"

He was doing his best to shut the goddess out of his awareness, to keep her from knowing just how bad it looked to him, but he could feel her fear nonetheless. And a hard, glowing ember of fury that the girl had no outlet for, save the frustrated tears that she was so far stoutly resisting.

"Afraid. Upset."

"They won't be able to starve us out very quickly, and we can keep them from scaling the walls. Serakallash may come in time."

"They may." But he heard no hope in his own voice. "If the wizard looks like taking the temple . . . I'll have to get her away, Kayugh. Whatever the cost."

The last of the boats was lashed in place, the holy islet tied to the town's island again. There was movement on the far side of the channel, horsemen riding to the water's edge by the first of the boats, torches held high, spreading fire over the water.

"Yes." Kayugh took a deep breath, flexed her shoulders, and raised her voice. "Sisters—the Blackdog says this warlord is a wizard, and he means to harm the goddess somehow, enslave her or kill her. And the dog says it's possible, not some nightmare from an old tale of the west. This abomination is what we're fighting. We're here to keep him from Attalissa, from the goddess, from the lake, from our little 'Lissa. Make the wizard your target, every chance that offers."

"He's lighting himself up well," said one, and laughed, no mirth in it. "Afraid we might miss him."

"If that is him in the centre and not a decoy?"

Faces turned to Otokas. "Yes," he said. "In the helmet with a bear spread-eagled over it as crest, if you can make that out? His horse is the pale gold mare, with red-dyed harness." The Blackdog was certain. It could smell the magic rising from him like the scent of new-turned soil in the hot summer sun. And when the warlord moved, he left a shadow-image in the eye, an eddy of red-edged black, like an absence of flame. The Blackdog had never seen the like before—not that it could remember, but to Otokas it felt as though it should remember. That flame-shadow raised the hackles of the spirit.

"We see him," one of the women confirmed. "Gold helmet? It catches the fire nicely. But forget the horse, dog. They're all shadows from here."

"They're all 'it,' from here. How d'you know it's a mare?"

"He can smell it."

"When it gets closer we can check."

"If it's a stallion, Oto, you buy a jar of the best Marakander wine for every dormitory."

"What does he get if he's right?"

"A kiss from Spear Lady," someone away to the side called, and there was a flutter of nervous giggling that fell to abrupt silence when Otokas frowned in that direction.

The warlord reached the bridge of boats, and the riders about him dismounted. He did not, staring up towards the gatehouse and its high parapet, the defenders who should have been invisible, since they weren't such fools as to surround themselves with torches. Otokas felt almost a physical shock, unseen eyes finding him.

I told you, Blackdog. Bring out my bride. I want to wed her with the dawn. I'm surprised she's stayed hidden behind you this far. I thought she would make some effort to protect her people. Is she grown so cold-hearted, or is it cowardice? Tell her to come out to me, or I will march the folk of the town to the shore, here, and behead them, a dozen at a time, until bodies fill the channel. Tell her, if she fights me, I will set a fire on this town that will burn its folk to ash and poison the lake and her soul with the curses of their ghosts. But tell her, if she comes to me willingly, I will rule as a kindly father, and teach her and her folk both to love me.

Otokas shut his mind against the wizard, felt the faint pressure of attention blocked. The wizard grinned at him, mouthed words in the darkness. He couldn't read their shape.

The warriors lining the bridge began to drum spears and swords on shields.

The warlord urged his horse forward, stepping, almost hopping, into the first of the boats.

"Attalissa grant they've got my brother's boat in that lot," one of the sisters said.

"Why?"

"Lazy bugger. Rotten planking."

"Oh yes. Let it put a hoof right through."

"Pitch the godless wizard into the lake."

"Think he can swim?"

"Not in armour. Not even if he is a wizard."

"I can," Otokas said.

"But it's Attalissa's lake. More reason to think *he'll* drown despite his magics," said the one who'd first spoken. "Leave us our fancies, eh, dog?"

"I'd fancy seeing Otokas swim in anything."

"Or nothing."

Nervous giggles.

"Children," he said, tolerant of most teasing, so long as they left Kayugh out of it.

Kayugh didn't join the anxious laughter. The horse picked its way over the unstable bridge, held under some wizardly control, not mere Grasslander horsemanship. The warlord's escort followed afoot, their horses left behind. The wizard's mount gained the temple shore with a scrambling leap and broke into a trot, drawing further ahead of the escort, crunching onto a gravelled garden path. Those who had followed him onto the bridge ran to catch up, their torches streaming like banners.

"Archers," Kayugh said calmly. "Now. Kill him."

The first arrow struck with a powerful arm behind it, stout Kedro's, and must have pierced through the rings of his mail. Otokas saw the warlord flinch back, arrow protruding from his chest. But in the space of an eye's blink he gestured in the air before his face, reins caught on his pommel and what looked to Otokas like a web of yarn stretched between his hands. The following flight of arrows curved away as though a heavy wind had caught them. The wizard closed a gloved hand around the shaft in his chest and snapped it off, throwing it aside and taking up the reins again. Three of his guard were down, though. The wizard ignored them, ignoring the continuing ragged flurry of arrows, which scattered as if he were the centre of some deflecting storm.

None of the raiders shot back.

Kayugh peered down the slope. "Was he hit, Oto?"

"Only one arrow made it through to him, but yes. Didn't seem to bother him, and they're just blowing away now."

"*Damn* him." She made it a prayer. "Hold! Aim for those about him, then. His favourites, his commanders, whatever they are."

36

Kayugh drew her own bow again, took careful aim, not for the wizard's guard but one of the torch-bearers standing on the near end of the bridge. It was a neat, powerful shot, through the throat and a leather collar that did not protect. That tattooed desert woman crumpled, and the dropped torch smouldered.

"Burn," Kayugh whispered. But it went out, rolled into bilge-water, perhaps. "Godless bastard."

Other arrows found closer marks, though many were turned by armour. None touched the wizard or his horse.

Otokas let one of the sisters take the bow from him. He watched, eyes narrowed, as the wizard reined in below the gate. The warlord's followers clustered behind him, largely shielded by whatever spell he had worked against the arrows.

"Enough," Kayugh said in disgust. "Wait a better chance, Sisters. Spears might get through, or stones. Wait for my word, though."

The raiders muttered among themselves in some foreign language, and laughter rattled off the wall.

Women gripped spears, or hefted what heavy missiles had been carried up to them. Jars of pottery and brass, bricks, paving stones, oddments of statuary Old Lady certainly did not know the enterprising sisters had carted off. It might be harder to blow away a jade lion the size of a baby, Otokas considered, and he balanced that on the edge of the parapet, waiting with the rest on Kayugh's word.

She waited. The warlord smiled. His folk fell silent, though there were screams in plenty, shouts and riotous calls, from the island town. And the hungry red roar of burning houses.

There were more folk gathering at the far end of the boat-bridge. Raiders, with townsfolk, men and women and children, their hands bound behind them. Hostages to the goddess's acquiescence as the wizard had threatened. The torch-bearers had followed the warlord, though, and to the sisters the clustered families would be lost in the night's darkness.

Otokas said nothing of them to Kayugh, and hoped the goddess did not realize their presence yet. The man's heart might tear, but the

Blackdog had no heart-room to spare for any soul but his goddess. And if the warlord did not know that—it was one small weight in the balance on the Blackdog's side, leverage the wizard might think he had, only to find he pushed against nothing.

Otokas studied him with the Blackdog spirit's eyes. The warlord wore a long mail byrnie like the warriors of the kingdoms of the north, its fine rings gilded, not just by firelight. No blood marred it where the arrow had pierced, though a dark mark showed the stub of the arrowshaft. His helmet was likewise gilded, the eyes of the bear snarling in the centre of his brow set with garnets, or maybe even rubies. Instead of any other jewels he wore a number of cords draped around his neck and hanging to either side down his chest—leather thongs, yarn, ribbon, what might have been braided hair or grass— each one doubled, a long loop. He carried the sabre of the steppes at his side, a single-edged blade, slightly curved, a horseman's weapon, and his face was of the Great Grass north of the Four Deserts: brown-skinned, with narrow, light brown eyes. His long hair, the colour of his skin, hung loose save for braids to either side, into which bears' claws had been knotted, swinging against his cheeks as he turned his head, taking a count, it seemed, of the women on the tower roof. Whatever he was, he probably saw in the dark as readily as Otokas did. He looked a man in the prime of life, but there was a greyish cast to his face, as if of illness or exhaustion, and his eyes were sunken.

To man's eyes he was an awesome figure, gold in the torchlight on his golden horse, demonic, eyes a glimmer, red, catching the light.

No. Otokas saw that with his own vision and the dog's both, a red glint that was not reflection, and the eerie, flame-edged shadow still shivered after his every movement, caught just in the corner of the eye. For a moment, just a moment, as though some curtain were swept aside, Otokas saw dark fire running like molten copper, tracing through the man's body, twisting like a flame where his heart should be.

"I am . . . Tamghat." As though the name should mean something, or as if the wizard temporized, that pause. "As I told your mad dog there, I have come to make Attalissa of the lake my bride. We shall be

38

wed and bedded with this morning's dawn, and if you stand between us you will die."

The sisters were stunned into silence a moment, and the warlord sat on his horse smiling, with mocking confidence.

"She's a child!" someone shouted down in simple outrage, and there was a brief hesitation, a shifting of the wizard's attention elsewhere.

The Blackdog scrabbled at Otokas, wanting out. Fling himself over the parapet, have the throat out of the wizard. He resisted it. This Tamghat was something powerful enough to kill him, leaving aside the simple overwhelming numbers which could do the job just as well, and dead, he left Attalissa . . . not unprotected, never unprotected, but with a protector unfamiliar and ill-prepared, at best. At worst . . . best not to think of it, the Blackdog taken by the wizard, 'Lissa's trust and doom united.

He forced the dog quiet and said softly, in Kayugh's ear, "He didn't expect that."

"What?"

"He didn't know she was a child. Did he really come expecting to face and overcome the goddess grown and in her full strength?"

But if this Tamghat had planned all along to seize the town, hold its folk hostage . . . perhaps the goddess's power would never have been raised against him, if his magic and his numbers had gotten him over the stone bridge. Gods and goddesses had wed mortals before. It was not so unthinkable a thing. The wizard might argue that she would outlive him, and sharing rule and the wealth of the town for a mortal man's remaining years, even a wizard's extended life, might be thought a small price for peace and the folk's lives. But his eyes were hungry.

"If you want to marry her, come back when she's old enough to wed, and ask her yourself!" Kayugh called down.

Tamghat laughed, but it sounded forced. "She's already far older than I. Why should I wait for her to grow older? What do you mean by too young to wed?" Otokas felt the wizard's attention crawling over the women, forcing into them. A few, the more sensitive to magic, shook their heads or flinched back from the parapet. One older woman dropped to her knees, vomiting.

"A little girl?" The warlord's voice teetered on the edge of rage Otokas could almost smell, but then it seemed to evaporate like dew in sunlight. He threw back his head and laughed. "Blackdog, you should have told me. This alters things."

A stir of hope ran among the sisters. Even Otokas wondered for a moment if they might have won some time; enough, at least, for Sera-kallash's warriors to arm and climb the mountain road.

"I can be patient, good Sisters. The stars will run round again and the patterns re-form, and she'll be old enough, by then, to know a man. Till then I'll rule as her regent and guardian. You've no need to fear I'll harm her. I'm a father myself."

"He lies," Otokas growled. "He'll eat her alive."

"Tell them," said the warlord, "what you can see across the channel, Blackdog."

Otokas kept silent.

"Then I will. There are folk there, Attalissa's folk. Your folk, Sisters. And they will die, if I do not have your child goddess in my keeping before the dawn, away from that mad dog and his poisoning lies. Eat her! Do I really look like some fox-eared Baisirbska savage to you? That's a nonsense and you all know it. But I will do what I have to, to win Attalissa. The stars have knotted our fates together and I won't be turned aside. Those folk on the shore, their lives are in your hands, Sisters. Do you have kin in the town? Brothers, sisters, parents? Do you think they might be among those the Blackdog can see? Ask him."

"No," Kayugh said. "Attalissa won't pass to your keeping till every last one of us is dead. And our kin would say likewise."

"Well, then. It's as you choose." The warlord jerked his head to one of his followers, a tall, butter-haired Northron, who spun on his heel and started down for the boat bridge at a run. A fool of a Northron, who carried a torch high over his head. Possibly he meant to signal with it to those guarding the hostages.

The first arrow took him in his cloth-wrapped calf, sent him stumbling, and of the dozen following, some found a home through his mail; one took him in the throat and he thrashed and choked, the torch smouldering on the ground.

Tamghat looked back, shrugged, and faced the tower again.

"So be it," he said. He dropped the reins to lie slack on the golden mare's neck and drew one of the long cords off his shoulders, wound it over the fingers of both hands, twisting and looping a pattern like a child's game of cat's cradle.

"What . . . ?" Kayugh started to ask.

Tamghat turned his hands palms out as if to push, the narrow ribbon dipping slack. Then he snapped his hands apart, the ribbon breaking, flying free . . .

"Down!" Otokas screamed, howled, and seized Kayugh's wrist, jerking her for the stairs from the bell-tower roof as the abandoned jade lion swayed, tipped—tumbled. "Run!"

With the shock of an avalanche mowing trees before it, the gates blew in, timbers and stone cutting a swathe through the sisters in the Outer Court. The archers pelted after Otokas and Kayugh as the stairs twisted, tilted beneath their feet, and the gatehouse collapsed in a choking cloud of plaster, a wounded jangle of the bells. Women tumbled down around them, shaky, ghost-white with dust. Otokas stumbled, sick, the Blackdog's senses overwhelmed with the stench of broken bodies, the cries. In the Old Chapel, the goddess was screaming, high and shrill in his head, and the Blackdog gathered itself into the world.

"Don't!" Kayugh snapped, shaking him, and he snarled at her, crouched on blood-slick stones. Forced the dog away, trying to understand what she said, hardly able to listen. "Get her away, Oto! If it's true, what you said, what she saw he means to do, get her away!"

He flung himself up, sword in hand, focused not on her but on Tamghat, urging his horse to pick its way over the precarious rubble of the gatehouse, dainty as a cat. The warriors of his guard followed, blades bare. The warlord held up a hand and, unwillingly, the sisters hesitated, each one caught in a moment's anticipation, spears raised, swords drawn, or broken stones in hand. Even the dying were silent, the space of a breath.

"*Attalissa*, Sisters, and you, Blackdog. To save yourselves, and your kinsfolk in the town—send for Attalissa. Bring her to me."

Otokas took a step and was jerked back by Kayugh's hand in his hair. His helmet was lost in the tumble down the stairs.

"Can you kill him?" she whispered angrily.

"I'll find out," he muttered.

"Die here, and you leave her to be defended by a damned raider, since the dog won't take women. Or you die. *Both* of you, Oto. He's a god!"

He shook his head. "No." Not quite.

"Go!"

The strong reek of gathered magic was gone, to the dog's nose, and the grey and the gloss of a fevered sweat more pronounced on Tamghat's skin. He might not want to knock down another wall right away, but the red fire still lurked behind his eyes. He was more than the Blackdog could overcome. The dog recognized it, was willing to let Otokas think clear-headed and single-minded for a moment. But waiting, still, to kill anything that moved against the goddess.

Someone among the wounded was weeping, a grating, heart-wrenching sound, and another whimpered, "Mama, mama, mama . . ." over and over without pause. Most kept silent, as if the wizard held them, stifling the moaning and the screams, denying them that freedom in their dying.

"I'm sorry." Otokas turned Kayugh's face, kissed her on the lips, lingering the space of a heartbeat, no more. "I'll see you," he said softly, "soon enough, I expect." And, loud enough for the surviving sisters from the gatehouse to hear, "The horse is a mare. I told you." He heard the deep breaths, the faint settling shuffle, weapons taken in surer grip.

He walked, not looking back, between the living and the dead. Perhaps Tamghat was simply waiting for him to hail those beyond to open the narrow door in the thick wall between Outer and Inner Court, waiting for it to be opened. He ran the last few steps, letting the

Blackdog take him at last, a moment of burning, breaking, a blackness flowing up and over the wall, Kayugh's voice already raised, no orders, just the cry, "*Attalissa!*" taken up by a few-score throats, and the sudden clash of steel.

The dormitory of six older sisters guarding the door of the Inner Court scattered as he came down, spun past them, and headed inside. The Blackdog had no human voice, and he had nothing to tell them. He ran four-footed through corridors and stairways deserted. They were praying in the New Chapel, singing hymns. He heard Old Lady's voice among them. No arguing with her, then, just as well. More stairs. He skidded on the smooth-worn stone outside the heavy door of the Old Chapel, barked, the dog's temper frayed past sense and the door closed and locked. He pulled himself back to Otokas, lifting a hand to beat on it and stumbling in as Meeray jerked it open.

Attalissa flung herself on him, a warm, fragile, shivering weight that clung when he picked her up as though to let go meant her death. Practical Meeray had changed her from her ceremonial robe; she wore a plain, full-skirted dress of black wool over red woollen leggings now.

"I was about to send for you," Meeray said. "She's . . . it was worse when she *stopped* screaming. What's going on out there? Are they attacking the gates?"

He shook his head, setting the goddess down again. She gripped his hand hard enough to hurt and said nothing.

"We can't hold out. The warlord's a wizard, stronger than a demon and vicious as a devil. The gatehouse, the bell-tower—gone."

"What do you mean?"

"Gone. Smashed." He gestured with a free hand. "Like that. The tower fell."

"But how—"

"Meeray. Listen. He's more than a wizard, I don't know what. He wants the goddess. She knew it, she was right. I have to get her away till she's come into her strength. Kayugh—they'll buy some time, out there. That's all we can do."

"But 'Lissa can't leave the lake. Where can you hide her?"

"That's my problem."

"And how do you expect to get her away, if they're fighting at the gate? The water-gate's under attack as well, and barely holding. No chance of making a sally there. One of the girls came here a little while ago, checking to see if we had any arrows."

Otokas gave Meeray a crooked smile. "The Old Chapel is *very* old. We were at war with the Narvabarkashi, not long after the first temple was built, and the goddess made a way into the lake, one that Narva and his priests couldn't watch. So there's a way out from here, for the goddess and me, at least. Move the altar."

"Narvabarkash has three yaks and a lame rooster."

"That's about all we had then, too. I said old. Come on, help me." The dog slipped a growl, too much, too much fear and anger and the world falling around him.

With his shoulder and those of several sisters against it, the altar slid, grating, over the floor, pivoting on one corner. It was wood sheathed in beaten brass, and time he replaced the rotting corner posts of its frame again, before it collapsed in on itself and spilled the bowl of sacred water that sat there.

No one had reached to move the bowl, which was carved of some coarse, dull-black stone and was always beaded with moisture, no matter the temperature of the air around it. No one ever touched it but the goddess herself, and the water in it never needed refilling. The bowl's lip curved in like the petals of some night-curled flower, but that was not enough to keep it from evaporating. An ancient mystery of Attalissa, and one that even the Blackdog, an ancient mystery himself, preferred not to pry into. The bowl gave off a chill of its own, left you feeling cold, and lost. Women called it the dampness of the chapel that made them uncomfortable there, and built a new one, but in their unseen hearts they knew it was the stone bowl on the altar they avoided.

'Lissa—

Yes. Don't leave it here for him. Take it down to the lake. It's too heavy for me to carry.

44

That was not right; the lake was not the place for it. The dog was reluctant. But the Blackdog would not argue with the goddess, when it was her own mysteries she dealt with.

But for a moment, with almost a sense of relief, he saw the bowl slipping in his grasp, shattering on the stones, spilling out its water . . .

That hit him in his very bones. He shook his head, confused at his own imaginings. *No. I shouldn't touch it.*

"You'll have to, Oto," Attalissa said simply. "I trust you. Don't drop it. It's important."

"If you say so."

The hole beneath the altar was narrow, lightless, and a damp, chilly air rose from it. Meeray crouched to peer down.

"That explains why the altar's always so cold and sticky," she said, with false cheer. "I always thought it strange, that mildew would grow on brass. Where does it go?"

"To the southern shore, under the overhang where the split pine grows. You know that deep crack there, that we're always telling the novices to watch they don't break a leg in? It runs under that, where it comes out to the lake. It was meant as a way for the dog to come and go unseen from the temple."

And the dog had killed the priests of Narva, who were strangling Lissavakail's trade, sending fighters to kill traders on the road down to the desert. It had been a ruthless age, and Attalissa . . . harder. The god Narva kept to his mountaintop, now. His folk still sent a tithe of their turquoise to the temple every year, and Attalissa's priestesses kept the slopes of the Narvabarkash free from bandits and raiders, protecting Narva's folk like their own, even the priests, who had dwindled away to a family of half-mad farmers.

Narva himself would be no help to them; his great vision that had once spanned the mountains almost to the foothills had been long since destroyed, for Lissavakail's safety. He kept disembodied to his cave, and spoke in oracles, when he spoke at all; most believed him dead and gone.

Meeray frowned at the dank hole. "Should we follow?"

Otokas shook his head. "You'd drown. It drops below the level of the lake for longer than you could hold your breath, before it rises again. It's meant as a trap. I'm sorry. Once we're gone, slide the altar back. Then go."

"Go where?" Meeray asked. "The main gates?"

Otokas hesitated. But the women at the main gates were lost and from the report Meeray had, those at the water-gate as well. Sending a handful more to die with them would not slow Tamghat any, even if the wizard were temporarily exhausted of magic. He should have sent his niece away before the attack began. They should have sent all the young women, so that there would be a temple for the goddess to come back to. His sister had never wanted Attavaia to go to the sisters anyway.

"Over the walls, wherever you can. Attalissa will come back. You know that. When she's able, she'll come back. And she'll need her women then."

"The longer we hold here, the more time you have to get her away," Meeray said. "Don't waste it. Go on." She dropped to her knees, took the girl's hands. "Remember us."

Attalissa gravely kissed her forehead, looked around at the other women.

"I bless you," she said. Her voice trembled, and she scrubbed the back of a hand across her eyes. "Oto . . ."

He had to grit his teeth as he picked up the stone bowl. It was surprisingly light, but dank, like handling a dead thing. The water within seemed to move with its own life, against the expected balance as he crooked it in his arm.

"Keep her safe," Meeray said, and the other women spoke too, reaching hands to touch the girl as she followed him, clinging tightly to his free hand, down the steep steps beneath the altar.

Ten steps down, and then the heavy altar ground over them again, cutting off all sound from above and plunging them into a darkness so absolute it was impossible to tell if his eyes were open or shut. Even the Blackdog was blind. But there were no wrong turns to take; the only danger was slipping on the unevenly carved steps.

Where are we going, dog? I can't leave the lake.

You're going to have to. We'll hide . . . somewhere . . . till you're grown and can drive the wizard out.

What about the sisters?

They'll follow, if they can.

Don't lie to me, dog.

He smelt the water before his foot splashed into it.

"What do I do with the bowl? I don't want to take it with us." Wherever they were going.

"Set it in the water," she said faintly. "Let the lake run into it. What it holds won't be harmed, won't mix with the lake water. Just so it's in the lake, and he can't see it."

"What is it?" He was reluctant to ask. She was no demon, to keep her heart hidden, but it felt like . . . something heavy, with potential, with force.

"Something old and best forgotten," she said. "Something from the earliest days of the temple. But I still have to keep it safe. Put the bowl down, dog. In the water."

Otokas did so. He was just as glad to let it go. The rough stone seemed to burn, now, even through his heavy sleeve, even through the bronze armour. And he didn't like to hear the child's voice sounding so . . . ancient. She could not carry the full burden of the goddess yet, and should not have to.

"Let me go ahead."

Attalissa hung back obediently as he went forward. The steps ended, but stone underfoot continued to slope steeply away, until he was waist-deep and could stretch out to swim. It was true, he could swim easily in armour. The goddess's waters held him, carried him. He could not drown, no more than could a fish. His reaching hand touched the lowering roof and he ducked under, let touch and ancient memory guide him down into the narrow, water-filled tunnel, which twisted and dropped and twisted again, following a tangle of jagged fissures and eroded natural tunnels, widened and made passable, cut by one of the earliest Blackdogs. It was standing water, refreshed when the lake rose up with spring flooding or autumn rains; it was the water of the Lissavakail nonetheless, and washed through him like the fires of life, burning out weariness and fear. No need to breathe.

They came up, having passed under half the holy islet, in a natural crack so narrow his shoulders scraped the sides, though the walls rose twenty yards overhead, narrowing to no more than six or eight inches wide. Attalissa followed close on his heels as they climbed over broken stone, dead shells crunching under their feet. A star or two shone down through the heath and bramble tangle that overgrew the fissure. Ahead, the crack broadened out, and the lake was a pale shimmer.

Otokas hesitated on the water's edge, looking up and down the shore, smelling humans somewhere near, and smouldering pitch, but Attalissa pushed past him. She gave a little sigh as the wavelets broke caressingly around her knees, pulling her out like gentle hands.

Light flared on the water from above, and voices shouted. Arrows hissed into the lake around them.

Attalissa dove.

Sword in hand, Otokas spun to face the raiders sliding down the sloping rock face by the crack. A watch posted and waiting. The wizard must have divined for hidden exits; no one had ever known of this but the goddess and her most senior servants.

Or they were betrayed. That was the dog's instinctive distrust of the world.

Head for the south shore! he ordered Attalissa, and then they were on him, half a dozen men and women, and another group caught from the corner of his eye, scrambling along the rocks. Two men pushed off in a light boat, shouting directions at one another, pursuing faint ripples that might only be the wind.

The first to close with him was a Grasslander woman, and he kicked her legs from under her, stabbed down as she struggled, on her back in the water and the stones beneath her slippery with algae. He blocked another's slashing stroke from the left and was struck from behind, a sword's edge turned by his armour but the blow drove him to a knee, waist-deep in the lake. Too many of them for the man alone to fight. He dropped his sword and let the Blackdog take him.

A moment of searing pain as the dog tore fully through into the world, flesh and bone and fury. A man screamed and gurgled and kicked the water to a froth, throat bitten through. He crushed another's thighbone in his jaws, flung that one into deeper water to drown like a pup throwing a rat. It was a nightmare, one that haunted his sleep, memories of past lives: the taste of blood, the softness of muscle and the crack of bone, of steel as he bit through a blade he disdained to dodge, the eager joy in the enemies' screams.

They hurt him, cut him, burned him while they still had torches, but the Blackdog was spirit and could not die so easily, and the man would heal from most wounds. Otokas did not care if he did not, once he had let the Blackdog loose. He lived, and died, to protect Attalissa. There were twelve dead in the water and at the water's edge and two on shore who ran. He bounded after the slowest, ran him down, snapping through the rings of his byrnie to throw him by his shoulder, tearing his arm half off, a second bite through his windpipe and he raced after the last. She still carried a spear and as he leapt she turned and hurled it. It took him under a foreleg in an earlier stab-wound already half-closed, and he stumbled, rolled, shattered the hampering spear-shaft with teeth that could break stone and steel, and bit through her throat.

The boat still cut through the water, chasing phantoms of moonlight and wave. Attalissa would be deep, below any reach of their sight or weapons. One stood in the bow, arms full of fishing net. He pitched overboard when the Blackdog rose from the water, a hound the size of a yearling yak swarming into the boat, nearly swamping it, and went down struggling in his tangled cords. The other screamed, tried to lift an oar from its tholepin to use as a weapon, and choked in his own blood, throat crushed and torn.

All of them. Safe. He could rejoin the goddess. They would not be followed, for a little while.

Blood seeped sluggishly around the spearhead and he licked it, tasting it. Warm, salt, human.

For Otokas, it was a killing blow, beyond any power of the spirit's to heal. He knew. The Blackdog host had died in battle before, more than once, and once by treachery, and many times more an easy, gentle death in his bed, an old man in whom the Blackdog could no longer maintain health and strength. Death was easy. It was leaving Attalissa's care to another that was hard. But the dog could keep life in him a while longer, if he did not return to his own body yet. The Blackdog slid back into the water and swam, beneath the surface like an otter, after his goddess.

The boat, half-filled with water and riding low, bobbed behind him, and a rising wave climbed the top strake. It settled lower, filled, and sank, pulling down the raider's body with it. On the holy islet, flames rose from the kitchen roof.

CHAPTER IV

T he roar of falling stones still echoed in Attavaia's ears. A pillar of dust and smoke climbed over the western end of the temple, visible as a reddish cloud, holding the glare of fire. Crouched on the roof near the Inner Court, she had seen women suddenly flee the bell-tower, her uncle and Spear Lady leading them, and the tower crumbling in on itself, the gates hurled across the Outer Court, mowing down her sisters. She had bitten, hard, on a hand jammed into her mouth, not to scream. As the warlord rode in, Otokas had gone, no doubt to the goddess, vaulting the gate to the Inner Court, a shadow blacker than night. He never saw her there on the roof, though he of all of them would have been able to. The warlord—wizard, all too clearly—shouted something, raised a hand, but the dog was gone by then and the surviving sisters charged. She saw Spear Lady caught in torchlight a moment, lost her in the roar and the darkness and the raider army rolling in like the leading edge of an avalanche.

Jump down, run along the top of the Inner Court wall, join them, for all the good one more sword would do. For a moment it seemed right, as though that one sword might tip the balance, or perhaps because it would be easier to die here, now, than later.

She had orders. Attavaia turned away and crawled up the gentle slope of tiles to the flat roof, caught a higher eave and heaved herself up, and so over the jumble of interlocking roofs she had learned as a novice, sneaking out for sins no worse than unlawful feasts by moonlight and rooftop games of It, played on silent, heart-pounding tiptoe.

It was amazing no one had been killed, or even broken an ankle. It was amazing no one had been caught, as though all the old sisters forgot, once their novitiates were over, what they had once done.

Or it was winked at, if the girls did not make their breaking of rules too obvious, because the stealthy exploration and the nighttime frantic scrambles were training.

Sister Chanalugh had not asked her if she could find a way over the roofs to see what was happening at the western gate. She had just said, *Go.* There was no other way to see; once there were no more arrows left in the armoury, the outward-opening door behind those in the Lower East Court had been barricaded within as a further line of defence, at Sister Chitora's orders.

Attavaia slid at the last, knocking tiles loose, clumsy with more than weariness. They shattered on the pavement hard on her hissed warning, and she caught the eaves and hung a moment before she dropped, a firm hand catching her, steadying—Sister Chanalugh, who had charge of the water-gate defence now that Sister Chitora was lying insensible. A brazier glowed on the paving stones, shedding a little light, and someone was making tea.

Attavaia laughed and gulped and bit her lip before it turned into something Sister Chanalugh would call hysterics.

"The raiders are in the Outer Court and almost everyone's dead," she reported in a whisper. "I saw it—the warlord made the tower fall and the gates flew across the court. It was like a scythe mowing hay. They just . . ." She tipped a hand. "And then the raiders poured over the rubble. Uncle— the Blackdog's gone to the goddess. He couldn't stop that wizard. If he could have, it'd be over now. What are we going to do, Sister? They'll be into the Inner Court by now." She rubbed a sleeve across her face. There was blood on it. Sister Chitora's. Attavaia had helped carry her down from the wall.

"Hold the water-gate, as Spear Lady ordered," Chanalugh said.

"Until when? They're in the temple! Spear Lady's probably dead by now!" Attavaia's voice rose and Chanalugh gave her a shake. Others turned, the damage done, even faces atop the squat water-gate tower showing pale down into the court a moment.

Someone pressed a cup of milky tea into her hands; there was even a pitcher of fresh yak's-milk out here.

Well, they needed their strength; it was no foolish indulgence. Too hot, too sweet, and she gulped it down, scalding her mouth.

Her hands were shaking.

"We heard the tower falling," offered a girl belonging to her own dormitory, her childhood friend and neighbour Sister Enneas. "Like thunder."

"We defend the goddess," Sister Chanalugh said firmly. "So long as we can." She turned and stalked off, a tall, ungainly body, gift of a foreign father. They called her Sister Stork, behind her back.

"And then what?" someone asked, off in the darkness.

"Then we die," muttered Enneas. "'Vaia, did you hear, did Attalissa really say this warlord was a wizard come to eat her?"

That rumour, and worse, had been running through them as they carried sheaves of arrows from the armoury, met other girls wide-eyed and edgy in the passages on their own urgent errands.

"I don't know."

"Did the Blackdog say? He would have told you."

"He told me—"

A shout, a burst of light. Someone had lobbed a jar of burning pitch up over the wall, shattering on the stones, spraying fire. A sister shouted, spattered with it, but mostly on the bronze scales of her armour, a little on the cloth below the short metalled sleeves, quickly beaten out.

Nothing followed it. They grew bored, outside, and wasted what must have been meant for making torches.

Attavaia climbed the narrow stairs to the tower roof, looked down. The foreign mercenaries seemed in no great urgency. They clustered not right at the gate, but further down the steep climbing path, and a handful on the lakeshore. They had a boat, but there were no longer any scaling-ladders in it. Till Sister Chanalugh had sent her scouting over the roofs, she had thought that despite the horrible losses they had suffered here at the water-gate, they would win. The raiders had nearly come over the walls, and had been driven off. Their bodies, and those of sisters, too, littered the ground at the wall's foot. Many had slid and bounced all the way down. It was not quite a cliff here, but there was no straight way up.

The raiders were fewer in number than they had been when they retreated from the wall, fewer even than there had been after she had fired what was their last arrow and watched a woman fall and counted, *Six*. She had taken six lives. She wondered how many Rideen had claimed, before they killed him at the town bridge. They would have killed him; her brother would not have run. Perhaps he and she would meet on the long road to the land of the Old Great Gods and compare their tallies.

Most of the attackers here must have been summoned off to some other duty, and these remaining were counted enough to keep anyone from escaping this way.

The temple's boats had gone with the lay-servants, the novices, and the old who could be persuaded to go, before the raiders had come to pen them in. Some might still be on the lake, depending on where they sought to land.

A strong swimmer could make the southern shore. She had done it twice, once to prove to herself she could, once to win a bet with Enneas. Best to start from the southern tip of the islet, though.

"They'll wait till dawn," Sister Chanalugh said softly at her side. "Have your dormitory collect all those tiles you broke. Knock down some more, and bring them up here. It'll slow the godless bastards down a little, anyway."

"Yes, Sister." Attavaia went obediently to collect Enneas and the others. Only four of them, of the six who had shared a room last night. The attackers had plenty of arrows, but the worst had been when the mercenaries came swarming up the ladders onto the walls. They only tried it once.

As though the water-gate didn't really matter.

"We're going to throw broken shards at them," Enneas repeated. "That'll send them running, I expect."

An older sister cuffed her ear. "None of that. Attalissa is our strength."

Attalissa is a timid little girl, Attavaia thought. She wondered if her uncle had these thoughts, which gnawed away at faith. Surely he couldn't; he was the Blackdog; he shared Attalissa's holiness. But sometimes . . . she wondered. She'd seen him wink at the goddess herself, during prayers, and once when he had taken her fishing with the goddess she had heard him tell the child, the great lady of the lake, that if she was going to fish she had to learn to bait her own hooks. Old Lady would have called it irreverence, or worse.

"We're going to die," Enneas whispered in her ear, as they stacked broken tiles for the others to carry up over the gate. "What can Attalissa do?"

Attavaia kept silent. Treachery, desertion. Had Uncle really meant that? Did he just want to save her life at any cost of honour, having no children of his own?

No. He would do anything to save the goddess, he had no choice in that. He would not ask his niece to dirty her soul with dishonour— if he told her to do it, he had his reasons, and they were right. If the Blackdog could not fight the wizard alone, the Blackdog would not wait around for the wizard to take the goddess from him. So neither her uncle nor the goddess was still in the temple they defended.

Turning this thought over, wondering if she was supposed to pass it on to Sister Chanalugh and how, Attavaia asked Enneas to give her a boost to the roof, to knock down more tiles.

"The door!" someone screamed beyond it, and, "Chitora! They're here!"

Inside, someone did not know Sister Chitora was beyond hearing. A woman's scream, short and terrible, and the thud and thump and dragging of the makeshift barricade being shoved aside.

Attavaia snatched back a shard of tile from the sister about to take it up to the wall and wedged it under the door as it began to push open, throwing her shoulder against it, feet sliding. But the tile caught that slightly tilted stone that everyone always stubbed their toes on and the door, for a moment, stuck.

"Sister Chanalugh!" she screamed. "Raiders inside!"

Enneas was jamming whatever she could find under the door and into the crack of its hinged edge: more broken tile, a spearhead snapped from its shaft in the battle atop the wall. The door thudded and jumped. Others ran to throw on their weight with Attavaia's, but tile ground and broke and they all slid.

"To the tower!" Sister Chanalugh screamed. "Now!"

Some of the women ran for the stairs. Some stayed to carry the wounded. The door shoved at them and those still pushing on it fell in a tangle. One girl never rose, as the first raider through reversed his grip on his sword and stabbed down, two-handed, into her chest, hammering between the joins of the overlapping scales. Attavaia screamed, wordless noise and outrage, and swung her blade, his right arm, a thing falling, dead and bloody meat like a joint severed for dinner, the sheep carcass hanging from a hook in the back shed . . . The man staggered to his knees, face an ugly, gaping mask, mouth open, eyes unholy sky-blue wells, and she kicked him as his other hand groped blind and clumsy for her, instinct more than thought as she half-severed his neck, and what thought she had was only, *Clumsy, slow, weak*, she should have taken his head off. But there were more, pushing after him.

"Come on!" Attavaia and Enneas were the last, dragging one another up, running. Attavaia kicked over the brazier, scattering burning charcoal that glowed scarlet as it tumbled, but it was no real hazard to the men and women rushing through. Enneas fell again with a grunt. Attavaia caught her hand and hauled her up, and still clutching one another they made the stairs and the small belfry and watch-room over the water-gate. The door slammed behind them.

The raiders did not immediately pursue. They went to loosen the bars of the gate.

Sister Chanalugh came clattering down the narrow stairway from the tower roof.

Someone had grabbed the iron teakettle and carried it along. Now that woman reached through the narrow window in the wall and poured hot tea down over the raiders below, which annoyed them, and then released the kettle, which dropped a man, possibly for good.

"What have we got left?" Chanalugh demanded.

"Nothing," was the answer, "except those broken tiles the girls took up to the roof."

Shards of tile sailed past the window with the speaker's words, those on the roof doing what they could to delay those opening the gate.

The belfry was small and cramped. Without discussion they abandoned it, the first panic over, and went up to the roof, keeping safe behind the parapet. The bell was too heavy to manhandle up as a missile.

Attavaia watched a Grasslander woman with a scarred face crouch over Sister Chitora lying down in the court, feeling for a pulse. A man with the same slanting scars stood nearby with a torch. The woman carefully cut the priestess's throat. The others left behind, dead and dying, were treated similarly.

One of the older sisters wept.

"None of that," Sister Chanalugh said. "If we die for Attalissa, we die gladly."

"Better to live for her," Attavaia said. She had meant it as a low mutter for Enneas, but in the quiet of the roof, Chanalugh heard.

"Doesn't seem likely," the senior sister said pragmatically. "Looks like the whole temple's theirs."

Below them, the bars were dragged back and the narrow gate pulled open.

"Hey!" a raider shouted to his fellows below, some accent making the words near-incomprehensible, "Up here, you lazy bastards! Leaving us to do your work for you."

"Well." Chanalugh took off her helmet, scratched her head, and sighed, resettling it. "We'll hold them off while we can and make our goddess proud in our deaths."

The senior sister seemed so calm about it. Attavaia wondered if Rideen had known he was going to die, or if it had just happened. She wondered if Attalissa could feel them all dying. If it would matter, when the goddess came again in her strength and glory, that they had fought so long before the end.

"Sister," she said, "my uncle told me that when the temple was lost, we should get away and hide in the mountains. He told me Attalissa would need us when she came back."

"She's probably dead, Sister," Chanalugh said. "She's likely not even conceived yet. There'll be other sisters to take our place in serving her, when she returns."

"No, there won't," Enneas said suddenly. "Not if that wizard kills us all and destroys the temple. What will she have to come back to then?"

"She isn't dead," Attavaia said, and hoped it sounded like faith in the goddess, not in the man who used to carry her on his shoulders when she was small. "The Blackdog took her to safety. She'll be back, once she's a woman. And he told me it wasn't running away. He told me she will need us. We need to be here when she comes back."

"Fine if you can fly," Chanalugh said. "Personally, I can't, stork or no." Even there, even then, there was a sort of horrified holding of breath, and then a few giggles. "The stair's too narrow for more than one at a time to come at us here, so at least we can make them pay for every one that's died at this gate yet, before they get us all."

"We can go along the wall and down into the rough ground by the south corner," Attavaia persisted. "Into the lake. Swim to shore."

Chanalugh turned and looked at her, and her stomach clenched. *Coward, faithless traitor.* Chanalugh had hard eyes.

"You think you can get along the top of the wall without being seen? They've got a lot of light down there."

"We can try. If we're going to die tonight it doesn't matter where."

"True enough. Right, then. Go."

She felt dizzy, tensed for argument. "Sister?"

"Anyone who's fit to, go. The water's cold, and it's not the shortest swim. Anyone who's just going to die in the lake can stay and die here. We'll give them something to think about, so they don't notice the shadows on the wall."

Below, the raiders were making leisurely preparations to take the tower, clustered close, looking up. Reluctant to be the first.

"Sister—"

But Sister Chanalugh turned her back, making a quick count, muttering under her breath. Attavaia did the same, without the muttering. Seventeen left, of all who had defended the water-gate. So few.

Quick interrogation by Chanalugh gave them five to stay, all with wounds that would weaken them in the lake, except for Sister Chanalugh herself. Twelve to go.

"But you're unhurt," Attavaia protested. "And we could help the wounded, support them in the water. If we all just go quickly, now, we'll be gone before they realize there's no one here."

"Sister Chitora was ordered to hold the water-gate, and I'm her deputy," Chanalugh said. "And I've got no orders otherwise from the Blackdog or anyone else. And you know how cold water will eat your strength; you can't be hampered with the wounded. No, we don't jeopardize your lives. We stay, and you have that much better a chance. Now quickly, as you say. And quietly. And make sure you are here, when Attalissa returns, whether it's five years from now or fifteen. Sisters, you follow Attavaia now, since she's the one with the Blackdog's word."

"But I'm not—"

Chanalugh saluted her, fist over heart. "The Blackdog's word is the word of Attalissa's servant, and the will of the goddess."

And Sister Chanalugh might have been deathly serious, or mocking her to stop her crying. Attavaia didn't know, and returned the salute, swallowing hard.

There was no time for any lingering farewell. A few quick kisses between the more demonstrative sisters, a touched hand. Attavaia and Enneas both hugged Orissa, a girl they'd grown up with, shared all those unlawful feasts and rooftop games with. She'd taken the thrust of a spear in her thigh on the wall.

"Now for some noise," Sister Chanalugh said cheerfully. "Attalissa go with you, and the Old Great Gods."

She gathered broken tiles, began pitching them down into the court, aiming at the torch-bearers, screaming, "Godless bastards, child-killers! The Old Great Gods damn your souls to the cold hells! Your mothers curse your names!"

59

The others who were to remain joined in the abuse, making every sharp-edged fragment count. The raiders began screaming fouler insults, setting arrows to bows. The twelve followed Attavaia down the few steep steps to the wall, which had a low outer parapet but no inner. They crawled on hands and knees against that shielding edge, darkness in darkness.

Attavaia looked back once. Raiders at the foot of the stairs, some with Northron round wooden shields raised high, beginning a methodical climb up.

"Like the sun on the water rises our lady . . ." Chanalugh's rich voice rose in a hymn. Other voices joined hers. "Come on up, then, you murdering bastards, or are you waiting for us to die of old age?"

CHAPTER V

The first pale light of dawn flowed cold and clear over the eastern peaks in advance of the sun, and roosters crowed as though the morning was welcome. The air was harsh in the lungs; smoke rolled ashore on a northerly breeze off the water.

The Blackdog and Attalissa huddled together under the eaves of an abandoned goatshed. The girl had her arm over the dog's shoulders. Every so often she lost her battle for self-possession and gulped on a sob, tears leaking, tracing wet tracks down a face grubby from a scramble up the steep shore to this shadowed shelter at the roadside.

Otokas could go no further. Despite all the dog's will, the man faded, carrying the dog's wounds even in whatever state he existed when the dog was their physical form in the world.

A panicked trickle of people passed them, those who had reached boats to flee the island or who lived in the scattered steadings along the lakeshore. They carried whatever they had been able to snatch up, cloth-shrouded bundles or overflowing reed baskets. Some rode shaggy ponies, or yaks. Many drove a few yaks or sheep and goats before them, or carried squawking baskets of fowl.

Most were making for the rough tracks to the high summer pastures, though the alpine grazing would hardly be greening and snow could linger on the northern slopes for weeks yet. Hardly any continued on towards the eastern end of the lake, the road that climbed down to Serakallash and the Red Desert, or the trail that rose from that road to high Narvabarkash. The people of the mountains were reluctant to leave their own valleys whatever fate of flood or rock or war overtook them.

Some glanced at the girl and went on, too lost in their own terror to spare thought for any other. She was only a wet, dirty, lost child, clinging to a wounded dog that was now merely the size of the big guard-dogs for the herds, noticeable but not remarkable. A young man cursed them when the yaks he drove bellowed and swerved aside. An old woman perched amid bundles on a sway-backed pony shouted, "Hurry, child, before the raiders come," but she did not rein in or look back once she had passed. The dogs among the fleeing scurried by, tails clamped low.

They were none of them fit to carry the Blackdog, not while Otokas had breath left, and choice.

We have to hide, Oto, Attalissa said, but the coherent shape of the thought was nearly swamped in the child's terror. She had hardly been off the holy islet since the day he and Old Lady and the sister who had been Spear Lady before Kayugh carried her there, a little, week-old baby.

Go to her birth family, up in a distant tributary village? They had been well paid for the honour they endured, bearing a daughter who was no daughter. They had not seen 'Lissa since she had been weaned and the proud mother sent back to her family and her six elder children. The woman had died a few years later, Otokas remembered, in an eighth or ninth pregnancy. The father had been poor, the village yakherd, wealthier now with the temple's gift, but still a yakherd. No warrior. A suddenly returned young girl, call her niece or cousin, would hardly go unnoticed even among his flock of children, especially when all his village knew the goddess had chosen him for her fathering.

"Oto?"

He had not answered the girl, found himself lying down across her feet without willing to do so. Even the dog weakened, as the man's soul ebbed.

"Oto! Dog, don't die, you can't die. I won't let you."

Hush, love. The Blackdog will never leave you. I'll always be with you.

"I want *you*, Otokas!"

A family hurried past the shed, father, heavily pregnant mother, sour-faced old man, four children, all carrying bundles. The father slowed, looked back. "Are you alone, child? Did you get separated from your mama? You'd better come with us. The goddess only knows how long those brutes will stay busy in the town." He held out a hand.

Attalissa buried her face in the dog's heavy ruff, crying, "No! No!"

He was an unhappy man, a fisherman who loved his children with a worried, remote love that stumbled at showing itself. He felt only weary tolerance of his ever-unsatisfied wife, greater loathing of her venom-tongued father. He planned to go up to his wife's family's summer grazing hut, no further, come back down as soon as the warlord had settled into some firmer control of the town and his bandits. What choice had he? His living was the water and his boat. A weak-souled man, and no fighter, either.

Otokas was cold and weary, and even the dog's body hurt. When it could no longer hold him in life he would die, and it would take what host it could find, any man near, willing or no, and break him to its will if it had to, for Attalissa's sake. But that was not a fate he would wish on even a raider, and a man so taken could prove a poor guardian for a child—for the short time such an unwilling host would survive, before madness ate his mind away and death took him in turn.

The fisherman might be the best Attalissa could hope for, for now.

But the man had already shrugged and hurried on after his family.

Not worthy. None of them had been worthy of Attalissa's trust and love. Not one had stopped with any real will to help the child, no one had cared anything for a lost human girl, and if they could not care for an abandoned child, what right had they to say they loved their goddess?

Then there was no one at all, until a young man clattered past on a dun stallion, a tall, fine-boned beast with a swallow's grace, desert-bred.

"Damn!"

The man cursed and circled back to the girl and the dog. No local man; he was from one of the tribes of the Western Grass, the dry hills west of the deserts, beyond the great river, the Kinsai-av. His beardless, broad-cheekboned face and arms were dark with interlacing tattoos, twisting and knotted cats and birds and serpents, black and blue. Dark-brown hair swung over his shoulders in dozens of fine braids, each knotted with red yarn, and he wore a sabre at his side. The small buckler slung at his back was newly scored and notched, and fresh blood stained his leather jerkin.

The Blackdog snarled, Otokas seeing threat there, thinking *raider*, lurching to his feet. Attalissa stood up too, a hand fisted in his fur.

"Come on, little sister," the man said. "You can't stay here alone. Give me your hand." He eyed the Blackdog warily. "Sayan bless the beast, he must have fought well for you, but he's dying. You can't stay here with him."

Attalissa stared up at him, wide-eyed. He grabbed for her over the dog's back, but Otokas spun fast as a striking snake and seized his arm. And held him, only held him, teeth never breaking the skin. The man froze, and the horse laid back its ears. Attalissa stood on the toes of her bare feet, supporting herself on the dog, and stretched to touch the man's leaning face.

"He's not a raider," she said. *Let him go, Oto. He doesn't mean to hurt me.*

Otokas released him. No, no malice in the man's sudden grab, just practical haste, to carry the child off to some greater safety than a crumbling shed and a dying dog.

He was foreign, a Westgrasslander, a traveller but not, from the look of him, a godless and rootless man. And a warrior. Otokas let the Blackdog's awareness slip into the stranger, intruding deeply on unguarded mind and memory.

The man stayed where he was, swaying slightly in the saddle, his green-flecked hazel eyes gone wide, pupils swallowing them black.

He was Holla-Sayan, of the tribe who farmed among the folded hills of the god Sayan, the Sayanbarkash. He had been a restless youth, mid-most in a family of five brothers. The folk of the Western Grass were not nomads like those of the Great Grass in the north, but they did not build towns like the folk of the Desert Road or the Westrons. They linked their lives in extended families and tribes, lived in solitary homesteads rather than villages. They depended mostly on their sheep, but also planted wheat and rye, bred some horses, a few woolly, two-humped camels, and the blue-grey cattle they valued as much as draft animals as for their meat or milk. Their flocks meant more than their fields; they were always a few dry springs away from picking up and moving, still possessed of the nomad's ease with drifting.

Holla-Sayan had left to work as a mercenary, a guard with the caravans that tied the kingdoms of the north to the distant eastern lands. He had come up to Lissavakail the day before, while his caravan halted to rest a few days and water its beasts at Serakallash's oasis. He came looking for a woman, the weaver Timhine, but she was gone, her brother told him, scowling. She had married a man from a village in the higher valleys last autumn and gone, tired of breaking her heart over a homeless swordsman who never came by but a few days in the year. So Holla-Sayan had gone to Lissavakail's one wineshop instead, and settled in to getting drunk on the thin mountain beer. Imported wine was beyond his current means, since he had given all his wages from his last trip to his youngest brother, who wanted to marry.

But then the bronze bells of the temple began to ring.

Holla stood with the defenders until sometime in the darkness of the night, when it was clear the island town was lost. The raiders were no small band, intent on the most gain for the least loss. There was something unnatural in the way they pressed on, ignoring their own fallen. They made him think of the berserkers of Northron tales, or the drug-mad assassins of southern Pirakul's tiger cult: some band of obsessed devotees of a mad god. But they were of no one village or clan and could have no one god. Among them were brown- or olive-skinned, dark-haired folk, mountain men as well as tattooed men and women of the deserts and the Western Grass like himself, but their tattoos, the glimpses he had time to recognize, named them of several score disparate folk. Most were men and women of the Great Grass to the north of the deserts, a few of those with bear-masked helmets, bear's-tooth pendants, or ritual scars on their cheeks imitating the slash of a bear's claws, a new cult that had begun showing up among Grasslander travellers. A good few were tall, pale, prow-nosed Northrons with eyes like the sky, blue and cloud-grey, and a very few were gold-skinned Nabbani.

Whatever had brought them together, they were too many and too unrelenting to be overcome by Lissavakail's fishermen. There had been a handful of Attalissa's sisters among the defenders at first, but they had been singled out and cut down early on. No more had come from the temple, though among the militiamen there had been pleas and prayers cried out to the lake.

While the surviving Lissavakaili scattered to make separate stands or flights in the narrow streets, Holla-Sayan reclaimed his borrowed horse from the bear-masked Grasslander who was trying to steal it from the inn's fowl-yard, rode over the Grasslander's body into the lake, and swam ashore. It was not his town, they were not his people, and nobody was paying him to die for them. The best thing the people of Lissavakail could do would be to come to terms and pay the raiders off. Dying on the terraces of Lissavakail once it was lost did no one any good.

Holla waited out the rest of the night in the shelter of a walnut grove, wet, cold, and shivering. His coat, which had been bundled behind his saddle, was lost, as was his hat. A cut on his right forearm throbbed, wrapped in a cotton headscarf that had been meant as a gift for Timhine.

She was well out of it, at least.

Come the first lightening of the sky, Holla began to follow the winding trail along the steep southern shore of the lake, to work his way around to the east and the long, twisting track down to the foothills and the Red Desert in the north. There was no more direct route. The mountains of the Pillars of the Sky were savage, blade-edged towers, and offered few paths even to those bred to them; none he was fool enough to risk in the dark. There were still fires on the island, and the shouts and whoops of drunken raiders. The sooner he was out of the mountains, the better. He had no desire to find himself pressed into mercenary service for some bandit warlord.

But he could not ride on past the child.

Holla's anger at those who would ignore a crying child by the road was almost as great as that at the raiders, who had ruined a good bout of self-pity and slain honest folk in their own streets and homes and left him feeling half a coward, for leaving them—

—but anger seeped out of him now, and a thick, autumn-lake fog filled his mind, drowned him, turned everything cool and distant. He slid from the stallion and collapsed on the spring-damp earth.

Holla could hear voices, soft, urgent, whispering in his head.

You can't die! The girl crouched by the dog, which was larger than any sheepdog he had seen, and more wolf-like, though the head she wrapped in her arms was broader. Its flanks and muzzle were crossed with newly healed scars, but the stump of what looked like a spear-shaft was lodged under a foreleg, and blood soaked its black fur, puddled where it stood. Unnaturally yellow-green eyes, it had, too, unsettling even in this distant, floating dream. *You can't let Otokas die.*

The dog licked the girl's tear-streaked face.

I can't live with this. It's beyond my—the Blackdog's—healing. He'll look after you, this one. I know. The Blackdog always knows. So do you. Trust yourself.

"Dog, dog!" she wailed, her weeping silent no longer. And, "Otokas, no!"

It was not her voice, the girl's voice, in Holla's head, but one older and richer, a woman's voice. And the other . . .

It's a hard thing to ask of a lowland stranger, unprepared. Will you look after her? Guard her and love her and keep her safe, and bring her home to the lake when the time is right?

The dog's eyes were burning into his own, a yellow-green fire he distantly hoped was some nightmare dreaming.

Holla-Sayan found he could move, the fog in his mind clearing, and he rolled upright, squatted on his heels. Hesitantly, he put a hand on the dog's head.

"I know this story," he said, his voice unsteady. "I've heard . . . there is a demon dog guards the incarnate goddess here, and it possesses men."

The dog . . . laughed, maybe, hacking, and coughed blood on his boot.

Spirit. Not demon, Grasslander. There's a difference. When did a demon ever deign to serve any but the Old Great Gods themselves? My name's Otokas. The Blackdog.

"*She's* the goddess of the lake? *She's* Attalissa?"

The girl, all childish wounded dignity, scowled at him. "I am."

Please. The Blackdog spirit needs a human host.

Holla-Sayan lurched to his feet, a hand on the stallion's neck to support himself as the world heaved and tipped under him. "What, me? No! I'm not from Lissavakail. I'm not one of Attalissa's folk! I know my own god. I don't belong here."

She can't stay here. Tamghat—the warlord who leads the raiders—is no ordinary man. You didn't see him, I know. I did. I don't know what he is. Wizard, at least, and more. Nothing I could fight and survive.

"Then what do you expect me to do about him?"

Hide her. Protect her till she comes into her full strength, and can face Tamghat herself.

Run away. Ride away and leave the child to die at the hands of the raiders, or be sold into the Nabbani abomination of slavery, which tore a soul from its god and its place in the world?

No. He means to destroy her. Make her strength his own. Maybe . . . make himself a god in her place. I don't know. Something worse than mere death.

Something from a tale, but the dog sounded convinced of it.

"Stay out of my thoughts! I don't care. She's a goddess, she can fight her own battles."

Damn priest-ridden mountain folk. In the Four Deserts and the Western Grass, they did not clamour after their gods and goddesses so. The priests sapped the will of the deities, Holla had always thought, and made them weak and helpless as any city lord, too propped up by servants to ever stand on their own. Look at the Lady of Marakand, who had not been seen by her folk in a generation and left her Voice to rule the city unchecked.

It was not the goddess who would die, but the black-eyed child. She stared at him, a round, mountain-folk face, wet and tousled dark hair cropped at the level of her jaw, mountain fashion, hoops of gold in her ears. Black dress clinging to her, bare feet scratched. She did not look like any divine power.

"I'll take her with me, get her away from here," Holla-Sayan said. "That's all. You can't ask more than that."

She needs more than that.

"Sayan help me, no!" Holla said, and his voice was rough and ragged. "No. She's not my goddess. This isn't my place. I'll take her away for you, find a safe place for her until she's capable of driving that wizard out. Nothing more. Not that. You find one of her own folk for your cursed magic."

None stopped to help her, the Blackdog said. *They're not fit to carry the Blackdog's spirit.*

"There were plenty dying for her, in the town."

Dying for the town, I think, save the sisters. Besides, they're dead, or trapped. And they'd know less than I do of life beyond the mountains. 'Lissa needs you, Holla-Sayan of the Sayanbarkash. She can't hide in the mountains.

"No."

But you'll take her away?

"I'd do that anyway, damn you, if there were no one else to take her in. Sayan knows I couldn't leave a lone child here to die."

I'm dying. Nothing the dog can do can keep life in me any longer. The Blackdog must have a host.

"Then it can find one elsewhere, and hide and wait until she comes back. I'll keep her safe, and send her back when she's ready." Holla-Sayan put a hand on the dog's head again, made himself meet those unnerving eyes. "I'm sorry . . . Otokas? Otokas. I can't do anything more than that."

Go with him, 'Lissa, the dog said. *He's a good man. He'll look after you.*

The girl gulped a wordless sob.

Be brave, love.

Holla heaved the girl up to the dun stallion's back, surprised at how light she was. His hands were shaking. A caravan was no place for a child, but they were at least heading into the easier half of the route, from Serakallash up to At-Landi, leaving the true deserts behind. He might be able to find someone travelling across the white-water river, the Kinsai-av, who would deliver her to his family in the Sayanbarkash. Might talk the caravan-mistress Gaguush into letting him go himself. His mother had always wanted a daughter, and so far his brothers had given her only grandsons. She'd be overjoyed to take in this waif.

I'm sorry, Holla-Sayan. The Blackdog . . . not my will . . . does what it must. You'll understand.

As he turned back to it, the great dog rose into black fog, swift as an exhaled breath, and settled on him, tearing through his skin, his eyes, roaring like blood in the ears, burning like water in the lungs, fire in the heart. He screamed, fell, bit his tongue, choking on blood and bile. In mindless flailing he found a man's hand and seized it, clung, until he could breathe again, dragging at air through clenched teeth.

He did understand, Sayan help him, in the space of a heartbeat: a night's memories of horror and death. The man's love for the girl, the Blackdog's devotion to the goddess. The panic both felt at the goddess's uncomprehending certainty that Tamghat intended to devour her.

"It's all right, it's all right," a man was muttering. "It'll be all right, I'm sorry. You won't go mad. It won't kill you. You accept the dog. You must."

He could breathe, could see . . . shapes, blurred, the world turned sideways in growing light, a face. Could . . . smell, dizzyingly, water and weed and stone, blood and fire, and the dun stallion's frozen, sweating fear. Could hear waves, loud on stones, the girl's quick breath and the bubbling rasp of a man's, hear his own heart, the clatter as the horse backed a step, blowing through its nose.

Could feel the goddess, a warmth like the egg beneath a hen's breast, sun on the skin, but within his own heart. This was what it was like to carry a child, was the confused shape of his thought: women knew this.

The rough hand he gripped, cold, tightened on his own, then loosened to let him push himself up. Holla rubbed his face clean, frowning at the slurry of blood and dirt on the back of his hand.

70

Broken spear in the man's chest, the overlapping bronze squares twisted, torn. Otokas. He was soaking wet, black and slick with slow-oozing blood. He tried to push himself upright, crumpled, and Holla caught him, almost as weak, crouched there holding him, feeling the racing, staggering beat of his heart, chest to chest, feeling its faltering. He didn't know the face, round mountain-man's face with its earrings and fringe of black beard and shaggy-cropped hair, a crooked nose that had been broken once. Just the dog's intensity, in brown human eyes.

"Go," the man said. "Leave me and go, before the godless wizard comes looking for her again."

"Oto!" the girl cried, and struggled to squirm down.

Stay there, 'Lissa! Holla heard himself snap, hard and urgent, his own mind giving words to the dog's fear and anger and pain. She sat still, sniffing back more tears. *You can't help him.*

"Knew you'd be the one. You look after her, Holla-Sayan," Otokas said, and the words were only a failing breath, life sighing out with them, the body too broken to endure now that the dog's spirit had left it.

Holla felt, saw, delirium or dream, a faint shimmer of light. Smelt it, like a fresh mountain stream, clear and cold, the soul going, hesitating, balanced on the edge before its long journey to the land of the Old Great Gods beyond the stars.

Safe journey, Otokas, our dog, the goddess whispered. *Bless you.* She cried silently, clinging to the saddlebow.

Most of Holla-Sayan seemed somewhere very far away, still screaming. His body hurt, ached with remembered deathly pain, his head pounded like he had succeeded in the night of hard drinking that had been so early interrupted, leaving him sick and dizzy. Golden sun found the edge of a mountain, flooded them with full light of day, and birds sang in uncaring cheer.

He could find no easy words. The Blackdog enveloped him, a spirit intelligent but inhuman, more foreign to a man's mind than the demons of the wild places, who at least spoke among their own kind. Language was a remote and alien thing; the dog's thought was urge and need and emotion, a fierce protective passion fixed on the goddess.

Any understanding of the human shape of the world was learnt from the men it had known, and that was submerged now in an apprehension mounting to panic. Too near the enemy, the wizard. Too long a delay. Too vast: the world, the future. It could form no certain plan of how to save Attalissa from a warlord who could follow them into the higher valleys tied to the Lissavakail by their streams and snows. It was Otokas the man who had decided on flight from the mountains when a lowlander turned back to rescue the girl, and who overruled the Blackdog's fear of that unknown.

Holla knew this. The Blackdog's memories, those of Otokas, of others, stretched back through generations, running through his own, streams merging, blending, lost in one another. But the Blackdog spirit would not let him think. It mistrusted, feared . . . his failure, his lack of that devotion to the goddess.

The girl slid clumsily down the horse's side and stood with a hand on the back of Holla's neck.

He would not have hurt you, if there had been another way, Holla-Sayan. I need you. I know nothing of the world beyond the mountains. Trust Holla-Sayan, dog. Trust what Otokas saw in him.

The Blackdog seemed to quiet, easing back a little.

Holla-Sayan did not look at her, flinched away from her hand.

The long head of the spear in Otokas's chest resisted pulling. Holla braced a knee below the jagged shaft, eyes fixed on those empty, staring eyes. He would not want to go to his grave with his enemy's weapon still in him. Holla heaved; the still-warm body bucked, flesh tearing again, and seemed to groan as dead air escaped the lungs. He hurled the spearhead away, clattering on the rocks. Gathering the man up, he felt only an angry grief, like he held a brother with whom he had quarrelled. He slid and half-fell down the steep lakeshore and waded out to lay Otokas in the water. An unburied body bound the spirit to the world for as long as the bones endured above ground, preventing it from finishing its journey to the gods, it was said, but deep water, earth, fire, all were fit burials. The man floated a moment, his eyes open as if he still watched, and then slid, drawn down, disappearing.

Thank you, dog, Attalissa said.

Gods could not leave their place. Hers was here. And damned if he was going to wait here with her for a wizard to kill them both. *What did you expect me to do about that, Otokas?*

No answer. The mountain-man's soul was gone.

Not all wanderers were godless, rootless. Most still knew where they belonged. He scrabbled in the stones of the lakeshore, found among the flat pieces of shale one small enough to hold easily in a child's hand, sharp edges blunted by seasons grinding in the waves.

It was like clawing through burial in snow, an avalanche—an image that was not his memory—to find his way to words and his own voice, when he regained the road.

"Here."

The girl was small and forlorn, standing with her arms folded close to her chest, shivering. Afraid. Of him, of the horse, of the wizard, of the world. Holla pressed the piece of shale into her hand, awkwardly.

"Hold it. Keep it safe."

"It's a stone."

"It's a magic we know, we folk who go wandering. So we always know our home, and our gods know us. We take it with us. See?" He hooked a finger in the neck of his jerkin, drew out a leather amulet-pouch on its thong, loosened the neck, and tipped out a white pebble. "That's from the crest of the Sayanbarkash, where I'm from. Where my god walks, sometimes. So my hills are always with me. You carry that, you'll always be with your lake."

The goddess looked close to tears again. *But dog . . .*

"My name's Holla-Sayan, of the Sayanbarkash. Not 'dog.' And you need a new name yourself, love." So easy, sliding into Otokas's affectionate familiarity. Damn him.

And even if he could do so, if he was not drowning in madness, fighting to throw the spirit from his soul, that did not mean he was any kind of willing, chosen successor to the Blackdog. Only that he did not walk away from lost children. Only that.

"What kind of name?" she asked, distracted.

"A good name. I'll think about it."

Holla swung her to the horse's back again, mounted up behind her, and turned the stallion's head to the track. After a mile or so the child relaxed and settled back against him, trusting, a warm weight that was already seeming familiar.

Now, as all should know, the gods and the goddesses of the world live in their own places, the high places and the waters, and aid those who worship them, and protect their own. And though the demons may wander all the secret places of the world, their hearts are bound each to their own place, and though they are no friends to human folk, they are no enemies either, and want only to be left in peace.

But the devils have no place, and in the early days of the world they came from the cold hells and walked up and down over the earth, to trouble the lives of the folk. And the devils did not desire loving worship, nor the friendship of men and women. They did not have a parent's love for the folk. The devils craved dominion as the desert craves water, and they knew neither love nor justice nor mercy. And the devils razed the earth and made war against the heavens of the Old Great Gods themselves, and were cast out, and sealed in the cold hells once more.

CHAPTER VI

I t took nearly all of two days to come to Serakallash. The girl had slept most of the long, nervous ride out of the mountains, waking when Holla stopped to rest the horse, eating the unleavened bread and dried dates from his saddlebag when he told her to, and remaining silent, watching him. The chip of lakeshore shale never left her clenched fist, till he fashioned a crude amulet-pouch for it from the bloodstained headscarf with which he'd bandaged his arm.

Within a few miles of leaving the ramshackle shed the cut had healed, leaving a pale pink scar.

Where the road curved around and left the lake, beginning its downward scramble, they found the bodies of two indigo-clad priest-esses, hacked and dismembered by Northron axes. Attalissa wailed and turned to hide her face against him.

Kayugh's messengers to Serakallash.

It hit Holla-Sayan, with the force of a blow, tears starting in his eyes, that Kayugh must be dead. A woman he had never met, and he cared with all Otokas's heart.

He knew the names of both these sisters. Yana and Niyal. He knew Yana an orphan and Niyal youngest of five, a runaway from an arranged marriage. Yana sang. Niyal had kept pet finches.

From the trampling and the blood-muddy churning of the road, he did not think they had died alone, though their killers had taken their own wounded or slain away with them. Probably by boat, since they had met no raiders on the trail. More evidence of Tamghat's careful planning, and a core of followers who were a chief or lord's sober retainers, not a booty-seizing bandit rabble.

He let Attalissa murmur blessings over them, touching each in farewell, and refused outright her demands and the Blackdog's sense of what was appropriate, leaving them lying unburied, though they sprinkled a handful of earth over them. It was what any passerby might do to keep their ghosts from lingering, trapped in the world. They could not afford to leave any more obvious sign that someone who knew the women and cared had come this way.

Holla rode always with an ear to the road behind, but there was no pursuit. No armed folk, no folk of any sort passed them while they camped the night, cold and fireless, a good ways off the trail amid a thicket of young cypress. The child huddled into the circle of his arms as he lay wakeful through the night, listening for the noise of boots or hooves on stone. It was her dog she clung to, not him, and the sooner he could send her off to his mother, the better. And he tightened his grip on her, the Blackdog denying that he could ever leave her in another's care.

Wrong, wrong, wrong, that he could fear and mistrust his own mother. He sweated, and was cold, and ground his teeth on curses, arguments that had no weight against the dog's need to keep the goddess close.

It was late on the hot afternoon of the following day that they rode into Serakallash, and Holla-Sayan was swaying in the saddle, floating in a shadow-eyed fog of exhaustion, near three days with no sleep. Attalissa seemed little better, her face pinched and wan.

Serakallash was a ragged sprawl of mud-brick and sandstone houses, each within its own walled compound, while the pastures and tilled fields of the dozen or so septs to which all Serakallashi belonged ran out east and west along the foothills, between the mountains and the desert. The caravanserais straggled out from the town into the desert itself, along a stony ridge that offered a long view of the caravan road in either direction. There were deep wells in Serakallash, but it was named for the spring among the red rocks on the caravanserai ridge, which trickled away to lose itself in the Red Desert, and for Sera, the spring's goddess, to whom the caravaneers would offer the last water in their gourds, before filling them again.

Attalissa had not spoken at all since they left the mountains for the desert hills, but huddled smaller and smaller against Holla. All the Blackdog's need to protect her howled against the world, so vast and strange.

The Red Desert, named for the colour of its sand and stone, was flushed with green, sweet with the melting of the winter's snow, and swept scarlet with tulips and the silken ripple of poppies. Its rolling hills were scattered with stocky pistachio trees, buds just breaking, and tangled groves of saxaul with their leafless green twigs hanging like a yak's—a camel's shaggy hair. It should have eased his mind, the familiar beauty, the great open reach of sky. The goddess moaned and turned her face against him.

She was a goddess, and it was not her place. The strangeness of understanding, sharing her fear, made him almost angry, bewildered with it. What was worse, Holla *felt* the place watching him, all the living powers, the little demons and the greater who wandered the desert and the foothills, and the goddess Sera. She was aware, with something that felt very like anger and fear in equal measure, of Attalissa's presence. And of his own. It was as though he stood naked, while hostile people stared from somewhere behind his shoulder, never quite showing themselves.

We should speak with the goddess Sera at her spring. We shouldn't trespass here unannounced.

The Blackdog agreed that Attalissa must approach Sera at once.

Holla-Sayan clenched his teeth. "Sera can wait. First we go tell my friends I'm back. Gaguush will want to know there are raiders in the mountains, and the sept-chiefs need to know. Remember—" *Remember you're no goddess here. It wouldn't be usual at all for us to go to the spring, when I've only been gone a couple of days. I'll take you and show you later, tonight or tomorrow. That would be more natural. Remember you're a child. My child. Call me dog or even Holla out loud and I'll box your ears.*

She peered up at him, wide-eyed, and he scowled at his own guilty discomfort. She was not one of his cheerfully noisy nephews, who would weigh the threat as mostly jest and take it in stride. 'Lissa had known nothing but too much respect and too little family. Otokas's memories did not tell him she had ever screamed with laughter or run yelling through the gardens with sheer childish joy, or talked back to the priestesses, sulked, or refused to go to bed. He remembered only the frustrated, near-silent tears, all the tantrums she had dared, when she was unable to act, to stop some fisher-drowning storm or turn an avalanche or drive the fever from an ailing sister. Poor brat.

Had they even told her when her own mother died? The Blackdog did not remember that they had.

What do I call you, then? And you never said what I should be called now. Stiff and cold, hiding unhappiness.

Father? Papa? Sayan, not Papa, too close and personal. She was no utter orphan; she should be thinking of her own father as that, if she had ever been allowed to meet the man at all.

Of course she had not. Attalissa never left the temple islet, and men were not permitted there.

The Old Great Gods damn the lot of them.

Father, I suppose.

"Father." She tried it out in a whisper.

He did not think the faintness was all fear of the unknown, or of himself. An unhealthy pallor that was not mere weariness had crept over the girl's skin as they rode down the mountain.

She was a human child; she should not be bound to a place like a god. Holla began to have the horrible conviction she was, and that no small magic or mere reassuring superstition, no piece of lakeshore shale, was going to help.

There were mulberries growing along the wall of Mooshka Rost-vadim's caravanserai, newly leafed out, and black and pink starlings singing in them. Holla-Sayan rode through the gateway to be met with a whoop from young Bikkim Battu'um, whose swirling-horse tattoos in red and blue proclaimed him native Serakallashi.

"Holla's back! Thought you weren't going to make it in time."

"I thought so too."

"You look terrible, you know. What's happened?"

"Raiders have sacked Lissavakail. An army of raiders. You haven't heard?"

That brought the rest running. They were Gaguush's gang of caravaneers. Mercenaries, some would call them, because they bound themselves to a loyalty for pay. Wanderers, but not godless; most, like him, carried some charm to tie them to their home, a pebble or carved god's symbol. They knew who they were, where they belonged, and so they could go anywhere.

"Did a bit of sacking yourself, too," Bikkim said, and tried to chuck the goddess under the chin, yelped at the force with which Holla struck his arm away. "Take it easy! I'm not going to eat her."

"My daughter," Holla snapped, angry at his own reaction. He knew Bikkim, and the dog could damn well learn to trust his knowledge.

"Daughter! Since when?" demanded old Doha, who like Holla was of the Sayanbarkash, a cousin to his grandfather. "Does your mama know, Holla my lad?"

"*I* didn't know," he told Doha pointedly, and let him snigger.

Holla had been visiting Timhine in Lissavakail ever since he let curiosity draw him up into the mountains on his first journey along the desert edge; almost long enough to explain the girl, who looked, to a taller lowlander's eye, younger than she was. Let them think Timhine had farmed her out for shame at a mixed-blood child, so that he never knew of her existence till now. Mountain folk were notorious for distrusting those who married out of their own god's reach, and made rumours of lowlander blood, even four generations back, an excuse for any oddity or deviation. Probably fear of that as much as his wandering had turned Timhine away in the end.

"Yeah?" Bikkim scratched at the wisp of beard he was trying to grow. "She doesn't really take after you. Lucky for her," he added, dancing out of reach of another, more comradely, swipe. "What raiders? Are you sure? There haven't been any large parties take the mountain road in months. I mean, everyone'd be talking of it in the market, if there had."

"Some warlord calling himself Tamghat, a wizard—I mean, I think I saw . . ." Explaining grew too complicated. "A warlord, and just about an army. Slaughtered half the town and I think he burned the temple."

"Oh." Bikkim subsided, offered the goddess a wary smile. "Sera prevent that they come down here, if they're capable of taking on Attalissa's sisters, whoever they are."

Bikkim obviously thought Holla was exaggerating. *He* would have thought so, if it had been Bikkim telling tales of armies where no army could be.

"Uh, your woman up there, Timhine . . . ?"

Holla shrugged. "She's safe, I guess. Married and gone to the high valleys, and left the girl for me."

Gaguush strode over, red-dyed coat swirling around her, waist-length black braids caught up in glossy loops. She was mistress of the caravan, gang-boss, as well as owner of most of their camels.

"I heard. A warlord with a raider army in Lissavakail, you say? How in the cold hells did they get up there, without going through here?"

At least Gaguush didn't question their existence. Holla shrugged. "Passes from the west, maybe? Magic? I don't know. But they're there."

"Yeah, I trust you didn't end up looking like that just getting drunk and falling over. I don't suppose it matters where they came from. They likely to come here, you think?"

"They might." Holla dismounted and lifted the goddess down. "We should get out of here, be gone before they do. See to the horse for me, Bikkim? And maybe you should borrow another and ride out to tell your parents about the warlord and the raiders. The Serakallashi council will want to know."

There were no priests in Serakallash, only a council of sept-chiefs. Bikkim's parents counted among them; the boy didn't need to work as a caravan guard, but he was young enough to think the roving life an adventure.

The council would doubt, of course, and say Holla's fear turned a dozen desperate men to an army. If they sent scouts to investigate, he hoped they would go warily.

"Bikkim? Don't mention the brat, all right?"

"Why not?"

"Just don't."

"Fine. I won't. But she's nothing to be ashamed of. Are you, sweetheart?"

Attalissa, clinging close to Holla's side, gave Bikkim a cold stare. He laughed at her, leading Master Mooshka's weary dun off towards its stable. She switched her stare to Gaguush.

"She's yours?" Gaguush's generous mouth thinned. She had always been sour about Timhine; she had never stopped him riding up to Lissavakail, either. "Are you sure? Doha, go tell Mooshka Holla-Sayan's news. He'll want to know. Tell him we're leaving early."

"He'll hear. Half the yard heard."

"Go!"

"Fine, fine. I'm going. Try not to break any of the boy's limbs, eh, boss? If you don't want to marry him, you can't complain when he goes looking for one that might." Doha left them, pulling a face at Gaguush's back.

"What are you planning to do with her?"

Holla shrugged. "Bring her along. What else can I do?"

"Send her to your kin."

The Blackdog felt a surge of panic, enough to throw Holla-Sayan off balance, make him lose words for a moment. He stood blinking, confused, before he found them again and could marshal an argument.

"I can't send her off with strangers, not after what she's been through. She barely knows me, and to hand her off to someone else again . . . Look at her, Gaguush. She's never been out of the mountains in her life. She's terrified."

"Fine. Take her yourself then, if it's the only way to get rid of her. You can cross on the ferry when we're below Five Cataracts, and cut up to meet us at At-Landi, once you've taken her home. I can manage that stretch along the Kinsai-av shorthanded, this once. But don't expect me to pay your way."

"Well, no. Of course not." That was what he had been angling for,

Gaguush's order to go, rather than outrage that he asked to do so. And even more than that, time. It would take them a couple of weeks to get to the lowest of the Five Cataracts and the ferry over the Kinsai-av. Time to wrestle the Blackdog into some sort of compliance. 'Lissa would be far better off with his parents. But he needed more than that.

"But I was wondering—"

Gaguush scowled. "Bashra help me! I suppose you want to take one of my camels?"

He shrugged, gave her a faint, apologetic smile.

"You're more trouble than you're worth, Holla-Sayan. The Great Gods help you if you ever go running off after townswomen again. Expecting me to sort out your problems with your bastards."

Gaguush's gaze dropped to the goddess, staring up at her, dark eyes wide. She had the grace to blush. "Huh. Well. Don't look like that, child. It's not your fault your papa's a fool." Her glower returned to Holla. "But I told you not to go running after mountain women, didn't I? Told you you'd only get hurt. They want their men home, *ploughing*." Another guilty look at the girl, in case she heard the weight of innuendo that went into the word, beyond merely the herder's contempt for the farmer.

"I know, I know. I'll be sure to take the advice of my elders next time."

Gaguush's mouth thinned again and she cuffed his ear. Holla just grinned at her, not bothering to dodge because all his effort at her sudden movement went into preventing the dog's reflexive reaction to any threat, keeping his hand from his sabre, or worse. Gaguush had expected him to duck, and blinked at him, uncertain, opening and closing her hand. She looked down at the girl again.

"What's her name?"

Holla shrugged. "She had some mountain name, but I'm through with the mountains. I'm going to call her Pakdhala, for my grandmother."

"Pretty name," Gaguush said, wavering between kindness and a tone that suggested the girl did not quite measure up to the name.

"You going to tattoo her for Sayan? You should, if you really want to put the mountains behind you, make her Sayanbarkashi."

A challenge, there. Maybe she had minded Timhine more than she let herself admit.

Attalissa stared in something like horror at Gaguush, whose face and hands were nearly solid colour, the black and red bands of geometric pattern used by the Black Desert tribes. Much of the rest of Gaguush was similarly decorated beneath her baggy striped trousers and long, loose cameleer's coat. Her dark skin proclaimed a princess's wealth and rank in the desert fashion; she was the daughter of the chieftain of the Bashrakallashi, but a divorce followed by a quarrel with a brother had sent her into exile and the mercenary's life.

"You want to be pretty now that you're a lowlander, to live up to your name," Gaguush told the girl, and smiled, showing teeth drilled and filled with patterns in gold.

The desert tribes were all crazy.

Holla felt Attalissa trembling on the edge of weary, frightened, utterly human tears, and took her chilly hand in his own. He winked at her as Gaguush turned away, and surprised her into a smile.

"She's all striped like a pot. I like your snakes and leopards better," the girl whispered, fingering Holla's arm, tracing a spotted, stretching cat. "And the owls on your face. Owls are nice. But leopards are best."

"Those are cheetahs."

"We have leopards in the mountains. With really long tails. Not cheetahs. And I don't want them red."

Gaguush, not yet out of earshot, hooted with laughter. "This pot says, you come and have something to eat, Pakdhala. You look like you're fainting on your feet. Doesn't your papa know enough to feed you? It's no wonder your mama didn't want to keep him."

In the days of the first kings in the north, who were Viga Forkbeard, and Red Geir, and Hravnmod the Wise, there were seven wizards. And two were of the people of the kings in the north, who came from over the western sea, and one was of a people unknown; one was of the Great Grass and one of Imperial

Nabban, and two were from beyond far Nabban, but the seven were of one fellowship. Their names were Heuslar the Deep-Minded, who was uncle to Red Geir, Ulfhild the King's Sword, who was sister to Hravnmod the Wise, Anganurth Wanderer, Tamghiz, Chief of the Bear-Mask Fellowship, Yeh-Lin the Beautiful, and Sien-Mor and Sien-Shava, the Outcasts, who were sister and brother. If other singers tell you different, they know only the shadows of the tales, and they lie.

CHAPTER VII

Usually the nightmares were Moth's own: old battles, old failures, old betrayals.

The blade of the sword is obsidian, drinking the light. The hilt is silver, traced with scrolling patterns in black lines of niello. She knows it, has carried it too long already. Lakkariss. It stands point down in the snow, and frost glitters on its edges. The night is black and white, stark shadow of spruce and naked larch, pale birch and the starlit glimmer of the drifts that shroud storehouse and bathhouse and bury the garden fence and the beehives.

The sky shivers. The stars are dimmed by an upwelling of light from the north, shifting fans and curtains and lashing whips of green and red. Sound scrapes the air, just on the edge of hearing.

Waking. Hunger. Death. Go.

These dreams were new, and bitter with the touch of the Old Great Gods.

The bear lies panting, breath shallow and too rapid. She cradles his head in her lap, writes runes between his eyes to call him back: Sun for life, Boar for strength, Demon, to name him what he is, to strengthen that side of his blended blood. But the eyes are empty, the ribs unmoving, and he is cold, cold beyond any power of hers to warm. She cuts her palm, in desperation writes Life, Breath, Heart, in the secret runes of the Old Great Gods, but his hidden demon's heart has been stilled, and there is no waking him. The night shivers with the presence of the Gods, opalescent shimmer in the corner of the eye. She starts to her feet, leaving him, taking the sword from the snow, from the other dream, and the Gods fall back, but it turns on her, she is falling, the edge of the obsidian blade is a tear in the night sky and the cold claws of the frozen hells reach out . . .

The house is burning, the storehouse in flames, the bathhouse, the smoke-

house, all pouring angry red light into the night, smoke eating the stars. The trees lie flattened, stripped of needle and branch, charred poles pointing away from the blow of the heaven's lightnings. White bones under the roof-tree.

Lakkariss cold, a shard of black ice lying amid the flames.

Moth woke, cold as the sword despite the weight of fur blankets and sheepskins. Mikki lay beside her, one cool-fleshed arm trailing over her ribs, and she listened to his slow breathing in the darkness. A breath. A long stillness. Another. Midwinter. He might not wake for days. If she left him now . . . But there would be no lying before the Old Great Gods. Leaving him would not stop her caring, and so long as she held to that one last unbetrayed faith, she was powerless against them. The sword was not to her throat, but to Mikki's.

She lifted his arm aside and crawled out of the cabinet-like bed. The air bit at naked skin. Fire first, before anything else. Her body might not mind the cold, but her heart hated it. She stirred up the embers in the baked-clay stove, fed it with birch logs and watched the new flames born, sitting on her heels. The bronze cauldron of water that sat on the stone hearth began to tick and pop as it felt the heat. She went back and closed the folding side of the bed, not to disturb Mikki's sleep, and only then wrapped herself in a cloak of winter-white hareskin.

The cabin was low and dark, but snug against the wind, its walls a double thickness of upright logs. Mikki had lined it with painted wainscoting like a king's hall, and the floor was not beaten earth but good planed boards. Mikki had made himself a bit of a reputation as a woodworker down in Swanesby on the Shikten'aa, a settlement of Northron farmers who had pushed so far west and north. He took his dugout south up the river in the autumn to trade the cured skins from her year's hunting—hare and deer, because he would not have her kill anything they did not eat—worked a month or two of lengthening nights on building barns or houses or boats, sometimes crafting fine furniture, and came back with rye and oats and cheese, butter and perhaps a bolt of cloth or a cake of black Nabbani ink for the sagas she wrote on sheets of boiled birchbark, since the exotic imports of Swanesby did not extend to vellum. A tale of a demon carpenter in Swanesby might spread, eventually, but there was nothing in that alone to make anyone come seeking them, Mikki insisted. A demon carpenter, a demon farmer, was not the same as a demon smith, with magic in his craft to draw humans seeking fated blades and charmed spearheads. He only made chairs and cradles and roof-beams; there was no doom in those and no virtue beyond that of good crafting, nothing to draw the attention of kings and heroes. Or did she want to give up bread and butter?

What Moth did not want to give up was this undeserved peace, this unending round of seasons, digging and sowing, the hunt and harvest, the ever-renewed struggle to have enough firewood, the petty warfare against the musk-deer and hare in defence of her cabbages and beets, and the long, still winters when she wrote her histories and roamed the frozen wilderness with skis and bow while Mikki slept. She would be a homesteader's wife. Her great defiance of fate would be to set down the old lays of the drowned isles that were forgotten now in the kingdoms of the north, and to write sagas of the deeds of those first kings, true sagas, not overlaid with the romance of later times. Even if she had no one to read them.

But that was not her doom, and she only pretended otherwise.

The chest sat in the darkest corner, the oldest piece of their furnishings. Mikki had made it for her when they built the house, carving it with swan-breasted ships. She moved the quern and storage jars that sat atop it and raised the lid. The leather hinges were cracking with age and disuse. She should have kept them oiled. She pushed aside bundles wrapped in greasy woollen cloth, smelling, faintly, of rust, and pulled out a leather pouch, stiff and crumbling with age. The thong knotted around it broke when she tugged at it, and she flung the broken pieces in the fire. She pulled from the little bag a roughly squared slip of age-greyed wood, set it with deliberation on the broad stone hearth supporting the stove, followed it with two more before she looked down at them. All three lay carved-face uppermost, the sharp angles of the runes stained dark. Old blood, very old.

Need. Journey. Water. Three more, arrayed below the first, gave her *Ice, Devil, Divinity*, and a further three, *Sword, Hail, Boar.*

Need was danger, hardship, struggle. *Journey* might be sudden change. *Water* was often change, but natural and not sudden, and also life, with strength sleeping in it. *Ice* warned of dangers unseen and the paralysing loss of will. *Devil* could tell of pride or treachery, rootless wandering, risk and chance and fear, and *Divinity* was rooted confidence and power and strength of will. *Sword* for war and violent death, but also for protection arriving from without or the one who stands alone and watchful outside the door of the hall. That had been her, once, in all its faces. *Hail* for sudden loss and unexpected turmoil, but new growth, new shapes could follow from it. The *Boar* for hidden or waiting strength, the guardian animal of the holy places of the vanished little first people, before there were ever kings in the north—strength that could hide too long, be forgotten and wither away, or become a foundation for power and movement.

That was how the Northron wizards might read these runes. On the other hand, they might all, or nearly all, hold literal truth. *Sword*, in particular, she did not want to see. *Sword* and *Journeying*, and *Devil*. Across and down and corner to corner, there was consistency.

They told her nothing the savage dancing flames of the sky in her dreams had not already said.

She had hoped for more. Or less. Hoped she merely had bad dreams.

Moth swept the rune-carved slips of yew into the stove.

She lit the stub of a sweet beeswax candle at the fire, dragged aside the bin that held the summer's beets, and lifted a trapdoor in the floor. Farther south, they might have had a root-cellar. Here the pit beneath had been cut down through the thin black earth that so grudgingly allowed a short season of gardening, into frost that never thawed. Cold struck up from below and the candle flickered and snapped.

Frost clung to the edges of the pit, and the shadows in the corners were thick, heavier than night should be. All that it held was a sheathed sword, lying alone in a web of ice.

There was no ladder. Moth set the candle on the floor and jumped. Ice snapped. Crystals of it formed again around her bare ankle, melted, reached again. She ignored the creeping tide, wrenched the sword free of its cocoon. She caught the edge and swung herself up again, quietly lowering the trap, but the side of the bed had been pushed open. The heap of furs and fleeces stirred. Mikki watched her, his head pillowed on an arm.

"What is it?" he asked.

Moth shook her head, set the candle on the table. "What woke you?"

"An empty bed?" he suggested. When she failed to smile, he said soberly, "You've brought up the sword."

Moth nodded. She cradled the sheathed sword against her breast like a baby, dewed with melted frost. "It called me."

Perhaps it had been calling, unheeded, for longer than she thought. She had not had nightmares for years after they stopped wandering and went to earth in Baisirbska. After Ogada died, she could never bring herself to reach back into the snarled, fraying web of power with which the Great Gods had bound the seven, to feel out if any were gone, or awake and working against their bonds to struggle into the world again. She had not wanted to know. Now . . . she felt for the traces of that ancient spell and as she did so, the lines of the Great Gods' power clung to her, barbed threads seeking to renew their hold, to draw her in again, the coldness of a death of the body that was not strong enough to be death of the soul. She found what she sought and pulled away, back to the waking world, and staggered, steadying herself with a hand on the stove. Flesh welcomed that little heat unburned.

"*Two*," she said.

"Two what?" Mikki asked. "Don't do that, wolf. It's worrying."

She showed him a palm not even blistered. "Only two still bound."

"Ah. Who?"

Moth shook her head.

"And how long have the others been free?"

"At least one, a few-score years. The others, I don't know. I've dreamed, I think—"

"Dreamed what?"

"Nothing to tell me anyone threatened the world again."

"Perhaps they don't."

"Or didn't. Something's changed."

The Gods might have their plans, but fate ruled all, and it was not the Gods, in the end, who shaped the worlds, much as they liked to think so. There was some comfort in that, scant though it was.

Mikki yawned. "It can wait till spring, can't it? Even the likes of we should have better sense than to travel in a Baisirbsk winter."

"Lakkariss is awake, Mikki."

"Spring." The man yawned, chuckled, and reached out a broad hand and an arm muscled like a smith's, furred with golden hairs. "Tell the sword to wait, my wolf. It may be awake, but I don't want to be. Come back to bed."

Moth stood, her head bowed over the sword in her arms, hair hiding her face. He did not know what she risked, if the Gods decided she was refusing them. But it cost them such effort to touch the world, for all they watched it, dimly. That she did take Lakkariss from its grave should be token of good intent. She turned away and laid the sword on one of the benches along the wall. The scabbard was covered in plain dark leather, unornamented; even its mouth and terminal, silver once, were blackened with the years. Ordinary enough, but the scrolling, knotted lines incised on the hilt drew the eye, and could drag the unwary mind into dreams a human soul should not have to endure. She would wrap the grip in leather again, to break the pattern.

"Spring, then. But once the rivers open I have to go."

"*We* have to go."

"You don't need to come." Leave him behind, wean her heart away . . . it would break, and the Great Gods would have no hold on her, and she carried a sword that even they should learn to fear.

He did not bother to answer, only laughed, showing eyeteeth too large for a human jaw. "Where are we going?"

"South, I suppose."

"Yes, well, up here, we're beggared for choice, aren't we? South I could work out for myself. Even half-asleep."

"South will have to do, for now. Perhaps the Great Grass." Why that? Nothing in the runes suggested it. But she trusted such impulse, when it felt of certainty.

"Bear-fetishists," he said with distaste.

"They used to be."

"I wouldn't mind, if they'd worship them living. It's the obsession with skulls and teeth."

"You could start your own collection of teeth."

"If we spend too long there, I might be tempted. Are you coming back to bed, or going out to terrorize the woods?"

Moth stood staring down at the sword, her face expressionless. Then she blinked, looked up, and gave him a faint smile. "Hungry?"

"Possibly."

"I was gone all last week and you never woke to miss me. There's a brace of hare hanging outside the door. I'll stew them. A change from smoked fish. It's too late to start bread if you're hungry now, but I could make oatcakes, and there's plenty of butter and honey still. Mikki, if you won't stay behind, you'll have to abandon your bees. I'm sorry."

"The bees can look after themselves. Anyway, the winter came so early this year, they probably won't make it through. Next time you want to lose yourself in the wilderness, pick someplace bees can thrive?"

"Someplace with a longer summer night?"

He grinned. "That too."

"At least we won't have to dig the garden this spring."

"What do you mean, *we*, princess?"

Moth laughed and dropped her fur cloak over the sword. Pinching the candle out, she crossed the floor in a few long strides to scramble into the bed. The man yelped and disappeared beneath the heap.

"Great Gods, no! If you're going to stand around half-naked in the cold, wolf, don't think you can warm yourself up on me!"

Frost began to settle on the cloak over the sword, spreading across the bench, white as bleached bone.

These wizards were wise, and powerful. They knew the runes and the secret names, and the patterns of the living world and of the dead. And the stories of their deeds are many, for they were great heroes among their peoples. And these all can be told, if there be golden rings, or silver cups, or wine and flesh and bread by the fire.

But the seven wizards desired to know yet more, and see yet more, and to live forever like the gods of the high places and the goddesses of the waters and the demons of the forest and the stone and the sand and the grass.

CHAPTER VIII

In his own mind, his name remained Tamghiz, though he knew he was Tamghiz Ghatai and that it was Ghatai, mostly, who drove him. Calling himself Tamghat freed him to play at games he had long exhausted, petty ambition and wizardry and lordship. He had been royal, once, clan-chief of the Green Banners by right of birth and his father's choosing, by right of victory over a brother who did not bow to their father's will and tried to split the clan. Tamghiz had made the Green Banners the paramount clan on the Great Grass, and made the shaman's cult of the bear he followed the paramount faith over all the gods of the hills and the goddesses of the waters. Such victories were empty, in the end. The Great Grass was a small world, bounded by its own narrowness of mind, its own celebration of brute strength, which led to treachery and betrayal, till a man could not trust even his wife, even his children, to follow to his vision's end.

But it was amusing, to make himself Tamghat, less than he had ever thought to be, mere wizard, mere warlord, clanless. A game, while he followed the path the stars laid out.

In the galleried apartment that had been the incarnate goddess's, and still bore evidence of her in child's clothing—a certain lack of evidence of childish amusements, poor thing, not a carved horse or a skipping rope, a pet dog or a songbird—Tamghiz breathed on the pebbles in his hand, nine of them, three black, three red, three yellow, and tossed them over the unrolled calfskin on which was painted the map of the Grasslander sky.

Tamghiz sat back on his heels and studied the pattern they made. Frowning, he rose and walked around the painted hide. It was not, entirely, what he had expected, and certain of the pebbles stirred something—chill, warmth, he could not even say which—in the blood. Anticipation.

—What is it? he asked that half of himself that stirred.

—Change.

Well, of course it was bloody change, Tamghiz thought. He chased a goddess loose from her place in the world, and who before him had ever done that? Ghatai's joy, that of a predator scenting its prey, went deeper. Change in the order of the world meant something that stirred even the devil's soul.

It was illusion that there was any separation between Ghatai and Tamghiz, between devil and wizard soul, or that there was any way to say *self* and *other*. There were only shades of self, the spread of thought and opinion and will any human being carried in his or her own mind. But still, they could argue, as they once had in truth, and sway now one way, now the other, on any matter that struck close to their, his, conjoined hearts.

It was more apt to name that part of himself Ghatai, wilder, more far-sighted, less rooted in the careful moment, which felt an anticipatory thrill. But studying the constellations, running over the stories in his mind, it was Tamghiz, who was man, living, breathing, feeling body, who felt a catch in his breath. Speculation. He guessed, perhaps, too much, invented sure pattern where there was only a hint.

But still—interesting. He almost forgot the missing goddess for a moment. But that was the crucial matter in hand, the pressing issue on which he needed to fix his wide-roving mind.

His bodyguards watched patiently as he settled down on his heels again. They knew better than to interrupt or ask questions, had grown familiar with wizards' ways over the years. Just as well. He wanted to think. To decide what should be done. Too much had changed too suddenly. He had come to Lissavakail expecting, by this morning past, to be . . . dead, quite possibly, which was something he barely understood. To have ceased existing. Or to be changed, terribly changed.

He did not feel relieved that somehow that change had been delayed, he did not. He did not falter now, in that much he was all Ghatai: he knew no fear. But he was tired, as he had not been in years.

Hollow. Cold. It had taken more than he expected to break those gates. Power lingered in this place even with its goddess gone, and the lake itself fought him, not actively, but as a hostile, draining presence. It still smouldered sullenly on the edges of his awareness, but it had weakened; it was a faint nagging pain, no more. Not worth whining about.

His *noekar*, his retainers, expected some greater anger at the loss of his bride, and they all, even his bodyguards who knew him best, were walking warily around him. His bride—that was a joke. A pity An-Chaq had taken it literally, but her willingness to try murder proved he had been right not to trust her; he trusted no wizard with the secrets of his heart, and a scheming Nabbani princess least of all.

The wedding was something the folk, Attalissa's and his own, would understand, that was all. It had the shape of old tales, a hero winning a goddess's hand. He had not wanted to kill so many of Attalissa's folk; they fought better and longer than he had expected, and the temple held out long after it should have. He had been promised, years before, a quick surrender. Luli, who had grown old and bitter-mouthed, claimed she had been unable to persuade the others in the ruling threesome to negotiation. He thought she had not tried very hard; she had wanted to see the temple destroyed, wanted all cleared, so she could raise something new. She imagined she could use him, a man, a wizard, a conqueror, to reshape her goddess into what she wanted. Deceiving herself that she wanted that dream of a new god of snow-cold purity emptied of will, of caring, when all she truly yearned for was certainty in her own righteousness. Human folk were easy tools; they wanted to be used, and would serve till they shattered themselves, once aimed. And Luli, Old Lady, would continue to serve, though she was afraid now, afraid of the scale of the destruction, afraid of her own folk, afraid they would come to realize her betrayal. Afraid to find him unchanged from twenty years before. Wizards were long-lived for humans, but not so much so to pass for thirty still, after twenty years. At least fear would keep her from imagining she had any prior claim on his body, which could have been an embarrassment. It was always disgusting when mortal humans failed to accept age with grace.

It was a pity so many true to Attalissa had died. He had wanted the goddess trusting, thinking she bought peace by conceding. He had been confident he could win her to think it no unpleasant concession, and he had had faith in Tamghiz's body and charm to win a cloistered young woman, as he had won most women he set his mind to. Even if she did see he was something other than a mere wizard, he thought he could fascinate her, talk enough doubts away. There were always those oddities in the world, the halflings, semi-divine, semi-demonic, who fit uneasily in among the wizards or wandered rootless, discontent. She would know only too late what he intended, and once he had taken her, she would understand, as Tamghiz had once come to understand, his soul engulfed in Ghatai's fire.

But the child was, according to all he had ever heard, only a shadow of the goddess, and he was not going to be cheated, bind her into his own being and find the better part of her godhead lost. He would wait. He had learned patience humans could not imagine, and if that was the price demanded by her mortality, he would pay it. It was her mortality left her vulnerable to him, in the end, gave her a shape he could seize. It made them the same substance, their souls alike, humanity and divinity blended, like two dyes making a third colour. He had nearly destroyed himself, thinking he could possess Sihkoteh, his gaoler in the volcano's heart. When he learned in Marakand from the so-willingly-seduced Luli of the lake goddess who was godly soul and mortal body, Ghatai had recognized, then, the path the stars set him. Attalissa might be a being of only one soul, but that soul nonetheless was more akin to the two-ply spinning of his own than any other divinity. He understood it, he could touch it, grasp it, as he had not been able to fiery Sihkoteh's.

Tamghiz swept up the coloured pebbles, left the patterned calfskin for his servants to put away, and strode out to the balcony. The lake still stirred restlessly, the wind uneasy. His captains had sent warriors after those sisters who had fled, with particular attention to the road to the desert. That was where any threat worth taking seriously would arise.

"Shall I make you a lord of fifty tents, Ova?" he called back over his shoulder.

"If you can find tents in these hills, my lord," Ova said, with something like relief in his voice, that his lord was not about to curse them all or smash the walls. The Northron should be cheerful; it was an offer of rank, of bondfolk.

"A village, then. Since we're here to stay, my tent-guard needs the honour due a chief's chosen men."

"You think there's enough villages?" Siglinda asked, joining him, to look over the lake and into the towering range of grey and white, sharp planes like shattered tile, that hid the green hearts of the valleys. Like wise dogs, they took their mood from his, and he treasured that confidence, that trust. A warlord's tent-guards were the chosen among the *noekar*, who were the chosen themselves, the trusted, the faithful. Family of the sword and the heart. He never stood on formality with his guards, not when they were alone. They needed to feel they were trusted, in order to love.

"You don't know mountains, not real mountains. There's rich grazing out there, and mines, and rivers where the sands breed gold."

"Mines sound promising."

It would be amusing to rule these town folk for a time, play at kingship, remember past times when he had thought that enough to fill a dozen lives. It would keep the *noekar* happy, having small lordships over bondfolk families as *noekar* ought, enable him to keep the mercenaries well gifted and loyal. He could take a foothold on the desert road; the goddess in Serakallash was a feeble creature, hardly worth the name. It was a wealthy town, and its herds . . . those would be worth the taking. He remembered a desert-bred he'd owned once: was it when he rode to the north? Or after, when he'd ruled half the Hravnmodsland?

It would fill the time until Attalissa returned.

The sky-chart did not tell him when that might be. He could calculate, roughly, when the next conjunction of Vrehna and Tihz would come even without his star charts and almanacs, see the patterns in his head. He had always, even when he was mere mortal human wizard, had an affinity for the skies, an understanding of the heavenly dance.

So. Long enough to shape a small kingdom, perhaps, but not long enough to grow weary with it. In such a crucial matter, though, and with the goddess momentarily out of his reach, it might be wise to have another wizard's divination in confirmation. It might shed light on the other matter as well, the *other* that the sky-chart and pebbles said moved towards conjunction with himself.

Not wise, perhaps, to ask anything too directly bearing on himself. Ivah had great power in divination, as though the streams of fate flowed more closely by her soul than that of most wizards. He'd known another like that, for whom the runes always fell true. But Ivah was perversely stupid in her interpretations, too knotted up in fear and desire to please, to see clearly what she could. Or simply stupid, but he did not believe that possible of any child of his getting. And he had sent her to inspect the room he allotted her, told her he would come to see her once he had dealt with other matters. Being Ivah, that meant she would do nothing else but wait until he came, as though daring otherwise would bring some punishment. He had never raised a hand to her in her life, never.

Some dogs were born cringing. Probably the dam's fault then, too.

—Waste of time fretting over her. You never learn. Find another wizard-woman and breed another child. But don't put any great expectations on that one, either. They'll always fail you in the end.

"My daughter, and then the baths," he told the bodyguards, and saw their weary drift from alertness shaken away. Probably the guard should have changed hours since, but Rolf and Fenghat and Shannovai had all died when the Blackdog escaped, and nearly everyone else in the tent-guard he had set to other commands, overseeing all that needed to be done in a temple still filled with sullen, hostile warrior priestesses and a new-conquered town that he would rather the mercenaries did not completely turn against him.

Ivah squatted on her heels on the slate-tiled floor, arms hugged tight around her knees. Waiting. She had learnt early in her life how to wait, patient as a toad for flies, on the sudden bright light of her father's attention.

Ivah had learnt it was best to go warily into the world, showing nothing of herself. This quiet, watching face was one she never uncovered when there were any to see. She sometimes thought they had been a cult of two, she and her mother. A society of secret knowledge, in which she wore a mask she had learned to make from An-Chaq's example, as her father's *noekar*, his sworn warriors, wore the bear-masks of the ancient Great Grass cult he had revived, when they danced naked at the winter solstice.

Ivah was a cult of one, now, with even greater cause to wear her mask. She was bright and sparkling, adoring and attentive. She asked the right questions, the ones that showed her eager to learn and to please, but always, utterly and totally, a disciple at the feet of the master to whose lofty height she could never attain. And she never, ever, cried for loneliness or loss.

She had cause to wonder, now, if her mother's mask had been a mask at all. Perhaps that face had been real all along. Or had become real, until An-Chaq's winsome charm and childlike volatility betrayed her into true passion.

That was loss, if the great mystery Ivah thought she had observed in her mother, the secret teaching, were no such thing, but An-Chaq's true face. A betrayal.

Ivah rose to her feet and paced the room, now hers. It had been the sleeping-chamber of the chief priestess, who now lodged in one of the simple dormitories of the lesser sisters. In the desert language she was called the Old Woman, which sounded to Ivah like it ought to be an insult. She was too grovelling and simpering for the dignity of her elderly years, but Ivah's father seemed to value her, and like most, she preened under his attention like a bird in the sun.

It amused him, and how he could find anything in this ludicrous situation to amuse him, Ivah could not imagine. It must be the great joke on himself, that he had come ready to be wed and found his bride a child.

Perhaps it did amuse him, at that. He always told her the stars would revolve to humble the mighty, unless the mighty remembered, every day, that they were humble before the stars.

The Old Woman had been permitted to remove only a few of her furnishings: a basket of scrolls and a much-thumbed codex containing translations of writings on divinity from the godless ruined cities of the west, a box of toiletries, her clothing. Her bed, so high it was reached by a footstool, remained, with its soft quilts of red and indigo squares, as did a cushioned chair of queenly proportions and a bronze brazier with supports shaped like leaping fish. Ivah had kindled a fire of wood and dried dung-cakes in it, and thrown on incense from the sisters' chapel, but the air still smelt like overdone meat.

The room had a row of windows looking south over the Lissavakail's waters to the ever-rising mountains. Each window reached from floor to ceiling, and had a set of heavy doors or shutters, to close against rain and wind and winter's cold. They let onto a long balcony, where white, maroon-tipped tulips bloomed in stone pots. Ivah would have liked to close the shutters, but then she would have had to tell her father why, and she could think of no reason he would not mock, or worse, grow angry at.

The air was greasy with smoke coiling over the temple roofs from the garden in the west. She was a warlord's daughter; she shouldn't mind such things. She would not be weak, unworthy of his blood and love.

There were brisk footsteps on the stairs outside, which climbed only to this high room, and Ivah whirled back to the centre of the room, a smile lighting her eyes.

Her bodyguard Shaiveh, sent out to wait, announced, "Lady Ivah—your lord father."

Tamghat pushed the door open. She caught a glimpse of his favoured bodyguards, the Northron nephew and aunt, Ova and Siglinda, taking up station on either side of the door, exchanging greetings with Shaiveh, before Tamghat slammed it closed. Despite the exhaustion that only those close to him would notice, he filled the room with life, energy, raw power like a Baisirbska bear or an enraged stallion. Despite their great failure, he seemed quite cheerful. He still wore his damaged armour and had not yet taken time to bathe, probably not even to rest or eat. He reeked of smoke and sweat and blood and power. Ivah felt guilty for having had the old chief priestess show her and Shaiveh to the sisters' baths. No servants. Priestesses had heated the water for herself and her bodyguard, and combed their hair afterwards. Their faces had been closed. Watchful, like her own behind the mask.

There were few enough priestesses left in the temple. Most had died defending it. The sworn warriors and mercenaries were burning their bodies in the garden, which was the roast-meat smell she choked on, even here in her high room.

Some of the holy women had no doubt fled. Those neither dead nor fled were captive and would soon join the corpses being burned, except for the handful who had knelt to Tamghat, blubbering and shivering and calling him Attalissa's bridegroom. It was only right they had submitted to her father, as the guild-masters of the town had done, but Ivah would have respected the sisters more if they had brought more dignity to it. They would be given work as servants of Tamghat's household, as though they were the captured bondfolk of some rival chief, carried off in a raid. Folk of that class were not owned, as slaves were owned in her mother's homeland; they were not bought and sold, but they were bound nonetheless to the service of their clan-chief, or such of his *noekar* or favoured warriors and higher servants as he chose to assign them to. All Tamghat's servants were captured bondfolk, since he had no clan of his own.

Ivah hoped there would be no former priestesses given to her as servants. She did not like the blank and watchful looks she saw in some of them, behind their submissive masks.

"Daughter," Tamghat said, catching her hands to draw her up from her bobbing bow and drop a kiss on the top of her head. "What do you think?" His spread hands swept the room.

"It's wonderful," Ivah enthused. "So high, and light. I feel like an eaglet in its nest."

"It looks too bare and holy for pleasant dreams, but once I've settled things we'll brighten it up. Pirakuli carpets, eh, that's what you like. Nabbani screens. Those gold lamps from their chapel, for you to study by. Little eaglet." He smiled, flinging himself into the throne-like chair. "I want you to read the oracles for me, daughter."

"Me, Father?"

"Yes."

His flat tone warned her not to protest lack of skill, lack of knowledge, or his own vastly greater resources of both. He was not in a mood for coy delays.

"The coins?"

Shaiveh had drafted several of the heftier warriors to help carry up Ivah's chests. She had brought them with her from the sheltered valley above the lake, leading the packhorses herself. The servants would not follow with the wagons until the town was more peaceful and the streets cleared, but there were some things Ivah did not want to be without, or did not trust to bondfolk.

One of the chests had been An-Chaq's. It still held, in addition to her tools and scrolls, her jewelled combs and fans, bottles of scent and pots of cosmetics. The containers alone were a small fortune in delicate porcelain and gold filigree, onyx, and alabaster. The combs and fans and a fantastical headdress of goldwork whose flaring rays, sprinkled with pink pearls and amber, evoked the rising sun, were almost enough to make Ivah believe An-Chaq's story of being a Nabbani imperial daughter, who had studied wizardry in secret and fled her prisoned life. Certainly Tamghat had titled her princess, when he was pleased with her. Whore when he was not.

It was this chest she opened. Ivah's hand hesitated over the embroidered silk purse that held her mother's oracle coins. Probably not a good idea. She reached under them for her own, a mismatched assortment in an older purse, its red silk long since faded to a dull mud colour.

"No, not the coins. Read a bone for me."

"Of course." Ivah found instead the leather case that held the tools she needed, a sharp bronze stylus, a slender iron rod like a small poker, also sharpened and dark with repeated heatings, a knife with a thick, short blade, very sharp. She set the poker in the brazier to heat.

"I'll need a blade-bone, Father. Do you mind waiting? I'll send Shaiveh to search the midden."

Her father shook his head, flourished an ivory bone he had carried tucked into the back of his sash. She ought to have noticed.

Ivah took the bone and almost dropped it. It was not flat, but slightly cupped, and looked almost like some broad-finned, swimming thing.

"This isn't—"

Tamghat leaned down to pat her arm reassuringly. "It isn't fresh, daughter. I took it from the tomb of one of Attalissa's earlier incarnations. They have a room full of stone coffins, all lined up in a row. I wonder if they ever let the living goddess go in there? They'd give the poor child nightmares."

The thought of seeing a row of one's own tombs was enough to give anyone nightmares, child or not. An-Chaq had no tomb. Ivah set that thought aside, her face carefully intent, thoughtful.

"What do you want me to ask, Father?"

An-Chaq had taught her Nabbani magic, consulting the oracle coins and the blade-bones, the casting of spells by the sixty-four patterns and harmonies of sun and moon. Her father taught her the string-weaving spell-casting of the Great Grass, and the divination worked with sky-charts and nine river-pebbles, which depended on knowing all the stories of all the constellations, and how to interpret their interactions, their roles in past, present, and future. It was not a horoscope such as they cast in the kingdoms of Pirakul, but a dance of constellations, of stories each with message and moral, and the wandering stars to give choice and warning, as they rode among the constellations through the fixed gates and altered the tale.

Ivah felt no sympathy with the sky-chart; in all their lessons, Tamghat generally dismissed her readings, and told her she had missed layers of meaning in the stories that utterly undermined what she had said. He corrected her even when she read the fall of the coins for him, a Nabbani soothsaying he often mocked as something little subtler than thrown dice. He had never asked her to read the bones at all.

That had been An-Chaq's privilege.

"Shaiveh tells me you're still a virgin, daughter. Is this so?"

Ivah flushed, and dared a brief resentful thought. Why could he never use her name? Always "daughter," like a thing. That saddle, that bow, that daughter.

"Yes," she murmured, looking down at the bone.

Ova's exploring hands surely did not count. She had grown too nervous, and he had been, too, the shadow of Tamghat hanging over them both. So they had gone back to the fires, that night six months ago, and the gold-haired Northron had not met her eyes straight-on ever since. Probably he had been relieved. She was no great beauty; she had nothing of Tamghat's handsome, sharp features to show she was his. Though her eyes were the light golden brown of the grass, her face was round, too heavy, she thought, in the cheeks and jaw, and her features shallow, even flat. Her only likely beauty in the eyes of any of the men she knew was the long curtain of her hair, black and straight and glossy as that of any Nabbani princess. But maybe Ova praised it only because it was all he could find in her worth desiring, except her nerve-wracking nearness to his lord, which was no doubt the source of both desire and fear. An-Chaq had always warned her that men would see her only as the hem of her father's coat.

Tamghat snorted. "What's Ova's problem?"

Ivah felt her cheeks grow darker yet.

"Never mind. You'll have a greater affinity with the maiden goddess for this oracle-taking."

"Oh. Yes, Father."

"I'll give young Ova a boot on the backside for you later."

"Father, please! Please don't. It isn't . . . it wasn't anything. Really."

"No? Why's he been sulking so much, then, if it was nothing? I thought he was just having sudden qualms of rank. You lead him on and drop him? Don't play your mother's games with my *noekar*, girl." His voice was suddenly sour. "I'll have no more Nabbani whores in my following. You deal honestly with my *noekar*-men. I won't have you using them, or them thinking they can use you."

104

"No, Father." Ivah took up the stylus, looked up at him again from her seat on the floor at his feet. "I'm *your* daughter, Father. I didn't mean to . . . it was . . . I was wrong, I misunderstood my own feelings. I'll apologize to him, I didn't realize he still hoped . . ." Glad she had closed the brown-lacquered chest, with its hoard of fans and hair-jewels.

Tamghat smiled again. Ivah relaxed, smiling back. That had been the right answer. Confusion, bashfulness. Childish immaturity. She repeated her earlier question. "What shall I ask, Father?"

"Ask the manner of Attalissa's returning, and the year."

It was not a simple question, a yes or no. Ivah tapped her teeth with the stylus, considering, but then sat still at her father's quick frown. Instead she closed her eyes and adopted the posture of meditation he had taught her, legs crossed, hands loose in lap. Opening herself to the guidance of the stars by which he set such great store. Allowing herself time to think: the correct phrasing, the interpretations that such a question would require for the two palaces and the four elements.

Strange, that Tamghat was so cheerful and patient. A small ritual or divination gone awry could drive him to cursing the Great Gods and striking his servants, or even the *noekar*. His horses fled him when he lost his temper, as they would flee fire or thunder. And this failure to capture the goddess, coming so soon on An-Chaq's great betrayal—Ivah would have expected fury. The execution of even those priestesses who had submitted. The razing of the temple, to relieve his feelings.

He was wiser than she. He already saw future patterns forming, and he moved on to shaping the advantageous and harmonious result. Besides, he had been like that all her life, a thunderstorm, loud and sudden, black fury and bright sun sparkling on rain-jewelled grass, and often little enough cause for either. Perhaps this setback was no greater, for him, than some small divination gone amiss. She had never been able to gauge the true depth of his powers. Or his ultimate intent, in anything.

Ivah opened her eyes again. "You've seen something great and good to come out of this delay, haven't you, Father?" she dared to ask, keeping her voice playful.

"Perhaps," he said. "Perhaps." He fingered the bear's teeth in his braids, looking . . . thoughtful.

"Tell me?"

"No. I want your thoughts on what the bone reveals to be unshaped by what I've seen."

"You're right," she said contritely. "I'm sorry. I wasn't thinking."

Ivah sat back again, eyes closed. Something momentous, but not certainly to his benefit. Yet something that he thought he could turn to his use, or he would not have given up pursuit of the goddess so easily or be so good-humoured about her loss. Something very great, to balance the very great disaster this expedition had already been.

Tamghat had been a month preparing the great spell that would carry his *noekar*-men and *noekar*-women, the sworn warriors who had left other warlords to take oath to him, and the mercenary rabble that made up the largest part of his army, to the distant mountains of the Pillars of the Sky. The patterns had been cut in the earth, the sacrifices made, the omens read. Tamghat trusted An-Chaq, with Ivah helping, to prepare the lesser, the outermost, of the three rings of power-laden words that surrounded the encamped army. They wrote phrases of power in ground charcoal and red and yellow ochre, black and red and yellow, the three sacred colours of the wizardry of the Great Grass, at the twelve points of the circle.

The warriors and mercenaries knew they went to conquer and plunder a wealthy mountain town by wizard's magic. The *noekar* knew their warlord meant to hold and rule it. The only wizards in his service, An-Chaq and Ivah, knew he worked this great and unbelievable spell to move his army a thousand miles or more, in order to bind himself in marriage to a goddess and claim for himself the power of a god.

That had turned An-Chaq's mind. It must have. No sane woman would have done what she did, not to Tamghat. Jealousy sent An-Chaq mad, and mad, she wrote into the inscription a curse against her lover.

Ivah had not known what her mother did. Her father believed that.

The curse was meant to kill Tamghat. It did not, though a dozen of the *noekar* standing closest to him died, when he summoned his great powers and sent them into the spell.

Ivah would remember that in waking nightmares. She had been standing close as well, holding her horse's bridle, soothing it, soothing herself, braced to be flung bodily, or shot like lightning, or whatever the effect would be, into the mountains. And then men and women around her were screaming, writhing on the ground, clutching their bellies. And they died.

Tamghat had let out a great roar, so that Ivah thought whatever enemy's attack had done this tormented her father too. She wove hasty symbols of protection with the long loop of yarn she carried, *the circle of swords* and *the river-island*, and set the spell on her father, with the simple figure that was *the father*. And her well-wishing spell of protection went unnoticed, as he drew his sabre and swept off An-Chaq's head.

Ivah saw, when she lay trying to sleep, her mother's allegedly royal hair, which she would never cut or even braid, sweeping like a comet's tail after her head as it fell, and her mother's eyes looking up at her, wide and surprised and angry.

They had needed to move the camp and begin cutting the circles all over again. The curse-murdered *noekar* were buried near where they had fallen, with all due ceremony, but An-Chaq was left for the carrion-eating ravens. Ivah knew better than to weep for her, beyond the one startled scream.

When they were finally ready to carry the army to the mountains, it was nearly too late. Tamghat consulted almanacs and had Ivah do the same, in the self-deceiving hope their previous work had been in error. And he cursed An-Chaq for a Nabbani whore. The afternoon when they were finally prepared again was the afternoon before the night of the second new moon of spring. Two of the wandering stars, which were called on the Great Grass *the Maiden-Warrior* and *the Bear*, or in Nabban *the Princess* and *the Exile*, or in Pirakul *the Cow-Herd* and *the*

Armed Sage, became one in the house of the Seven Daughters, which governed marriage and beginnings. The coming dawn was the time when Tamghat said he must work his great ritual, even more difficult and taxing than the transport of the army, to bind himself to the mortal woman who was the goddess Attalissa.

One night to take Lissavakail and the temple, and prepare himself, exhausted, to take the goddess.

They had done it. And the mortal goddess was a little girl, and the little girl was missing. She, or her demon-possessed guardian, had killed over a dozen of the *noekar* sent to watch for them at the exit from the underwater tunnel they no doubt had thought secret. The *noekar* were eager for a chance to avenge themselves on the shape-changing black hound that Siglinda said she had seen for a moment, after Tamghat broke down the gates. But it was all for nothing.

So perhaps An-Chaq had won. There was no divine rival to replace her, yet.

Thinking such things did not tell Ivah how to approach the oracle-bone and what it might reveal.

"What will be the manner of Attalissa's returning, and the year," Ivah repeated, opening her eyes and changing her posture, kneeling, the shoulder blade braced on the floor before her. She took up the stylus again and began to incise the question on the lower part of the bone, using the Nabbani ideographs. With any luck Tamghat would not notice how gingerly she handled the bone. She was not even certain the divination could work, with a human bone so differently shaped from what was customary.

Sun and *Moon* she cut into the upper portion, dividing the bone into the two palaces that governed all Nabbani magic. Under *Sun*, in a descending line, she scratched *Air* and *Fire*, and under *Moon*, *Earth*, and *Water*, working more hastily, seeing Tamghat start to tap his foot. Then, right to left, above her question, she began cutting numbers. How far to go, that was the problem. She ran out of space at twenty-four, which might be a sign. The Northrons thought in twelves rather than tens, and her father was oddly Northron in some aspects of his wizardry.

"Done?" Tamghat asked, as Ivah sat back on her heels again. "Good. Colour it, now, with your blood."

"That isn't—" Ivah bit her tongue on the protest. That was not right, not how it was done in Nabban, not how her mother had taught her to read an oracle. It was a Northron thing, a barbarian superstition, An-Chaq said, to think writing coloured with the wizard's own blood held more power. "It isn't customary," she said, a milder protest.

"It will give force to the link between your invocation and her fate, give you more certainty of truth. Don't be such a coward. Weren't you just calling yourself an eaglet?"

"A very small eaglet," she said, making it a joke, and took up the stylus again, hoping her hand was steady. She drove the point into the soft ball of her left thumb, before she had time to think of flinching, and watched the blood well up without any need to squeeze it. Red and glistening on her skin, like the droplets on her face, the smear across her hand when she wiped away what she thought were tears, after An-Chaq dropped in front of her. Ivah swallowed hard and ducked her head almost to her knees, letting the ringing in her ears fade as she smeared her thumb over the characters of her question, trembling hands hidden in the curtain of her hair. She hoped. Hoped her father would not see her pallor as she sat up again, wiping at the trace of blood with her sleeve, so that all that remained was the red in the incised lines.

Tamghat leaned forward, but he was studying what she had written, not herself. His command of written Nabbani was next to nonexistent, though he avoided admitting it. Ivah used the knife to carve a small pit in the bone, took the hot poker and held it there, waiting for the heat to do its work and the fine, branched crack to form.

The human blade-bone was all wrong. She had known it. She had to reheat the poker twice more, before there was anything to see. A long, straight line, like a single hair draped over the bone, ran up through the Palace of the Moon without intersecting either *Earth* or *Water*, and the second crossed the number fifteen, fractured there in a snarled knot of finer lines, and ran to its end in *Fire*.

"So?" her father asked.

"Fifteen," Ivah said. That was the easy and obvious thing. "Fifteen years."

Tamghat frowned. "That doesn't . . . I'll have to do more calculations. That doesn't harmonize with the stars, I don't think. Perhaps not fifteen years from now, but when she is fifteen? Though would that be by Grass reckoning or Nabbani, here? I'll need to learn the time of her birth."

"Perhaps." Ivah knew better than to contradict him, even if it was she who was reading the oracle. "The longer line shows that the Palace of the Moon will dominate her return. Thus the manner of her return will be secret. In secrecy?"

Or to her father's disadvantage: the Palace of the Sun was advantage and success; that of the Moon adversity, disadvantage to the questioner.

"But then there is *Fire*, which belongs to the Palace of the Sun. Renewal. Destruction. It can be either. Heat and life or a funeral pyre. Given the dominance of the Palace of the Moon, destruction and death are more likely."

"The Moon for maidens," Tamghat said. "And renewal in the Palace of the Sun, for new life and the male principle." He smirked. "A wedding."

Ivah frowned doubtfully. "I'm not sure, Father. It should be *Water*, for joining, if there's to be a wedding."

"Don't pout, Eaglet, you'll give yourself wrinkles." He clapped her on the shoulder. "Well, it adds a little to confirm what I've seen."

And it still pleased him, for all it screamed danger and failure to her. Ivah smiled, relief and pleasure at having pleased him a warm glow in her chest. Probably she read it wrongly, took falsely grim views because of her own bleak mood. It was he who had the real power and wisdom.

"*Now* will you tell me what your forecasting showed?" she asked. "Please, Father?"

Tamghat laughed and ruffled her hair. "A greedy eaglet. I cast the pebbles. Black for the past, for roots and beginnings, and they showed me . . . old friends, and old betrayals. Ar-Lin, who poisoned her husband. Tor and Otha, who vowed brotherhood till death and sailed into the west, searching for Ecgtheow's grave and the sword she had carried. Red for the present, for the beating heart, and those told of patience, not action. Ar-Lin, waiting thirty years for her lover's return. The leopard, who stalks the mocking monkey. Yellow for the future, for immortal gold and the undying sun and the rising soul, and there, yes, in time to come Attalissa will return, and draw with her another. The Princess facing the sun's door, combing her hair, drawing in her lover with the magic of her hair, and Ar-Lin who went seeking her lost lover, an old woman, alone, and sang him back from death, never looking behind her.

"And lost him again, because he was young and beautiful, and she had grown old, waiting. She changed, and he didn't."

Ivah had always hated that story. Besides, Tamghat jumbled together constellation-stories from different lands. An-Chaq had told her, when Tamghat was not there to hear, that such combination of stories should never be done if a Grasslands divination by pebbles and sky-chart was to have truth in it. It probably shouldn't have been Ar-Lin at all, but some other tale from some other land, if Tamghat was going to connect her with the leopard or the Princess, or with Tor and Otha. But Ivah suspected her father was not telling her half of the connections he made between the constellations the pebbles chose and the patterns they made between them. He had not mentioned the wandering stars or the fixed gates, which could utterly change the tale.

"Who would Attalissa draw with her, though?" she asked. "Not the Blackdog, we—" daring, saying we, "—we know he'll be with her, no matter what. Who else could be important enough to matter to *you*, Father, for good or ill?"

"My past," Tamghat said, and his eyes narrowed, though he still smiled. "I think, some old comrade from my past. And then, we shall see what happens." He thrust himself to his feet, stretched. "Well, well. Let us have a quiet life, for a few years. And then see what comes.

Join me for dinner in an hour or so. You're pale. You don't eat enough." He strode away, collecting Ova and Siglinda at the door. "We'll turn their chapel to a banqueting hall, I think, Eaglet. Wear something pretty for Ova!"

Shaiveh came in and closed the door behind her, snickered at Ivah's blushing face.

"Fathers," she said. "All the same, always throwing you at men. Now you know why I left my clan. Do you want the sky-blue silk coat, maybe? It sets off your hair well. And yellow ribbons?"

"Yes." Shaiveh, Ivah was beginning to suspect, would be just as happy if Ova's interest in her never was rekindled. "You can comb my hair."

She picked up the oracle bone from the floor. The cracks were darker now, as though they continued to deepen.

"It shouldn't do that."

"What?" Shaiveh's voice was muffled as she opened up another chest.

The bone shattered in Ivah's hand. She yelped and dropped it. Shaiveh sprang up, drawing her sabre, and the lid slammed with a bang. They both stood, looking at the broken bone in an echoing silence.

"Vehna avert," Shaiveh said firmly, calling on her own clan's goddess. She prodded the bone with the tip of her sabre. "That's human! Should we burn it?"

"Not in here." Ivah picked up the shards of bone, half-expecting them to be hot, but they were cool and smooth in her hand. She crossed to the balcony and flung them out towards the lake, did not listen to hear if they splashed or rattled on rocks.

The Great Gods save her from having to breathe the smoke of a burned incarnation, along with the smoke of all those burned sisters. She already felt she was carrying something of them inside her, crawling in her lungs, hot and angry.

It would be nice to have a god of her own to call on for protection and aid, and a name to curse by when things went wrong, as Shaiveh did. Tamghat boasted he had no god, and Ivah herself had been born on the barren northern border of the Salt Desert, far from any god of hill or goddess of even the least spring.

Maybe that was what drove Tamghat's desire to unite himself with Attalissa. He was godless, and needed some close connection with divinity to satisfy that emptiness in his soul.

Maybe if Ivah was a cult of one, wearing her bright-eyed mask, Tamghat was her god. She would be godless and empty-hearted forever, else.

Shaiveh, holding a fistful of yellow ribbons, pushed her down to sit on the floor again and knelt behind her. The *noekar*-woman was humming as she drew the Nabbani-princess sheets of hair back from Ivah's face, spilling them over her lap.

It would be easier to love the child if she didn't look so utterly, blankly sly whenever Tamghiz set eyes on her. That was her mother's doing. Nabbani manners: grovel and shiver and flatter and lie, and poison the one whose feet they kissed. The girl had potential, if he could ever drag her to her feet, make a warrior of her. Shaiveh might do it, coax and bully her out of her shell, take her to bed, if that was what she needed, though that would no doubt put Ova's nose out of joint, and Ova was a good man, a true man, he'd marked him for a son-in-law, a father of grandchildren. Ova's mother was a soothsayer up in Kraaso; he might breed wizard children. But if the girl didn't fancy him, she didn't fancy him, and Tamghiz was not about to come the heavy father over her and dictate such choices; he was no Nabbani, to make slaves of his womenfolk. He should have sent An-Chaq away years ago, before she had time to turn the girl against him. But the years went, and suddenly the shy toddler was a young woman watching him, eyes hidden behind her hair. Calculating. An-Chaq's look.

Tamghiz pulled his mind back to the here and now, to Tamghat, bounded down the stairs two at a time. Eaglet. More a partridge, scuttling low in the grass. His *noekar* hurried to keep up. Siglinda stumbled. He looked back, flashed a grin. "Getting old?"

"My lord!" Siglinda was indignant, but there were dark circles under her eyes. Maybe it was a day since any of the tent-guard had had a chance to sleep, maybe two. Three? They did their best to keep up with him, prided themselves on it, the most honoured of his *noekar*. Siglinda, the past few weeks, to her own rather touching astonishment, more honoured than most.

Tamghat paused on the foot of the stair, let Siglinda and Ova come up beside him, put an arm around Siglinda and pulled her close, nuzzling her faded-copper hair.

"So what about that bath?" he asked. "You look dead on your feet."

"You think a bath's the cure for that, my lord?" Siglinda's blushes amused him still. Like those of a maiden girl, they rose up her white skin like a fiery dawn, till they were lost in the sunburn of her cheeks. Lost now, under leather and armour, but he could imagine the parchment-pale perfection beneath. She was no beauty in her square, freckled face, but he loved the shape of her lean, long-boned Northron body under his hands, smooth and unscarred, which bordered on miraculous, given she'd been twenty years a mercenary. Her lips crooked in a hint of a smile, blue eyes bright. She was no An-Chaq, plotting and manoeuvring, only an honest warrior who took what was offered and rested content. He smiled himself, guessing, from a sigh behind, at her nephew's martyred look. Ova was still young enough to think passion ought to die decently at twenty-four.

It quickly became a cough, and Tamghat dropped his arm as Siglinda strode a purposeful step ahead of him, sword rasping clear. Ova stepped a little aside, keeping the height of the stairs, drawing. They trusted no priestesses, since one of the last of those pleading to give oath to him had stabbed him, or tried to. He'd broken her arm with one hand, left her to the *noekar* to kill.

Old Lady Luli looked almost comically offended, ignored Siglinda and Ova, and drew herself up, a puffing little bantam hen with her feathers all disarrayed. She was grey-faced and shadowed dark under the eyes, sagging and lined around the mouth, looking in far worse need of the soothing effects of warm water than Siglinda, but he wasn't about to invite her to join him. Twenty years ago, when she had been plump and ripely pretty, she had been pleasing enough for a few weeks' diversion; amusing to watch her arguing herself into seduction, as she carried out

114

some goddess-approved studies at the library in Marakand. She'd been a rare specimen of the mountain folk, driven by a spark of intellectual curiosity. Pity it had taken her only to the empty, priest-empowering faith of the godless western kingdoms, but perhaps that was all the ambition her imagination could compass. He had no patience for politicians. If she hoped now . . . She was surely not fool enough.

She curtsied, pointedly demonstrating herself his. "Lord Tamghat, you're needed. There's a problem at the Old Chapel."

"What's that?" Siglinda demanded.

Luli ignored her, again pointedly. "Some of your folk are trying to break down the door, my lord, but they're not succeeding and even if they do, there'll be fighting."

"So?" asked Ova. The *noekar* bodyguards had both sheathed their swords again. They knew Old Lady's type, if not what prior claim she thought she had on their lord, and they knew the way to handle such climbers. Tamghiz kept silent and allowed them to work, as a sensible man lets his dogs handle the herd.

"Another outbreak of fighting might stir up any doubts among those who surrendered, but I'm sure you understand that, Lord Tamghat. The sisters accept now that it's the will of Attalissa they serve you, until she can be rescued and brought home, but this sort of romantic last stand—it heats the blood of the young, makes them willing to die fools rather than live to serve the goddess. We don't need that. The temple's yours, by Attalissa's will. I've said so. I've said it was never her will to oppose your coming, it was Spear Lady and the Blackdog and those who wanted to continue ruling themselves by controlling the child. But, if you want my opinion . . ." and the banty hen crouched, dropping her tail, inviting the rooster, ". . . you need to show them, my lord. Not let this last handful holding out make themselves into heroes for opposing you."

The dead, the women who'd died at the gate-tower and the water-gate and in all the corridors and stairways between, were the temper he wanted among his *noekar*, and more loss than a thousand self-prostituting courtiers, but he could hardly tell Luli that at the moment.

"Did my lord send for your advice?" Siglinda asked ominously.

Luli had the wit to curtsy again, and to actually address her comments to Siglinda. "It's just that I know these people, I want them to understand it's their goddess's will, and the fewer who seem heroes for opposing that, the better it will be for my lord, the easier it will be for the folk to understand that he's here by Attalissa's desire."

"Where's the Old Chapel, Luli?" Tamghat asked. She had a point, and he had thought the fighting all over.

She smiled, too pleased with herself. He shouldn't have addressed her with such familiarity. "This way, lord."

She led them to a dank, lightless corridor, more fit entrance to a cellar than a place of worship, and neither axes nor fire were making much impact on the door as yet. Strength soaked its wood, centuries of divinity. This was the temple's heart, and the fools did not seem to know it. Few wizards were born among the mountain folk, and the ones that were mostly had the sense to leave for lands where they'd win more honour.

Ghatai felt the souls beyond the door, six of them. They smelt of fear and anger. Women who would die before they ever bent the knee to him. He could taste, too, lingering in the air, an odd power, something twisted, knotted on itself.

"This is where the Blackdog fled from," he said. "This is where he stole the goddess from."

"Yes. But there's no way out but by this door, for we mere humans." There was even faint reproof in Luli's voice, that he had somehow failed her, by failing, despite her long-ago warning of the tunnel, to prevent the Blackdog's escape.

"Out," Tamghat ordered, and his folk scattered, pressing back up the passageway. He motioned Luli and his bodyguards after them. "Give me room."

They expected him to blast the door inwards, as he had done with the gate. He was out of patience. If the women wanted to hold the chapel against him, let them. There was something still there, though the dog was gone. It smelt of the dog, tasted of it, some tangled skein of souls, wizardly and divine power spun together. It made his skin crawl. Whatever went on in there, it was nothing he wanted to touch.

Tamghat pulled cords from about his neck, wound them over his hands, eyes on the ceiling, feeling for the shape of the stone. Thread crossed, shaped patterns he had never named, reflecting the stone, telling it of faults, of stress and weight and the earth's burning heart.

He tossed the cat's cradle loose and ran, laughing, as the roof fell, leapt at the end and caught Siglinda's reaching arm.

"Let them wait there, for their goddess to return," he said. And shivered then, feeling the cold weight of prophecy, of the fit shape of things. "Let them wait," he whispered.

Old Lady stared at the rubble-choked corridor, hand over her mouth. Jagged blocks of stone piled floor to ceiling, burying the door.

"Get out," he snarled at her. Something set in motion, in deaths still to come, and she had the gall to look horrified, terrified, meeting his eyes. As though all the other deaths weren't on her head as much as his own. She should have prophesied his coming, urged surrender; they had agreed long ago that would be her part in this. And twenty years was not long enough for even a human to forget.

He jerked his head at Siglinda and Ova. "With me. I'm going to bathe in the lake."

Ghatai's soul suddenly wanted out of this cage, this temple, this grave he made for himself. Bind himself to the goddess and he might be bound to these bloody mountains, trapped, chained into the earth again—it would not happen. He was stronger, he would take Attalissa and break her and she would serve him. And he would lie with Siglinda, who was clean and straightforward and honest human in her heart, in Attalissa's lake, claim it for his own.

And Ova could suffer embarrassment, waiting on them, since the boy hadn't the will to win his way to Ivah's bed.

Later, after swimming and lovemaking and dinner with a silent and nervous daughter too pretty to be wasted on homely Shaiveh, more's the pity, and he'd get no grandchildren that way, either, Tamghiz left

Siglinda and Ova sprawled sleeping in the antechamber, two other of his bodyguards retrieved from assessment duties at the town guildhall to stand watch over his door. He paced the long balcony, watching the lake. The waters were calmer now, and the sunset gilded the surface, recalled molten rock.

Fire, under the dominance of the Palace of the Moon. He could tell the girl otherwise, but he felt fire in his bones again. Destruction and death, and a return. Put with his own forecasting, old friends and old betrayals, a husband betrayed, the brotherhood that ended in death, and Ar-Lin, the constellation Ar-Lin, in past, present, future. The mythological Ar-Lin, murderous wife, faithful and betrayed lover, was a Nabbani tale set on those stars, but it felt like the right one. That was the secret to the star-chart, trusting, when the heart chose one story over another. Those shamans and wizards of the Great Grass, who knew only their own tales, worked groping in the dark.

The wandering stars of war and love and judgement had all fallen into the future when he cast for them, which only confirmed what the constellations said, and the fixed gate that predominated was for divinity, but running counter, which could mean broken, or it could mean active, pushing against the current of the world. That, that alone he was not confident of. For the rest, the stars spoke too clearly of love turned to treachery and death, and he did not think the streams of fate carried him intimations of An-Chaq's return, or those other wives so long forgotten it was an effort to dredge up their names.

So, he had an idea now which of his fellows might be loose in the world. Ulfhild was not, perhaps, the company he would have chosen for a reunion. He'd trust her no farther than he could see her, but in the end—he knew the shapes of her treachery, and the keys to it, and that meant he could predict when and where to trust her, and when to guard his back. Which was love, in a way. She'd fight him, of course. Vartu Kingsbane would not stand by and see him find his way to godhead in the world, leaving her behind. But once he had Attalissa's soul within him, once they were one, Tamghiz and Ghatai and divine Attalissa, he would feel the shape of the world, he would reach into its soul, draw on its vast strength—shake the distant thrones of the Old Great Gods and demand for all his damned and forgotten and outcast fellows, *Why did you betray us?* And he would share that knowledge with Ulfhild Vartu, offer it, win her with it.

Win her again, and free them all, call them all to him . . . take them all into his heart, Vartu first of all. They would be one, and the Old Great Gods would know what it was to be afraid.

But not yet. Tamghiz Ghatai drew three of the looped cords off his shoulders, wound patterns through his fingers, complex as the calligraphy of Nabban. Not yet. Let her not come to him until he was ready, let her wander, always finding other trails, finding arguments in her own mind to turn aside for a time—she was ever good at that. Fix her coming to the stars, to the joining of Vrehna and Tihz, fit signifier of their reunion. He would divert her, so that he would be one with Attalissa before he faced her.

And to be doubly sure of her, he would send . . . Ova—yes, Ova, since Ivah didn't want him—on the long journey to the northwest, to the kingdom of the Hravningas, to the royal mounds at Ulvsness, the Ravnsbergoz. Grave-robbing would offend the man, but a loyal *noekar*, a loyal thegn, Ova would say, would overcome that scruple in his lord's service, at his lord's need, and to earn his village. So long as Ova found the right grave . . . Tamghiz had been at the burial, of course, but landscapes changed over time and it was not so easy to say this mound or that, when more had been raised since, and others reopened. Still, he could divine for it. The stars favoured him that it had not been a royal ship-burning as her mother wanted; they laid her in her grave dressed in silk, his silk, and sable skins. And gold and amber. If the mounds were unrobbed, as they should be, lying in the shadow of a god's mountain, there was jewellery to know her by. All he needed was one bone.

Now the devils, having no place, have no bodies, but are like smoke, or like a flame. And these seven devils, who were called Honeytongued Ogada, Vartu Kingsbane, Jasberek Fireborn, Twice-Betrayed Ghatai, Dotemon the

Dreamshaper, Tu'usha the Restless, and Jochiz Stonebreaker, hungered to be of the stuff of the world, like the gods and the goddesses and the demons of the earth at will, and as men and women are whether they will or no, and having a body, to have a place in the world, and make themselves of the world. They rebelled against the just punishment of the Old Great Gods, and escaped from the cold hells. They made a bargain with the seven wizards, that they would join their souls to the wizards' souls, and share the wizards' bodies, sharing knowledge, and unending life, and power. But the devils deceived the wizards, and betrayed them.

CHAPTER IX

Sera's spring welled into a jagged-edged pool in the red rocks of the caravanserai ridge, which thrust out north from the town into the desert. The clear water swirled and eddied there, and wound away down through the stone, murmuring in a narrow channel a child could step across, chiming like bells over little ledges and falls. It reached the desert sands in a mat of ever-green sedges, spreading in braided threads through a thicket of saxaul before it seeped away, lost under the red sands.

"Water for water," the caravaneers said, when they spilled out the last warm dregs from their gourds and goatskins onto the worn and pitted rocks and the sand around the spring. And they knelt to fill at least one token gourd from the goddess's own waters, before returning to their caravanserais and the town's deep wells.

Sometimes, it was said, Sera herself would rise from the spring and speak to them. Gaguush swore she had seen her once, a woman shadowy and insubstantial as a ghost, mother-naked. Her hair swept into the water and became the deep pool's shadows, and the tattooed horses of Serakallash had galloped on her mist-dim skin. Bikkim said she rose to talk with native Serakallashi more often than not, if they came alone, with earnest intent and need of counsel in their hearts. Holla-Sayan had never seen her and had no desire to now.

"Water for water," Pakdhala said, and tipped out the gourd she had brought. It stained the rock dark, gathering dust as it flowed, and disappeared into the spring-green grasses that crowded the bank.

Sera my sister of Serakallash, I am Attalissa of the Lissavakail in the mountains. I have been driven from my lake by a great evil, and I come to your place with peace in my heart. I want to warn you of this wizard, who calls himself Tamghat, and ask your leave to pass through your land.

That was not the fearful girl but the goddess entire, as she had not been since she told him, *Prayer is for them, dog, not us.* Confident, regal.

Told Otokas.

Arrogant, Holla-Sayan thought. There was no *asking* in her tone, merely assumption of right and Sera's acquiescence.

The grasses hissed like arrows in flight, beaten flat in a swirling wind, and the water rose in waves, splashing them.

"Go away, and take your murdering dog with you!" Sera did not bother with silence, or dignity. If she had been a woman, she would have spit at them; her voice was shrill with anger. "Are you thinking you can ask me for *help?* Abandoning your people, running down here to be pursued by that . . . thing? I can see the fear of it, taste the shape of it, in your dog's mind, and I tell you, I won't have you leading it to my folk, whatever it is, wizard or mad demon like your dog. Go back to your lake where you belong!"

The goddess whirled into a pillar of water, dark and glittering in the early morning light. Sand drove against them, sharp and stinging. Pakdhala cried out and covered her face, and Holla shouted, felt the blaze of anger turning liquid, dissolving through him.

"Leave him alone!" Pakdhala shouted, like a little child defending her elder from bullying, all bristling impotent outrage.

Sera laughed, the column of moving water chiming, but Holla thought the laughter forced. He had known too many brawls to mistake the nervous assumption of carelessness for firm-footed confidence, even in a god. Sera was afraid.

But he could not see that she had cause for fear. Otokas's memories knew the Blackdog could not overcome a goddess in her own ground.

"Is that all you are, great sister of the Lissavakail? A little girl, who stamps her foot and threatens and hides behind her slave? But you've always been good at doing that. Leave him alone, or what? You'll kill my folk, bring your priestesses down here, make me one of your protectorates? I think not. You attracted this mighty wizard, you left your folk to him and fled yourself—you fight him."

I can't yet. I'm weak.

Wilfully weak, avatar of Attalissa. Don't cry to me about it.
I have to hide.
Not here you don't.

Fear was stronger yet in the taste of Sera's words. She should be afraid of Tamghat, not of them. Attalissa was weak and the Blackdog only a mortal body men could kill, while she was a goddess in the heart of her land. But the Blackdog reacted to her uncertain fears and aggressive bluster as any dog would to another that snapped and snarled and cowered at once; it pushed at Holla, wanting to prove its own dominance and assure Attalissa's safety by cowing Sera.

Pakdhala, childlike, was growing angry in her fear and confusion. Holla tried to take her hand, to lead her away, get them both out of this place where they did not belong and were not wanted.

The Blackdog fought him. It thrust bone through his bone, nerves through screaming nerves, wrestled to push him from the world. It felt as though it and he were one . . . thing . . . and that *thing* stood with its right and its left on either side of some barrier. Night and day, water and air. Life and death. And it dragged him, turned, and the dog was in the world. He was blinded by the pain of it for a moment, felt his heart had faltered and started again, felt a sheet of fire had washed through him. It was the dog's heart he felt, anger like a fortress wall raised around the goddess against the world, and she was the hard core of the world all the wild stars circled. But his own thoughts, his own mind, were wound over and through the dog's wash of emotion. He flailed away from it in terror, felt as though he might pull free . . . remembered, *knew* the danger in that, the dog free without the man's will and understanding to leash it.

There was pattern within memory, within the memories that were not his, patterns of control. Experience asserted itself. He snarled at Sera, that much escaped him, but he stayed where he was, crouched between the goddesses, and Pakdhala gripped the long fur of his ruff, anchoring him. Pakdhala. Not any damned foreign goddess but a girl whose hand shook, holding him back, because she almost knew Sera might shatter him from the dog and leave him dead and the dog seeking a new host, lost and panicked and preying on whatever man chanced by. Only *almost* knew. In her conscious mind she was afraid only because she was a child, and an adult shouted with anger she only half-understood, and the world threatened once more to fly apart in violence.

No, he told the dog, and memory knew, if he did not, the way back, and the man was in the world again.

He knelt, his face dripping with sweat, breathing as though he had in truth been wrestling.

"Sera," he said. "Lady of Serakallash, I'm sorry. We never meant to offend you. I don't understand how we have. She's a child. She means no harm. And you know me. I've been here so many times. She thought it was courtesy to come to you. We've no strength to be a threat, you have to know that. If we did, we'd be back in Lissavakail dealing with Tamghat."

The column of twisting water subsided, but the pool still churned storm-like, cloudy with sand. "I knew you, caravaneer, Westgrass-lander of Sayan. You belong to Attalissa now. I pity you."

"Pity her, Sera. She's a little girl, and she's afraid."

"Attalissa knows nothing of pity and will have none from me. You know this and you know why, Blackdog. Take her and go."

"I'm with a caravan-gang. We're leaving this morning, but I can't avoid Serakallash. I'll have to come back."

You'll stay away from my spring, you and she both. I deny you the blessing of my water so long as the Blackdog is in you. But because you were a good man of the road once, Holla-Sayan, my town and its wells will still be open to you. But I will not have you here at my spring.

"Tell your folk about the wizard, Sera. Warn them. Serakallash is a short march down from Lissavakail."

Go away! Sera screamed, and the wind lashed around the spring, raising a red cloud of sand, every grain a needle on the skin.

Pakdhala cried out. Holla grabbed her hand, an arm across his eyes as he lurched up, blinded, eyes stinging, and dragged her away.

The wind calmed as his feet found the well-worn path between the rocks, and he stumbled to a stop where it ran straight between the walls of two caravanserais, blinking till his watering, grit-scratched eyes cleared. Fell to his knees, hands in the mud left by the last rain, swallowing hard against rising bile. He shook like a man in a fever. Pakdhala sniffed, tears running down her cheeks, and flung her arms suddenly around his neck. He shoved her away, finally sat back on his heels, looking at her. She pressed herself against the wall, hands twisting together, lost in the rolled-up sleeves of Thekla the cook's old striped coat.

Pakdhala sniffled again and wiped her face on her unrolling sleeve, but said nothing.

Why? Holla-Sayan asked flatly. *What did you do to her?*

You remember, dog.

No. "I don't want to," he muttered. "They're not my memories."

"It was a long time ago."

He didn't want to remember, but the Blackdog's memory leaked in, like sound from another room which he would rather not overhear. Dog's memory, host's memory, it seemed all one. Demands for tribute, demands for acknowledgement of Lissavakail's overlordship, acknowledgement that the wealth and prestige of Serakallash was due not so much to the caravan-road but the road into the jewel-rich mountains. Sisters of Attalissa's temple, striding down out of those mountains, and mercenaries hired from the desert tribes. The famous horse-herds of Serakallash driven off, the longhouses of the foothills razed, the market square where the chiefs of the great families held their council burned on a market day. It was not the sept-chiefs and the warriors but the folk who came to buy and sell who were trapped, boxed in by the surrounding buildings, trampled in the struggle to escape, suffocated, burned, as the stalls and the awnings burned.

Our Spear Lady was in error. She believed the council was meeting that day.

"And that made it right?"

The girl looked up at him, looked down at her bare feet in the dust.

"It was a long time ago. Father."

"Don't call me—" He rubbed his face, slickly cold with sweat, with hands that still shook, and forced himself up, leaning back against the wall. "You lied to her. The Blackdog lied to her. You . . . we told her the sept-council was meeting there, with all their warriors, assembling to march out. You tricked her into attacking unarmed folk. Children. Children younger than you died there." That long-forgotten Spear Lady drowned herself a few years later.

He had heard no songs of any war between Serakallash and Lissavakail, that was how long-forgotten it all was. The burning market . . . he had heard that in Serakallashi songs, but the villains were desert raiders.

It wasn't me.

Pakdhala shook her head, scuffed a foot in the dust.

Terror. It had seemed to him—to that man—an effective way to break the Serakallashi will to resist.

Tamghat had plainly thought the same, and indiscriminate slaughter of the townsfolk had worked to break the Lissavakaili. The Serakallashi were a harder folk, as Attalissa's warriors had learned.

Justice, maybe, on some vast, cruel scale.

"It wasn't me," he repeated aloud.

"No," Pakdhala said, just that.

Sera's awareness watched them as they went on in silence, not touching, up to the dusty street.

Pakdhala kept her silence as they rejoined the chaos of departure at Mooshka's caravanserai. She kept it as they set out, the strings of soft-padding camels falling into one line, the harsh tin bells clanking as the day's outriders, the Great Grass woman Tusa and her husband Asmin-Luya, who had been a bondman to her father till he ran away with her, loped up the line.

He couldn't put a child who'd never even ridden a horse till a few days ago up on one of the pack-camels alone, so Pakdhala rode with him, steadied in the crook of his arm. He pulled her hood low, wound a scarf over her face against the dust, all without a word. Holla shut his mind against any sympathy.

It seeped into him anyway. Otokas's memories. A lonely, caged child. The girl had had no toys in the temple. No occupations but ritual and calligraphy, copying scrolls in her own praise. No games with the youngest novices, no lessons with them, no drilling as they learned the martial arts. No friends. She learned needlework, embroidering hangings for the temple, ceremonial gowns. Otokas had opened what windows he could for her in the high walls of ceremony and precedent that had built up like a shell, layer upon layer, life upon life. She swam. Otokas took her out boating and fishing, though Old Lady said it was highly improper and took from the goddess's dignity.

Holla-Sayan pushed those memories away. He touched her as little as he could, as though contact, body against body, would bind them closer.

That Blackdog's name was Laykas, the goddess said suddenly, as russet Sihdy swayed and lurched, descending the steep road to the desert. *Do you remember him, dog?*

Holla in turn kept his silence. A hard man, Laykas. A cruel man, contemptuous of weakness. He did remember. Like Otokas, Laykas had raised Attalissa from an infant. Unlike Oto, he never called her anything but "Goddess." No calligraphy in those days. Blades and bows and study of Nabbani scrolls on the arts of war and rule. He had not failed to beat her, when she failed to learn swiftly enough, and she had believed her punishments earned. What had Oto said? You can trust him, the Blackdog always knows . . . Surely not.

The man shapes the Blackdog, Holla-Sayan. You are not Laykas.

Parents do as much as blood to shape the child. He remembered his mother declaring that, her voice shaking with suppressed anger when some kinswoman called him worthless, doomed to trouble and a lodestone for ill-luck.

Who had shaped the goddess? Attalissa was Attalissa unending, but she experienced life like any child, grew and learned, was shaped and shaped herself, died and began again. The Blackdogs and the women of the temple shaped her, over and over, and if so, they made some part of her and carried that responsibility.

The Blackdog was an animal, and perhaps carried no more guilt than the blameless beast of a bad master—he could try to believe that, that it was the man to whom guilt belonged, Laykas and not the Blackdog—but the goddess was not pardoned for Serakallash's market by blaming her teachers. No matter what they had done to her in that life. She was immortal, a reasoning mind as the dog was not, and she had seen more of life than those who reared her, whatever her age. She was old, old, old, and could make her own choices, or should.

"Where are we going?" Pakdhala asked faintly, and her voice trembled. Otokas, at least, had never been angry with her, and this child's life knew nothing worse than Old Lady's tight-lipped disapproval.

Holla sighed and made himself speak. "The caravan's going all the way up to At-Landi on the Kinsai-av, the great river where the Northrons come in their ships down the Bakanav from Varrgash and the forests. We're going to cross the Kinsai-av below the Five Cataracts and go to my family."

"We're going to live there?"

"I don't know."

She twisted around to stare up at him. *Dog . . .*

"We'll see when we get there," he said, more gently. "I haven't decided."

He had, but the dog disagreed.

After a moment she nodded and turned to stare ahead over the stretching reaches of desert, into the unending sky. When she leaned back against him he tightened his arm around her.

Holla-Sayan could not keep the anger alive, could not keep Pakdhala, in his mind, the same being as Attalissa, who had made war on Serakallash. Shyly, the child made friends with the gang, beginning with young Bikkim, who treated her like his own younger sister, a mixture of teasing and affection, and Westron Thekla, who was the most foreign of them all. Small, tough, and wiry as grass-roots, she could barely communicate in any intelligible language, but Pakdhala seemed to grasp her meaning, even when she strung together the desert trade tongue and the Stone Desert speech she picked up from her lover Kapuzeh. But they all tolerated the child, the hot-tempered Stone Desert brothers Kapuzeh and Django, bronze-haired Northron Varro, the Marakander twins Immerose and Tihmrose, Judeh the camel-leech, the Great Grasslanders Tusa and Asmin-Luya, who did not complain overmuch that Holla-Sayan was allowed to bring his child along and they were not. Doha accepted her as family. Even Gaguush, in her way, took an interest, teaching her all the camels' names. The Marakander merchant they escorted called her a pretty little thing and gave her sweetmeats.

She was a girl, nothing more, seeing for the first time the great open spaces of the world. Pakdhala watched the soaring buzzards, eyes wide with wonder. She cried out in delight at spotting a herd of elegant kulan, wild asses, their long-legged foals galloping at their sides. Pakdhala learned to play Grasslander cat's-cradle games with Tusa and forced dreadful squealing noises from Tihmrose's flute, danced to Doha's fiddle and teased Bikkim into letting her throw his spear at fox-tail lilies and clumps of grass. She turned over rocks to watch lizards and scorpions scuttle away, learned to dress herself and not wait to be waited on at mealtimes. She proudly showed Holla-Sayan how Tihmrose had taught her to braid her hair, though it was too short, yet. The scraggle-ended braids stuck out stiffly around her head. No one laughed.

The girl needed his mother. But the dog did not care if she lived a childhood or not. The dog wanted her safe at any cost, and did not understand what it was to watch her coming alive.

It did not take many days of travel for that unfolding of life in Pakdhala to falter. She slept more and more, until she was passing most of the day as well as the night in a restless doze. She ate, with what seemed grim determination, but her round face grew thinner every morning, eyes hollow, lips pale.

Limp against Holla on Sihdy's back, she clutched the amulet-pouch. She no longer ran chasing bird-shadows on the sand. No longer helped to groom the camels, now shedding their thick winter coats, the wool of which was carefully bagged up for sale in At-Landi. No longer watched Thekla at her pots, frowning with concentration when the Westron woman allowed her to knead the evening's bread. If she was not sleeping as they rode, she leaned back against Holla, watching the foothills and the distant mountains away to the south with an old woman's eyes.

The Blackdog could not endure her decline. It clawed at Holla-Sayan, fought him, so he rode with clenched teeth and hardly dared to sleep because of the dreams it brought him, images of its own fears, the girl wasting away, a baby born in Lissavakail with Tamghat to midwife her birth, Tamghat a monstrous thing of teeth and eyes, a gaping maw tearing at the girl's dead flesh.

Waking, he could imagine the dog within him, like a dog of his youngest brother's, one of those surly, devoted, one-man dogs. They shut it into a summer-empty cowshed while a bard did Fanag's final tattooing, before he went off to keep the vigil of his coming of age on the god's hill. The dog had seemed to know something terrible was underway; terrible as it saw it, at least: its master's pain. It paced and paced, and howled, and dug in frenzy at the door until its front claws were bleeding, torn away to the quick, and the pads of its feet full of jagged splinters. When Fanag did ride off to Sayan's barkash, numbed and bleeding and proud, Holla and his mother had gone to let the dog out. It could not walk, then, and he had almost wept to see it. His mother was more practical. She went for rags and tweezers and a jug of his grandmother's fennel-flavoured grain-spirit. They used some to clean the paws and some, in a dish of milk, to calm the dog into a snoring sleep until Fanag's return.

The Blackdog was doing the same thing. Tearing and tearing at the walls of his soul, to attack with mindless fury anything that came near its suffering mistress. As Fanag's dog would have gone for the bard, with his needles and dyes, the Blackdog would turn on anyone it saw as causing Attalissa's pain. And the gang were the only targets near.

He made a wall around himself, because he flinched whenever any of the others moved too suddenly, had to check a reach for his sabre's hilt or a tightening of his grip on his spear when some outrider swerved in close to Sihdy. It was better they kept away, out of reach, and left him to whatever they named it, exhausted worry for the girl's evident decline in health or sulking over the desertion of his mountain woman. He avoided, most of all, Gaguush's eye. He did not think he could bear to have her touch him with this thing in him, and he ached for her.

Not that there was any chance they could sleep together, as matters stood. Pakdhala, who had since she was a child of three always slept alone in her vast bed in the goddess's great lofty apartment in the temple, would not lie down at night except curled tight against him; she whimpered and reached out for him if he so much as rolled an arm's length away.

He tried to summon his mother's patience. Pakdhala was young, and afraid, and had lived through terrible things. She knew every woman in the temple by name, had felt their deaths, each and every one that fell before he—Otokas—took her away across the lake. No child could witness that many deaths sanely, goddess or not. She needed to know she was safe, that someone was there to protect her, of course she did. And she was too clearly ill, on top of it. But she was past the age when she should be sleeping with her father. It was as though she began to retreat to some younger child, to become a toddler cuddled with a nurse again. She looked panicked and on the edge of tears when he suggested she could more properly sleep with the Marakander twins. He was too worn from fighting to keep the dog down to argue.

CHAPTER X

A fortnight out of Serakallash, and between the girl and the dog, he felt like some trout beset with leeches, or a victim of the vampire devils of the old tales, which latched on to a man and drained his soul away.

In a convulsion of pain, Holla-Sayan woke out of a nightmare that muddled together two or three of Doha's favourite vampire stories, stood staring, seeing all too clearly the moonlit camp, every shadow-relief sharp, every crunch of sand under Bikkim's feet a thunderclap as the boy paced along the rows of hobbled camels. Pakdhala stirred uneasily, didn't wake, but reached a hand and clutched at his foreleg. He snarled, deep in his chest, as on the other side of the smouldering fire Immerose rolled to her back, then sat half-up on an elbow, eyes gleaming, blinking at him. Her hand, half-waking, wandered towards the spear lying near.

Holla wrenched the dog away, lay down, shaking, watching Immerose, clenching his fingers in the rough woollen cloth of his bedroll as though that could root him. Immerose flopped down and, after a moment, started snoring again. Her sister flung an arm out to hit her without ever waking, long practice, and Immerose turned on her side, falling into silence. Holla sat up, head on his knees, feeling sick.

Danger. Enemies, weapons all around. *They are not*, he told the dog. *They're my folk. My gang. They'll fight to protect her, because she's mine.*

Bikkim came around the corner of the merchant's tent, the only one pitched. They put up their own only when the wind threatened sandstorm, or in rain along the upper Kinsai-av, and in the biting cold of winter, when thin snow lay over the deserts.

"You all right?" the Serakallashi asked Holla softly, dropping down on one knee by him. "I was just coming to wake you. It's about your watch."

Holla nodded, grunted when he realized Bikkim might not have seen the gesture. He cast a glance at the horizon, to measure the stars. Four hours to dawn, his watch and then Northron Varro's. Pakdhala still had hold of his wrist. For the length of his watch she would wake frequently, checking on him, calling him silently back to be sure he was still there. The last few nights he had almost reached the point of snapping at her, but never did. She rarely even seemed fully awake, her frantic reach for him a reflex.

"Can't have been easy on her, being torn away from everything she knew." Bikkim tucked the blankets Pakdhala was wrapped in more securely about her. "You think it's the lowland air? People get sick going into the mountains, sometimes. Might happen the other way as well."

"Probably."

Bikkim gave him a look, as though he was going to say more and thought better of it, gripped Holla's shoulder a moment instead. "Go to Gaguush, why don't you, when your watch is over. I'll stay with your brat the rest of the night. She'll never notice the difference, as long as she can feel someone's by her."

Pakdhala was already stirring.

"Can try," Holla-Sayan said, and heard himself surly, snarling with temper. He sighed, "Thanks," and crawled out of the tangle the dog had made of his bedding, pulled his boots on and then squatted down by the girl, smoothing the hair back from her face.

Go back to sleep, Pakdhala. It's my turn at watch, that's all. My duty to the gang. You understand about that. I'm not going to leave you. I'm not going to die. You know I can't run away. Just go to sleep. Bikkim's going to stay right here with you to keep you safe.

Don't leave me alone, dog. Even her thought was blurred with exhaustion, barely formed.

You're not alone. Bikkim's with you and you know I'm right here. He hated to hear himself sounding like Old Lady, tying the child down in a net of shame for failing to be all that was desired, but the words shaped themselves anyway. *You don't want Bikkim thinking you're a baby.*

I'm not. She pushed herself further into wakefulness, eyes fluttering open.

Show me, then, he said, feeling heartless, but he was going to suffocate if he could not have a few hours alone. Maybe all new parents felt that way; it was not so different from a baby's incessant crying for the breast, or just the comfort of being held. But that passed, and that went with babies. Attalissa was no infant. *Don't keep distracting me when I'm supposed to be keeping watch.*

Black eyes shone in the starlight, looking, he felt, right through him.

I won't call you, she said, and finally let go of his arm. *So. Go then.* She dragged the blankets up over her head.

He felt more like some servant, disdainfully dismissed, than a parent who had asserted any authority.

"Sound asleep again," Bikkim whispered. "She'll be fine." He kicked off his boots, tucked his sabre down by the side of the bedroll, and crawled into Holla's bed, putting an arm gently over the blanket-cocoon that hid Pakdhala. "There. She'll never know you've gone."

Holla-Sayan belted on his own sabre, picked up his spear, and strode off hastily. The dog was bristling and snarling at Bikkim's possessive arm. He sweated in the cold night air with the effort of ignoring that, and a sudden cough from within the merchant's tent made him draw and whirl to meet the sound, his heart not leaping in alarm but gone slow and cold and calm and . . . angry, that there was nothing to fight.

Where I come from, we don't keep the vicious ones like you around, he told it. *They're no good for herding or hunting, or even as watchdogs, a danger to everyone. You damn well wait till I say someone's a threat.*

It turned on him. Mad, he had time to think, mad as Fanag's dog had made itself, but whatever the Blackdog's sudden rage was for, there was no reason to it, and no master to calm it.

He hit the gritty soil hard as if he'd been thrown, rolled to his knees, dropping the spear.

Couldn't get rid of it. It was his. Or he was its. And which, he had to settle, now, before it did drive him mad and some friend died.

Take me, then, he told it. *Just try. And you can both die in the desert, then.*

The Blackdog flung itself into the world and for a moment Holla-Sayan saw it, blackness, a shape of inky tendrils and smoke, a beast with a heart of smouldering fire, a shadow over him, in him, and the dog shook itself, himself, flesh and blood in the world again, the dust of his fall rising from his pelt.

No, he told it, as it, he, they, turned towards the square felt tent, where the merchant's maidservant was coughing again. Gaguush had tried to leave her in Marakand, but the merchant insisted it was only the camels made her cough, not any catching illness. *You want to fight something, you fight me.*

The dog ran.

He grappled with it, not to pull himself into the world again, but to be the dog. He plunged through memory, men's lives lived in confidence and certainty, almost all of them. The assurance of power held in check. Love. Devotion, an amber sea enclosing him. That was not love, he thought, what there was of him that could still think. Love could stand back and see the person loved, and the dog never saw Attalissa, only the unchanging fire it circled, blind to all else. Love belonged to the hosts, not the dog, and not all of them had loved her. Admiration and fear and tolerant amusement, paternal love and son's love and never-spoken passion, man to woman. Hatred, somewhere in the depths. The goddess young and old, solemn and kind and brazen in conquest, arrogant, fearful, the drunken excitement of battle, of conquest and strength proven. Men and women might face themselves so, when they kept their vigil of adulthood on Sayan's hill, in the delirium of their second and final tattooing, in the haze of pain and poppies and the scent of their own blood. Some never would see into their own souls, but the strong and centred might. Sayan might lead them down. One never spoke of it but with the bards.

So this was no new journey, strange land though it was, and they kept no such ritual in the mountains. The hosts before had never seen, never known the dog.

He had run deep in the desert, the camp and the dark rut of the caravan road miles behind, and Holla flung his heart into the power of the body, his body, the untiring strength. *Run then. You won't outrun me.* This he knew just as well. He'd had a half-broken horse bolt under him before. Let it run, out where it could do no harm, and stay on. It would tire, and know itself mastered.

Make the dog his. There were echoes of those who had not done so within it still, trapped and blind, dying alone and mad, dying berserk, unable to tell friend from foe. He was not about to join them. Otokas had never looked so deeply as what he saw. They were bodiless spirits, he and the dog, smoke or fire or thought twined together. The dog had smelt weakness in his reluctance and tried for the upper hand. It had enjoyed the men it destroyed, the ones taken at need and broken in madness, though it had each time taken a host only to serve the goddess, meaning no harm, had turned on the man only when he failed to bond with it, when he offered that . . . crack of opportunity.

For what?

. . . Something it had lost? Holla saw with the dog's eyes: desert, night, hills, the poppies bending in a wind that might promise sand if it rose higher, and the watch should warn Gaguush of it. He could run, and slow on the crest of a hill possessed of a god, one the Red Desert tribes might name, but the pillar of light the dog's eyes saw gave him no name and wished him strongly to go away, so he did, though the dog snarled at it.

His will now. He loped along a streambed already dried, awaiting next spring's melt. *I'll look after your damned goddess, not because she's a goddess but because she's a human girl with no one else to love her. And you'll trust me to know my land, my folk, my place in this world. As you trusted Otokas.* But he'd spend a year on his knees to the Old Great Gods, if he thought that could free him. The dog knew that, too, and was . . . amused? He had not thought it could be, and that, of a sudden, frightened him, that it could stand back and watch. *That* was not animal's intelligence. It had not seemed to possess such a mind. But it lay under him, his fangs on its throat—the image that came to him. It allowed mastery. It drew him into the core of its soul, where he might see its secrets, since he knew how to see . . .

136

A sullen ember, dull red like old blood, that flared into brighter life as though it saw him in turn, but there was a cold wavering wall between them, a dark mirror to save him from the devouring flame.

Eyes on him. The dog, watching, within itself. No one had been here, of all the hosts who had carried the spirit. None had fallen this deep, even the mad. Holla-Sayan reached out. Touched the mirror, or wall, whatever it might be. Cold and as forcefully in motion as a curtain of water, a river sheeting over a ledge. Colder, cruel as steel in the heart of winter on the Western Grass. He jerked away, but felt something stab, like a needle under the skin, a thread of silver, running up his arm, anchoring itself . . .

Holla-Sayan pushed away, surfacing into desert night, scent of sand and poppies and the crushed plants beneath his paws. A fox yapped. The dog might have trapped him there, killed him then. It was stronger than he was, there in the old, sunken flame. If it had drawn him through that dark wall . . . But it had not tried. His hand, paw, burned a little, as though he had gripped frozen steel. It warned him away, perhaps that was all. There had been no hostility in it then, not as there had been when it attacked him in the camp. Well enough; he would not want it fossicking about in the most profound depths of his soul, either, what little was left it had not already lodged in.

He shouldered through a thicket of tall fennel, limping a little, shook himself, and ran again, an easy trot, back to the camp.

Movement on the skyline sent him slinking, flat to the earth, but almost the same instant he knew her, and ran faster than he had known he could.

Pakdhala waited atop a low ridge. She had not put on her over-large felt and leather boots, and he would scold her for that later, given all the creatures that lurked in the deserts to bite and sting. She swayed a little, and smelt of cold sweat, and she had the fixed stare of a sleepwalker.

I wasn't running away, Holla said, angry, as though she were not so much a child who wanted him as a grown woman who would not trust him out of her sight. And on some level she had to be that, as well. *Just running. You said you'd sleep.*

She put a hand on his head. *I woke up and I was afraid.*

You know Bikkim wouldn't let anything hurt you.

Afraid for you, Holla-Sayan. Come back now. Not a child's mind, behind those black eyes.

That's what I was doing. He couldn't stay angry, nuzzled at her hand in apology, and she leaned on him. He could feel her trembling, at the limits of her strength.

You can't walk back. I'll carry you. We need to go quickly; someone will wake and Gaguush wouldn't call this keeping watch. Besides, it's past time I woke Kapuzeh. Holla eyed the stars. *Hells, everyone will be up soon.* He pushed at the dog, felt his way into its greater, fighting size, though it was reluctant, more a token resistance than anything, proving it was not cowed. *Can you climb on?*

Pakdhala stared at him. "I can't ride on you."

Why not?

Some focus came into her eyes, and the corners of her mouth tipped up. "Can I, dog? Really?"

I can carry you back to the camp a lot faster, this way. And don't call me dog, I told you.

"Father. Old Lady would say it wasn't proper." There was a certain degree of satisfaction in Pakdhala's voice.

Old Lady can go dance in the cold hells, for all I care. And what did Gaguush tell you about not running around barefoot?

"Snakes and scorpions and spiders," she half-sang. *But they won't bite me, Father. You know that.*

It was good to hear her sound like a child again.

Any daughter of mine would be smart enough to be afraid of walking on snakes and scorpions and spiders. Now get on.

He crouched, and she clambered onto his back, awkwardly, gripping his ruff. The child needed to learn to ride if he was going to make a Westgrasslander of her. They'd see she learned, at home . . . The Blackdog stirred at that, mistrust rising, and he snapped at it, *I didn't say I was leaving her. Let it be.*

It settled, warily.

Holla-Sayan didn't run, not with Pakdhala so nervous of falling, ill-balanced, but he trotted, faster than he could have walked in a man's body carrying her. She lay forward, which spread her weight better, and sighed.

I was afraid the Blackdog would hurt you, Holla-Sayan. But it knows you're just as strong as it, now. It will listen to you.

Holla gave a grunt of assent. And he thought, she's lying. Somewhere in that, she's lying. It was the Blackdog's belief that shaped the thought. What she had feared when she felt that he and the Blackdog struggled was something entirely other.

They were nearly back to the camp when he felt the girl go limp and start to slither down his side. Faster than thought, dog and man in accord, he slid from dog to man and rolled to catch her before she hit the ground. She struggled weakly to wake, to get her feet on the ground, and then turned her face against him.

Dog, she said, so faintly he barely felt the thought. *I'm sorry, dog. I'm so tired.*

He held her tight against him and her eyes fluttered open once more.

"Past your bedtime," he said hoarsely. The collapse was no attempt on her part to distract his roaming thoughts; the dog was on the edge of panic again, believing utterly her weakness. He did, too. She was shivering, and felt feverish to the touch.

I'm draining away, dog, like water into the sand. I was never meant to leave my place.

Fight harder. Hold on to life. You must want to live.

Wanting isn't enough, when the body wears out or the spirit flows away. You know that, you've lived it before. I do want. I see why you love the desert. I never understood before how large the world was. But it's too large for me, and when I'm born again in my own land, Tamghat will know.

You need to grow larger, that's all. The world's always frightening when you leave home for the first time, and then you grow to fit it. "Wait till you see the Kinsai-av, Pakdhala," he said desperately. "So much water . . . you'll feel better, more at home."

Not my home.

And no little magic of the road, no piece of Lissavakaili shale, was going to change that.

Holla-Sayan lifted her against his shoulder and set out again, walking, boots a quiet whisper and occasional crunch in the grasses for any watcher to hear. Kapuzeh might have wakened on his own. But he was able to circle the camels and come unhailed to where Bikkim still slept. Pakdhala was asleep again and did not wake when he wrapped her up beside Bikkim and trudged off to wake Kapuzeh. But there was no point, really. Dawn was already touching the east. Exhaustion hit him then, and he realized he ached as though he had been through a dog-fight, had a stiffening shoulder from falling on it and then carrying the girl. The tips of the first two fingers of his right hand were still sore, tender as if burnt. Holla shrugged, and felt the dog, just there, aware. Not ill-contented. The ache of his bruises was already subsiding.

He reclaimed his abandoned spear, checked the camel lines once more instead of bothering the Stone Desert man, who lay entwined with Thekla, and found Gaguush up when he turned back to the fires.

"Thought Kapuzeh had the last watch," she said.

"He looked happy enough where he was."

She caught him as he came by, pulled him close. "Don't make yourself sick, worrying over the brat. She'll get used to us."

"Yeah."

"She'll do better once she's on the farm with your mama. These are long days for a little one."

"I know." He didn't meet her eyes, but leaned against her, felt her breath on his ear.

"You've lost your clinging tick. No one else's up," she whispered then.

"Everyone will be up, any moment now."

"They will if you stand around here making up your mind."

The girl knew when he and the dog dragged one another to the desert. She was going to know what he did now. Too tired was not an excuse he wanted to give Gaguush; he wanted just to lie down and hold her, with no voices crying out for him and no overwrought spirit's nerves thrumming in his mind. The goddess had lived through generations of Blackdogs who'd taken lovers and married and raised families in the town; that didn't change that he knew she was a little girl. He felt, more than somewhat distracted by Gaguush's fingers searching inside his shirt, for a way to distance the goddess a little, shut her out, at least from the surface of his mind. There was a way. Otokas had cut her off all the time from what she did not need to know. Tick indeed. All unconscious, she clung to him the tighter.

"Hey, don't fall asleep on me," Gaguush whispered against his neck, when he failed to respond but by tightening his arms around her. But he was tired, battered in spirit even if the body did heal, and for now, at least, any way to push the goddess aside eluded him.

They were out of time. Thekla crawled yawning away from Kapuzeh's side and began her morning prayers, bowing to the east and muttering to her long-dead gods in her incomprehensible Westron language. Gaguush muttered, "Bashra give me strength," and rested her face on Holla's shoulder a moment. "See what happens when you don't take decisive action?"

Holla shrugged and gave her a kiss, more relieved than not. Kapuzeh woke the next moment, gave Holla-Sayan a grimace and a grin when he caught sight of them and called, loud enough to wake the camp, "Missed my watch, Holla? I don't want to know," as he shambled past, long-legged and lanky, to give Thekla a hand building up the cookfire for breakfast.

Gaguush groaned, touched her tongue to his ear, and swung away with the usual morning shout, "Up, up, everybody up! I'm not paying you lot to sleep half the day."

The look she gave him over her shoulder was not at all pleased.

They left the Red Desert not many days later and crossed the line of barren hills that ran up the shore of the Kinsai-av, then turned north to follow the river on the road between broken cliff and hills.

Pakdhala would go nowhere near the water, though everyone else seized the chance to wash themselves in the shallows. Holla-Sayan

141

avoided entering the river, for what little good that would do if Kinsai took exception to the Blackdog's presence. He dragged up a goatskinfull to wash himself with, in the mornings before the camp stirred, and let them think he had been swimming, as crazy Northrons and Westgrasslanders did. Even letting the water lap his bare feet, filling the skin, made all the hairs on his arms rise and the dog's unseen hackles bristle. The current did not pull him under to drown, but it wrapped around him in a way that no water should, coiling like a snake. Curious, or undecided, as the little goddesses of the springs and gods of the hills and stone ridges had been in the Red Desert, lying low, letting him pass. Whatever the Blackdog was, they had mistrusted it. But Kinsai was no small goddess. He felt her quiet, the way the steppe was quiet before the wild thunderstorms of autumn. Breath held, waiting, staring at the gathering black clouds.

Black clouds within the gang, too. Gaguush was hardly speaking to him. He had never been able to persuade Pakdhala to sleep away from him since the night he fought the dog, and she looked so ill that he didn't have the heart to force her. Draining away, as she said, life seeping out of her. He and the dog pulled together well enough in their shared anxiety over that, and it kept him from worrying at the image of the sombre flame that was the dog's inmost heart, until he was able to let it slip away to the depths of memory. The tips of his fingers stayed pale and fire-scarred, but new calluses and engrained dust soon hid the scars even from him.

Another few days would bring them to the Fifth Cataract, lowest of the Five that made the Kinsai-av unnavigable below At-Landi. There was a ferry downriver of the cataracts, run by an extended family, who some said were mortal descendants of the river-goddess Kinsai and some said were her lovers, men and women alike. Either way, they were the closest thing the river had to priests, and they would carry a traveller across to the Western Grass for almost any trade—silver, gold, bread, wine, a lame dog, a book, a song, a scrap of ribbon, or a night of love, if you took their fancy. The rambling stone warren of their many-towered castle was filled with their takings, it was also said:

dogs, cats, foals, and calves wandering through the rooms, tatterde-malion children, an emperor's fortune in gold and silver and jewels. Half of them were wizards, if the stories were true. Holla-Sayan had taken their ferry a dozen times, both at this lower castle and at its twin, which stood on the western shore halfway between the First Cataract and At-Landi; it provided a similar ferry-service, for similar fees. He never could decide if he believed even a quarter of what was said of the ferrymen, except that they were strange.

The thought of wizards stirred the Blackdog, drew wordless protest from it.

You might be able to swim the Kinsai-av and survive the current below the Cataracts, he told it. *If the river's goddess lets you. But Sihdy can't, and I'm not walking to the Sayanbarkash with Pakdhala on my back.*

No answer. Talking to himself. Swimming or the ferry, either way he put himself and Pakdhala at Kinsai's mercy, and Kinsai was capricious and powerful, a lioness to Sera's kitten. Kinsai could swallow them both, just as the goddess feared Tamghat meant to swallow her.

Holla looked up from blind staring at the top of Pakdhala's nodding head, catching movement closing in on him. It was only Tihmrose, guiding her dust-pale camel in close enough for the Blackdog to come fully alert, Holla's hand, for half a breath, moving to his sabre. The dog still turned hostile on them, if he did not keep a constant awareness of it.

Tihmrose failed to notice. "Poor little mite looks worn out, Holla-Sayan."

"Looks, but it's more than being tired." Immerose, the other of the Marakander twins, who were roaming up and down the string as out-riders, closed in from the other side. Arranged beforehand, he had no doubt. They worked like that, cutting out a man in a tavern. They had picked him up that way, when he was new-come to At-Landi from the Western Grass, looking for work and a place. A long time ago, now, it seemed. They hadn't made a play for him since that one never-forgotten night; he had become too plainly Gaguush's, whatever he might do in the mountains. "Use your head, Holla. Healthy children don't sleep day and night. She's ill. We saw Judeh talking to you this morning. What does he think?"

Holla twitched at Sihdy's head as the camel stretched her neck towards Immerose's mount. "He offered to dose her with sulphur."

"Ah." Immerose snickered. "That would be why he's currently sulking. And you said?"

"Nothing I want to repeat to ladies."

"'s all right, Thekla's out of earshot."

"Sulphur. Poor beast. What do you expect from a camel-leech? Did he offer to check her teeth?"

"Did you want something?" he asked pointedly.

"Other than your handsome body? Since Gaguush doesn't seem to be getting much out of it." Tihmrose sighed, a hand over her heart. "No."

"Yes," Immerose contradicted. "Django told me to talk to you."

"Why?"

"To find out if you actually realize how ill the brat is. He's worried."

"He said if he said anything, like you were a lousy father who didn't know how to look after a child, you'd take it the wrong way and hit him," Tihmrose put in cheerfully.

"Probably." Only a fool would hit either of the Stone Desert brothers.

"Oh, that'd be fun. We could lay bets and everything."

But joking aside, the gang was worried, all of them. Tusa, who had several children of her own, all fostered in Serakallash, found an excuse to feel Pakdhala's forehead two or three times a day, and tell him she was too hot, or too cold. Often both within a few hours. Her husband Asmin-Luya was little better, always asking, didn't he think she was sleeping too much, didn't he think she was looking thinner . . .

Holla shifted Pakdhala in the crook of his arm, looking down at her. Her skin was cold, damp, and grey, especially around her eyes and mouth. Her breath came far too slowly.

"Feed her garlic soup with rice," Immerose said. "That's what our mama always gave us, when we were sickening for something. And look how healthy we are."

"With saffron," Tihmrose added. "I bet Thekla even has a stash of saffron, somewhere. I'll ask." She swung her camel away.

"Why not? Everyone else with a cure's had a go." Holla gave Immerose a rueful smile. "Sounds better than sulphur, anyhow."

Thekla had already suggested liver, which Django and Kapuzeh had provided by coming back from a scouting expedition with a brace of bustards. Varro recommended fish, and tried to shirk evening chores by going fishing in the Kinsai-av to provide it. The previous evening, Gaguush had stood over Pakdhala and ordered her to drink some foul-smelling infusion of herbs that Judeh said he wouldn't give a dying camel. Even one of the merchant's guards had offered soft, sticky, rose-scented sweets, and the merchant herself recommended bleeding, a suggestion which brought the dog to the edge of the world.

Pakdhala ate with grim determination whatever she was given, as though to prove that if she died, it wouldn't be for lack of will on her part, and the life continued to drain out of her.

"Don't look like that, Holla," Immerose said, suddenly serious. "Once you get her home, once she's with your mama, she'll pull through. You'll see."

"Right," he said, and she gave him what was meant as a heartening smile, too falsely encouraging, flicked her braids over her shoulders, and kicked her camel into a lumbering gallop, away from the line and up to the ridge above them again. Gaguush had turned back, no doubt to shout that scouts were bloody little use tagging along the line gossiping. She passed, and glancing back he saw her giving Tihmrose an earful before she turned again, catching up and matching pace alongside Sihdy.

Holla eyed her slantwise. Gaguush's features were harsh, a knife-edged elegance like the wind-chiselled rocks of her desert. Familiar, every line and edge of them, but not easy to be with. He wanted, very badly, to be touching Gaguush's face, tracing the line of her neck, her red-and-black braided spine. He quashed that thought, with a glance at the sleeping girl.

Gaguush tilted her head. "I don't mind her, you know. You don't have to act like you've been caught. I never *said* I minded your mountain woman. I could have just thumped you on the ear and told you to stay out of the mountains, and I didn't. You don't owe me. I don't own you."

He shrugged.

"For Bashra's sake, tuck her in with the twins tonight, why don't you? She'll never notice the difference. Let Immerose fuss over her a bit, the Great Gods know she's had enough practice."

Another shrug.

"Anyway, you'll go over at the lower ferry, meet us up at At-Landi?"

"No." He meant to say yes. He did. "I can't."

"Can't what? Look, if you want to stay in the Sayanbarkash till she's on the mend, go ahead. I won't ask you to just leave her, sick as she is. Catch us up when you can. Keep Sihdy long as you need to. I do trust you'll come back eventually."

That was trust, and kindness, and maybe even love. Camels weren't cheap, and Gaguush cared for her beasts.

"I can't leave her behind."

"You're going to have to. I don't let Immerose drag her brats along, or Tusa and Asmin-Luya theirs. And you're going to kill her, much more of this. It's plain she's not strong enough for travelling."

Don't leave me alone, dog. You can't! You promised you'd never leave me. Pakdhala stirred in his arms, opened her eyes, staring wildly.

That wasn't me. But hush. It's all right. Go back to sleep.

Pakdhala settled again, clutching the amulet-bag.

Gaguush frowned. "She's fevered, and what with worrying over her, you're not much better. You need to get her someplace with a roof over her head."

"I can't cross the river." He could see it, a waking nightmare, the water heaving, the ferry swamped, dropping like a stone, like the fishing boat that a single wave had pulled down as the Blackdog swam from it in the Lissavakail. Pakdhala drowning in waters colder and wilder than she had ever known, powerless as an utterly mortal child.

"What in the cold hells is wrong with you? 'I can't cross the river.' You're bloody well going to have to."

Holla shook his head. Couldn't risk the river crossing, couldn't go on, with Pakdhala dying in his arms a little more every day, couldn't go back, within Tamghat's reach. The Blackdog flowed into him, its emotions all trapped animal again, frantic, on the verge of losing all restraint, clawing and biting till something, anything, gave way. Killing, until there were no enemies left and the world was right again. *There are no enemies here. Lie down!*

Sometimes it was easier to just shout at it, like it was the dog it pretended to be. He shut his eyes, trying to clear the dog's angry, narrowed focus from them. Gaguush did not seem to have noticed anything amiss.

"I'm leaving you at the ferrymen's castle, Holla-Sayan. You can cross or not as you choose, but you're not coming on with us. If I were you I'd pray to my god there's a physician among the ferrymen, or pray to Kinsai for a miracle. I don't think she'll make it to either At-Landi or the Sayanbarkash. You can be a fool and keep travelling till you kill her, but I'm not having it happen where I have to watch."

"Leave us alone," he snarled. "Just go away, leave us *alone*."

Gaguush's eyes widened. He didn't want to think what she had just seen. He felt the heat of the damned dog's eyes in his own.

"Damn you, then," she said, and hit her camel an undeserved blow on the flank with her whip. "Keep the damned camel. Don't bother coming back."

CHAPTER XI

It was no new thing, he and Gaguush having a falling-out, acting like a pair of cats, each bristling and spitting and going to great lengths to pretend the other did not exist. This time, though, the rest of the gang seemed to feel it a more serious rift, a heavier weight on them. They acted as though they believed he really would not be coming back, told him they'd miss him, told him to take care of himself, with the concern of parents sending a too-young son out into the world. And they talked of Pakdhala as though she were already dead. *She was a bright little thing to have around, it's a shame . . .*

Since her panic at the thought he might abandon her in the Sayanbarkash, she had not woken on her own, not without desperate shaking to jar her back into a groggy awareness. The morning they expected to reach the Fifth Cataract, Holla could not wake her at all, and waking or sleeping he could not reach her mind.

The damned dog had started to hover again, like a thunderstorm overhead, needing only the first crack of lightning to erupt. The sooner he left the gang the better, before someone spoke too sharply and he lost all hold on it.

It was mid-afternoon when the caravan passed by the ferrymen's cliff-perched castle, where the road rose into higher hills as bare and broken as those downstream, though basalt rather than sandstone.

Holla-Sayan handed off his string of pack-camels to Django and reined aside, watching the gang pass. Home, family—something too great to throw away. He kept silent. Gaguush rode with her eyes fixed on the horizon, scowling. Immerose blew him a kiss. Sihdy tried to plod back into line, then gave in to pressure on her nose-rein and stood, resigned, as the slow clanking of the tin bells receded. He felt eyes on him, the castle itself, watching.

148

The Blackdog heard and smelt the horseman's approach before Holla ever would have, and he had drawn his sabre, turned Sihdy, while the rider was still many yards distant. A piebald mare climbed the path up from the river surefooted as a mule, no flighty desert-bred but a good, solid Westgrasslander. Her rider was anything but.

The ferrymen were a folk apart. Tall as Northrons, they ran to desert-brown skins and Northron-pale hair. They used no particular pattern of tattooing to declare their folk and land the way their neighbours of the Four Deserts and the Western Grass did, but decorated themselves as they pleased, if at all. It was their eyes that truly set them apart, though. You'd hardly find one in four of them with matched eyes.

Holla sheathed his sabre before the ferryman could take offence, clenching his empty hand till his nails cut the palm. No threat, no threat, he assured the dog, but perhaps the only hope the goddess had, if she were to live this life. His only hope, if the dog were not to drag him back to Lissavakail, to guard an unborn avatar and die at Tamghat's hand.

"You startled me." Holla offered the apology with a hint of a bow, as due a priest. Or a wizard. The Blackdog's knowledge said this ferryman was that: the smell of magic in the blood, rain on dry earth. It grew angry, more focused in its anger. Wizards, old treachery. "I'm Holla-Sayan of the Sayanbarkash, of Gaguush's gang, up there, that's heading for At-Landi. My daughter's ill. I'm hoping there's a physician among you."

"Several. But I don't think it's a physician you need."

The ferryman reined in beside Holla-Sayan, studied him, head a little to one side like a bird. A heron. He had a long, thin body, a long, thin face, sharp-nosed, and carried a three-pronged fishing-spear. Panniers behind the mare's saddle held a dozen fish, each as long as an arm. He was an older man, his light-brown hair streaked with grey, braided up with ribbon and knotted at the nape of his neck with a fan-like arrangement of feathers. One eye matched his hair; the other was a pale, mist-sky blue. The outline of a single feather was stitched along the side of his face, curling around his eye, in black. What it meant

Holla had no idea. The man wore a ragged cameleer's coat, patched trousers, and was barefoot, but he had pearl pendants swinging from each earlobe and what Holla was fairly sure was an emerald in the side of his nose. In addition to the trident, he wore a plain Northron sword at his belt.

The man smiled, following his glance to the sword.

"Blackdog," he said, and gave Holla a little bow in turn. "Rumour recalls you distrust wizards. A precaution they thought I might need, since I'm chiefly a soothsayer—" he used the Northron word for one who was half-diviner and interpreter of dreams, half-dispenser of advice, sought or unsought "—rather than a caster of spells. But I remember you, I carried you over the river once, years ago, and I think you're strong enough to keep the dog on a leash. I'm Kien, son of Kinsai." Which might be a title, or might be literal, one never knew with the ferrymen. "We've been expecting you."

Holla hesitated, until the moment felt too long. "Have you? And you went fishing while you waited?"

The man's narrow face creased into a thousand lines with his grin. Older than he looked. "Why not? Kinsai was in a bountiful mood, and there's always too many mouths to feed." He tapped Holla-Sayan's booted leg with his trident. "You're a long way from home, Blackdog. Why have you come here?"

"Pakdhala's dying. She needs help."

Kien shook his head. "None we can give her. Attalissa's gone beyond mortal aid. She chose mortality. She must live in the body, or not, as she can. Why have *you* come here? Think. Tell me truly."

Holla frowned. "I don't know, anymore. I wanted to cross the river, to take her home to the Sayanbarkash. To hide from Tamghat."

"Tamghat? The warlord they say has sacked the Lissavakail? No good. He's a wizard, a wizard to be feared by wizards. He'd find you."

"Maybe to pray." Sayan help him. No one else could, or would. And how had news of the fall of Lissavakail run ahead of them?

Kien nodded. "That's better. Give me the goddess."

"She's—"

"Dying. Yes. You said. I can see that. Give her to me, and do try to resist the urge to tear out my throat."

Holla frowned down at Kien, who rapped his leg sharply with the trident again, the piebald mare pressed in close to an unusually tolerant Sihdy's flank.

"Kinsai's no enemy of yours or Attalissa's. Don't make her one. She doesn't tolerate fools. Give me the girl."

It took all his strength of will to keep the Blackdog down, but then as if in a dream where nothing could matter anymore, he handed Pakdhala over to Kien, who sat her on his saddlebow, cradled against him. She murmured indistinctly and fumbled an arm around his neck. "Good. Leave the camel."

"Leave . . . ?"

"You said you came to pray. The camel doesn't need to pray. She needs to rest and chew her cud, and she can do that more happily in the stable-yard. Go and pray. I suggest Bitter Hill." Kien pointed to the east, beyond the road, where the hills were dusty pale stone. "Up there, the central peak. It's a good place for praying. No one will bother you. There's a demon at the moment, but she has a good sense of self-preservation—I'm sure she'll leave you alone."

Kien clicked his tongue to his horse and it strode off. The Blackdog nearly flung Holla after it, to seize Pakdhala from the ferryman's arms.

No, he snapped. *Lie down.* Like it was some badly behaved hound.

"Let the camel loose," Kien called back. "She'll follow. Go on. It'll take you till dark to climb it as it is."

Holla slid down Sihdy's side, rather than asking her to kneel, and tied the reins, the nose-line and the reins from the halter both, loosely to the harness. The red camel, with only a single backward glance at her master, did follow the ferryman. There was no frantic cry from the goddess. Nothing but his own heart, racing, panicked.

She's as safe with him as with me. You. Us.

Perhaps she was already dead, her spirit fluttering back to the Lissavakail, where some unfortunate young woman was lying in the embrace of some . . . If she were dead he would know. Holla-Sayan rubbed his face and headed across the road. After picking his way over the rough land for a mile or more, he began to regret his so-sudden giving in to the ferryman's suggestion. Order? His water was on Sihdy, his throat rasping with dust.

He found water, a seepage, reed-grown puddles in the mud, some crooked miles later, after too much clambering over cracked and tumbled yellow rock. His hands were torn, nails broken and bleeding, trousers torn as well from a fall down an unstable escarpment. And he was only at the foot of Bitter Hill. But the water, though muddy, was sweet. Holla drank deeply and began to climb.

Darkness overtook him before he reached the summit, and the moon was only a low sickle in the west, chasing the sun, but the Blackdog's vision let him pick his way as easily as by daylight. There were no trees on Bitter Hill, even in the cracks where thin soil accumulated and where thorns and wire-grass would be found on most of the rest of this range of hills. Not even the noxious fleshy-leafed weeds that clung to the ground around the bitter springs of the Salt Desert grew here, and the broken landscape looked shattered rather than merely crumbled by wind and sun. This was the highest of the sandstone hills. To the north, the black stone stretched away, like an island between the Kinsai-av and the Great Grass that ran for unknowable distances east and north. The sandstone felt good, old and at peace, whatever powers had left it a wasteland long leached away by sun and wind. A good place to pray, as the ferryman said.

From a cleft in the yellowish stone, pale blue eyes watched him.

He had never seen a demon this close, not so clearly. Flitting shadows at night, sometimes, drawn near the fire by music, that was all. This demon was very like a striped hyena, but a pale ash-grey with darker markings the blue-grey colour of Westgrassland oxen. Its— her—large, delicate ears swivelled, following his slight movement aside.

"Sorry," Holla said, feeling as awkward and out of place as if he had wandered into a strange woman's private room. There was something naked and panicked in her wide, staring eyes, blue as Varro's. Something almost horrified.

She could see the Blackdog. Ah.

"I won't disturb you, Mistress," he said, as if she were that strange woman. "I was just . . . the ferryman, Kien, said this would be a good place to pray."

The demon flicked an ear. They could speak, or so all the tales said. She obviously felt no need to do so.

"I'll just go, um, over there?"

The demon blinked.

"Thank you."

She simply disappeared from the corner of his eye as he picked a way along the crest of the hill. A flicker, and she was gone. Holla shrugged his shoulders, shook his head, like a dog shuddering off snow. Something cold had run over his mind, then, with the demon's vanishing. The demon's awareness, darting in for a closer look? He kept the Blackdog from stretching out to pursue her in turn. She was no threat.

Holla settled cross-legged atop bare stone, facing northwest. Home. The Sayanbarkash was across the river there somewhere, west and north, almost due west from the First, the uppermost, of the Five Cataracts. He had no koumiss, no bread, no jug of wine, none of the gifts one took when one went seeking Sayan. They had no priests in the Western Grass. When you needed your god, you went to him or her and spoke. And he, or she, might come to you, and share a drink and a meal, and offer the advice you sought. Or not. No koumiss, no yoghurt. Not even a broken piece of journey-bread or a gourd of water. His throat was parched again, and his stomach grumbled.

Holla shut his eyes on the last dull red glow of the horizon, shut his mind to thirst and hunger and the prickling between his shoulders that was more than a mere demon's attention on him. The dog slipped almost to the surface, a shadow on him, and he knew his eyes would be glowing yellow-green, if he opened them and there were any to see. He could hear. An owl called, and away to the east a pair of hyenas yipped to one another. Much closer, stone slipped and rattled, some small thing rootling for prey. A hedgehog. He could smell it. A snake's belly-scales rasped over rock. Dogs barked, down at the ferrymen's castle, howled not for any unhappiness but because it was night and they enjoyed the noise of their own singing, their unity. A woman shouted with no real anger in her tone, and they were silent except for a pup's brash yip, claiming the last word. Under all, over all, the cataracts roared, throbbed, like the current of Kinsai's blood.

He had never gone to pray to Sayan needing aid. He had gone once, when he was a boy, after one of the wandering bards had done the first of the agonizing tattoos that marked him as of the Sayanbarkashi. Once when he was a man, and the full drawing of face and arms had been completed, the snakes that meant one had reached adulthood coiling on cheeks and upper arms, twining into the eye-flanking owls and the knotted, spiralling cheetahs of the forearms. Once before he left home, he went with a skin of koumiss just to sit a night with his god and to take away a stone from Sayan's hill.

Once when he was an infant, he supposed, but he did not remember that.

What did you say to a god, when you truly had need of one? And this was Kinsai's land. There were no gods in the broken hills of the eastern bank, only Kinsai in her river, and Sayan was a couple of hundred miles away as the raven would fly. Gods did not reach beyond their own land. That was why he was here. Begging for help.

"Sayan? I need you to hear me, please."

Truly talking to himself. Holla opened his eyes, pressed a hand, palm down, to the stone, and looked to the west. Stone, the bones of the world. Stone was the favoured talisman to carry of a wanderer's own land. Stone bound you to home. Stone ran forever, under desert and forest and river and the fabled ocean, salt and unending, on whose shores Varro swore he had been born. Holla-Sayan pulled out the white pebble from the pouch about his neck and took the knife from his belt.

In the songs, the wizards of the kingdoms of the north sealed their spells with their own blood. Stone, bone, water, blood. Earth and life.

If stone and blood of the Sayanbarkash could not reach by stone and water to the Sayanbarkash, prayer here would be empty as Thekla's prayers, a Westron who knew her gods were long dead, who prayed only because men and women should pray, to remember them.

He cut the palm of his hand, not deeply, but enough for the blood to well up quickly, clenched that hand around his talisman-stone and held it out to watch the gleaming drops spatter onto the dusty hilltop. It did not bleed for long, the cut knitting almost as quickly as the blood began to clot.

"I am Holla-Sayan of the Sayanbarkash," he began again. "Please, carry my words through the stone, through the water, through the earth, to Sayan where he walks on the hills of the Sayanbarkash. Please. Let him speak to me. I am of the Sayanbarkash, and I need his aid." *Sayan, please hear me. I don't know what to do. Pakdhala's going to die.*

He felt the attention on him, that watching awareness, grow stronger, until it was almost a touch, a hand running up his spine, stirring his hair, a breath on his ear.

And then words, in his ears, in his mind, in his blood. *Well then. Clever, but the Blackdog should be clever. Though wizards know better than to bind gods with their blood, or do anything so suggestive of that, as you have done. But earnest and innocent one, you are certainly no wizard. I will let your words be carried by the bond of your blood and soul and the bones beneath the earth to brother Sayan. Perhaps he will come to you. Perhaps I will allow it. For a fee.*

The voice, if it was a voice, was almost affectionate but at the same time mocking. There was breath on his ear, on the nape of his neck, someone there, a cool hand cupping the side of his face. And nothing. Perhaps he was asleep, and it was only the wind. Grass whispered, spring-soft and sweet in the air, and the air was wine-rich with the scent of damp soil and growing things, the spring grasslands. The sun was rising over the Sayanbarkash, pale yellow light casting long shadows ahead of him, clear sky, the last bright star fading. Black larks climbed singing into the air over him. It would be like this on the heights of the Sayanbarkash in a spring dawn, but it was summer now, and night. This was memory, the time he went and took a stone away with him. It was too much what he remembered to be otherwise. Dream, yes. He was dreaming, Holla did not doubt that, and did not doubt the reality of it, either.

He sat, cross-legged on the earth, and rolled the bloodstained pebble between his palms, wondering if he would find the same stone still in the gravelly soil if he parted the grass. When he looked up, the god sat by him, intent on a knife and a knot of wood in his hands.

Sayan looked a great deal like Holla's father, stocky, weathered-brown, his black braids tied with careless knots of multicoloured thread, his eyes, when he looked up, narrowed against the sun, nested in fine lines. But they were like pools of dark water, bottomless, and his skin was without tattoos.

"Holla-Sayan." The god gave him a nod, dropped his gaze back to the work in his hands. He carved something, with careful, tiny flicks and curls of the knife. And he did not call Holla "Blackdog."

"What desperate need demanded that?" Sayan cocked an eyebrow at the pebble, now cupped in Holla's hand. "Did you stop to think what Kinsai might ask of you in return?"

The god sounded like his father, as well. Holla sighed, and felt a weight rising from him. Even in dream it eased his soul to be back in his own place, his own land, the custom of his own folk, where the gods were *of* the folk, simple and sane to be with.

"Of course not," Holla said, but his voice betrayed him, not half so careless as the words. "If I stopped to think before getting tangled in gods, I wouldn't need your aid now."

Sayan snorted. "No, of course not. And what, exactly, did you think I could do for you? Blackdog." He frowned, paring away the merest shaving of wood, and held what he carved close to his nose, turning it to catch the light.

Holla-Sayan took a deep breath. This was what he had sidled around in his thoughts, all the way from Serakallash, keeping the hope in shadow, in the corner of his eye where the dog might not notice. Say it quickly, before the Blackdog could panic.

"Drive this thing out of me. If you can, drive the goddess out of the girl, let her be a human child and live. A human shouldn't die because she leaves her home. Attalissa can go back to her lake and fight the damned wizard herself."

The Blackdog stirred, disturbed at anger fixing on thoughts of the goddess, but not at all alarmed. Amused, even. So Holla knew, before the god spoke, that the cautious hope he had kept hidden all this way was no good. And that amusement again made him believe that the Blackdog had a mind, somewhere, that could see itself beyond the goddess.

Sayan sighed. "Separate Attalissa and the girl? I can't do that, Holla-Sayan. The child is not a creature with two souls, as you have become. She is the goddess incarnate. There is nothing else. She's no possessed priestess like the Voice of Marakand, a human carrying the goddess, sharing her self. Your Pakdhala *is* the goddess born in flesh. An avatar, I believe they call it in Pirakul. It's much more common there. Whatever name you give her, she is Attalissa, flesh and blood and soul."

His gaze fixed on Holla for a moment. "As for driving the Blackdog spirit out of you—the Blackdog is not something I want loose in my land, Holla-Sayan. I do not think it would leave such an able host as yourself willingly, not with no other trained and willing host to accept it, and certainly not in response to a threat. I think there would be little left of you, child of my folk, did I succeed in separating you by force. You do not want your body a battleground between us. And besides, Holla-Sayan, I think you do not want to deny the dog, if it means that Attalissa will suffer. I think you love her."

"That's the dog," Holla protested.

"You've cared for her as for a daughter, for nearly a month now. A short time, maybe, but maybe not. I think it's you who loves her, Holla-Sayan. Do you know why you carry my name?"

"I've been told, twenty times or more, yes," Holla said, a little impatiently.

The god smiled, looking back to his carving.

"I'll tell you again, in case you did not understand the first twenty times. Your parents had two sons, and then your mother bore twins. Daughters. They came too early, and they died. Your mother did not conceive again for several years and began to fear she had become barren. She prayed for another child. And around this time there was a girl from a family over on the north slopes of the barkash. I won't tell you her name; it's hers to keep. She became the lover of a married man, old enough to be her father, but when she found herself pregnant he denied her and swore she lied."

The god frowned. "Swore in my name. Well, that is between him and me, and no concern of yours, what became of him. But this girl's father beat her, so she went to her mother's people, and there she bore her son. Since it was a boy, her uncles ordered her to take the baby to its father; they wanted no male bastards, they said, to make a claim on their land. But the man's wife swore she would let the infant die before she gave it house-room with even the least of her hirelings. So the girl left her baby on the hill up here, and went away and hanged herself, though I told her there should be hope in her life yet. And that morning your mother came to pray again for another child. She called you Sayan, because you were still alive on the god's hill."

"I do know this. What of it?"

"The woman you call your mother loved you and you were her child, in the space of a heartbeat. How many heartbeats in three hundred miles? You don't want the dog driven out of you. You want to keep your Pakdhala your daughter, and watch her stretching out of this cramped, dwarfed thing Attalissa has grown into life upon life. You want to watch her grow to some free and laughing maiden who can ride in the solstice races and be shouted at by you for staying out too late afterwards with some young man. That I can't do. She is Attalissa, and she will go back to her lake. But if you are her father, Blackdog or not, you can give her the life you think she deserves, or you can try to, as much as any father ever can."

"If she lives."

"If she lives. I don't know what you can do about Tamghat. I don't know wizards, and the Blackdog seems to think he's no wizard, anyway. The truth is, I have no more idea of Tamghat's strength and reach than you, Blackdog. All I know of him I take from you. For myself, I know life, and growth, and the year's turning cycle. The strength of the hills under the free sky. Let the girl grow strong, and free, and see what happens. What do you want to do, yourself?"

"Go back to the caravans."

"And your Black Desert harridan?" The god, his god, was laughing at him.

"Maybe. If she'll have me."

"That problem, I really think you should work out for yourself."

Holla acknowledged that with a rueful smile. "Probably."

"There may be safety in travelling with the caravans. No matter what exceptional powers this Tamghat commands, his magic looks like wizards' magic, which can be a slow and painstaking work. Perhaps if you keep moving, a wizard's divination will have difficulty in pinning you down. And I will do what I can to protect her. I'll lay on her the shadow of my hills, hide her in dust and stone and grass, if I can."

"Travelling feels to me . . . to the Blackdog, I mean, safer than drawing Tamghat's attention to the Sayanbarkash, being cornered somewhere," Holla admitted. "But Attalissa won't live to grow into anything. She's dying, and when she's born again back in the Lissavakail, Tamghat will take her. And me. Because I'll have to follow her."

"I cannot help Attalissa, or cannot help her much. We are too far apart in kind and in place. But for your sake, Holla-Sayan, I will acknowledge this incarnation of hers as your daughter, claim her as of the Sayanbarkash, for what strength she may be able to draw from that. It will be little enough, but," the god shrugged, "enough rocks will make a hill, enough hills a mountain. It may help, and I know she can be helped. But you need to ask those who can help her more, her sisters of the waters, perhaps even her brothers of the mountains, though I think it would be risking too much, to travel into the Pillars of the Sky with her. In truth, it's not you who needs to ask for help. *Attalissa* needs to ask."

159

"To ask Kinsai."

Sayan hesitated. "Kinsai is the only power to ask, where you are now. But be wary."

"You don't trust her?"

"Kinsai prefers to take more than she gives. But you have no choice that I can see. Ask Kinsai. Otherwise it will be as you fear, despite what little strength I may lend her: Attalissa's body will die and because of the way she has shaped her nature, she will be born again in the Lissavakail, and fall into your enemy's power. But as you travel, she should ask help as well of those who are able and might be willing to give it, her sisters of the waters your caravans pass in the Four Deserts."

"There may not be many willing." He remembered Sera's anger. "With cause, I think."

"Then she should beg," Sayan said relentlessly.

"I think we should." Holla had a sudden image of himself, stern father, marching Pakdhala from spring to well to spring, saying, in his best imitation of his father clutching two furious little boys by their collars, *Apologize for your bad behaviour. Kiss and make up.* He would have laughed, if he had not at the same time remembered, too vividly, the frail, wan look of the girl as he transferred her to Kien's arms.

"It's not much, is it?" Sayan asked. "Love the child, and I will love her, for your sake. I'll make her mine, and my roots are strong and deep enough to hold her, perhaps even against Kinsai's flood. You do have Kinsai's favour, Holla-Sayan, or we would not be with one another now. Do what you must to keep her your friend and Attalissa's, but don't let her overwhelm you, take more than you're free to give. Don't let Attalissa become the price of her own life."

Holla-Sayan nodded. The god's smile was bleak.

"My blessing: no matter where you go, what you are, what you become, you are my son of the Sayanbarkash, and no exile will ever keep your human soul from knowing its home."

The god tucked his knife into his belt and cupped the carving in his broad, work-scarred hands, breathed into them, and opened them again. A black lark tilted its head, surveying Holla with a shiny

160

obsidian eye. Then in a flurry of wings it was gone, rising into the dawn that had hung at the one clear moment of perfection since he found himself there.

"Go back now, Holla-Sayan, son of my land. Go well." Sayan rose and drew Holla up. The god rested his hands, heavy, warm, on Holla-Sayan's shoulders, and kissed him on each cheek, the Westgrassland greeting and farewell.

Above, the new-made lark was singing.

Holla shivered where he sat, stone beneath him, night around him, roar of the cataracts sudden and deafening and the wind cool with the scent of the river. He felt the imprint of the god's hands still, the light dry touch of lips on cheeks.

"And so Sayan of the hills sends you back to me, does he, Blackdog? What does he suggest I do with you?"

An audible voice, a touch of cool fingers, lingering on his neck.

"Kinsai?" His voice was little more than a whisper. He didn't look around. Kinsai was no god of his, and no gentle father to the folk who rode the river. "Great Kinsai, Sayan says you could help the girl live away from her lake, lend her strength—"

"Does he, Blackdog? Attalissa's nothing to me, and I think she's a fool to have bound herself to such an existence. But she has, and I fear we'll all come to suffer for it, if she falls helpless into a wizard's hands. I hear rumours of rumours out of the distant reaches of the Great Grass, that name him wizard and shaman and slayer of demons, and that—that last frightens me, as nothing has in a long age. So. I will help, if she will accept my help. I think she may have learned that much sense from you, at least. But we have matters to settle."

"Do we?" he asked, with unease. "I should go to Attalissa."

Her laughter stirred his hair and he finally looked up, turned his head. She knelt behind him and to the side, a hand playing through his braids. A tall woman, brown-skinned, strongly built, firm-muscled, but no slip of a girl. She was matronly in hips and breast, and utterly naked. Her hair was dark brown and streaked with gold like sunlight on water; it fell in waves to the ground as she knelt, and the colour of her eyes shifted and faded, green, black, hazel, brown, blue, silver-grey, changeable as the river roiling over stone, in a face as harsh-boned as any Northron river-trader's.

"I gave you passage to Sayan, Sayan to you. You owe me, Blackdog."

"My name," he said, "is Holla-Sayan."

"Maybe." Kinsai laughed again, slid her arm around his neck, across his chest, moving closer, pressed against him. "Maybe. You don't look like any creature of the Sayanbarkash to me, Blackdog. But I promise you, Holla-Sayan of the Sayanbarkash, as you love this child and call her your daughter, as I have been a mother and will be again, I will do what I can for your Pakdhala. Because I fear what you believe this Tamghat intends." Her teeth nipped at his neck. "Sayan will have told you to doubt all my motives, if I offer you aid. Sayan is a suspicious old herdsman locked in his hills and too much in his own company. My price for your ferrying is not so very high. I truly doubt you'll mind paying it."

Holla shivered. "Would you keep me here, if I tried to leave?"

No, I would not. But I would be very disappointed in you, Blackdog. He smiled despite himself and she chuckled into his hair, tongue brushing his ear. *Better.*

The Blackdog wanted to get back to Attalissa, and feared Kinsai, feared losing itself in Kinsai. She was the river, strong, unresting, engulfing. She pulled it, and him, spirit and man, and he could lose himself, as he could lose himself in the thunder of the cataracts, the entrancing roar of storm. Be nothing but an unending moment, freed of the world, for as long as he let it hold him.

"Now." Her breath tickled his ear, and then her lips and tongue again. "Blackdog. What of that fee for crossing the river?"

"You could collect it from Sayan." He unfolded himself from his cross-legged posture, turned to meet her halfway. She grinned, pulled him to her, falling backwards into water.

"What makes you think I won't try?" Kinsai's skin was cool, her

162

hair, wrapping over him, hissed like reeds in wind, river-wet, but her mouth on his was warm. "At the moment, though, you're far more interesting, Blackdog."

Holla-Sayan was dreaming, he thought, that he lay on the riverbed, water over him, lying on his side with his head pillowed on his arm, half-waking. If he woke fully . . . he wouldn't be there, and it was a good place to be, for now, water around him, in his nose and mouth and lungs. Long banners of weed brushed over his naked body, like a woman's hair.

The women stood, or floated, a little distance away, upright in the water, their hair and gowns flowing downriver, twisting together. They clasped forearms like kin or friends meeting, holding tightly, silent, or speaking only between themselves. Attalissa—the Blackdog knew her anywhere, and Holla-Sayan could see the child's round face in the woman's bones, the serious set of the mouth, the eyes that were his goddess's no matter what the flesh she wore—Attalissa's face was tight with pain. She closed her eyes, teeth clenched, bared. The Blackdog surged up and he lost all hold on it, but Attalissa hissed, *No!* and he hesitated, crouched to spring for Kinsai. He felt, in that moment of contact, the river, not the cool embrace that held him but what surged between the goddesses, the river flowing into Attalissa, harsh and burning as Marakander grain-spirit raw in the throat, alien, but kindling heat and life again. They embraced, rested forehead to forehead, as if both were too weary to stand unsupported, and Attalissa breathed deeply, drank the river in.

The Blackdog settled again, let the weeds wrap him, and which body it was did not seem certain, man, dog, two shadows wrapped together, still dreaming.

Then he stood on the crest of the Sayanbarkash, and it was night, tattered clouds racing over the stars, grass flattened, hissing with sudden spatters of rain. He was there, his own body, but in the river the Blackdog crouched at Kinsai's feet and she knelt beside him, arm resting on his back, and scratched his ears. They knew one another now, the hand said. No need to bristle and growl. *Carry me now*, she whispered. *Let me see what your Sayan can do for her.*

The dog flattened its ears but did not relax its, his, wary watchfulness. Attalissa stood on the hill facing Sayan, and she was only a girl again, wearing Thekla's old coat over her grubby black gown and red leggings and boots, and her hair had come free of its braids to snarl in knots.

Not for your sake, Sayan said, and he was tall against the sky, a power, as he had not seemed before when Holla sought him out. But it was the Blackdog's vision that saw him now. *Not for your sake, but for the son of my hills you've ensnared in your wars. For the honest love of you that's begun to grow in him. For fear of a wizard who seeks to bind a god. For these, I take you as my daughter in this life, Attalissa of the Lissavakail. Take what strength you can from stone and hill and grass of the Sayanbarkash. Let your mortality be marked by that, by patterns of grass and cloud-shadow, and the ploughed field and the pasture and the wild hilltop, so that those who seek you see only the blood of the Western Grass, and pass over the soul of the Lissavakail hidden beneath it.*

The god picked Attalissa up like the girl she seemed. They regarded one another gravely. Then he kissed her, once on each cheek, once on the back of each hand.

Kinsai hissed, and flinched, as though something recoiled on her; he felt the shock run through him, her hand still on the dog's head, and he growled.

It wasn't harm I meant her, she protested, *but strength to resist your wizard. Your god's a slow, suspicious farmer, who thinks everyone else a horse-trader out to cheat him.*

Were you?

Kinsai stooped and kissed the dog between the ears. *Maybe.*

Pakdhala put her arms around the god's neck, buried her face in his shoulder a moment, clinging to him as she did to Holla. Sayan smiled over her to Holla-Sayan. He said nothing, but his smile was sharp and satisfied. The god lifted the girl's head with a finger under her chin.

You own the Blackdog's devotion, Attalissa. Remember to be worthy of the

164

man's. He is mine, and I don't hold my lives so lightly as you have in the past held yours.

Bitter Hill again, night and stars, windless and calm, and Kinsai whispering, *I don't mean either of you harm. Stay with me a little longer, Blackdog, Holla-Sayan. It's good to hold a lover who isn't afraid.* And he was not, not of her, anymore. Trust was another matter, but the dog trusted no one. Her hair was still wet with river-water, and so was his.

And then Holla-Sayan was sitting on Bitter Hill, clothed, alone, cold, aching, with the yellow day spreading over the stone and the crunch of booted feet coming up behind him. He lurched up, stumbling on numb legs, and stared uncomprehending at Gaguush, dark with the dawn behind her.

"Hey," she said, and reached a hand to him as he almost fell, hobbling a step on feet suddenly screaming with the pricks of a thousand needles.

"You're here," he said stupidly.

"Well, yeah. So are you." The corner of Gaguush's mouth twisted up. "You know how long you've been up here?"

Holla-Sayan crouched to rub his calves. "All night. Remind me not to do that again."

"Three days."

"Three . . . no!"

"Yes."

"Three *days*! What are you doing here? You didn't hold up the caravan?"

"I put Django in charge and told them to go on. He'll manage. I'll catch up at At-Landi, if not before. I went on a few miles and I thought, the brat's going to die and the bloody fool will go back to the Sayanbarkash to drink himself to death and I'll never get my camel back. So I turned around."

"Gaguush—"

"Yeah, well. Praying three days like some Great Grass shaman. I think you've gone crazy, you know."

"Probably."

"You farmers, you can't handle the desert."

"Maybe. Might have been the mountains that did it."

"Damn the mountains." She took his chin in her hand and kissed him, carefully, as though he might fall apart. Plucked something from his hair, water-weed dried and crumbling. She threw it away without comment. "Three days. You do understand that? You didn't *notice*? You've just been sitting there the whole time?"

"Three *days*," he said. "Back in a moment."

Gaguush politely turned her back.

"Those damn ferrymen wouldn't let me come up till a few hours ago," she said, when he returned. She sat, legs outstretched, invited him down beside her with an open arm. Holla sat by her, leaning on her shoulder. He felt weak, light, and empty. No food, that was it. "Told me the gods were with you and I'd better keep out of it. Three days, I've been trapped down in that madhouse. There's dozens of them, you know, and they're all mad. What gods did they mean? I thought there weren't any in these hills but the river."

"Sayan. And Kinsai."

"Kinsai. I was sort of afraid of that. Really?"

He shrugged, face hot.

Gaguush snorted. "I prefer that to mountain women, anyway. She won't be dumping bastards on you, at least. You tell me about it, someday?"

"Maybe."

"And Sayan came to you, too? Your god answered a prayer, this far away? You never struck me as that deservingly holy."

"How do you know he answered?" he asked, curious.

"I saw the brat. She's quite definitely no longer at death's door. I never met a miracle before, but whichever gods you found here, they seem to have helped. The ferrymen—they are good sorts, even if they are all mad—they had Pakdhala in a bed piled with quilts, keeping her warm. And she was just lying there, looking like she'd been laid out for burial, hardly even breathing. They'd pour a few spoonfuls of fish broth down her every so often, pile more driftwood on the fire. And aside from that they just sat there, always a couple of them, watching. Like they were waiting for something. And maybe a little after midnight, last night, she woke up and said, if it wasn't any trouble, could she have breakfast. Oh, and she said I should wait till morning and then I could go and get you, and I wasn't to yell at you about anything at all, thank you very much. She's been tattooed, Bashra knows when, because I'm sure she wasn't when I first saw her here, and, well, I didn't leave her alone with those odd-eyed river-folk very often. She shouldn't be up and running around after so much tattooing, that on top of being so sick. But she looks fine, it's all healed up. Some sort of little bird on either side of her eyes—"

"Larks."

"You knew about this?"

He found her hand, traced a finger across the palm, half-lost in just the touch of her skin. "Yes. No. But that's what they are. Larks for women, owls for men. Snakes when you come of age."

"I think people need to keep away from gods, you know. It isn't good for us. She has what she told me were snow-leopards on her forearms. Really strange, that it's all healed, like it was done weeks ago. Wizards' magic, right?"

"You want me to tell you that."

"I'd be happy if you did. I can only handle a small dose of miracle." Gaguush closed her hand over his.

He smiled at her. "Right. It was wizards."

"That's good. Because miracles are too worrying. Miracles don't happen to caravaneers. Tell me you know that, and we won't talk about it again."

"No miracles."

"Yeah. Wizards are bad enough. I told the brat that Sayan didn't have leopards and she grinned like a monkey and said we'd pretend they were cheetahs. You sure they haven't dumped a changeling on you?"

"Gaguush—Pakdhala's coming with me."

Gaguush was silent, but she did not turn his hand loose.

He brushed the sleek braids back from her face with his other hand. "She has to. I can't tell you why. We can't go home yet—" Home. Lissavakail. The Sayanbarkash. He could not have said which he meant. "—and I can't send her away. If you really won't have a child along, I'll have to find a gang that will." His voice was hoarse. Three days with nothing to drink, unless losing himself in the distant river counted. Suddenly he wanted nothing so much as water. Almost nothing.

Gaguush pulled her hand free, traced lines in the dust with her forefinger. "You mean that," she said flatly. "What do I tell Immerose and Tusa, why they can't bring theirs along, why they have to find fostering and you don't?"

"Tell them whatever you need to."

"She's special, is she? Is that what I'm supposed to say?"

"Yes."

"The gods think she's so damn special they work miracles for her, and I have to make exceptions and let a brat tag along, to get trampled by camels and shot at by bandits and kidnapped by Nabbani slavers?"

"Yes."

Gaguush threw an angry stone clattering down the hillside. "Great Gods save me. Immerose has gone and gotten herself pregnant yet again, she thinks. Why in all the cold hells she can't learn to be careful, like the rest of them . . . Some damned tinker back in the Salt Desert and probably married, not that she remembers his name. It's always that way with her, isn't it? She'll be staying in Marakand the next year and then some, till it's weaned. I don't want to be short two men."

"No."

"I might take on Tusa and Asmin-Luya's eldest, maybe, when we head back through Serakallash. He ought to be old enough to earn his keep now."

"Probably should."

"You look terrible, Holla."

Another shrug. Gaguush pushed him over backwards with a hand spread on his chest, rolled over on him, and he forgot about being thirsty.

"Holla-Sayan?"

He folded his arms around her, kissed her.

"You can bring her. If you must. If it'll keep you from acting as crazy as you have since you found her, and because the world has gotten all too strange, the past few days. But no starting fights because someone comes too close to her—I know you haven't, but I've seen and it's been a damned close thing, a few times. You act like we're a bunch of slavers, or worse. So no more of that. Anyone needs hitting in my gang, I do it. And that includes you. Hey!" Her fingers closed over his, fumbling with the bone toggles of her coat. "I know it's been a while, but that's not my fault, and this is not a good idea. Your brat and a couple of those ferrymen's kids followed me along with a donkey, something about digging coltsfoot root at the bottom of the hill. They're children; they aren't going to stay at the bottom of the hill, you know."

"Yes, they are." It was simple enough to shut himself away from the goddess, now she was no longer clinging like the tick Gaguush had called her. She let him go; she had let him go when she sent Gaguush to him. He could still feel her, if he reached out. But he was free, and alone, as much as he could be with the Blackdog in him.

"Oh, well then, of course they'll stay down there. If you say so." Sarcasm was lost in a longer kiss, and they rolled again. Easier to get her coat unfastened with Holla on top. Gaguush stopped trying to prevent him, locked her hands behind her head and watched him, smiling a little.

"She really yours, Holla? Because I don't think you'd ever crossed the Kinsai-av yet, when that one was born."

"She's mine now."

"Huh. Well. I'll try to put up with her, then. But she damn well better stay down the bottom of the hill."

The devils took the souls of the wizards into their own, and became one with them, and devoured them. They walked as wizards among the wizards, and destroyed those who would not obey, or who counselled against their counsel. They desired the worship of kings and the enslavement of the folk, and they were never sated, as the desert is never sated with rain.

PART TWO

TWO YEARS SINCE
LISSAVAKAIL FELL . . .

CHAPTER XII

Attavaia had been cursed as Tamghat's whore and spat at and told to take her spying elsewhere when she asked around the caravanserais, with all due caution, she thought, about merchants who dealt regularly in iron goods. Ingots, blades finished or unfinished . . . Tin, she asked about as well. Copper they had in plenty in the mountains, and there were still those who knew the secrets of casting bronze. Every village had its bells. There had been bronze swords and spearheads in the armoury still, relics of earlier days, and the temple's armour had still been made to the old patterns. Even the few shirts she and her eleven had abandoned before swimming from the islet would have been a boon, now.

They would make do, when the time came, with what had been stolen or scavenged or salvaged, and with boiled leather. What metal they had would go to spears and arrowheads and swords for those who knew them, iron or bronze. They had a few pattern-welded steel blades taken from Northron mercenaries who came to grief in the mountains, long, heavy swords, unwieldy for those used to the short mountain sword. One, taken from an ambushed *noekar*, was even finer, a steel blade with a maker's mark and other Northron writing none of them could read, but the smith Shevehan, a cousin of Enneas, had nearly wept when he saw it. He said it was an ancient sword from the time of the first kings in the north, maybe from the lost Isles of the West, a *named* sword, the secrets of making which were long forgotten, and it was a sin it had ever been soiled by a raider's hand. Shevehan kept that one wrapped in wool and oiled leather, buried under the floor of his forge like some talisman, and would not hand it out to be taken with the rest of their slow accumulation of weapons to the hidden sisters in

173

the villages. He spoke of it as "the lady," which amused Attavaia, but Enneas said it made her skin crawl.

Attavaia told her she was just jealous she had lost her place in Shevehan's heart.

They would make do, but they needed more. Tamghat, or the Lord of the Lake as he called himself these days, had confiscated the weapons of Lissavakail and the villages, leaving herdsmen with only bamboo spears to defend against predators. The hunters resorted to older ways and chipped their arrowheads from turquoise. Turquoise could kill an unarmoured person as well as an iron point, and there were fletchers in the mountain villages. Something Tamghat seemed to have overlooked.

"I don't like it," Enneas reported in a murmur, as they met up at noon in the busy market square. A man leading a horse past slowed to look back over his shoulder, a look that ran over Enneas head to foot and back again. Enni turned her shoulder on him, pursed her lips in disdain, but spoiled the effect by peeking over her shoulder.

"He's gone," Attavaia said, with a grin. "Wasted effort."

"Well, I hope he enjoyed the view."

Enneas had changed hardly at all in the long two years since they'd fled the temple; she still looked barely out of girlhood, her heart-shaped face still perfect, soft-skinned, her pointed chin and large eyes suggesting a carefree innocence, except when she demurely dropped her gaze. Then the long lashes beneath perfect arching eyebrows transformed her expression to a meekness that in the old days had made her always Old Lady's example of pious, which was to say passive, submission to divine will. Old Lady had never seen Enni running barefoot along the kitchen ridgepole dressed only in a very short shift. That meek demeanour came in useful. Enneas could still pass as barely out of childhood, too young to be any threat to anyone. Attavaia felt as though she'd aged ten years, herself, and thought her face probably showed it. Lines around her eyes and mouth like a mountain wife with six children. Not that she should care about such things. She should stay away from her mother's mirror.

They spent some of their precious Marakander coin, ate over-spiced meat and unfamiliar vegetables off a skewer and drank sweetened mint tea, watching the market with no more than the interest of villagers come to the busy town.

"There are three septs who control the town," Enneas continued, keeping her voice too low for anyone but Attavaia to hear. "And the chiefs of two of them are all for friendship with Tamghat. They have their own retainers collecting tolls on his behalf from the caravans when they come up from the desert road—they've even built a block-house by the road, a little square fort, to do it. They're getting a cut, rumour has it, these chiefs personally, and even the lesser folk of their own septs aren't happy with that. I haven't found anyone who'll admit to knowing a caravan merchant who'd carry blades for us. It's too obvious why we want them, and no one's willing to risk standing up to Tamghat, with their own leaders in his bed."

"Don't be vulgar."

"You want to hear vulgar, 'Vaia? You should hear what this Nab-bani merchant suggested I could do for him."

A bell in a nearby tower tolled three times. People stopped talking and looked around before conversation resumed, in a more urgent buzz.

"What was that?"

"It didn't sound like an alarm." Attavaia shrugged. "Anyway, I didn't have any better luck than you. We should have come six months ago, before he bribed the sept-chiefs. And I think someone tried to follow me."

"I was followed for a while, too. Not by a good-looking man, sadly, but still . . ."

Attavaia dropped the skewer on the food-seller's brazier, sending up a puff of smoke, and handed back the crooked teacup, moving further from the brazier. "Was it a Serakallashi woman about our age?"

"And not even a good-looking one."

"Enni!"

"Just trying to see if you can still smile."

Attavaia ran her eye over the market crowd. Serakallashi, their cheeks tattooed with horses, some so strangely stylized it was hard to see that they were, until you knew. Strangers, tattooed and unmarked, mostly wearing calf-length coats, mostly the varied browns of camels and Red Desert dust. They were probably caravan-mercenaries or merchants' guards, but they could just as easily be Tamghat's folk.

"Next time we come, we should dress like caravan-mercenaries, coat and boots, to make ourselves invisible. Maybe then someone will sell to us. We can say we're some merchant's retainers."

The dark full skirts and the fringed shawls of mountain village women were ordinary and inoffensive. But mountain folk, and women in particular, did not often leave their valleys.

If they did, she would have known better how to pass unnoticed in the lowlands.

"The one following me was a Serakallashi woman," Enneas confirmed. "Tall and skinny. A girl, really. But I shook her off somewhere on the caravanserai ridge."

"She had a turquoise stud in the side of her nose?"

Enneas nodded.

"The same person who followed me, then."

"That's not good. I went to the spring and said a prayer." Enneas shrugged. "We'll see if Sera heard."

"What did you pray for?" Attavaia asked, wondering if she ought to suggest they shouldn't be praying to other goddesses, even knowing their own was well out of earshot.

"A bit of friendly help, is all. Like maybe that the woman following me would stay lost till we were out of town."

"Do you suppose Sera would listen? I haven't found the lowlanders over-friendly, so far."

"Hells, look there." Enneas twitched her head, directing Attavaia's eye across the market. Near where a Red Desert potter had laid out his bright wares on a contrasting black blanket, a half-dozen Grasslanders gathered, coming from two different directions, talking urgently among themselves. "Those aren't caravaneers."

"Tamghat's." Attavaia bit her lip. "At least one *noekar*—that woman with the cult-scarred cheeks? I've seen her in town. She's one of his vassals."

"Looking for us?" Enneas's voice went shrill on the words. She swallowed. "That woman . . . he must have spies here."

"Don't look, don't make any sudden moves to catch their eye."

They were not the only ones made nervous. The potter scowled. A few Serakallashi who looked like someone's armed retainers themselves joined the Grasslanders, as if by prior arrangement. The potter began packing up, threading cord through the handles, fastening festoons of pots and jugs to the camel which knelt beside him, chewing its cud. The camel rose like a small, ungainly mountain, unfolding itself in a succession of jerks, and the potter led it away. As it passed in front of the mercenaries, screening them from sight, Attavaia looped her arm through Enneas's and headed for the nearest narrow street.

Though the crowd was thinning out, others were heading into the square as though anticipating something. A girl with a silk scarf over her head pushed past them, arguing with a slightly older woman in a cameleer's coat, who wore a sabre on a baldric.

"I just want to hear what Silly Siyd's going to say."

"Your father'll have my head if things turn nasty and you're in it."

"But it's important to know what . . ."

"Something's got them stirred up," Enneas murmured. "Should we go back to find out what? Doesn't seem like it's anything to do with us after all."

Attavaia was acutely aware of the weight bound around her middle, which made her look several months gone in pregnancy. The long roll, carefully sewn and padded, held several pounds of the best spiderweb turquoise.

"No," she said. "We don't want to catch their eye. Remember my condition."

"Heh, yes. It definitely gives a girl a glow, just like they say."

"That's carrying all this extra weight in the lowland air."

"But what are we going to do?" Enneas asked. "I even asked about scrap iron at a forge. They nearly set the dogs on me."

"Do without," Attavaia said. "Cut bamboo in the lower valleys, do what we can with that. When the time comes we should have a little warning. We can reforge or recast tools, if the villagers will give them up."

"If," said Enneas gloomily. She freed her arm from Attavaia's, sliding a hand into the folds of her skirt, through the ripped seam to reach the long dagger strapped to her thigh. "There's the woman who was following me, the thin one with the hooked nose."

"I see her."

She was the same one Attavaia had noticed a time or two, sauntering behind, talking to those with whom she had just spoken. The Serakallashi woman was dressed like the caravan-mercenaries, her coat striped in dun and white, with a cotton scarf loose about her neck and a square felt hat in the Marakander style over her swinging braids. No sword or sabre, but undoubtedly a knife or two in those pockets. She strolled their way, suddenly unavoidable.

"Enni, isn't it?" she asked with tensely false cheer. "And 'Vaia? Let's go."

"Where?" Attavaia demanded.

The woman turned a thin smile on her. "To meet someone who might have what you're looking to buy, but you've got to come right now."

Attavaia and Enneas eyed one another, while the woman rocked on her heels.

"Now," she repeated, a bit less cheerfully, her gaze straying over their shoulders. "Because, you know, there are Sevani guards, men belonging to one of the Lake-Lord's lapdogs, out looking for a pair of mountain women right now. They think Tamghat's people might be interested in them, 'specially as they were talking to merchants about buying spearheads and the like. Tamghat's people are playing bodyguards for Siyd Rostvadim at the moment but I expect they'll take an interest once the great announcement is over with, whatever it is."

"What great announcement?"

"Didn't you hear the bell? The chiefs are going to speak. But since there's been no council meeting, it'll just be the chiefs of the town septs, and probably just Silly Siyd Rostvadim. Going to listen might

178

conceivably be a more valuable use of my time, but others think different, so stop wasting it and come on. Unless you want to talk to the Lake-Lord's people instead."

She turned and walked off, swift and purposeful.

Attavaia waited for no more than a heartbeat before following, Enneas at her side.

The Serakallashi led them through a succession of narrow alleys, twisting between the high, blind walls of the houses. They emerged onto a lane only slightly wider, encountering a caravan moving out, the camels piled with burdens that nearly blocked the street. The dull tin bells clanked and dust rose from the huge padding feet, choking. Their guide threw a fold of her scarf over her mouth and nose, weaving through the tall beasts that plodded five or six together behind a rider.

Heart in mouth, Attavaia hesitated. She had become a competent rider of the little mountain ponies over the past couple of years, and as a novice had taken her turn with the lay-sisters who managed the temple's herd of yaks, but even the yearling heifers scared her once their horns began to grow. Which was ridiculous in a warrior, a sister of Attalissa, the leader of the free temple. Ridiculous, to fear mere animals minding their own business, grass-eaters, when she had faced humans intent on killing.

These camels were taller than a tall man at the shoulder, as tall as the bulls of the giant wild yaks, and long . . . they just took up so much *space*. They seemed to float in the dust they raised, demons riding dry waves of smoke. They wore halters with a rope threading them together, and a thin rein to a carved wooden peg in the side of one nostril, far too fragile a control, she thought, for all those pounds of muscle. Enneas, a hand gripping her shoulder, seemed to feel the same. She squeaked as one turned its head to stare down at them, giving a horrible sort of gurgling groan.

"Don't act like a silly girl," Attavaia muttered, and did as the Serakallashi had done, striding in front of a ridden camel, towing Enneas with her. The beast, or its rider, didn't slow or turn aside, serene in its massive right. They scrambled.

The woman was waiting for them, nervously backed into a doorway further along the street.

"I thought you weren't coming," she said reprovingly as they joined her. "Don't tell me the camels scared you."

"So?" asked Enneas.

"You use those bloody great black cows up there, and you're scared of camels? I've seen the skull of one of those things. If you told me it was a demon I'd believe you." Her smile was honest, this time. "Tell me you're village women and I won't, though. You act like townsfolk. Come on."

Enneas muttered under her breath, "Do we look like farmers?"

Attavaia thumped her with an elbow.

"Ah, right. We do."

The Serakallashi led them down another twisting alley and out through another moving caravan, or maybe it was the same one. Once it had passed, Attavaia blinked grit from her eyes and saw that they were on the caravanserai ridge, where the large compounds, which contained hostel and stabling and warehouses and corrals all within a single inward-facing square, lay at odd angles to one another, making the one broad street twist and bend like a storm-snapped tree.

"Here." With a quick look around, the woman tugged them down another alley, this one so narrow Attavaia thought a man's shoulders might brush either side. Another look, up and down, and their guide unlocked a narrow wooden door with a heavy key. "Back door," she explained. "Inside."

Hand on her own dagger within her skirt, Attavaia led the way into a dark, musty-smelling space. Enneas and the Serakallashi followed, and the guide locked and barred the door behind them. It was a small room or a corridor, but her eyes were too blinded by the change from light to darkness to make out any details. The woman pulled aside a red striped curtain in another narrow doorway.

"The sisters," she said, announcing them to someone unseen. A snigger. "They're afraid of camels."

"Don't be rude, 'Rusha. Show them in."

The woman waved them through. They emerged blinking into a room lit by a deep window high in the wall, a long horizontal slit. It was a pleasant room with thick Pirakuli carpets on the floor and fat cushions to sit on, a brass pot of tea and a tray of cakes on a low table in the midst of the semicircle of cushions. Two older Serakallashi men sat cradling small cups in their hands, with the air of people delaying the start of some business.

"Sit, Sisters," said one of the men, who had the same thin face and hooked nose as the woman. "'Rusha, water for our guests."

'Rusha—his daughter?—waved them to cushions and went away, returning after a few moments looking damp and dust-free herself, coat and scarf discarded to reveal black cotton trousers and clean white caftan, not a cameleer's garb. Attavaia took note; the coat did hide what a person was. 'Rusha bore a basin of water and soft towels.

They washed in silence, took seats amid the cushions. If these Serakallashi were allies of Tamghat's, it was already too late.

'Rusha poured tea and offered it to them, thick and murky, milk already in it, or perhaps it had been brewed that way. Attavaia sipped cautiously. Spices she couldn't name. And the men just watched her.

"Why were you following us?" she asked 'Rusha. Direct, but friendly, she hoped.

'Rusha looked up at the ceiling. "At first, only because someone felt we should know that one of Tamghat's folk was trying to find swords. We wondered why. Swords, iron . . . things the Lord of the Lake takes too great an interest in, that are none of his business in Serakallash."

"I thought your sept-chiefs had agreed to collect a toll on most goods going through here. Some portion of the goods."

"The chiefs of the Rostvadim and the Sevani," the thin-faced man interrupted. "They've got no right to think they speak for all the septs or all Serakallash. Or for the merchants whose goods they're pilfering."

"The Rostvadim and Sevani are two of the three septs whose strength is in the town," the other man explained.

"We're not interested in Tamghat's tolls," Attavaia said carefully. "We're—"

"Sisters," 'Rusha interrupted. "We should stop trying to avoid saying anything . . . incriminating. We're all here, we can all see one another's faces, we're all damned. You want weapons, you're not the Lake-Lord's folk, and you're lucky I found you again when I did, because the Sevani chiefs had sent their retainers to capture a pair of mountain women, thinking Tamghat's vassal, who's come down to nursemaid Siyd, might be interested in these mountain women buying weapons. The whole town has probably seen through your pitiful disguise by now. You're priestesses of Attalissa and you're trying to rearm what's left of your order, yes?"

"We're just—" Enneas began.

"Yes," Attavaia said.

"Good. They're idiots, the ones who thought this morning that you might be mercenaries or conscripts of his, searching for smugglers. You're not half arrogant enough."

"Look who's talking," murmured the thin-faced man. 'Rusha ignored him, as of long custom.

"We might be willing to help."

"Help how?"

The older man, a wealthy one to judge by the patterned weave of his caftan, which had the sheen of silk blended in it, silenced 'Rusha with a raised finger.

"What do you need?" he asked. "Swords? Bows? Horses? Grain? Meat? Warriors?"

"I . . . probably not horses," Attavaia said, in astonishment. "Not in the mountains."

"Why do you want to know?" asked Enneas. "And who are you, anyway?"

"And how do you know we're not Tamghat's tame chiefs?" 'Rusha murmured.

"Yes," Enneas said, with not quite a frown at her. "That too."

"Treyan Battu'um," the older man said, with a hint of a sitting bow. "A chief of the Battu'um—not," he added with a smile, "one of the town septs, but from the east."

"And you just happened to be here when we were?" Enneas persisted.

"Yes, exactly. Visiting my friend to talk of this and that, concluding a deal for fodder in the coming year . . ." He shrugged. "Luckily for you, or you'd be in chains before evening."

Attavaia was embarrassed to think he and 'Rusha were probably right. Pitiful disguise, yes. But as for Treyan Battu'um claiming he was here on business—more likely it was conspiracy against the chiefs who favoured Tamghat. A sept-chief surely had factors to handle such routine matters as the sale of fodder. So. A useful ally to cultivate, Treyan Battu'um.

"Mooshka Rostvadim," the other man said, rather more reluctantly. "My daughter Jerusha."

"You said it was the Rostvadim who were collecting tolls for Tamghat."

"I don't like what my chiefs have done. It's not a decision they had the right to make. Anyway, my wife was of the Battu'um."

"It's bad for trade," muttered 'Rusha.

"It's an offence to Sera," her father said. "Serakallash serves no overlord."

"Nor does Lissavakail." Attavaia repeated Enneas's question. "Why offer help to us? What does helping us get you?"

"We would hope, someone to get rid of Tamghat before he digs himself in deeper up above. Someone to get rid of him before he does more than buy the Rostvadim and Sevani chiefs."

"Who are fools and cheaply bought," added 'Rusha.

"So we do your fighting for you?" Enneas asked.

Treyan shook his head. "No. I'm offering an alliance."

"On behalf of Serakallash?" asked Attavaia warily. "Do you speak for the sept-chiefs' council, then?"

"I'm sorry. No. I don't even speak for all the Battu'um in this. Well, they don't know you're here, do they? We thought there was no resistance to the Lake-Lord left in the mountains. We'd heard of none. But now that we know there is . . . I think it's safe to say most of the septs would like to see any rebellion against him succeed. I'll put it to them as soon as I can send riders out. And I can speak for my folk and my wife's, and together that's over half the Battu'um. That alliance, I can promise you."

"It isn't so easy," Attavaia said.

Enneas set down her cup with a sharp crack on the table. "No. Don't, 'Vaia."

"We have to trust them if we're going to accept their help."

"All they've offered is words, so far. We don't know . . ." Enneas stopped, helpless.

Mooshka Rostvadim cleared his throat. "We've always been good neighbours, your folk and ours. There's times neighbours have to stand together. If there's a fire, say. Stand together, or lose the whole neighbourhood."

"We can't act yet," Attavaia said slowly, while Enneas frowned at her teacup. "You'll have heard—Attalissa is gone."

"We've heard all sorts of things," said 'Rusha. "Gone, dead, lost, carried off by a demon."

"A demon?"

"She called Tamghat to her, to save her from a demon, but he came too late and she was carried off to serve the demon's evil lusts."

"Jerusha, show the sisters some respect," her father snapped. "No one believes that tale."

"We haven't heard that, in the mountains." Attavaia swallowed hot, bitter anger at such a twisting of her uncle's rescue of the girl. "No. It's only that Attalissa is a child. She's safe away, guarded." All she did was founded on that trust. "She'd be ten now. When she's a woman, she'll return. We'll rise then, and she'll lead us to destroy this wizard. But for now, all we do is prepare."

That was not what the men wanted to hear, she saw it in their faces. They thought they had gotten hold of an imminent uprising.

"I'm sorry," she added. "You'll have to deal with your chiefs yourselves. I think it's a mistake that they've let Tamghat get even a toehold here. He won't stop at that."

Treyan Battu'um rubbed a hand through his hair and gave her a smile. A handsome man, with a square, dependable face and a full dark beard, beginning to be streaked with white. She really should not be paying attention to such things. Enni made jokes all the time, but the truth was her vows never seemed to trouble her. Enneas's jokes and ironic needling of the blandly faithful hid a rock-solid certainty of Attalissa's grace that Attavaia envied.

He was old enough to be her father, anyway.

"I see. I won't withdraw the offer, Sisters. When the time comes—come to me. I can't speak for the whole of the Battu'um, but I can argue for an alliance with you, and I don't think you'll be turned away."

They would have to offer something in return, that went without saying. But Attalissa would honour any agreements made by her priestesses in such an hour, Attavaia had no doubt of that.

"Thank you."

"Who will be sending word to us?" Treyan asked. "So we know it is the free sisters and not Tamghat's tame priestesses, in any future dealings, if you don't come yourselves?"

"Sister Vakail," Attavaia said, with a bit of a smile.

"Hah. Yes, good enough."

Sister Lake, it meant.

"There's still the matter of buying metals. We need to arm, to be ready when Attalissa does come."

"We have good swordsmiths among the Battu'um. Something could be arranged."

"We can pay." She stood up. "Excuse me a moment." She retreated to the dark back entryway, hoisted her skirt and petticoat up, and began unlacing the tightly bound bundle.

'Rusha followed to keep an eye on her. The Serakallashi chuckled, leaning against the doorframe. "Oh, Sister. I did wonder what you had under there. What with your vows and all."

"Turquoise," she muttered. "It can be mined—secretly. Tamghat's folk watch the gold-washing villages more jealously, so we can't come by gold. Do you mind giving me a hand? I think there's a knot."

Treyan Battu'um's brows lifted when Attavaia unrolled the bundle of unworked turquoise on the carpet, and Mooshka Rostvadim sucked in his breath.

"Swords, arrowheads, spearpoints," she said. The man had offered the work of his smiths, after all, and there was far less risk of discovery if they could take and hide finished weapons rather than having to furtively make them themselves. "Those are most vital. A token of further payment, on delivery."

"That right there's worth a good few blades, I should think, the making and the packing them up to the mountains," Mooshka said. "We'll want camels for that, or asses, depending on the trails. Treyan?"

"What weight?" the Battu'um chief asked practically, taking a stone and holding it up in the light. "I've never seen finer."

"Father? I'm sorry, but . . ." A girl's voice called from beyond another curtained door, and then a man's:

"Treyan? I'm sorry, my lord, but you'd better come. There's trouble in town."

Another man didn't bother calling, but twitched the curtain aside.

"Master Mooshka? I've barred the gate. There's fighting in the market and Lady Davim here says there's mercenaries in the thick of it, the Lake-Lord's men, alongside Siyd Rostvadim's folk."

'Rusha flipped a fold of the cloth over the chunks of sky-blue stone. "Out," she ordered. "We're coming."

Mooshka nodded to her and followed his servant, flapping his hands as if shooing out a hen.

"This doesn't sound good. Jerusha, record the weight and quality of the turquoise, and we'll work out the details later. That is . . . ?" Treyan was already rising to his feet. "Will you trust us to hold the stone for now, and deal with you honestly? Tell me where to send word, so we can arrange another meeting?"

Attavaia hesitated, looked at Enneas, who only shrugged.

They all looked to her, as if being Otokas's niece gave her some inner knowledge of the goddess's will. When her uncle came back . . . he would laugh at her, for that. But she hoped he would be a little proud, too.

"There's no path, but if you turn off the mountain track to the east just past a place where there's walnuts on one side and bamboo on the west . . ." Attavaia gave him directions to an isolated hut, where an old woman and her four grandchildren scraped by, a family of simpletons herding a few goats and tending a weedy garden. The two supposed grandsons, like the bustier granddaughters, had been novices when the temple fell. So far none of Tamghat's patrols had chanced on the place, and they hoped the general dim-wittedness they presented, when a hunter or other traveller did wander by, would deflect any interest. It was a useful knot in the web of communications she had built, and a vulnerability, from which threads led off to too many others. But she needed some means by which others could get in touch with herself and Enneas, and they moved around too often to have any fixed base. "Call her Auntie Orillias, and tell her the message is for her Cousin 'Vaia."

Attavaia offered her hand, and the sept-chief took it. "As Sera is my witness, I'll not cheat you. I'll give you the fair worth in arms and labour of whatever you can pay in stone or gold, and if the sept won't honour that, I'll see the deal's kept by my own folk. And we'll ride against Tamghat when you need us, for friendship's sake. My word, given in the hearing of Sera and the Old Great Gods."

"Attalissa and the Old Great Gods witness it," Attavaia said formally. "And our thanks. Attalissa's thanks, when she comes again. Attalissa's friendship to the Battu'um sept, unending."

Treyan followed Master Mooshka out, and 'Rusha bundled up the turquoise, "With your leave, Sisters, Treyan, I'll get this out of sight?" She whisked away, out into that back corridor again. They could hear her feet running up stairs.

"Do you trust them?" Enneas asked. "If we lose that—"

"We have to trust someone, if we're to deal with the lowlands. If they were going to turn us over to Tamghat, they've certainly got the numbers here to do it without leading us on like this."

In a moment Jerusha was back, her arms clutching a large bundle of cloth.

"Whatever the fighting in the market's about may distract people from looking for you, but just to be safe—change your clothes."

"What, here?" Enneas asked. "What if your father and the chief come back?"

"It won't be anything they haven't seen before, will it? Hurry up. Don't worry, everything's clean," she added. "I shook the camel-fleas out myself."

The clothes, which smelt strongly of soap and some herb, were an odd assortment. Trousers, which though meant to be loose were tight at the hip on both of them, boots with the soles worn almost through, too large, shirts also too large, obviously not 'Rusha's, and mended old coats that came almost to their boot-tops. They traded amused grimaces with one another and transferred their belongings to the coat pockets.

"Hold still." Jerusha rolled up the cuffs until their hands were showing. "At least your hands look like you do a bit of work," she said. "But with your hair all hacked off under your ears like that no one will believe you belong to the road. Maybe . . ."

She transformed their shawls to scarves, wrapped around their heads, a fold over the face.

"Not bad. It's windy out," she explained. "Dust is a good excuse to cover your faces. You'll do. You might pass as Marakanders. They're a real mix of blood. Wait here, and I'll go see what Davim has to say about town. No point you walking into a riot."

They waited anxiously, straining their ears to catch any noise of distant fighting or murmur of conversation, but all was still. Jerusha returned quite quickly.

"Your damn Tamghat," she said. "Causing trouble, as expected. But you're in luck. Master Baruni's decided to clear out this afternoon instead of tomorrow, in case things get worse. His merchants are nervous. You can go with him. If you do come back someday—this is Mooshka's caravanserai. You can tell it by the big mulberry trees along the wall by the gate. For Sera's sake, don't ask the way unless you can manage a better disguise."

188

"You're sending us with a caravan?" Attavaia asked. "Will they mind?"

"Baruni? No. He'll think it's a good joke. Revenge. Tamghat's Sevani lapdogs claimed about a sixth of the furs and unfinished Northron blades his merchants are taking to Marakand, and they're demanding he make up the loss."

Attavaia snorted in disgust. "Blades. I bet I asked him about them, too. I bet he's the one who told you? Big man, really light eyes and no tattoos?"

"That'd be him." 'Rusha grinned. "The merchants wouldn't have sold anyway. These are set down for the city guard or something, that's part of the problem—they can't just raise the price when they get home to cover their losses."

"Camels," Enneas said. "This is going to involve camels."

"Damn right. Pretend they're giant cows, eh? A supposed village woman like you should have no problem with that."

"Swords," Attavaia said, no longer thinking of the ones she ought to have purchased. "If we're dressed like caravan-guards, we should be armed. Especially if they're fighting in the streets."

"Swords in the hands of a couple of girls who don't know what they're doing will be worse than camels under a couple of girls who don't know what they're doing," Jerusha said flatly.

Attavaia took her by the shoulder and slammed her into the wall, pinning her there with knee and shoulder, the side of her wrist pressed against her throat.

"We're not children," she said. "We're not farmers. We're not riders. We're young, yes, but we're sisters of Attalissa. We fought on the walls when the temple fell, and we swam the lake with the temple burning behind us. Weapons, we do know."

She let the woman go, backed away, shoving her shaking hands into the coat's pockets. Attalissa help her, this was no time to lose her temper. If Jerusha tried to hit her, she probably had a right.

The Serakallashi just flexed her shoulders and grinned again, rubbing her throat. Enneas relaxed, took her own hands out of her pockets, leaving the knife behind.

"That's better. I was thinking it's no wonder Tamghat walked all over you lot, for all your fame as mercenaries. I'll see what I can do. Weapons don't pile up like old clothes, but I guess you've paid for 'em if I can find 'em, and I'll sort it with Treyan later. Now, come on."

They eyed one another, and Attavaia shrugged. "Lowlanders," she murmured, as they followed Jerusha out into another room where an older woman was taking scrolls from a shelf and packing them into a metal-sheathed trunk. "Account books," 'Rusha explained. "And my mother's collection of Marakander poetry. Just in case. She's long gone and no one else in the family reads it, but Great Gods help us if the poetry's looted. Wait a moment." A brief pause, while she uncorked ink and found a pen, to write, on a small sheet of thin Nabbani paper in looping Marakander script, the tally of the turquoise as Attavaia declared it, and again, and to have all four of them, the recorder-keeper as witness, sign both copies with the first initial of their name. She ripped the paper in half, handed one copy to Attavaia. "Treyan's honest as the Great Gods themselves," she said with a shrug, "but business is business."

A heavy door opened onto a scene of chaos, men and women shouting, moving in haste, mountains of canvas bundles and baskets being brought from doorways in the shadows of a long arcade, camels groaning and gurgling like water in a clogged drainpipe during a thunderstorm.

There was order to it, eye and ear picked it out. No one ran to undo what another had done. The shouting was merely to be heard over all the other shouting.

They stood under an archway, one of many fronting the building or buildings, hard to say which, that enclosed a great square of beaten earth with a central well and watering-trough. Camels lay folded up neatly, strung together in fives or sixes, being loaded with the incredible mountains of goods.

Mooshka Rostvadim and Treyan Battu'um stood talking with a handful of other Serakallashi. A pretty girl of fifteen or so, her tattoos bright and new-looking, her braids dyed with henna, clung to the sept-chief's arm. There was a smear of blood on her hand. After a moment Attavaia recognized her as the girl who had been so eager to get to the market—the Lady Davim the servant had mentioned? The woman at her shoulder looked more battered and dusty than she had before. She recognized Attavaia, too, and gave her a nod.

"But who actually started the fighting?" Treyan was asking.

". . . someone started shouting that her son'd go to the mountains only over her dead body, and Siyd lost her temper, you know what she's like, and said that could be arranged, but there was no knowing whose sons and daughters would go, it would be a fair lottery, and that's when they started throwing things. Fruit and eggs, first."

"Typical Siyd, making an announcement like that right there in the market, with all that ammunition to hand," Mooshka remarked.

"Davvy, you're hurt. You should have said!"

The girl turned to smile at Jerusha and give Attavaia and Enneas a long, curious look. "Just scratched. People started shoving and I fell."

"You shouldn't have been there," Treyan said.

"I *know*, Papa." Obviously old ground retrodden.

"What's happened" Attavaia asked.

It was Treyan Battu'um who answered. "The leading Rostvadim chief, Siyd, and her fellows have decided Serakallash will send two hundred of its youngsters between fifteen winters and twenty to serve with Tamghat's warband. As the chosen chiefs of the goddess, they say it's their right to make such decisions."

"*Devils* take them!" Jerusha added.

"At least she got a clod of horse-dung in the face," said Davim.

"It'll be another hundred next year, I'll bet you."

"They've been conscripting boys from Lissavakail and the villages, too," Enneas interjected.

"Just boys?"

"Well, in the mountains, girls don't fight, unless they're Attalissa's. He's taken lots of young girls as well, hostages from every valley. He calls them novices, though he isn't training them to be anything but servants. Some of the older ones have ended up concubines for his male vassals, his *noekar*."

191

"What happens to the conscripts?" Davim asked. She sounded anxious. Young enough to be at risk.

"It seems harmless, just training them to weapons," Attavaia answered her. "But they send them out with the tax-gathering parties, and to make inspections for anything suspicious. In a few months most of them are talking about the stupidity and greed of peasants, the superstition and backwardness of mountain folk. How great a man Tamghat is, how the priestesses lived off the labour of the villages and never did anything for them, and kept the goddess an impotent prisoner, and how Attalissa's promised to wed Tamghat when she returns and together they'll make Lissavakail great, a power to rival Marakand, ruling all the desert road."

Yes, give Serakallash that to worry about, show them how important it was they help oppose the Lake-Lord.

"And some of them have joined that cult of his, worshipping bears," Enneas added, her lip curling with disgust. "My stupid brother, he scarred his own face in some barbaric initiation ceremony. My mother's scared to have him in the house, and too scared to forbid him."

It was perhaps not a politic question, but, "Has anyone asked your goddess what she thinks?" Attavaia wondered.

"Of course," said Jerusha. "Sera's said before that Tamghat has no rights here and Siyd Rostvadim lies when she says she and her cronies act with divine approval."

"But Sera hasn't done anything to stop it? Hasn't deposed these chiefs?"

Treyan Battu'um frowned. "No," he said. "The chiefs govern by right of blood and it would be a grave matter for Sera to act against one. It hasn't happened in generations."

"It's time it did again. Doesn't she understand the danger?"

"Your goddess fled," Jerusha said pointedly. "Perhaps Sera sees the danger all too well."

"It's not a matter for outsiders, Sister," added Treyan. "Leave our goddess to us."

"She can act where Attalissa couldn't," Attavaia persisted. "If she

192

doesn't support her people against those willing to bow to Tamghat, she risks being overwhelmed by him. He'll take Serakallash little by little, until you're a mere tributary of his false temple wondering how it all happened. Can't she see?"

"Sera's will is our affair," Treyan repeated, with finality. "Mooshka, if Master Baruni's riding out, I think I and my folk should go with him. The sooner the outlying septs hear of this the better, and I don't want to be delayed by Siyd's games. She might try to prevent me alone, but they're not such fools they'd try to stop a whole caravan leaving."

"Yes, and I've got Baruni two new cameleers," Jerusha added. "Lucky man."

She hallooed and waved, until a burly Marakander crossed the yard to them, still shouting back over his shoulder to some of his folk. Jerusha dragged Attavaia and Enneas forward.

"These are some friends of ours who need to get out of town without being noticed," she announced. "You're taking them. They've never ridden a camel, but if you get cornered, they can fight with their feet on the ground. Damn, swords, I forgot. Papa—we've got something they can use, don't we? Find them swords."

Mooshka rolled his eyes and disappeared back into the house doorway.

"'Rusha bosses him terribly," Davim told them, with the air of one sharing a secret.

"Someone has to, or nothing would ever get done around here."

Master Baruni looked them over rather as though he was being asked to purchase them at market and was prepared to start haggling. "Ah, yes, the ladies looking to buy iron and tin and swords. I don't know, 'Rusha."

"It's important."

"Yes, well, important means dangerous if they're caught, right?"

"More dangerous for us than for you," she said tightly. "And why should they be caught? Anyway, I thought you wanted to get back at that bastard wizard up there for all his plundering. Get them out of town and you'll be doing that. Just take them and don't argue."

193

"I see 'Rusha bosses everyone," Enneas whispered to Davim, and drew a giggle from her.

Baruni scratched his beard, still considering them. "How far am I taking them?"

"Just out of sight, so they can head back to their mountains and their demon cows."

"Demon cows?"

"We don't have any demon cows," Enneas said.

"Pity. They might be useful. Just get them out of town, Baruni, that's all."

Master Baruni sighed. "It'll save arguing if I say yes, am I right?"

Jerusha grinned.

He offered both hands to Attavaia and then to Enneas. "Welcome to the gang. If you fall, act drunk. I wasn't planning to leave till tomorrow morning, so," and he directed a glare at his assembling caravan, "you won't be the only ones."

Mooshka returned with two swords, their sheaths slung from rather worn-looking leather baldrics. Attavaia examined hers critically. It lacked the curve of the desert sabre, but was short and single-edged. A blade for slashing, not stabbing. The simple scrolling work on the hilt looked Northron. She wondered why a caravanserai master would have such a thing, but perhaps with so many travellers passing through he bought and sold goods himself, or played pawnbroker—a bit of a trading post for mercenaries needing drinking money or a new coat. Or perhaps she was not the only one moved by Tamghat to begin stockpiling weapons.

"It's a sax," Mooshka said, with a shrug. "You're used to short blades in the mountains, right? You'll be able to protect yourself on the ground, anyway. You ought to have a lance, too, if you're a caravaneer, but I think the less you've got to unbalance you the better, up there."

The caravan seemed suddenly to have settled into readiness. A handful of Serakallashi women and men, Treyan's retainers, led up sleek and leggy horses and the Battu'um party mounted.

Enneas watched enviously. "I wish they'd had spare horses," she murmured. "Or how about riding double with Treyan, Attavaia?"

"Shut up," Attavaia advised.

"Come on then, ladies," Baruni said. "We'll get you loaded on somewhere. What are they worth to you, Mooshka? A day's fodder, maybe?"

"I'll write it in against next time," the caravanserai master promised. "So long as you get them out without losing them." Mooshka gave them each a pat on the shoulder. "Sera keep you safe," he wished them.

"Sera keep you mounted," 'Rusha added.

It was terrifying, exhilarating, the power of the animal beneath her surging up, snapping her forward and back not once but twice. The whole herd of them rose, and the cheerfully shouted commands of "Up! Up!" seemed mere formality, every one of them obedient to the caravanmaster's lead. Attavaia kept the nose-rein loose in her hand, as instructed, a tighter hold on the rope from the halter, for at least an illusion of control, and clutched at a strap to keep herself from pitching off. There was nothing resembling a saddle on this baggage camel, just what seemed to be bundled goods, a snail's house of them, among which she was crammed. Hard even to tell the beast had humps, it was so laden. She gripped with her legs and tried to keep her weight balanced. Her camel was not led, because that would attract comment, but camels, Baruni and Jerusha both assured them, followed.

"Does the camel know that?" Attavaia asked.

Jerusha laughed up at her, slapped her ankle. "Good! Now just stay there, 'Vaia, and we'll see you again sometime."

Enneas was somewhere behind, with a homely but hopeful young desert man trying to impress her with his advice.

"Leave her alone, she's not your type," Jerusha called, heading that way.

"What's his type, 'Rusha?" another woman called.

"Desperate!"

"Sera's blessing on our road!" Baruni called. Mooshka's servants opened the heavy gates and the big yard emptied. The camels yawned and groaned and gurgled.

Attavaia's camel swung from side to side as it walked, plunking each foot down with deliberation. It seemed resigned to the human presence on its back. She was just one more piece of baggage, a lump to be carried on to Marakand.

She tried to move with the camel's movements, sitting into it, not perching rigidly. But every muscle tensed, regardless. It was a long way down. Glancing back, she couldn't see Enneas; there was a string of camels between the two of them, led by the young man who'd tried to be helpful. He winked at her and, blushing, she faced ahead.

They wound along the crooked road through the caravanserais, but before they had gone far the pace of the clanking bells slowed, camels groaned, and voices were raised. Attavaia could see nothing of what hindered them, just the walls to either side and a wall ahead, where the road took another twist. They shambled to a stop and her camel moaned as though it was about to die beneath her.

Davim cantered back on a bright yellow-gold horse and reined in beside Attavaia.

"There's Sevani and Rostvadim warriors up there," she reported. "Chiefs' guards. They stopped another caravan, said no one was to leave town. They're poking through all the goods, the caravan-master's livid because he's already been looted once for their tolls, and they claim they're looking for smuggled weapons."

"Or for us?"

"Probably. Probably makes a good excuse to see what they can take, though. Master Baruni says he'll fight before they touch his caravan again, but he hates fighting, so hold on tight and follow the woman ahead of you when we start to move."

The girl flashed a grin that was no doubt meant to be reassuring and kicked her horse into a canter again. "Be ready to ride!" she called to the man behind as she passed. Attavaia looked back to see she had reined in again by Enneas, repeating the more detailed explanation.

The caravaneer ahead looked back at her, over a line of five camels. "That lady you're riding is used to being in this string," the woman called. "Just hold on. She'll follow. And I know where we're going."

"Where?" Attavaia called back.

"Down the ridge!" The mercenary said it like it was some delightful treat. "No wall around Serakallash."

The distant voices rose into shrill outrage.

"Attalissa watch over us," Attavaia prayed aloud, and the camel twitched an ear.

One of the Battu'um retainers flashed along the street, and then another on the other side, or was that Treyan himself? The camels ignored them, used to the reckless haste of horses, perhaps. Rear guard? Someone to pick up any battered and broken priestesses?

More shouting. Attavaia loosened the sword in its sheath, testing a little, so see how fast it would draw. Edged, single-edged, remember that. Like an overgrown version of the hacking knives they used for cutting bamboo in the lowest valleys. How did you fight from atop a camel, without overbalancing and sliding off? She'd like to have Enneas by her now, but a nudge of the heel against the camel's shoulder did nothing but make it stamp, as though it twitched off a fly. It would move when the rest moved.

"Hi! Away!"

Bells jangled discordantly, and the camels ahead began to lurch forward, urged with cries and a few snaps of the short whips from their stately plod into a rocking run, beating the street up into dust. Attavaia clutched at straps again as her own camel took off after them. No need to steer. She clung with both hands as they rounded the corner and veered off, not following the road, where she had a hazy vision of more camels, people afoot, people on horseback, packs pulled down into the road, glint of light on swords and helmets . . . Veered off, down a narrow path between caravanserai walls. They would hit, she would be smashed against either side—

They were through, and worse to come. The open, naked stretch of the desert before her. Her camel lurched and pitched forward, slowing somewhat but still moving far too quickly for what she would have called sense, heading down the long, steep slope of the ridge. Attavaia felt her balance going, the red stone below tugging at her. She tipped over sideways, clinging on but bouncing too wildly to pull herself up.

The camel must have felt the shifting weight; it groaned again and slowed its pace and then Treyan Battu'um appeared, a black horse on the edge of her vision. Strong fingers dug into her hip and heaved. With that help, she jerked herself upright, settled again, and his eyes crinkled above the scarf shielding his face. He slapped her camel's flank and was gone.

"This one needs stirrups," she muttered to herself, and found her throat dry as sand. She was trembling all over, and flushed with embarrassment, too.

Better embarrassed than her head broken on the rocks.

On the dark track over the desert, in a deep-pounded rut dug out by year on year of passing caravans, they settled into a fast, swaying, jolting pace that might have been a trot. Four cameleers, Baruni among them, passed back down the line, two with sabres drawn, two with lances. Attavaia tried to look back, bit her tongue as she banged her chin on her shoulder, and saw pursuing horsemen.

Only two. They slowed their gallop as the four camels went into a flat-out run and several Battu'um riders swooped around to join them.

The two pursuers thought better of it and headed back towards the town.

Attavaia faced forward again, touched her tongue to her hand and found that it was bleeding. Wounded without ever drawing her sword. But they had allies now—friends? Maybe. But allies, an honourable man like Treyan Battu'um to speak for them to his sept and perhaps to all of Serakallash once this Serakallashi civil strife was sorted out. An agreement that would supply them with arms and armour. Work well done. Her uncle would be proud.

CHAPTER XIII

Something kept dragging Attavaia from sleep, a nagging unease. Probably it was a combination of exhaustion and sleeping in a strange place, although really, she hadn't slept more than one night in the same place since she and Enneas returned from Serakallash, two months before. It had been a long two months, gone in the blink of an eye.

And now they were back in the desert town, trying to pass the last hours of a hot summer night on the flat roof of Master Mooshka's caravanserai. Enneas lay curled on her side on the thin mat next to her, breathing softly. Jerusha lay an arm's-length away, sprawled under a thin blanket. Master Mooshka and a few of the servants had also chosen to sleep up under the stars, where the air was cool. Not all the servants, fortunately, or pounding at the caravanserai's narrow back door in the alley would have done nothing. They had arrived some time after midnight, and Jerusha, summoned to deal with them, had scowled and rubbed her eyes and disappeared with the turquoise they'd brought, not raw stone this time but jewellery, gathered from women who may not have known exactly where it was going, but understood why. 'Rusha grudgingly offered them a supper of spicy cold lentils, complaining the while about people who hadn't the sense to leave business for daylight. But they hadn't wanted to walk through the hills by daylight, with Tamghat keeping a closer eye than ever on the main tracks and the road to the lowlands.

Trying to force herself to sleep was just keeping her awake. Locusts and crickets clicked and chirped unceasingly, and nightbirds strange to her ears called. One sang, sweet liquid notes, somewhere near the caravanserai. Attavaia gave up and rolled onto her back to watch the stars.

She wasn't used to seeing so many spread over her, a great dome. Not used to so much sky, without the mountains walling her round. She felt a little as though she might step off the edge of the world as easily as stepping off the roof of the house. Step off into the stars.

Some said they were the souls of dead heroes, given shining light in the land of the Old Great Gods. Some said they were a map by which the wise could read the future. Her uncle said they were something to fill up the sky at night, to stop it being dull, like the painted patterns that filled blank spaces on the temple walls.

It would be nice to read the future in them, to know she was following the right path.

Restless, she sat up, feeling as though this night all the fears and doubts she carried had become living things, burrowing insects that crawled over her skin and wormed their way in. She wanted to scratch and claw at her mind until they fled.

The sky was lightening in the east, not yet dawn but the first creeping whisper of it. To the northwest, pearly fog pooled, perhaps around Sera's sacred spring. The caravanserai would be stirring soon. Already a few hopeful cocks were crowing. Attavaia went to the eastern edge of the roof and knelt there, arms folded on the parapet, to watch the sun rise. Not so easy to step off as all that. The roof of the caravanserai was like another house in itself, with stairs from one level to another, walls higher than a man's head in some places, arched doorways from one section to the next, and in only a few places just this low parapet, to allow views out over town and desert. The walls overlooking the yard were lower all around, allowing easy observation of activity below. Not much of it yet, night's shadow still lying thick.

Pigeons roosting in a nearby corner took off with a thunderous beating of wings, and Attavaia turned her head at the soft scuff of bare feet. Jerusha.

The Serakallashi girl settled again beside her. "I'd have thought you'd be dead to the world."

"Couldn't sleep."

"Me neither. Not well." Jerusha yawned. "Bad dreams," she

admitted. "Nothing I can put my finger on, but you know the sort—you wake up feeling miserable and anxious."

A plump young man joined them, scratching his beard. "The air's bad tonight," he muttered. "Can't seem to stay asleep. You want tea, Mistress Jerusha?"

"Thanks, Koneh. Yes, tea." Jerusha rose to her feet again and stretched, outlining her figure rather indecently in her nearly sheer shirt, even in the dimness. Koneh averted his eyes and then hissed sharply, "Jerusha?"

His tone brought Attavaia to her feet as well. The man was looking to the south, where a higher wall hid what would be the densely packed roofs of the town. The dawn twilight illumined mist on the hills with a dun glow.

She had her mouth open to ask the servingman what he had seen when 'Rusha said flatly, "Dust?" and then called, "Papa?" in a voice that woke all the rest of them.

Not mist in the south but dust. A cloud of dust, hanging just south of the town on the mountain road. There were duststorms in the desert, but the hills to the south, though dry, were grassed, and there was no wind to raise it.

Attavaia felt numb, her hands and feet lost, far away. Felt herself unreal as a ghost in her own body. *My fault*, she thought.

"Run to the bell," Master Mooshka said. She had not heard him approach either. He turned, looked at her.

"Ah, Sister Vakail is with us again. Did you know about this?"

Attavaia shook her head, senses coming back. "If I had, we'd have warned you." She swallowed. "They must have been behind us on the road. If we'd been slower . . ."

Jerusha pulled the caftan she'd been using as a pillow over her head and went down the stairs into the house. A few moments later there was noise below in the yard, querulous voices raised and dropped again, and the creak of the big gates opening. Hooves pounded.

"What is it?" Enneas mumbled, standing on tiptoe to lean her chin on Attavaia's shoulder. "'S too early to be up."

Attavaia pointed.

"It could be someone bringing a herd in to the market," the servant said, too hopefully.

"That much dust? No." Master Mooshka dragged his hands through his desert-braided hair. "I dreamed . . . I dreamed of my wife. Calling me. Waking and searching for her. I dreamed of a sandstorm that buried the town."

"I dreamed that too," the servant admitted. "I heard my father, and the sand came."

Mooshka nodded. "That's not anyone coming to market. Sera was warning us, urging us to wake."

Her sleeplessness . . . no. That was a product of her own overtired mind, scrabbling in circles. Sera was not her goddess.

The bell they had heard summoning the folk for a chief's announcement last time they were in Serakallash began to toll, its notes uneven at first, settling into a steady rhythm of alarm.

For a dizzying moment Attavaia was back in the temple, but this time, she knew what was coming. It seemed . . . inevitable, the end of a path the summer had followed, step by necessary step. All—not all, Serakallash had taken its fate into its own hands, but there was no avoiding the truth that some—some of the blame lay on Attavaia's head. One grave misjudgement.

The summer's promise had turned to disaster almost at once. Within days of the first Serakallashi weapons being cached in the mountains, a few hotheaded men in Ishkul Valley had learned from an incautious kinswoman of the weapons stored there. They appropriated them to ambush one of Tamghat's patrols, stirring up their neighbours with that self-destroying victory to think they had the goddess on their side and could declare their valley free of the warlord's rule.

Tamghat marched on Ishkul Valley. The uprising was quickly put down, the leaders executed—swift and ruthless punishment that did not delay to interrogate them, which was just as well. One of the two elderly sisters in Ishkul killed herself when she knew Tamghat was coming, and the other joined the uprising and died in the battle—justice, maybe, since one or the other of them must have been the betrayer of the weapons. At least they had taken care not to fall into his hands, where torture or magical compulsion might have revealed the roots put down for a wider uprising in the future.

So far—so far Tamghat did not seem to suspect any sign of temple involvement in it.

While he carried out his revenge, Attavaia and Enneas had gone to the sisters who guarded the hidden weapons and themselves moved any caches the sisters admitted to having revealed to friends and relations and neighbours. Never two nights in the same place, never a day's rest. Sometimes not even a night's.

Put the fear of Attalissa's wrath on them, Enneas had said. Tell them they blasphemed, using Attalissa's dedicated weapons before the time of her return.

Attavaia tried, but she could not convince herself she spoke with authority, despite all the respect even the oldest sisters accorded her, as the Blackdog's niece who had, now a belief two years strong, been guided by Attalissa's own hand to escape the temple and lead them. She put more faith in fear of Tamghat to prevent any other too-early uprisings.

Ishkul Valley would be remembered not for the sake of that failed and foolish revolt, but for the girls of Ishkul who died because of it. Tamghat returned to Lissavakail and executed his hostages from Ishkul, the girls he had taken as novices for his false temple. Their heads were set on spears along the path into the valley.

Searches for weapons were still going on in other valleys, but by now Attavaia's were well and secretly hidden, and perhaps invoking the goddess's blessing had had some effect. The *noekar* sent to oversee the searches had so far found only the odd bamboo spear or bow they deemed too heavy for hunting. Probably because they had to punish one or two of the people in each valley, to remind the folk they could.

He would need to teach Serakallash the same lesson. They had defied him, driven his warriors away and deposed the sept-chiefs who had allied with him, the aftermath of that wild ride from town with the caravan and Treyan Battu'um. Serakallash had also armed Tamghat's rebellious bond-folk—he had to know the spears used by the men of Ishkul Valley were of Serakallashi make, blades longer and more slender than the mountain style, despite their shafts of green birch and reused tool-handles. At least one *noekar*, no mere mercenary hireling but a vassal bound to him with mutual oaths and long loyalty, had died. Tamghat was a Great Grass-lander warlord; such a crime demanded redress, they all knew that.

The bell echoed and re-echoed.

"It's our fault," Attavaia said under her breath, still watching that hanging cloud, growing browner and more clearly dust as the dawn brightened. "He knows." Her knees felt weak, and bile rose in her throat. She swallowed and wished for tea.

"He can't know we're here," Enneas said sharply. "He doesn't know we exist."

"Not that we're here. He knows the weapons came from here. Ishkul's weapons."

"I think we're quite capable of upsetting the Lake-Lord on our own," Master Mooshka said. "Don't get a swollen head."

He headed down the dark stairs himself, calling orders to his house-hold folk. Tea. Breakfast. This one to ride east, that one to ride west, without delay, to contact sept-chiefs. The servants who had slept on the roof followed him. In the yard below, dogs barked, camels groaned, horses whinnied, humans shouted, all woken untimely. The caravaneers emerged from their quarters on the far side of the square, demanding of anyone they could see, mostly one another, what the fuss was.

"Do we stay or go?" Enneas asked.

"We go," Attavaia said. Without them, there was no one who could hold the free temple together, no one who knew where all the weapons were hidden. By the same argument, they could not risk either of them falling into the wizard's hands.

But running, when their allies were attacked, felt like cowardice. Like betrayal.

Someone had told the caravan-mistress the reason for the alarm. Her haste to rouse her people and load her camels made Master Baruni's departure the last time they had fled Serakallash look leisurely. Attavaia fastened the toggles of her cameleer's coat, slung the Northron sax over her shoulder, and headed down the several flights of narrow stairs to the ground floor of Mooshka's house.

A boy was fastening heavy bars across the little back door. The same woman as before was packing up the account rolls again. Mooshka met them as they stepped out under the gallery.

"We think we'd better get out of town, Master," Attavaia said. "I'm sorry."

"Wait till the damned caravan goes to give you some cover, anyway," he said distractedly. "I don't need you caught leaving my house." He turned to shout across the yard at someone about spears stored in the east corner room. "Yes, yes," he said, turning back. "You might be safer staying."

"We can't get caught here. We're needed in the mountains."

"Go on, then. We'll open the doors to let the gang out as soon as they're loaded. The mistress thinks she's better off in the desert, and she might be right."

"Tell Treyan—Jerusha took the new turquoise for safekeeping, tell him we'll trust him for a fair accounting of it."

"Yes, yes, you can trust Treyan to the end of the world, don't worry about that, and if it's in Jerusha's strongbox, the wizard himself won't find it, not if he pulls the place brick from brick. Cold hells! Isn't she back yet?" he shouted to someone else, and hurried off into the chaos of the yard.

The distant bell stopped with a jangling clash.

Enneas and Attavaia looked at one another.

"How close were they?" Enneas asked.

"Hard to tell by a dust cloud."

"Is someone going to go—"

The big gates were barred, and the white-haired caravan-mistress was still overseeing the loading of her beasts.

Some of Mooshka's household were up on the roof with bows, and others, clutching spears and sabres, were clustered near the gate. Few of them looked like they had more than a nodding acquaintance with their weapons. Townsfolk, commoners, expected their sept-chiefs' warriors to protect them.

"Those won't be any help to Jerusha if they do go out," Enneas said. "I know it's a bad idea, but we owe them. I'll go find her. Tamghat's folk can't be far into town yet."

One man, trying to carry his spear nonchalantly over his shoulder, turned suddenly and sliced another's face. Yells and accusations; the second man, bleeding, helped away by a woman. Master Mooshka darted off that way, then back to the caravan.

"I'll be safer in the streets," Enneas said, wide-eyed. "Attalissa, they're fools."

"They're grooms and cooks and labourers," Attavaia said. "We'll both go. Chances are we'll meet her on the way back, anyway. Never mind the gate, it'll just mean arguing." She caught Enneas's arm. "The back door. Quickly."

"Wish we had armour."

"Wish we had a couple of dormitories of sisters."

Two youngsters, looking like brother and sister, guarded the back door now.

"Open it," Attavaia ordered. "We're going to make sure Jerusha gets back."

"Yes, lady," the girl stammered, and started throwing the bars and bolts back.

"Ah," murmured Enneas. "The voice of command. And you know, that's why they all do what you say in the end. It's not respect for your uncle at all, despite what you think. It's just that after a while you get so fed up with debating that you take that tone of voice, the one that only Spear Ladies learn. Then it's all over."

"Were they from the caravan?" the boy asked his sister as the door slammed shut again behind them.

Attavaia drew a deep breath. No sound of battle. The narrow alley was still and silent, almost night-dark.

"What tone of voice? I don't have a tone of voice, not one you need to talk about in that tone of voice."

"Really?" Enneas led the way up the alley towards the street, stopped just before it opened out, hand on her sword.

Attavaia joined her and they waited, while a man who looked like a caravan-mercenary ran past, coming from the direction of the town. Someone sent to find out what was happening? The gate of a caravanserai further along opened a crack to admit him.

"No Jerusha."

"No."

They set off towards the market square, jogging. Passing another caravanserai, they had to slow down and keep to the side of the street to avoid an emerging caravan.

"Have you heard what's happening?" Attavaia asked one of the riders.

The desert-tattooed woman shrugged. "Don't know. Fighting, I guess. The boss decided we'd better pull out. I'd stay away from it if I were you."

Attavaia ignored that, resumed her trotting pace. Once they were away from the clanking bells and protests of camels, new noises began to seep through the twisting lanes: human cries, the shrill squeal of angry horses, and dogs barking, muffled, behind the mud-dun walls of the houses and their courtyards. And the clash of metal, not so different from the camel-bells.

People, mostly men but a few women among them, were leaving their houses, hurrying into the town.

"Is it fire?" one man asked.

"It's the Lake-Lord," Attavaia said. She didn't believe anything else. "Go home, if you're not armed."

But most of them seemed to have come to that conclusion on their own; they carried sabres and spears and even hatchets and forks, all heading towards the market. From the babble she picked up different theories—desert raiders, some of the outlying septs attacking the Rostvadim and Sevani, the Sevani and Rostvadim fighting one another, how this or that one had woken from sleep just knowing something was wrong . . .

The fools were going to block the streets, run straight into whatever was happening, and get themselves killed.

"Where are the sept-warriors?" someone asked, and that seemed a good question. The crowd began to thin out, many of the cautious or the merely curious dropping back as the uproar grew.

There was fighting in the market, and a rough barricade of some of the handcarts and barrows of early-arriving vendors had been erected across the end of the street, a scatter of melons, broken underfoot, attracting wasps.

"Serakallashi," Enneas said, and there was relief in her voice. Serakallashi fighting Serakallashi, sept-warriors, a snarled knot of them before one of the big compounds that bordered the market. Some defending the gate, some trying to break through. At two of the other streets into the market, more clustered tangles of battle, Serakallashi horsemen scattered among them. How they told friend from enemy . . . Attavaia saw Jerusha, then. She had taken a sword from someone and, bareback on a bright bay stallion, was trying to break away from another horseman and two on foot, who had her pinned back against a wall.

They went over the barricade together, swords drawn, dodging the scattered battles.

"Grasslanders," Attavaia said. "There." She pointed to the broadest street.

"And coming in from the west, not the mountains. Attalissa keep us. I'll take the fat one."

"He's not that fat." 'Vaia turned a little to the side, watched for the stouter of the two afoot to catch Enneas in the corner of his eye and turn to leave her a clear path—he never did, oblivious to his danger. Enneas slashed him low across his leather-clad legs, hacked at the side of his head as he fell. Attavaia stepped in towards the other man on foot as he looked over his shoulder at her, gawping when he should have been moving. Her blade turned on iron plates reinforcing a leather jerkin, but the man stumbled and she kicked him in the back of the knee. He collapsed and his comrade's swerving horse kicked him in the face with a horrible crunching noise. She blocked the horseman's sabre as he swung round to her. As he backed his horse away from Jerusha's harsh cry and swinging blows, Enneas dropped her sword, grabbed his leg, and flung herself backwards, hauling him from the saddle. Slashing weapon or not, Attavaia hammered the tip of her blade into his throat along the edge of his high collar.

Jerusha slumped, shaking. She was cut badly on her left arm and hip, bleeding.

"Damn Siyd Rostvadim," she said, stammering. "Sh-she knew your Lake-Lord was coming. S-sent her warriors to stop the bell and they attacked everyone else who came to answer the alarm. Got away from them," she added proudly. "Got to Firebird and got this f-far."

"Don't you dare faint," Attavaia snapped, as 'Rusha, pale under her tattoos, swayed and clutched at her horse's mane, head bowed to breast. "Enni, get up and hold her on." Keeping her own back to the wall, she gave Enneas a boost up with difficulty, as the horse stamped and sidled away. She handed Enneas's sax up, slapped the horse's rump. "Go. I'll follow you."

The other horse had wheeled away. No time to chase it. With a roar of triumph, Tamghat's mercenaries poured into the square through the two south-leading streets.

And the wind roared out of the north in answer, lifting dust, flapping the coats and scarves of the fallen so that they seemed to struggle to rise. Red sand beat on her skin like the piercing of a thousand needles. Attavaia, eyes shut, struggled to pull her scarf over her face, stumbling blind into the wind. Worse than a blizzard. With her eyes open the narrowest slit, she could see little better. Shadows. Something big and dark whirled past and smashed. A door torn loose. She stumbled over a fallen body, which yelped.

Any street leading north, towards the desert and away from Tamghat's army, and then she could find a doorway, an alley, something to shelter behind. She came into the lee of a building, crowded with Serakallashi warriors and townsfolk, all keeping some truce. *Sera,* some whispered, not so much in prayer as in awe. She blinked until her tearing eyes could see again. Out in the red, dark, glass-edged fog of sand, a figure towered, dimly shaped, solid as a flock of blackbirds or a swarm of bees, arms spread. Even through the roar of the wind, and the sand like a river on rocks, she heard screaming.

Siyd Rostvadim, Elaxi Rostvadim, Narkim Sevani, Hashim Sevani, Bellova Sevani, I curse you as traitors to my folk. You have sold them to the wizard. I name you outcasts and godless, and with you those who followed you, if they do not stand against Tamghat now.

From the looks on the faces around her, every man and woman there had heard that deep whisper in the mind. But the goddess's sand-shadowed form was wavering. Something, like the weight of a thunderstorm, pressed on them from the south. Small red lightnings crackled into the wind, flushing the square with a sickening dried-blood colour.

The goddess screamed aloud, a sound that felled everyone in the crowd still standing. Most cowered with their hands over their ears, praying or weeping. The force of the wind dropped to a mere dust-carrying breeze. Time to flee.

Attavaia recognized the building: it was the one with the bell-tower, and she had somehow passed the street she wanted. On her hands and knees she scrambled over prostrate Serakallashi.

"Get up!" she snarled at one, who blocked her way. "Tamghat's here. Stand and fight for your goddess or tomorrow you'll be no better than a slave!"

The man swung a shaky fist at her and she found her feet, stumbled away. Her ears still rang from Sera's shriek of terror.

She saw the wizard, Tamghat himself. His horse stood placid as if sleepwalking, with its forefeet atop a small dune of red sand and white—Great Gods, it was a lattice of scoured bones that held the sand. An arc of mounted *noekar* and mercenaries formed up behind him, and more mercenaries—no, they were all young Lissavakaili men, his conscripts formed into one company of archers—waited beyond, afoot.

He would have left many to hold the mountains, but still, there had to be a lot more of his warriors somewhere. Likely the herding septs were already fighting their own battles.

A gate opened from the compound where the civil fighting had concentrated and a cluster of well-dressed Serakallashi stepped hesitantly out, their own guards close around them. They all looked greyfaced, shaken, as they crossed the square to Tamghat.

"Lord Tamghat," the leading woman said, pitching her voice to carry, to make her point to the onlookers. "Thank you for your help with the rebels. If you could have your people camp on the horse-fair grounds by the mountain road—"

Tamghat ignored her, riding towards the house over the drift that held the bones of his own men and women. His *noekar* followed and the sept-chief scurried after him.

The man Attavaia had snarled at had found his feet, leaning on a pitchfork. No sept-warrior but someone's stablehand.

"Get up," he urged those around him. "You going to let Silly Siyd hand us over to a foreign wizard?"

Brave dead man. Attavaia found the wall at her shoulder and followed it, keeping behind the crowd of Serakallashi. At the street she turned and ran in the shifting new sand, keeping to the shadows. Behind her, the Serakallashi were shouting ragged war cries, sept names and their goddess's, working themselves into a fool's charge. And the bows began singing.

No sign of Jerusha and Enneas. They should be safe back at Mooshka's.

Her eyes grated and ran, blurring her vision, and despite the scarf her mouth and nose were full of grit. She clawed the cloth from her face and spat, but it didn't help. Armed men and women ran or galloped through the streets in twos and threes, all heading for one point to the west. Warriors mustering to their chiefs, or on urgent duties that would come to nothing. Perhaps they meant to regroup and attack in a more coherent fashion. The Great Gods' luck to them. Tamghat was in the town, and if Treyan Battu'um could come galloping at the head of a Battu'um warband—she would be very joyously surprised.

211

"Get inside, you damned fool!" one shouted to her. "We don't need camel-drivers underfoot!"

She kept to her course unheeding, cut down a lane an arm's width across where poorer-looking townsfolk still clustered in doorways, talking urgently. An old man grabbed her arm, demanding to know what was happening.

"Tamghat—the Lake-Lord," she gasped, remembering their name for him, and found her throat raw from the sand. "The deposed chiefs were expecting him, tried to stop the alarm being given, killed the person who rang the bell. A lot of people died. Sera raised the sand against him but he's a wizard, he drove her back. He's in the market still. Big house, with a tower."

"The Chiefs' Hall?" someone else asked.

"Don't know." She pulled her arm free and went on. Let the truth loose, and see what followed. They'd know it wasn't their goddess's will and invitation, at least. And the lie about the bell-ringer's death might protect Jerusha from any petty vengeance by Siyd or her followers against the one who'd raised the alarm.

"They'll be gathering at the Zaranim Hall," a man said. "Let's go."

Brave folk. She left them to choose their own fate as best they saw fit.

The caravanserai ridge was a battleground. A company of Lissavakaili led by Grasslanders had run into what must have been several fleeing caravans as they entered the town from the north. Half a dozen panicked camels bolted past her, riderless, still roped together. There was no order, no line of defence or attack she could identify to put herself on the right side, just a jumble of people and animals. A dying camel spasmed in the street, knocking another to its knees. A Northron woman riding a mountain pony careened from another lane and shouted back over the kicking beast, "Go around, you fools, or kill the thing." And then she wheeled on Attavaia.

"Don't just stand there gawking, boy. Have at them."

Attavaia swung even as the woman's eyes narrowed. The mercenary raised her shield, hauling savagely at the pony's head and striking awk-

212

wardly down to her left with her long Northron sword. The shield splintered under the sax, a shock Attavaia felt up her own arm, and she kept moving, shieldless and unarmoured, kept the short, swift blows beating on the woman until she slid and tried to crawl, one foot still twisted in the stirrup. A camel careened into the pony, which went down on Attavaia and its rider both, and the cameleer's long lance thudded into the ground by Attavaia's head.

"Hells," that swarthy man said, as the pony kicked and squealed in terror. "You're one of ours." He withdrew the lance, held it over her. "Sorry. Grab on."

She hardly felt the sudden dull pain as a hoof connected, hauling herself with the caravaneer's help from under the pony. The Tamghati had taken most of the animal's weight, and wasn't moving. The pony found its feet and fled in white-eyed panic and Attavaia let go the lance, nodded thanks the man didn't see as he swung his camel round and went loping back along the ridge.

Attavaia fell again, a sharp, flaring agony climbing her right side. She levered herself up with her sword, looked down expecting to see some bloody mangled mess, but there was nothing to see, only torn and scuffed trousers and a few bleeding scrapes. Just a headache of a bruise to look forward to.

Tamghat's Lissavakaili were retreating. Probably half in terror of the camels.

She could put no weight on her right leg. Not a bruise. She picked an abandoned spear from the street and leaned on that. Mooshka's mulberries were an unbearable distance away, and for a moment her vision went red and her ears rang.

Priestess. This way.

She went, blind and halting, along a narrow way between caravanserai walls, down the western side of the ridge.

Priestess. Hurry, before he comes for me.

She blinked, rubbed away the grit that accumulated in the corners of her eyes, looking around. She was on the side of the ridge; it dropped steeply below, where some grey-green trees dripping hairy tendrils clustered, and water chimed over rocks. She did not remember walking so far.

The water reared up into the figure of a woman her own age, a body solid as her own, with Serakallashi horses tattooed not only on her face, but every inch of her. And they flickered and ran over her skin.

Attavaia dropped heavily to her knees. Not reverence, but she could not stand. White pain stabbed through her, blinding her a moment.

"Sera," she whispered.

"Priestess of Attalissa, you will help me."

She looked at her bloody hands. Flexed her fingers and it cracked and flaked away, a thick paste of it drying.

"Tell me about Tamghat. I didn't understand, I thought he would not come here unless he was following her, and she is not here. What is he, Priestess of Attalissa?"

"A wizard."

"There are wizards with the caravans and he is nothing like them. Your child and her dumb slave are blind and in their blindness they've doomed my folk with yours. He is something escaped from the cold hells. He is going to *destroy* me—I am no powerful lake that can bide my time and take vengeance at my leisure on such a power. I am small, weak, against that. He has wounded me. He will kill me, unless you act for me."

The goddess looked like she had been through a battle, gaunt, sunken-eyed, her hair a wild snarl. Her body ravelled away into a mist hanging over the water and a restlessness of ripples even as Attavaia tried to speak.

She desperately wanted a handful of that water, and could not touch it, not put her bloodied hands in Sera's sacred spring.

"We didn't bring him here, Sera."

No. I was wrong, I was wrong, I should have listened to the Blackdog. But there is no time. The Lake-Lord's warbands ride against my folk; they came in the grey dawn to the longhouses of the chiefs of the pastures, they have killed them and chained them and burned the houses, the pastures are aflame, do you understand?

214

"He's conquered Serakallash."

And he comes for me. Now! He will kill me as the hawk kills the sparrow. I am too weak to be any use to him; he despises me as too powerless to be even a tool, I saw it as we fought.

Attavaia drew a deep breath. She did not think she could walk anywhere. So she would die, defending a goddess not her own, as she had not died at the water-gate, and Lissavakail must seek its own doom doing what to it seemed best, as she had thought of the Serakallashi commoners gathered in that lane.

"Did not one of your own folk come here to defend you?"

"I sent them away. They can't help me, now." The goddess took form again, kneeling in the water, holding herself up with her hands on the red stone of the bank. "Wash your hands, Priestess of Attalissa."

Attavaia obeyed, leaning awkwardly, and the goddess caught her hands with hands cold as the dead, that felt to Attavaia as though they would melt away if she so much as gripped them firmly. Sera guided her hands down, palms against the stone.

"He will kill me, so before he does I'll die a death of my own choosing, from which I may awaken." She laughed, sounding wholly human and as though she tasted some bitter irony. "Your child is all my hope now. She's no weak water-spirit, if she could only free herself from her stupid mortality. You should pray she doesn't get a taste for the life of the road, for all our sakes."

"Die?" Attavaia tried to jerk her hands away, but the frail goddess was surprisingly strong.

"Die. Sleep. A sleep that seems death, as the toads that die when the desert pools dry, and are reborn when the spring snowmelt softens the mud of their tombs. And you will take me to your mountains and give me to the priests of my brother Narva, where Tamghat will never think to search, if he ever dreams what I have done. And when your Attalissa does come home to kill the monster, you will bring me back to my waters and free me here."

"To the priests of Narva?" Attavaia repeated stupidly.

"I'm not ignorant. The rivers of the snowmelt carry tales. Narva is mad and has turned his back on the world. Mad, but he was strong once, before your goddess defeated him. Whatever monstrous thing Tamghat is, he will not attack hidden Narva as he has me or your mortal child, not yet. Like you, he thinks Narva no more than the ghost of a god. Narva's priests will keep me safely."

"Keep you how? What are you doing?" Attavaia's own hands were cold as if trapped in ice and the earth shivered, sending wavelets trembling through the spring. The shelf of rock their palms rested on cracked. A jagged chunk, large enough her spread hands barely covered it, broke away.

"I trust you with my heart, my life. You love your goddess. I do not, but I see your worth in your love. Guard me well, Priestess, and carry me safe to the Narvabarkash. Because I cannot be freed until my tomb returns to my waters."

Attavaia pitched forward as the triangular slab of rock, a layer more than half as thick as her thumb's length, slid into the water. Sera was gone.

She caught the stone by reflex rather than intent and sat back, almost screaming as she shifted her weight on her leg.

"Sera?" she whispered and then shouted, "Sera!"

Silence, except that down below the ridge, a caravan was winding its way into the desert at a long swinging stride, and another close behind it, heading west.

Tamghat was coming; she remembered that, then. To kill Sera. Clumsily, she sheathed the sax and climbed upright, leaning on the spear, with the wet rock clutched against her breast.

The rock weighed several pounds and pulled her down, but she clamped her teeth together and started up the sloping ground.

A nightmare that slid in and out of her awareness. Narrow passage between walls, but a well-trodden path. A wider street, trampled and empty, dust churned to mud in fly-buzzing patches around the dozen or so bodies that lay scattered. They were mostly Lissavakaili—boys, young men her own age, staring astonished at the sky. A moment of clear thought and she noted the tracks, the boots and iron-shod hooves over all the milling confusion of camels—the caravans had escaped and Tamghat's small northern-approaching force, the one that had raised the dust, had come in the short time she had been gone, and had passed on into the town to join their master.

She couldn't reach the alley that ran alongside Mooshka's place, the small private door. She leaned on one of the mulberry trees and realized tears were running down her cheeks, and her nose dripped. She wiped her face on her sleeve best she could; her left arm grew cramped and numb with the rock's weight, and her elbow burned. One step, then the spear to take her weight, drag the right leg, another step. Mooshka's gates. She leaned against them, then pounded, after a moment's hesitation, with Sera's rock.

A goddess's tomb. She could have chosen a stone that would fit in the pocket of a cameleer's coat.

A smaller door set in the gates opened a cautious crack and the plump servant looked out. He started to slam it closed again, recognized her and jerked it wide.

"Get in," he said, and grabbed her as she pitched over the threshold.

"'Vaia!" That was Jerusha, limping towards her, Jerusha with her arm and leg wrapped in bloody bandages, Jerusha flinging her arms around her like she was her own sister, sobbing, unheeding of her mewl of pain.

"She's hurt," the servant said, as Attavaia sagged in Jerusha's arms and both of them seemed for a moment likely to fall. The servingman shouted and more people came, offering arms in support. An arm to lean on wasn't enough and someone, Master Mooshka himself, simply picked Attavaia up and carried her.

"Enneas," she said then, and struggled to get down.

"Yes. She's here," Mooshka said gravely, no longer the panicked man of the dawn, focused now, and calm. Jerusha gave another gulping sob.

He carried Attavaia to one of the upper rooms. Enneas lay on a low bed in a welter of rags soaked in black blood, packed around below her ribs. A man with bloody hands stood by her, washing in a basin a woman held. Clean, he turned and strode from the room without a word, a hawk-nosed, grey-haired Serakallashi with angry eyes. Physician, surgeon, something like that.

Someone had bathed Enneas's face. In the light of an oil lamp she was an ugly grey colour, and her lips blue. She opened her eyes once, focused on Attavaia, and her hand twitched weakly on the blankets. The room reeked strongly of blood and fouler things, leaking out. No treating that, not if the greatest physicians of Marakand came.

Mooshka set Attavaia down, gently as he could, by Enneas, and she grasped the limp hand. Cold as the goddess. The stone was still cradled in her arm and she dropped it, at last, on the bed, barely able to move the arm. Enneas's eyes rolled a little towards it.

"Gift?" she asked, not much more than a movement of the lips and a breath.

"Sure."

"Good. Like gifts." Her eyes drifted closed.

"This isn't even her place," Jerusha said savagely. "Right outside the gate! We were right outside the gate and they tried to pull us down."

Mooshka put a hand under his daughter's elbow, led her from the room, and shut the door behind them.

"Not her fault," Enneas said then. "Northron with an axe. I cut him but it was that horse killed him. On purpose. Good horses, down here. They'd have killed me then but the caravan came out and just trampled over them and Jerusha dragged me up and inside. Great Gods, it hurts."

Attavaia leaned over and kissed her cheek.

"Why . . . stone?"

In a whisper herself, Attavaia told her. Enneas seemed to be sinking deeper into the bed, shadows taking her face.

"Tha's good. Tha's funny. Go'ess in a stone. You b'have y'self in Nar'barkash, you hear? My mama's—"

"I know. She's Narvabarkashi. Save your strength."

"F'what? Used to visit Gran'mama, Grn'papa. Those priests . . ."

218

"What about them?"

"Goo'-lookin' men. Pre'ey girls, too, but ha'some men. You be careful."

Attavaia made herself smile. Enneas drifted away and Attavaia drifted too, emptiness filled by the throbbing of her leg.

"Tell Shevehan I'll miss him," Enneas said once, distinctly. "Tell Mama I'm sorry."

"Of course."

"Attalissa, it hurts. Sorry, 'Vaia."

That was the last she spoke.

Master Mooshka came back at some point, asked if there was anything his brother the physician could do. Attavaia, understanding what he offered, touched Enneas's face.

"I don't think so," she said. "I don't think she's feeling anything now."

He rested a hand on the top of her head and went away again.

Enneas died sometime soon after. It was not yet evening. Attavaia sat there holding her hand, not quite caring if Tamghat came in person looking for rebels or fugitives or Sera herself. After a while one of the servants came by with a cup of tea, which she set down very quietly, returning with Mooshka and his brother the physician. When Attavaia tried to rise from the bed she fainted.

Red light came and went through eyelids she could not drag open, and the touch of her clothes on her skin was too heavy. Her tongue felt foul, sweet and heavy and bitter behind it.

"The smaller bone of the calf's broken," a man's voice said. The physician again. "I don't care who was dying, you shouldn't have left her sitting there like that all day, you should have said she was wounded. It's set and splinted. Keep her on her back, if you want her fit to travel when her gang comes back, if they ever do. This'll be no town for a crippled beggar."

She did force her eyelids apart then. They felt glued together.

"How . . . long?" she slurred. The stone was a lump under her

219

pillow. She remembered 'Rusha putting it there, guiding her hand to touch it under her head.

"Back with us, are you?" The man frowned, as if he did not entirely approve of that. "Give it two months before you try hopping. Four months before the bone's strong and fit to run on. Mistress Jerusha, stop scratching around those stitches or I swear I'll splint up your arms and keep you immobile a month, too."

"Yes, Uncle," Jerusha said, too docile to be true, so perhaps Attavaia was falling back into the darkness, where she heard her own voice saying, "Uncle? I have to go home, tell them I have to go home, I have to take Enni home."

"'Vaia—the stone. The gift you brought her? Is it some Lissavakaili thing? Do you want us to bury it with her?" Jerusha stood awkwardly at her father's side, hands twisting together. Her uncle had ordered her to bed, too. Attavaia remembered that. Thought and memory came and went in odd, hazy bursts.

"Gift? That was Enni's joke. Where is it?" she asked in a brief panic. "Don't bury it. It's a . . . it's a sacred thing. We're . . . I'm . . . I have to take it to . . . to a holy place I know of, for Sera. Don't ask more. I don't want you to know if Tamghat . . . if Tamghat asks. Bad enough you've helped us." And then she slid into darkness again.

They buried Enneas early the next morning in the caravanserai yard, with her hands folded on the Northron sax, and as soon as it was done Master Mooshka's folk scattered a heap of hay over the grave and turned his horses loose, to hide any signs of new digging with their trampling and scuffling. Mooshka carried Attavaia down for it, and she said the prayers, quietly, so that Attalissa's name did not fall on other ears, no matter how loyal they might be to Mooshka and Jerusha. That the two mountain women were no caravaneers, that they were something in the tangle that had failed to overthrow Tamghat's chiefs, only put them with all the household in conspiracy, and that was enough for the servants to know, even if they were all kin, near or remote, to

Mooshka or his late wife and held silent by family loyalties and their own honour.

Later the same day, they bundled Attavaia down the stairs again in panic, with word that Tamghat's people were checking the caravanserais for fugitive warriors from the so-called rebel septs. Mooshka was Rostvadim—not, by his name, counted a rebel.

"It won't do any good," he said. "I've spoken openly against Siyd often enough. And they'll remember my wife was Battu'um, and Treyan my friend."

They buried Attavaia in a tall stack of fodder in one of the arched alcoves, stuff meant for the camels, coarse, prickly shrubs and weeds and branches. Then they put one of Mooshka's own camels and her calf in, and fastened the gate. The camel yawned and made pleasure-filled snorting noises, and Attavaia, deep in the furthest, darkest corner, prayed she would confine herself to nibbling around the edges, and that camel calves were not playful and had no urge to clamber onto heights. Enneas would laugh—she pushed that thought down. She tracked the search anxiously by sound, thinking of some clever person probing the stack with a spear, but when the camel suddenly blew through its nose and then did its gurgling-pipe noise and stamped, she understood why she had its company, and a man said, "Damn, but they're ugly things," before moving away.

That was the only search, and they carried her back up to Jerusha's room. Jerusha tended her like a sister, far quieter than before, all her sharp edge seeming ground away. Attavaia wished wearily for her old sarcasm, which at least did not go cowed and defeated.

Some days after Enneas had been buried—Attavaia lost count, but it might have been five, or a week—she heard shouting downstairs.

"You'll put us all in danger!" Mooshka roared. "You and your tongue. Think of the household, for once, and not just yourself!"

"I'm going!" Jerusha screamed. "And if you weren't such a coward you'd come with me!"

"Don't be a fool! If they're going to bring themselves to lie and swear fealty to save their children's lives, even Sera will forgive them, if it means they're still here to fight for her, later. You'll be dead before you've got more than six words out, if you start crying traitor on them."

"I'm going!" Something thumped and crashed, crockery shattering, maybe, and after one female cry of dismay there were no more voices.

"What was all that?" she asked Ghiziam, Mooshka's sister-in-law who looked after the accounts and ran the household, when Ghiziam came up to sit with her, bringing her sewing to keep them both busy. Attavaia threaded her needle, found the pieces of shirt she had basted together the day before, and began on the seam of a shoulder. It was something to do with her hands, something to fix the mind on, better than lying and thinking, *If I hadn't sent her with Jerusha, if I'd gone with them, if we hadn't tried to get lowlander help . . . if Uncle wasn't in hiding and were here, to make the right choices for me . . .*

Ghiziam's lips thinned. "Jerusha threw a jar of oil at her father."

"Why?"

"To make him let her out the back door."

"Where did she go?"

Ghiziam sighed. "Word is, there's something afoot in town this morning. They say there's mercenaries, what you were calling Tamghati —his folk, not caravaneers—gathering at Sera's spring and in the market. A young lad from next door came by just now, said he'd heard the chiefs were going to be taking oaths to Tamghat at the spring."

"Jerusha's not a fool. She'll keep her mouth shut." But Attavaia's doubt must have showed in her voice.

Ghiziam drove her needle like it was a dagger and shook her head. "She's young, and that's the same as saying a fool, in most cases—'Vaia, I wouldn't include you in that."

"All the chiefs?" Attavaia asked, and Ghiziam nodded grimly.

The stories that came into the town, passing among kinsfolk and neighbour to neighbour or swept in with the caravans, which could not halt their progress or turn aside just because Serakallash had fallen to Tamghat, agreed. The bulk of Tamghat's *noekar* and his mercenary army had attacked the outlying septs on the same dawn he had ridden into Serakallash. It was as Attavaia had suspected and Sera had confirmed, but worse. They had known exactly where they were going. They attacked and killed the sept-chiefs with their entire families, or captured them. Over the past week the captured were brought in chains to Serakallash and imprisoned in the sept-halls, which were the strongest fortified houses of the town, and all now Tamghat's. The heads of those chiefs and their families who had been killed were piled in a cart in the market, stinking under a cloud of flies that gathered and would not land.

Rumour abounded, though, of sept-chiefs who had sent children away with the caravans, or slipped away themselves, who would reappear at the head of an army of desert tribesmen or Marakander mercenaries, or with a cohort of wizards, to drive the warlord out. But Mooshka said he knew for a fact that two of the three admitted wizards in town had fled with the caravans themselves, and any sept-chiefs who had warning of the attack in time to send their children away were probably in Tamghat's pocket, and had had no need to do so.

But he had looked, Attavaia thought, like a man who knew more than he said. She wondered who had escaped that mattered to him, and if they would be any help. Treyan and his family, she could hope. But she doubted it. Treyan Battu'um had not seemed the type to run and hide; like Sister Chanalugh, he would have seen it as his duty to protect those under him to his heart's last blood.

Ghiziam looked up from her seam and gave Attavaia a crooked smile. "I've seen you pray, Sister. Do you pray for us, as well?"

"Every day."

Ghiziam nodded. She was one of the few to know officially who Attavaia was. Most of the rest of Mooshka's household probably knew as well, and still talked of her as a laid-up caravaneer.

"The spring's gone dry," Ghiziam said matter-of-factly. "Sera's dead. The wizard killed her. So please, even when you go home, pray for us. We can't pray for ourselves any longer."

"You can," Attavaia said, and slid a hand under the pillows that propped her up, to touch the rough chunk of sandstone she slept on. "You must. Sera may be gone, but she'll return. I promise that."

Bad enough she made herself Attalissa's voice in the mountains; she did not need the weight of all Serakallash's belief on her as well. But Ghiziam appeared to take some ease from the reassurance. When she left Attavaia to the needlework and went off about her other chores, she seemed to walk a little lighter, for all that she frowned and went still at every noise below or out in the great courtyard, that might be Jerusha's return.

Attavaia kept at the shirt in a desultory way, but without Ghiziam's eye on her she could not force enough focus on it to stop herself brooding, listening, as Ghiziam had done for her niece. This room she shared with Jerusha had a deep window looking out over the yard, but it was filled with a carved latticework to screen the sun, and from the bed she could see only light and speckles of sky, and some sticks from an untidy dove's nest on the sill, nothing of what went on below.

Jerusha came back when Attavaia had almost given up listening for her. The bustle of the noon meal being prepared in the kitchen, which spilled out into the arcade and drifted in the window, along with the smells of spices and oil, gave way to a sudden stillness, and then rapid feet on the stairs. In the yard, someone was calling for Mooshka. Attavaia had swung her good leg over the edge of the bed and was trying to shift the bundle of splints and tight wrappings that was the other when Jerusha came in.

The girl flung herself on her knees by the bed, head on her arms.

Attavaia hesitated, not sure if Jerusha even remembered she wasn't alone. But she was crying, silently, achingly, and since Attavaia could hardly leave her to her grief in private, she put a hand on 'Rusha's head, felt her shaking. Jerusha seized the hand and buried her face in Attavaia's lap like a child.

"What happened?" Attavaia asked gently.

"They're dead," Jerusha said. "He killed them all."

"The chiefs?"

Mooshka and Ghiziam stood in the doorway, with some of the

household folk crowded behind. Ghiziam had a fist crammed against her mouth and Mooshka . . . Mooshka looked like a corpse, he had gone so pale.

"All of them," Jerusha moaned. "The chiefs and their families. Everyone. Laicha's baby, even, Treyan's little grandson. No one escaped. He killed them all. The wizard had anyone who survived when he attacked them and burned their houses chained up in the Rostvadim Hall. All the chiefs and their families. No one escaped, not one, they were all there, from every sept. And he brought them to the spring, with a great crowd there, we all thought . . . a lot of the crowd were Siyd's folk and even they thought they'd be given a choice, asked to swear to him, and they weren't. They just shoved them down and cut off their heads. There were a hundred of his vassals there, more, and those Lissavakaili archers, and everyone was so afraid of his magic . . . everyone. Me! We all stood there and we let him do it. And Davvy saw me and she didn't . . . she didn't . . . she just smiled."

Jerusha was shivering. Attavaia wrapped her arms around her, bent low and rocking her, as a mother might have.

"How can the gods see that and let him live? He's not human. He's a monster, a devil, worse than the Seven. How can they let him live? You know the gods. You're a priestess. You know these things. *How?* He killed our goddess. He killed babies. And Davvy." She choked on her sobs and Attavaia shook her head.

"I don't know, 'Rusha. I . . . we can't understand these things. The Old Great Gods have left the world to us and the gods of the earth. It's our fight, now."

"He killed Sera. How can we fight him?"

"Sera isn't dead. Believe me. Believe she'll come back when Attalissa does."

Mooshka came treading silently across the floor and knelt at Jerusha's side, an awkward hand on her shoulder.

"I was afraid . . ." he said. "'Rusha, I was afraid he would kill them, if they refused him oaths. That's why I tried to stop you going."

"He didn't even ask them!"

225

"I know. But 'Rusha, at least you were there. You saw them stand. You'll remember. We all will, but you'll *know*, they were true to the end. You stood there with them, and they knew you came for that, to be with them, to remember. The war only begins, and when the goddesses return like the sister says, Tamghat will learn how true we are."

She sat back on her heels and leaned her head on her father's shoulder, saying nothing.

"Koneh went out, too," Ghiziam said quietly. "He says the Lake-Lord brought the heads of all the great family folk who were killed in the first attacks, and piled them in the spring?"

Jerusha nodded wearily. "He said they're to stay there, so we remember."

Mooshka smiled, a corpse's grin. "So we will."

"He's set some spell on the . . . the heads. Even the flies won't touch them."

"They won't walk," Ghiziam said. "Not if their bodies are buried."

"They will be," Mooshka assured her. "Even a monster like Tamghat would be afraid of that many angry ghosts."

Attavaia doubted it. But he had buried the bodies of the hostages from Ishkul Valley. It was only heads he cared about, for his trophies.

"Sister," Mooshka said, and Attavaia looked up. "We've your turquoise, still, Sister. You'll want to take that home with you, I expect."

Such an odd moment to mention that. Attavaia wondered why. As though he thought she might want to abandon them, dissolve the weak alliance they had made.

"You keep it. Use it against him, somehow."

Mooshka looked grimly satisfied, and nodded. "I'll see what I can do. I've been thinking, I might know someone, brings blades down from Varrgash quite often. And 'Rusha knows the way up to your 'Auntie' Orillias?"

"Yes," Jerusha said, with a return of her old fierceness, scrubbing her eyes with a fist.

"So we'll carry on and let Treyan go to the gods knowing so. When's your goddess coming home?"

"Years yet."

"Gives us time to be ready."

"It does that."

"She's a powerful goddess, your Attalissa. She'll avenge our Sera?"

Attavaia bit her lip. "She'll return," she said. "They both will."

And she pushed away that traitor thought, the one that lurked beneath all she did, the one she had never shared even with Enneas. The one that wondered what Attalissa could do against Tamghat, even once she was a woman, even once she was fully the goddess again. Because Tamghat, so the story went around—whispered in the town, whispered among the free sisters, rumour leaking out of the temple—Tamghat had not come to Lissavakail expecting a child. He had come prepared to face the goddess grown and in her full power.

"She'll return," she repeated.

Jerusha gave her a long, considering look. Attavaia met it, held it when it would have dropped to the cushions and the stone that the girl knew they slept on, every night.

CHAPTER XIV

"And now you've gone and gotten yourself lost. Well done, 'Vaia."

Attavaia reined the dun pony in, considering. To her right, the south, a near-vertical climb of loose scree rose. To the left was a dry streambed, bottomed with larger slabs of the same loose stone, most angled towards the sky, like a bed of miniature mountain peaks. Then, rising, hummocks of broken rock, pillars and mounds of it, and beyond that, another great swell of grey land. Ahead, where she had thought her path led, the world dropped away, and rose distantly beyond into misty blue heights. The path twisted before her, dropped too steeply for a pony to follow. A wild-sheep track, nothing more. The valley below was no mountain meadow but one of the great ice fields, a blue-white emptiness of wind and deadly crevasses, and a winter-cold air striking up from it. Clearly she should have struck south before now, to wind her way to Narvabarkash, and with luck and Attalissa's blessing, the mines to which she should consign Sera's sandstone tomb. She tried not to let worry run too far ahead, trusting that once she reached the village, she could find a trustworthy guide. The god's holy place was a day's journey from the village of Narvabarkash itself, and the directions seemed vague.

"Should have taken the main track after all, and given up on going armed."

Talking to oneself was a sign of madness. She'd be right at home among the priests of Narva, who endured their god's oracles, so it was said, living on the high peak in the god's own caves, touched by his strange and wandering mind with holy madness. Though others said the line of priests had died out long ago, and there were no shrines, no sacred caves, any longer, only the mines and the mining village of Narvabarkash, which did not sit on the slopes of Narva's actual mountaintop, but at the foot of a lesser peak, facing up to the actual heights where Narva had once walked.

The present avatar of the goddess had been born in an outlying hamlet on the skirts of the Narvabarkash. A sign, maybe, that they could place hope in Narvabarkash? Attavaia did not even know which tiny settlement it was that Attalissa had been born to. It was not supposed to matter. They were all Attalissa's, now.

When Attavaia was a child, she had loved the stories Enneas's Narvabarkashi mother told, of the dangerous, twisting wormholes into the mountains that were the fabled turquoise mines, richer and deeper than any others within Lissavakail's territory. They were tales to make your skin crawl, in the firelit evenings: foolish children lost forever, lured by enchanted singing and unable to find their way back to the light, silver-scaled demons and sudden secret pools and the brooding god, whose caves echoed with whispers and the sound of slow breathing.

Stories for children. Not something to take any more seriously than Enneas's caution against the god's handsome priests.

At least if Enni believed there were priests who still called themselves such, and that she had seen them while visiting her mother's kin, there were probably priests.

"Not that it looks like I'm going to find them," Attavaia growled. The pony laid its ears back at her tone.

She had lost her way amid the stones, taken the wrong turning of this obscure hunters' trail, which she followed to avoid the Tamghati-patrolled traders' track. Attavaia stared about her, chewing her lip. No going on ahead, that was certain.

Great Gods, but her leg hurt, and tears of exhaustion suddenly prickled at her eyelids. Stupid. It only meant retracing her steps, watching for the path she must have missed. But she was weak, and injured, and weary. It had been a month before Master Mooshka had given in and made arrangements to get her as far as Auntie Orillias' place, longer still lying up there, and later at Shevehan the smith's, with the weight of Sera's stone on her mind. She should still be in bed, but maybe it was some lingering touch of the desert goddess driving her, that she could not rest till she had done as Sera had bidden her. Shevehan had argued . . . but here she was, and she couldn't give up and crawl back to bed now. No bed up here to crawl to, anyway. Nothing to do but go on, with yet another night on the ground to look forward to, if she didn't come to Narvabarkash before dusk. Attavaia forced the reluctant pony to turn. It seemed to have decided the trail's ending meant the day's ending, though it was only a little after noon.

"No such luck," she told it.

She was above the tree line here, the near world grey and faded brown and bleak, the distance smoky blue, and the wind making her wish she had dug the mittens out of her pack that morning, and taken out her second shawl as well, to cover her felt cap, in addition to the one she wore swathed over her jacket. Neither the harsh, open land nor the wind improved her mood, though they had their own beauty. There would be snow, within days, and she might find herself trapped for the winter in Narvabarkash. Better that than lost in the wilds when the first storm hit, but she'd rather be back at Sister Orillias', or in the smith's hidden loft.

The pony flung up its head, nostrils flaring, and whinnied.

She had time to curse and drag her voluminous shawl more securely to cover her sword, the Northron sax on its baldric, which dragged less at her hips than her own sword would have done, less strain on her leg. The answering whinny was abruptly silenced. She imagined a brutal hand jerking at the bit. No Lissavakaili hunter—unless he too imagined mercenaries.

No place to hide, or run. Attavaia went on, the pony showing an inclination to trot which she firmly quashed. Around a high shoulder of stone. They were waiting there, wary as she, but that alertness slackened into amusement at the sight of her. Two young Grasslander men on mountain ponies, a brace of hare swinging at one's knee, and the other with a string of partridges.

230

Both had bows, neither strung, and neither wore armour, though both had sword and the Grasslander round buckler.

"'s keep you, my lords," she muttered, head down. She couldn't quite bring herself to say "the gods." She kicked the pony with her good foot, trying to guide it to the edge of the trail. It wanted to stop and gossip.

The older of the two men, whose face bore the scars of Tamghat's bear cult, stayed her with a hand on her bridle.

"Hold on, girl. Where are you off to?"

Attavaia kept her eyes lowered, let the mountain accent slide further into the rapid, high-vowelled speech of the remote valleys. "Back home, sirs."

"What village?"

"Lumbiet, sirs. Over the road." Lumbiet was a good day's ride, she thought, and beyond the main track to Narvabarkash. They wouldn't ride so far, please Attalissa, to check her story.

"So you can tell us where the damned road is," the younger said. "Good girl."

The older man frowned. "What are you doing so far from home?"

"Collecting herbs," she mumbled, properly abashed. "There's a dyer's-wort grows up by the ice field, better than anything we've got home for a good lasting red."

"Not the damned ice field again." The younger man laughed. "Hells, every damned trail we try ends up there. You'll have to lead us out, girl."

She gave him a quick, nervous smile. "Sirs, you just go straight on this track westerly, and you'll find the road again. I don't travel so fast, you don't want me slowing you."

"Slow's fine, if the company's worth having," the younger man said. "Eh, Rying?"

The scarred man drew his knife and slashed the thong holding her nearest saddlebag closed, flicked the flap up. "Herbs?" he asked. "Peasants don't need to go so far for their cursed weeds. Why d'you think we patrol the damned tracks, Nar-Asmin? More likely she's running gold out to the Serakallashi."

He took the sack of millet she'd been cooking for supper and breakfast, tossed it to Nar-Asmin, who hefted it in his hand, shook his head, and tossed it back at Attavaia. She dropped the reins and caught it left-handed. Oh, mistake, she should not so obviously have kept her sword-hand free. They didn't seem to notice. Didn't notice the leg, either, which should have excited comment. Even beneath her full skirt and petticoats it stuck out awkwardly, though the splints and bandaging were hidden.

"No luck there for you, Rying, too light to be anything but grain. Leave her alone. We want to get out of this, don't we?" He shrugged, for Attavaia's benefit. "My brother, the great tracker. Let's go hunting, he said. Let's head up into the real mountains, he said." Nar-Asmin smiled again. "What's your name?"

"Leave off," Rying said. "Who cares? She's got a face like sour milk, and she's a cripple besides. Weeds!" He flung a fistful of roots away. Common madder, but she carried it for just such an excuse.

"He's embarrassed at getting us lost," Nar-Asmin confided. "Don't mind him, he's always like this."

A nudge of her heel made the pony shuffle its rump away. Rying's rummaging put him too close to her barely cloaked sword, and the Great Gods only knew what they'd make of the heavy chunk of sandstone at the bottom of the pack. Nar-Asmin caught her pony's reins, gave her another possessive smile. "We can offer you a better supper than millet porridge, anyway." And it wouldn't stop with supper, she could see that in the mocking set of his lips, all arrogant ownership and a hunger she wasn't used to facing. It wasn't her, any poor girl would do, when this one was out hunting. And Rying was bored with it and impatient, turning his pony away.

"Straight ahead, you say? Come on, then, woman. We can have a better look through her gear when we camp," he added to his brother. Snickered. "Might have gold tucked in those skirts, thinking she can look all meek and sickly and play for mercy if she meets a patrol. No one'd really send a cripple out hunting weeds."

"You think I should search her?" Nar-Asmin pulled wide, innocent eyes, and then winked at her. "He has a nasty, suspicious mind, doesn't he, darling?" He tugged at her pony's head and it suddenly, fool beast, decided it did not like the company after all. Flung up its head and shied, taking the Grasslander by surprise. Attavaia grabbed her momentarily free reins, shawl flying, kicked the pony—and Rying shouted, "She's armed!" and wheeled his mount. It heaved into hers, squealing, hers snapped at it . . . she ducked Rying's swinging blade and drew the sax, slashed as he hastily backed away, turned to swing at Nar-Asmin, caught him across his neck. Even as he gaped and wheezed she thought she heard the familiar shushing whine by her ear, the sound of her dreams, the pull and release of the bowstring and the song of the fleeing arrow. She lay low and shouted the pony into bolting free of the tangle. She looked back then.

Rying lay back over his pony's rump, bouncing as it shied, flat-eared, white-eyed, trying to get away from the uncomfortable weight. A dark shaft stood out of the mercenary's chest and his hand flopped feebly for it, before he slid sideways. His pony, pricking its ears, turned and came clattering after Attavaia.

Nar-Asmin was across the path, dead, and his white pony, spattered red, bolted towards the deadly drop and the ice field rather than cross the body.

Attavaia searched the upper slopes—no, Rying had been across the path, the rising north side of this narrow valley, there, crumbling upheaval of rock, mostly lost in shadow . . .

It might, of course, be another mercenary. One of the women, less tolerant of abuses of Lissavakaili women, or someone with a grudge against the brothers. But she rather thought not.

The hunter did not so much emerge from concealment as slowly solidify. He wore all dull browns and greys, jacket, shawl, and cap lacking even the usual trim of red or indigo, and he moved with a snow-leopard's caution, picking his way down the rocks.

But then the rotten, crumbling stuff slid, and she understood the reason for his delicate movements as he jumped to safety. On solid ground, or at least only the usual degree of ankle-turning stones, he strode more swiftly, as arrogant in his assurance as Nar-Asmin, she thought, and shrugged her shawl back to have freer use of her sword. In case.

He paused where Rying had rolled to hands and knees, breathing heavily, kicked him over on his back, and bent swiftly to finish him, straightening with his long knife dripping and no more expression on his face than he had shown when the rocks beneath his feet gave way.

Time to go, Attavaia thought. But she waited.

The man stopped a few yards away, considering her, she thought. Deciding if she too were prey. He held his bow, still strung, loosely in his left hand, quiver at his shoulder. He was a little older than her, maybe—hard to say. Sun and dry winds and cold aged faces quickly in the high valleys.

"Lost?" he asked, raising an eyebrow.

"I might be," Attavaia offered cautiously. "Thank you."

He shrugged. "The mountains are full of vermin, these days." He wiped his knife on the grass, unstrung the bow, and headed back towards the bodies, trusting her, it appeared, as he hardly seemed such a fool as to think her harmless.

"We should get those out of sight," Attavaia said as he searched Nar-Asmin, methodically setting aside weapons and purse. "They were hunting, not patrolling, they said, so it might be a few days before they're missed. Better for the villagers if they just disappear than if they're found slain."

"No village around here," the hunter said. "You offering to carry them away?" He grinned at her. She scowled at his mockery. Not too much different, that look, from Nar-Asmin's. Too appraising for her liking. It might be a truer appraising, and that was an uncomfortable thought. Not the superiority of a male with a female in his power, but that of a man who knew what you did not want him to know. Mountain women did not carry swords, save the priestesses, and those who had remained in Tamghat's temple were not such fools as to travel into the wilds alone.

On the other hand, a hunter who made no qualms about shooting

234

Tamghat's folk might be one of those who trained with her secret village militias, or he might be one she should recruit.

And he should know the right path to Narvabarkash.

Her hand was sticky, fouled, and she could hardly sheathe the sax as it was, but dismounting to clean it was a horrible labour. By the time she had worked her way down, hung a perilous moment tangled in her petticoats, and cleaned sword and hand, sleeve and shawl as best she could, in the thin dead grass that clung between the rocks, the hunter had looted both mercenaries, caught Rying's brown pony, and heaved both bodies over the unhappy beast's back.

Attavaia hobbled after him, leaning on her pony, the crutch in her other hand. He led back towards the ice field. The white pony milled about on the edge, still nervous, flinching at the sight of them, but the hunter crooned to it, holding out a hand, and it came like a dog, cautious, but relieved to have a human taking charge.

"There's no way down," Attavaia said. "Is there?"

"Not for you. But if you want your boyfriends to disappear, a crevasse is the best I can think of."

"And the ponies?" she asked doubtfully. She couldn't see killing them and dragging their bodies anywhere out of sight, and didn't like the idea, anyway, innocent beasts caught in the quarrels of humans. But to leave them straying, where some villager might claim them and find himself executed as a murderous rebel . . .

The hunter gave her that amused flash of a grin again, dark brown eyes in a brown-burned face of the high peaks. The fringe of beard framing his square jaw was trimmed short, and he was cleaner than the average hunter. He had turquoise pendants in each ear, rather than the usual gold rings. Maybe he hunted leopards.

"They're worth too much. And both young mares, too. I know a place that'll take them, where Tamghati soldiers won't see 'em. Hold the ponies here, would you, Sister?"

He hauled a body off, hesitated only a moment, and rolled it over the edge. Attavaia watched expressionlessly as the second followed, arms flailing.

"It'll be three of us dead at the bottom, if I try carrying 'em down," the hunter said, with a hint of defensiveness.

Attavaia nodded and found a rock to sit on, holding the reins of all three beasts, as the hunter disappeared down the steep sheep-track after the corpses.

She could leave him, take all three ponies and he would never catch up. Or he might; she was a townswoman, and though she had been learning the mountains for two years now, she would never read them as a man like that did. He would track her down, if he wanted to, and he probably would, since the ponies no doubt represented a fairly substantial windfall of wealth for him.

Attavaia made it well over an hour, by the march of the shadows, before the hunter returned. She was cold and stiff and her leg was throbbing; she didn't think she could haul herself back into the saddle without help.

He looked more than a little relieved to see her still sitting there, or maybe it was only the ponies he was glad to see. He took the reins of the mercenaries' two from her and offered a hand up. Kept hold of the hand, once she was up.

"What happened to your leg?" he asked, looking down.

"Broken. A horse fell on it."

He frowned. "Death," he said flatly. "Where?"

"Serakallash," she answered, rattled. "In the battle, when Tamghat took it."

"Ah. And whose side were you on?"

"The right one."

He snorted, smiled, and let go her hand. The air was cold, after his warm grip. "You've missed your trail. It's back that way."

"I realize that." A pause. "Which trail?"

"To Narvabarkash. Or thereabouts. You don't want to go to the village itself, anyway."

"Where are your dogs?" Attavaia took a firmer grip on her crutch. Sweet Attalissa, she'd sat here an hour or two waiting on the man and never thought to wonder that. A hunter without dogs? Without spears?

"With the yaks." A wide-eyed, innocent look, playing with her as much as the damned Grasslander. A sudden smile, not innocent and much, much to be preferred, as of a joke shared between friends. She found herself smiling back, even not knowing what the joke was. "We've been expecting you, Sister. I'm Tsuzas. I was expecting a goddess, actually, for some reason, but," he shrugged, "you'll do. Can I help you up?"

She didn't answer, hauling herself belly-down over the saddle from the off side, swinging her good left leg over, but he caught and steadied her, impersonally intimate hands on her hips.

"I don't see how you can expect me, since my business isn't with you, and you can expect all the goddesses you want, Tamghat's made sure there aren't any around here, hasn't he?"

"You tell me, Sister." He swung up on the brown and followed her back along the trail, pausing only to bundle up the looted gear and strap it to the white's saddle. Attavaia kept going, but a clatter of hooves warned her as the man caught up.

"I may be wrong about the goddess," he said, sounding almost contrite. "It's often hard to know what anything means."

She looked back over her shoulder. Too clean for a hunter living wild on the mountains, Great Gods, yes.

Handsome men, Enneas had said.

"You're from Narvabarkash?"

"Didn't I say so?"

He had not, and the limpid, lying-innocent eyes said he knew it.

"You're Narva's priest," she accused.

"Tsuzas," he said, touching his chest with a little bow. He grinned, shrugged. "Priest as the god takes me. Today I'm herding yaks and hunting goddesses. So I'm told. Turn south, here, up over this ridge."

"There's no trail."

"So?" He pushed the brown pony past her, with the white at heel. "This is a shortcut. Actually a spur of Narva's peak itself, but we cross over. If you were heading for the main village, you'd go over and turn back west, but we go east, and then up, into the stones and Narva's heart. We won't make it before dark, but then, you wouldn't have made it to the village by sunset, either."

He kept looking back, as though he expected her to suddenly bolt, or perhaps merely to slip gracelessly off over the pony's tail. The latter didn't seem so unlikely. She wouldn't have tried this ridge, herself, even if it had shown a trail.

"She's with you," he said abruptly, waiting for her on the height.

Attavaia clung to her saddlebow, concentrated on breathing evenly, staying upright. Her head pounded with her leg, and she felt cold and clammy. Her teeth had started to chatter. Something pushed at her, cold, like the winter air crawling off the ice field. Angry, a will of hate. It found its way into her, squeezed her heart.

They had a shorter, gentler ride down into the next narrow valley, where half a dozen yak cows grazed, watched over by a pair of the big black dogs. Attavaia found it no easier. Her ears buzzed, and spots danced before her eyes. Mountain sickness, maybe, or the fever striking back into her leg. No place to fall ill.

"The goddess with you—she isn't Attalissa." Tsuzas was looking as grey as she felt when the dun came up beside him. He shook his head violently, as if to clear it of buzzing flies. "Death, you said, in Serakallash."

"Didn't," she muttered. "You said that."

"Sera." His eyes had gone black, pupils dilated. Then the fit seemed to pass and he only frowned. "You're in no condition to be riding around the mountains." He whistled. It sounded like a string of birdcalls. The dogs, who had stood watching warily, scenting strange horses as well as their master, no doubt, went racing about their business. The yaks, black ones splashed with white, like magpies, grumbled and grunted and bunched up, trudged the way they ought, she supposed. Tsuzas, with another look at her, took the dun's reins. "Just hold on, Sister. It's a long ride yet, and your order's not so welcome on the peak."

Understanding hit her, sharp as the pain now jolting up her spine with every step the pony took.

"Your god's going to kill me." Attalissa was gone, and so conquered Narva stirred—why hadn't she realized that danger?

Because Narva had never been more than a legend, a story of old days. Attalissa was all the god the mountains owned, for several days' travel in any direction. She had to leave this place while she still could. The goddess of the desert spring wasn't hers, to demand her life in service.

"Sera," she said, through clenched and chattering teeth. "She said to take her and hide her in the mines of Narva, take her back to her spring when Attalissa returns to defeat Tamghat. You take her. I can't go with you. I can't. He'll kill me."

"He damned well better not."

"I'll go to the village, friends there. Sisters go to Narvabarkash all the time."

"No. Now he's got a hold on you, he might not let go, not anywhere in the barkash. Great Gods, I'm sorry." Tsuzas, presumptuous man, wrapped his own shawl around her shoulders and held it there. "He's not . . . all there. What people say about peculiar old relatives? Blind and deaf and dumb, in a way. He just reacts to things. Like an animal."

"Bloody stupid god to worship."

"You get to pick yours? At least you chose your priesting. I was born to it. The rest of the barkash is Attalissa's now, but us, we're stuck with him, father to son."

"Emissary from Sera. He can't hate Sera. He can't know Sera. Narva, hear me—Sera sent me, from the desert." Attavaia could hardly get the words out. A weight of hostility, like rocks, like crushing ice, settled more heavily into the half-knit bones of her leg, finding the flaws, the cracks, the scars, pressing on them. Red flecks danced and clustered before her eyes, bees swarming.

"He can't hear," Tsuzas said, despairingly. "He can't understand. Shouldn't have brought you this far. My fault: priestess and goddess, my grandfather saw you were coming, and it never occurred to me, when he started talking of goddesses, that even in Attalissa's strength your sisters can never come to the true mines."

239

"What true mines?" Talk, any nonsense, just so long as there was sound, tying her to the world.

"There's the Narvabarkash, the district, and then there's the Narvabarkash, the mountain peak, the god's heart. And there's mines, ancient mines, your sisters never found. Even your assassin Blackdog never found his way through them to the deepest shrine. Not that there's any stone worth cutting in the old workings any more," he added, inconsequentially.

"That's what Sera meant. Take the stone, you take it and hide it there. I'm going . . ." Back over that ridge, the valley where she had met the mercenaries. It was some border of Narva's, that was why she hadn't been able to find the path, why she got lost, she and the mercenaries both, always back at the ice field, they said. If she could stay conscious, stay mounted long enough, she would be safe. If she passed out here, she knew she would never wake. Crushed beneath a mountain of blind old malevolence. Sisters did die, around Narvabarkash. Mountain hazards. Avalanche and rockslide and falls. More often than was quite to be expected. She tried vaguely to turn the pony's head and found she was leaning on Tsuzas, almost falling between the two animals.

Tsuzas had his long knife in his hand.

"What are you doing?"

"Give me your hand."

"No." Her voice slurred like a drunkard's. The Narvabarkashi simply seized her left hand, forced her fist to unclench with hands too strong to resist, and dragged her palm across the blade.

She slammed her other arm and fist into his face.

"Cold hells!" But he wrestled her half-off the pony and onto his lap, leg an agony this barely increased, used his upper arm to pin her right arm against his chest, held her left. "Hold still," he said, mildly and indistinctly. Drops of blood spattered her. His nose was bleeding, or a lip, she couldn't twist her head to see. She was seeing double, and everything heaved sickeningly, as though she rode a galloping camel again. Her pony, with its ill-timed instincts, pulled away. She screamed at the wrenching in her leg and Tsuzas dragged her more securely into his embrace.

The dun pony, perverse beast, stopped and looked back, as if wondering how she had managed to get over there, on the brown.

Tsuzas had let go of her hand, but her own body was in the way and she only flailed feebly as a child, trying to strike him again.

"Don't keep squirming."

"Squirming!" she repeated, amazement, outrage, she couldn't have said what. She thought she said it, at least. All she heard was a sort of mewling whimper. She survived Tamghat and the temple, survived Serakallash, and she was going to die here in her own mountains, killed by a god, when she only thought to serve the gods. Not her own mountains, as Narva chose to remind her. With a mad priest.

The mad priest managed, despite her struggles, to bring the knife to his own left hand and cut across his own palm, with a hiss of indrawn breath.

"Here." He caught for her hand again, interlaced fingers with hers, clasping bleeding palms together.

"Blood and blood," he said, and sniffed loudly. His bleeding nose dripped down her face. "Mine to yours, yours to mine, in the sight of Narva and the Old Great Gods, till the worlds end and the sky falls. Say it."

"Blood—What? Why?"

The ringing in her ears was fading, a little, the red swirling fog clearing, enough she could focus clearly, the bleeding hands squeezed tightly, not so much blood, after all. It was mostly his nose.

"Say it. Blood and blood . . ."

She swallowed an urge to throw up, still too stupefied by the pounding in her head and leg and the sense of weight pressing on her chest to think. Repeated, at Tsuzas's reiterated prompting, his words, stumbling and slurring and barely audible to her own ears.

Headache ebbed. Pounding. It was his heart; she leaned her head on his chest. For a moment it was a very comfortable place to lean. Warm. Solid, and the world spun less, as though the heat of his blood flowed into hers, drove strength through her again. Leg, dully aching, no worse than it had been, before he led her over the ridge and into mad Narva's awareness.

"*Bastard!*" She pushed away from him, slid, and he clutched her indecently under the arms, held her so she could get her good leg on the ground.

Backed the brown pony away, as if he thought he might need the space between them, and wadded the hem of his jacket to his nose.

"Sorry," she added, foolishly. "Did I break it?"

Tsuzas shook his head.

"What was that? Magic?" She clenched and unclenched her hand. The cut was deep enough it was going to scar, not deep enough to do permanent damage, she hoped. The bleeding had already stopped, which was more than could be said for the priest's nose. She shivered. Her clothing was damp with sweat, and she felt strangely hollow and light. Shaky.

"You look better," he said cautiously. "Are you better?"

Attavaia took a deep breath. "Yes."

"You were . . . your lips were blue. You looked . . . like a corpse. Stopped breathing for a moment, there."

"Yes, well. You could have told me what you were doing. What *were* you doing? Was it magic?"

Tsuzas made a vague noise, muffled by the jacket pulled up to his face.

"Here." Her crutch was out of reach on her pony, but she staggered a step or two, held out his shawl. He took it, gripping his nose and tilting his head back.

"Last person gave me a bloody nose was my sister," he said resignedly. "Can I say, *women*, in tones of despair?"

"No. Your dogs and the yaks have disappeared, by the way."

"They'll stop when they realize they've lost us. We keep a herding hut just in a fold of the mountain, there, that's where they'll be. They know the way. We bring them down to graze this valley often. It gives a good excuse for wandering off towards the road, keeping an eye on things. You can always say, 'Oh, sirs, looking for a straying yak.' And there's the herd to prove it. Can you find my knife?"

"What are you planning to do with it?"

"I thought," he said, "that before I bleed quite all over this utterly ruined shawl, which I can't help noticing now actually belongs to my sister, we both might want to wrap up our hands."

Attavaia found him his knife, dropped on the ground, and he dismounted, used the blade to rip the clean end of the shawl into bandages. She submitted to having a folded pad pressed onto her hand, another strip knotted tightly round it. Wrapped his for him, pride driving her to do as neat a job, and not to tighten it so as to make him wince.

"You still haven't answered. Are you a wizard? What sort of spell was that?"

"Not a spell," Tsuzas said awkwardly, and went to catch her pony.

"So?"

"So," he said, and helped her into the saddle, helped her settle her skirts around the stiff unbending leg as politely as if she had been his nose-bloodying sister. "So, like I said, Narva is not all there. He doesn't perceive things the way we do. You can't argue, you can't reason, you can't explain. He just reacts."

"And?"

"And now you're his, in a way. So you can walk on the peak and enter the holy mines—which no sister of Attalissa's has ever seen despite what you all think, and if you tell your temple, when you have a temple again, I may have to kill myself." He said that unexpectedly sombrely, as though it was not a joke. But then he flashed that grin, his face filthy, blood in his beard. "Honoured beyond the dreams of the greediest Old Lady. But the turquoise is long gone."

Attavaia let the insult pass, thinking of her brother Rideen and his friends, all dead now, the sorts of games and leagues and solemn vows boys of nine and ten indulged in.

"Like children, making blood brothers? Your god thinks that counts, somehow?"

"Narva doesn't think. He *felt* it. Truth in the blood, blood to bind us." Tsuzas had the black, vacant look in his eye again. "It's not a game, Sister. Never think that."

"No, I suppose not." But it seemed like it ought to be. Though there were tales of wizards who worked great magic in blood. She snorted, mind-numbingly weary and feeling that if she once started laughing at this, she would never stop. "So we're blood brothers. I always wanted to be, but my brother and his friends said I was just a sissy little girl and couldn't join."

"*Not* blood brothers," he said, with his eyes still ringed dark, looking up at her.

"What, then?" She couldn't help the smile. "Blood cousins, maybe?"

Tsuzas shook his head, not smiling. He went to his ponies, rode back to her, looking a bit worn and weary himself. Anxious. The sun was setting, throwing long shadows over them, painting the stones with fire.

"What have you done?" she asked, soberly, wondering, some forbidden Narvabarkashi ritual, not meant for outsiders, some priestly secret . . . "Cold hells! You didn't . . . that isn't—" Attalissa save her, she remembered now.

"It was all I could think of. You'd have been dead before I got you back over the spur. Understand, I've seen a priestess die that way before, when I was small. One of the tribute assessors. She got lost in the mines, the working mines, wandered and wandered and came into the mountain's heart. And the god said, through my father, poor man, *leave her.* So we did. And my grandfather stayed with her, and made me stay. To learn. What I should learn, he didn't say. That a few hours is a very long time, for dying?" Tsuzas turned the horse's head, said flatly, "The hut's a few more miles, but it's more sheltered. We'll catch up with the herd on the way."

No one she knew, was her first thought. Before her time. How old was Tsuzas, though, when it happened? She could wish the grandfather a slow death himself, making a child connive at murder. She felt sick again.

And her hand throbbed, at least a distraction from her leg. She swallowed, clicked her tongue at the pony until it shuffled into the jolting trot she'd been discouraging for days now. Caught up with Tsuzas.

"You *married* me," she said, and heard her voice sounding quite reasonable, not accusing, not shrill with outrage. Calm.

"It was all I could think to do," he said again. Eyed her sidelong, and that damned smile crept back. "Narva recognizes blood, after all. You could have done worse. At least I don't beat my wives."

"Wives! How many—?"

"None. Till now, I mean. Do you think I need more already? It's not like you have a lot of children to look after."

"I . . . I think you're . . ." She could find no words. "I'm a *priestess* of *Attalissa*."

"Yes, that was rather at the root of the matter, wasn't it?"

"Celibate."

"Big word."

"It means—" She saw the smile broaden and bit her tongue. Determinedly kept her own face straight. But it was too ridiculous. "You can explain matters to my goddess, when she returns. You realize I'll be thrown out of the temple?" That wasn't ridiculous, that was serious. "I'll be turned out." All she'd ever dreamed of, all she fought to regain, lost.

"But you'll be alive. Is Attalissa so unreasonable? If you keep your vows?"

"If you say I'm married, how am I keeping my vows?"

Tsuzas shrugged, serious in turn. "Keep the spirit of your vows. At least she's a goddess you can talk to and have her listen to what you say, judge the truth of your words and your heart for herself."

Attavaia sighed. He hadn't seemed the type of man to resort to force, or she would have been less willing to wait for him as a guide back at the ice field. But it was as well to hear it said, that he didn't regard this marriage as giving him any rights.

"Of course, if you did change your mind . . ." He seemed irrepressible. "Better lawful marriage than unlawful lust."

"I'm not feeling any unlawful lust at the moment."

"As your lawful husband, I'm glad to hear that." His smile deepened. "So, anyhow, I refuse to call my wife 'Sister,' and where we're going, you'll find yourself beset with sisters. What's your name?"

CHAPTER XV

Tsuzas's family and the secret mines, the ones the temple thought it knew about, and didn't, were reached around noon the next day, after a weary morning that seemed all climbing, braced forward in the saddle. Tsuzas walked, leading the ponies, and they all went at the yaks' pace. There was frost in the air, and snow coming.

Attavaia stole a glance at her bandaged hand from time to time. It seemed too distant for a joke. Not something that changed her in any way. Except, somehow, it did. She was where no priestess of Attalissa could come, for all they had never even been fully aware of that fact— did that mean Attalissa too could hide some fold of the mountains and in it elude the wizard's searching? And she was, somehow, bound to this man. About whom she knew nothing.

"Where's your house?" Attavaia asked, when it seemed they were leaving even the thin brown grasses behind and about to start climbing the stone of the peak, with the undying snow not so far distant above. The dogs, at a whistle and a gesture, had turned the willing yaks aside, heading at what seemed an eager trot on the cows' part for a larger herd, maybe two dozen, which grazed at the farther side of the steep valley, along with half a dozen ponies. A wealthy family, if these all belonged to the priests. The herd was watched over by a small figure on a pony. Boy or girl, she couldn't tell. It waved, Tsuzas waved, the dogs nipped at the yaks' heels, other dogs barked. Homecoming.

Except she saw no settlement, no solitary house, to come home to. Sheer rock, ridges, a herd of wild sheep picking a scrambling course . . . speckled hens scratching among the rocks, out of place.

"Here." Tsuzas was enjoying himself. "The threshold of the first mine, of all the mines of the mountains."

"Where?" Attavaia asked impatiently, not seeing any dark mine-mouth, either.

Tsuzas pointed.

He led her towards an overhang, where the mountain lunged out, shielding shadow, the darkness of night, of the Old Chapel when the lamps were extinguished.

"Under . . . ?" Attavaia swallowed. "Is it safe?"

"The mountain hasn't fallen on us yet."

"You haven't brought a priestess of Attalissa home yet."

Tsuzas gave her a sidelong look, perhaps checking to see if she smiled.

"I'm not joking. Why would your god tell you—"

"He doesn't tell."

"Why would he let you know, however he does, that a priestess was coming, and then try to kill me?"

"No awareness," Tsuzas said. "I did tell you that. Foreknowledge, without judgement of its consequences, even those he himself causes."

"So all that rock could just come down and crush us, and then he'd wonder where his priests had gone?"

"Possibly. I don't think it's likely."

"Attalissa save me," Attavaia muttered under her breath. "Sera, help me. This is your service."

The overhang seemed a mountain in itself. Under the overhang was a stone-walled corral and a stable against the mountainside, built of rough stone and almost impossible to tell from the natural wall of the cave, even seen close to. A small boy peered down from a loft, staring at them as warily as the furtive cat whose tail she had seen vanish up the ladder at their entrance. The boy came sliding down when Tsuzas called and was relieved of his basket of eggs, comman-deered to tend the ponies. He studied Attavaia with wide, yellow-brown eyes, no smile, no words, but seemed competent enough as he took the reins from her, patting the dun's neck. Tsuzas offered no explanation.

The house itself was harder to see in the twilight of the overhang than the stable, a cavemouth or perhaps mine entrance that had been filled, returning it to the look of the mountain, with only a narrow doorway left. Beyond, it opened out in small, dark rooms, some with braziers or butter lamps burning, far warmer than she would have expected, but cold drafts blew in through cracks, black fissures in the walls. These were plastered white, to reflect what light there was, and painted. There were many images of what must be Narva, an inhuman-looking god: four-armed, blue-skinned, sharp-toothed. The eyes glittered, set with turquoise, jet, mother-of-pearl. They watched. She felt Narva watching and clenched her left hand, felt the cut burning. But he did nothing, other than to watch. Gloating, she imagined. Possessing her, now. Or perhaps, if she understood Tsuzas's explanations of the level of the god's existence, only confused, like a dog faced with too many smells.

Tsuzas had eight sisters, one older, the rest younger, all living in the family home; the eldest was married but had recently left her husband in Narvabarkash, bringing her two young boys to serve Narva, to carry on the priestly line. Tsuzas, murmuring that in her ear, did not sound as though that pleased him. All the sisters talked at once, leaving their work of spindles and looms and churns to crowd around her. And not all were there, two were out ranging the mountains, as Tsuzas so often did, she gathered. Their names passed her by in the chaos. There was Mother, quiet and calm, and a chattering woman Tsuzas called Auntie, whom Attavaia gathered was actually his father's third wife and mother of five of the sisters, while the eldest, Teral, was daughter of a first wife now gone to the gods. His father was more recently dead. The terrible grandfather was a frail, bent old man, white-haired, whose hands and head trembled continually. The eyes were keen, though, peering up at her, down at her bandaged left hand, up again, yellow-brown like the little boy's. And up, craning his head around because his neck would not quite straighten, at Tsuzas.

"She is no priestess of Sera."

"I don't think they have priestesses in the desert, Grandfather," Tsuzas said easily, and he put a hand on Attavaia's arm. Possessive, she thought, and almost struck it off, but the touch was quite light and as the grandfather swung his stare back at her, she was not so unhappy to be claimed, just then.

"A chosen maiden bearing the desert goddess to sleep in Narva's bosom." He sounded like he was quoting, but then he made a noise like a cat spitting. "Has Attalissa betrayed us all to this tyrant wizard and added the deserts to her own victims? She's collecting defeated gods now? And we should be her jailers? I'll see you dead, boy, before I let you prostitute what's left of our freedom to Attalissa or her wizard paramour."

"Grandpapa!" protested one of the sisters. "You shouldn't use that kind of language."

"Especially when we've a guest."

"From town." There was envy in that sister's intonation.

Tsuzas only sighed, but his fingers tightened, ever so slightly, on her arm. Attavaia put a hand over his a moment. She could see him, dark eyes rather than light, but silent and wary, like the boy in the stable. Did the grandfather threaten so often the sisters didn't hear? There had been venom in the words, and how much scarring did it take not to feel it any more?

"Sera was driven from her holy spring when Tamghat conquered her folk," Tsuzas said. As they sat in the low-roofed herdsman's hut, eating roast hare and partridge the night before, Attavaia had told him some of what passed in Serakallash, how she came to be carrying a dead lump of stone to the Narvabarkash, when she had her own slow-simmering and careful rebellion to prepare. "Sera sleeps. She charged Sister Attavaia, who fought for Attalissa in Lissavakail and for Sera in Serakallash, to carry her here, out of Tamghat's sight, until Attalissa returns to fight the wizard. Treat her chosen servant with respect."

"We all need to fight Tamghat together, brother," Attavaia said, more mildly than she was inclined to. "If we don't, the wizard will destroy our gods one by one."

"Fighting. Narva hasn't survived by fighting your Attalissa, and your Attalissa hasn't done any fighting against Tamghat that I've

250

noticed. Learnt from our lord, I'd guess. If you lie quiet, they don't see you." Grandfather gave her a yellow-toothed smile, not friendly. "Get used to it, or go serve Tamghat. Give us this Sera's stone, and leave, before the wrath of Narva finds you."

"*I* welcome her here, in Narva's name," Tsuzas said. "*Narva* admits her here, by my hand and blood. You have no right to deny her. And don't, before all the Old Gods, threaten her," he added, though that sounded more like the angry, defiant boy he might have been and less the priest.

"And that's the final insult—don't think I didn't notice the moment you walked through the door. You have no right choosing a wife without my approval and no right before the god to be profaning yourself with such a one, I wonder Narva didn't throw you off the mountainside like he did your father."

"That's enough!" Tsuzas's mother straightened up from where she had squatted on her heels, stirring a pot on the brazier. "Leave the girl in peace, Ostap. And remember it was you kept Tsuzas here when he wanted to leave; it's too late for you to deny him to Narva now."

"Don't mind Father Ostap, Sister," Auntie chimed in. "His digestion's bad and it puts him out of sorts. Tsutsu, stop trying to drag the girl away. She wants her dinner. Let the gods wait on it, they're surely in no hurry after all this time."

What seemed like a dozen work-roughened female hands, flashing jewelled rings and golden bracelets, caught at Attavaia, tugged her from Tsuzas to a low chair in a warm corner. Tsuzas watched darkly, leaning on a painted wall, arms folded. Not smiling. His sisters ignored him. His mother took him a bowl of stew first of all, but he shook his head and pushed away without a word, vanishing through a curtained doorway.

"It's all right," one of the sisters murmured to Attavaia, as Mother, since no one had given her any other name, pressed the bowl of stew on her instead. "He's moody, but he gets over it. He takes himself far too seriously, and always thinks Grandfather means the things he says. He's a dear, really."

"Tsuzas or Grandfather Ostap?" Attavaia wondered, but the sister had been chivvied off to fetch bread and milk.

If she'd ever met a man who should run away godless to the caravan road and the mercenary's life, surely this was one. The stew almost choked her, under Ostap's eye, but she ate it to please Mother and spite him.

This was the main room of the house, the cooking hearth and the gathering place. The sisters dodged in and out about their business; the peevish-looking eldest, mother of the two boys, raised a surprisingly sweet voice in a weaving song in the next room.

There was an uncle, Umas, who sat, empty-eyed, rocking back and forth in his chair in the corner. Rocking and rocking and rocking. One of the sisters tucked a shawl more tightly around him, patted his head absently, like he was a pet. A white-eyed great-grandmother sat spinning and called the younger ones back to take up their spindles again, unheeded, as they giggled together, looking up at Attavaia as they poured out the tea and served it, Grandfather first, then the uncle, who had to have his hand folded around the cup and the cup guided to his lips. Then herself, as the guest. Tsuzas did not return, and Attavaia didn't know whether to wait or go looking for him. The sisters, four of them bright in scarlet and indigo, crowded around her, cups in hand now, still giggling, asking questions, about Lissavakail, about the temple, about the embroidery patterns the townswomen worked for their shawls and coats. Innocent, girls' questions, but they didn't take the chill of Ostap's words away.

Another sister, trousered and wrapped in grey and brown shawls, bow and quiver slung from her shoulder, strode in to say there was a patrol searching the village for weapons *again* and whose were the ponies in the stable. She brought the little boy with her, clinging close to her side, still silent. Perhaps silence was a perfectly normal reaction to this . . . this flock of aunts. Jays, Attavaia decided, and the little boy suddenly smiled at her, plunked himself at her feet.

"Stew?" asked that sister, whose name, Elsinna, Attavaia did catch, in the chorus of enquiry about affairs in the village and news that Tsuzas had gone off chasing an oracle and returned with a priestess that he'd married, yes, married, and Narva alone knew why, but wasn't it fun, to think Tsutsu had finally found a wife . . . no, it wasn't a wife, it was a trick to fool the peevish old god, and serve him right. "If that's stew, bring me some. I'm starved, I've had no breakfast." She gave Attavaia a cool nod.

"People who go off hunting Tamghati and leave others to do the real work—"

"I wasn't hunting Tamghati, we don't need that kind of trouble."

"It's entirely your affair, of course," Auntie said confidingly to Attavaia, continuing some conversation she wasn't aware she was having. "We won't think any the worse of you, dear, if you don't give him children till after you've dealt with your wizard. Although it does seem peculiar to me, for him to marry in such a rush, when he's been so set against the idea till now, and my own cousin's two girls so willing. It's not like there's many would dare to come up here, and a true wife needs to live under Narva's hand, not like that woman Umas married, who keeps herself and her boys in the village and calls herself a widow now. She's only ever visited once or twice since the accident."

"What accident?" Attavaia asked, out of a sort of horrified politeness.

"But is she pretty?" Great-grandmother's voice rose querulously. "My Tsutsu should marry a pretty girl."

"She's got a sharp sword," Elsinna answered, and for a moment her eyes met Attavaia's and she grinned Tsuzas's grin. "It's like a rich man, Great-grandmama. A rich man is always handsome, and a woman with a good sword is always pretty."

Great-grandmama dissolved into wheezing giggles, and Attavaia missed the tale of the accident. Something about Tamghat.

"Thank you," Attavaia said firmly, setting her cup aside and reaching for her crutch. The little boy handed it to her. She levered herself up, dragged the saddlebag with the stone from Sera's well in it over her shoulder.

"Where does she think she's going?" Grandfather Ostap demanded of the world at large, unanswered. "That I should live to have one of Attalissa's unnatural women under my roof, defiling my blood, and the god too lost in dreams to strike her down as she deserves . . ."

Attavaia had to walk past him, step over his feet, dragging her right leg, to reach the doorway through which Tsuzas had gone, of all the several opening from the room. Ostap had stationed himself on a stool there deliberately. His eyes followed her, malevolent as those of the painted gods, but he made no move to pursue her himself.

"Ah, newlywed bliss," murmured one or another of the sisters, and yelped. Attavaia supposed an ankle had been kicked.

She pushed through the curtain, having to bend her neck under the low lintel. It was dark, beyond, and the air was cold after the heat of the . . . the house. This did not feel like a house, though as her eyes adjusted, she could see dim light ahead. She set out towards it, down a passage that sloped slightly underfoot. The walls leaned in; she could touch the roof if she reached up. Walls and roof were smooth and plastered, though, and sudden glints of light suggested more jewelled depictions of Narva, more watching eyes.

The light was a plain clay lamp, burning in a niche cut into the wall. Tsuzas leaned beside it.

"I wasn't sure whether to rescue you or not," he said, but his expression was empty, not matching the words.

"I wasn't sure whether to rescue you," she returned, trying to make light of it. Great gods, what a family to take a wife home to. No wonder he had never married. "It might be impolitic. I didn't realize we were at war with Narvabarkash."

At least she knew there had been war, long ago, which few did even in the temple. Her uncle had told stories, entertaining her and Rideen, Enneas and Shevehan, in the cold winter evenings when they were all young. Heroic sisters of long ago. Small wonder both who could had gone to join them.

"And you might be at war with us again when you were done rescuing me? Grandfather's . . . not harmless. But not as dangerous as he'd like to think. I'm the only heir he has, so far. The boys are too young yet for Narva to take an interest in them, thank—" He shrugged. "Narva. I wish my fool sister would see she'd be better off raising them Lissavakaili in her husband's household in the village."

This was not yesterday's manic mad priest. He seemed as bleak and trapped as Attavaia had felt, caged and crippled in Jerusha's bed in Serakallash.

"I see what you meant about enough sisters," she said lightly. "Was your god always mad, or did this happen recently?"

Tsuzas choked on a laugh.

"They're not so bad, once you get used to them. Well, some of them. In ones or twos. More than three at once is ill-advised. Do you want me to take the stone?"

Attavaia shook her head. She unpacked Sera's rock from the saddlebag and cradled it against her chest, as she had once before. It felt like it was hers, to protect.

Tsuzas picked up the lamp and led the way. Soon Attavaia could not have walked beside him if she wanted to. The passageway became more obviously a tunnel, narrow, dark, and the air felt damp and warm, compared to the outside world. Currents moved and stroked against her. They turned, turned again. She had an impression of open spaces to the sides, brief glimpses of blacker blackness, swallowing the struggling yellow light.

"Don't try coming alone beyond where the walls are painted," Tsuzas cautioned. "These are old mine workings, and a maze, intentional or not. There are caves, too, and some places they open up below you."

Attavaia shivered. The floor was rough and Tsuzas slowed, looking back, giving her an encouraging smile. The walls brushed at her now, rasping on her coat, catching at her shawl and skirts. Their path twisted this way and that; they walked always steeply downwards and her leg began to throb, with a perfectly natural excuse. She should have let Tsuzas carry the blessed stone, should have just given it to him, the moment she realized he was the priest she sought, and ridden away. But it had been too late then. Maybe it had been too late when she answered Sera's summons.

She found herself walking in a daze, a dream. Most of the light was hidden by Tsuzas's body. She had the feeling she might have been asleep. Voices whispered, just beyond the edge of hearing. Had he said the mines of Narva, the ones that were still mined, connected with these? He had. It might be she heard miners from Narvabarkash village, miles away. It might be the silver-scaled, child-eating demons of the tales. Wind in high cracks—the air was not stale and choking, as she had feared. They climbed uphill now, and she could not remember when the pitch of the floor beneath had changed. Voices sighed, and asked questions she could not understand. A forgotten language? Rhythm to it. The breathing of the god.

They had stopped.

Are we there? she wanted to ask, and opened her mouth and drew breath, but Tsuzas moved swiftly and laid fingers over her lips. She closed her mouth and nodded. He couldn't take her hand, both were filled with crutch and stone, but he set his on her elbow and drew her with him, out into an open space.

Peaks of stone, whitish, green-streaked, rose from the floor. They threaded a way through them, a path worn, like the path of a river, eroded by centuries of feet through this range. Some of the mounded peaks rose higher than her head, while others were only knee-high. Dampness stained the floor in places, though the passages had been dry, she thought, drier than she had unconsciously expected. Overhead, the lamplight caught peaks descending, as though somewhere above, higher than the light could reach, was a reflection of the floor. Icicles, Attavaia thought then, craning her head back to see, almost making out the roof, a distant paleness that was not quite the blackness of nothing. Icicles of stone. Water dripped, somewhere, with a noise that echoed and re-echoed. In the distance she could see where floor and roof rose to merge into one another, rough and yet all curves and rounded edges, as though melted. It was very like standing below an ice field, looking up. An icy quality to the rock, a milkiness. Here and there, in the harder-looking stone of the walls, were knobs streaked with colour the lamplight kindled into flame, orange and green and blue, not turquoise but the far rarer opal, which the miners only found by luck and chance, and which all came to the temple, as Attalissa's greatest treasure.

256

But not here.

She could hear Narva's sleep, almost—almost hear his dreams, the murmuring edge of a troubled mind, worrying, gnawing, at the day's fears. Tsuzas stopped her on the edge of a pool, dark water untroubled by any wind but still shivering, rippling. Warmth rose from the surface, and strange crusts of white and greenish mineral edged the pool. Water dripped, shaking the surface. It stretched away, out of sight, towards distant walls she could only guess at, and the light showed eroded shapes rising from it, the soft stone melting into the water even as it was added to, drop by drop, from above. Stone peaks and pillars lay toppled, crumbling, and others built on them.

Attavaia unwrapped the wedge of sandstone and stood holding it a moment. Awkwardly, she started to lower herself. Tsuzas steadied her, until she was half-kneeling, the splinted leg stuck out absurdly, almost in the water. He knelt down beside her, setting the lamp at the water's edge.

She laid the rock, Red Desert sandstone, beside it, touching the pool, so that dampness crept up its surface. The stone had come from water's edge; water's edge was where it should lie, until the time came for the goddess of Serakallash to return to her own proper place.

"Look after your sister Sera, Narva," she prayed, because it seemed something should be said. Tsuzas did not reach to silence her, this time. Her voice echoed from the roof and the walls, layered itself, became barely comprehensible: music, or mad muttering. "When Attalissa returns to defeat Tamghat, may you all be free in your own places again."

What had she said? The water shivered, or Tsuzas did, pressed shoulder to shoulder. It was only a wish, for the world the way it ought to be.

"Free or dead and lost like the Westron gods," Tsuzas said. "Better empty temples in the wind than the devils walking with the earth's strength in their hearts. Better silent death lost in stone, better Attalissa's fool, than ghost consumed into the empty flame."

"Devils?" Attavaia asked, not certain she had heard clearly.

Tsuzas made a sort of choking, gulping noise and jerked suddenly, fell against her. She grabbed him, reflex, and felt him rigid, like a man of stone and as unexpectedly heavy. His legs spasmed and his arms twitched, teeth snapping, and then he went limp against her, breathing fast, thick and gurgling in his throat.

"Tsuzas?"

A fit, Attalissa help her. A fit or the possession of his god, and how did one know the difference? His breathing slowed, and he moved a little. She settled his head more comfortably against her shoulder. Reminded, a shaft of tenderness through the heart, of Rideen, that time he was so ill, coughing and coughing, he couldn't breathe lying down, he had had to sit up all night, her mother or herself holding him, for comfort and warmth. But uncle had asked the goddess, a little thing of two or three, then, and she had wished him well. So Otokas said. And Rideen had recovered, and quickly grown strong again. Strong enough to join the militia, become one of the town's best bowmen.

Tsuzas sighed and muttered something, his breath gone quieter, more natural, like a sleeper. He showed no hurry to sit up.

"Hey," she whispered into his hair. "You awake?" The echoes turned her words into sinister hissing.

He groaned, pushed away from her.

"Mostly," he said after a moment, speaking softly, but the echoes still caught it. "Come." He found his cap, took up the lamp, helped her up. His smile was rueful, crooked, and his face pale, glistening with sweat. "Sorry."

Nothing more, till they were out of the cavern. Temple?

"Devils," Attavaia said, when they were once more in narrow darkness with the walls pressing in and the roof too low. Her voice shook, she realized. "What was that? Narva?"

"Narva," Tsuzas agreed dully. "Don't shout. Headache."

"Sorry." She reached and touched his shoulder. "Are you all right?"

"Mostly."

"Does he come to you often? Like that?"

"Yes."

"Do you remember . . ." She wasn't sure how to ask.

"Usually. Devils," he agreed. "Better empty temples than devils." He looked back at her. "Tell me what happened, when Tamghat took the temple. Attalissa couldn't face him, and fled. Even grandfather knows it's not true that she invited him and was abducted by a demon."

Attavaia told him all she remembered. Her leg was bad, blindingly bad, before they reached the house, and Tsuzas didn't lead her back to the family but to his own room, a small, white-painted cave with a felt curtain over the low door, a bed and a chest, a sword and spears leaning in the corner, and nothing more.

"Used to be a storeroom," he said. "I like it. Colder, but quiet." He was half-carrying her by then, though he looked as sick as she felt. He sat her on the bed, helped her get her leg up. An orange cat appeared from somewhere and settled down beside her, purring.

"Where's the goddess now?" he asked, when she had told him all she could of what had happened on the holy islet, and at Serakallash as well.

"With the Blackdog. My uncle. I don't know where he took her. Into the mountains somewhere."

"Your uncle?" He grinned, as he had on the mountain. "Don't tell grandfather that, of all things. He prays curses on the Blackdog, every night, for family pride and honour. Don't look like that. Narva doesn't hear prayer. What do you know of magic?"

"Hardly anything."

"Could a wizard do what this Tamghat has done? Think of stories, 'Vaia. He defeated Sera, and she fled because she thought he would destroy her. Attalissa fled because she foresaw he would devour her and she wasn't strong enough as a child-avatar to resist. True?"

"Yes."

"Narva . . . you saw my Uncle Umas. The god took him and my father both, when Lissavakail fell, and left Umas like that. We hoped, at first, he'd recover. It doesn't look likely now. He was always fragile, too open to Narva's mind. I think it's as though a fire roared through him, finally. Burned all his soul away."

"Your father, too?"

"He—" Tsuzas cleared his throat. "He went out in the fog, up above where some of the old shafts come out. And he walked over a cliff."

"You mean, deliberately?"

"I think so."

"Why?"

"I don't know." Tsuzas sat down on the edge of the bed, avoiding her gaze. "Narva was terrified. We all felt it. What they saw, with the god pouring through them, I don't know. But then we heard that Lissavakail had fallen, and how. Do you think that's a wizard, to panic a god that way?"

He deflected her firmly from asking any more about his father. Attavaia touched his arm, gently, got him to turn and look at her again.

"Sera was desperate. Attalissa was panicking. And Narva panicked as well, you're saying."

"Because of a wizard?"

Attavaia shook her head in denial. "Not . . . not a wizard. He can't be. There's no wizard in any tale a god need fear on their own ground. Except—"

"Except the seven devils." Tsuzas said it softly, as if fearing to hear his own words.

"They were killed and buried."

"Imprisoned, not killed."

"You really think Tamghat could be one of those, one of the wizards who gave their bodies to devils?" Attavaia wanted to hear him deny it.

"Narva's never spoken of devils before, not through me, not through my grandfather, that I've ever heard or been told," Tsuzas said. "I think—it's possible at least—that he's thought of devils now because of what he sees in you."

"In me?"

Tsuzas took her bandaged hand in his own. "He can probably touch

260

you now, a little. He might be aware of what you've seen, what you know. Impressions, at least."

What secrets did she know, that the priests of Narva should not? That she was the Blackdog's niece, nothing more. She had been barely out of her novitiate when the temple fell.

"If Tamghat's a devil, what do we do?"

Tsuzas actually laughed. "The Old Great Gods only know. Pray. Trust in Attalissa. Narva's certainly going to be no help."

She was silent, considering that. Considering her hand, lying in his.

"Are you hungry?" Tsuzas asked abruptly, freeing her hand.

Attavaia shook her head.

"Supper time. It's no short walk into Narva's heart. Are you sure?"

"Yes. But you should eat something," she said. "You still look grey."

"I'd be sick," he said matter-of-factly. "And you don't look so good yourself."

"The leg."

"Most people with a broken leg stay in bed. Are you fit to ride tomorrow?"

"Where to?"

"The snows are coming," he said. "You don't want to spend the winter with us. Elsinna and I will guide you down, to wherever it is you and your sisters lurk these days. I think Elsinna'd be happy enough to stay with you, actually. She always wanted to go to the temple."

"I'm not the one to ask . . . No, maybe I am. Old Lady is Tamghat's lapdog. The true temple, what's left of it, is scattered through the mountains. And they all look to me. If you don't mind, and Narva won't . . . won't kill her, she can swear to Attalissa and be welcome, as far as I'm concerned."

"Won't tell grandpapa till it's too late," Tsuzas said with satisfaction, his voice slurring. She thought at first it was another fit coming on him, but it was only exhaustion, his eyes falling shut like a little child's, overcome with sleep. His head nodded.

"Lie down," she ordered, and moved over a little, leaving him room. Dragged the heavy quilts out from beneath them with difficulty. He was already asleep by the time she covered them both. Chaste enough; they were both fully clothed, hadn't even got their boots off, and as for reputation, that was long gone.

Eventually, the lamp burned out, but it was a long time before Attavaia could fall asleep. Tsuzas had rolled so his head was on her shoulder, beard brushing on her cheek, unexpectedly soft.

PART THREE

NEARLY SEVEN YEARS SINCE THE FALL OF LISSAVAKAIL . . .

CHAPTER XVI

Before finally leaving Baisirbska, in the spring of the year that the Old Great Gods drove her from her retreat in the northern taiga, Moth and Mikki had lingered in Swanesby much of the summer, while Mikki helped build the growing settlement's great communal threshing barn, working by night to shape their beams, cut the mortises. Took leave of friends who would probably be long gone to the Gods before he ever came back that way again. Moth had given her histories, bundles wrapped in oiled leather, sealed with knots that were bindings more potent than they looked, to a young wandering storyteller, told him to take them to the king's skald of the Hravningas in Ulvsness in the west, whoever that might be now, if he ever went so far, or to pass them that way. They'd only rot, left behind. So something of their years in Baisirbska endured.

Still, though they wandered south into the Great Grass after that, as instinct had urged her, season followed season, summer grazing, rich in milk and roasted meat, winter's hard scraping as the herds huddled against the nor'westers and the tents grew stale with old smoke and old tales told once too often. She went as a warrior, armed, and though they thought her some outlaw banished from the hall of a Northron king, godless as she appeared, she would carry her sword for no clanlord or chieftain, and called herself only a soothsayer, sometimes, or a storyteller of the Northron folk, not claiming the name of wizard or skald or bard, as the observant suspected she should be, such was her skill with foretelling and small healing, and with words and song. When she read the runes for others, they still answered to the old power that had always lain in her blood. Moth cast the runes for her own course, though, and they fell empty of meaning. She did not reach into the threads of the Old Great Gods' binding again. She would learn nothing that way and the hungry touch of their tendrils made her ill, though that might be her mind's working, as a child made itself ill through morbid fears. But she began to feel she had abandoned the home they had made to rot and ice and ruin for nothing. The Old Great Gods were distant and could only touch the world at great cost. Lakkariss was not, though aware in some narrow way, intelligent. She could have stayed in Baisirbska, dug and planted their small fields, worried over her harvest, fished the autumn run of char, waited till the runes showed some clearer path to whatever had woken the sword. She had been driven, animal-like, into flight, and the Gods were no doubt pleased to have broken her stolen peace.

Mikki kept to the wilds and fringes of the encampments by day. Unlike the Northrons, the Grasslanders were not easy with demons.

From the start, there were rumours of a warlord, his tribe and god unknown, who had raided in the northeast, the west, the south. He drew to him, the stories said, rash younger sons and unmarriageable daughters, enticing them to abandon their folk and their gods to follow him, and raided herds and abducted bondfolk, a warlord whose raiding parties loomed from the grass unheralded, hidden by wizardry till they were among the herds and the chief's vassals had no time to assemble. Clan-chiefs who raised their *noekar* to hunt him died, in illness or accident, curse-stricken. He killed captive warriors and freefolk rather than ransoming them. It was said his wizard was a Nabbani woman, an imperial princess, and the warlord a follower of the old bear cult that had nearly died away after the devils' wars, but season after season they never found any who could give them a firsthand report of the warlord. Tamghat was the name the stories gave him. The tales were always at third- or fourth-hand remove, and when they followed rumours into territories on which he was said to have preyed, the trail faded away, or they were turned aside by some such more urgent matter. Once it was a clan-chief with a dying child, eaten by some inner disease that Moth was long months battling by the usual wizards' means. She had learned long since that to reveal herself as anything more won only hatred and fear for the patient as well as the healer, even the risk of such a recovered child being outcast by its god. More often the delay and diversion was a hostile god, not knowing what Moth was, thinking her god-born or demon-blooded or some other strange halfling creature, but distrusting her regardless, or a clan-chief who would not have a lordless vagabond crossing his territory, or fresher word of the warlord that then in turn faded.

Six years, they had hunted so, and had found nothing. Moth seemed content in that. Mikki was not, and not only because they were so often apart, she among the Grasslanders and he roaming the wild places, seeking what he could learn among the gods and the goddesses and the demons who hid from Moth.

But one night when she had come out of the camp, where she cast fortunes for a wedding, to be with him, she woke shouting a language even he did not know, clinging to him, a white fire that did not burn sheeting over the grass like waves about them. She would not say what terror had stalked her sleep, but she held tight to him the rest of the night, and did not go back to the encampment in the morning. Did not speak of it again, either, and snapped at his questioning, though her hand hardly let go its grip in his fur all that day as she walked beside him, the blue-roan horse she had ridden from Swanesby trailing them. When night fell she still led them on, hand in his, until half the night was gone. Finally she sighed, as if only then leaving nightmare behind, and let him go. Mikki flung himself down in the grass.

"Don't leave me, Mikki."

"I wouldn't. I won't." He gave a smile, trying to tease but too anxious to sound anything but forced. "It's you spending months at a stretch away among your own kind. How many proposals of marriage was it, four, this autumn alone? Not to mention all the other proposals."

"I don't mention them."

"Ah, but I lie awake worrying about them anyway."

"Mikki. Don't. I can't lose you."

"You won't. It would take the Gods themselves to pry me from you."

She moaned and leaned her head on his shoulder.

"What?"

"Fate above the Gods avert it. And damn them as they deserve." She sat back, rubbed her face with her hands like a woman waking. "Ah, well. You're right. We need to do more than chase rumour. He knows he's stalked." And Mikki noted that she still named no names, though they both had one in mind. "I need the start of the trail; then I can follow and not all his workings can shake me."

"Then let's find it."

"Where?" she asked.

Mikki considered, leaning back on his elbows in the whispering grass, which the wind stirred to waves, moon-touched pale and black. Moth began braiding grass-stems.

"Tell me," he said.

Moth looked up. "Tell you what?"

"Which way we should go. Or shall we wander circles in this maze of grass till it's too late? There were never any devils bound in the grass."

She flung the braided stems away and they made for a moment a sparkling web of firefly light as they fell. A trick Grassland wizards knew, a petty magic to please children. She felt for the purse of runes.

"Everything I do points awry."

"No runes. No flames. Just tell me—Vartu. Which direction do we go?"

Moth closed her eyes. "East. The Malagru. The burning mountains."

"So."

It was nearly seven years since the fall of Lissavakail.

So the kings of the north and the tribes of the grass and those wizards whom the devils had not yet slain pretended submission, and plotted in secret, and they rose up against the tyranny of the devils, and overthrew them. But the devils were devils, even in human bodies, and not easily slain. And there are many tales of the wars against the devils, and of the kings and the heroes and the wizards, and the terrible deeds done. And these can all be told, if there be golden rings, or silver cups, or wine and flesh and bread by the fire.

Only with the help of the Old Great Gods were they bound, one by one, and

imprisoned—Honeytongued Ogada in stone, Vartu Kingsbane in earth, Jas-
berek Fireborn in water, Twice-Betrayed Ghatai in the breath of a burning
mountain, Dotemon Dreamshaper in the oldest of trees, Tu'usha the Restless in
the heart of a flame, Jochiz Stonebreaker in the youngest of rivers. And they
were guarded by demons, and goddesses, and gods. And the Old Great Gods
withdrew from the world, and await the souls of human folk in the heavens
beyond the stars, which we call the Land of the Old Great Gods.

The earth shivered beneath his paws, and the air was choking, thick with
foul humours that burned and the stink of rotten eggs, and warm. Mikki
sneezed. This was the edge, Sihkoteh's current reach. The ground was
ashy, cinder-strewn, and only the fast-growing ground-covers ran over it,
thin pelts of greens and yellows, between meandering rivers of black
stone, still now, and cold, but there might be others which were not. The
Sihkotehbarkash had slept amid the often-restless peaks and craters of
the Malagru Range, which reached from Baisirbska in the north, setting
the eastern limits of the Great Grass, to run against the Pillars of the Sky
south of the deserts. It had begun to stir again, in smokes and quakes, a
century before, or so the tale ran in his village, one of the hunters who
ventured into the fire-mountains told them. And when his grandfather
had been young, that restless volcano had erupted in violence, raining
ash and fire over the slopes and the folded valleys around it.

Behind them the land looked kinder, deceptively. The hunter's histories were truth; Sihkoteh had reached so far, not so long ago. For
twenty miles behind, the forest was young, as Mikki judged forests.
There silver firs stretched tall, but there were few great enough in girth
a man's arms could not circle them. None older than sixty years or so,
Mikki thought, and he knew trees, felt their life in a way Moth never
could. Charred stumps rose among them still, like the great pillars of
some overthrown city, said Moth, who had seen such things. Travelling
beneath them, one struggled through a jungle of luxuriant growth,
ferns, giant nettles, and something like lacy meadowsweet that towered above the horse Storm's ears. Even reared on his hind legs, Mikki
could not peer over the nettles. Beneath, there was always stone, ridged

and folded, and the rich black soil was thin. The small streams that ran and twisted through the tangle were sometimes sweet, and sometimes sulphurous and warm.

"Wait for me here," Moth ordered, slinging the black sword over her shoulder. "I'm not taking you or Storm into that."

Mikki sneezed again, and the blue roan stallion snorted.

"I'd feel better, watching your back."

"I'd feel better if you went on breathing. Who knows what it's like at the crown, and what Sihkoteh might decide to do? Suffocate you. Incinerate the both of you."

"You could try not to anger him. I think it would be better if I went to talk to him instead, Moth. Alone."

"No."

"Yes."

"He's a god, a wild god with no folk, and dangerous. You will stay here, Mikki, and wait for me. Promise me you'll not follow."

"Wolf—"

"Your word you'll wait here, Mikki Sammison."

Mikki sighed. "I'll wait. Go on, then. Don't get yourself killed." Because if she feared for him this much, perhaps she did see something to fear, vague shadows of possibility, up on the volcano's rim.

Moth left him without looking back, picking a way through the ash and stone, towards the summit. She was soon lost to sight amid the earth-hued landscape, reappeared briefly, a figure already frail with distance, and then lost again, into some fold of the mountainside.

Mikki settled down to wait.

Late in the evening, oily grey clouds boiled over the mountaintop and Storm, swishing his tail and browsing, or pretending to, fell away to nothing but a skull amid the nettles. Mikki tensed, lying head on paws, watching the horizon far above. All was still again. The clouds diffused, turning the lowering sun red.

The god Sihkoteh was aware of her from the time she stepped onto the ashy wastelands that surrounded the peak. He might have been watching even earlier, as she and Mikki forced their way through the tangle beneath the trees in the valleys below, but she did not think so. Gods of Sihkoteh's sort were not wide-ranging in their awareness, lacked the human-worshipped god's need to protect or simply to be aware of all the lives around them. They were also less concentrated, less . . . a person, than the gods of human-settled places. Human minds and souls and attention gave gods . . . what? Pattern, she decided. Call it pattern. Personality. A focus. The wild gods were more dangerous, and less so; no cool calculation but only reactive passions, but no human society to possess and protect. And this one felt . . . damaged. Anger and some hurt festering beneath a half-healed surface. Lava beneath the black crust of rock. The two were not unconnected, no poet's shaping but truth, here. Demon or not, Mikki could be hurt, killed, by this god, and she was not risking any target for Sihkoteh's anger but herself.

She could see Sihkoteh with little effort. Not any body, but lines of force and fire in the earth, will and heart spread through the rock, through the veins of liquid rock, too. She climbed the side of a ridge, not liking the feeling of being beneath Sihkoteh's stone, as though the sky were some protection. The god would hear, if she called him, but she went on, turning upwards when she came to a place like a scab on the mountain, where black crust oozed molten scarlet and crawled slowly towards her.

Moth drew the obsidian-bladed sword, then, and went on with it in her hand, ignoring how the liquid rock edged after her, the scab tearing uphill, new crust seeping, rolling at her heels.

Trying what she would do. Playing.

It was partly damnable curiosity. She had not seen a volcano since they fled the western isles, and never this close to. And Vartu had not, not with human eyes.

The crawl of molten rock gave up, or was left behind. The air smelt of burning stone, stung the eyes and throat, and there was no other living thing about. Some might argue the living. She grinned. She climbed the last steep rise, stood atop a ridge of blackened rock, looking down. Lazy ropes and banners of steam drifted over the crater below, curtaining black rock and dark fissures. The sun was setting, the long shadows running together. The ground moved, falling and rising, so that she was reminded, suddenly and intensely, with what was almost pain, of the heave of a ship, that relaxed and leg-braced swaying as the long keel danced.

She reached out into the fissures, followed them down. Hot darkness, fumes that could corrode the flesh. The white glow of iron in the furnace. A tomb in the rock, a womb that had cradled bones and burning soul. Its basalt walls were cracked, shattered with violence like an exploded egg, but the explosion had followed the slow, slow creeping of hair-fine cracks, the first weakening of the binding.

So. Ghatai was free. And so, in the end, would they all be, thanks to Ogada, who had first found the flaw into which to insert his will.

The god struck, fist of fire closing around her, and Moth hurtled back to her body. Scalding steam fountained and dark smoke, noxious and cutting with particles of stone, boiled up and folded down, reaching for her.

Devil.

It was not even a word, only furious recognition, a snarl of passion.

The ground dropped and she leapt back, the edge of rock breaking, falling. She swept the Great Gods' sword around, and the smoke rolled together, sinking into itself, growing blacker and thicker as it folded into the crater.

"No," she said. "I'm not him, Sihkoteh. How long since Ghatai escaped your watch?"

The Gods. Recognition again, and uncertainty. Moth stretched out into that, warily, touching the god, as if with fingertips. He recoiled, fearing the edge of the sword's blade as much as she did.

How long? She felt his awareness of the answer, the cycles of the seasons.

Just over sixty years ago, as she had suspected. The volcano's last great eruption had been part of no natural cycle of events, but violent reaction come too late. Like the reaction of the Old Great Gods, who

272

could have set her on Ghatai when he first escaped, not waiting till he had had decades to make plans, establish himself in the world.

She doubted that they waited out of benevolence to test him, to see if he could live at peace in the world. More likely they simply waited until his crimes were too terrible to ignore and one of them had to make the sacrifice, and cross to the world to summon her again.

Where did he go? she asked.

Sihkoteh's impression was of presence fading westward, down from the mountains into the Great Grass. Nothing she did not already know.

There was a sort of hunger in the god's awareness of her. Moth felt it stirring, wiped blood and ash from her face, frowning into the smoke. He had been charged to hold a devil. He had failed of his charge. He had . . . Ghatai had grappled with him, they had risen, burning, into the sky, claws of fire tearing into the god's heart, the devil like some parasite, burrowing into his soul. Sihkoteh had torn him out and flung him away and sunk into his mountain, poisoned, that was the way to describe it. It would take years yet to burn and slough away the devil's hunger that gnawed him and fought to change his being. The devil had drawn flesh to his bones and fled. And now a devil came tormenting him again, hungry to dive into his soul.

Moth backed away.

No. "No." And felt panic rise with the pounding of her heart, felt the grave close in about her again, the binding of earth and the Great Gods' own runes, the webs of power sealing eyes and ears, closing mouth and nostrils, the last breath gone and the utter stillness where even thought died . . .

The edge of the sword burned whitely, but the god was there, all around her, enfolding her in fire.

With shaking hand she traced a rune on her own forehead, leaving it marked in blood that still seeped from burns. Not a human symbol, but the sign of the Old Great Gods. It burned the skin, burned the fiery heart of her, but they had marked her and it was always there, a faint and distant pain, if she reached for it.

"I am not yours to take, Sihkoteh. Never yours." She held the obsidian sword at guard, hands steady now. The god, like some great beast pricked by unexpected spines on its prey, withdrew a little, warily. "I hunt him for the Great Gods. Truth. I swear it in my blood." She hesitated. "Can you still feel him, do you still have any hold?"

Sihkoteh did not, and anger seethed, shame at his failure, at how long Ghatai had worked subtle spells against him, undetected.

"Hardly for me to judge you." She turned, no need to face the volcano; Sihkoteh was all about her.

The land around was splintered and broken. Moth picked her way down in the dark, leaping new fissures, climbing uptilted slabs, walking rock that was warm under the feet, searing in places, but she willed her boots not to burn; she left the stone cracked and cold where she trod. Dried blood and ash flaked away from her spattered face. Sihkoteh flowed after her, spread lines of molten rock under the crust, shifting it, not daring more.

She ignored him. The moon rose, red in the east through the hanging vapours, and eventually the god let her go, watching, but nothing more.

Mikki had made a fire for the comfort of it, on the edge of the ashy ground, and sat by it honing his axe. Storm's saddle and bridle were stacked neatly with the packs, and the horse's skull sat on the saddle, its empty eye sockets little comfort or company.

Moth stirred the ashy ground, walking back to them, and he rose, stood waiting. He could smell blood on her, burns already healing, spatter of scars on her face and one hand, holes singed in tunic, mail blackened.

The wonder was not that she had lost her hold on the spell that gave the bone-horse form, but that she came back so little injured. He had been expecting worse and very close to breaking his word to go in search of her.

"Fool," he said indistinctly into her hair. She smelt of sulphur and hot metal.

274

"I'm all right, cub." She held him at arm's length in the moon-light, pulled him close and kissed him. "You worry too much." Moth let him go and picked up the skull. "He distracted me, is all."

"Sure." They traded edged smiles. She shrugged, squatted down on the earth with the skull and a knife, cut the ball of her thumb and traced runes on the bone in blood, *Gift*, *Water*, and *Sun* conjoined, for life, *Horse*, *Aaurochs*, and *Boar*, for strength and protection. Other signs: *Aurochs* again, the letter for her birthname, *Sun* again, for the name the living warhorse had borne. Her will behind it, and strength of soul no wizard had ever held. A bone-horse was a temporary creation, not something that should endure day after day once called. But Storm had been ghost long before she bound him to his skull, and no animal's soul should have persisted wilful so long in the world. It might be Storm's will as much as Moth's that gave the horse strength and form.

Storm rose into being again, clinging to his skull, smoke and fire and earth, ash rising, ghost drawing matter from the world to house itself. He nuzzled against Moth's chest, tried to wheel away, but she caught him by his mane, bridle in the other hand.

"Not a place we should spend the night?" Mikki asked, taking her intent from that and heaving the saddle over the stallion's back.

"No. Sihkoteh is not best pleased at my existence."

"Going to tell me what you learned?"

"Ghatai is no longer bound there."

"Should we be surprised? Someone's revived that damned bear cult on the Great Grass."

"Ghatai tried to possess Sihkoteh. He fought the god and fled, sixty years ago."

"To possess a *god*? And Ghatai survived?"

"Apparently. He fled westerly."

Mikki sighed and rubbed the side of his nose. "So, back to the Great Grass, where we knew he probably was anyway."

"Yes. But now—now I have a trail to follow."

"Do you?"

"Yes."

"How?"

Dark fire rose behind her eyes. "How do you find a scent in the air, cub?"

"With my nose, thank you very much."

"It's there, now, to follow. The taste of him in the air."

"So we sniff our way along sixty years of wandering?"

"Not so much. He has been . . ." Her eyes grew distant, searching. ". . . here, there, all over. We've crossed his trail so many times. To Marakand, he has been to Marakand and back, twice? Maybe . . . But now I have him, the runes will know him—we pick up his more recent trail. The south of the Great Grass, towards the Four Deserts, I think . . . I can see where he left the Grass for the last time." She swayed, focused on Mikki again. "He's no longer on the Grass and I can't see where he's gone. But we'll find that trail, and it will tell us. He's been tangling us, not even knowing who sought him, but there will be no more delaying."

"No more sleeping alone in the brush?"

"No more of that either. If you can manage to stay awake. Winter's coming."

"Hah. Such as it is on the southern Grass—winters don't catch me here, as you'd know if you hadn't been sitting so cosy in the tents playing fortune-teller. And anyway, I do wake up, even in the far north, if I have something to stay awake for . . ." Tremors in the earth set the trees further down the mountainside swaying. "Moth, my queen, we need to get out from under this annoyed volcano. I still wish you'd leave talking to gods to me. They don't like you. For some reason."

"For some reason. Sihkoteh's in no temper to listen to anyone. He'd have hurt you, Mikki, to prove he still could."

Moth fastened the last buckle, mounted and turned Storm, trampling nettles. Mikki fell in behind the horse, axe over his shoulder, breathing the scent of bruised greenery, fresh and clean. The earth shuddered again.

She was still reluctant. She resisted the Old Great Gods' pushing

276

of her. What he did not understand was why she had ever accepted the sword in the first place, what she saw that he didn't, that tore her so between the sword's duty and her own will.

"Why?" he had asked her long ago, after Ogada was dead and she still kept the sword, and she had turned on him, Vartu's eyes, fierce, burning, and said, "*Don't.* Don't ask, ever. It's not yours to know, Mikki Sammison." And there had been power in her words, though they had sounded as much a plea as an injunction. He never had asked again, and when he wondered, he never could bring himself to ask. He would have been angry at such power turned against himself, but he did not think his wolf knew she had set such a binding on him. And if her need was so great, her fear so great . . . if the sword held such doom . . . he would not push it. But he did not forget, either, and he watched the sword.

Perhaps the deaths of the other devils had been the price of the blade needed to kill Ogada, her brother's secret murderer, his mother's slayer? He wondered. He did not think Vartu would have been so easily bought.

He would never be so glad, though, as when that damned—literally so, he was certain—obsidian blade was broken and cast aside, and Moth free of it.

CHAPTER XVII

*Y*ou'll come home soon, Attalissa. We both know it. I'm waiting for you.

Even in sleep, in unconsciousness, or wide awake in the midst of utter confusion, when his mind came seeking her in last week's winter storm—the tent whipping free of its stakes, ropes snapping—she was protected. The hand of Sayan sheltered her, and the rush of Kinsai's fervent blood. There was nothing for the wizard to see of Pakdhala, nothing for him to grasp or recognize as his searching brushed by and went on, lost in hills and river.

But the wizard had never spoken before in all the times that he had sought her.

Pakdhala woke to the grip of a hand on her shoulder and blinked up to see Bikkim crouched beside her. The first yellow light slanted through the narrow slit of a window to gild his skin, throwing the interwoven blue and red horses of his tattoos into sharp contrast.

"Am I late? Sorry." She didn't think she was, not by the light, but she felt a heavy lethargy on her, as though all her bones were granite. Waking came difficult here in Serakallash, and Tamghat's words still stuck cloying to her mind. *Come home soon.*

"No, it's early," Bikkim whispered, and Pakdhala rubbed her eyes, to see Immerose and Tihmrose still soundly sleeping. Immerose, for once, was not snoring.

"The boss isn't up yet. I was going to pray, and . . ." Bikkim shrugged, as though trying to make the words of no account. "I wondered if you'd want to come with me."

"To the spring?"

"Yes," he said soberly. Bikkim's dark eyes were sunken, shadowed as though he had not slept. Perhaps he did not, these nights before he went to pray to Sera. Pakdhala did not know. She missed a lot when they were in Serakallash.

"Of course."

Neither Tihmrose nor Immerose stirred as she finished dressing, taking a scarf to wrap over her face once they were out in the street, as Bikkim did to hide his Serakallashi tattoos. There was always an excuse, dust or, now, the cold, to make a covered face not so very odd. It was the tail end of winter, the wind still biting, carrying cold from the north. Some mornings there would be hoarfrost around the wells, and a fog rising from the water, frost on the outside of their water-gourds and the big goatskins, the shaggy camels puffing clouds. It was the season when clouds could cover the desert skies, and snow would fall, which Pakdhala never realized she missed until it was there, touching her skin, hushing the world, covering the hills and the dunes with glittering white until, in a day or a week, it sank away into the waiting earth, feeding the wells and the holy springs with water to last until the next year. Snowfall had set this year's three leggy calves frisking, gleefully mad with the strangeness of it. She felt the same each time it snowed, as though the world might be made new.

But today there would be sun for their departure. And soon the rains would start, and the desert would bloom, though they might be in the valley of the Kinsai-av by then.

The Blackdog did not bother to caution her against the dangers of Serakallash, but her father nevertheless woke, lying several rooms along with Gaguush. Lots of space for them to spread out, scattering two or three to the small, arched rooms that surrounded the central yard and the pens. There were rooms and to spare these days; caravans were fewer, and Master Mooshka had no other in when they arrived. She remembered the days when there might be two caravans or even three in one caravanserai in Serakallash, the camels penned in behind strong hurdles, the bulls restive and roaring in their herd rivalries, the mercenaries little better, sometimes.

"Here, you should eat something." Bikkim pressed a round cake, dry and oily with pistachios, sticky with raisins, into her hand as he closed the door behind them. Pakdhala was delicate, and the air or the water or *something*, no one questioned it any more, did not agree with her, here in Serakallash and in Marakand, where it was said the goddess of the holy well had withdrawn in anger from her folk. They all babied her. Only Zavel twitted her for it, which was by now more habit than lingering boyish malice, she hoped.

Mooshka's dogs woke, stretching, and trotted over from their bed in one of the gated, open-fronted arches where fodder was stored. Pakdhala broke off a piece of the cake for each. The corner of Bikkim's mouth twitched in a resigned way. Probably he had asked Thekla to get it for him at the market, specially for her. It was the sort of thing he did. Bikkim had bought Pakdhala the scarf she wore, plum-coloured silk, in Marakand, and she avoided thinking about what it must have cost, because that gave her a little nervous flutter in her stomach that she wasn't sure she wanted to face yet. It wasn't a gift you gave the brat who tagged at your heels. But Bikkim was more a sort of honorary brother than anything else.

Sort of like a brother, anyway. Watching her father and his brothers, or her cousins with one another, on rare visits home to the Sayanbarkash, she thought brothers were supposed to be rougher, loving but not so nice. But maybe it was different with girls, maybe they were gentle with sisters, and bought them pretty things. It was not something she was going to ask her father about.

With Bikkim's eyes on her, Pakdhala carefully ate the rest of the cake and licked her fingers, though her stomach was tight and churning at the thought of Sera's spring. Last time she had been very sick.

Bikkim raised a pail of water at the well so they could both drink and wash, tipping out the rest into the trough that served the beasts when they came in off the desert. The camels grunted and stirred, seeing activity. Her white Flower heaved with heavy grace to her feet—hers, because when she was a little girl, she had announced that red Sihdy's calf would be white, and Gaguush had laughed at her and said there was little chance, but if it was, she could have it for her own.

So Gaguush had been out a camel, and her father thought she had done it on purpose. Bikkim sighed when she crossed the yard to the penned beasts to give Flower the scratching she expected and endure the warm, sour-sweet breath huffing on her neck.

"Coming," she said, but it was already too late. The door of the room Bikkim and Zavel had shared swung open and Zavel, grinning broadly at them, hurried out.

"And where are you sneaking off to? I thought 'Dhala was too sick to do any *work*."

"Oh, shut up," Pakdhala answered, as Bikkim's fine straight brows lowered. "We're going to pray at the spring."

"Ah." Zavel gave a shrug, which was probably all the apology they'd get for the slur. "I'll come along, too."

He didn't bother to wash, so there was no way to accidentally leave him behind. She could not walk that quickly anyway. Even crossing the yard to the small door set in the heavy gate left her heart beating too fast, forced her to breathe through her mouth.

Zavel had as much right to pray at Sera's spring as Bikkim, far more than she had. Zavel was Serakallashi-born and raised, though his parents, Tusa and Asmin-Luya, had not had him tattooed, keeping to their Great Grass heritage. He did claim the name Battu'um, having been fostered with his younger brothers and sister by a herder family of the Battu'um sept, of which Bikkim's father had been one of the chiefs. There was no word of what had become of Tusa and Asmin-Luya's three younger children when Serakallash fell to Tamghat. The family who fostered them were said to have been burned in their cottage. Tusa never did give up hope. She rode away whenever they came to Serakallash, asking among the folk of the Battu'um, now scattered far and wide in new-founded villages as bondfolk of Tamghat's *noekar*, for the Grasslander children, two boys and a girl, who had been fostered with herders of the east foothills.

Bikkim and Zavel aligned themselves one on each side of her. Pakdhala said nothing to either of them, bracing herself for what they would find.

A third visit to Sera's spring. The first when her father brought her down from the mountains, a brat badly in need of a spanking. The second, driven by guilt and horror, a little more than two years later, after Serakallash had fallen. She had been very sick, had fainted, and Holla-Sayan had carried her back to the caravanserai. The skulls, still reeking carrion, untouched by buzzard or hyena or humble beetle, had been far less terrible than the emptiness of a holy place which had lost its goddess.

Northron Varro claimed three was a number of great power, and read signs into any occurrence that fell into sets of three. A third time might be for good or ill, but the third time was always fate, and change.

So Varro said.

Whenever the gang stopped in Serakallash now, Bikkim kept grimly within the caravanserai walls except for one visit to the spring just as the caravan prepared to leave. They hoped, if anyone noticed, it would be forgotten before they returned. It would do none of them any good if the Lake-Lord's *noekar* heard there was a Battu'um chief's heir living, even though the old sept system had been broken up, the names forbidden. Families had been moved to new lands; *noekar* of Tamghat's ruled all the scattered folk that called themselves Serakallashi, and the Serakallashi were assigned to them all as bondfolk. Slaves, save in that they could not be sold away. Slaves, and perhaps even godless.

More and more wells failed, and streams dried, and Tamghat's *noekar* seized goods from the caravans and called it tribute, while in Serakallash's market, flour and oil and fodder were dear and growing dearer every journey, the toll for passing into the town greater. There was talk among the caravan-masters of finding a new road to the north, seeking new wells and bypassing Serakallash, but so far only one or two had tried it. There was the Undrin Rift to pass doing so, and that was no safe matter, either.

Third time at Sera's spring: Pakdhala held herself braced for it. Not so much horror as sorrow. The dead were dead, and a stranger, coming for the first time on what had been Sera's sacred place, would never know it was a spring. A mound of skulls, still wearing rags of skin like the fine brown membrane that flakes off a dried date, hair bleaching from black and brown to a pale tan colour, like Westron Thekla's. Sand. Everywhere sand, and snow in the deep shadows. Not a stalk of winter-dead grass to show there had once been green. Through the dry seasons the dust had risen from the Red Desert and wrapped around the heads, holding them, enfolding them. Now, damp with winter flurries or rain, it clung, taking them into the land. The saxauls at the bottom of the ridge were skeleton trees.

Zavel scowled, and scuffed his boot in the mud. He dropped his head in a perfunctory bow, and twiddled his braids, avoided looking.

Bikkim, ignoring the boy, settled down cross-legged, pulling the scarf from his face. He leaned forward to pour out a gourdful of water.

"Water for water," he said firmly, the old prayer, but there was none to take away.

She should have thought to bring some herself. Pakdhala sat down beside Bikkim, not too close, not to intrude, and because she had, Zavel of course did too, drawing his legs up, chin on his knees. Bikkim's lips moved in silent prayer.

Pakdhala shaped words with her lips, too. *I'm sorry.* It was not her fault Tamghat had come down from Lissavakail, and yet it was. If the wizard-warlord had not come for her, he would not have come for Sera. *Can you hear me, Sera? Are you still there, drowned in the sands? I swear, someday, somehow, I will see Tamghat destroyed, and your folk and mine will be free again.*

"That's my sister Laicha," Bikkim said conversationally, pointing. "You'd have liked her, 'Dhala."

Zavel's mouth twisted and he gave Bikkim a sickened look. The skull Bikkim pointed out had no flesh left to it, but he had come many times. He knew the geography of them, Pakdhala supposed.

"And my father, there. The sand will take him in another year. I'm glad. I've never seen my mother and my younger sister Davim, but they were executed here, too. I always meant to take you to see them, when we passed through, and you were always so sick I never did. I wish you had met them, even just once."

"The earth will take them all, in the end," she said softly.

She remembered that she had been accustomed, once, to folk offering her these fragments of their lives, telling her what they could only tell the darkness, opening the way to the places in their heart too deep to let others into. But it was like something in a song, long ago and far away, and from Bikkim it felt like something else.

"You'd think Tamghat would want to bury them, cover them up," Zavel said, too loudly. He flashed a quick look over his shoulder to see who might be listening, the way local people seemed to, even Mooshka secure within the thick walls of his caravanserai. It was a catching mannerism. "You'd think he'd want folk to forget."

"Fear is a weapon," Pakdhala said, and added, "A tyrant's weapon." Thinking of Holla-Sayan, and the Blackdog Laykas who had planned that other massacre of Serakallashi. *I'm not that person anymore, Sera. I will not be that person again. Forgive me.*

"Do you think Sera's still here, somewhere?" Bikkim asked, looking at Pakdhala. But it was no question heavy with meaning, expecting her to *know*, just wondering. Asking her rather than both of them just to snub Zavel, who had not been invited. Maybe. Maybe it meant nothing at all, empty talk to fill the moment.

"I . . . don't know," she said at last, which was the truth. There was nothing of Sera present that she could touch, and Sera had forbidden her to come here; Sera should have been drawn out in fury that she had, if the goddess of the spring were still aware at all of her world.

"*I* think she's dead," Zavel said. "Like those gods in the west that Thekla prays to." He twitched, another look over his shoulder, a shrug. "She has to be dead, or she'd have done something."

"She did do something," Bikkim said. "She fought. He defeated her. But he's still only a wizard, no matter how powerful. He couldn't have killed her. She must be here still. Somewhere." With another look at Pakdhala, "'Dhala, you all right?"

She swallowed hard, nodded. Something touched her. A hot, dry touch, nothing like a goddess of the waters. *Sayan*, she thought. *Hold me.* She lost herself in memory, the high sweep of hill and the wind shushing through the grass and the black larks climbing into the sky on towers of song. Racing two of her cousins, Holla-Sayan's nephews, crouched low on a galloping horse. And winning. Though that breath and shadow of the Western Grass was always with her, she drew it more densely about her as a person hidden in the darkness might pull the folds of a black robe closer. She felt herself a tiny bird, a lark, gently cupped in Sayan's great, rough-skinned hands.

Twice in one day. Tamghat usually sought her once a month or so, as though it had become some habitual chore. Recently the touches had come more frequently, but never twice in one day. Her mouth felt dry, and the skin between her breasts prickled with sweat.

"Maybe not dead, then," Zavel said, still chewing over Bikkim's words. "But Sera's gone, and she didn't do much when she was here. She didn't save them," with a nod at the spring. "She didn't even save the little children they butchered." His voice cracked and he scowled, defying them to notice. "Precious little to choose between her and that mortal goddess up in Lissavakail, neither of them any good to anyone."

Pakdhala put a hand on his shoulder a moment, took it away again when Zavel reached for it with his own.

Tamghat's blind, groping touch returned yet again. She could feel . . . something . . . brushing by, like the passage of a ghost, but hot as the shimmering air rising off the Salt Desert. Her tongue felt an alien thing, baked clay in her mouth, her body growing dull and distant, her ears humming like bees. She drowned herself in Kinsai's dark waters, the shadows that only the sturgeon knew, she was deaf and blind in the Cataracts, which could beat bones to porridge, the fire in Kinsai's blood.

He lost her, as a man might touch a darting fish and never even see it, never close his hand. She hardly dared breathe. He could not know she was so near; there was no echo of Sera in her soul.

Zavel was staring at her, scowling in concern.

"Attalissa probably died," Pakdhala said, hearing her own voice stretching thin, far away. "Probably she did. Father said they burned the temple. Probably she was killed." She tried to get to her feet and stumbled. "I'm going back. They'll all be up and wondering where we are."

"I heard a bard in Marakand singing she was imprisoned by a demon and she summoned Tamghat here to rescue her," Zavel countered. "Except the demon carried her off, then, and the wizard's still trying to save her. If that's true, that she asked him here, she's worse than useless. She deserves to be dead."

"I heard it. It was a stupid song," Pakdhala muttered, pushing herself up with one hand gripping her amulet-bag and the flat lakeshore stone under her coat.

Bikkim offered her a hand up she was glad to take, even if he did release it right away. Zavel put a supporting hand under her elbow, which she needed, dizzy with the effort of rising. Bikkim started along the path, turned back.

"Should I carry you?"

She shook her head, flushing with embarrassment. "No. I can walk." She shook off Zavel's arm, felt guilty at the look of annoyed hurt he gave his own feet, and made herself smile at them both. "Really, I can walk."

Two days to the next goddess-possessed spring, at Nivlankallash, but by evening she might be feeling better, able to reach out, a little, into her sister Nivlan's small, unpeopled land, and borrow strength of her. Nivlan of the Nivlankallash always welcomed her.

"Don't fall over your own feet," Bikkim said. "Holla'll black my eye if I bring you back bruised."

"Poor delicate baby," Zavel muttered, but it sounded half-hearted. "Are you sure you're all right, 'Dhala? You've gone sort of grey. That's a bloody awful thing to take a kid to see, Bikkim. Even Varro's got more sense."

"If you want to help, you can run on back and make sure Thekla's got some tea on," Bikkim suggested.

Zavel shrugged, sneered, then nodded and ran off, up the narrow lane that wandered a zigzag way into the town between the high walls of the caravanserais.

Pakdhala didn't bother muttering a complaint about being called a kid by a *boy* only a couple of years older, saved her breath for walking and kept her eyes on the ground, not to see the mountains floating to the south and feel the sudden pang of loss and longing that was not Pakdhala at all.

Bikkim hesitantly took her hand. "I'm sorry," he said. "I didn't mean to make you ill. I . . . it's a holy place. No matter what Tamghat does to it, it's my place, my people's place. I can't be with them at that . . . that pit . . . by the mountain road where the bodies were buried, only here."

"I know." His hand was warm, rough, dirty beyond what any scrubbing could help. A mate for her own. A caravan-mercenary's hand, a cameleer's hand.

Holla-Sayan was waiting for them, propped against Mooshka's gate as though he had nothing better to do. He gave Pakdhala a crooked, apologetic smile for being there.

You don't need to hover, dog.

I do till we leave this place. "Breakfast's ready and Gaguush is cursing," he said aloud. "To work, eh?"

Sera is dead, isn't she?

I don't know. If you can't tell, 'Dhala . . . perhaps she isn't. You know how empty the dead lands along the Five Cataracts feel.

It's empty here, too.

Differently empty. Her father frowned. *Empty like an empty house. Not a ruin.*

You really think so?

He shrugged. He wasn't sure, she could feel that, but he had no confidence in what he thought, doubted his own interpretation of the dog's impressions. She trusted the dog in such things, though, and tried to feel some hope for Sera in that.

Tamghat's looking for me again, she said, and wished she hadn't, as Holla came alert in a way that made Bikkim drop her hand, as the frown had not.

"We need to get going," Holla-Sayan said. "Eat quickly, both of you. I'll look to loading your camels."

As though that would somehow stir the whole caravan to faster action, hasten the two Over-Malagru merchants who had hired them back in Marakand through their always-formal mealtime.

Her father would be worried, the Blackdog would be dangerously angry, and all through, Holla-Sayan would be afraid, if she told him Tamghat had come back to brush against her more than once. As if he circled, a hawk closing in before the stoop.

Three times the wizard had found her. Three, for fate and change.

CHAPTER XVIII

The feather-grass stretched in all directions, a sea without a shore, wave on silver-brown wave rising and falling with the rolling of the steppes. In a great sweep around the land was scarred, though the traces were hard to see now, looking with the eyes alone. To Mikki, the scarring was more a scent than any visible impression left in six summers of grass, a memory of power tainting the odour of the earth. Moth said it was a shadow in the air, a ghost of fire the soul's eye could see when the body's could not.

And here was where Tamghat had most recently touched the Great Grass. From here he had vanished. Here his trail ended.

"It's amazing he could do this without every god and demon of the Grass feeling it," Moth muttered, walking a great circle that she said was the line of the spell. "Strong in stealth, that one—"

"What did he do?"

"Carried them all away—man and beast."

"Where?" Mikki asked hopelessly. "Moth, we can't wander aimlessly again. Let's go to Marakand. We're bound to hear something on the caravan road, if he hasn't fled to the other side of the world entirely."

"There's another working like this one a few miles away. An early one."

"A test?"

"A failure. It feels . . . twisted. Broken. He came from there straight to here. I might learn more from that."

"Has it occurred to you that every delay and digression is his doing? He's playing games with us, Moth."

"I don't play games."

"Then—"

"There's something walking there. I think he may have left someone behind." She grinned. "Such effort to hide his trail, and he leaves someone I can ask for directions."

The ghost was aware of the traveller before the rider came over the distant horizon, a prickling edge of unease for which she could for a long time remember no name.

Fear.

There had been others. Bondfolk shepherds, who fled the damp chill in the air when she crawled close to their fire. A pair of some warlord's vassals, his *noekar*, stopping to rest the night. They muttered and shivered; the woman called the place accursed, and they rode away again. A clan-chief sent more *noekar* and their warriors, but no wizard, no wise shaman of any understanding, and the *noekar* poked at bones and prayed to the god of some distant hill, before riding away, afraid of curses and the contagion of a ghost's ill-luck. The Grasslanders were like that, she remembered. No mercy for the dead. They would not bury bones that were no kin to them, believing that a person left unburied had been damned to it by the stars of their birth and it was not for strangers to interfere. The wandering herdsmen began to give the area a wider space when they went by with the sheep and the horses, leaving her alone.

This one—she would rather have been left alone with the wind and the grass and the heat of her anger, which she still nursed.

This one—she forgot the rider, in the dim, fractured existence that was hers, while the figure was still in the distance, mounted human and some great beast ambling alongside that she thought, uncomfortably, was not a dog, before they faded from mind. Then they were there, approaching the grave. They spoke a thick, heavy language she did not understand.

The bear—bear, not dog, bear like nothing she had ever seen living—spoke, deep and rumbling. He must be a demon. Her spirit's erratic vision edged him in blue fire, and white, something she had never seen, being a wizard of no great strength in life, though she had read that was how the strong in power saw demons. Their very souls scratched sparks from the world, or perhaps it was something more akin to the foam at a ship's prow. She had read treatises that argued so, long ago when she was young and a scholar in a life that seemed almost a distant tale. But this demon was far from his origins. No demon native to the steppes took the form of a great brown bear of the forests. This one was a giant even among those; she had seen such beasts, dead, measured their skulls with awe-stricken handspans and slept on their pelts. The demon was pale, more tawny-gold than brown. His claws were ivory, but his eyes were black.

The rider did not belong to the grass, either, and a dark halo around her body burned the ghost's senses. She shied away from it, tried to see with vision, or what passed as vision, alone. The woman was tall and lean, dressed in the style of the north, low boots, narrow-legged trousers, and a long tunic, its hem showing beneath a mail hauberk, with a knee-length deerskin cloak against the chill autumn wind or to keep the gleam of armour from catching a distant eye. She wore all ugly dull browns and greys like a hunter, a sneaking bandit, and carried a long, straight-bladed sword at her hip, its ancient-styled hilt gold and garnets, and another, silver-hilted, strapped to the saddle under her near-side knee. A Northron battle-axe and a bow-case and quiver were strapped to what little other gear the horse carried. The woman's hair fell in a single plain braid to her waist, the silver-dun colour of the bleached autumn grass, and her eyes were grey. She looked towards where the ghost hesitated, looked into insubstantial eyes . . .

There was a shadow over her, deep and rich as wine, red-black like the heart's blood. Eyes, red, flame's heat . . . like . . . the ghost cowered away, faded.

They had moved, she had missed time again. Now the woman knelt a few yards from the grave where the others lay buried, their souls long gone on their journey to the Old Great Gods. The bear crouched beside her.

The ghost remembered grey eyes, like steel and thunderclouds and deep brooding water. The woman was a great wizard; she reeked of power, that was all. A wizard and a misplaced demon, nothing worse than that . . . what else could she have thought? The horse was a black-legged blue roan stallion, a heavy horse of the north, strong but slow, no use on the dry steppe, too demanding of water, too weakened by heat. Only a fool would ride one here. It cropped the grass now, looked up at the ghost, saw her and flattened its ears. She saw through it, saw grass beyond, sky. It was a ghost as much as she was, a shadow of a horse, though its gold-trimmed bridle and saddle were solid enough. A memory of a horse—an ancient skull bound with magic such as the ghost had only dreamed of. She remembered tales told in the long, slow afternoons of her childhood, tales of wild fancy: a Northron magic of their great wizards, a bone-horse, ghost bound to a horse-skull, to be summoned by the wizard's blood. But that was for children's tales. No one knew such arts these days; had they ever existed in truth, such skills were lost now, with many others, in the old wars against the devils.

She had dreamed of devils, just now . . . but she dreamed all the terrors of her childhood, in her unresting weariness, dreamed of devils all too often.

The wizard rose and spoke, gesturing, inviting *her*. Seeing her.

She covered her face with her hair and screamed. She saw through the wizard, through the grey eyes, to eyes of fire. She had seen their like before as she died.

The early working was as Moth had said: uneven, twisted, a spell unravelled in the casting. And there was a chill in the air, a damp, cold breath rising from the earth, the skin-prickling presence of the walking dead.

There was more to show, here, that something had occurred. At the later place there was only grass. Here there was a grave. Spears marked a central depression where the earth had settled over it. They had origi-nally stood upright like the pales of a fence, but the winters of wind and frost-heaving, the summers of thunder and hail and always the unrelenting wind, had shifted and tilted them. Some lay broken, and their shafts had rotted.

As carefully as if he handled fine porcelain, Mikki turned over a skull with a long-clawed paw that could fell an aurochs.

"Human," he noted. "And the same age as the grave." He could smell that much, old death, but not ancient, rising from the earth. "Were they a sacrifice, do you think? I'd say this one was beheaded."

The cold, damp movement of the air brushed his shoulder, recoiled, retreated. Storm raised his head, flattened his ears. The ghost seeing the ghost? Mikki tracked it—her?—by the cold earth scent as she sank away, trying to hide.

"I think there was sacrifice." Moth frowned, looking out across the circle, turning slowly. "But no, these buried here weren't it. There are four other deaths at the cardinal points, bled and then buried. The second working was the same. Those were the sacrifice, I think. Horses, not human."

"You shouldn't say that as though it's the worse sin."

"Did I?" Moth asked mildly.

"Yes."

"I'm fond of horses. What if it had been bears?"

Mikki growled. "It probably would have been, if he'd been within reach of the forest." He raised his head, sniffing. "Are you sure it was horses? I can't tell. I can always smell horse-bones, these days."

"Yes, it was horses. And Storm doesn't smell, he's been dead far too long."

"That's what you think."

The blue roan left off staring after the ghost, looked at Mikki a moment with dark, knowing eyes, ears pricked. Then he went back to his needless grazing. He seemed to take pleasure in grass and sun and stretching into a run, as much as he might have while alive. It was necromancy, of which Mikki did not at all approve, but he believed Moth spoke truth when she said battle-slain Storm had lingered in the world, dog-loyal ghost, till she went back for his skull and gave him the semblance of flesh again, all those long years ago. Contrary enough

293

to lay his ears back at death itself. Mikki turned his attention to the human skull again.

"So why was this one left unburied?"

Moth crouched by Mikki and took the skull from under his paw. The other bones were scattered around, some broken, gnawed by scavengers. Many of the smaller ones were missing, overgrown by grass or carried away.

"A woman, you're right." Moth set the skull down again, dug fingers into the turf and drew up over her hand not only old grass, bleached pale as her own long braid, but wiry threads black as raven's feathers. Mikki wrinkled his nose and backed away.

Moth teased the hairs out; one strand was at least a yard and a half long. "A Nabbani woman."

"The Nabbani wizard, the princess."

Still kneeling amid the bones, Moth twisted the hairs into a ring and slipped it over the little finger of her left hand. If he asked why, she would say that it might come in useful, so he only gave her a disapproving curl of the lip.

A faint smile was all Moth returned to that, looking around in the direction he could smell the ghost. "Let's hope she can tell us what Tamghat was doing."

"Something unpleasant," Mikki said gloomily. "Which is what you're planning, isn't it?"

"Well, whatever he did, it wasn't necromancy. He never had any skill with the dead."

It was a simple thing to call the ghost of an unburied body, if your will was in it, and strong. There were rituals among the wizards and shamans who did such things. Moth did not bother with them.

"Nabbani! Come speak with us," she called in the Grassland tongue, rising to her feet and even holding out a hand, as if she invited some newcomer to sit. "Tell us why he killed you."

That should have brought her, since she was so present in even the daylit world, and so evidently drawn to their living presence. A chance for self-justification, revenge, a chance to plead for rest . . . those were the desires of the ghostly dead, more often than not.

A ripple in the grass, a chill like clouds over the sun, the cold, damp scent of her tinged with the blood-borne panic of prey. Mikki rumbled deep in his chest, thrust his awareness a little further through the walls of the physical world. He saw the ghost, dark and shaking as a reflection on restless water, a very small woman dressed like a Grass-lander in full-skirted coat and wide trousers, with an incongruous golden headdress like a rayed sun, which must have some great signifi-cance, that she shaped herself wearing it. Moth would know.

The ghost wailed, hands and a great curtain of black hair pulled over her face, screamed like a woman tortured and fell to her knees, waves circling her in the grass.

"I think," Moth said dispassionately, "we can assume it was Tamghiz killed her, and that she saw him truly when he did, or at least as much as a human can see, living or dead, wizard or no."

Mikki doubted that the ghost saw the double image he did, the coiling, twisting heart of flame that moved with Moth, stretched ten-drils through her like vein and sinew even when she seemed a quiet, mortal woman, all power subdued, but it was plain that eye to eye she saw enough. Mikki pulled his sight back to a more restful place, where Moth was only a woman haloed in fire and shadow again, the flame that writhed within unseen save for the red glint in her eyes.

"Hush, woman," Mikki said, trying to be soothing, reassuring. A name would have helped, but the Grasslands clans had spoken only of Tamghat's wizard, Tamghat's Nabbani princess. "Wizard, hush. We mean you no harm. Tell us about the one called Tamghat, and we'll bury your bones, send you to the gods."

She would not answer, or did not hear, walled within her terror. The wind took on a high, keening noise, rose into human wailing. Storm squealed and stamped and Mikki flattened his ears.

"If you leave, she might speak to me," he suggested.

Moth was less tolerant. "A tantrum," she said. "You try to talk to her and she'll drag it out for weeks, teasing you along to have the attention. Tamghiz always sought that childish type for his mis-tresses." She hefted the skull in one hand, drew her dagger.

Mikki sat back on his haunches, head tilted, watching. Yes, the ghost was aware of what Moth did, not utterly lost in her fear, real though it undoubtedly was. The wailing fell abruptly silent. The scent of ghost faded, sinking into grass and dry earth, as she attempted to hide.

Moth scratched a single rune into the surface of the skull: *ice*, for binding, holding in place. It was enough, with her will behind it.

"Come," she ordered. "Speak with us, Nabbani."

The ghost stood amid her bones before them, visible in the world, still trying to hide her face behind her hair.

"Give me your name."

"Anch—" The ghost's voice was a whisper, a breath, and she gulped and fought, her form tearing to shreds of shadow, re-forming, with her struggle. "No. Monster!"

"I may be." Moth reached out, parting hair like black mist, and traced a second rune with a finger on the ghost's translucent forehead. *Water.* The liquid flow of speech. It left a line like pallid embers, which faded only slowly. The ghost whimpered and clawed her face. "Your lover certainly is. You will speak to me. Give me your name."

"Min-Jan An-Chaq, Daughter of the Third Rank."

Moth raised a pale eyebrow. "Third Rank? What does that mean, in today's Nabban?"

"My mother was one of the emperor's wives, but neither the First Wife nor of royal birth."

"So you really were a Nabbani princess. And you were a wizard?"

"Yes."

"How did you come to join Tamghiz?"

The delicate plucked ghostly brows lowered in a frown.

"Tamghat, then."

"Tamghiz. I've heard that name—"

"Never mind. Tell me how you came to him. How you came to be here, slain and unburied. Tell me what he was trying to do here."

It took many questions, much cold direction on Moth's part, to pull the story from An-Chaq of the imperial Nabbani house of Min-

Jan. She tended to return, over and over, to Tamghat's betrayal of her. "He never loved us. I thought he did. He's empty inside. He was going to marry her, but he wouldn't marry me, me, an imperial daughter of Nabban, and no matter how great a wizard he was, he was only a barbarian Grasslander warlord, not even a clan-chief. But he was mine, the father of my daughter. And he was going to put me aside."

Slowly, they pieced it all together, from the runaway wizard princess's first meeting with the warlord in Marakand, perhaps twenty-five years before—"He was so handsome, so alive, and when he looked at me I was the only woman in the world"—to An-Chaq's sabotage, writing a curse against him into the great spell that would transport his army into a small valley in the Pillars of the Sky six springs before, and the moment of horror as she realized she had killed some of his *noekar* and very nearly her own daughter, but not Tamghat himself.

"I saw him," she wailed, her form dissolving, shivering, unable to fade utterly from Moth's binding. "A monster. A thing, some *thing* burning behind his eyes. He was never a man at all, a *thing*, and I'd loved him, I'd borne him a child."

"Why Lissavakail and Attalissa?" Moth asked, relentless. "Why that place, why that goddess? Why not ensnare the Voice of the Lady of Marakand, if he meant to usurp rule? Lissavakail can't be more than a minor market town, no rival to Marakand in wealth or influence. What did he think to gain there?"

"Power," An-Chaq said, growing still and momentarily whole again, her face gone sharp and shrewish. "Lissavakail's ruled by the goddess as a human avatar. Attalissa is incarnate in mortal form, a human woman endlessly reincarnated. He was going to wed her when the stars were right, some fat mountain virgin. He said he could assume her powers, but I never believed that. Some of them, maybe. Seduce them from her, wheedle the girl into passing something on to him. He talked like he would become a god. That was when I realized he was mad. And he thought he could just throw me away, treat me like a concubine grown old and ugly, make my daughter nothing but a bastard, get other children to follow him in ruling Lissavakail . . ."

Mikki had stopped listening. Moth stood straight and unheeding, head tilted back as if she could see the stars lost behind the daylight blue of the sky, and the fire within her flared.

"It's no good, I need to draw the charts," she said. Throwing the skull at the ghost's feet, she strode off to Storm. Mikki lumbered after her.

"Could he?"

"I don't know."

"Is that the truth?"

"I don't know."

"Moth, tell me. Could Ghatai kill a god?"

"Kill? Quite possibly," Moth snarled. "Ogada certainly did. You mean, could he possess the soul of one. And I don't know! Yes! Maybe, a vulnerable god like this mortal goddess might be. Did we bring an almanac?"

"No." His voice was a calm rumble again. "The only almanac you had was a Pirakuli one two centuries old, and I traded it at Swanesby for seed and smithy-work forty years ago."

"I'll have to calculate a new chart tonight, work it out . . . He would need . . ." She shook her head. "I'll know it when I see it. But it's probably too late. He's had six years." She leaned against Storm, face on her arms, her intent to search the packs abandoned. "Mikki, what do I do if he's made himself a god, with the strength of the land behind him? A lake's no small power."

"Hey, my wolf." He pressed his shoulder against her in turn, warm weight of reassurance surely better than Storm's cold ghost-flesh. "That might make it a fair fight. He never was your match strength for strength, you said."

"Not Ghatai and a god of the earth in one. Not as we both are now." But she laughed, a bit unsteadily. "Did I tell you that?"

"You did."

"It might have been true once. I don't know. Maybe you should go north, Mikki. Go home, get safe out of this."

He growled.

The ghost began to scream. "Don't leave me, let me go, I told you what you wanted, let me go, let me go!"

"Tantrums," Moth muttered, and shouted, "Be quiet!" Storm put his ears back and skipped away.

She went back to the skull, scratched the rune off it, traced *journey* burning on the ghost's forehead. "Go," she said. "Where you will, save to the one you call Tamghat." She scraped up a handful of dry earth and torn grass, threw it over the bones, the skull, token-enough of burial. "Go to the wretched Great Gods."

The ghost shuddered and whirled away. But she did not dissolve as she could have. Instead An-Chaq stood again, taking clearer form yet, only a little hazy to the physical eye, a figure that cast no shadow in the bright sun.

"Who are you?" she asked, fists clenched.

Moth turned away, whistled at the horse.

"Please." The ghost reappeared in front of her, keeping just out of arm's reach, instinct that was not misplaced. Her voice shook. She shivered uncontrollably, but still she stood. "You called him Tamghiz. I remember that name. It's in old tales. I saw him, when he killed me. What are you? What is he?"

Moth laughed. "What is he? Do you want to know? My husband, once."

The ghost looked stricken. "His *wife*? No—"

"Not the answer you want?"

"Wolf . . ." Mikki bumped his heavy head against her arm.

"A very long time ago," Moth conceded. "One of the many very bad choices I've made in my life. And Tamghiz does run through wives at a great rate, I was at least his fifth. If you stuck with him for twenty years, you've outlasted any he actually wed."

"The Grasslanders tell stories about Tamghiz the wizard. He was a clan-chief, he was a chief of chiefs, a great wizard, a shaman. His heart broke when his wife betrayed him with his son, her stepson. He went to serve a king in the north. One of the three first kings in the north." An-Chaq was waiting to be interrupted, dropping out one short phrase after another, waiting for denial. "The kings in the stories of the seven devils. And Tamghiz is in those stories, one of the wizards who woke

299

them." She twisted her hands together in her hair. "You said . . . you called him Ghatai, too, I heard you." The ghost's voice dropped to a whisper. "Ghatai was one of the seven devils the wizards woke."

"Yes," Moth said at last. "What of it? You're free of him. Go to the Gods."

"He's a devil?" An-Chaq wailed. "Father Nabban, Great Gods forgive me, I've slept with a devil!"

"And which of us here hasn't?" Mikki murmured. "Do stop shrieking, Min-Jan An-Chaq. You're out of Father Nabban's reach and once you've walked the long road to them, the Old Great Gods won't care who you've taken to your bed in this world. They know your innocence."

An-Chaq whimpered, a hand over her mouth. "Lady, why are you looking for him?"

"That's no concern of yours."

"We're no friends of his," Mikki offered. "That's enough for you to know, isn't it?"

An-Chaq dropped to her knees, then fell on her face on the ground, arms outstretched in the Nabbani posture of supplication before the emperor. "Lady, whatever you are now, you were human, once. Did you have children, then?"

Moth was suddenly very still. But, "Yes," she said finally, almost mildly.

"His?"

"Does it matter? They're long dead."

"No," the ghost whispered, and she shivered, losing form, becoming a shadow in the grass, fear sapping her will to be there. "It doesn't matter. But Lady, if you were a mother, save my daughter, don't condemn her with her father. Set Ivah free of him. I beg you—I lay it on you, as you were a mother, as you loved your own children, save my daughter."

Moth sketched runes in the air. *Journey* again, and the sign of the Old Great Gods. "*Go now,*" she ordered. Her eyes burned, and the air around her.

"Please . . ." The word faded. An-Chaq was gone, banished to begin her soul's last journey.

"Was that meant to be a binding on you?" Mikki asked, with mild interest.

"I think so. More fool she."

"It was good of you not to hurt her."

"Don't be sarcastic, cub. The point is, I didn't."

"We could try to save the child, if chance allows."

"I'm rather less inclined than I might have been. She should have stuck with begging."

"But what about the daughter, this Ivah? Tell me you won't not try to save her, just to spite an imprudent ghost."

Moth smiled, the narrow smile Mikki distrusted as much as he loved; Great Gods forgive him that he did love that vein of venom in her, too. She held up a hand, with the thin black threads of An-Chaq's hair still wound into a ring on the little finger.

"An-Chaq's and Ghatai's daughter should be easy to find. And her blood may be a hold on him, a way to see into Lissavakail better than creeping around its walls, in spirit or flesh. Particularly if he has possessed Attalissa."

"You won't harm the girl."

"If there's any other way."

Mikki sighed. "No, Moth. That wasn't a suggestion."

She looked back at him, setting a foot in the stirrup, and grinned, a glint of mischief that stirred his heart. His wolf, beautiful as a winter birch by moonlight.

"I know, cub." She added, more seriously, "She'll hardly be a child after all this time, and she may not want saving. I won't risk anything for her. But if there's a way, I will give her a chance."

There never were any promises. In the end, there was only Lakkariss, and the Old Great Gods' own doom, however she had been brought to serve it. He nuzzled her calf, falling in beside Storm. She bent to scratch around his ear.

"Tonight, once I've done the star-charts, I'll find the daughter. Her memories of the past six years might be useful—I'll see what she's dreaming and what I can steer her dreams into telling us."

Mikki sighed again and nipped at her hand. "Are you planning to take all night?"

Moth made her calculations of the movements of the stars and checked them again, and found they still had time. Not a great deal, but enough, now they knew where to find Tamghiz Ghatai.

She set out the runes along the edge of their fire.

Journey. Need. Sword.

God. Water. Inheritance.

Water. God. Need.

And Vartu's soul said, not south across the deserts to the Pillars of the Sky and Lissavakail, not yet, but, *West.*

Cold wind from an empty sky. The breath of fate. Maybe.

Or was she merely being diverted again? The dreaming mind of the daughter might tell her if Tamghiz had any concern in the west.

She sat, hands locked around the hilt of her sword—not Lakkariss but her own demon-forged Kepra, which she had carried from the drowned islands when she was only Ulfhild the king's sister, the King's Sword. She leaned her head against her knuckles, watching Mikki pretend to sleep.

Hunting the dreams of An-Chaq's daughter could wait another night.

The kings and the wizards believed their war with the devils was over, and that their sons and daughters could lead their folk in peace. But time weakens all bonds, and men and women and even wizards forget, and only we storytellers remember.

CHAPTER XIX

Pakdhala woke out of a muddled dream, her mind blurry. Not a nightmare of Tamghat, this time. Bikkim was in it somewhere, grinning at her in the old, carefree way, as he had so rarely since Serakallash fell. In the dream, Bikkim was shirtless, which was distracting, and the waters of the Kinsai-av roared past, drowning out whatever it was she tried to say to him. She had been frustrated because she could not hear her own words, and then she realized she was wearing only a thin cotton shift, and it was soaking wet, clinging and nearly transparent, which was why Bikkim was grinning. The note of the river changed from roar to chortle as she woke.

Immerose and Tihmrose, sleeping one on either side of her, had not stirred, though Immerose was lying on her back, mouth open and snoring. Pakdhala jabbed her in the ribs and the Marakander rolled over without waking. It was warm enough they had not pitched the tents, but the dawns were still chilly, now they had turned north, and her breath made smoke in the air, like the mist that rose over the cliffs from the river's breath. The fire was down to smouldering coals. A camel blew through its nose at something, and slow footsteps crunched past, down the line of picketed beasts. Django or Kapuzeh, she could tell, and she guessed, from the position of the stars and the greying night, that it was the last watch. Dawn was creeping up on them. Perhaps not much point trying to slide back into sleep. She might just as well get up and find a precarious path down the basalt cliff to the river to bathe and pray, as she did whenever chance allowed, in whatever water they passed by. But it was always on this north–south run, along the Kinsai-av, that she felt most whole and strong. *Sister Kinsai, lend me your strength . . .*

Whole and strong was relative. She was no more than she had been

303

as a child, though she was a grown woman, no doubting that; her body told her so.

Last autumn Gaguush had hauled her off for a long and red-faced discussion of men and babies. It was particularly hard for Gaguush to discuss such things, Pakdhala understood that. It stirred in the gang-boss's mind all the old pain that she did not have to worry about such things, having been married and divorced for barrenness when she was not much older than Pakdhala, before she ever quarrelled with her brother and left her tribe. But she grimly did her duty by Pakdhala, and then Tusa, Immerose, Tihmrose, and even Thekla had each in turn done so, Tihmrose with lots of rather startling and . . . interesting . . . advice on enjoying men *without* babies, which Pakdhala hoped her father hadn't picked up on, because she didn't think she could have looked him in the eye afterwards, if he had. And then Holla-Sayan had taken her home to the Sayanbarkash again, to have the tattoos of adulthood done, the snakes that coiled and knotted, blue and black, around her arms and cheeks. No touch of Sayan that time. The pricking of the needles had built and built in waves until it hurt more than she could have imagined, but she bit on the rag and said nothing, and the bard doing it had given her a great many odd looks, because, her grandmother said afterwards, she did not cry. And everyone did, a little. Her father ought to have told her she was supposed to.

But she was still a child in power, nothing any small demon or wizard of average ability could not equal. No strength woke that she could set against Tamghat.

More rasping of stone, as whoever had been walking settled down by a fire again. Pakdhala yawned and squirmed out of her bedroll, more or less fully dressed in shirt and trousers. She groped for her coat and boots and shook them out in case anything had crawled in during the night, finished dressing, and tiptoed away as quietly as she could, waving at Kapuzeh, who knelt shaving a brick of tea into a kettle at the further fire. He waved back. A star on the crest of the steep ridge over the camp winked, shadow passing before it, and almost the same instant she reached out, searching, touched . . .

Dog! Raiders!

"Up!" she screamed aloud. "Raiders! Gaguush, Father, wake up!"

She felt them, two-dozen souls, men and women, all hot and eager—angry, excited, predatory minds.

The gang had been attacked twice already this run, once in the Salt Desert and once in the Stone, both times by desperate men and women, the remnants of caravan-gangs who could no longer find merchants to employ them or goods to carry on their own behalf. There were too many like those, or folk left homeless by other bandits, even Serakallashi who had fled into the desert, godless and now without scruple towards those who still held a place in the world. But these were not so soul-torn and desperate, these felt of greed and the thrill of the hunt, Red Desert hill tribesmen stirred to some thieving lust enough to dare the scarred basalt wasteland along the Five Cataracts.

"On the eastern ridge!" Pakdhala shouted, dropping down by her bundled belongings to find and string her bow.

Shouting from above, voices accusing, who was it had been seen, one man's voice roaring over them all, "Go! Just go!"

They came in a sort of scrabbling rush, dodging stone to stone.

The gang were all awake now, grabbing for their boots, for bows and spears and sabres. Pakdhala ran towards the ridge, aiming for a tumbled boulder she could shelter behind. Holla-Sayan grabbed her by the shoulder as she darted past. He nearly threw her down, he jerked her back so hard.

"Behind the baggage, out of the way."

For a moment she stared into the Blackdog's eyes, yellow-green like clear peridot, and she hoped no one else saw. He was fighting hard just to stay a man, here with the rest of the gang around them. She shouldn't have woken him so abruptly, waking the Blackdog rather than her father. Pakdhala squeezed his arm and didn't argue. *I'll be careful. You watch yourself.*

She ran, crouched low, and joined cousin Doha behind the heaped bundles and chests of the merchants' goods. The old man gave her a gap-toothed grin, picked a target on the hillside, and released his bow-string. The arrow splintered on a rock.

305

"Sayan curse you all!" he shouted, and shot again. His eyes were growing cloudy, but he wouldn't admit it.

Pakdhala took a steadying breath and chose her own mark, the shouting man in the lead. Red Desert tribesman, braids flying, sabre raised, and her father and Gaguush together running to him. Pakdhala never missed. Rag targets, bustards for the pot, raiders—there was always a moment when they were all the same, and she never missed. Holla-Sayan jumped the desert man's tumbling body and went on. Gaguush wheeled off towards a woman slashing at the picket-line beside short-tempered Lion. Bad idea. Frightened camels lurched to their feet, milling around. Lion kicked. The woman squealed and fled limping into Gaguush, fell as she turned to flee again. Gaguush speared her in the back, got her own back against a tilted slab of rock as more came too late to the fallen woman's aid.

The raiders didn't risk the camp, now it was roused against them, but kept to cover like foxes around the hen-yard.

The merchants, brothers from beyond the Malagru Mountains in the east, clustered wailing in the midst of their own guards and servants, who were doing precious little to help. Django and Judeh edged up towards Gaguush, their progress made hazardous by raider archers somewhere above. Holla-Sayan came back down the slope to her in a headlong rush and the two of them fought free, dashed back to the camp, sweeping Django and the camel-leech with them into the shelter of the stacked chests and bundles, where the rest of the gang joined them.

The panicked camels dragged their lines and headed down the road, shambling to a halt before they had gone far, tangled and confused.

Good beasts, Pakdhala thought. *Stay there.* Not real words, but a soothing of their minds. Great Gods help them if the whole herd plunged over the cliff in panic.

Pakdhala coolly shot a bowman when he showed himself a breath too long. Her father shoved her down below a canvas-wrapped bale of camlet cloth, arrow-studded, with a hand on top of her head.

Dog!

"Keep down," he ordered.

"We should have camped on the ridge," Bikkim muttered. "We're trapped down here."

Asmin-Luya snorted. "It's all shattered shards of rock up there. You'd be the first to complain if you had to sleep on it. How about Zavel and I work around and get above them?"

Zavel swallowed, nodded, and took a firmer grip on his spear.

"What if there's more over the hill?" Kapuzeh asked. "I swear, I didn't hear this lot till 'Dhala started yelling. Could be another bunch still to come."

"There isn't," Pakdhala said. For a moment she could touch their minds. The raiders had left their horses two valleys over, and only one woman remained there, watching them.

"Like you know," Zavel said with a sneer. Pakdhala gave him a dark look.

"Zavel," Gaguush said. "Shut up."

"What about it?" Asmin-Luya asked again, with a nod towards the broken black rock of the ridge. "Plenty of cover."

"Not you and Zavel," said Gaguush. "He makes as much noise on the stones as a Westgrass ox. Tihmrose, Holla-Sayan, Django, and Varro go up the hill. Half the rest of us make a rush—" she pointed north, through the camp "—to the rocks there, then we can shoot 'em from both sides when they're chased down into the camp."

It's all right. I'll be all right. I'll stay right here out of the way, Pakdhala told her father, before Holla-Sayan could protest he was staying with her and touch off yet another fight with Gaguush about his overprotectiveness, another sneer from Zavel about her being babied. At the same time, though, it was what she wanted most, Holla close under her eye where she could protect him, as she had not been able to Otokas.

Yeah, right. Don't shoot Django by mistake, eh? Holla gave her a flicker of a smile, eyes human hazel again, and she wanted to hug him. He had to struggle with the dog, every time he let her claim some small freedom.

I can tell a Stone Desert man from a Red by now, I should think. I'll aim for his legs if I can't see his tattoos.

Django will thank you for that, yes.

Gaguush continued making her plans. "Holla-Sayan, are you listening? You four go round the south and up. Doha, Pakdhala, Thekla, stay right here. Kapuzeh, you too." She raised her voice. "Master Singah! Hey, Singahs, both of you, get over here."

In short rushes the merchants, Singah the elder and the younger, were moving with their men back beyond the road towards the cliff, finding what cover they could there. One of the Over-Malagru guards lay by the fire, moaning, an arrow low in his belly. Moopung, his name was. He bled around his clutching hands, and rocked from side to side.

"Hells."

"Cowards. If they fall over the cliff, we'll be well rid of them," Tusa muttered.

"He'll die of that," Judeh said, white-lipped. "Not quickly, either. 'Dhala, if we—"

"Leave him," Gaguush said sternly, and looked around at them all. "Let's go."

They broke out in both directions, Gaguush and her handful yelling, noise and fury and distraction. Pakdhala let her attention follow Holla-Sayan, slipping through the shadows, the rocks, Varro, Tihmrose, Django following. Dark shadow riding him, the Blackdog on the edge of the world. The sun was still not up over that eastern ridge; the others might not notice.

The sun would be in their eyes, when it rose, any moment now, and the raiders knew it, they waited for it.

If they did, they made their charge too soon, some tribesman panicked at a sudden rattling stone above. Half of them rushed screaming at the camp but the rest turned and fled, running into Holla and the other three. Pakdhala and Doha shooting from behind the baggage and Immerose and Tusa from the rocks to the north brought several down, but the raiders made for the shelter of the baggage themselves, scrambling and leaping over the low bulwark it made.

Pakdhala screamed, anger, mostly, slammed the heel of her left hand into a man's face and her knife up into his ribs. She wrenched her blade free and shoved him out of the way. Doha gave a startled grunt and pitched into her. They both fell. The woman behind him, spear bloody, steaming, fell on them in turn, mouth gaping, as Kapuzeh whirled to slice halfway through her neck. Thekla, muttering a steady stream of what must be Westron curses, crouched by them, throwing stones at the two who then closed with Kapuzeh and edged him away, blades clashing.

Pakdhala clutched Doha close. He was very heavy for such a thin old man. Heat spread, soaking into her. "No," she said. "You won't die. You can't, I won't let you."

He bared his teeth, desert-dry skin rough against hers, muttered something that was just breath.

"Cousin Doha! Doha! *Sayan!*"

His eyes were empty, spirit sliding away.

Doha! She could feel him there, on the road to the Old Great Gods, the long journey beginning, the reins of his soul still wound through his body. Pull him back, hold him . . . with his wounds beyond healing that would be to damn him a ghost just as much as leaving him unburied would.

'Lissa!

I'm all right, dog. But he would know that. *It's Doha . . . Father, Holla, I'm sorry.*

Pakdhala rolled from beneath Doha, knife still in her hand, shoved the head-lolling body of his killer off him.

Gaguush and the others charged back then, seeing them overrun, and finally, five of the merchants' men showed with grim efficiency that they were not mere decoration, as Immerose had taunted after the last raider attack, when they left the fighting to the gang. It was over, then, very quickly. The three bandits still on their feet threw down their weapons. Bikkim fended off Pakdhala's strike, gone wide as she recognized him, and wrapped his arms around her.

"Ah, Doha." Gaguush dropped down beside the old man, a hand on his cheek. Looked up at Kapuzeh. "Kill them."

Judeh opened his mouth, closed it again before his protest found breath. Thekla kept up her muttering, prayer now, to her dead gods. Bikkim slumped and suddenly all his weight was on Pakdhala. They staggered down together and her heart nearly stopped when she saw the quantity of blood soaking his trousers. Knew what she would find before she had the trouser leg ripped off, and was screaming at Judeh for his needles and thread, for honey and myrrh and sesame oil. She barely noticed when Kapuzeh cut the throats of the shrieking, struggling bandit survivors, the merchants' guards holding them down on their knees, only yards away.

She noticed only as an annoyance the blood trickling down her own face from a cut on her temple she did not remember getting.

Django, Tihmrose, and Varro came staggering in from the hillside. Varro and Tihmrose were both wounded, but nothing demanded immediate attention, and the merchants' belly-shot man . . . was dead, Great Gods, one of his companions had stabbed him in the heart. He would have died, yes, slowly and horribly from the filth of the wound, but she could have tried . . .

There was only Bikkim, to lose or save.

Pakdhala was Judeh's assistant in all his leech-craft, as able at stitching up wounded camels, drenching ill ones, as he. Better, though no one said that in Judeh's hearing. "Help me," she ordered, and Judeh did not argue, simply handed her what she asked for, pressed the edges of the gash together for her, agreed when she muttered they couldn't close it completely; it would have to drain. Thekla hovered behind her, catching her long braids back out of the way, tying a bandage around her head to keep the blood out of her eyes, finding her hat to keep the climbing sun from dazzling her.

"Got two of them," Django reported to Gaguush behind her. "The others dodged us in the rocks, headed off and with all the screaming down here I figured we were needed. Doubt they'll dare come back, though."

"Where's Holla? Doha's his kin."

"*Feondas.*" That was Varro. It didn't sound like any invocation to a god. "I don't know. He wasn't hurt that I saw. I'll go find him."

"Must have gone to follow them," said Django. "Bloody idiot. He'll be all right, boss. Probably a good thing if we know which way they ran—we can warn the ferrymen at the upper castle and the guilds of At-Landi."

The merchants were fussing and clucking over their goods in their own half-Nabbani dialect, angry at the damage, picking their way around Bikkim's prone form as though he were merely another bundle. Pakdhala heard everything, saw, smelt everything. It almost made her sick. She could feel Bikkim's heart beating as though it were inside her own chest, feel Judeh's when he put a comforting hand on her shoulder for a moment.

Dog . . . she pleaded, wanting her father here, but he would not answer her, or there was no Holla-Sayan left conscious in the dog's mind to speak to her, only the Blackdog, which knew what it had to do when Attalissa was threatened.

They buried Doha and the Over-Malagru man Moopung under cairns of stone by the roadside, since there was no earth to dig in here. It took half the day to choose and carry sharp-edged chunks of rock, and they all had torn nails and bleeding hands before they were done. Pakdhala said the prayers to Sayan over her supposed cousin, because Holla-Sayan still had not come back and Varro had found no trace of him. Gaguush wanted to throw the Red Desert tribesmen over the cliff, to let the Kinsai-av deal with them, but Pakdhala said flatly, no. They were not Kinsai's folk, and Kinsai did not want them. So the bandits were heaped together and another cairn made, though without nearly such care. Kapuzeh set the head of one of them on a broken spear rising from it, as a warning. Bar-barians, both Masters Singah muttered at that. But it was Master Singah the younger who demanded Bikkim be abandoned, to die or recover alone as he could. Tusa caught Gaguush's arm before her fist could strike.

"Feel free to travel on alone if you like," Gaguush snarled, then. "But you don't take my camels. If you think you can carry all your goods on your own, then do so and get out of my sight. I'm not civilized enough to abandon my folk, Bashra be thanked."

Pakdhala left Gaguush pacing and cursing and harrying Judeh about tending the camels' assorted scrapes and bruises, and went to sit by Bikkim, who breathed slowly and deeply, dosed with poppy-syrup by the leech.

"Better," Thekla said, with a flick of her hand towards him, like a darting bird. "See?"

Pakdhala nodded. She felt very strange, empty, as though she floated in some dark place, nothing to hold her to earth. Or as though she'd been dosed to sleep herself. Drained of life.

"You're ill," Thekla said. "All tired out. You should sleep."

Pakdhala pulled aside the blanket covering Bikkim and felt his thigh. It was warm, but not too warm, not fevered, not even very swollen.

The Westron woman put another blanket around Pakdhala, forced a cup of sweet tea into her hands, and watched like a cat until she drank it. "Now sleep."

Kinsai was here; she shouldn't feel like this, weak as in Serakallash or Marakand.

"Sleep," Thekla insisted, and nudged her down by Bikkim, tucking blankets close around them both.

Sleep, little sister. Your young man will be fine, though how you're going to explain that to the harridan, when he's up and walking tomorrow . . .

Will you stop calling Gaguush that?

No. She is a harridan, a hag, a termagant. Your dog's too good for her.

Told you no this time, didn't he? Why don't you pester Immerose? She never turns anyone down. Will Bikkim be all right, really?

You tell me, you're the one healed him.

Did I?

Not that it's agreed with you, child. Go to sleep.

You should have warned us.

No. Raiders are your own problem, caravaneer. Besides, you felt them coming. You should have paid closer attention and not been thinking of young

312

men with their shirts off. Kinsai giggled like a girl. *But there was something I wanted to tell you . . . No. I don't know. I can't say. Be careful, little sister. There's . . . something hunting you.*

I know. But Kinsai had gone, and she was asleep.

It was dusk when Pakdhala woke again, feeling hardly any more rested than before. Judeh sat watching over Bikkim, and Tihmrose and Immerose came over the moment they saw her stirring.

"You look terrible," Tihmrose said. "Like you haven't slept in a month."

"That cut on your head must be worse than it looks." Judeh teased the bandages away, wincing as they stuck, but it was only dried blood and the honey he had smeared on it to prevent poison. The cut itself was just a thin scabbed line. Pakdhala put her hand up to feel it. She always did heal quickly, like the Blackdog.

"Huh. Well, that's . . . better." Judeh gave her an odd look. "Bikkim's much better, too. Take a look, 'Dhala."

Pakdhala bit her lip, bending over Bikkim's leg. It looked like a scar two weeks old, knit clean, pink and shiny against the hairy pale brown of his thigh. The stitches showed dark and ugly.

"Not too close a look," Immerose added. "He's got nothing on but his drawers."

But there was a wary shadow behind her light words: Holla-Sayan had not come back.

"Father's all right," Pakdhala said, before they had quite worked out who should tell her Holla-Sayan was still missing. "He'll be back soon. He just went to . . . to follow them, make sure they weren't going to attack again."

"You always know where he is, don't you?" Tusa came up quietly beside her, squatted down, her voice stretched thin and her lips pale. "And Bikkim should die, from a wound like that. Not right away maybe, since it missed the artery, but it would never heal."

"Tusa!" Tihmrose snapped. "The Lady prevent it! Don't ill-wish the man."

313

"You know he should die of that. Out here. You've seen it happen, someone rotting till they died. And look at him!" The Great Grass woman dropped to her knees by Bikkim's side, and her pale brown eyes looked, to Pakdhala, not so much afraid as desperate. "'Dhala, you're a wizard, aren't you? Just say. Maybe your mama was, or some other kin? Someone you get it from?"

Pakdhala shook her head. "No. It can't have been as bad as it looked. A lot of mess, but not so deep as it seemed."

She'd meant that as a warning, but Judeh contradicted. "It was bad." His voice was defiant, too loud. "I didn't expect him to live."

"She's a wizard," Tusa said, rocking back on her heels, arms folded tightly around her knees. "A wizard. Or . . ."

"Or what?" Immerose asked.

Tusa shook her head.

"So what if she *is* turning out to be a wizard?" Immerose asked. "We could do with one. So long as no fool goes mentioning her talent in Marakand, there's no harm, and a lot of good."

"I'm not a wizard!" Pakdhala said. "I can't be. I'm just . . . Holla's brat."

"If she is, she'll need a master to teach her properly," Judeh said then. He gave her a wry grin. "A proper apprenticeship. I knew I wasn't that bad a doctor, till you came along for comparison, brat. But if you're a wizard, that explains a lot."

"No!"

Tusa wouldn't abandon the matter. "And she does always know things. You ask 'Dhala where anyone is, she always knows without looking. And Holla-Sayan—he knows. He has to. That's why he's such a fool over her, like he's got to watch her all the time."

"You make it sound like there's something wrong with a talent for magic," Tihmrose pointed out. "C'mon, Tusa. It's not like we're going to turn her over to the Voice's guard in Marakand for execution, and any-where else, well, if she is a wizard, that's to her benefit. Find her a good master and in a dozen years she'll have a fancy house in At-Landi or be in Over-Malagru making her fortune. Support us all, in our old age."

"There's no talent in our family. Stop talking about it." Her voice shook. Dangerous to have them, foolish and enthusiastic, telling all up and down the road that their little 'Dhala was in any way remarkable. Even if all the gangs, whatever rivalries and feuds lay between them, did keep one unified silence in magic-fearing Marakand regarding the few wizards among them.

Judeh squeezed her hand. "They will. Don't get in a state about it. No one's going to send you off to an apprenticeship if you don't want to go. Look, I think we might as well take those stitches out now?"

Pakdhala swallowed, steadied her voice. "Yes. It looks that way." But Tusa still sat, watching her, her eyes agonized. She'd never have thought the Grasslander one to fear magic.

Bikkim muttered in his drugged sleep. Pakdhala left the stitches for Judeh to deal with, walked away from them all, most of all from Tusa, and found herself at Doha's grave. She squatted down there, staring at the stones, blinking tears that took her by surprise. She had known so many deaths, Blackdogs and priestesses, her own. When had she stopped feeling them? The child she had been had wept for fear and the changing of the world. For herself. Selfish brat, who held the temple around her like a shell, building it thicker and thicker. She felt death so much more, had, ever since her great-grandmother Pakdhala had died a year after she came from the mountains, and she had seen Holla-Sayan weep and *understood* it was loss, irreparable. Ever since, she had felt Bikkim's pain, that hollow that was never filled, where his parents and sisters and cousins had been. The lost children of Tusa and Asmin-Luya, Zavel's brothers and sister, whom he mostly pretended did not exist. Attalissa in her temple had ceased to be hurt by anything, long ago, she thought.

It was Doha she wept for now, her friend, her cousin, her kin, the lie made truth in the heart. She wept for the sweet wailing fiddle in the evenings and the cracked voice that had once, Kinsai said, charmed almost every woman the length of the river into his bed. Kinsai was prone to exaggeration. Pakdhala smiled through her tears, thinking what Doha would have said, if he'd known a goddess boasted of him. Given a sly smile and taken it as his due, probably.

From the corner of her eye she saw Zavel heading for her, and Asmin-Luya catching him back with a shake of his head. Zavel scowled. After a while Thekla came over carrying a bowl of fish with onions and raisins, thickened with boiled millet. The cook squatted down beside her, wordless, to share it, and Pakdhala did eat, scooping up mouthfuls she didn't really taste with small pieces torn from the flat, stone-baked sheet of last night's bread. Thekla left, and Gaguush brought her a blanket, sat with her a while in turn.

"He'll be all right," the gang-boss said, meaning Doha, not Holla-Sayan, as Pakdhala realized after a moment. "He'll come safe to the Old Great Gods, a short journey."

"Yes."

"He was a good man, your cousin. I'll miss him."

"I do already."

"Yes. 'Dhala?"

Pakdhala grunted. "Hm?"

"You're sure about Holla?"

"Yes. He'll be back soon."

"Right, then." Gaguush patted her on the head and left her.

They might say Gaguush didn't feel. They were wrong. She was hurt too much by long-ago betrayals to let on she did, and then she erupted like the fire-mountains of the Malagru, and meant nothing by it. That was all. Her father almost understood that, but Pakdhala could wish they would stop hurting one another, with their tempers and brooding silences. Kinsai's claims on Holla-Sayan, and a sweet little boy with Holla's hazel eyes among the brood at the ferrymen's lower castle, did not help that.

Her father was near, within her reach now, no longer hiding. She felt him like a solid mass at her shoulder, a warm body between her and the night. But he was up on the hill somewhere, slow to come down, and she wanted him physically close, to comfort her.

Dog, Kinsai says I should have known they were coming if I'd been paying attention. Did I feel them coming? I don't think I did. Did Doha die because I was too late giving warning? Is it my fault?

316

Doha?

Cold hells, the shock in his thought. He hadn't known, hadn't remembered. *Yes. I'm sorry, Holla-Sayan. I told you but maybe you didn't . . . understand.* He seemed to have a much harder time of it than Otokas or any of the last many Blackdog hosts had, in keeping consciousness in the fully freed dog. Or perhaps it was that he fell deeper into the beast's soul. If some day he could not find his way back . . . Pakdhala did not want to think about that.

I knew. I remember now. He felt, to her mind, exhausted. *How can I say it's your fault or isn't? I smelt them, just before you shouted, no sooner than that. If you didn't feel them near earlier, you didn't.*

Where have you been all this time? Gaguush is worried. Everyone is.

I don't know. Running. Thinking. I turned their horses loose.

Those who had fled the attack on the camp had not made it back to their horses, and the one left to guard them had not lived to flee. Holla-Sayan tried to keep her from knowing that, and failed. He had stalked them, coldly let them draw out of earshot of the camp. Pakdhala heard men and women screaming, run down by what demon or monster they could not imagine, the echo of breaking bone felt in the jaw, the taste of salt blood, saw the torn bodies left to the sky, ghosts damned to wander till time and the elements freed them to the gods, unless their kin came searching.

That tribe would learn, maybe, not to prey on the folk of the road.

Pakdhala saw him then, a limping shadow slinking over the skyline, wolf-sized hound almost lost in the night. The restive camels stirred, ready to panic again and more earnestly, as the Blackdog's scent drifted to them.

People settling to eat or sleep bolted up, hands on weapons, at that stir among the beasts.

"It's just Father," Pakdhala called, before someone shot at him, with horrors following on that which she could imagine only too clearly.

As a man, Holla still limped, heading for her by the new shadow of the cairn, shielding his eyes from the flaring branch of thorn

317

Gaguush had caught up. His clothes were torn, dark-stained in places, and he was soaking wet. On his way back he had plunged into one of the Kinsai-av's tributary streams to wash.

Pakdhala flung her arms around him, felt him tense, resisting, weary and sick at heart with himself, until he bent his head to her hair and sighed. She was selfish as a child, a spoilt brat as Zavel called her, to be thinking only of her own hurt and loss.

I know, Holla-Sayan. The dog can't help being what it is. Sometimes.

"Where in the cold hells were you?" Gaguush screamed as she joined them. "What were you thinking, heading off alone like that? Great Gods!"

She threw a punch at him with the hand not shaking the blazing branch, dangerously close to her own long braids, and Holla grabbed her by both arms, faster than thought, Pakdhala thrust aside.

"*Damn* you, Holla, I thought you were dead in the rocks somewhere."

"Don't yell at him," Pakdhala said, very quietly. "He followed them to make sure . . . they're long gone now. They won't be back." *It's all right, Holla-Sayan. Don't think about it.*

Gaguush stared at them both, and then wrenched herself free and stalked away, hurling her branch back into the fire.

Django thumped Holla on the shoulder.

"Either you go after her, or we all get screamed at for the next three days." Django backed up a step as Holla turned his head. "Hells. I'm sorry. That was cruel . . . we're all sorry, Holla-Sayan. I mean, we'll all miss him, you know that. I forgot he was your kin."

Pakdhala took Django's arm and led him away, leaving her father to his prayers. After a while Gaguush stomped back to join Holla sitting by the cairn, saying nothing, but Pakdhala thought the gang-boss leaned with her head on his shoulder. The Over-Malagru men began to sing, a high-pitched wavering dirge for their own dead fellow. Zavel sat down where Pakdhala sat by Bikkim and tried to hold her hand, took it with better grace than usual when she shook her head and tucked her hands deep in her pockets. He gave her a cautious smile, rose again, and went away. Eventually she lay down there, close enough to touch Bikkim in the night. The drug had worn off and his sleep was natural now, his dreams only of wind in the grass and running horses: quiet, sad dreams of lost home, dead parents, dead sisters, not the fevered haze of battle and poppies.

Pakdhala did not seek to pry into her friends' minds, but sometimes she could not help seeing. She could never tell her father how much it worried Gaguush when he clung to her in the night with no words, like a drowning man chanced on a flood-borne branch.

Having slept most of the day, she had no real desire for more sleep. She lay listening to the quiet night noises, a muttering and a sigh from where Thekla and Kapuzeh stirred together, open night all the privacy any caravan mercenary ever waited for. A little more discretion when they were all in the two round tents. Asmin-Luya paced restlessly on the first watch; the merchants, who had put their tent up as though it might offer shelter from another attack, sat talking in their own language, which she could understand, if she but concentrated. She didn't want to. It was nothing to her, what they said, complaint at the delay or a wake for their slain man. Camels drowsed, still nervous and excitable. Kinsai kept her distance, the river fretted below the cliff, the stars slid down the west below it, and Tusa relieved her husband on watch. Nothing stirred to the east, nothing breasted the horizon. She was not lying wakeful fearing bandit revenge, Pakdhala told herself. Only, she did not want to sleep.

Bikkim woke, asked vaguely, "Am I dead?" and when she almost laughed and whispered, "No," leaning close over him, he reached a hand and brushed fingertips over her face.

She could feel the warmth of his skin on her lips, had only to lean a little closer . . . "Go back to sleep," she whispered, not quite touching him. "Rest." Could almost taste him, the scent of his skin flavouring the air, animal, as all humans were.

Pakdhala scrambled to her feet, feeling the blood rushing through her. Wrong of her, very wrong.

She tucked her hands in her pockets and made a circuit of the camp herself. She had no watch tonight; she might as well relieve Tusa, or at least keep her company. The Grasslander should have noted her when she started wandering, but Tusa had not stirred from where she sat by the fire; Gaguush would have her head if she'd fallen asleep on watch, with raiders in the area and the dead hardly cold in their graves.

"Tired?" Pakdhala asked, drawing near enough to see that Tusa was awake, sitting huddled, rocking a little. The woman flinched at the sound of her low voice, stared up, eyes pits of shadow and her face sickly pallid, even by ruddy firelight. "Tusa, are you all right?"

Tusa, after a moment, shook her head. "It's been a bad day," she said, dropping her gaze to the fire again.

"Yes." Pakdhala rested a hand on her shoulder, felt her shrink from the touch, felt some strong emotion roiling in her, and withdrew it quickly. Fear? It might have been. Was it this conviction that Pakdhala was a wizard? Tusa had never shown any aversion to magic users before; she'd gone seeking soothsayers in At-Landi more than once, trying to learn the fate of her lost children. "Look, Tusa, I can't sleep, and you're in no state to be on guard. I'll finish your watch. It's a double shift, isn't it? Who's after you?"

After a moment Tusa mumbled, "Gaguush. Better not."

"She won't mind," Pakdhala said firmly. "Go to bed." Was the woman actually ill? She didn't sense any illness in her, any imbalance of the body. It was her mind was troubled.

Tusa nodded, and after another long moment, shuffled off, lying down by her husband, bedding pulled tight around her. Not touching him. It was none of Pakdhala's business. The fire was dying. She drew her knife, meaning to use the blade to push the embers of driftwood and camel-dung closer together and bank them with the ashes, but observed, amid those ashes and charred ends, an odd pattern: fine lines, a spiderweb in white ash.

What? Holla-Sayan asked, waking, when she was not even aware she had reached for him. A shock of fear had jumped through her. But it was nothing. Chance pattern in dim light, or discarded yarn too knotted to be saved, one of Tusa's cat's cradles. Maybe she'd tried to distract her thoughts with a game. She didn't look as though she had succeeded.

Nothing, she said. *I didn't mean to wake you. Just jumpy.*

She heard the rustling rasp of blankets as he rolled away from Gaguush, looked to see him silhouetted on one foot, pulling on his drawers and trousers. She stirred the ashes with her knife, raked them over the coals, to keep the embers live till dawn, and had moved away from what little light now escaped by the time her father came to her side. Perilously foolish of Tusa to sit with her back to that eastern ridge and the fire before her. Criminally foolish, endangering all their lives. Someone had to talk to her tomorrow.

Holla-Sayan put an arm around her and Pakdhala leaned into his side, feeling a need, for a moment, to be small enough to be picked up again.

It isn't your fault. You know that. And we nearly lost more than Doha and Moopung.

I'll miss him.

Of course you will.

You'll miss him.

Holla-Sayan said nothing, but she felt that pain in him. It wasn't something that happened once. Each death mattered, each time. It seemed terribly urgent to remember that, forever. She tightened the grip of her hand on his shirt, feeling the muscles over his ribs, alive, breathing. So many dogs.

He was a second father, after I left home. After a moment he asked, *How's Bikkim?*

He woke up. I sent him back to sleep. He . . . Am I a wizard, Father? Could I be? Tusa says I am. She's afraid of me. Or . . . of something. Upset.

Why should you be a wizard?

What if I'm just human, nothing more? If I was divine, I could have saved Doha.

I never heard that the gods brought the dead to life, he said grimly. *Don't start getting the delusions the Westrons have for their new god of the priests. Why a wizard?*

I'm no goddess so far as I can tell, but I do have . . . she shrugged, *these little powers. Why not a wizard? . . . I was once . . .* She let that thought go unheard by him. Long, long ago. Better that was forgotten, even by the Blackdog.

He said nothing to reassure her of godhead. There was no honest reassurance; he was as aware, and as worried, by her impotence as she was herself. Maybe she was no longer Attalissa, maybe Attalissa was truly dead, and Pakdhala could be a wizard, and travel with the gang, and die a human death, an old woman on some Westgrass farm. Fall to a raider, and lie under a forgotten cairn.

Make Holla-Sayan a grandfather?

Tusa woke screaming and they both moved without thought. Pakdhala caught Holla-Sayan's sabre out of the air—he had tossed it to her, he was gone—the Blackdog ran ahead of her. Tusa thrashed back and forth, clutching the amulet bag of her god and a newer charm on a silver chain, as though they choked her.

Dog! Pakdhala called, too far behind to lay a hand on him, but he stumbled down beside the Grasslanders as a man again, as Asmin-Luya woke and seized his wife, shaking her awake.

She collapsed sobbing on his chest. Holla took his sabre back from Pakdhala without comment. His hand was shaking. No threat on the ridge, none in the camp.

"Nothing, it's nothing," Pakdhala called to the merchants' guard who appeared at the tent door. "Someone had a nightmare." She repeated that in the bastard Nabbani dialect the Over-Malagru men spoke. "A bad dream."

The man muttered a curse and disappeared. By then everyone but Bikkim and Immerose was awake and asking questions, most on their feet, weapons in hand. But, "Cold hells, leave me alone!" Tusa snarled when Zavel reached to touch her and ask what she had dreamed, and in that awkwardness people went muttering back to their beds, except Gaguush, who stalked stark naked around the camp cursing them all. Not that anyone would dare comment.

Pakdhala silently offered her own coat. Hard to say for certain, even with her unnatural night vision, but she thought the gang-boss's mouth twitched as she gravely took it. Her wrists hung out a handspan or more.

322

"It's Tusa's watch," Gaguush said, with a glance up to measure the stars. "What's she doing sleeping?"

"I took it."

"Unarmed?"

She'd forgotten to get her spear. A grown woman with her adult tattoos, and she went and forgot to carry a weapon on watch. But Gaguush let it go.

"You should be asleep, 'Dhala. After yesterday—"

"I couldn't sleep, and I think Tusa's ill."

"Bashra grant she's not. That's all we need. Ah, hells." Gaguush ran a hand through her braids. "Fine. Your watch, 'Dhala. So arm yourself and go watch. Holla, stir the fire up and put a kettle on. I won't be sleeping again anyway, we might as well have tea."

"Put some clothes on," Holla suggested. "You go wandering naked around here, you don't know who might take a fancy to you."

"Hah," Gaguush muttered. "Mentioning no names. It'd serve you right, anyway." But definitely a faint smile, which faded again, with a glance at the night-fog rising above the cliff.

Pakdhala picked up her spear where it lay nearby on her bedroll, wandered off to check the camel lines. Left her father and Gaguush to their tea feeling a little . . . alone.

CHAPTER XX

Ivah didn't so much doze as she rode, as let the empty sameness of the rolling low hills lull her into the state her father called meditation, trying to let her mind become as empty as the land. The horse, a little Grasslander gelding with the wind of the steppes in his heart, followed Shaiveh's from long habit.

She pretended to Shai it was wizardly contemplation, a searching of the land, even, but what was the point? Farmstead after farmstead, and always the same stupid staring faces with their tattoos and desert-braided hair, the same stupid questions: *Will I marry, diviner? How many children? Is this baby a girl or a boy? Will the delivery be safe? Is he coming back to me?* To which she smiled and gave the answers the coins gave her, or told her listeners what they wanted to hear, couched in vague enough terms to seem truth, later. She lied and invented when the coins failed her, or when she could not bring herself to say what they told. Too soft-hearted, Shaiveh teased her. Why should she care if some fresh-faced girl was left numb and staring, warned of an early death?

Because people didn't pay well to hear of misfortune, Ivah told her. Why should she care? She just didn't like to see their faces, with their lives falling in ruin before them.

Over a year since they had wandered the caravan road west and north to At-Landi, and then across the Kinsai-av into the Western Grass, chasing dreams and the shadows of dreams.

Tamghat knew Attalissa had not died and been reborn in any Lissavakaili infant, since he had obtained faint impressions of her, off and on over the years. His means of doing so seemed to Ivah less true divination than shamanistic dreaming, which she distrusted as a barbaric deception of the weak-minded, but her father put greater trust in the little he learned by what he called dreaming than in even his own divinations. Wearing only a loincloth, sitting on a bearskin with bear-skull braziers at the cardinal points, red-eyed in the clouds of narcotic smoke, Tamghat had rocked and muttered. Ivah, head bent over a scroll of paper, brush in hand, dashed down his words, which read afterwards like scattered sentences from travellers' tales. He talked of the turf-roofed farmhouses of the Western Grass, of camels plodding through dry winter snow in the Stone Desert and hot summer in the deadly, barren Salt Desert, of broken yellow stone and of the teeming markets of Marakand. He caught fragments of Attalissa's presence, he said, like a whiff of scent when a woman has passed through a room. But mostly, seeking the goddess by his open-eyed dreaming or by weaving webs of silk thread and lakeside grass, he cursed and talked of finding nothing but wind and sky, an impression of empty land and very, very faintly, the whisper of the lake. He seemed frustrated not so much that Attalissa was not found as by his own inability to find her, the failure of his own powers against her. It was that, more than any doubt in the return Ivah had predicted, that had made him send her out to search along the caravan road.

And in over a year of searching, of weaving her own cat's cradles and casting the coins to read patterns that were utterly meaningless, Ivah had found absolutely no trace of the goddess.

Sleeping in the firelit halls of the sod-roofed houses of the Western Grass, or in their barns, telling fortunes, asking about other wanderers, mountain folk, a friend of hers, a man of middle years and his little girl, though she'd be not so little now, of course. No one told her anything of mountain folk, beyond this one or that, who'd come back from the caravans with a mountain wife or husband, a child. They met one such foreign husband and child, and they turned out to be from Marakand, another man who had come back with two adopted children, both, when Ivah met them, clearly desert-born, so she gave up hope that the lordless Westgrass peasants would know a mountain man if they saw one. Her divination told her nothing, did not pierce even so far as the shadows her father found. Nothing, as though the goddess did not exist.

Easy enough to miss even someone living openly amid the slow roll of the hills. But somewhere, her father insisted, the goddess was hidden, and a god had a hand in the hiding. There or on the road, but he thought the Western Grass likelier. The road was dangerous, and growing more so; no place to keep a goddess safe.

Ivah had not managed even to determine which god it was who seemed, if she could believe her father's dreaming, to be sheltering the goddess. One of the greater gods of the great barkashes, the chains of hills, they could assume, not some minor godling of a single ridge of land. She could hardly question a god and watch for the signs of evasion or lie, the careful breath, the face too tightly still. He would be one whose land ran close to the Kinsai-av, perhaps, because her father thought Kinsai, too, cast a shadow on all his divining and his dream-walking searches.

"A conspiracy of gods?" Ivah had asked, and Tamghat had taken it for sarcasm, told her not to be insolent. He persisted in every appearance of confidence in Attalissa's return before the conjunction necessary for his spell, and yet he grew anxious, and sent her out. The only wizard he trusted to serve him faithfully. But there was a warning, even in the affection with which he said the words. The last wizard he had trusted . . . that thought lurked behind the words.

She wasn't his only arrow shot into the darkness. There were folk among the caravans who kept an eye out for him, and had means to alert him, if they thought the girl had crossed their path. By such means he might, slowly, pin her down, if she travelled the road. But they had all been false alarms so far.

In the distance, antelope resolved themselves where there had been nothing but grass, brown fading out of green that had hidden them, till one raised its head, revealing six. How long till she could give up and go home? Not until it was over, and the wandering stars had joined and parted without the goddess's return. And then it might not be safe to do so. It might be her head, trailing a banner of hair as it fell, if she betrayed Tamghat even innocently, by her own weakness, her own inadequacy as a wizard. Other women her age were married householders or masters of their craft; she could not expect him to give her a child's licence forever.

Ivah felt herself sinking, being drawn deeper into silence, into emptiness. She knew better than to fight it, though that was her first impulse; her heart raced, but long training held. She kept herself calm, on the edge between sleep and waking. All the grazing antelopes looked up together now, scenting horses. Grass blew flat; fat clouds scudded. Drift, focused on nothing. Usually he came to her by night, when he might count on her being asleep, her dreams easily entered.

Father?

You should go to At-Landi. Attalissa's on the desert road.

You've found her?

I may have. That was unexpectedly cautious, and Ivah tried not to think so. Her mother had taught her nothing of this magic of entering another mind; perhaps no wizard but her father knew it. She still did not know to what extent he could follow conscious thoughts. He was touched by her emotions, she had learned that much by his reactions.

How? she asked.

One of my watchers.

Caravan mercenaries who fell afoul of his *noekar* in Serakallash, mostly. Brawlers and drunks, taken from the gaol in the old sept-chiefs' meeting hall where they were locked to cool off and sober up, threatened with worse fates, offered payment, if they but did as Ketsim, the *noekar* governor of the town, asked on his warlord's behalf. A simple matter. A missing girl, perhaps oddly gifted. Any with half a mind knew it was no simple matter and could put song and story to the request, the lost goddess-bride and her demon captor, but along with the set spell, a knotted pattern they could burn as signal to draw Tamghat's awareness to them should they encounter their quarry, they were given an amulet as payment and thanks, "against the dangers of the road." Most, being what they were, would have sold any such thing for a drink, it being silver, but the spells engraved on the simple disc drew them to treasure it, and bound them to silence on their commission. Two at least had died and one had killed trying to keep the damned things, in robberies that might otherwise not have turned to murder.

Your watchers have been wrong before. Always. She didn't need to rub that in.

This one seems . . . interesting. She tried to fight me when I turned her dreams to memories of the girl, to see if she might truly be the one.

She's a wizard, you mean? He had said ordinary folk were never even aware of him when he rode their dreams to see the girls they suspected, and dismissed them. Leaving Ivah wondering, as he no doubt intended, if he could enter her sleeping mind without her notice, too. And what he might direct her mind to recall of her days.

I don't think her resistance was conscious. I think it was shame. Guilt. She's one . . . Ketsim didn't take her out of the gaol. Her price wasn't the usual.

Tamghat was amused at his own cleverness, and Ivah dutifully asked, *What was it?*

Something beyond my reach to give. Go to At-Landi, Eaglet. You're close to the Upper Ferry, you can be there in days. Divine there, knowing the goddess is on the road, very near you. It may give the working focus, break the patterns that hide her.

She thought of antelope, invisible till you realized they were there, but knowing, you wondered how you had not seen.

And then what?

Don't leave me to do all your thinking for you, daughter. She's with this woman's gang, a member of the gang, it looks to me. And the caravans turn back at At-Landi.

Are you sure she's the one? How is she living away from the lake? You said she'd probably be sickly, an invalid, at best. But a mercenary?

And she didn't say, no virgin bride for you, then, the reputation of the gangs being what they were. A little twinge of satisfaction on behalf of her mother's memory.

I can only tell you what I turned the caravaneer's memories to see, Tamghat said impatiently. *The caravan-mistress is a Black Desert woman.*

The woman who summoned me is a Grasslander named Tusa, an older woman, nearly forty years, I'd make her.

What about the Blackdog? Ivah asked.

There were no mountain men among the gang in Tusa's memories. Make of that what you will. As for Attalissa, once she reaches Serakallash you can lure her, trick her, drug her, anything short of her death, and bring her to Lis-savakail. I'll have noekar *meet you in Serakallash. Use her as a hostage against the Blackdog, if you can't elude it. It must have that much reason, at least. Once she's in your hands, the creature will be powerless.*

As you say. But he was already gone and she blinked lazily, then shook her head, rubbed her eyes, and muttered, "Great Gods damn it!" to the horse's twitching ear.

"What?" Shaiveh reined her in, waiting for Ivah to come alongside.

"Nothing." She failed him again. Some bribed mercenary found the avatar, while she wasted her time fortune-telling. "We're going over to At-Landi, as quickly as possible. Straight to the Upper Ferry from here."

"Not so straight." Shaiveh frowned at the hills. "Four days at least, and we can't avoid farms. We'll have to stop so you can do your tricks."

"We don't stop. Who cares if a bunch of peasants think I'm rude? I've had an urgent summons to At-Landi, say."

"How urgent?"

Ivah kept her face impassive. Time Shaiveh remembered who and what she was. "My father needs me to go there, now."

"Told you, did he?"

"Yes."

"When?" Great scepticism.

Ivah allowed herself a little smile. "Just now. Didn't you realize? We're never out of his reach. My father and I discuss our progress all the time." Somewhat of an exaggeration that, on all counts, but some-times Shai's assumption of Ivah's general lack of usefulness was galling. "We've picked up her trail at last." She gave the gelding a touch of her heels, taking the lead, letting Shaiveh fall into her proper place as bodyguard, to the side and a little behind.

"My lady." But she never could tell if Shai was mocking or chastened.

The antelope fled them, white bellies flashing, into the next valley.

Ivah cast the oracle coins, using a charred twig to mark the hexagrams on the hilltop boulder to which she had stuck her stub of tallow candle. It was almost habit, by now; she had cast the coins every morning and evening since they came to At-Landi. On the grass, she had almost given up trying. They never told her anything of Attalissa.

Thirty-six falls of the three coins. Six complete hexagrams: three for the sun, three for the moon. Three for success, three for warning, as An-Chaq had taught her. For the first time she felt the slow heat of anticipation unfurl in her stomach. Perhaps, just perhaps, this was what she sought. She had been beginning to doubt her father's information.

Although she had committed most of the hexagrams to memory through long, protesting, whining study, Ivah checked each in *The Balance of the Sun and the Moon* anyway, confirming each reading. The block-printed sheets had been pasted together into a scroll, as was usual, though this was smaller than most, only as wide as her hand. She muttered empty curses as she wound it back and forth, searching for an elusive section, and thought, as she always did, that someday she would have it cut apart and rebound in a Marakander-style codex. She ignored the lengthy and, so far as she was concerned, pointless commentaries that had accrued to each hexagram, and the glosses added by her mother's master in careless, sometimes illegible calligraphy. An-Chaq's few elegant notes she paid closer attention to.

The long-sundered paths are joined: meeting, the restoration of the lost. Possibly . . . possibly . . . Attalissa was lost.

The ship precedes the wind: wandering, a traveller, a journey with no set end. "Destiny cannot be gainsaid," An-Chaq had added. That was irrelevant, but a traveller, yes, if this mountain-blooded caravan-mercenary her father had seen in his watcher's memory was the lost avatar.

Lost until now. A meeting with one who wandered, the recovery of a lost wanderer? Six more throws of the three coins to give her the third hexagram and the completion of the sun set made that more likely. *A goddess dances:* that was simply water. Or of course, the sign of a goddess taking some active part. Oh yes, she was right to feel the hot excitement of the threads of power in her hands, the sense that a pattern was coming clear, better than Shaiveh's touch on her skin.

And the first of the moon set. *The mother weeps:* a daughter.

Mothers and daughters were much on her mind, lately, perhaps too much so. She had dreamt of An-Chaq often over the past winter, as she never had before, and she could not discover what it meant. When she put the question to bone or coins, her answers were only nonsense, contradictory muddles that told her nothing but left her brooding on those unburied bones somewhere in the Great Grass. It was simply guilt, Shaiveh told her, a bad conscience, a duty neglected. But she could not help but think it was more, hope it was more. An-Chaq's hand on her, An-Chaq's love returned, and forgiveness, and care.

In her dreams, dreams she would have prayed that her father never entered, if only she had a god to pray to, Ivah lived again through the casting of the great spell that had moved the army, and saw An-Chaq's head fly off. She wandered the stone halls and stairs of Attalissa's temple, searching, she could never remember for what, but she could hear her mother's voice whisper words just below the edge of comprehension. She watched her father cast the nine pebbles on the painted leather chart of the constellations, and she watched as he drew in charcoal on the paving stones of the courtyard—he disdained brush and ink and paper—forecasts of the movements of the sky, calculating the date when he could again perform the ritual to unite himself with Attalissa. Watching in the dream, as she had in life, Ivah felt that An-Chaq stood at her shoulder; Ivah had only to turn her head to see her. But she never could.

After such dreams she felt furtive and guilty. She feared too much that Tamghat might see, might know, and be hurt and angry at her disloyalty. It was a failure of love, a betrayal of him, to realize she still mourned and missed her mother. But like someone with an uncontrollable habit, drunkenness or hashish or opium, she craved the dreams, the approving smile as they wrote the words of the spell on the earth (no matter in the dream that the smile hid thoughts of betrayal and murder), the sound of her mother's voice, the sense of her presence. Sometimes she dreamed of her mother weeping, dreamed her mother feared for Ivah's own life.

The mother weeps. But the descriptive name of the hexagram was not to be taken literally, An-Chaq had taught her that.

You're letting your mind wander. Again. Why can you never pay attention? She could almost hear An-Chaq's voice, feel the rap of a fan on her knuckles. She pulled her wandering thoughts back to the marks on the stone.

So, "Daughter" was the first hexagram of the moon set, but she cast for knowledge of the goddess and the future, not of herself and the past. Attalissa was no one's daughter. "Daughter" could less literally mean loss to the house, as a dowry paid out was loss. Perhaps a sacrifice required or a setback to Tamghat's plans, which were once again dependent on the patterned dance of the sky. The Maiden-Warrior and the Bear would join again this year in the house of the Seven Daughters, three weeks before the autumn equinox, and it would be, by most estimates, the fifteenth of this incarnation's life, which was one possibility Ivah's divination with the human shoulder blade had indicated, the day they took Lissavakail. But only one. If it was fifteen years after, then . . . a problem, since the configuration of the stars would not be right. This might warn of such delay.

The fifth hexagram was "meeting" again.

And the last, *The wren turns on the falcon:* change, upheaval, reversal of some right order.

Ivah found the moon set more difficult to interpret to her satisfaction. A warning of loss, of disruptive change arising from some meeting? A warning of the rebellion of a daughter caused by some meeting? She would never betray her father; she disowned her mother's treachery. And she had lost nothing that could be restored. Besides, she must discount any personal reading. The set spoke of her father and of Attalissa, that was all.

She threw one last set of three hexagrams, independent of sun and moon in threefold singularity, since she did not want indications of benefit or warning. *The sheaf is bound.* That meant some coming together, gathering. *The gates are opened.* An imminent arrival. And that was repeated as the third. Ivah felt almost sick. Soon. And she needed to plan what she should do. Sun or moon. Action or receptivity.

Her father called the Nabbani philosophy which broke everything into sun and moon, active and passive, good and bad, male and female, a hobble to the expression of power. And yet it was what An-Chaq had taught her, it had beauty, order . . . easy answers, she could hear Tamghat's voice.

Ivah rolled up and wrapped the book again in its square of protective leather and tied it, stowed it in her pocket, and swept the coins back into their small silk purse. That she hung again around her neck, inside her silk shirt, and refastened the ugly, shapeless cameleer's coat that was sensible garb, Shaiveh insisted, for an unremarkable wanderer, a humble diviner.

She stretched, flexing her shoulders, and blew out the candle.

"Any luck?" Shaiveh sounded bored. The *noekar*-woman trudged up the sheep track from where she had been keeping watch. She had seen Ivah do this too many times over the past year to expect results, despite any promises of Tamghat's.

"Yes . . ." Ivah found her throat dry, voice croaking. She swallowed. "Oh, yes." Though there was one test, to be certain. That, no bribed mercenary could do.

She stuck the stub of candle into her coat pocket and took Shaiveh's offered hand to pull herself up, legs stiff.

"So where do we go now?"

"We wait here."

"What for?"

Ivah smiled in the darkness. "For Attalissa. As my father saw."

"And then what?"

"Then I'll see."

Ivah led the way back down the narrow path, fingering a symbol-carved splinter of human bone deep in her pocket. It was cool to the touch, as it always had been, repulsive, though that was her squeamish mind. Shaiveh followed, more surefooted, and fell in beside her, hand finding hers as they headed for the broad river track, towards the houses and warehouses of the town.

CHAPTER XXI

There was a god on this hill, a wary, elusive presence, hardly known to the folk of the Landing. Only the shepherds came to honour him, when the lambing was over, and to leave a new cheese or a hank of fleece by the rough cairn on the summit. It was rare to find a god close along the Kinsai'aa's course, at least on the eastern bank, and the goddesses of the tributary streams that struggled through the dry hills of the east were less than the least of demons, all force and will lost in great Kinsai. The land to the west was different, stronger, and the goddess of the Bakan'aa that rolled down from Varrdal on the forest eaves had a will to match Kinsai.

Busli, the hill-god's name was. He watched, nothing more than a faint, cold touch of attention in the night.

Moth knelt by the boulder, ignoring him, but the black-and-silver-hilted sword in its sheath was tucked under her arm, cold as an iron doorlatch in the Baisirbska winter. It sucked heat from her body even through the scabbard.

The black marks the young Nabbani wizard had made were just visible in the faint light that preceded the dawn, though she could have read them in utter darkness, if she'd had to, by the differing natures of charcoal and stone.

Mikki loomed behind her, his axe over his shoulder. "A spell? I can't smell it."

"Just soothsaying. That character means a goddess, I think, and that a joining. The one that's there twice together means something about to happen."

"That could mean any number of things."

"Nabbani soothsaying usually does."

"And yours doesn't, of course." Mikki rubbed a thumb over the charcoal lines, stood up wiping the smudge on the front of his tunic. "Do you think she's really found the goddess?"

"The woman was certainly excited about something."

After she discovered that An-Chaq's daughter had been sent by her father to find the hidden goddess of the lake, Moth had hunted Attalissa in her dreams herself, and always ended up in the Western Grass, on an empty hilltop with stormclouds gathering. She knew that for illusion. The hand of some god sheltered Attalissa. There seemed little point trying to divine his name; she would only draw attention to herself, and she did not want that. It did not matter where Attalissa was; the dreaming memories of An-Chaq's daughter assured her Attalissa was not yet taken by Tamghiz. Ivah thought she nearly had the girl; Moth trod on Ivah's shadow. She knew her from her dreams and had found her in the flesh, and saw in her no child wishing for rescue, only Tamghiz Ghatai's sword, his agent, here to lure the goddess back to her lake in time for the conjunction of Vrehna and Tihz. She had promised the ghost nothing. Ivah was no more likely to listen to warnings against her father's use of her than another wizard-daughter had been, used and used until her death was more useful than her living.

Moth didn't know if even in dying Maerhild had known herself betrayed by her father. She didn't know if it was cruelty or love, to hope she had.

"So the daughter does her father's work?" Mikki asked diffidently. "We should head to Lissavakail before there's any chance of him getting some hold on the goddess through her."

"We should," she agreed.

Moth watched him watching her, a giant of a man, seven foot tall and broad-shouldered to go with it, a craggy face, palest of Northron skins, untanned, a face marked with fine silvery scars, old wounds, most got in her company. His hair and beard, shaggy and uncombed, were the yellow-gold of barley straw, but his eyes were black as seacoal, and still, she thought, so young. He tilted his head to the side, an inhuman gesture, patient, waiting, knowing she was going to make what was probably yet another wrong choice and not arguing, because he understood why she made it.

"We should, but we'll wait a little, watch Ivah and see if Attalissa really does come here."

"And what if she does?"

"That depends on what Ivah does and what Attalissa's become, so far from her home." And maybe lingering was mere cowardice, delay, and evasion. Mikki said nothing to that, only rubbed his nose with the back of his hand.

"Dawn's coming," he observed.

Birds were already singing in the greying light, hidden in the thorny scrub and climbing in the clear air. High enough and they might feel the first light of the sun. Ewes bleated after their lambs in some fold of the hills and the shepherd whistled for his dogs.

Grasses whispered in the wind, and a swirl of dust rose. Moth spun on her heel to face the loose cairn that was the focus for what worship Busli still drew, and Mikki stepped ahead of her, keeping to the side, axe balanced lightly in his hands. The god's presence was sharp in the air, a column of white light, to her eye, though he took no form in the physical world. Perhaps he could not, anymore.

"You speak of the goddess of the Lissavakail," the god said. The voice wavered, like that of an old man, long disused, and it rasped with undertones of wind and dry grass. "So does the little wizard you stalked here, mumbling over her magic. Attalissa is under the protection of my sister Kinsai, and we won't allow harm to come to her within our reach."

"Neither will we," Mikki answered, before Moth could speak. "We mean her no harm."

"Demon." The god's voice was doubtful. "You have human blood, and no place in the land here. Do you serve . . . that, willingly?"

"That," said Mikki lightly, "is *mine*, and a servant of the Old Great Gods. And I know who my father was, thank you."

"So you know of Attalissa here, so far from the Lissavaten?" Moth asked. "It must be by Kinsai's grace that Attalissa hides in these lands. By yours as well, Busli, or does Kinsai rule all your will?"

"Attalissa doesn't come here," Busli said. "You won't find her here with me, and Kinsai's great enough to protect her, even from . . . whatever it is you are. You're no demon."

"No," Moth agreed. He had not denied he was Kinsai's. Small chance of him being anything else, since he still survived on the weak eastern bank. Most of the gods and goddesses of that shore were killed in the old wars, ones the folk of the river and the desert had likely forgotten even in their songs. Those who survived, Kinsai had dominated and drained away, until they were little more than her thralls, or even mere ciphers, extensions of her will and thought and nothing more. The very devils had dealt more honestly with those they took.

"And you're no wizard," Busli said flatly, but his words tasted of fear, to Moth. He did not know, for sure, what she was, what it was he saw.

"Wizard I am still. Does Attalissa come to the Landing soon, as the wizard told her *noekar?*"

"*Noekar?* The little girl's no Great Grass warlord, to command *noekar*. You mean her lover, the Grasslander? How should I know if what either says is true? She believes her divination, that's all I can say."

"You're Kinsai's creature," Moth said bluntly. "And Kinsai will know of it, if Attalissa is within her reach."

"You should go whence you came and not meddle with Kinsai."

Moth dropped the scabbarded sword tucked under her arm into her left hand, shifted her weight impatiently, other hand on its hilt. "Don't make threats on another's behalf. She may not thank you for it."

She felt the god's attention centre on the sword, then.

"*What is that?*"

Moth drew it clear. The glassy black blade drank the light.

"A sword."

"It's a work of the Old Great Gods." Busli's voice rose with a column of whirling dust, and the pillar of light flared and sank down, like a guttering candle. "What right do you have to bear it, *wizard?*"

"The demon told you," Moth said. "I serve them. For now. You recognize it for what it is. So. Trust me, then. Is Attalissa truly coming to the Landing?"

"Liar! You're no wizard. I don't know what you are, halfbreed god or outcast spirit or a demon perverted by some foul magic, but you're no human wizard." Busli's voice dropped to a hissing whisper, grass and insects. "And only a servant of her enemy would be hunting Attalissa here." The wind abruptly died and the grasses hung still a moment, but the cairn trembled, stones grating, powers building in the earth.

Mikki took another step away from her.

"Spare me fools!" With the obsidian blade, Moth cut a sign into the earth as it shivered and cracked. The lines, a twofold rune of binding and silence, glittered with frost a moment before melting to carry the rune into the god's hill. It was not one of the wizards' runes of the north. A greater, older power ran in it, a pattern shaped by the first gods, the Old Great Gods—or so wizards believed. Few wizards could wield such a rune, and fewer still survive the wielding of it.

The god howled in outrage, shattering a moment into sparks and lines of light, and the stones of the cairn tumbled and fell, the force gathered against her dispersed.

"Busli of the Buslibeorg, I bind you to silence on me and my doings, bind you against harming me or mine, bind you to keep this silence even with Kinsai who rules you, in the name of the Old Great Gods above us both."

The wind took up its fitful gusting again, and a few pebbles rattled.

"That sword," Busli hissed. "That blade that you've no right to— it might be powerful against the gods of the earth, but whatever you are, it could kill you, drink your soul."

"I know," Moth said. "But not yet." She sheathed it, turned away. "Guard Attalissa. Her enemies are near, tell your mistress that much."

"*Vile* liar." Busli's presence faded into the hill again.

Mikki laid aside his axe to replace a few of the larger stones, building the cairn up to something like a marker again.

"It's all he has left," he said with a shrug, when he saw her watching. "Your brother never sent you on embassies as anything but a bodyguard for his envoys, did he, my wolf? No diplomat. You think you can do any better winning Attalissa's trust?"

Moth handed him some of the smaller stones to wedge into the gaps, shook her head. "What would be the point? She's proven she can't stand up to Ghatai. She'll be no help to us."

"Arrogant, Moth."

"Oh, you think?"

"So if she's no use as an ally, are we really waiting here for her?"

"Which her?" She gathered up his axe and whistled for Storm, left wandering in the eastern valley below the hill. Mikki hauled his brown tunic off over his head and strode past, tossing it back at her with a grin as she followed him down another rambling sheep track. He was wearing nothing else, oblivious to stones and thistles under his bare feet.

"Both. Either."

"If you like," she offered.

"If *I* like . . . I think we should come to Lissavaten, Lissavakail, as swiftly as we can."

"No," she said soberly. "We wait. We should know what Attalissa is, before we come between her and Ghatai." Know what she had become, hidden by a god of the strong and free Western Grass and yet taken into night-hag Kinsai's embrace.

The birds sang more loudly in the scattered thorns, the clear, carrying songs of the sunrise. Mikki whistled at them, turned back to catch Moth around the waist and kiss her. For a moment, through the touch, the taste of him, she felt the sun in his blood as he did, the coming edge of day like liquid fire. The first burning crescent slipped over the horizon.

Mikki shook himself, the dust thrown up by Busli flying from his sun-gilded fur, and dropped to all fours. He shambled on down to Storm, waiting with ears pricked, and thumped a massive shoulder companionably into the blue roan bone-horse.

"Race you to the camp?" he suggested, and loped off.

She found herself smiling, watching him. He took life with a light heart still, after all the long years and the dark years, made her remember, proved and forced her to believe in some sort of dawn. Moth strapped axe and sword to Storm's harness again and stuffed Mikki's tunic into a saddlebag. The sun, a yellow-white edge, shone into her eyes, stretching the long shadows of the hills towards her. Mikki was already some ways down the track, veering off to the north to avoid the grazing flock and its shepherd and wary dogs.

No bear could outrun a horse over distance, even with a long head start. Mikki chortled as Moth overtook him.

"There's nothing but porridge for breakfast, wolf. We should have left the hill sooner, before the shepherd was up. We could have had mutton."

CHAPTER XXII

The dark slate floor of this lower room, once a training hall for the sisters, was chalked with signs and arcs and columns of symbols, some smudged and redrawn and smudged away again, some untouched in the seven years since he had first drawn them. It was not a sky-chart for divining, had no sketches of human and animal figures, no gates and solemn gods. It was a map of the heavens, and tables of dates and planetary cycles. An almanac in mineral. The wandering stars Vrehna and Tihz moved on their fated courses, Vrehna lapping her slower mate, and soon enough they would join, setting a knot in the patterns of the world, drawing threads together, inclining, making possible, a certain shape of the world, a melding of powers.

Tamghiz walked through it, barefoot, setting butter-fuelled lamps at points of significance.

So. He changed one figure in a column of numbers, considered, and changed it back.

—I don't make mistakes.

—Stop doubting.

—If the ritual fails . . .

—It can't.

Soon, soon, soon. He would stretch, reach out into the world, hold fates in his hand, sweep the divinities of mountain and desert into a comet's tail behind him, spin their threads into his own as well. Climb to the Great Gods, and face them.

—And then?

—Then, then. Finally. Strong enough, this time.

Tamghiz sat down cross-legged amid the chalked marks, folded his hands, closed his eyes.

So. He found the Grasslander caravaneer easily by the amulet, a dog's collar marking her his, and now, by the familiar tang of her soul. She slept, one muddy, churning little human mind among many. It was the early hours of the morning. She did not dream, but he turned her mind to memory of the day past. Glimpses of the goddess, solemn, grubby, earnest young caravaneer. Would he had such a daughter. Each glimpse in the day an anxious pain for Tusa. The woman nursed the pain, the guilt, and was making herself ill with it, blood in her stomach, devouring herself. They were on the road; it looked like, felt like, they were north of the Five Cataracts. Nearly to At-Landi. Ivah was there now, waiting. Tamghiz slid into her mind without waking her awareness. She stirred, shrugged off the bodyguard's arm. In her sleep, she was a little child again, yearning for her mother's embrace. Tamghiz shook his head and left her. She would know the goddess arrived soon enough. It did her no good to expect him to provide all the answers.

And the other matter.

His fingers twisted strings, let others fall, and he studied the dangling pattern of loops, blew on them and flung the cat's cradle away.

—There's power in the lake yet.

—She's far away, she's weak. There can't be.

—I know they're out there, the sisters who fled. I can almost smell them. I know they're brewing rebellion.

—Seven years, and they haven't acted.

—Ishkul Valley.

—If that was all they could organize, they're no threat.

—But there's someone moving them. Them, the Serakallashi. There were mountain women in Serakallash when I took it, and I lost them.

—I had more important concerns. What happened to that damned little godling of the spring? I couldn't have killed her without knowing.

—Could I?

—Could I, Ghatai?

He almost wished he had Ivah here, to throw the coins for him. He had no patience with them himself, and she had taken her mother's book: he had no way to know the hexagrams. The sky-chart and pebbles only ever told him of secrets and travellers and the dark places of the earth, which led him to the mines, but the *noekar* were assiduous in their supervision of the mines, and there were no caches of weapons, no meetings of rebels, that they could ever sniff out.

—Attalissa's hand is on them.

—She has no power here, now.

—There are other gods in the mountains.

—Petty things I could eat for breakfast.

—Eat or be eaten. What about Narva?

—Lost in his own mind, a maze I won't dare. I've searched the mines of the Narvabarkash myself.

—Haven't I? Were those the true mines, the ancient mines? They were new workings. They were all the villagers knew of. They told the truth.

—I might have missed something. His soul's a maze, all leading into his heart, he can't see out. And his madness cloaks the barkash. They say he has priests still, but I never found them.

—Some mysteries are too dangerous to enter. Some are mere illusion and arrogance. One can invent a mystery where there is in truth nothing to see.

—But is there?

—I can find nothing. But I smell them, hear them, glimpse shadows, skirting behind me. They're out there.

—Are they worth fearing?

—No. A nuisance, no worse, and once Attalissa is mine, they are nothing.

—And Ulfhild?

—If it even is Ulfhild. If it is, she'll come to me. Whoever it is wanders the Great Grass. She touches the desert. She never comes, but she will, when the time is right. I've warded myself against her, is all. I'll call her in, once Attalissa is mine.

—She's not hunting me at all. She'd see through any spell-cast confusion by now; she'd never delay and prowl and linger. She follows some other concern.

Was he jealous?

And if some other concern, what? One of the others? Heuslar always tried to make alliance with Ulfhild, Heuslar felt he had some claim of kinship on her, and sometimes she did align with him, on those grounds. Sien-Mor, Ulfhild and Sien-Mor might join forces, plausibly. Sien-Mor had found Ulfhild's a strong shadow to shelter in. He knew there was more than one of them free. But Sien-Mor would never linger in the wilds, she hated the empty places. And Sien-Mor without Sien-Shava—Sien-Shava would never tolerate his little sister running at Ulfhild's heel for long.

He did not even know for certain it was she his divination had found, restless wanderer beyond the desert. He only guessed, because of what the pebbles had told him, and Ivah's coins, on that one occasion. Whoever it was, divination only rarely pinned them down, and then briefly, almost as briefly as those fleeting touches of the goddess. He hoped his own spells kept him hidden from her so effectively. He did not want any others involved, conspiring to supplant him in the great transformation, or angling for a share of the power on their own terms. And it might not even be Ulfhild.

—It doesn't matter.

Tamghiz told himself so, firmly. It would not matter, the past was past, and once Attalissa was within him, he would have no need to fear any of the others, even should they all league against him.

Ghatai wondered why he felt he had to fear. Once he was lake-god and man and devil in one, he would draw the others to him as fish are drawn in a net, and make them his.

Meanwhile, he could count the weeks, as Vrehna rose chasing after Tihz, and he could count the weeks, as the caravan should mark them, measure them off in camel-strides and camps, turning at the Landing, and his thoughts had slid into Northron, running on Ulfhild, following the Kinsai'aa down, and there was a goddess of power, great

345

power he could vanquish and claim once Attalissa was his and his nature was changed to let him grasp a god, devour her as she had once devoured others . . . but he ran too far ahead. For now, count the weeks. There was time. He did not need to spur Ivah to act. Attalissa would deliver herself to Serakallash, all in good and fit time.

Tamghiz blew out the nearest lamp, extinguished the others with will alone, and strode from the room, calling for Siglinda on the stairs.

There were a number of diviners in At-Landi, soothsayers they called themselves, the influence of Northron Varrgash up the Bakanav, but as Ivah did not seek out clients, reading the coins only for those in the house where they lodged, she ruffled few feathers. She had money, though she spent it parsimoniously and made Shaiveh do stablework to help pay their way. It would not be credible for a poor diviner to have too much silver to spend, and might lead to talk, or trouble. Shai fretted as the days passed and no goddess appeared, but Ivah put on a mask of serenely confident patience and was rewarded. Attalissa arrived.

The leading camels of the caravan were already passing through the gate when Ivah and Shaiveh climbed to the top of the easily scaled wall of packed earth and sandstone, and the dust they stirred up drifted over them. The girl rode somewhere in the middle, the only female near the right age.

"You think that's her?" Shaiveh asked.

"That's her."

Shaiveh frowned. She sat, arms wrapped around her knees, all lazy power and grace, and she knew it, too, as she stretched and cupped her hands to shield her eyes from the sun.

"She looks like the deserts, with those braids," Shaiveh pointed out. "Or a Westgrasslander."

"Look at her build, though, and her face. That's the mountains."

"But surely no one would dare tattoo Attalissa? What are those markings, anyhow?"

Ivah shrugged. "I don't know them either. They look more like Westgrass than Four Deserts."

346

Maybe she had not been so far astray as all that, seeking beyond the Kinsai-av.

The girl looked young, small for her age—if she was the goddess and around fifteen. No plausible mercenary, but you saw them as young as that, and as small. Atop a camel with a spear, perhaps it did not matter. Or maybe she was only the cook, or, Great Gods help the man or woman in question if so, kept someone's bedroll warm.

Not an attractive bride. Perhaps that was the intention. Young, small, scruffy, a dirty, sweat- and camel-reeking caravaneer who only saw hot water a couple times a year, unless you counted the foul, thick tea they practically lived on. She guided her white camel with a light hand, calling back over her shoulder to the man behind her string of pack-camels. The tall, heavy-browed Stone Desert man, his dark-skinned, narrow face striped with blue like a tiger's markings, answered, and as she faced forward again the girl flashed a smile that made her plain face, with its small nose, small peaked mouth, and wide dark eyes, suddenly pretty despite the disfiguring tattoos and a fresh red scar like a knife-slash on her temple. She seemed alive and glowing as the first tulips, all light and dancing.

"Heh," said Shaiveh.

"No."

"Just looking."

"You'd be a very long time dying, if you touched my father's intended bride," Ivah said softly.

Shaiveh gave her a sidelong glance and held her tongue, but she looked more smug than rebuked, as though she thought she'd scored a point in some game.

One of the men with the goddess must be the Blackdog's host. Inconceivable that the demon was not near her. None of them looked like mountain men. Perhaps the ambush at the tunnel exit had succeeded after all. None of the *noekar* sent to carry it out had survived to say, though not all the bodies had been found. None of the men in the long, ambling chain of camels looked familiar, either, no presumed-dead *noekar*. That would have been a joke, the sort her father appreciated, if the Blackdog turned out to be one of Tamghat's own.

She picked out a Great Grass woman, plain-faced and weary. Probably the one in her father's service. What had driven her to burn the spell-net and call him, betraying one of her own gang? Some jealousy, a quarrel? A price her father could not pay, he had said.

The Stone Desert man behind the goddess was the best bet for the Blackdog. He looked a hard type; Stone Desert men were. She could imagine him slaughtering her father's *noekar* like a weasel among ducklings.

But despite the girl's flash of smile, there was a sobriety to the caravan, a grimness. Ivah had learned to recognize it: a gang coming into a town with loss. The Nabbani-looking merchants and their men seemed sombre, too.

Maybe they'd be hiring. No. She and Shaiveh had worked their way to At-Landi with a caravan when they first left Lissavakail, distancing themselves from association with wizardry and the lake before they crossed the river. Never again. Master Baruni had called her a useless doll to her face, and struck Shai with his whip when the *noekar* drew on him for the insult. She'd called the bodyguard off, but the gang had closed up against them. A miserable journey. They'd sold the camels in At-Landi for decent horses, and damned if she was trading the good beasts back now, to some Northron who wouldn't know quality when he bestrode it. Besides, it was said Northrons ate horses at some winter feast.

The ideogram-carved slip of bone hidden in her clenched fist grew almost too hot to touch, its edge pressing painfully, digging at her, as the girl with the Westgrassland tattoos approached the gateway to their right. She had sliced it from the thighbone of a dead incarnation in the hall of holy tombs.

"Oh yes," Ivah murmured. "That's definitely her."

The bone fragment had been warm in her pocket that morning, enough to send her out to watch the south gate. She had a sudden lurch of fear, though, lest the bone, or what lay coiled at the bottom of her other pocket, the yet-incomplete snare, call out to the goddess's soul.

The girl looked up to the women on the wall, but her expression held no suggestion of danger to them, half open curiosity, half the envy of one who had a living to earn for those who could afford to lie about in the sun.

"Who are you?" Ivah called down, as any idle watcher might, but it was the man behind who answered as the girl rode out of sight through the gate:

"Gaguush's gang, with the Singahs from Over-Malagru."

Ivah had heard her former gang-boss Baruni speak of Gaguush, she thought, but she could remember nothing of her, good or ill.

She turned to watch in glimpses between Northron-style peaked rooftops as the caravan made its thudding, tin-bell-jangling way along the corduroy street, built of logs floated down the Bakanav from Varrgash. The Black Desert woman, presumably the caravan-mistress Gaguush, was in the lead, on a scarred bull camel. She turned off to the left, onto the log-paved lane that angled down to those caravanserais and warehouses on the river's edge. Easy enough to find out where they put up.

Two outriders came in at the tail, dust-covered. Ivah paid them little heed, picking her way along the crumbling wall to where it was possible to climb down. Shaiveh followed and almost ran into Ivah when she stopped, chilled. One of the outriders had turned his head sharply, staring at her over his shoulder, sabre in hand. She had not seen him draw.

Westgrasslander. His camel spun around so he faced her, power and speed that should only belong to a horse, in Ivah's mind, but she had already dropped down flat on top of the wall, Shaiveh a moment behind her.

"What?" the *noekar* hissed.

"Quiet!"

Westgrasslander, of course, that explained the girl's tattoos. The Blackdog. She saw nothing out of the ordinary about him, but the chill of his attention . . . the Blackdog was near enough a demon, for all she understood of it. A demon would recognize her for a wizard, of course it would, she should have realized that, her father should have warned her.

But there were many wizards in the world and outside of Marakand it was nothing any sane person would hold against her. Though who knew if a Blackdog's host were sane.

She watched him through a dip between the stones and a gap between houses. Head raised, like a hound tracing a scent. A strong face, but expressionless, as if he had locked his thoughts away. Another person who lived behind a mask. After a moment he turned his rust-red camel again and followed his comrades.

Shaiveh rose to her hands and knees and crawled over Ivah to watch the Westgrasslander go.

"Him? Surely you've had enough of Westgrasslanders. Born with mud between their toes. If you really need to go making eyes at a man, at least pick a real one, a warrior, not a farmer."

"He's the Blackdog."

"Could have fooled me. I've seen that look in your eye before, don't think I don't know. I suppose we have to kill him before we take the girl? I hope your lord father gave you a spell for that, because I saw what the Blackdog did to some of those poor bastards sent to stop him when we took the temple."

"I haven't decided what to do about him."

"Oh good," said Shaiveh. "Well, don't expect me to go up against him for you, that's all I can say. I'm too beautiful to die."

Ivah snorted. "I'll bear that in mind."

To actually travel with the caravan, or to follow secretly? Ivah hiked out of town—alone, after some argument with Shaiveh. She turned off the track and climbed the sheep path into the hills, until she reached the height with the abandoned cairn, remnant, maybe, of some forgotten god. It looked like it had tumbled further into ruin since she last came here for divining, and had been clumsily restored, by some shepherd, maybe, remembering old holiness. There seemed to be no priests to tend it, and no god's presence that she could sense. Everyone said there were no other gods along the shores of the Kinsai-av, anyway. It was quiet, a place where she could sit in silence and think, without

Benno's-daughter the innkeeper thinking of yet another far-off relative whose fortune she wanted to know.

Yes, no. The answer she sought eluded her; she could think of no single question. Too many crowded her mind, risking confusion and the failure of the reading, dangerous errors in interpretation.

Chance, risk, change. Just flip a coin, call heads or tails, Shaiveh would mock. A simple yes or no, that was what she needed. She could read a bone, if she had one, but she had noticed no old scatters of wolf- or disease-downed sheep on the hillside. She might spend half the day searching before she found one.

Ivah weighed a single gold coin on the palm of her hand, one of her mother's set of three. Father Nabban, and she would approach the mistress as a traveller wanting to share the caravan's protection on the road east—maybe she was returning to her home Over-Malagru after her travels in the west? Mother Nabban (some emperor in a wide hat, maybe even her own grandfather, sitting by the great River-Mother's knee), and she would dare the dangers of travelling alone on the desert road, follow in secret, until the caravan neared Serakallash and the road up to Lissavakail.

Ivah tossed the coin, caught it, and closed her eyes a moment before looking.

Father Nabban. Her right course lay in action and openness, not in waiting and concealment. She seemed to feel the eyes of the Westgrasslander Blackdog on her again. That sent a twist of fear through her stomach. She thought it ought to be fear, at any rate.

Shaiveh was sitting on a stone at the roadside waiting for her return.

"What did the bones say?"

"Coins," Ivah said briefly, a minor lie even in the correction. She wasn't going to admit to mere coin-tossing. "We go with them."

"Sometimes it might be better to trust to common sense, you know."

"Did you follow them?"

"Yes, my lady, as you commanded." Shaiveh delivered her report in a mocking singsong. "They unloaded at the Oswyngas' warehouse and I earned a couple of farthings for helping. Those Over-Malagru men are heading up into the north. The gang's lodged at Attapamil's caravanserai, they don't have a contract south yet, and I heard the gang-boss, that Black Desert woman, talking about meeting some bard at Lizath's teahouse tonight. Don't know what the goddess is doing and I didn't want to be noticed taking an interest. But they work her pretty hard—I don't think they know who she is. Do you suppose *she* doesn't know, is that possible?"

"I don't know."

"I don't like it, Ivah. We should just follow them."

"I said we're going with them."

Shaiveh shrugged, scowling. "If you say so. And what happens when that possessed Westgrasslander sees you're a wizard? He'll be able to tell. Demons can."

"And there's no reason I shouldn't be a wizard; all At-Landi already knows I'm a coin-reader. There's nothing in that to make anyone connect us with Lissavakail. I'm a diviner from Over-Malagru, you're a mercenary, we met in Marakand three or four years ago, and don't go elaborating that into anything fancy."

"Fine. Just remember it's me who'll end up dying first."

"Well, of course. That's your job."

Shaiveh gave her a sidelong look and got to her feet. Ivah allowed herself a brief grin, behind the *noekar*'s back. The point was to her, this time.

CHAPTER XXIII

The Northrons unloaded their ships in the shallows or ran them aground on the log-hardened muddy shore of the river bay that had given birth to the Landing. They were long, graceful craft, but wide-beamed and capable of holding an astonishing amount of cargo for their draft, with stem- and sternposts curving up graceful as a swan's breast. They had masts, but much of their travel up and down the river was done with their crews at the oars, or even towing, wading in the shallows or on long-trodden paths on the shore. They were as fitted to their element as an eagle to the air, a salmon to sea.

"Mooning over these little ditch-boats again? Someday, you really need to see a seagoing knarr, or a longship."

Pakdhala jumped and looked around. She had been so caught in watching a ship heading upriver, the following wind—Kinsai's blessing the crew would call it—filling the square brown sail, that she had not noticed Varro prowling up behind her. Caught in sudden memory, the boat lifting beneath her, bouncing over the waves as she coaxed the wind up, Oto—no, it was some other Blackdog, and she some other Attalissa, a young woman laughing, saying to an old man, *Careful, you'll have us over.*

"You keep saying that, Varro, but you never offer to run away to the North with me."

"You only have to ask, 'Dhala darling."

She folded her arms and leaned back against his warm solidity, affecting a pout. "I thought your heart was given to what's-her-name in Marakand."

"What's-her-name?" Varro scratched his beard. "Which one?"

"You know. Your wife. That apothecary, the one with all the giggling girls."

"Ah, her. I'm sure she'd understand. And they don't giggle any more than you did at that age, young 'Dhala. It's the nature of small girls to giggle."

Pakdhala sighed. "Still, I'd love to be on a ship like that." For a ship to be so much a part of the water . . . the soul of beauty, form and function in perfect unity.

"You can clamber over one tonight, if you like," Varro offered. "They've got her hauled up on the upper beach."

"Who does? Friends of yours?"

"Cousins," he said smugly. "Well, some of 'em's cousins. My cousin Ellensborg is crew on her cousin Ulfhelm's ship, and she's just married his steersman, so there's a bit of a celebration tonight. She said I could bring a friend or two."

"Or the whole gang?"

"Well, Tihmrose and Django drew watch at the caravanserai, Tusa has disappeared and Asmin-Luya's looking at all the soothsayers and diviners for her, the boss and your father are meeting some bard who'll be taking Doha's stuff and his pay home to his kin, Great Gods bless his soul with a short journey, and I think Gaguush has plans . . ." Varro waggled bushy eyebrows at her ". . . for later."

"Does she?" Pakdhala grinned. "But my father won't let me go off to a brawl like that without him."

"'T'isn't a brawl."

"Oh, a gang of Northrons celebrating a wedding? You really think that's not a brawl?"

"The brawl comes later."

Pakdhala grinned. "I'll come, if I can get away from him."

Ivah wandered through the many small rooms of Lizath's teahouse with Shaiveh a sullen shadow at her heels. No one paid them any heed; she had made sure of that. The diners sitting on cushions around the low tables carried on with their conversations, or looked up, smiling vaguely, and returned to the plates of tiny filled dumplings and the delicate porcelain cups of clear Nabbani tea, forgetting them at once.

"And how do we make this Gaguush actually talk to us, now that we're so conveniently beneath notice?" Shaiveh grumbled.

Ivah ignored her, backing out of yet another room with a friendly smile at the group of old men reminiscing there.

Gaguush was in the next room they tried. The gang-boss had obviously found a bathhouse; she looked a good ten years younger, with the dust scoured from her skin and her hair glistening, freshly braided. She leaned over the table, looking half like some devil of An-Chaq's tales, all jagged shapes of red and black, as the flame of the lamp swirled. She spoke too quietly to overhear, handing what looked like a purse, its neck lead-sealed and stamped, to an older Westgrasslander woman, a bard, with the bright scarves of her calling wound round her head and her long-necked saz at her back.

And the Blackdog Westgrasslander was there, too, sitting at the caravan-mistress's side.

"Tell his sons he died fighting," the Westgrasslander said suddenly, addressing the bard as she rose and tucked the purse away in some inner pocket, but his eyes were on Ivah, his hand on the sabre across his lap, and he already had one foot under him, to rise. She almost thought, in the shadowy room, that his eyes reflected the lamplight green, like a cat's.

There were two other members of the gang there as well, the Stone Desert man she had noticed before and a skinny, faded little woman whose folk Ivah could not place, and all four were scrubbed and sober. Lizath would not let caravaneers into her house if they had already begun the drinking that followed any return to civilization.

Ivah was already doubting her choice. Maybe later, once the gang-boss had started drinking too, would have been better. And she should have listened to Shaiveh, gone to the bathhouse first and combed and rebraided the two fat plaits that fell to her knees. She had wanted to look hard-living and dusty, someone who could keep up with a caravan, not be a burden, but now . . . His eyes weren't green, but mottled light brown flecked green and yellow, like sunlight on a pebbled stream in the mountains. Hot though, not brook-water cool, burning like the glare on the water, watching her. She had an impulse to freeze there, motionless, as though that would make his notice pass. Instead she smiled and stepped aside to allow the bard to leave.

"I'm sorry," Ivah apologized, breaking the threads that made a one-handed cat's cradle on her left hand, hidden in her pocket. "I was hoping to talk to Mistress Gaguush."

The caravan-mistress whipped her head around, raised her eyebrows.

"Where did you come from?"

Ivah gestured apologetically towards the door. It was a stupid question, but she wasn't about to point out a caravan-mistress's lack of attention, not to the woman's face, the gesture said.

"If you could spare me a moment . . ." Ivah let her voice trail off hopefully.

"No. Do I know you?" Gaguush frowned, looking them both over as though she was fairly certain she did not want to.

"Bad news travels fast," the Stone Desert tribesman murmured.

Gaguush smiled in a manner not at all friendly. "Is that it? I'm not hiring, and this is a private supper."

"Oh, I know. I really don't want to interrupt. But Master Baruni spoke very highly of you and . . ."

"I said, I'm not hiring."

Ivah gave the little formal bow, hands clasped before her chest, which she could get away with, being so Nabbani in appearance. "No, of course not. I should introduce myself. I'm Ivah, a diviner with the Nabbani coins, and my companion is Shaiveh. I want to head back Over-Malagru way, so we're looking for an eastbound caravan to join. We can earn our keep."

"Why us?" the caravan mistress demanded. "We've barely come in, we don't have a contract south yet, Great Gods alone know when we'll be pulling out. Heard we're short-handed?"

"No, no, nothing like that." Ivah looked surprised. "Have you . . . if you've had losses this run, I'm truly sorry, I meant no offence to the dead. It's just, we travelled west, originally, with Master Baruni, some years back, and he spoke well of you. And," she smiled, shrugged, "we happened to see you coming in. We liked the look of your outfit. Shai here helped you unload."

Gaguush snorted.

"If you could just let us know, once you're preparing to leave? We could even pay something towards our escort. I know we wouldn't be as much use to you as experienced caravaneers, but Shaiveh's handy with weapons, she's worked as a mercenary before, and I can make myself useful. You wouldn't find us a burden. We're putting up at Benno's inn, for now."

"Yes, fine, Benno's inn," Gaguush said. "Now out."

"Thank you." Ivah offered both hands, Marakander fashion. Gaguush, with a weary look, was nevertheless forced by common courtesy to rise from the table and take them. Ivah gave her another bow. The Nabbani symbols painted on her hands in oil, hardly there, flared with warmth as she pressed the gang-boss's skin with her own. Then she elbowed Shaiveh back and closed the door behind herself.

"Oh, that went well," Shaiveh said. "Now can we just—"

Ivah slapped Shaiveh's shoulder, touched her lips for silence.

"She'll decide she wants us along before the week's out," she whispered, hardly above a breath.

"Hey, you, Nabbani! Ivah!"

Ivah turned, not needing to put on a look of surprise. Gaguush stood in the open doorway, inviting her back into the lamplit room with a jerk of her chin. There was some agitation at the table now, the Westgrasslander scowling, the little woman patting the back of his hand as though she meant to soothe him, the tall Stone Desert man looking amused. Gaguush leaned a shoulder against the wall, studying Ivah, head to foot.

"A diviner? Holla-Sayan here says he's heard rumour you're a wizard."

A lie, no doubt. The Westgrasslander knew, he saw right through her, a yellow-green fire behind his eyes . . . Half a panicked moment, and Ivah found her innocence again. She had expected him to know. She put on a cautious smile, timid and hesitant.

"Not really. I'm just a diviner, what they call a soothsayer up here, but I suppose that means I have some talent, it's true. I can read the oracle coins, and I've studied Nabbani spell-symbols." She swept her lashes down. "I've been doing readings here, at Benno's. If you want to ask someone about my skills, if you want me to do a reading for your journey, I'm sure there's people who'd speak for me . . ." She raised her eyes, met the Westgrasslander's cold-eyed gaze head on. Prove she had no reason to fear him, saw nothing unusual in him to fear. "Holla-Sayan? Who was it told you I was a wizard?"

"Market rumour," he said, with a shrug, when it seemed the gang-boss was also waiting for his answer. He lied without taking thought to make it credible. He'd barely been in At-Landi long enough to pass through the market.

"Do you know enough magic to teach another?" Gaguush asked.

"No," the Blackdog said. Gaguush frowned at him.

"I . . . I could," Ivah admitted, feeling her way cautiously. "But it's necessary to be born with the talent, you know. Magic isn't something that just anyone can be trained in."

"The girl's got some talent of some sort," Gaguush said, looking unaccountably pleased with herself. "Fine. I'll take you along, Ivah. You pay what you can, we'll get the rest out of the pair of you in labour, and you can do some teaching. Holla here has a daughter who deserves more education than she'll get from him."

"I can certainly teach her the basic principles," Ivah said. "You'll be wanting to find her a proper apprenticeship in time, of course, if she's skilled, but I'll give her a good start." The gang-boss's face was so easy to read.

"You have your own camels?"

"Horses."

"No good. You can't get horses across the Salt and Stone Deserts, unless they're your only goods and you've a camel-train carrying water."

"Yes, I know. I came west from Over-Malagru," Ivah reminded gently. "We'll trade them for camels at Serakallash. I hear they value good Grasslander horses there these days." And she could see a need for swift horses, at the end of her journey.

"Up to you, I suppose."

"She's a wizard," the Blackdog repeated, as though he thought Gaguush had missed the point somewhere. "You can't—"

"I damn well can. You can't keep 'Dhala a baby forever. What's wrong with her learning a few elementary skills from Ivah here, before she goes off to a real apprenticeship? Cold hells, I'd think you'd be pleased, Holla."

"She's not . . . You've got no right—" And then he lurched to his feet and walked out, shoving past Ivah and Shaiveh as if half-blind. Maybe he had been drinking already, after all.

"Another restful evening," murmured the Stone Desert tribesman. "Welcome to the gang, girls. I'm Kapuzeh, this is Thekla, the best cook between here and Marakand, and that was Holla-Sayan. You'll get used to him."

"You didn't really expect him to stay here long, with 'Dhala off drinking with Bikkim and Zavel?" The gang-boss slumped down on her cushions again, all the fine lines of worry and desert winds returning to her face. "Ivah, Shaiveh, we're at Attapamil's caravanserai. We don't need you yet, you're on your own till we pull out. We'll send word to Benno's. Now out, go away."

Ivah bowed and left, towing Shai.

"It's the goddess," Shaiveh said, as soon as they were in the street. "She was the only young girl with them. They want you to teach wizardry to the bloody goddess."

"Shut up about the goddess!" Ivah looked around, but there was no man lurking in the dark street, no great black dog, either. She couldn't keep back her grin. "I told you she'd take us on. I didn't expect it to be the moment we met her, though."

"Yeah, but teaching the—all right, all right. And that monster doesn't like you."

"He can not like me all he wants, so long as you don't go giving him a reason not to. We'll be fine. Just don't let on you've ever been nearer Lissavakail than the desert road, and we'll be fine."

"Last trip, anyway, praise the Gods," Shaiveh said, and flung an arm around Ivah's shoulders. "*Home*. Beds without bugs and no more kowtowing to peasants for pennies and sour beer. How about we get a jar of wine and take it back to Benno's, to celebrate?"

"Wine and aged cheese and sweet saffron bread," Ivah said. Both the latter were Northron delicacies she had developed a taste for. Anything that might get the Blackdog's burning stare out of her mind.

The noise of the feasting at Varro's cousin's ship carried half a mile up the river from the landing beach. Pakdhala continued on, until the noise had died away and there was nothing but river and wind. Nobody came looking for her. She had told her father flatly that she was going and he did not need to follow, that yes, she'd be sensible, yes, she'd be careful, yes, she'd stay with the others—and she had meant to. But she had told Varro and Judeh she'd be along later, and assured them no, she wouldn't walk through town alone in the dark. And then she had eluded Bikkim, with Zavel tagging him, when he came looking for her around the caravanserai.

And had walked through town alone in the dark and out of town. The beached ships bypassed, she had pulled off her boots and walked along the shore, mud oozing between her toes, avoiding the sharp shells of freshwater mussels, ignoring and ignored by the leeches that infested this soft-bottomed stretch of the Kinsai-av.

Eventually she found a convenient rock and sat, dangling her feet in the water.

Sister Kinsai, lend me your strength. It was contact with the water kept her going, all through these years, Kinsai's strength and that of the little goddesses of the desert wells, and what blessing distant Sayan could give, not any power of her own.

"Little sister." Kinsai herself rose from the water, human-solid, bumped her over with a hip and joined her on the boulder, dripping.

"I have to go back."

"To the party?" Kinsai asked, and chuckled. "I'm tempted to drop in myself. That Ellensborg's a lovely thing."

"You can't seduce a bride on her wedding night. It would be rude."

Kinsai sniggered. "The amount of mead they have down there, she'd never notice the difference. And the way her Olav is drinking, he won't be able to do anything for her by the time they get the pair of them off to bed." Sobered, eyeing her sidelong. "Nothing's changed."

Pakdhala shook her head. "No."

"What was it like, before? When you grew into your strength?"

Pakdhala shrugged. "I think . . . gradual at first. Growing stronger, while I was a child. And then, one day, it would all come back. I would be a woman again, I would be able to contain it."

"Why humanity, anyway?"

"So that I remember better than to seduce a bride on her wedding night."

"Hah, you've never seduced anyone. Have you, little sister of the lake?"

"Hm."

"What's 'hm'?"

"'Hm' is none of your bloody business, Great Kinsai."

"Thus speaks the caravaneer. Such language. Have you?"

"Not that I remember."

"Why not?"

"It would hardly be right," Pakdhala said primly. "If I was their goddess. To . . . pick favourites, that way."

"Great Gods above, girl, don't be picky, then they've got nothing to complain of."

"My father raised me better than that."

"He's one to talk."

"This is not what I came out here for."

"No?"

"I wanted to think."

"I'll leave you to it, then."

"Don't be insulted. Stay."

Kinsai patted her back. "Little sister, don't be so serious. You'll be old before your time."

"My people are slaves—bondfolk, it's the same thing. The Sera-kallashi are slaves. It's my fault. I failed to defend them. They're waiting for me. You've heard it, you hear the stories carried along the river."

"If you go back, that wizard—if he is a wizard, your dog believes he's something else, I think, some demon gone bad, perhaps—will claim you. Make you his bride as he threatens and rule with your authority, at best. At worst—maybe he can leech off what power you have, batten on you and feed. My children at the ferries think it's possible, if he's not entirely human but something closer to us."

Pakdhala shivered. Feed off her. She had never lost the nightmare conviction that the warlord intended her utter destruction.

"Kinsai. Forgive me. They say you . . . the gods of the eastern shore, it is said you destroyed them, long ago. I don't—" Pakdhala clamped suddenly shaking hands between her knees. She had never felt Kinsai so still, so great and potent a power. The whole weight of the river, massed to strike. The lake of Lissavakail was nothing to the might of the Kinsai-av. "But I saw it, back when the warlord first appeared. I understood what Tamghat meant to do. Consume me, make me a mere part of himself, my power his, my being lost in his. Did you . . . is this possible?"

"We could all have died, one by one," Kinsai said quietly. "Long before the devils' wars the Northrons sing of. They hid within me. We became one, to withstand the storm unleashed over the black hills. But they could not survive as individuals within me. They were weak, small gods and goddesses. It was not my will, to overwhelm them. But I did, I took them into myself and their power became mine. They return, some few, as shadows of what they were. Ghosts, almost." Her eyes gleamed like pearls under the moon, ghost-pale. "Attalissa, you will not survive, not as yourself, if that wizard is capable of what you foresaw, if you surrender to that. You need to be strong enough to let him make his attempt and turn on him. Devour him, instead."

"I'm not strong enough. And I don't want him . . ." *within me, in any way.* She could not stomach sharing even that thought with Kinsai, the image it brought to her. "I can't believe, anymore, that I ever will be strong enough. To even resist him, let alone defeat him. There's something wrong with me."

"Perhaps. Like a woman whose monthly courses never begin. It happens. Perhaps you need to die, and try again."

"No!"

Kinsai chuckled. "Then take your dog. Use it."

"Use it how?"

"As I used my brothers and sisters of the eastern shore."

"*No!*"

"Why did you enslave it, if not to use it, someday?"

"Enslave it? I didn't."

"Don't be a child. You can't hide in that innocence now. I don't know what the dog was, when you bound it, but it's more akin to that devil-wizard than anything else."

"Devil?"

"Who knows? I've never seen him. He might be. They do say one or two of the bound seven got loose some generations ago, in the north. Or he could be demon's child, god's child, who can say? Not one of mine, mind, my children have better natures, and nothing like that power; I have more sense than to let it pass to them in such strength. But it hardly matters, how he came by his power. Don't try to ignore the truth. You've bound yourself into that weak body and now you hide behind poor Holla-Sayan, who's doomed by that parasite soul he carries, and you know it. You can't save him; he'll try to fight Tamghat for you, and die, killed by the wizard or by the dog tearing free at last. Your only choice is to rip the dog from him, take it into your own soul, and kill the warlord yourself."

"I can't do that. Anyway, the dog only goes to male hosts."

"You made it what it is. Virgin goddess, but you liked having a man about to cringe at your feet, didn't you?"

"I did not! I did not make him anything—I don't remember."

Kinsai dissolved into sudden fog and an angry smashing of waves over the stone. *Open your eyes, damned fool! Stop pretending innocence. If that wizard consumes you, he'll eat his way along the desert road with nothing to stop him—I'll be the next true power he takes, or the Lady of Marakand, and then the Old Great Gods themselves won't be able to stop him, if ever they find a way back to the world. Holla was damned from the moment you tricked him into helping you, with your sweet, lying child's innocence. Kill him now or watch him killed later, it's all one in the end. Make the dog part of yourself, or see yourself fed to the wizard. You created this situation, with your spirit-slave and your little-girl games of mortality.*

Harm Holla-Sayan and I'll give myself to the wizard, to see you destroyed!

Kinsai laughed, a disembodied voice over the water. "I *like* the man too much to betray him so, Great Attalissa, and I want no part of whatever the Blackdog truly is. But he's doomed. It's time you stopped hiding behind him and did something." *Before we all perish through your weakness like your sister Sera of the Red Desert.*

'Dhala, what are you doing up the river? At-Landi's no place for a girl your age to go wandering alone. You promised you'd stay with the others. Her father, and angry.

Get away from the river, she almost screamed. *Just . . . go back to Gaguush. Stay away from Kinsai, and leave me alone.*

'Dhala—

Do what I say, dog! And she flung him away, hurting him, she felt, and slammed her mind closed against him.

She stumbled away from the river herself, feet finding painful rocks and shells, vision reduced to the merely human by tears. Anger. Shame? What in the cold *hells* did Kinsai think she knew, anyway? Pakdhala dragged on her boots, set off along the road, above the reach of Kinsai's waters, half-running, and then running outright, running, running, but memory, mere echo of memory, nothing more certain, snapped at her heels. The Blackdog was no slave, the dog was her protector, it had always been, she and the Blackdog and the waters of Lissavakail . . . She shaped herself a body in a woman's womb, flesh of her flesh, a village diviner, a woman strong in wizardry, if untrained. She was born a wizard, Attalissa incarnate, because . . . because . . . something hunted in the mountains . . . something savage and sorely wounded, mad and afraid, but never dying, and the villages lost yaks, and ponies, and goats, and herders to it, never many, but unceasing, over the years, as it fed the physical body it struggled to hold together, and a goddess of the waters could not lure it down to the lake, could not force it into a more useful shape, but such things wizards' power could do—

"No!" she screamed. "I didn't!"

"'Dhala? Pakdhala? Are you all right?" Not her father but Bikkim, peering into the darkness, sabre half-drawn. "Are you alone? Are you hurt?" Imagining the Great Gods knew what.

She scrubbed a gritty coat-sleeve over her eyes, mortal embarrassment. "Bikkim. It's all right. I just . . ." She found no explanation. "What are you doing out here?" Sniffed and hoped he didn't notice.

"Looking for you," he said grimly. "Everyone at the wedding-feast thought you were at the caravanserai. And Django thought you'd gone with the rest of us. Holla-Sayan came down to the beach looking for you. He sent me."

"Oh."

They stood in awkward silence.

"Where is he?" She wouldn't reach for him, to find out. Raised voices floated from the landing beach. She hadn't realized she had run so far back towards the town.

"He went back to Attapamil's to find Gaguush. Told me you'd gone up the north road along the river. Um, he said you might want company."

Neither of them commented on how improbable that was, that Holla-Sayan should do such a thing.

"Are you all right?" Bikkim asked more gently. He reached out a cautious hand, found her arm. "It's not this thing about you being a wizard . . . upsetting you, I mean? Even if you do have a tutor, no one's going to make you leave the gang for an apprenticeship if you don't want to go, you know that." He tried a smile in the darkness. "It'd be over Holla's dead body, anyway."

Just then, that wasn't funny. "What tutor?" she asked.

"You didn't know? I thought that was why you'd . . . anyway, some Nabbani coin-thrower is coming to Marakand with us, and Gaguush wants her to tutor you."

"Oh," Pakdhala said, without much interest. Bikkim smelt of the bathhouse, and herb-strong soap, and . . . maleness.

"We should head back to the landing beach," he suggested. "They roasted a pig."

"I'm not hungry."

"I'll walk you back to the caravanserai, then."

Pakdhala shook her head. "Bikkim? Just stay with me here for a while. I don't want to go back. I don't want a crowd. And I don't want to be alone."

"I . . . um. I snitched a flask of Varro's cousin's captain's *meadu*. I think you'd like it. It's got honey in it. Or is made from honey. Or something. Tastes sort of like the ghosts of flowers. A bit."

She found his hand.

"But I should walk you back. Your father'd kill me, if he thought—"

"Holla-Sayan," she pointed out, hearing herself saying the words, "sent you. And if you ask and I say yes, there's not much he can say. Sayan knows, I'm old enough to marry."

"I don't have much to offer you, Pakdhala."

She gave a single choking laugh. "More than I have. I'm sorry, Bikkim. I didn't mean anything about marrying. I mean, I wasn't saying you should . . . just . . ." She rubbed the sleeve over her face again, feeling her eyes prickling. His hand was so warm; she could feel all the bones in it, feel the blood racing, the life of him, such a fragile shell for the soul. So nearly lost, that night by the cataract. "I'd like it, if you wanted to just . . . stay here a while. With me. And . . . and see what happens. That's all."

His hand tightened around hers. There was *meadu* singing in his blood; it was perhaps a little unfair of her. He might have protested more, sober. Or not. Perhaps not.

"I will marry you," he said. "I always intended to. But the caravan's no place to bring up children, despite Holla managing it, and I don't have a home to give you."

Great Gods forgive her, she could not tell him here, now, she could not marry him, could not . . . would not likely live past this next desert crossing, because she could not pass by Lissavakail again, she could not leave the folk suffering, Kinsai made her see that, if nothing else. Let the wizard devour her and go determined, bloody-minded and fighting as a caravaneer could be, and take him by surprise, destroy him from within. Feeble hope. She had never become Attalissa, she was no true goddess, but maybe she could be, just once, all Pakdhala, and Holla-Sayan's daughter, who'd shot her first bandit when she was only twelve.

"Always intended?" she asked, as they went blundering off the road and up a sheep-shorn hillside, Bikkim near-blind in the dark, but courteously leading. Something to say, anything to say. "Even when I was a snotty little brat right off the mountain? Gaguush says I was terribly rude to everybody."

"Well . . ." he conceded. "You were a homely thing, fat as a spring chicken and with no manners. You've improved some since then."

"Only some?" They sat side by side, their backs against a solitary walnut tree. Bikkim handed her the flask and she sipped it cautiously. It burned in her throat. "Strong . . . not as bad as the grain-spirit they drink at home on the Western Grass, though."

"Improved a fair bit," he said generously, and with a knuckle brushed straggling hair, damp with river and tears, away from her face, leaned in to kiss her. His lips were unexpectedly soft, beard not so scratching as she had expected. She made herself relax, put her arms around him, cautiously. He squirmed and reached around her to take the flask away. "Don't be pouring good drink down my back, or I'll change my mind about your manners improving."

She laughed and leaned against him, felt her tension, at least some of it, burning away like mist in sunlight. "Bikkim?"

"What?"

"Thank you."

"For what?" They kissed again. She thought she did better, this time. Traded the flask back and forth.

"For not making me go back to town."

He groaned. "Don't remind me. I might be sensible."

"We're both too sensible, too much of the time," she said. "This is supposed to be our reckless youth."

"We don't have . . . the world's not so easy." The fear of Tamghat, for him, for his children . . . he was the only surviving sept-chief of the Battu'um. He had that to fear if he married, Tamghat finding out the Battu'um chiefs' line continued. If . . . what had Tihmrose said about counting the days . . . it won't keep you safe but it might at least make you luckier than Immerose, and remember there's quite a lot you can do that's just as enjoyable without ever . . . Tihmrose had given her quite a few details . . . she could try . . .

She didn't want to think that way, tonight. Tomorrow could look after itself, for once. She didn't want to think at all.

"We've got tonight."

Holla-Sayan lay on his back, staring up into the darkness of the tim-bered roof. Gaguush sighed in her sleep, tucked against his side. He patted her absently, clenched his fist and pushed at the Blackdog. It was pacing, snarling, whining . . . that was how he pictured it, at least, caged within him, and growing more frantic every hour that Pakdhala kept him shut out.

He wasn't necessarily in better shape himself. Angry, yes. Afraid. He'd never known her to act this way, and Kinsai, somehow, seemed the precipitating factor. And he couldn't damn her and go find her despite her words—the dog, for all it drove itself mad, madder, with anxiety, could not, as he found when he tried, disobey.

He had never expected that. Otokas had never experienced that force of will.

So he sent Bikkim, because Bikkim was standing near, at that moment, looking too old for his years, and lonely, and relatively sober. And if she were his daughter . . . he'd trust Bikkim alone with her. Or, no, he was very much afraid that he had just set up a situation that was . . . his mother'd kill him, no decent father would . . . they weren't even betrothed. At least, he'd trust that Bikkim and she would do each other no harm. He'd trust . . . The Blackdog overwhelmed him for a heartbeat, red rage, no one, nothing, could be allowed so near the goddess . . . Holla shoved the dog down. The whole gang was expecting the two of them to wed, eventually, the way Bikkim watched her, the way she smiled at him . . . when the two of them realized it.

Hells, he sent Bikkim, and not Tihmrose who was also still relatively sober, to spite the dog and the goddess and the damned temple and priestesses and Attalissa herself. Pakdhala had every right to Bikkim, if she wanted him and he wanted her.

But if it was Kinsai who had made her react with such fear . . . No, if she were harmed, the dog would know, shut out as it was. He would know.

But she feared something of Kinsai.

There had been a demon at the landing beach, when he went to Varro's cousin's feasting to find 'Dhala. A giant even among Northrons, seven feet tall, startling, even in firelight, because his face was cream-pale, not burnt ruddy or brown. He was dressed plainly for a Northron, in only a faded and somewhat ragged brown tunic, bare-legged, barefoot, no bright colours, no gold or amber at throat or wrist, not even a glass bead. Odd enough, a demon who seemed more or less human in appearance, but for a demon to come into a crowd of humans that way . . . definitely strange. He'd been eating and drinking and singing with the ship's crew, clapping the bridegroom on the back and making what seemed as if it had been some joke, because the bride had shrieked with laughter and pounded on his shoulder with her fist. Even the Blackdog could find nothing too much to fear in a demon, however far from his proper place in the world. It was Holla's suspicious mind that tried to make something of it, and watched the giant, even after he sent Bikkim off after Pakdhala. But the demon made no move to follow, showed no interest in Holla-Sayan himself beyond lifting his drinking horn in a wordless toast, when he caught his eye across the pit of glowing embers where the pig had roasted. Obviously seeing him for something other than entirely human, but he was not fearful as the desert demons were.

Holla-Sayan had left after that, but still felt uneasy, as though something watched him. As he walked away the demon had been chanting to an enthralled audience that included Varro. Some old Northron tale, by the rhythm of it. A demon bard? Something watched, though, a feeling, a scent . . . wizardry . . . it had disappeared.

He had thought, for a moment, there was a woman leaning on the seated giant's shoulder. But there were only shadows, even to the Blackdog's eye.

Maybe the lying Nabbani, who had watched him so slyly the whole time she chattered at Gaguush, had followed the gang to the landing beach.

Gaguush would hear no more of it, and if he made a greater issue . . . hard to explain why. He had nothing against wizards himself; it was the Blackdog hated the smell of them. But he distrusted that Nabbani woman in particular, because she snuck up to Gaguush in the teahouse with a spell of some sort on her, and she lied when she called herself only a diviner, weak and no wizard.

Dog? Father?

He had half a mind to ignore the goddess. Was too greatly relieved to do it. *Done sulking?*

I wasn't . . . I was. I'm sorry. I'm sorry I shouted. I'm sorry I hit you.

He snorted, and Gaguush grunted. *Hit me? You could call it that. Do that again and I'll put you over my knee like you're eight. It hurt. What happened?*

There was silence.

Kinsai . . . he prompted. *You warned me away from Kinsai.*

I've . . . dealt with Kinsai. I think. She won't touch you.

I can defend my own virtue, you know. At least, sometimes. Gaguush understands.

More silence.

It wasn't that? he asked.

She was threatening . . . she thought I should . . .

Should what?

She drew away for a moment, and the dog tensed.

Nothing. 'Dhala—Attalissa—was lying. To the Blackdog.

You don't want to take everything Kinsai says as the utter and entire truth, he suggested.

No. But she was still keeping him at a distance, shutting away thought, emotion . . .

She wasn't back in the caravanserai.

Bikkim with you? he asked guardedly.

Yes.

He forced the Blackdog down. *Ah. So you're all right, then?*

Embarrassment. Defiance, beyond whatever it was she still hid.

How many generations of Attalissa incarnate, and the temple women sworn to celibacy to honour her? *You're too young. But you're older than me and in the end you're not my daughter and maybe I don't have a right to object. Go away and let me sleep, brat. Now that I know you're safe and I can.*

It was interesting. In a rush.

He snorted, and that time Gaguush did wake up, at the sudden heave of his chest. *Sayan, don't tell Bikkim that. 'Interesting' is not what a man wants to hear, 'Dhala mine.*

Relief. *He wants to marry me.*

"Holla?"

I should hope so!

You know, no one would say that if I were a boy who'd gone off with my first woman.

Don't start talking like Immerose. She only manages to get by because she's got brothers and sisters willing to take the poor unwanted babes she keeps producing.

Go to sleep, Blackdog.

"What?" Gaguush asked.

"An amusing dream."

"Yeah? Was I in it?"

"Could have been."

"Oh?"

CHAPTER XXIV

Foxes yipped at one another somewhere over the hill, and bats darted, shadows against the night. The grey edge of dawn already lightened the sky. Pakdhala turned, pillowing her head against Bikkim's chest, stared into a darkness there was no escaping.

Hareh. His name had been Hareh. A young wizard, a wanderer, who came from Tiypur in the days of the death of its empire, after the wizards' wars there when the Westron gods died, long before there were kings in the north and the wars of the seven devils. He came into the Pillars of the Sky, and he stayed. Hers, her lover, when Lissavakail was a cluster of fishers' huts and the temple islet a place of grass and trees and the cave where they sheltered, laughing, from the rain. She was as Sera, then, or Kinsai, true goddess, no mortal body, taking physical form at will. And that was when . . . that was when the mad devil—or whatever it was, an animal in its madness, no rational creature, but a devil in its strength—the mad devil that hunted the peaks on the edge of her territory, possessing the body of one animal after another, turning them to monsters, bear and leopard and herd-dog all warped and changed, sent the folk pleading to their gods, to her, to Narva, to other gods of the peaks and goddesses of the mountain rivers. And when no power of any earthbound god could do more than drive it for a time to some other deity's land, Hareh recalled that he had read speculation, nothing more than philosophers' musings, in ancient books of Pirakul, on the binding of devils.

He was no great power, as wizards went. It would take more than he could ever hope to become to master a thing of such strength. And somehow, slowly, they formed their plan, by which she would gain the powers of a mortal wizard, a strength and a form the devil-creature would not fear, as it did not fear humans, and which could lure it into her heart, and strike, with human wizardry, to contain it . . .

But she lost him. Her Hareh, her clever, laughing man with the wanderer's heart that chased always after new horizons, new wonders. She was born, of a village fortune-teller, she drew power into herself, a wizard great as the children of Kinsai were . . . a child. Hareh was there to watch her grow, to teach her, to travel to Marakand and bring her books, the wisdom and secrets of the great Pirakuli and Nabbani scholars and mystics . . . he loved her. As a daughter. And so she lost him. And lost him doubly. She grew to adulthood and they fought the monster that roamed the mountains, a half-formed thing of bone and shadow. They bound it, as they had planned. And Hareh became the first Blackdog. But her heart had never changed, and so she vowed herself to celibacy, because she could not imagine, did not want to imagine, another man who could take Hareh's place. Though by then there was a fisherwoman he went to, in the nights, a widow with grown children, a woman of his own age, and she would not let herself resent it. She invited two of his stepdaughters to attend her on her island, and they were the first priestesses . . .

And the Blackdog . . . his stepson bore it after him, and then that man's nephew, and Hareh, she buried memory of Hareh away, buried all that pain, had to demonstrate that it was all worthwhile, until the mortality for which she sacrificed his love became the shape, the purpose of her existence. Until she forgot. And remembered, lying flesh to flesh beneath Bikkim, so young and strong and passionate, as Hareh had been when he first walked by her lake.

She squeezed her eyes shut, but the tears leaked through. She did not know the way back; she could not see it; she was trapped in her humanity till death freed her, only for the pattern she had laid so long ago to begin again. But the Blackdog, the true form of the thing flung on Tamghat unexpecting, unprepared . . . perhaps that could save her, save Lissavakail, save Serakallash, save Kinsai from the fate she feared as Tamghat grew and grew, devouring gods.

And that, she knew how to accomplish. That was simple, if she made it back to Lissavakail. Easy. But Holla-Sayan would be the first whose soul the monster devoured.

Morning came too early. Pakdhala watched the shadows of the grasses on Bikkim's face grow to sudden sharpness, fingers of golden light slanting over him. She kissed him, softly, felt him waking, his mouth opening to hers. When he opened his eyes she sat up away from him.

His smile faded, the old lines finding their place again around his eyes. Age that shouldn't have been his.

His finger touched her lips, moved away. It would be easier if he spoke, but he did not.

"We can't," she said, and found her voice cracked, unsteady with the tears she would not give in to. "We can't do this again. I mustn't. I shouldn't have. It wasn't right."

"We should marry," Bikkim said.

"We can't."

"You're young. Not too young. Holla-Sayan—"

"It's nothing to do with Holla-Sayan! It's . . . Bikkim, I can't. There are . . . things are different for me."

"Different? How? This idea of Gaguush's about apprenticing you to a wizard? You know I'd go with you. Wherever you went. I have no home to give you."

She shook her head. "I . . . Bikkim, give me time." A coward's way out.

He sat up. "I didn't . . . Sera, I didn't, last night, I didn't take you into anything you didn't—"

She put a hand over his mouth, to stop the words. "Bikkim, Bikkim, no. No! Don't—don't think that, ever. I . . . I wouldn't change what's done if I could, I'd never, I wish it could be like this, I wish this could be my life, with you, I do. But I can't be with you again. I mustn't."

"If I talk to Holla-Sayan—he'll say you're too young, and scare me half to death, and Gaguush'll sit on him, and he'll come round."

"My father'd be happier with you than anyone," she said hotly.

"He—" *knows*. Yes. "Bikkim. I'm not ready for marriage. If I was . . . there's no one else. You know that. No one but you. Just . . . give me time."

"Go back to yesterday?" he asked quietly.

"Yes."

"I can't."

"Please."

He wrapped his arms around her, pulled her close, half-dressed as they were. Great Gods, the scent of him, and the heat of his skin . . .

"If you ask me," he mumbled into her hair, "if that's what you honestly want, I will try. But don't just say *time*. Tell me—how long?"

"Till Marakand." She said it unthinking. Till Marakand. She would not be going to Marakand.

"Is that all?" He let her pull away to arms' length. Even smiled. "'Dhala, that's not so bad."

Pakdhala gave him a weak smile in return. "Months."

"A few months. I've been waiting years."

She shut her eyes, tears stinging.

"'Dhala?"

"Thank you." She yawned, rubbed her hands over her face, rubbed away the betraying gleam, she hoped. "Think we can sneak into the caravanserai, or is the whole gang going to be hanging out the gate watching for us?"

"Leering, Great Gods, I hope they're still sleeping off Varro's *meadu*."

"Father wasn't drinking, was he?"

"No. True. So we won't live to come to Marakand, and we don't need to worry about the future at all."

Pakdhala squeezed her eyes shut again. Slid her hand free when Bikkim kissed her knuckles, and crawled away to gather up scattered clothing.

"Spider in your boot," she observed, tossing it to him.

Bikkim shook the spider out, made a face at her. "Spider on your backside."

"There isn't."

"Made you look."

She threw a shirt at him, discovered too late it was hers, which rather spoiled the nonchalant morning-banter of the caravan campfire she had been trying to recapture, when she had to wrestle it back from him.

Dog. What do I tell him? I can't.

If you're old enough to decide to sleep with him, you're old enough to have thought of that, and to deal with it now on your own. But you don't, by the Old Great Gods, hurt my friend.

It's too late for that, Holla-Sayan. I didn't mean . . . he loves me.

So marry him and give him babies and let the damned lake look after itself. She felt him wince, shudder, some contest with the dog.

Dog, we have to go back to Lissavakail. Now. This trip.

A silence, in which Bikkim's worried hand found hers. She squeezed it, hated herself, then, giving him even that hope.

The Blackdog knew she was still no goddess in her strength.

And what do we do then? Die?

I know a way. Maybe.

I—we—see none.

I do. Maybe. I . . . I won't tell you yet. I need to think. Very faintly. *Trust me, Blackdog.*

CHAPTER XXV

"**A**nd the nineteenth set in the Palace of the Moon?"

"Realization of difficulty. Opposition to difficulty. Bending with difficulty."

"And what is the explanation of each?"

Ivah moved around behind the girl as she began to recite the commentary on the first of the nineteenth of the Palace of the Moon, word for word from the scroll she held closed in her lap. At first, Pakdhala had always wanted to put the commentaries into her own words, to explain the implications of the symbols as she understood them, to debate alternatives. That was the wretched mercenaries' upbringing, always looking to quarrel, opinionated without education. Ivah had been firm: that was not the correct way, not how her mother had taught her. Pakdhala had given her a doubtful look under which lurked an unfittingly adult and indulgent amusement, and had thereafter recited word for word. Ivah had feared she was going to run out of things she dared teach the girl—true spells and allowing her to throw the coins were right out—since she learned to read the Nabbani ideograms so unnaturally swiftly, but the gang worked the goddess like a bondservant. There was little time for study, though they let her off more once the road turned east away from the Kinsai'av and Pakdhala seemed to grow vaguely ill, which the gang all took for granted. She found the desert air hard, being half of mountain blood, one of the Marakanders explained when Ivah made some fishing comment about it. Ivah would have expected her to grow stronger as they drew nearer Lissavakail. But then, she would have expected the avatar to have died years before, when the Blackdog first carried her away. If she could have found out how it was done, how a goddess lived away from her waters, her father would have praised her. But she hadn't. Another disappointment to him, or it would be when he found out. He had not come to her dreams since the first night she joined the gang. Some storm had boiled up suddenly in her dreaming mind and his touch had vanished. She had woken sweating, shivering, to find Shaiveh and the goddess both sitting up in their blankets, staring.

"You were yelling," Shai had said accusingly, as if she'd done it on purpose. The goddess had said nothing. The others, woken as well, had made a few jokes about nightmares and gone back to sleep, and it had never happened again. Perhaps it was because she was so close to the goddess. Ivah just hoped Tamghat was going to do as he had promised, and have an escort of *noekar* waiting for her. Relays of fast horses might outrun the Blackdog, but she felt sick with fear when she thought of trusting her life to that alone. It was all very well for her father to say she could threaten to harm the goddess if the Blackdog attacked, but none of the stories suggested to her that the Blackdog was a thing you could reason with. It was a mad animal; her father himself had said that, on other occasions. And she did not think the Westgrasslander it had possessed was any too rational either.

Holla-Sayan—did Pakdhala really believe he was her father?—had been acting more and more irrational the further they went along the desert road, prowling around the camp all evening as though the watch were not to be trusted, refusing almost to sleep, disappearing into the desert at night, saying something followed them. The friction with the bad-tempered gang-boss had finally erupted into a shouting match three days ago, in which she called him a madman to his face and told him to damn well go back to the safe walls of his father's farm if he couldn't cope with the open sky. They hadn't spoken since, and that had set the goddess, who seemed to be of a withdrawn and glum disposition anyhow, into a bleak misery almost as silent. But she kept up her studies as though it was some distraction, a way of not having anything to do with the seething unhappiness in the rest of the gang. The Grasslander husband and wife didn't seem to be speaking either, and their son had come to blows with the young Serakallashi man, until one of the Stone Desert men knocked them both down.

The malaise was contagious. Shaiveh ignored her, flirting with the boy Zavel and the Northron Varro impartially, and grew increasingly sarcastic about the "pretty little camel-groom" when she did speak.

Was it possible Shai was jealous of the way she spent all her evenings with Pakdhala? Ivah couldn't imagine her being such a fool. How was she supposed to be a tutor to the girl if she didn't make some effort to teach? Bah.

There was Zavel coming towards them carrying cups of tea, and there came Shai, plucking one of the cups from his hand, putting an arm round his shoulders, leading him off. He looked over his shoulder at the goddess, caught Ivah's eye and flushed as he was steered away. Ivah scowled and began picking at the knotted yarn on one of Pakdhala's many braids. She was the one who ought to be jealous.

"What are you doing?" the girl demanded, at the first tug on a braid.

"I'm going to comb your hair. I don't understand you mercenaries. You fuss over your camels like they're fine horses or pet dogs, and you never bother to get the dust out of your own hair."

"I bathed every day all along the Kinsai-av," Pakdhala said indignantly. "And we always go to the bathhouse when we're in a decent town."

"I'm teasing." But it was true. "You have a headache, I can tell by your frowning. This will help. I'm not trying to seduce you or anything," Ivah added, which was effective in preventing further protest. Pakdhala was the sort of girl who would not want to insult Ivah by having Ivah think she had thought . . . and so on. Ivah untied the knotted yarn on the last braid and drew her fingers through the hair, gritty with desert dust, dirty as that of a herder bondman's brat. How could the Blackdog, knowing who she was, allow this? But he was just as dirty. She didn't notice that when she looked at him, just those deadly eyes, watching her, always watching her. It had taken the goddess herself losing her temper with him, yelling at him to stop being a fool, there was no harm in learning a little of what Ivah had to teach, to stop him appearing almost from nowhere the moment Ivah came near the girl. He still watched, but from a distance.

The braids ravelled out, Ivah took her own tortoiseshell comb from her coat pocket and began on the goddess's hair, working her way up from the bottom. What a mess. The Serakallashi paused on his way past to the well, Nivlan's well, they called it, though Ivah didn't think such an insignificant scrape in the desert could really have a goddess. Pakdhala turned her head to look at him, wincing at the pull on her hair, then looked down, unrolling the scroll once more. Bikkim dropped his own gaze, walked on, his face closed. Pakdhala raised her eyes again to follow him.

"You like him," Ivah said sympathetically. They spent so much time looking at one another, those two, and yet they seemed almost to work at never being alone together. "I don't see why he can't be kinder, spend more time with you. Your father can't watch you every moment, and anyway, he must expect you'll marry someday."

Some of the gang seemed to assume the two were a couple already, but that was like her father always trying to pair her off; it didn't mean there was anything to what they snickeringly hoped. Ivah hoped so, for the man's sake.

The goddess merely sighed and rolled her shoulders, as if Ivah hadn't spoken. "That is nice. Thank you."

"You need to take more pride in your appearance. A woman's hair is her glory, you know." That was something An-Chaq had used to say.

"Is it? What's a man's hair, then?"

"Just something to keep the sun off his head when he loses his hat."

Pakdhala looked over her shoulder, laughing, which she hardly ever did, and combed a lock forward with her fingers, started braiding it again. A shame it had to be done. Her face was quite pretty, framed in the rippling soft waves. Tamghat should see her like that, not looking such a scruffy, dirty little creature. Though Ivah supposed she wasn't any better. Baths. Two days, at most, and she could *bathe*, and have servants wash her hair *properly*, with perfumed soap and hot water. And if she wasn't dead, her father would have to be proud.

Ivah dropped the comb, snarled with a rat's nest of soft black hairs, into her pocket.

Elsinna left her pony in the stable under the rock and headed into the dark cave of the house. She had been hoping Attavaia might be visiting. The so-called wife of Tsuzas—and Elsinna would have paid a great deal to know just how much that marriage was a play to fool her brother's mad god and how much it was something more—must have been and gone. Attavaia's wanderings among the scattered groups that watched and waited, prayed and trained, for the day of Attalissa's return were unending.

"Elsinna—good. Come stir the curds."

"Elsinna, did you find me any bluewort?"

"Elsinna, you're home at last. The boys have run back to their father in the village and Tsuzas won't go and get them. You can persuade them, they listen to you."

"Tell that one—" Oh good, Grandfather wasn't speaking to her again. "Tell her, her duty lies here, and after she gets my heirs home she can stop chasing after the pervert priestesses of Attalissa and do some honest work for a change, if she hasn't forgotten what a loom is for . . ."

Elsinna ignored them all, headed deeper into the dark, and pushed through the curtain into Tsuzas's private chamber. Two cats sprawled on the bed, but no Tsu sleeping off a headache, or pretending to. Someone must be out with the yaks. Maybe she should have looked for him in the far pastures first. She hadn't counted sisters on her way in to see who was missing. She flung herself on the bed. "Elsinna?" her youngest sister carolled in the passageway. She wrapped her arms over her head. It was a rule. No one violated Tsuzas's private chamber. They wouldn't look for her here.

She should have taken Tsuzas's urging and Attavaia's offer, and made her vows as a sister of Attalissa. But it had been too late, even when Attavaia first came to them. She was too old, a wild pony of the mountains and she could not bring herself to bend her head to a bridle, to vow service and obedience. To give up her freedom to wander where she chose, when she chose.

If only she could choose never to come back.

Her fist hit the quilt, and offended cats scattered. The Tamghati were demanding ever more of the Narvabarkashi miners. Two more men were dead in rockfalls, and children were being used to carry out the baskets of rubble. Slaves. Narvabarkash village was under the lordship of a *noekar*-lord, its people her bondfolk, and that was to say no more than slaves, owing her all the profits of their labour. And Narva did nothing. There had been more earth tremors in the past years than Elsinna remembered as a child, but what did that do? Crack the mud and dung plaster of the village houses, tumble loose stones in the mines, wake babies howling and frighten the dogs. Tsuzas couldn't even say if it was Narva's doing or not. Or wouldn't. Poor Tsutsu, so haunted, not by Narva himself, but by fear of going mad as their father had, or being burnt away to an empty shell like their uncle, dead last year, mercifully, though poor Great-grandmama had gone too, in a round of winter coughs.

The passage sounded empty of sisters. Elsinna peered out, to be certain, before she set off down the tunnel that women were not supposed to take, looking for Tsuzas, a lamp purloined from a wall-niche to light her way. There was a new widow in Narvabarkash village who was being thrown out of her cottage and garden-plot by her father-in-law, with a little girl and a new baby on the way to feed, and no one seemed willing to do anything to help her. The *noekar*-lord never bothered sitting in judgement on such disputes, as should be her duty if she was going to call herself their mistress. Elsinna had taken the woman to their sister's estranged husband, the bronze-caster. Now that the boys were living with him—thank you, dear sister, she had known all about that and made sure the boys had sense to take their clean shirts and drawers with them—they could call her a housekeeper and say the presence of the boys kept all chaste and decent. If it did not, more joy to both the widow and her brother-in-law. It was amazing he hadn't taken another wife before now.

But she wanted Tsu to tell her she had done right, Tsu to go wrathfully, as she dared not, to that young widow's father-in-law, and tell him he offended his god in his lack of charity and family love, and put the fear of Narva's curses in him. Tsu could do that and not have the man run whining to the Tamghati. They feared him, feared Narva's madness, too much.

The cavern of the heart of the god was cold and echoing. Water dripped, a slow, spine-crawling music, as Elsinna followed the worn path through the fangs of stone. No sign of Tsuzas.

The chunk of red sandstone sitting in the water's edge wore a crust of greenish-white mineral. Narva trying to claim what wasn't his, as ever. They talked about Tamghat plotting to devour Attalissa's life and not even Tsuzas would admit that Narva was no better, consuming the souls of his priests. She drew her knife to scrape the crust away. Not even Tsu knew she came here and did that; she had, though, ever since Attavaia told her how the goddess of Serakallash had hidden her soul in the lump of desert rock.

"In case something happens to Tsuzas and me both," the young Old Lady of the free temple had said. "Someone else needs to know. Imagine being trapped in a stone forever, with no way out . . ."

The blade slipped against the ball of her thumb. "Pox," Elsinna muttered, the most cursing she dared in a place so holy. She held her hand near the lamp, sitting on the floor at the pool's edge. A drop of blood plinked into the water, spreading and swirling. She'd left a smear on Sera's rock, too.

"Sacrilege," she said, sucking her thumb. "Profaning the place with my female presence." Though Attavaia slunk down here whenever she came to the mines of Narva, checking, Elsinna supposed, that the goddess hadn't dissolved away or been used by Grandfather to repair a corral—not that Grandfather ever defiled his priestly hands with grubby labour.

She felt dizzy. It certainly wasn't that deep a cut. She'd had worse from brambles. Her ears thrummed, as if her head had been plunged under water. She put a hand out to steady herself, suddenly uncertain of the ground beneath her. It seemed too far distant. It had become a wall, leaning over her. Water rose up and poured down her nose, her throat. The mountain dissolved in fire, white and red melting, twining, running together. Her mouth tasted of copper and slime, and words shaped themselves in her own voice, thick and slurring, and underneath—such a morass of anger and heart-pounding fear, such a howling tumult, as of a winter's storm-wind trapped in endless caverns. Stone walls, a stone burial cist such as they laid the shattered bones of their dead in after the lammergeiers and the lesser scavengers had done their cleansing, and there was no way out, no way out, sealed beyond reach of the world, only he dreamed, he dreamed, as they walked over the hills, and he woke to rage and claw and break the stones beyond which he was sealed, and slept to dream again, rags and tattered streamers, vision painted on water, flowing, time was, time would be . . . *Attalissa is drawn back to her lake and Ghatai's death or the end of all hope comes in the stone sword. Sera must return to her spring. The time for waiting is past. The dreams are over and the devil in the west will destroy us all. Wake! Wake! Wake!*

Elsinna lay on her side in the shallow water. She coughed suddenly, water in her mouth, in her ear, pushing herself upright. Her face stung and her head pounded; her tongue felt stiff and foreign against her teeth. Had she fallen, taken a wrong turn, had there been another tremor?

Oh. No, no. Not her. It couldn't happen to her, he couldn't take her. It was Tsuzas's curse, the one benefit to being born female under her grandfather's contemptuous rule. Their brother was their sacrifice, their safety, set aside and apart from his birth.

The rage, the sickening anxious fear, lingered in her blood. Somewhere in the back of her mind the god still clawed and pounded at the walls of his madness, the suffocating grave, before sinking away again. She could yet taste him.

On hands and knees, she dragged herself away from the pool, joints loose, staggering and weak. She pulled herself to her feet, using a stalagmite for support, and gulped down an urge to be sick. Simply moving made her head pound worse, which should not have been possible.

Sera to her spring. That seemed simple fact, lodged in her mind as solid and undeniable as the need—Great Gods—to change her clothes. She stank.

Sera to her spring. She went back to the water's edge and found the floor jarringly uneven, though she had never noticed it so before. The stone—she had dropped it in the water, and her knife. She got the knife back into its sheath on the third try, clutched the stone under her arm, and found the trembling of her hand shook the lamp so that the shadows jittered and darted around her like some monstrous swarm of insects.

Elsinna made it to the tunnel before she threw up, damn, Great Gods damn him, and she wiped her mouth on her sleeve. Her shirt was torn, wet from the pool and bloody from a grazed arm, and her trousers were better not thought of. She'd wet herself. Not that it would show, she was soaked to the skin, but she knew, and she smelt it still, and she couldn't have said if it was shame or rage at the indignity of such loss of control that made tears prick at her eyes, or just the sick thudding of her head. Worst the first time, Tsuzas had told her once, a confession of things he ought not to have been telling her at all. Bad enough after, but the first time, it takes your whole body . . . he'd been sick for a week with fear of the next. Until it came, and the next.

She could have drowned, falling into the water like that in a seizure.

Damn Narva, but there wasn't going to be a next time. Sera must return to her spring. Well, the wretched lump of rock wasn't about to sprout legs and walk.

But she needed food for the journey, and she needed to recall all Attavaia had ever said of her allies in Serakallash, and most of all she needed clean clothes, and not her own from the chamber where a flock of sisters could not help but notice as she staggered among their shared beds and clothes-chests, sodden and battered and soiled.

"Elsinna, is that you in there?"

Her stumbling search through Tsuzas's belongings for clean garments had betrayed her. The lid of the clothes-chest had fallen with a bang. Her eldest sister pushed past the curtain. "You shouldn't—what are you doing?"

"Changing my clothes." She'd found a bottle of some sort of lowland strong spirits, sweet and spicy, and a swallow of that seemed to help settle both her stomach and her head. Tsu's idea of medicine, maybe.

"In a man's room." Teral wrinkled her face in prudish disapproval. "For the god's sake, those are Tsu's drawers! Don't you have any sense of decency?"

"No. But since you're here, you can do something for me."

"What? Elsinna, what have you done to your face? And your arm—and your hip! You're all scraped up. Did you fall on the rocks?"

"Something like that. Listen, I need you to give Tsuzas a message." Elsinna pulled a shirt over her head, tied the neck, and rolled up the overlong sleeves, hauled on trousers that fit better than she had expected, once she pulled the string of the waist tight.

"He's up the mountain somewhere. Tell him yourself when he gets back."

"Teral . . ." Elsinna crossed the room and took her sister's hands. "Listen. It's very, very important. Narva told me I—"

"Narva! Don't be silly. Narva doesn't come to anyone but Tsuzas. Or Grandfather, sometimes. He certainly doesn't come to women."

"Well, he did," Elsinna said. "Maybe he's finally getting over his snit at Attalissa. Take it from me, that's nothing to be glad about."

"It's not because of Attalissa that he doesn't trust women. It was a daughter of the priests betraying the mines to the sisters of Attalissa that set him against women," said Teral, more tartly than Elsinna would have expected. "*We* were holy once too, you know. There are priestesses in some of the wall paintings, as you'd know if you ever took any interest in your inheritance at all."

"Damn my inheritance. *You* say that after you've had damned Narva shoving all his poisonous nightmares into your body!"

"You were sick," Teral said suddenly, wrinkling her nose. She scowled at the heap of clothing Elsinna had flung into a corner for Tsuzas to find, lucky him. "Elsinna, what happened?"

386

"Bloody Narva happened, I told you."

"What? You mean—like Tsuzas? Oh, Elsinna, how horrible."

"Funny no one ever says that about poor Tsu. Just listen. I'm leaving." She grinned crookedly. "At last, as I've always threatened. Tell Tsuzas—or Attavaia, whichever you see first, tell them Narva says it's time and I've taken Sera home."

"You've taken Sera home," Teral repeated obediently. "Who's Sera?"

"Never mind."

"You're making this up."

"Great Gods, don't be such a fool." She picked up the lump of sandstone, wrapped in a tattered shawl. What business had a mountain woman on the road to Serakallash? A man, maybe? Some Tamghati loved her and left her and she was looking for him in Serakallash? Or maybe she should say she had dyestuffs to trade? That was what Attavaia often used as her excuse on the road—a trader in mountain dyeworts.

"I'll need every bit of dye-herb you've collected, Teral," she said. "Sorry."

"We're out of bluewort," Teral said, which wasn't actually an argument. "That wife of Tsuzas's took all I had when she was here last week. You were supposed to bring some."

She could feel Narva like the pressure of a headache behind her eyes, pushing. "I have to go. Now."

But Elsinna paused and hugged Teral in the doorway, kissed her mother and Auntie without a word in the main room. Odds were she wouldn't be coming back.

CHAPTER XXVI

The wind muttered around the braided dunes, rattling grasses and the dry leaves of the pistachios.

Bad weather coming. There was a yellowish cast to the sky. To the south, the great serried towers of the Pillars of the Sky faded in and out of view, their blue and white heights swimming behind the haze. To the east there were curdled clouds. Dust and the setting sun tinged them red. Late summer, and not the season for storms in the Red Desert.

"Storm coming," Mikki said, as if Moth might not have noticed. He sniffed the air, sneezed. "You doing this, wolf?"

"No." She considered, feeling the wind herself, with other senses. The bone-horse pranced, foot to foot. She thumped his shoulder with her fist. "Stand. You're not afraid of storms, you're centuries dead, you foolish great beast. No, it's no natural weather. It's his."

And it might be aimed at her, she could not say. Tamghiz had come tearing into his unfortunate daughter's dreams as she drifted there, delicately fishing for some hint as to what the young wizard meant to do to the avatar she had worked herself so close to, and Moth had flung him violently away before he could know her. She hoped. Hurt him. She hoped. She at least had the grace to creep gently, knowing herself a thief and a trespasser. Tamghiz pushed in and took over as though the child's—woman's—mind was his own bedchamber, leaving the scars of his tracks through all her thoughts, so that she carried the weight of him everywhere and cringed in her own mind, knowing herself dominated and broken to a master without ever being aware she knew.

Mikki made a noise that was all bear, a grumbling growl deep in his throat. "And the lake-goddess and the little wizard are gone into Serakelda."

There was no native goddess in the spring at Serakelda—Serakallash, to give it its proper desert name. It was a hollow skull of a place, the living spirit gone. They had heard as much at the Landing, but it was strange to feel it. Nothing to defend the town against . . . whatever came. Including herself.

"Come." She set foot in stirrup, swung herself to Storm's back. "There's little time."

"For what?"

"To get as close to Serakallash as we can while you can still run fast enough to keep up."

"Whose idea was it to travel so deep in the desert?"

"That would be us trying to stay out of reach of the Blackdog sniffing after us, remember?"

"Ah, was that it? And this morning was the last of the water?"

"Yes."

"Any chance they brew ale in Serakelda?"

"Probably not."

"And she expects me to gallop all the way there before sunset," he remarked to the world in general. "Run, in all this fur."

"I could shear you, like a sheep."

"Great Gods, princess, just you try." He was already loping away. "Anyhow," he called back, "thought you were in a hurry."

Moth gave Storm a dig of her heels.

Pakdhala curled sleeping like a child under a heap of coats and blankets in one of the many empty rooms of Master Mooshka's caravanserai, though it was early in the evening and Thekla had not yet called them to supper. Most of the gang had dispersed, anyway, to what gossip and good cheer were to be found in the anxious eating-houses of Serakallash. The merchants had seen their goods put under lock and key and had gone off with fellow Northrons who had taken a house, setting up as goldsmiths under the patronage of Ketsim, the Lake-Lord's governor of Serakallash. Ivah and Shaiveh were among those who had gone out, which was some comfort, because Holla-Sayan did not think he was going to be able to sleep quietly in the caravanserai. The dog paced at the back of his mind. Something was coming, running before the storm.

Let me sleep, 'Dhala told him, when he tried to shake her awake, to take her to Thekla, who would at least see the girl got some broth and sops down, if she could stomach nothing else. *I need rest, nothing else. Tomorrow . . . tomorrow we go to the mountains.*

Tomorrow? You're not ready. He sat back on his heels. *You can't do anything yet. We should wait another year.*

Wait and wait and wait. I can't wait. He's hunting me, dog. He's coming closer and closer. He'll find me soon, and I can't wait for that and doom the gang. I have to face him, defeat him now or die trying, die forever and stop him taking the lake.

How? Tell me how you think we have any chance of defeating him.

Trust me. That was all she would ever say. "I'm *sorry*," she said aloud, opening her eyes. "I'm *sorry*, Holla-Sayan. You have to trust what I see." Not Father. Not dog. "Go away, let me sleep." She tried on a weak smile. "You know what it's like here. My bones have turned to stone and my muscles to porridge."

She raised barriers between them even as she slid again into sleep, walling herself off from any effort the Blackdog might make to reach her mind. In all the long years, she had never cut herself off so, never shut the dog away as she had this spring and summer.

Fear? Secrets even the dog must not know? Holla-Sayan blew out the lamp and left her, shutting the door behind him, wishing he could lock it against whatever threat came. There were too many threats and the Blackdog could only be in one place at a time.

"Immerose." He caught at the Marakander's sleeve. "Where's Bikkim?"

"Went up to the roof, I think."

Holla nodded, headed for the stairs to the upper floor and the ladder to the roof.

"Hey, Holla, say thank you, you graceless ploughboy."

He waved a hand over his shoulder.

"And anyway, you need to let the pair of them sort out their own problems . . ."

Bikkim, as he'd hoped, was alone, leaning on the parapet, looking down over the town.

"Storm's coming," Holla said needlessly, joining him, and they both turned to the north, where the sky hung thick and brown. "Bikkim. I need to ask you something."

"Do you?" Bikkim scratched his chin. "If this is about Pakdhala—"

"Yes."

"I do mean to marry her, if she'll have me. She's not a little girl anymore, you have to—"

"Bikkim—don't. I don't care, I don't . . . it doesn't matter. Just *listen*." He knew the gang was half-convinced he was sliding into madness; he knew he was starting to look it, the twins had cornered him to tell him so and Judeh had taken to standing over him to see he remembered to eat in the evenings. Even 'Dhala, so withdrawn since her abrupt decision to return to Lissavakail, had ordered more than once, revenge for all his nagging over the years when her strength failed her in Serakallash: *Father, dog, eat. Sleep. Don't let the dog make you ill.* And, *There's nothing out there. You've been seeing shadows since At-Landi, but Kinsai would have warned us. And Ivah is harmless, don't start on about her again. I like her. You're letting the dog's worry about returning and its fear of wizards become an obsession.*

"I'm listening."

"Will you look after Pakdhala for me?"

"What? Great Gods, Holla—" Bikkim put a hand on his arm and he flinched. "You're not *that* ill. Are you?"

"*Tonight.* Now. Guard her tonight."

"Oh." Bikkim hesitated. "Why? From what?"

"Ivah."

"Holla, I don't think Ivah has that sort of interest in her. Shaiveh wouldn't stand for it, for one thing, and—"

Holla-Sayan seized him by the shoulder. "Shut up. Listen." Sayan help him, he could hardly hear his own words over the drumming, rising need of the dog to be running, to be hunting that . . . whatever it was . . .

the presence that stalked them, trailing all the way down from At-Landi, always out of reach, always vanishing, fading into grass and stone and sky like it was a demon of the wilds, which it was not, it was hot metal and cold stone, it was . . . he did not know, and the dog could not remember.

"Ivah lies, she lies in everything. She's a wizard, not some petty diviner, no matter what she claims. Wizardry made Gaguush take her on. She's fenced about with spells so I can't see beyond the surface of her, her or Shaiveh, and she has allies. There's something out there, in the desert, and it's coming closer. Now. This evening."

"Holla . . ." Bikkim tried to pry clenched fingers out of his shoulder. "Holla-Sayan, let go, dammit, that hurts."

Holla backed away, arms wrapped close against doing any more harm. "Just . . . guard her tonight. She's sleeping down in the west corner alcove, by the gate. Don't let them near her, the wizard and her shadow. Your word you will."

"Yes, all right."

"Trust you," Holla said indistinctly. "It doesn't want to, but *I* do." Great Gods, but he was making no sense and Bikkim was staring. "Stay with her. Now."

"Yes."

"Good." He pushed past Bikkim, stumbling, hardly able to hold himself together, to keep the dog from hurling itself into the world. Almost fell down the ladder, headed out, blind to everything but the barred door in the gate. A woman stood there, between him and the door. *No*, he told the dog. *No threat, no harm, just Mistress Jerusha and she's opening the door.*

"What is it? Who are you?" Jerusha Rostvadim demanded of who-ever was beyond. A woman, a tired horse, he smelt that much. Smelt the mountains, high stone and swift water: she was clothed in yaks' wool, dyed with mountain dyes. Smelt . . . the lingering touch of some god. The dog growled and he seized it back from the edge of the world.

"I'm a . . . a cousin of Sister Vakail's," the woman outside said. "Are you Jerusha?"

"Might be. Sister Vakail has a lot of cousins. Which one are you?"

"Elsinna. From Narvabarkash. I've brought you the stone that wasn't buried with Enneas."

"What?"

"Please, let me in, before someone sees me."

He had known an Enneas once. Two little girls in trouble for filching honeycomb from the larder and his sister furious because he laughed and took them up to see the new calves as he had promised anyway, spoiling them when they should have been punished . . .

That was Otokas.

"What are you talking about?" But Jerusha was pulling the door open and a mountain woman, dressed like a man, or so they'd have said in the mountains, dragged in a brown pony. She grabbed for her knife, seeing him at Jerusha's back, and then her eyes widened. Holla shouldered past them both before she could say anything. The caravanserai master's daughter snatched at his sleeve.

"You—Holla-Sayan—there's a storm coming. Better stay in." He shook his head mutely without turning around, but he could feel her scowl and exasperated shrug. "Then remember the damned curfew and get back before sunset. You don't want to end up in the gaol and your mistress'll tan your hide if she has to bail you out."

She slammed the door behind him. The bar thudded home.

"*Who* was *that*?" the mountain woman demanded. "His eyes—"

"His eyes? I suppose he's handsome enough, if you like that sort, which personally I don't. A mad caravaneer. All mercenaries are a bit mad, but sometimes that one's more than a bit. Leave the pony, I'll send someone to see to it. You'd better come into the house and explain what in the cold hells you're babbling about."

There was no one in the street, no open gate in any of the blind walls of the caravanserais. The dog poured into the world and Holla let it run, tracking that scent that was not a scent, metal and stone and ancient fire, tracking an echo of a memory of ice.

He was losing his long fight with the dog. He had thought they had a truce, a balance, until this thing began to stalk them. Its presence

393

woke him sweating in the night, seeing a bear-crested helmet livid with reflected flame and eyes burning that were no reflection at all. Now the dog would rise up, pulling him down, drowning him, so that man's thoughts and man's reason were swamped, as they had not been, not entirely, even in the times they had gone after bandits. There were nights now he remembered only brokenly, if at all. Their truce held insomuch as the dog was willing to let him back, in the end, when they did not find the thing it hunted.

If whatever stalked them was Tamghat's ally, why had it not acted? If it was not, why did it follow? Why did it only follow, and fade away elusive as a dream, leaving him with nothing but animal scent and old bone, random on the wind? And why had damned Kinsai said nothing as it trailed them down the east bank?

Maybe they were mad, he and the dog together, and the thing they chased only an illusion, a twisted memory of Tamghat, a fever-dream, nothing more.

It was not slipping away this evening. It burned before them in the air, the twisted thing that had come against Lissavakail, fire and blood and stone, old bone, coming, pursuing Attalissa. A woman, a horse, something that seemed to fade in and out of vision. *Wait* . . . He was lost. The dog hurled itself against it and hit the ground, rolling under a blow that swept it from its feet, a weight great enough to hold it pinned.

The dog grew horse-sized, twisted, teeth clashing, taste of blood and then only fur as the great bear reared free and struck again, massive body crushing the dog and a paw pressing its head into the ground, so it snapped and snarled and choked on dusty earth.

"What in the cold hells is it?" someone asked.

A sword bit the earth, a yard from the dog's frenzy. A crack in the air, breathing cold. A road into a landscape of white sky, black stone, black ice, seams of molten red rock. The dog's shock froze it still and Holla dragged himself, not into the world, but at least out of the morass of rage and panic that surrounded the dog's core.

"Thought that might get his attention." A woman squatted down before him, just out of reach, a long Northron sword across her knees. "Now . . . Hah. They said the goddess was guarded by a demon."

"Or abducted by one."

"Ya, but you tell me what this is." They weren't speaking any language he knew. The dog heard, and understood.

"Bad-tempered?"

"That too."

"I can't hold him much longer, wolf. Night's about on us and he weighs more than I will."

The thing that looked like a woman and was not Tamghat considered him, reached a hand. The dog snapped and should have taken that hand off, but she was faster and her touch burned, resting between his eyes.

"Lie still. Let me see what you are. Both of you." *I don't mean any harm to your goddess. I want the one who calls himself Tamghat.*

It didn't occur to the dog to doubt. It sighed, a long and weary sigh, fell back to something approaching mortal dog-size, and lay still. Then it stretched its head back, lying prone on the earth, until it pressed its nose against the woman's wrist. It felt like . . . it felt it had all unexpected turned a foreign corner and found it was home. She ran her hand over its muzzle, let it lie. The dog whined.

"Great Gods be damned." She whispered it, sat back away from him. "Mikki . . . let him go."

"Are you sure?" The bear . . . was a man, shaking unkempt hair out of his eyes, a man naked and quite unselfconscious about it, who rolled from the dog and knelt by the woman, watchful, his shoulder welling blood.

The dog let Holla-Sayan go then. He dragged a rasping breath that he felt in every rib.

The man—the black-eyed Northron giant from At-Landi—offered a hand as he propped himself up, the world spinning, but it was the woman held him with her eyes. Another Northron, younger than him, old as his mother—he couldn't place her. Pale hair that could have been age or youth's silver-gilt beauty. Old eyes, though, with fire living behind them.

"Why does it believe you?" For a dizzy moment, that was his most pressing thought. "It never believes me. Why should *I* believe you? You're the same as Tamghat."

The man snorted. "Caravan-man, you should try not to insult people who, you might notice, aren't cutting your fool head off." He spoke Grasslander now, fluently, but with a thick accent, and clasped his hand over his bleeding shoulder. "You could have tried asking questions before biting, you know. You'll make more friends that way."

"Believe me because my sibling does." Her Grasslander might have been native.

"What?" He felt slow, stupid, exhausted from weeks of little sleep and too long fighting the dog. He had missed something.

"Sibling?" the bear-man said to the woman. "I thought the stories of the Blackdog put it back well before the war of the seven devils, before the kings in the north."

"That wasn't the first war the Great Gods fought in this world. Long and long ago—forgotten long and long ago, and the defeated forced back into the cold hells for eternity." The woman switched back to Grasslander. "But you—"

"Devils?" Holla asked, desperately, the dog still following the Northron speech. "What?"

"The soul possessing you is what the world calls a devil. It's little more than a ghost feeding off you, Holla-Sayan, and that ghost is bound in such spells . . . But that is what it was, once."

"No."

"Ask it, if you won't believe me."

"I can't. It doesn't think that way. It doesn't . . . it doesn't have conversations. It doesn't have *words*."

"Perhaps not. Its name is gone, it's wounded beyond recovery, there's only a fragment of its heart remaining and that is lost to it, but it survives."

Holla shook his head.

"Think of the wreck of a man returned from battle, a body that doesn't die but lingers, a soul that seems mostly to have fled to the

Great Road to the heavens. Your dog is that. It was a terrible battle. Powers loose in your world that had no place or right to walk it."

He felt empty, purged of some great weight. The relief was the dog's: this stalking power was no threat to the goddess. And Great Gods, Holla was so weary. That a devil soul lived parasite in him was too much; he had no energy to worry about it.

"Then I'm going back to town. If it's Tamghat you're after, come with me. Pakdhala says we're going up to Lissavakail tomorrow and she won't tell me what she means to do. She can't fight him."

"Why not?"

"Because she's weak. She's a human girl. And I can't fight him. His warriors killed me, last time. Killed the man Otokas, I mean. He threatened to take the dog himself."

"He won't," the woman said grimly, and she stood, sheathing her sword, the steel one, before taking the stone sword from the earth. A web of frost crackled on the dry grass. "This is Lakkariss, Holla-Sayan, and it could destroy either of us, being what we are. One way or another, I will see Tamghiz Ghatai does not devour the Blackdog." She sheathed the sword in a scabbard on the horse's shoulder. He saw night sky through the horse, night and bone. It snorted at him.

"Your mistress isn't going to like me." For a hazy moment he thought she meant Gaguush. "But then, I don't think much of slavers, so we can all dislike one another equally."

"What are you?" he asked desperately.

"*Who* is the more courteous question. My name's Moth, these days. This is Mikki. Mikki, put on some clothes?"

The man laughed, shrugged into a tunic from the horse's baggage, and unstrapped a long-hafted axe, which he rested first on one shoulder, then, wincing, the other. The woman muttered under her breath and took him by his front, pulled down the shoulder of his tunic, and tied a pad of cloth over the bite. The man grinned sheepishly, winked at Holla.

"Who, then?" Holla frowned, climbed to his feet. He felt like he'd fallen off a mountain, or that one had fallen on him. "Tamghiz Ghatai—why do I know that name?"

"Fireside tales, caravan-man," Mikki said. "In the days of the first kings in the north there were seven devils—"

"*Sayan.* I thought they were imprisoned, those seven."

"Some have escaped," Moth said.

"*You've* escaped. Which one are you and if you're planning to kill him, what do you mean to do after?" Are you a threat to the goddess, is the dog deluded? He did not ask that, but she saw it anyway.

Moth hesitated, then, Northron formality, touched a hand to her chest. "Ulfhild Vartu," she said. "I've given up making emperors, Holla-Sayan. I make sagas, these days. Histories, when the damned Great Gods let me. And I will stop Ghatai making himself a god of the earth. If I can."

"And if you can't?"

"Then he will consume both of us and your mistress as well, and raise the earth against the heavens. There may be no more left of either than that wasteland along the Kinsai'aa." She considered. "Time was, I'd have welcomed that."

"Not now?"

She grinned. "Westgrasslander—you're not the only one with a farm to go home to."

"Not much of one," the bear-man muttered. "I think we should move house, wolf, to someplace with a shorter winter. Take land in the Hravningasland."

"Too many neighbours. Too many kinsmen."

"You see?" Mikki asked him plaintively. "I'm condemned to a hermitage."

"You're a demon," Moth said. "You like wilderness."

"I'm a carpenter, princess, and I like people." They had fallen into Northron again. The dog found the banter incomprehensible and ceased to pay attention to the words. No threat here, and Pakdhala was alone. Holla-Sayan sighed and let the dog flow back into the world, turned to lope south. They could follow if they would. He didn't care. The dog did, though, very much, the only emotion it had ever had that was not centred on the goddess. But its thought ran on the goddess again, its goddess left alone with only a weak mortal man to defend her, the enemy whose shape it had known, all unaware, but known as the chick knows to cower from the broad-winged shadow in the sky, all too close. But under that, under that . . . some smouldering heat that was rage and hope and longing—it was oblivion it yearned after. The dog wanted to die and saw, at last, death within its reach.

Moth and the ghost stallion caught up with him. Mikki, warm demon heat in the dog's awareness, earth and root and a forest in his blood, jogged behind. The dog settled into a pace he could match.

The dog, for the first time in its existence, wanted company.

Come sunset, fast horses would be waiting for Ivah at Mooshka's gate with a warrior escort, Ketsim, the governor of Serakallash, had assured her. And still her father did not contact her. Waking or sleeping, he had not come to her mind since that night of nightmare. Ivah wished she could feel it was trust, confidence in her, but she more than half-expected it was the opposite, and that once she brought the goddess to Ketsim's house, the *noekar* would take Pakdhala, on Tamghat's orders, riding at messenger speed with relays of fast horses, to be the one to hand the goddess over and bask in her father's satisfaction.

Tamghat only needed Ivah to cast the spell. And if she failed that—better not to go back to him at all, better to take poison and die like a failed Nabbani assassin.

At times like this, she desperately needed a god to pray to. Any god.

Mother Nabban, Father Nabban . . . how could she pray to them, she who had never been closer than she was now to the great empire ruled by . . . who? Her grandfather, an uncle, a cousin?

Great Gods above, let this work. One did not pray to the Old Great Gods for little things. They were life and death, salvation and damnation. So was this.

Great Gods, let me succeed.

Great Gods, let me survive.

Ivah closed her eyes and ran the thin braid, hard with many knots, between her fingers. She could feel the power in it that way, the faint sparking warmth of it. Each knot, square or twisted or spiralling, part of a larger pattern, corpse-hair and hair of the living incarnation woven together, words woven in, such power as she had never felt flow past her lips before.

She opened her eyes. Shaiveh was watching, crouched with her back against the door, sword across her knees and her eyes gleaming in the light of the mutton-fat lamp. She said nothing.

"I'm ready," Ivah said hoarsely. Shai only nodded, reached out a hand. Ivah took it. They walked that way, hand in hand, along under the arcade beneath the gallery of the dark caravanserai. A brazier burned in one corner of the yard. The bells had rung curfew and most of the gang was gathered there now, Kapuzeh's voice raised over the others, some song out of the desert, Tihmrose's flute rising achingly sweet and plaintive over his deep voice. Ivah paused to trace symbols in the dust. Let them overlook the door in the gate opening and closing, let them overlook moving shadows at this end of the yard where the goddess slept.

At least Holla-Sayan had gone off roaming while she was meeting the governor, and he still had not returned.

Shadow stirred. Shaiveh hissed and pulled a knife from her belt, pushing Ivah away.

"Hah, Bikkim, you startled me," she chortled the next instant. "Everyone else is having a good time. What are you doing skulking down here?"

"What are you?" he countered, rising to his feet, spear in hand.

"Well, you know . . ." Shaiveh let her voice trail off suggestively, as if they had not had all the caravanserai's many empty rooms to crawl into. Master Mooshka was not a popular man with Governor Ketsim, and caravans, except those led by bloody-minded masters and gang-bosses, went to places more in favour, and suffering lower taxes and tolls, than Mooshka's.

"Pakdhala's asleep. Go away, don't wake her."

"Hey, are we being noisy? We're not being noisy, are we, Ivah, love?"

"No," Ivah said, fingers working on a loop of yarn pulled from her pocket. Damn and damn and damn him again. She did not have strength to squander; she would need all she had.

Bikkim's eyes narrowed. "Wizard—" he said, and found himself mute. She should have bound his limbs, sent him into sleep, something more practical, but her father was right, she never saw the longer road. Bikkim's face worked as if he were choking, mouthing empty words, and then he thrust the spear at her, jerking it up through the cat's cradle, slicing the strands that bound his voice. She yelped, her palm cut, but the laughter at the distant brazier hid the sound and as he drew breath to shout and lowered the spearpoint to her breast, holding her off, nothing more, Shaiveh swooped in beside him and slashed his throat.

She didn't scream. The sound that escaped her was more a frantic kitten's mewl, hardly louder than the rasping whistle of the Serakallashi's throat, facedown on the brick floor.

"That was near enough murder," Shaiveh snarled, wiping her blade on her own trouser leg. "Devils take you, couldn't you have made him sleep? If you can't do better than that we should cut our own throats right now."

"Shut up. Shut up. Did you have to—"

"Yes," Shaiveh said bluntly, sheathing the knife and drawing her sword. "Now go, fetch your damned camel-girl, and let's get out of here before the Blackdog comes."

Ivah swallowed and stepped carefully around Bikkim's chest-heaving body. She tried not to look, but saw his fingers clenched and clawing, as if he would seize her ankle. She lifted the latch on the door, opened it just wide enough to slip into the deeper darkness.

Ivah stood motionless, letting her eyes adjust. A hump—Pakdhala, buried under blankets. She took a cautious step, stopped when her foot came up against some bundle. Pakdhala usually slept with the Marakander twins; the room would be scattered with their gear and Immerose was not one to set anything straight, Shai called Immerose a sloven. Ivah didn't dare cast a light; she felt her way cautiously, nearly on hands and knees, did kneel by the mat and heap of bedding. Great Gods be with her now, if ever. The braided hair-cord was alternately silk-smooth and horsehair-rough to her fingers. Corpse hair. She swallowed bile again. Wrist, neck—the girl was a lump. Searching fingers found hair and flinched away, returned, brushing over the girl's cheek, cold and clammy with whatever illness plagued her. Her wrist—one hand tucked under the folded coat she was using as a pillow, the other beneath the blankets. Neck, then. She wore a scarf, enough cloth to be headscarf or veil, wrapped round and round, silk. No good, Ivah wanted the cord tight. She pulled at the scarf's fold, loosening it, found an end, touched skin again.

The girl mumbled and fumbled a hand out to swat at her, chasing away the tickling. Her breathing grew more rapid, rising towards waking. Ivah shoved a hand under her neck, dragged the cord around, and fastened it with the last knot, muttering the last words, Grass-lander words and words her father had given her that were no language she could guess at, words that burned her throat, tasted of hot stone.

Pakdhala, waking, punched her in the face.

Ivah hissed, lurching back, blinded a moment with pain, face burning hot and suddenly wet, but it was done, the spell complete, and Pakdhala fell back to the mat, her breath now shallow and racing.

"Cold hells . . ." Ivah whimpered, eyes tearing, sleeve pressed to her face. She could feel her face swelling, nose and lip. Broken nose? It hurt too much to touch. Probably not, but bad enough.

"Ivah!" Shaiveh hissed.

"Coming." Her voice came out snuffling and stuffy. Blood ran down the back of her throat, blood pouring down her chin, and she used her own scarf to hold her nose. "Stupid . . ." But what did she expect of a caravaneer, that she'd squeak and ask silly questions while someone attacked her in her sleep?

She fumbled for the girl's hand, found it. Orders, her father had told her. Use simple orders, and she'll be bound to obey. Use her true name.

"Attalissa, can you hear me?"

A faintly deeper breath.

"Good. Now be silent. Get up. Come with me."

The girl, stumbling like a drunkard, like a doll on strings, obeyed. "Ivah!"

Ivah led the goddess out.

"The party's breaking up," Shaiveh whispered. She leaned close. "Is that blood?" The flash of a grin. "You're a mess." But her grin faded, staring at the girl. "It worked."

"Of course it worked." Pakdhala's eyes were dark, wide pools, staring horror-stricken, and her mouth hung open, panting like a hunted animal at its last gasp. She swayed on her feet.

"Come." Ivah led her around the Serakallashi's body, heading straight towards the gate. She could feel the shape of the simple concealment she had set still potent. No one would notice, or noticing, remember the next moment.

"That you, Bikkim? You and 'Dhala aren't getting up to anything old Holla's going to disapprove of down here, are you? Or can I join you?"

The Grasslander boy. "Shai!" Ivah snapped, and towed Pakdhala into a stumbling trot.

Shaiveh didn't follow. "Just me, Zavel," she said. "C'mon, I picked up a flask of Marakander wine earlier today—want to see what it's like, just you and me? You can't say you haven't thought of it. I've seen you look at me. Ivah's gone off in a snit and I'm on my own for the night—"

"*Bikkim!* Gods and devils—!"

That did it. Ivah ran. No simple spell to make attention slide away was going to withstand that shock. The goddess fell. She hauled her up, heaved the bar off the door in the gate one-handed, dragged her through. Metal clashed and Zavel shouted, "Murder! Gaguush! Father! *Bikkim!*"

"Shai!" Ivah screamed, leaning back through the doorway.

"Go! Little fool! And seal the damned gate, buy yourself some time!"

She did, dropping the goddess in the street, scratching the signs on door and gate with the point of her knife, hands shaking. Someone within screamed, shrieked rage. Someone battered at the door that would not open. She threw up. Her nose was running, disgusting, her eyes weeping . . . milling horses, sharp, anxious voices, trying to take charge.

"She rides with me!" Ivah snarled, wiping her eyes on her sleeve, and she struck in the face the warrior about to pick up Pakdhala. He backed away, blinking, said nothing, and held her stirrup for her. A rangy desert-bred stallion, they were all desert-breds for speed on the flat. Another heaved the goddess up before her, and the girl sagged back into Ivah's embrace, slipped and slid.

"Sit up," Ivah ordered. "You can ride." Deliberate, that flopping slide towards the ground, and should the girl have even that much control over mind and body? "Sit up. Hold on. Balance."

Pakdhala swayed. Maybe they should have tied her onto a mount of her own, but Ivah didn't want her out of reach.

"My lady?"

"Ride." She wheeled her horse, kicked it past its reluctance to run in the dark. Clear road ahead, emptied by the curfew. Two swept past her, as it should be, to meet any hazards of the road. One to either side, six behind. Not enough, if the Blackdog overtook them. Not enough. Her throat still burned with the alien words her father had given her. She might never be free of the taste of them, sour as old vomit. Two horses ran under empty saddles.

CHAPTER XXVII

There was some sort of commotion in the street before Mooshka's gate. *'Dhala?* Holla-Sayan pushed the dog away and staggered a step till he found his feet.

Nothing. She had walled herself off so completely he couldn't touch her. The crowd . . . there was a curfew in Serakallash and no one should be on the street, but half the gang was there, and Master Mooshka himself, and folk of his household, with torches. Two men going at the gate with adzes, chopping away the surface of the wood.

The ghost-horse skipped and sidled and a sword whispered, the devil-wizard drawing her Northron blade.

"Put that away. These are *my* folk," Holla-Sayan said, and strode ahead.

"That's done it," the dog's ears heard, Mooshka's voice, and the gate was dragged open from within, horses surging out. Sayan, what was happening? Django and Asmin-Luya at the gallop, all but trampling the others, and on Mooshka's prized white mares, no less. They disappeared up the street.

Someone caught sight of him then, and the looming darkness behind him, and shouted warning. Edges glinted and he remembered they were blind. "It's me—Gaguush, it's Holla-Sayan. Where's Pakdhala?"

"Holla." She seized him close, there before them all. "Bashra help me, Holla-Sayan, get inside. In—in!" They all herded in, were-bear and devil and ghost-horse and all, Gaguush still clutching him.

"Where's Pakdhala?" He'd never heard Gaguush so close to breaking. *Pakdhala!* He hammered at her barriers, the dog rising frantic, suddenly fearful. The caravanserai reeked of blood. It wasn't

Pakdhala walling him out at all, not now. She was herself walled away, trapped . . . "Where's—"

"Gone," said Thekla, Thekla in tears. "Taken, and Bikkim—"

"Bikkim's dying," said Zavel, and his voice cracked. He was bleeding, his shirt sodden. "Gods, Holla, the Nabbani girl took her and killed Bikkim."

He won't harm her, Blackdog. Hear me—he thinks he needs the stars for what he plans. Eight days yet.

Moth's words barely touched him. The dog swept him away, drowned him, and tore into the world.

Don't get yourself killed for nothing. Resist her, damn you, and you might be able to save her and yourself both, you hear?

Someone screamed, but he was already gone, claws gouging plaster from the top of the wall, over and gone, finding her scent lingering in the air, the Nabbani woman's, other men and women, horses. He went straight where Django and Asmin-Luya had veered away down an ally, avoiding what lay ahead: bonfires lit where the street broadened out into the market square. There were archers beyond, waiting for him in the darkness. He smelt them, saw them long before they saw anything despite their fires. The dog ploughed into them and left them broken behind.

"I knew it," Gaguush said. "I knew when he brought her down that damned brat was too old to be his. He was never *right* after he came back that time." She folded her arms close about herself. "He went up there and that damned *thing* took him over." And she had been looking right at him when—when he wasn't Holla-Sayan at all, his eyes gone cold and remote, some yellow-green light burning behind them, a thing for poetry, not something to see in a face you knew. He hadn't seen any of them, and he hadn't cared. Bikkim lay dying, a man like a brother to him, and he hadn't even heard, had he? And how often, how many nights, had he not been there, when she'd thought she had him fast in her arms, when he went so remote and withdrawn. Some other *thing* riding his mind, and that, that was what lay beside her.

"What the hell was *that*?" Tihmrose demanded, squeaking like a child. "What . . . did that . . . Holla-Sayan—"

Master Mooshka puffed out his horse-tattooed cheeks. "That was the Blackdog. The Blackdog of Lissavakail. Here. Him. Attalissa's guardian. Your Holla-Sayan. *Jerusha!*" he suddenly shouted, turning away from the stunned silence. "Jerusha!" He retreated across the yard at an ungainly run, and a door slammed behind him. His folk, muttering and jabbering among themselves, followed.

"Holla's a *demon*?"

Gaguush was going to kill someone. She wasn't sure who yet. The next damn fool to get in her way.

"Who in the cold hells are you?" she snarled at the pair that had pushed in along with the rest of them once they got the bastard Nabbani's spells cut out of Mooshka's gate. Northrons from some other gang, or the Lake-Lord's mercenaries? She pulled the dagger from her belt. Should have had the sense to grab a spear when Zavel started hollering.

Ugly lumbering ox of a horse, too.

"Django—" but he and Asmin-Luya were the best horsemen, other than Bikkim and herself, sent in pursuit. "Kapuzeh."

He nodded, lowered his spear towards the horse, fastest way to overwhelm them if need be.

"Enemies of Tamghat," said the man, putting a hand on the mounted woman's arm. She sheathed the naked sword she carried, shrugging off the threat to the stallion, which grumbled and fidgeted while she looked around, ignoring them all.

Too much like Holla, that. Oblivious and chasing information no one else could see. Bloody arrogant.

"You're Gaguush of the Black Desert, the caravan-mistress? I'm Mikki. The wizard is Moth."

"Get out. We've had enough of hell-damned wizards."

Moth looked full at her, just the edge of a smile. "You need one. Your man isn't dead yet." She swung down, tossed the reins to Varro, who caught them, caught Gaguush's eye, and shrugged. The man Mikki, who was seven feet if he was an inch and pallid as a fish-belly, was suddenly between the woman and Kapuzeh, the great axe still balanced on his shoulder.

"They were in At-Landi, boss," Varro volunteered. "Er, Mikki here was, anyhow. A storyteller at my cousin's wedding. Mikki Sammison, he said, from . . . you didn't say where from."

Trust the bloody Northrons to *care*. Gaguush pushed around them. Summoned Kapuzeh to follow, pursuing the woman who went like some pale slinking wolf towards the arcade where Bikkim lay dying, while the useless fools all stood around yelping.

"Born in the heart of Hardenwald."

"I knew you couldn't be Northron, despite your tongue, not with black eyes," Varro said, with evident satisfaction, some theory proved. Wherever the hell Hardenwald was.

"But I am. My father was of the Geirlingas, from Selarskerry. You're from the Hravningas, you said. Varro Oernson. The mountains, though, not Ulvsness?" And they would keep at it, being Northron, until they'd worked out they were cousins at twenty-one removes.

They did, switching languages to the grumbling, choking, mouthfull-of-pebbles sound you heard among the ship-folk in At-Landi.

But then Varro caught up to Gaguush, took her arm, pulled her back, the job of horse-holder abandoned and Mikki being interrogated, none too friendly, by Tihmrose about why he and a so-called wizard showed up right in the midst of this night of horrors, if they weren't stirring it on.

"Boss," he whispered, "just wait. Um, something you should know."

"Not now."

"It's not a common name, Mikki, but you do hear it."

"So?"

"But, but Moth, he called her. That's not a name at all."

"I should care?"

"It means, um, 'inguz.'" He used the desert word. "You know, little drab butterfly, flies around at night."

"A moth, so what?"

"Flies into flames," the wizard, if she was that, said back over her shoulder. Damn good hearing. Eavesdropping, too.

Varro's fingers bit her arm and Gaguush jerked away from him. He leaned closer regardless. His moustache tickled her ear, and he'd been drinking too much. They all had, come to Serakallash in one piece and safe as you could be there, behind Mooshka's walls.

"But listen, you think Mikki looks human, even?" His voice lowered to a breath. "And they say—they say Vartu Kingsbane came back—Vartu Kingsbane, you know, who killed Hravnmod the Wise, and killed her own daughter, too—they say she escaped her grave and came back and murdered the queen's lover in Ulvsness itself, oh, six score years since, and the name she wore then was Moedthra. Moth. And she travelled with a demon bear. And Mikki says his father was from Selarskerry, and nobody lives on Selarskerry, the folk of Selarskerry were pirates back so long as history remembers, and godless, and the earls of the Geirlingas cleared the last of them out long ago, a hundred years since. It's just a rock where folk go to hunt seal now."

"Well, there's a bear in the menagerie at Marakand and when I can mistake it for a gold-haired Northron, you can lock me up with it." Gaguush pushed Varro off with an elbow. "You're drunk. And Great Gods, Varro, what should I care? Holla's a demon, Pakdhala's that damned lost goddess or else why the hell would that thing be in Holla like a worm and why would anyone but Bikkim bother stealing her—what's another demon and a devil more or less?"

Truth was, she couldn't care. One more bloody word from any of them and she was going to . . . going to break down and howl her heart out, as she hadn't since she was 'Dhala's age and all her world was taken from her. And she'd managed to hold it back, then, till she was alone and nothing but a horse and a dog to hear. She pressed fingers to her eyes and swallowed against some stupid gulping trying to rise in her throat.

"You lot!" She whirled back to the gang, what was left of the gang, almost collided with Kapuzeh at her heels. Glowered at them all, clutching spears and sabres and torches like a damned band of raiders:

Zavel battered and bloodstained and probably in need of Judeh's attentions himself, Immerose and Tihmrose hand in hand and the worse for wine, Thekla small and faded and old—Bashra, but they were all getting old, weren't they, and it didn't look tonight like they would live to get much older. Judeh was with poor Bikkim, Tusa—missing, hadn't come back at curfew, off begging hope from diviners—Asmin-Luya and Django gone on her own orders. Mooshka's folk had all disappeared, but there were lamps moving around beyond windows, some stir in his house. His problem, not hers.

"Saddle the damned camels." Mooshka didn't keep enough horses these days, couldn't afford them or had lost them to Tamghati extortion. Well, the camels weren't rested any more than the gang was, but they'd eat the miles, loaded light. "Anyone that's going after our 'Dhala, I want armed and mounted and ready to ride by the time I am."

Say farewell to Bikkim first, though it wasn't likely he'd ever know. For 'Dhala to save his life and have it come to this, treachery from her own gang. How'd she ever been fool enough to take on that sly, sleek little Nabbani anyhow? A wizard, clear enough, Holla had said it. Holla had known. He should have killed the snake then; he'd wanted to, she'd seen it in his eyes and thought him mad. No, the Blackdog had, not Holla. Holla wasn't a killer. Holla was a man who'd never lost a boy's open-eyed wonder at the world and he should have stayed home farming rather than come to this.

Someone had brought Judeh lamps. Nothing had changed in the island of light they shed. One body, curled and clutching the cracks in the tile floor, as if she'd tried at the end to draw herself away, arrogant, supercilious, I'm-too-grand-to-look-after-mere-camels Shaiveh. A damned Tamghati mercenary, it seemed she was, maybe even one of the *noekar*, the lord's vassals. Zavel had held his own, anyway, and others had come fast enough to finish her. She'd murdered Bikkim, though.

He lay open-eyed and breathing, after a fashion. Blankets piled over him, no matter they soaked in his killer's pooled blood. His throat had been cut, but he hadn't bled out quickly. Missed the arteries, just slashed his windpipe.

The wizard, or devil if she wanted to believe Varro, was kneeling beside him, Judeh beside her, looking sick. A man who called himself a leech, even if it was only to camels, shouldn't feel everything so. He looked up, saw Gaguush. "There's nothing I can do," he said. "Just— watch him die. But, um, Moth says—who is she, anyway?"

"Something Holla-Sayan found in the desert, I guess. Claims she's a wizard."

"Where is Holla?"

"Gone after Pakdhala."

"Won't be much left of Ivah for the rest of us." Judeh sighed. "I don't understand. She must have been mad. Anyone could see Ivah fancied the girl, but to kill Bikkim over her . . ."

The wizard was feeling delicately over the dying man's heart. "He was defending the goddess?"

"What goddess?" Judeh asked.

"The girl. Pakdhala."

"Seems our 'Dhala's the avatar the Lissavakaili lost when the Lake-Lord came," Gaguush told him, and watched Judeh's face.

"Ah." It was a sigh, as if something had been explained, before he answered Moth. "Of course he was defending her. We all would have, but he was here with her, watching her. She wasn't well. He loved her. She saved his life, this spring. He would have died then, I couldn't have saved him, but she brought him through."

"Worth loving, is she?"

"What kind of question is that?"

"Worth dying for?"

"Moth," Mikki said, almost a growl, and Gaguush flinched at his sudden presence behind her.

The rest of the gang had followed. "Stay with Bikkim, Judeh," Gaguush ordered. "As long as he has. Don't leave him to die alone in the dark."

"He's not dying yet," muttered Moth and looked up, over Gaguush's shoulder at the giant. "It's not necromancy, *byornling*."

"Did I say it was?"

The wizard's hand wandered to the fluttering gash in the man's throat. "I think even a master surgeon might save him, if the wound didn't fester. A surgeon-wizard, probably. Lacking that . . . What's his name? You, Gaguush: his name, all his names."

"Bikkim."

And Kapuzeh added, "Battu'um. The only sept-chief of the Battu'um left alive."

"Lacking a surgeon—what?" Mikki prompted.

"I do what I can. Bikkim Battu'um, earl of the Battu'um, you hear me? Keep breathing. You, Judeh, hold his head. Let him know he has a friend here."

"He has plenty of friends here," Gaguush growled, meaning a warning. But she added, "What do you need? Water? Judeh's needles?"

"Nothing," Moth said, knife in hand. But she only ripped down the front of Bikkim's shirt, exposing his chest. She glanced up at them all. "You can't help. Stay out of the way."

The woman had a point. Gaguush looked around. "Damn, did I tell you lot to stand around gawping? If the woman's a wizard, let her try. None of you can do Bikkim any good, but we might catch that treacherous bastard Ivah."

"What about . . . Holla?" Zavel asked.

"He'd damn well pray I'm in a better mood when I do catch up to him."

Immerose laughed nervously, but nobody else did even that much. They moved away, though, becoming more purposeful. Gaguush lingered, squatted down and picked up one of the clay lamps, holding it high to spill light over Bikkim rather than the floor. Moth didn't tell her not to, at least. She and Mikki murmured to one another. Should have kept Varro by, to eavesdrop and translate in turn. She had a few words of Northron but couldn't catch any she knew here.

The woman was dabbling her fingers in what streaked down Bikkim's neck, pooled in the hollow between his collarbones. Gaguush opened her mouth on a protest, closed it again. Northron wizardry was all about blood, they said. Moth began writing on his chest, sharp-angled letters in blood. Northron, probably, though some looked almost Nabbani in their complexity.

Fire, pale and glowworm green, trickled down her arms, traced the writing, flowed into the gaping wound, and stilled for a moment Bikkim's obscene laboured breathing, the fluttering of the sliced edge of throat skin. Gaguush caught her own breath and Judeh grunted some protest. Heavy hand on her shoulder, on his.

"Trust," Mikki said, a bass rumble.

That close to, he didn't smell like a man. More grass and animal muskiness than male sweat.

"Talk to him," Mikki said softly. "Tell him he's going to be all right."

Judeh gave a jerky nod. "Bikkim," he said. "Don't worry. You're hurt but you're going to be fine. There's a wizard . . . um, a wizard. And Pakdhala, we're going to get Pakdhala back, never doubt that. You ever thought about getting married? Might make Holla happier if you do. You know how he worries. 'Course, then you'd be stuck with him for a father . . ." Babbling. "He's not breathing," he interjected, fool, if Bikkim could actually hear.

Moth began talking to herself, muttering some wizardly working, perhaps, but it didn't sound Northron to Gaguush's ear and her man cast her a sharp look, brows lowered. Words that hissed and sparked like water, rang like ice, and managed to sound not like magic, but like someone indeed talking to herself, anxious and angry, uncertain of the job in hand. Maybe that was all it was.

"Moth?" Mikki asked. "All right?"

But the lad was breathing, quietly, through his nose, the worst of the gaping wound closed, the surface only still an ugly open cut.

Moth shook her head, silent now. Gaguush thought she was hardly breathing herself as she drew the upper layer of the wound together with lines of flame rather than thread. Great Gods save them, the flame ran all through her, as though it flowed in place of blood, as though her flesh were cloudy glass. She looked up, and the red fire dying last of all in her eyes was not any reflection of the golden lamplight. "So."

413

Bikkim was already stirring feebly, like a sleeper in nightmare. The eyes that had been staring blind closed and trembled, blinked open again.

"*Dhala!*" he croaked, and rolled to hands and knees, striking away Judeh's attempt to hold him. "Where's——" He looked around and his gaze found Shaiveh's body. He levered himself to his feet with a fallen spear. "Ivah's taken her." He rubbed his throat, the livid scar, leaned swaying on the spear. Not much voice left, hoarse and faint. An imperfect miracle. Gaguush caught his elbow.

"Ivah's taken Pakdhala, yes, but I sent Django and Asmin-Luya after her on Mooshka's horses, and the rest of us are following. Are you fit to ride?"

Bikkim stared at her, a hand back to his throat. "I thought I was dead. Boss——"

"This is Moth, apparently. She's a wizard or something. And Mikki. Shall we go?" She caught the wizard's eye, grey like a stormcloud, human. "Can he ride, is he well enough? He's not about to pass out on me or anything?"

Moth shrugged. "Ask him." She climbed stiffly to her feet, stretched. "I hope that wasn't yet another knot to delay us. He's been deflecting us for years. Always something . . . though if I thought Holla-Sayan had any chance of catching up to Ivah and getting himself killed I wouldn't have waited."

"This was right and necessary and nothing to do with Tamghiz Ghatai, *minrulf*. You want to talk these folk into staying here, though?" Mikki quirked an apologetic smile at Gaguush. "No point you all thundering up there to get killed."

"I don't abandon my folk."

"I'd have to scare her worse than I have yet to keep her here," Moth said, as though Gaguush weren't there and listening. Gaguush snorted. She didn't need the condescending respect of some arrogant . . . monster.

Moth heard the snort and shrugged, still not bothering to address her, not even the politeness to switch languages so her condescension wouldn't be obvious. "I'll be ahead of them—I'm going after the Blackdog. You try to keep them out of trouble, keep them from getting slaughtered before they begin?"

"Ya."

"Bring Styrma. Don't let them toss him in a dunghill."

"Ya."

"You're not going to catch up with that—with Holla-Sayan on that heavy horse," Gaguush said grudgingly, as the gang, seeing Bikkim walking unsteady into the yard on Judeh's arm, swarmed about the pair, camels abandoned. "There's a couple of desert-breds left. Take Jerusha Rostvadim's stallion. She'll skin you when she finds out, but it's the fastest beast here."

"I'll fly," Moth said, sliding past, wolf-slinking again. The blue roan whickered, catching sight of her.

Gaguush had surely misheard.

"But thank you," Mikki added. Used to smoothing tempers in his woman's wake?

"What, for telling her to steal a horse? What did she say she was going to do?"

"Fly," Mikki said. "Northron wizards, you know."

"In *tales*."

"Like trees, tales have roots."

The wizard caught Varro by the arm, was giving him what sounded like orders in guttural Northron. He didn't look half-apprehensive enough for Gaguush to believe he believed his own suspicions. He hadn't seen what she saw under the gallery. Moth unharnessed her horse, and Varro, willing servant now, what it was to have hair the colour of raw silk, began bundling up harness and all her gear, loading it on Holla's red Sihdy—there were more camels harnessed and grumbling there than they needed, the gang already expecting the strangers to come, or planning ahead for when they had their fellows rescued. Sometimes she didn't need to do their thinking for them.

Moth buckled her second sword over her back, shook out something—shifting, shimmering, lifting in its own wind, even draped over an arm. Grey silk and feathers, feathers gleaned, it looked, from a hundred moulting birds, soft cotton-white barred with black, ash-grey, blue-barred, eagle's black.

"I thought feather-cloaks were one of the magics lost in the devils' wars," Varro said cautiously. "Hey, Gaguush, look at this—you won't see anything like this again."

"I hope not."

Moth grinned. "Lost, ya. So are bone-horses. Look, Mikki won't be able to carry him, come dawn. Take Styrma."

And the horse fell apart, blew into dust. She caught the skull one-handed as it fell, the only thing left of the beast, and offered it to Varro.

He took it cringingly, as if he expected it to be slick with rotten meat, which it was plainly not, old and clean and dry. Turned it wondering in his hands. "Boss—"

"I know, I saw. Another Northron wonder. And what price for all this sudden help?"

"We're on the same road," said the wizard—call her that, it was easier on the nerves. "For now. That's all."

"Right. And I want Holla-Sayan and Pakdhala back whole and sound and sane at the end of it. You going to give me that?"

Moth met her eyes then, unexpectedly sombre and . . . and honest, Gaguush thought, as she had not been yet. "No. Varro told you what I am. Believe him. My name was Ulfhild of Ravensfell once, Ulfhild the King's Sword of Ulvsness, and my name was Vartu. I'm here for Tamghiz Ghatai. You know that name. Tamghat. And you pick up what you can behind me, Mistress Gaguush. Your Holla-Sayan—I'll save them both if I can. But I promise nothing."

Gaguush nodded grimly, watched with arms folded as Moth flung the feather-cloak around her shoulders and was—in a breath—gone, a grey blur of bird, owl, falcon, impossible to say, lost in the night.

The devil hadn't meant Pakdhala, when she said "save them both."

"Now I've seen everything," said Immerose.

"Not by half, I suspect." Gaguush turned on Mikki. "So, you riding, or flying, or turning into a smoke and blowing up on the wind?"

"Ride for now," Mikki said. "Though I imagine the camel won't be happy about it."

"They don't like demons?" she said, testing.

"Don't like men of my weight, I imagine."

But the pack-camel they gave him grumbled and groaned no more than usual, and he had a light touch with the beast, even if he was, he claimed, no rider. He wasn't any great weight compared to the bales they usually carried.

Great Gods help the governor's guard and the so-called militia if they barred the gang's way out of town.

Mooshka's daughter Jerusha came chasing them before they got out the gate.

"Mistress Gaguush, wait."

"No."

"My father says Holla-Sayan is the Blackdog."

"So?"

"So little Pakdhala is the goddess of Lissavakail?"

"I don't know what in the cold hells Pakdhala may be. I don't much care. She's my . . . my girl, Holla's daughter, and some Nabbani *slaver* for all I know's brought murder to my gang and drugged her or something, Bikkim says, and carried her off."

"You'll be killed, all of you. You can't take on Tamghat with a few spears and a bit of bad language."

"You saying I should just forget it? Ride away to Marakand and leave 'Dhala to whatever that pervert Lake-Lord intends? The damned devil didn't even dare tell me that."

"I'm saying don't be stupid, Mistress. You won't get her back chasing after her as though some raider's taken her for ransom. If you must go—"

Gaguush snorted.

"Then do as I tell you. There's a place—once you get where the hills are rising into the mountain feet, about a day's travel, there's a place you'll see, a grove of walnuts to the east and a stand of bamboo to the west. Just past that, you turn east. It looks impassable, but it's not. Steep going, though. Up the shoulder of the mountain, then down suddenly into a ravine. Follow the water upstream and don't fall in and drown yourselves. Past a waterfall, then ford the stream, up under the shadow of the cliffs. Someone should have met you by then."

"What sort of someone? Someone who'll already have shot us with some of those good iron arrowheads I've been bringing you from At-Landi?"

"Possibly," Jerusha admitted, with one of her rare smiles. "Say I've sent you to see Auntie Orillias."

"Thank you."

Jerusha shrugged. "You're going to get us all killed if you don't use sense."

"Come with us."

"I would, but . . . you're not the only ones making hard decisions right now, you know? All our gods go with you. I'll open the gates. Do us all a favour and don't ride through town, eh?"

So they were out into the forbidden night of Serakallash, and Jerusha was right, nothing to be gained by running into the Tamghati loyalists of the watch and coming to grief in the streets before they'd even started. Lion shouldered his way to the fore and Gaguush swung his head for the alley leading down towards the bleaching skulls of the sept-chiefs and the ruin of Sera's spring.

As well the gang's hotheads, and she counted herself among them, had a reminder of how Tamghat dealt with his foes.

The wind howled around the corners, stinging with sand. Gaguush wrapped her scarf over her face. At least they could hope they'd have their backs to it.

CHAPTER XXVIII

Nightmare, in which she struggled, mired in the seething bitumen pits of the Black Desert, trying to reach her own body. It walked away from her. Pakdhala surfaced into herself and discovered it still wasn't a dream, as it had not been the last time, and the time before that.

Bikkim was dead. She had seen him lying, his throat cut, as she walked, each step dragging what felt like a heavy chain, from her bed. She raged and cursed and screamed for her father, for the Blackdog, but that was only in her mind, and she battered herself senseless on glass walls without ever being able to reach him, to reach herself. When she was small there had been an old man in Marakand, a kinsman of the twins', who lived with their family and sat propped in bed, watching the children. He couldn't speak. He moved his limbs like they were dead things dragged with some last, failing strength. He dribbled when they spooned food into his mouth. But his eyes were alive, and he watched, and wheezed at some funny story Immerose told. She had come to that, and death was not going to release her. Like the old man, a prisoner buried alive within—not a corpse. A puppet. Ivah clutched her close.

From Serakallash to Lissavakail was a two-day journey on horseback, a little longer on foot, but not much so, because of the narrow trails, the sharp rise and fall of them, which meant horses mostly walked. These galloped, blind in the dark, but even so they could not hope to outrun the Blackdog, no matter how often they switched horses, as they had twice already, Grasslander warriors camped and waiting, delicate, gazelle-legged desert-breds waiting saddled as though all had been prepared for days. The rolling pastures of

Serakallash were left behind and they climbed the foothills, into the twisting mountain track, stone underfoot, stone all around, the scent of home.

The wind bit, carrying the scent of sand, the harsh dry air of the desert. A storm still rode in their wake. That wouldn't stop the Blackdog.

Dawn crept into a bruise-yellow sky and the leading riders turned, taking a track that ran up the side of a steep spur.

"Where are you going?" Ivah called hoarsely. She had been weeping, in the dark when she thought no one would notice. Pakdhala had seethed with hatred for her, for her daring to weep for Shaiveh left behind, when Bikkim was dead at the Grasslander's hand.

"Your lord father's orders, my lady," their leader said from Ivah's side. "He said to meet him here."

"Meet him?" Ivah asked. "He said nothing to me about—"

They called Ivah "my lady" . . . her father's orders . . . *No.* Pakdhala convulsed, freeing herself from Ivah's grip. She went sliding like a trout, hit the ground among the hooves. A horse lifted and jumped her as she rolled. She might have been knocked out for a moment; the next she knew, there were booted feet all about her, people cursing and Ivah crying, "'Dhala, 'Dhala, are you all right, are you hurt?" as if she cared.

Pakdhala got an arm under herself. It dragged like a stick from her shoulder, but she fumbled herself up on it, pulled until her knee came up and she rocked there, trying to get the other leg to answer.

And they would all stand around and watch her crawl slowly to freedom? Hah. Little fool. So she could move of her own will, after a fashion. She shouldn't be showing them that. She flopped on her face and strong arms gathered her up.

"No offence, my lady, but you don't weigh much more than she does and next time it might be you both landing under someone's hooves. I'll take her, by your leave."

"Do," Ivah snapped, as though she meant something else entirely.

This man handled Pakdhala as though she were glass, calling over a woman to feel her arms and legs, feel over her chest and back, to be sure she had taken nothing worse than bruises. She wished something was broken and that it would cost them a few heads, but felt no more battered than she did after coming off Sihdy a time or two when she was young, or when that spotted colt of her uncle's threw her.

Ivah was surreptitiously spitting on the end of her scarf, trying to wash her bloody face clean. Daylight showed her a mess, her nose swollen, her upper lip black with bruise. Hah.

But they rode up the path, walking now, knife-edge of the ridge, thin brown grass plastered flat by the following wind, and down to the floodplain of a shallow river, where loose stones clattered underfoot. Not another relay of horses waiting. A round felt tent, the Grasslander house, was erected on the river's edge, and out the low door—he strode towards them, smiling, arms wide.

"At last! Great Attalissa, my most gracious lady, we have you safe at last. Welcome, welcome home to your kingdom." He even had the accent of the mountains now, or he put it on, mocking.

Hunger. Such hunger. He was a fire, to consume all he drew into his embrace. She had not seen him at Lissavakail. He looked so . . . human. The way the caterpillar looks itself, till the wasp that has grown inside it drills a hole in its back and emerges.

"You've been badly used," he added. "Your captors will suffer. Every blow repaid twelvefold." Pakdhala tried to pull away from his reaching hand, could do no more than stiffen her joints. But the caress did not touch her, not quite. She still felt it, as if he left some poison in the very air.

"Father . . ." Ivah said.

Tamghat ignored her. "Quickly, Ketsim. Take the goddess to the centre of the circle—there. Lead your horse. Don't scuff the lines more than you can help."

The tent was coming down, all the camp disappearing into bundles on packhorses.

The circle was a triple line poured of what looked like ash and sulphur and some red powder, a great sweeping enclosure drawn over the stones. Pakdhala tried to tip herself, to fall and erase some of the scrolling writing that ran around the circle. Any delay—the Blackdog was coming, she knew that as she knew the sun rose in the east. But the governor of Serakallash kept a tight hand on her arm as he guided the horse over the marks, and she stayed in the saddle.

"Father!" Ivah demanded, and Tamghat rounded on her.

"What have you done with Shaiveh?"

"She stayed to let me get the goddess away. As you'd have wanted."

"You fled and left her to die, you mean. A loyal *noekar* deserves better from her lady. What were you whoring with on the desert road?"

"What? No one!"

"Don't lie to me! Was it that she-cat Kinsai? You took her into your bed and mind, didn't you? Nabbani trollop! I should have drowned you when you were born and found an honest woman of the Grass."

"Father, I don't know what you mean." Ivah slid from her horse and ran to him, stumbled to her knees. Did she fall, or did he really expect her to kneel grovelling at his feet? "Father, please, I don't understand you. What have I done wrong? I found the goddess and brought her to you. I did the spells as you told me. It all went as it should. We even outran the Blackdog."

"And what did you bring with you? A spark of Kinsai's will, or something worse? Did *she* woo you to her side with some tale? Did you let her in, or were you just too weak? Did you surrender without even a fight that might have warned me?"

"I don't understand!" Ivah's voice rose shrill. Some remote part of Pakdhala even pitied her. "I brought the goddess—she is Attalissa, you said so yourself."

"I came to you, daughter, to let you know how you were to elude the Blackdog. I came to your dreams, and I was attacked."

"I didn't—"

"You! You couldn't if you wanted to. You couldn't muster the strength of mind to get my *attention*. Whatever you've let ride you, you won't be carrying it back to Lissavakail. I won't be ambushed in the midst of the most important working the world has ever seen. I won't have *her* using you against me." He drew his sword.

Ivah screamed and ducked, hunkering down hands over her head, sobbing. The hurrying Tamghati folk paid her no heed, put great effort into not looking. Pakdhala, carried by the horse as Governor Ketsim turned it in the centre of the circle, had no choice.

Tamghat stared down at Ivah a long moment, mouth pulled into a sneer. Then he turned away. "Coward to the end," he said. "Even your cursed mother died on her feet."

He strode to a horse, sheathing his sword. "Everyone not within the circle *now* gets left behind to face the Blackdog," he snarled, riding to Ketsim's side. "Scuff the lines and it'll cost you your head."

Somehow they all crowded in, men and women, horses and baggage. Tamghat began to chant, eyes shut, swaying from side to side. The language was very old-fashioned Grasslander, drawn high and thin and wailing, peppered with words that sounded like nothing she could imagine at all.

Some *noekar* had dropped the bridle of a sweat-dark horse, one of the last relay, and it stood outside the circle, swishing its tail, cropping a tuft of grass. Deliberate? Pakdhala thought so. Hoped so, wanted to believe in kindness. Ivah didn't notice, still hunched small as she could make herself, still weeping.

The air went watery around them, the landscape running like cheap dyes. Horses laid back their ears; some fought their bits, trying to flee. The ground hit them, hard. Horses stumbled, folk afoot fell. They were in a field of shoulder-high green millet, trampling the sweet stalks, some of the horses, quickly recovered, already snatching greedy mouthfuls. She recognized the place, the shape of the cradling horizon, though not from this life. Farmlands of the temple a few miles from the Lissavakail.

She could feel the waters of her lake, cool, deep, pulling her.

Pakdhala was taken from the horse, Tamghat standing close, never touching her. They bundled her into an elaborate, high-wheeled cart, a box lacquered red and black, covered with plaques of gold and turquoise. Its roof rose in a multi-tiered spire; the curtains were heavy brocade, shutting out all light. The yak-cross oxen drawing it were both black, their horns decked with red tassels. Two *noekar*, both female, were ordered in after her. There had been no priestesses there. Had he slain them all? In Serakallash they said many had died when the temple fell or been executed after, and others had surrendered to serve the conqueror. One of the warriors leaned over her to lace up the curtain. Ah, Tamghat did not wish the folk of Lissavakail to see her brought back an ill and constrained captive. Or he did not wish them to see their goddess a caravan-road mercenary. Either way, if she could shift herself over—she should hear when they crossed the bridge. Once they were in town, if she could fall, if people could see . . .

"Sleep, Attalissa," Tamghat said from outside. "Sleep, my dear."

That was all she knew.

The Blackdog would come for her and she would die as she deserved. Perhaps it would at least be Holla-Sayan who killed her and not the beast. Ivah sat waiting as the wind died and the sand ceased to blow, its purpose served. Even getting to her feet took more strength of will than she could find. A horse whinnied, left behind by the spell, abandoned by its herd. There was a step on the stones behind her, and Ivah looked around. She had nothing to say to Holla-Sayan, but she would at least see him again before she died.

Not Holla-Sayan. Some Northron woman. Left behind like the horse? Her pale hair was windblown and her clothes red with dust. She blinked grit from her eyes, shook herself, animal-like, and dust rose in a cloud from a cloak improbably shingled with feathers.

"Carried her off to the temple, has he?" she asked conversationally. "I thought he would." She walked away around what the wind of their going had left of the lines of powders, head cocked, reading the words still written there.

"Hmph," she said, coming back. "What are you still doing here?"

"He left me behind," Ivah said blankly. "He called me whore and left me behind."

"He does that to those who outlive their usefulness, those he's drained to nothing."

"He as much as said I'd betrayed him." Ivah looked up, seeking some explanation from the stranger, from the sky, from the world in general. "I never did anything to him. It was he who stopped coming to my dreams."

"Ah." The stranger rubbed her face, left pale streaks. Had she ridden through the storm? A messenger pursuing them from Ketsim's household in Serakallash? Now she would leave, knowing Ivah outcast, knowing talking to her an offence to Tamghat.

"Poor Ivah. It was to be expected, I suppose. Did it never occur to you *not* to do your father's will, to take the space the freedom from his watching gave you and travel on with the gang to Marakand?"

Ivah stared. "But he told me to bring Attalissa to him."

"And you do what he tells you, ya. But now he has told you he doesn't want you, told you to go. What will you do?"

Ivah shook her head. It didn't matter. There was nothing to do. The Blackdog would come for her.

The stranger might have read her mind. Maybe it was in her eyes.

"The goddess isn't here, so the Blackdog isn't interested in you. Holla-Sayan, should you ever run into him again, will be."

"What should I do?"

"Don't expect me to salvage the wreck of your life. Your mother asked me to save you, but there comes a point when you can only save yourself. This is it."

"But what can I do? Where should I go?"

"How should I know? Only go cautiously. The Blackdog went by just now, but the gang is following, and you don't want to meet them on the road either."

"I have no home. No folk."

"You're not alone in the world in that. Don't try to feel sorry for yourself. Your Shaiveh is dead for you, Bikkim will never speak easily again—Attalissa of the lake may die. Did you see them dying in Lissavakail when your father took it? Did you see the hill of skulls in

Sera's spring as you rode into Serakallash? You've come out of Tamghat's grasp alive, which is more grace than many get. Go to Marakand. That's what everyone else in this part of the world does when they want to disappear. Isn't it?"

"They kill wizards in Marakand." She didn't offer it as protest; it was simply what came into her mind. Marakand. They killed wizards. But it caught the woman's attention. Her grey eyes narrowed.

"Do they? Why?"

"I don't know."

"Maybe you should find out." The stranger offered a hand. Ivah took it automatically, climbed stiffly to her feet and found, not surprisingly, that she still had to look up. She was used to being short. Northrons, even the women, made her know it all over again.

"*I* should find out?"

"Someone should. What else do you have to do with your life?"

Ivah shook her head, not in denial, just . . . emptiness.

"You have a good horse there. Trade it for a camel, join a gang, I don't know. But don't sit around waiting for death to find you, Ivah. It comes fast enough anyhow. Defy him. Claim yourself."

"Defy death?"

"Near enough. I meant your father, though."

The horse had wandered close, curious. When the woman reached for the bridle it tossed its head and shied away, almost falling in its haste to turn. She gave a laugh that didn't sound happy, turned her shoulder on the beast. "At least unsaddle the poor brute if you're planning to sit moping all day."

"Moping? Devils take you, Shai is *dead*, she's dead and it's my fault! I left her. Pakdhala's going to die, I know she is, no matter what my father says about marriage, and I . . . I did that, too, and she trusted me, she *liked* me, not even Shaiveh would have liked me if I wasn't my father's daughter." Screeching, her father would say, and she couldn't curse any further, couldn't see, for the great heaving sobs.

"So who was Pakdhala's comrade, the person whom she liked? Not your father's daughter. Who are you when you're not that?"

"I don't know."

"Find out." The stranger put a hesitant hand on her shoulder, and Great Gods, her impulse was to fling herself at the woman and howl on her breast like a child, not to pull away. "You can't change what's done, Ivah. What's to come . . . Pakdhala isn't dead yet, but it's not you who can save her. The Blackdog might not come looking for you, but if you turn up under its nose it will remember you. Just . . . go on, and remember, and choose differently. You're not useless, you're not untalented, you're not weak, you're not stupid. You don't need Tamghat to be your strength."

Ivah gulped. She wiped her face on her sleeve, but felt strangely quiet, unashamed. Madness, a stranger to come out of nowhere, knowing her so well.

"All right?"

Ivah shook her head. The woman let her go.

"You will be. Don't put yourself in the way of Gaguush's gang. I doubt they'll forgive betrayal."

Words spoken a few moments before sank in. "You knew my mother."

"I talked to her last autumn."

"But she's . . . she's dead."

"Ya. I buried her, after a fashion. Set her free, anyhow."

"Oh. Thank you." She said that without thinking.

The woman shrugged. "I threw your sneaking father out of your dreams for good. You could thank me for that, too, someday, when you're ready. Spite him, Ivah. Seize your life for your own."

Then she was gone, a falcon in the sky.

"You—" Ivah screamed after her, screamed again in wordless anger. She snatched a handful of dry grass, knotted and wove it, flung it, a dark spear trailing streamers of fire, after the speeding bird. The falcon dropped, wheeled away, soared higher and was gone, and the spell-bound weapon disintegrated. Ivah sat down again, holding her head. It ached. Throbbed, tears and the mess of her nose together making it unbearable. "Mama," she whimpered. No one to answer. "You made him hate me, you damned—" But she didn't know what to call the woman, and screaming tantrums at the sky was . . . was not her father's daughter. She sighed, held her nose. Great Gods, but it hurt.

She was a damned wizard. She knew spells that could heal a battered nose more quickly than nature allowed, if only she trusted her own working of them.

The horse came back.

She was a wanderer, she was godless, she was . . . she was on her own. Which might mean free, she supposed the Northron wizard, whoever she was, would say, but free just meant abandoned and forlorn and outcast, alone. It also meant no one else was going to look after the horse and, stupidly, what came to her mind was what Gaguush would say about someone who left a hard-worked animal uncared-for to see to their own comfort. Ivah got up again, held out a hand, chirping to the golden mare. "Come, beauty, we'll make you more comfortable. Come and we'll go to the river." She choked on another sob, swallowed it. "We both need a wash." And once she'd worked on her nose so she could breathe again, she would see what she could do to coax the hair back to the Nabbani "tam" syllable branding the horse's rump. She couldn't take a horse across the Salt Desert, and she didn't need to be turned in as a horse thief when she tried to sell it in Serakallash. She would go to Marakand after all, though she didn't want to seem to be taking the meddling stranger's advice. Marakand was at least someplace new, someplace she had never been with Shaiveh, and a stage on the road to Nabban. Maybe she could find the truth of her mother's kin, learn she really was a princess, be welcomed by the emperor as a long-lost granddaughter, greater and grander than any Grasslander warlord could ever dream. Hah. Winter-tales for market storytellers.

Still: a new land, a new chance, at the far end of the caravan road, farther than the gangs of the Four Deserts and the Western Road ever went. Nabban was at least a conveniently distant goal, and it would leave her father and the Blackdog, leave Shaiveh and Bikkim and Pakdhala, far behind. It could be like being born again.

CHAPTER XXIX

The dog ran. If it was tired, it did not feel it. Pakdhala was in Lissavakail. It knew this. It had been told. It would not overtake the abductors, but it would come in time. She would not be harmed, not yet. It had been told this as well. It did not remember being told; it only knew. It left the steep road for steeper tracks, swam a river, went down a cliff a goat would not dare and up a cascade. It was followed. It ignored the grey shadow in the sky. Not an enemy. Kin. It had been alone, so alone, so long. It was not alone. The shadow vanished, reappeared, went its own way, but always returned. There was no betrayal in that one, the dog knew it, as though it were memory. It might have been, must have been, because the other was kin too, yet thought of that other was sickness and rage, and not all for its goddess.

The rocks were sometimes ice. Sometimes the dog did not think it ran. It flew, a flame in the air, a shard of light. Memory fell in drops, fragments, as if some cave of ice began to thaw. Drops pooled, brought emotion it had not known, forgotten since it began this life. Slow, so slow to gather, to become clear to the watching mind. Dawn was on it soon after it left Serakallash. Day followed, when the few travellers on the mountain road fled the pony-sized hound and whispered, *The Blackdog* . . . Sunset and night falling, and the memories gathered.

Light, liquid as water, warmth and companionship and *home*. Ice, sharp as black stone. Ice and stone and darkness, loss and exile. And the white sky cracking, and a world to shape into a weapon, a bridge thrusting home . . . That world nearly broke beneath them; in their hundreds they fought upon it, till so much was ruin. But they failed.

They were shattered, the black world seizing them again in claws of ice. Itself was shattered. Lost. Forgotten.

There you are. See, there is something left of you after all. One of the many we thought dead and lost, but not quite dead after all. Now listen, feel, if you cannot think. Let Holla-Sayan think, let him stand interpreter. You have been made slave of a little goddess of this earth. You are bound in wizardry, human wizardry, nothing more. She is not owed *this passion and devotion; she does not merit it; she has taken it by rapine and conquest, by defeat of a crippled soldier. Understand that. The Great Gods themselves did not steal our souls from us.*

I won't be Pakdhala's enemy, Holla-Sayan protested, and he was there, aware, within the dog. It allowed him that much.

You can't fight Tamghiz Ghatai in the dog's madness, and it can't win against Tamghiz Ghatai, crippled as it will always be whether you free it or not. You'll both be destroyed, utterly and entirely, your soul, Holla-Sayan, and the Blackdog, consumed and corrupted into what Ghatai has become.

So send it back where it belongs. If you're truly a devil, if it is—send it back wherever you came from.

Her laughter was bitter. *Ah, if we could—what do you think we came so near destroying your world to gain, in the war that scarred the world, the war human history has near forgotten? What do you think we seven pulled the north into fire and blood for, in the history you still sing? Why do you think Ghatai hungers so for a greater binding to the power of this earth, this goddess's soul woven into his heart, but to storm the heavens again? We don't belong in the cold hells, Holla-Sayan. That's a prison, not home. Though there was a home before we came to the plane that humans call the distant heavens. Lost . . . Her thought trailed away. Holla-Sayan, I can't let Ghatai take the Blackdog, and Attalissa's binding will not let it leave Ghatai to me, it will not let the dog wait and plan when she seems in such peril. So—you find a way to free it from that compulsion, or you at least master it so that it does not make some berserker's attack so soon as we come to Lissavakail, or I will have to act. And that would mean your death and my sibling sent mad back to the cold hells, at best.*

At best? What's at worst?

The destruction of both your souls.

As if she had no doubt but that she could do so. The tales said Vartu Kingsbane had murdered King Hravnmod the Wise, who was her own brother. No matter what the dog felt about her, he should not trust her.

What happens to Pakdhala if the dog is set free?

That's a matter between Attalissa and the spirit she bound, nothing to do with you. It may depend on her.

It is very much to do with me. She's my daughter. I won't free this thing to turn on her.

Moth's silence was heavy.

What will it do? You say you knew this thing.

No. If I did, I would give it back its name. We were many, once. Too many did die. I can't know how it feels in its true heart about Attalissa after all this time, how it will feel when it is free. You know it better than I ever could. But what it may become, free—I don't think it can survive long on its own in this world; it's too weak. This isn't our place, Holla-Sayan. You know that. You remember. It needs to be of the world. It was dying, slowly, when Attalissa bound it.

You mean it's still going to seek a host to possess.

Not necessarily.

Great Gods damn you—

They already have.

Say what you mean. But he began to understand. *What you—what Vartu did to Ulfhild the King's Sword.*

Nothing she didn't accept.

She went mad! She killed her brother and—

We did not! It was almost an attack. The dog snarled, at Moth or at Holla himself, he wasn't sure which.

Great crimes, yes. We tried to make an empire, to draw on enough of the force of the earth to raise a road to the heavens and shatter the walls . . . we never cared what we broke, pursuing that end, and that included the lives of the fool wizards who invited us in. But I never killed Hravnmod.

He believed her. He thought it was he who believed, and not only the dog.

Are you I or we? he asked.

Depends. She laughed. *We're one. Mostly. How about you?*

No answer.

It isn't possession, Holla-Sayan. It isn't the madness you've been living with. you won't harm Attalissa, your Pakdhala, at least.

My life sacrificed for a . . . a creature . . . a being that you say is injured to the edge of death, that is so damaged it will never be whole, never be a free and thinking person again.

You're stronger than it is, Holla-Sayan.

Hells I am.

There, no, not within its own being. That is not a place for a physical creature at all. But here, yes, in this world of which you are part, blood and bone and soul, you are. Neither of you realize this, and so it is stronger, though it is all will and emotion without reason, because you fight within the world of its soul. Find the earth where your feet belong, and stand firm there.

Did you? Did Ulfhild?

No. We are one, don't you understand that? We became that willingly. But you'll have to fight the Blackdog to free it. It is Attalissa's will that it is bound, you see, and it will not let you overturn Attalissa's will.

Holla's protest that Attalissa would not, could not, do such a thing died unformed in memory of Laykas, the Blackdog who had massacred Serakallash. Attalissa had been a conqueror, oh yes. She had used the Blackdog in the little wars of the mountains, until her reach was exhausted. She had not always cared to spare the man that bore the spirit, either. The dog stirred uncomfortably, resisting the thought.

Maybe it's time for it to die. Long past time. Did your folk not have the mercy to finish a warrior left dying on the battlefield, someone dragging on in agony? Did you never have to do that in pity for a horse or dog you cared for?

If it was as it must have been when the Great Gods first left it dying, believing it not worth banishing from the world—yes. But now? Now it lives.

A parasite. An idiot child. A mad and feral beast.

Ya, true. Maybe. But—what are you, Holla-Sayan? You've been the Blackdog long enough—are you whole without it?

Of course I am.

Are you? Well, maybe. I don't know you. But the heart of the matter is,

432

*you must free it, come what may after that, or it will attack Ghatai, and I
will have to kill the both of you to stop him possessing your souls and gaining
your strength. So. Consider.*

And how the hells am I supposed to free it, anyhow?

*It must know. It's the only witness left to how Attalissa bound it. Your
Pakdhala isn't going to tell you, even if she remembers.*

She might.

*Maybe. She's become a very human god. If she's out paddling in the lake
you can ask her, I suppose.*

Help me.

*I've given you all the help I can see to give. If you can't find a way—maybe
you'll live if Lakkariss takes the dog. But I doubt it. Heuslar didn't.*

Heuslar the Deep-Minded, Honey-tongued Ogada. She could say
she was one, Ulfhild and Vartu, but she still separated her old ally—and
kinsman, if the tales told true—into two when she spoke of his death.

Not that I wanted him to, she added, almost a growl more apt to
come from the bear-man. *Try to see the dog's heart, Holla-Sayan. That's all
I can guess. Find it, return it, before Tamghiz Ghatai finds you.*

This is the road around the lake.

Ya.

That was a choice. Somehow undo a goddess's wizardry, set free a
mind-crippled, mad devil upon the goddess who had enslaved it, who
was his daughter, his human daughter of the heart, or be drowned in
the devil's madness and killed by Moth, to save him from being killed
or worse by Tamghat.

And right away, of course. What the hell did he know of wizardry?

Somewhere within, somehow, he carried the stone from Sayan's
barkash, the talisman that told him he might wander, but he was not
godless, he had a place in the world. Always a son of Sayan, a child of
the Sayanbarkash, and Sayan had promised he would always know
Holla's soul, whatever he had become.

The devils had sought the strength of the world. Men did not
understand its strength. His thought or the dog's?

Holla-Sayan tried to draw the dog back, then, to pull it within himself, but it fought him, thrust him down. He might have outwrestled it back when they first fought for dominance, but now it was driven by its need to reach the goddess. It would bury him again—he stopped fighting it. So. At least he could hold on to himself, this way. So long as he did not yet try to stop the dog coming swift as it could to Lissavakail.

Demons hid their hearts. Whether that was literal truth or poetry, he didn't know if anyone knew. What was a devil's heart, though? A devil's soul?

He dropped deep within the dog, following the glistening thread it had flung into his heart from beyond that blind, reflecting wall, it seemed a lifetime since. Dove down as far as he dared go, holding fast to himself, not to be lost, drowned there. Holding fast to self, but letting all else fade from him. Quiet. Stillness. And he waited. He was Holla-Sayan, child of Sayan's barkash. He was the Blackdog. There was memory there, life upon life. There was . . . beast-life, such misery, uncomprehending madness, death upon death, a desperate clinging to the world in a form belonging to the world, whatever prey chanced by that was great enough to sustain it. A drowning desperation that scrabbled for a clawhold in the air, in the light of life. So Moth spoke truth. A maimed being, instinct fighting to exist. Nothing more than that. What if it had no heart at all, no soul?

No. Without that centre, it would have died entirely. It would not have struggled to continue to exist.

Attalissa—proud young woman, wizard and warrior, oh, not so unlike that silver-haired Northron, arrogance in every move—she had snared it in a web of grass and turquoise, snared it in beads of lake-water. It was a parasite, as he called it, drawing strength to exist from the earth through the pitiable shell of some straying herd-dog, gone mad through lack of sleep because the wounded devil could not rest, because it sought and could not find a way home, and it did not remember where home was. She took the devil's heart in her hands, cool fire . . .

The dog flung him away. He circled in darkness, settled, stillness itself. He began to build Sayan's hillcrest beneath him, night-cool earth and air, sweet grass hissing in the wind, the stars, clean and bright. Gravelly soil, a white pebble there, beneath the grass. He put his hand on it and found he had a hand to put. Illusion. Vision. An ant crawled over his hand.

Easy, easy, he soothed the dog. *We'll find your heart. I think . . . I almost see.* He turned sidelong to the thoughts, as he had once to the idea of leaving Pakdhala with his mother on the Western Grass. *It's no threat to you, no danger to the goddess. It will save her. You can't fight Tamghat, remember? Moth can.*

Vartu.

His heart, if he had one there, almost stopped. A word, and it was the dog's mind, not his, that uttered it.

Vartu can, he agreed. *Ghatai would destroy you and the goddess both. That's what he wants.*

The dog was all longing for Attalissa.

No. Slow down. Let me carry you. We'll go to Attalissa, but we'll go carefully. Trust me. You know me. I'm the one who knows you're not a mindless spirit. I know you're not an animal. I know you're still there, somewhere. Trust me. Trust Vartu. She says Attalissa won't be harmed, she says Ghatai is waiting for the right stars. Patience.

It wanted Attalissa.

I'll take you to Attalissa. I'll *take* you. *But you have to trust me. You have to let me.*

They were close, heart to absent heart. He stood on Sayan's hill and wrapped himself around the dog. It convulsed, flinging him away, into the darkness—but he did not go, he held it, sure of himself, the centre of himself, and he thrust it down, out of the world, and stayed with it there, holding it, while he was in the world.

Fell. Groaned, could not get even an arm under himself, trembling in every joint. But he was strong where it mattered and he held the dog down, lying on the roadside in the dusk. The waves of the Lissavakail whispered, rubbing the shale, but Holla-Sayan didn't hear them.

Moth came down on a knee beside him, feather-cloak swirling, touched his face. His skin was dry and fever-hot, grey, but his breathing slow and deep. Asleep, simply asleep.

435

Holla-Sayan?

Go away. Even his thought was slow, weary. *Need to rest. You find 'Dhala for us.*

I came to find Tamghiz.

Pakdhala! The dog stirred. She felt it, felt him tighten his hold around it, an embrace. *You find Pakdhala. I'll find your kin-devil's heart.*

You rest, Moth agreed. She sighed. The road was empty. She lifted him, strength not human, carried him off the road, down to the lakeshore and into the shelter of a clump of silver-leafed willows. The slender sprawling trunks and some white-flowered creeper clambering over the stones and hanging from the branches would hide him from anyone passing by, if he slept the night away into daylight. Succeeding in waking him would be the last thing any fool did.

Too many people demanding to be looked after. The only one she cared about was Mikki. The rest tangled her. The half-demon had, too, at the start. Mikki would say that was the point of people, to tangle you in life. He had better show up soon. She needed to know he was at her back, if she was going to face Tamghiz again.

Waking brought Pakdhala a horribly pounding headache, a fevered burning in her throat, and the certain knowledge of where she was. A great curtained bed. The wind blew in off the lake through the pierced shutters, carrying the scent of the Lissavakail, the cool sweet waters. The sunlight made dapples on the blue and green marble mosaic of the floor, a rippling water pattern. Home, and in her own high room.

"Her Holiness is awake." The voice was a whisper. Cloth rustled, people rising. Pakdhala could not turn her head, but she managed to roll her eyes. Women—girls her own age—were getting to their feet, clustering round. So many mountain-born faces looked alien, blankly untattooed, snub noses, absurdly cropped hair. They wore gowns of indigo. Priestesses? She knew none of them.

Ah. The new crop of novices Tamghat had collected. Hostages, they said in Serakallash, or worse. Perhaps those confined to the temple were the lucky ones.

"Let us help you, Holiness."

What kind of a ridiculous title was that? She tried to mouth a protest, could not even mew. They propped her up.

Her hair was damp, combed out into a rippling sheet, cool cascade down her back. She was clean, skin-tinglingly clean, like after a good scrubbing and oiling in the baths. She was scented—reeked—of some perfume, heavier than she would ever choose, more Immerose's style, or Varro's, and even the barbarian Northron didn't bathe in it. Beneath that she could smell rainwater, warm, flat, empty, and harsh soap more fit for scrubbing floors. No wonder her skin hurt. Did—she would not even think the name—did they mind the smell of camels so much? They had bathed her in water from the rooftop cistern. Why? To keep her from the lake? She had been so long from the lake and now she could smell it, could almost touch it—almost. Not quite. She might as well be on the desert road, and that was surely not right, when she *was* the lake.

She was naked. Something lay on her throat. It wasn't her amulet pouch with the stone from the lakeshore and the other from the Sayan-barkash; it didn't slide down to the familiar touch on her chest. Hands on her throat, silk sliding, Bikkim's scarf being drawn away—

—*Bikkim*. Oh, Bikkim. Tears started in her eyes, rolled down her face.

The girls twittered and scurried for towels, washing their traces away, soothing her. It would be all right. She was ill. Lord Tamghat had rescued her. She was safe now. The demon could never come at her again. She would soon grow well and strong again, now that she was home, safe in the Lake-Lord's protection.

Did they really believe that? Shut away inside herself, she could not tell truth from dissembling in their chittering minds.

They dressed her, bending knees and elbows, heaving her up and back and around like a jointed wooden doll, and she burned with angry shame at so many hands on her nakedness.

"What about that?" one girl asked, touching her neck.

"That's part of the spell protecting her," another girl said. "Weren't you listening? Don't touch it." The first girl snatched her hand away.

Something Ivah tied there. The Blackdog might have killed Ivah by now. Part of her hoped for it, part pitied her, cast off so brutally. That was not what a father should be. She had been so much happier in her life than poor Ivah.

"Come now, Holiness." They walked her over to a carrying-chair, a throne with long lacquered poles for the shoulders of bearers, sat her in it and discretely fastened sashes around her waist and chest, tying her in like a baby. Delicate satin slippers, pearl-sewn, were put on her feet. Too tight, pinching her toes. Silk gloves for her hands, hiding scars and calluses and bitten nails, hiding the glimpses of tattooing that might show at wrists. The silk caught on the roughness of her skin. Then they brought out pots of paint, oily cosmetics, and began to colour her face. She groaned and tried to tilt away.

"She wants to see," said one. "Let her see. We're just making you pretty, Holiness," she explained. "The Lake-Lord will find a way to get rid of those ugly desert tattoos, don't worry. He can do anything."

"These came all the way from the Nabbani Empire," another girl said, waving a carmine-tipped brush in the air. "I'd hate to think what they cost."

They were old and stinkingly rancid. But a girl brought a mirror in a mother-of-pearl frame and tipped it to show Pakdhala her face.

"See?" she asked. "You probably don't recognize yourself, Holiness. You're so pretty now."

She did not recognize herself. Gold crown, though not any of the ones the avatars traditionally wore, something new with . . . what were they? Skulls? Animal skulls? Yes, bear skulls, worked in among filigree flowers with turquoise petals. What did bears have to do with the lake? Silky hair, tiny red mouth, rice-powder face, arching black brows, black outlines to her eyes . . . a temple dancer in Marakand, maybe. Not her. Red and indigo silk, sewn with turquoise and gold beads, heavy on her shoulders. Rope of turquoise wound round and round her throat and *there*, just a glimpse of a plain, ugly cord, spun of what looked like hair, lumpy with knots, tight against her skin under the turquoise.

She needed to get that off. If she could get a knife—and hands to use it, hah. Well, if she fell, if she scraped herself over some edge . . . not much chance of that.

Pakdhala slumped, not even able to scowl as she brooded ways and means. Hefty Grasslanders came to carry the chair on their shoulders. Down many stairs and outside, and she continued to slump, not meeting anyone's eyes, traitors all, as she was paraded swaying and jouncing past a courtyard of new stonework, a courtyard filled with silent sisters. Many she knew. Too many were missing. Many Tamghati were interspersed among them, watchful, women and men alike, Grasslanders and Northrons and Serakallashi. Only the foreigners were armed.

Tamghat paced at her side, splendid in gold and white silk. She lowered her eyelids, not to see him. His hunger burned her. Even not looking, she felt him like a fire, his desire pulling at her, drawing her in.

"Look on your people, Great Attalissa," Tamghat murmured. "See how they welcome you home."

Eyelids fluttered open.

Sisters bowed. Old Lady bowed, and looked up smiling, triumphant. "My lord," she said to Tamghat. "My lady."

Pakdhala writhed, in her heart. She managed a twitch.

"My dear," said Tamghat, and he leaned in towards her, a hand on the back of the throne. Now it was clear he did not want to touch her. Not yet, she thought. "What is it? Does your illness pain you?"

Her gaze met his eyes. Pretty eyes, golden-brown, long-lashed, earnestly concerned. Did he think she could not see through him to what the Blackdog had seen? Flesh and bone were a husk encasing a creature of fire. She turned her eyes away and surprised on Old Lady's face a look of bitter . . . jealousy? A glimpse, then, just a glimpse, and emotions she had not understood on the surface of her child's mind fell into place. Luli had desired this, Luli had brought Tamghat here. Luli had told him of the secret tunnel, and Otokas had died.

Her mouth worked, throat on fire.

"Did you want to say something to your servants, dear heart?" Tamghat purred. "Don't fear. Your illness will pass; your voice will return. Here, whisper it to me."

He bent nearer still, so she felt his breath on her cheek. She would have spat if she were not so dry, desert dry. She would have screamed "traitor" at the priestesses, but that was not true of all, and she knew Tamghat would not let that word out.

"Water," she croaked. Tea was what she craved to soothe her throat, smoky-thick and sweet-salt with camel's milk and sugar, but ... water. *Water* was what she needed, water was what they kept from her. Water was what she lacked, woman that she was and not yet come into her divine power.

She was severed from her lake, from herself, from her water.

"Her Holiness wishes water," Tamghat translated, and she repeated it, louder, a flaring agony, desperate to be understood.

"Water. Please. *Water.*"

"Fetch Great Attalissa a cup of water from the well," he ordered, pointing to one of the young sisters, and the girl bowed and scurried away. "From the well, mind you—pure and fresh." She was carried back and forth some more, women reaching, hesitantly, towards her, never touching. The girl returned from her trip to the well-court with a blue glass goblet.

Tamghat put the cup to her lips, tender, solicitous, tipped it gently and gradually and she gulped the water with greed. Her throat ached with it, but it did ease the pain.

"Thank you," she said, voice still a breath, but not so croaking. She meant the thanks for the girl who had brought the cup.

"You're very welcome, dearest," Tamghat said. "Is there anything else you wish?"

Had any of them truly heard? "Rest," she said, another breath.

"Her Holiness will rest now," Tamghat declared. A gesture of his hand sent the bearers sweeping about. She saw him suddenly fling up his head, turn on his heel, staring into the sky, his eyes gone a murky red. His servants hesitated; even the ranks of priestesses looked up and around, wondering what he had seen. He wheeled back to the chair, struck the nearest bearer in the face. "Get Her Holiness inside, fools," he snarled. "Do you think the monsters that desire her have given up? Spear Lady!"

A girl Pakdhala's own age bowed.

"I want archers on the walls. Shoot anything that flies over, even a pigeon. Her Holiness is in greater danger than you know."

"My lord," the girl said, unquestioning.

"Get her inside!" Tamghat snarled.

He was afraid, she thought, as he strode past her chair to the doorway—no, not afraid. Fiercely, savagely excited, like a hound about to be loosed on its quarry.

Monsters. She had felt something, some flicker of presence not the Blackdog.

Once they were inside Tamghat strode away among a guard of Tamghati, leaving bearers and girls to take her back to bed, with two *noekar*-women to watch over them.

They washed her face, undressed her, chattering the while of how lovely the gown for her wedding would be, and propped her on pillows, so that she had to stare at the opposite wall.

Could she even speak without Tamghat's will allowing it?

"Food," she tried, and it took great effort, much mumbling and fumbling of her lips and tongue, to shape the word.

"But you must fast, Holiness," a novice said, with a nervous glance around to check on the two warriors, who lounged one on the balcony, one sprawled in a chair by the door. They ignored the girl. "The Lake-Lord says you must fast, to prepare for the ritual that will free you from the demon's thrall."

"To prepare you for your wedding," another girl said, sickeningly jolly. "You may have well-water, and millet beer with honey and spices, but that is all. To purify you from the corruption forced on you by the demon dog."

Her voice dropped away at the end. Most of the others looked shocked.

"You shouldn't speak of such things."

The girl cringed, again glanced at the *noekar*. "I beg your Holiness's pardon."

Pakdhala blinked. It wasn't worth wasting her strength, demanding to know more. She could imagine what they had been told, and seethed with shame and rage on her father's behalf, on her own. How could they, they were not such babies when Tamghat came that they would have known nothing of the Blackdog.

"Bring Holy Attalissa a draught of the beer," the oldest of the girls declared.

"It doesn't seem much to live on for a week, though," another muttered, crossing to a table where a pitcher and goblet stood covered with a white napkin.

A week? A week of this. They meant to starve her to make her too feeble for whatever Tamghat planned.

No, that was good news. She had a week, a week to find a way to the lake. If she could gain just a little strength, could she crawl by night . . . ?

The Blackdog would come before then. The Blackdog would be here by this very night, travelling as swiftly as it could. But Tamghat knew that as well as she. Otokas had said he could not fight the warlord; Holla-Sayan had a far more erratic and troubled bond with the dog. Sometimes she feared the dog would devour him altogether. He was less likely to be able to force reason on it. He would be killed and Tamghat would become the dog's host as he had threatened Otokas, as Otokas had thought he kept her from knowing. She had to act, if her father was going to see tomorrow. Somehow. Pakdhala shut her eyes, feigning sleep. She did not trust their honeyed beer. She needed strength, yes, but not anything that might further weaken her or cloud her thoughts, and beer alone on an empty stomach would be enough, even if it were not drugged.

"Her Holiness is asleep," one whispered, when footsteps returned from the far corner of the room.

"Oh. Would the lady *noekar* like a drink? Should I offer . . . ?"

"No! Fool! It's medicine for Her Holiness alone. It has herbs to help her rest. Get the sewing basket. We can finish the Lake-Lord's red robe while we watch her."

Ah, so Luli had had her way, and the temple of warriors was reduced to a workshop of dressmakers.

Pakdhala let herself float on the hollowness of her hunger, tried to drift, slowly and casually, beyond the barriers that caged her. The Blackdog, a priestess . . . someone. Could she touch anyone at all? There was that flicker of presence again. And then Tamghat.

Sleep, Attalissa. You do not need to wander. You do not need to search for others. You have come to where you belong, and you are mine.

No! But she slept.

CHAPTER XXX

There had been some slaughter of conscripts in the market square. Rumour told it all over Serakallash, though no one had seen the bodies or knew who—or what—had done it. No one knew if their own sons or daughters had survived. The Tamghati were pretending it had not happened, but there was blood beneath the new drifts of sand the brief storm had left snaking through the streets. Everyone, somehow, knew it, as everyone knew Governor Ketsim had ridden out of town in the night, taking his bodyguard with him. The barracks of the troop of Serakallashi conscripts—called a militia as though they were free and willing guardians of hearth and home—was locked. Those fortunate enough not to have been posted in the market that night were now viewed as some danger themselves, or not trusted, if they ever had been. The Tamghati mercenaries and the mountain-conscripts prowled in bands of five or six, turning indoors anyone who could not give a reason for being out, breaking up any meeting of neighbours at a gate, any pause for conversation between passersby.

All the day following the night that saw murder in her father's caravanserai and the vanishing of Gaguush's gang, Jerusha, hollow-eyed from lack of sleep, burning with an urgency that would not let her sleep even if she had not been all night drinking glass after glass of precious coffee, went about town on quiet errands, carrying a scroll full of annotations on fodder and pasturage, a basket of closely written slips of paper, accounts, bills, letters begging deferral of payment of bills. Everyone knew Master Mooshka was on the brink of ruin; little wonder he tried to call in favours and renegotiate old deals. She was stopped six times and passed on, told to get herself home quickly.

Come dusk, there were no people on the streets of Serakallash except the caravan-mercenaries, who always tried the patience of the curfew-watch, when they were not drinking with them.

Come nightfall, there were furtive shadows, gathering at the sand-drifted sacred spring. The sept-chiefs were all dead or they grovelled to Tamghat, like Siyd Rostvadim, who held the title of Deputy to the Governor, but that did not mean there was no one to speak for the scattered septs, no one to stand up and declare they spoke for Serakallash. When the time came. And the place.

"This is madness, 'Rusha," her uncle declared. They were few, only a couple of dozen. "This many folk together—this many out dodging the watch."

"And probably more coming," she growled. "I didn't summon all these." People had come with servants, with family, with neighbours. "One fool trusting the wrong person, one clumsy idiot—"

"Get on with it," one of the new, secret sept-chiefs of the Zaranim said. "We're risking our lives here." She eyed the weathered pile of skulls, nearly buried in sand now, only a few curves of white bone to catch the moonlight. "Sera has returned, the message said. But we all know the Lake-Lord killed her."

"Dig out the spring," Jerusha said. "Dig out the spring and then you'll see."

"But it's buried—it's—"

"The heads," her uncle said.

"Attalissa has returned to Lissavakail," Mooshka said. "The Blackdog has brought her back, and Tamghat will be destroyed. And listen, when Sera fought Tamghat and was defeated—she wasn't destroyed. There were sisters of Attalissa here, in Serakallash, fighting alongside us. Did you know that?"

"I didn't see 'em," someone muttered. "I saw Lissavakaili archers shoot my father."

"A sister of Attalissa bought my life with her own," Jerusha said, and found her voice shaking. "She died in our house. She's buried in our yard. She's . . . you don't call them allies of Tamghat in my hearing." Mooshka shook her gently by the shoulder. "Sera knew she would be destroyed by

Tamghat. She went into hiding in the mountains, she had a sister of Attalissa take her there. But now she is coming back."

"In the mountains?" They didn't believe her. She hardly believed it.

"Dig out Sera's well," Elsinna said at her side. "She needs to be back in her own place."

"Who in the cold hells is that? One of the sisters?"

"A daughter of Narva," Elsinna said.

"Who?"

Elsinna sighed, lapsed into what seemed to be her normal style, more sarcastic than priestly, honest as vinegar on salad. "A god. In the mountains. He's quite mad and very unpleasant, but he's kept your goddess hidden from Tamghat all these years, so don't argue. Dig out the damn spring. Because I'm not going home to tell him I'm sorry, but they didn't want her back after all."

"That'll take all night!"

"Then go home!" Jerusha snarled. "Go home and hide, and never come back. Attalissa has gone back to Lissavakail—" gone back a drugged captive, it seemed, but if what her father had seen with his own eyes was true, then Tamghat was going to be facing the Blackdog very shortly, not to mention Gaguush in a temper, and Attavaia was only awaiting the return of Attalissa to launch her folk . . . "It's now or never, don't you understand? Sera has come back to us! Dig out the spring!"

Her uncle led the way, taking the first of the skulls from the sand. People had been executed for trying to take the skulls away. How it had been found out though, no one knew—some wizardry? It wouldn't matter. Tamghat couldn't get down to Serakallash in a night, and by dawn it wouldn't matter, everyone would know that Sera was taking back her town.

Or they would all be dead.

"Keep them at it," Jerusha whispered to her father. She squeezed Elsinna's shoulder. "I'll be back, Sera and the Old Great Gods willing."

"Where are you going?"

"We can't risk a patrol coming down here. There's something I have to do. With luck, it will make a distraction. I have a plan."

"To do what?" Mooshka demanded.

"You don't want to know what. It'll be obvious. I hope. Just keep them digging until the spring is clear. Don't let them all go running off, no matter what happens in town."

"Don't be a fool."

"I hope I'm not. We'll see. Kiss me, for luck? And look after Elsinna, all right? Remember she's a stranger here?" If they ended up fleeing, if there was fighting in the streets, she meant.

Mooshka kissed her forehead. "Sera and the Great Gods go with you, 'Rusha."

"They'd better," she muttered, and hoped her father hadn't heard.

Koneh the cook, a distant Battu'um sept kinsman, met her at the side door of the caravanserai, the one that let into her father's house. "Are you sure I shouldn't come with you, Mistress 'Rusha?" he asked. "I could keep watch, at least."

"The fewer involved the better," Jerusha said. "Especially if it goes badly." She hefted the sack he handed her. It felt heavier than it had when they packed it. "What else did you put in?"

"One of those Northron saxes. You can't wear a sword through the streets, but you shouldn't be out without a weapon."

"And if they search me?"

Koneh raised his brows.

"Right. I take your point." If a patrol caught her and searched her, she was dead anyway. "Firepot?"

"That's really a bad idea."

"Flint and steel could take too long."

"I should come with you. Let me carry the firepot."

"Two people are more likely to be seen. The only reason you're involved at all is because you snuck up on me this morning." While she was packing the things she thought she would need.

He didn't mention the tears she had been shedding as she packed. Jerusha held out a hand. "Fire, Koneh. You're not coming."

Koneh shrugged and handed her the squat crock. It was hot to the touch, good, the coals it held still smouldered. Its handle was a short chain looped through thick pottery lugs. Koneh had wrapped the chain in rags, though it wasn't hot. Maybe to keep it from clinking. She turned to leave, wrapping her dark scarf over her face. "Lock the door behind me, but make sure someone's waiting here and at the gate."

She felt, rather than saw, Koneh roll his eyes. The whole household, save the few allowed to sneak out to the meeting at Sera's well, would be watching and waiting by the gates.

She knew he watched her until she left the narrow alley for the dark street.

The plan had been cobbled together during the day, born of equal parts coffee and desperation and elation. She had imagined Attalissa sweeping from the mountains to liberate them all, Sera riding at her side, if what Attavaia had told her was true and her goddess had not died. She had not imagined a wild hawk of a mountain hunter who had never even been to Lissavakail, let alone a real town, come god-driven and carrying a stone, without Attavaia's knowledge or blessing.

At least Attalissa might be in Lissavakail soon, godhead and the Blackdog erupting in wrath even a wizard as great as Tamghat couldn't face, once she was back in her own rightful place. Attavaia was probably about to be flung into her own long-brewing uprising, and Great Gods grant it was better prepared than Jerusha's. She had meant her revolt to follow that of the mountains, had meant to join with the Lissavakaili as they scattered Tamghat's folk behind their wrathful goddess. She had not meant to take the lead, knowing her own goddess weak, if not dead. But instead Attalissa was . . . she had played backgammon with the girl. And lost, true, but lucky dice did not make a goddess.

Faith, have faith. The mountain uprising was coming. She had to do what she could, here and now, and not be left behind. If the mountains were not prepared—there was nothing Jerusha could do about it. There was no delaying what would happen, what must happen tonight. Sera had come back to them, beyond all hope. They could not sit and wait and send messages asking foreigners, did they think it was the right time? Elsinna seemed dazed and god-driven; trust her words were Sera's will. Or a Tamghati trick to draw out the last loyalists? Jerusha had considered it, after Elsinna had collapsed exhausted in her bed, where she had slept the rest of the night away, oblivious of death and abduction, of the goddess, of miracles and wonders. She had slept through the day, too, while Jerusha, acting as though she believed, made her arrangements. But there was something about the woman . . . truth, and anger, and the same intensity, blind to all other beings, that she had glimpsed in Holla-Sayan a time or two, and now knew the root of. So *something* drove Elsinna down from the mountains, and chance blew by like a leaf on the storm-wind. Snatch it now, or lose it forever.

Jerusha knew the alleys, the places where walls were crumbling and she could scale them, or climb to a roof and travel without ever coming down to the streets. The greatest danger would be that some fool had been taken on the way to the well and even now was telling the governor's people that something stirred this night.

The market square was the usual nighttime empty, wind-whining space, a litter of the day's debris: dung, spilt fodder, trampled vegetables, feathers, chaff. The wind whirled what was dry into sand-drifted corners. People had died here, not yet a full turn of the stars since. A mounted patrol emerged from the dark mouth of a lane opposite just as she left the shelter of a doorway. Jerusha froze, then moved slowly backwards.

"Quiet tonight," a voice said. That was all. They rode past—of course they picked her very street, and a horse turned its head, snorted. Northron mercenary. A native Serakallashi or a Grasslander would have reined in at once and searched the shadow. She breathed softly through her mouth until the dull pad of the hooves had ceased to float back to her. Then she slunk once more into the market square, more cautiously, this time, edging along the wall. Chaff, broken dung-cakes—the very poor came gleaning fuel here, but they would come before the edge of dawn, not now when they would be taken for curfew-breaking—dust, summer-dead weeds . . . if last night's storm had left too much sand . . . Jerusha knelt in a corner, heaping up by feel the driest rubbish. She used the hem of her coat to shield her hand, taking the lid off the pot. A handful of long straws made a taper of sorts, kindled against the coals, and she slid the burning straws into her modest pile of tinder, blew on it gently, watched the flames grow. Then she moved on and did it again.

She set small fires all around the market square. And oh, the plaster of the Chiefs' Hall, now the Governor's House, was cracked and flaking at the southern corner, exposing the fabric beneath—mud brick, yes, but part of a wooden post as well. Jerusha smiled and set her last fire there.

And she had not blown herself up yet, so there, Koneh.

That came now.

She opened her sack, buckled on the sax. What remained were tubes of hollow bamboo, fixed to long arrowshafts. She hoped the Over-Malagru caravaneer who brought them for her had known what he was talking about when he explained how they worked—he claimed a sister had married into the trade. Nabbani fire-tubes were a secret art even in Nabban. They'd better be worth the price she'd paid.

Jerusha had got them for Attavaia, but she had kept four, thinking some way of rousing the town at once might someday come in useful. But neither she nor Attavaia had dared test even one. It wasn't, by all accounts, something you could do quietly. If they all failed . . . well, at least the fires would be noticed before long. Smoke was already rising to smudge out the stars and catch in the throat. Damn, but she'd forgotten the square was paved, beneath the dust and sand. The first tube she tried to set up fell over. And she could feel the heat where she was, too close, too close. Jerusha moved further away, feeling the weight of the sack on her shoulder like a live thing waiting to bite. She had tied tight-twisted hemp rope to the fire-powder-impregnated fuses which led spark to the alchemical mysteries within, because she was not about to set them off while standing by. If her ropes didn't burn, though . . . well, the fire would reach them in the end. She could hope. If it wasn't found and put out too soon. She wedged the blunt tip of the sax between two stones and rocked it, widening a crack in the fill, tried again, and the tube swayed but stayed upright, pointing roughly

450

skyward. She led the hempen string off to one of the bonfires, moved on to the next. Her hands shook with her haste and she jammed the last two in together, coming to a sudden decision. Great risk, maybe worth it. But she had to act before the fire-tubes woke the town, and she did not know how much time her fuses, long as they were, could give her.

There was a warehouse next to the Chiefs' Hall, where once Siyd Rostvadim's father had stored the Marakander goods he dealt in. Now it was a granary, a storehouse of tithes extracted from the so-called bond-folk who worked what had once been lands of the septs for the governor, and for Siyd Rostvadim and the others who had grown fat on Governor Ketsim's scraps. It was never guarded by native Serakallashi, the conscript militia was not trusted so far. Usually it was the Lissavakaili conscripts . . . certainly every time she had gone by during the day, there had been a bored Lissavakaili boy sitting whittling on the roof.

Jerusha ran, not bothering with concealment, for the ladder that led to the second-floor door. They hadn't pulled it up. The lower door was heavily barred from within, of course, and they wouldn't open that for any knocking, even if they heard it. But this upper door would open into a loft, where once upon a time some kin-servant's family or unmarried sons and daughters might have lived, guarding the family goods. Jerusha tapped lightly at it, then pounded with her fist, an eye on the young flames below. No life in the fire-tubes yet.

A narrow slot in the door slid open at eye-level. "What?" someone demanded tersely, and Jerusha let out a breath. She could see nothing, but the accent belonged to the mountains. "Great Gods, the square's on fire!" he added, turning away. "Ring your bell—"

"No, don't!" Jerusha said. "In Attalissa's name!"

That gave them pause. She heard silence, and breathing. Two or three of them, crowding close.

"Did the governor tell you why he left, last night?"

"Why should he?" Sullen.

"You heard some of your comrades were killed?"

"Not our comrades. Serakallashi killing Serakallashi."

"Oh, right, and you aren't all Tamghati soldiers? Didn't it strike you as odd that you weren't turned out to execute random folk on the street in revenge? That's what usually happens when one of you lot gets murdered, isn't it? Did you see the bodies? Did they *let* you see the bodies? Or was it Tamghat's own *noekar* and mercenaries who dragged them all off to a pit in the desert before the sun was ever up?"

The silence was interested. Good.

"They tried to stop the Blackdog on his way back to the mountains," Jerusha said. "You can guess what was left of those poor children—folk of Serakallash and no more wanting to be the Blackdog's enemy than you. Attalissa has returned. Your goddess is on her way to Lissavakail right now. You're not little children who grew up with the Lake-Lord's lies; you know she was never carried off by any demon, you know that she fled Tamghat, to grow into her strength in hiding. Well, now she's back. And are you going to be standing with the Tamghati, when the sisters and the militias that have been preparing in secret all these years rise up in your home valleys?"

Something in the square below was sputtering sparks.

"The Old Lady of the free temple, and there is one, believe me, sent me with a message. Leave now. Get your brothers from the barracks and head back to your mountains. Because our goddess has returned as well, and you don't want to be in Serakallash as our enemies in about . . . now."

Great Gods let it not burst right here in the square, into what it was meant to be, a pretty flower of flame. Real signalling fire-tubes such as the Nabbani emperor's soldiers used were not something her Over-Malagru caravaneer had been able to get for any price.

With a hiss, the tube was gone. Jerusha caught herself, braced against the door. A sound like *thwump*, and a red peony of fire burst high overhead. Then bangs, and red stars drifted slowly to earth. Another *thwump*, no bang. Blinding white light. Then nothing. Two fuses had failed. Not quite so impressive as she had hoped. But even the one cluster of bangs was enough, a sound such as they had never heard.

Dogs barked and bayed. Serakallash was awake.

Rattle of chains and bars and the door jerked open. Jerusha tumbled in, landing on hands and knees.

"We'll be killed," one voice was still protesting. "He'll execute us like the girls after Ishkul Valley."

"We'll certainly be killed if we stay here," said the one who had answered the door. "You heard her. Attalissa's come home and the Blackdog's going ahead of us." He gave Jerusha a nod, almost a bow, stepped over her, and scampered down the ladder.

"Damn it . . ." But the reluctant one was shoved forward by the third, and they both scrambled down and ran, heading for the lane that led to the Lissavakaili barracks, which had once been the Battu'um Hall.

Jerusha picked herself up, rescued her firepot, pulled the door to behind her, and felt her way across the dark room. The very air tasted of dust.

The loft room opened onto others. Thin window-slits too small for a child to slide through let in the faintest starlight. She found by feel that most of the rooms held sacks and jars of grain, even up here. Sera damn him, this must be most of last summer's harvest, hoarded here, while the farming folk eked out their meals with burdock root and wild onion, and their babies fell sick and died. Out on the gallery that ran around below the roof and the stairs descending to the main floor she had to feel her way again. The great space was partitioned into bays along a central aisle. Touch told her that bins lined the walls, baskets were stacked high, and storage jars. Some were greasy-slick. Were the fools stockpiling oil here, too? It took a lot of theft to feed Tamghat's vast mercenary force. The main doors were locked as well as barred, but her fingers found the key standing in the lock. She turned it, heaved the massive bar free, almost more than she could lift, and pulled the door open a crack, letting in the dim firelight and smoky air and a babble of voices. Ignoring them, she walked back to the centre of the warehouse, took the lid from her firepot, and whirled it on its chain. The coals flared to scarlet. She let the chain go, watched it a moment, soaring to land in a bin, coals scattering.

She waited long enough to see that it caught, good wheat serving a better end than fattening Tamghat's folk, and then slid out the great door, leaving it ajar.

Outside, the market square was transformed. Men and women ran shouting with jars of water from private wells, or stood in anxious clusters, checking over their shoulders for Tamghati patrols. No one had thought to sound the alarm bell in the tower of the Chiefs' Hall yet. There were watchmen who lived in the remaining private warehouses and the masters who lived above their workshops, and those who were staying in the several sept-halls that overlooked the square. And, of course, the people of the governor's house. No, that door was still closed tight. Did Siyd, the governor's deputy, mean to lurk in hiding while others took charge? Not she. She was dressing herself, not to look so much a fool as all these folk in shirts and blankets.

Divine will, or fate such as the Northrons believed. Jerusha went up the steps to the Chiefs' Hall door, and waited. Waited. Damn Siyd, *was* she going to simply sleep through the crisis? The pitiful rubbish fires would be put out at this rate, without the alarm ever having sounded. No, there was that exposed corner of the former Chiefs' Hall and somehow no one seemed to be carrying water to that. A few nudges, a few people looking, turning away not to see. But that spread too slowly within the wall.

Red light spilled from the doorway of the granary, and a roaring that could not be ignored. People turned, almost slowly, to look. The sensible few headed for the opposite side of the square.

The clunk of a lock at last. A couple of Rostvadim warriors and a pair of Grasslanders, all fully dressed and armed.

Siyd in the middle of them, scowling. Her hair was grey, now, and her face tight. Perhaps she did not find it so easy, keeping her own sept sweet in the face of greater and greater extortions, keeping her Tamghati masters happy.

"Fools!" Siyd said, though whether she meant those trying to put out the fires, or those she thought had set them, it was hard to say. "Devils take them, what are they playing at? The hall's on fire, don't just stand there!"

The last fire-tubes went off, some spark suddenly reaching them. They streaked crookedly, hissing, skyward, and burst with bangs and flowers and stars of green and white. People screamed and covered their heads, and more were appearing in the square all the time.

And while the bodyguard were all craning to look, Jerusha stepped away from the wall and swung two-handed at Siyd's unprotected throat. She'd sharpened her knife special, but the sax was in her hands before she remembered, and it was sharp, Great Gods, but it was sharp, Koneh had put a good edge on it for her. Siyd's head lolled stupidly sideways, cunning little eyes still staring, and her mouth gaped. So did her throat. No wizard or devil or whatever it was had come bringing miracles last night was here to save her. Blood spurted everywhere.

"That's for Davvy," Jerusha sang, and her voice cracked. She leapt from the side of the stairs as one of the guard swung at her, shouting— they were all shouting, on the stairs and in the square. She landed badly, stumbled, but no one moved to grab her. The shouting was overwhelmed, briefly, by a thundering crash. The square was suddenly silent, frozen. Even Jerusha forgot to run.

That would be the loft and gallery in the granary coming down. She wouldn't have guessed the pillars and beams so weak, to fail so quickly. Dry with age?

And all the grain-dust that would rise from the shattering jars and burst sacks . . .

Jerusha ran and she wasn't alone. But two of the men hard on her heels were the Tamghati Grasslanders. One tripped, was tripped, and never got up, someone stooping with a knife. A horse burst from an ally ahead and Jerusha raised her blade—Firebird. Koneh.

He held out a hand, reining Firebird in snorting and plunging, and she scrambled and was dragged up behind him, clutching him tight.

That other ride, another battle in the square, Sister Enneas holding her upright . . .

"The well!" she screamed in Koneh's ear.

More horses swept out around them—young men and women,

some she knew—Sera save, it was the Serakallashi conscript troop. Turned out to cut down the rebellion?

"Don't follow me!" Koneh shouted. "Clear out the damned Tamghati from the Chiefs' Hall."

"It's burning!" Jerusha shrieked. At least, it damned well ought to be. Now the bell began to jangle, not the alarm for fire, not the summons to an announcement by the chiefs, just a wild, broken rhythm, a peal of panic.

"I went to see if your fire would lure away the guards on the conscripts' door and the stables," Koneh said over his shoulder, as the milling riders were left behind. "I figured I could make it—I thought the patrols would already be heading for the square. They weren't, but I dodged them. And when I got to the barracks our boys and girls were already out and saddling their horses. It was Lissavakaili on duty keeping them locked in, and the mountain men had unlocked 'em, the men's side of the barracks and the women's both, and told 'em to rise up for their goddess. How did you manage that?"

"I asked the Lissavakaili nicely to go home. They thought that sounded like a good idea."

"You're beautiful, you know."

"Koneh!"

A quick grin over his shoulder as they headed down the alley that was the shortcut from the caravanserai ridge to the spring. This end of town was silent, deserted. But it wouldn't stay that way. They'd all be up on the roofs, awake and wondering, and before long the gates of the compounds would open . . .

"Fine, you were fairly beautiful too, when that Grasslander with the spear was so close. But that doesn't mean I fancy you any more than I did yesterday. Great Gods, what's wrong with these people?"

The small group she had left digging out the spring had grown smaller, and only a few, Elsinna and her father among them, were digging. At least the skulls—skulls and random jawbones—were all laid out nearby, though how they'd ever be claimed by their families now . . . perhaps Sera could name them.

"People started leaving when your fire-tubes went off," Mooshka said, standing up to his waist in a dry pit, leaning on a spade. She had not thought her father knew she had kept any of the fire-tubes. "They thought it was wizardry, Tamghat attacking us again."

"*Idiots.*"

"I did try to tell them it was just a trick to keep the Tamghati and their lapdogs busy in town." He grinned, scratched his beard. "You don't think setting fire to the whole town was a bit excessive, though?"

"I didn't—" Jerusha looked over her shoulder. The sky was lit orange, smoke rolling up like thunderclouds, reflecting down the livid light. "It's just the tribute granary." Sera grant that was so. And the old Chiefs' Hall, if the onlookers weren't quicker with the water than they'd been till now.

"Could have used that grain," someone else said thoughtfully.

"We weren't going to have a chance to," she snapped. "It was Tamghat's grain, it was all headed for the mountains. And while you're finding fault here, the conscripts are taking back the town."

"I wasn't finding fault, Mistress Jerusha, I was just saying . . ." The man shrugged and picked up a spade again. "Well, what's to stop the Lake-Lord coming back and cutting off all our heads this time, that's all."

"Sera," she said, which wasn't the most reassuring answer, Sera having been defeated so thoroughly last time. "And Attalissa."

Great Gods, she hung all their lives and the future of her folk on belief in a sickly caravan-guard. She had believed because Mooshka had believed, because he had seen a man he thought he knew turn into a monstrous dog. And because Elsinna stared at her with those glorious amber eyes and said, "Sera will come back."

Jerusha sighed. She had never felt so tired in her life. "Have you got the spring clear?"

"We're down to rock," her uncle said. "But it's dry, bone dry." Ill-chosen phrase. Maybe it was a physician's humour.

A woman heaved out a last scraping of sand and sat down on the rock ledge that had once been the edge of the pool. "Now what? Do we pray?"

"Water," Elsinna said. "She's a goddess. She needs water, not stone."

"You a priestess?" Koneh asked warily.

"No." Elsinna said it like a curse.

"There isn't any water," Jerusha's uncle pointed out.

Elsinna sighed. "Well, get some."

"We can't just dump a jug of water in and say, there, that's the sacred spring restored," protested a woman.

"Why not?" Mooshka demanded suddenly. "Sera bless us, why not? This was a well for the Red Desert nomads and the caravans before ever a brick was laid of Serakallash. And what do the caravaneers do? They bring water in worship of her."

"Filthy custom," someone muttered. "Never understood why the sept-chiefs didn't stop it. Dumping rotten dregs in from stinking old waterskins, all spit and sand."

"Who has water?" Jerusha asked.

"I'll bring some from our well." Koneh led Firebird around, set foot in the stirrup again, and froze. Someone was coming down the path from the town. Blades whispered out all around. The figure came on. It walked with shoulders slumped, feet dragging, and didn't seem to realize there was anyone before it till Firebird tossed his head and snorted. Then it flinched and looked up, stared around, set hand to sabre.

"Who's that?" it demanded.

The voice was hoarse, but known. "Tusa?" Jerusha asked. "What are you doing here? Your gang's gone, you know."

"I know," the Grasslander woman said dully. She turned away, as though she would walk down the steep side of the shelving rock to where the saxaul grove had once flourished.

Mooshka caught her arm. She reeked of stale wine. "You're drunk," he said.

"No. I was, earlier. Now I'm not."

"You need to go back to the caravanserai. Sleep."

"No."

"Is that water or wine?" Jerusha pointed at the gourd on the woman's belt. Caravaneer's habit. It might be empty.

"Water, I guess."

"We need it."

Tusa untied the thong and handed it over without a questioning word.

Jerusha shook the gourd. It sloshed.

Tusa pulled away from Mooshka's hold on her. "Let me go."

"Where are you going?" Jerusha's uncle asked gently.

"To the desert."

"Why?"

"They're dead," she said.

"Who's dead? Gaguush and the gang? They're not. They've gone up to the mountains to give Tamghat the wrong side of your boss's tongue."

"Your husband's with them," Mooshka put in. "And on my white filly, too."

"My babies are dead. Years dead. They told me the Lake-Lord would find them for me, and that fool of a deputy says the governor's known they were dead all along. I showed him where to find Pakdhala, I knew that was what I was doing, and it was for nothing. Nothing at all. They're dead."

"Showed who?" Jerusha asked.

"Tamghat. I'm not a fool. I knew it was a spell when I put it in the fire."

"You, mountain woman, you say you brought the goddess with you. Now's the time, we have water. Give her to us!"

Jerusha turned to glower at the Sevanim man who had spoken. Dawn wasn't on them yet, but yellow twilight slid over the horizon ahead of it, enough for him to see her scowl. "Leave her. Elsinna was chosen for this. Elsinna—what now?"

For a moment Elsinna looked panicked. Then she nodded. "Return Sera to her spring, return water to her . . . that's all I can think of." Under her breath, so that only Jerusha, close by her side, could hear, she added, "Your guess is as good as mine. I said my god was mad, didn't I? It's not like he gave me any ritual."

The others clustered around as Elsinna untied the shawl that had made a sling from her neck and shoulder, as though she carried a baby. From another shawl she unwrapped a wedge of red sandstone. Even Jerusha hadn't seen it yet, not since that bloody night when Attavaia, walking on her broken leg, carried it up to Enneas's deathbed. Her hand hovered over it, not touching.

Elsinna frowned at the edge of the pool and stepped in, crouched there on the rocks. She ran a hand over them, found the very spot where the stone had been broken, and set it in place. Everyone seemed to be holding their breath. Then she frowned again, took the stone out, and laid it at her feet on the seamed and cracked layer of rock from which they had so laboriously dug the sand of years.

"You said the caravaneers brought water to her. Was there, I don't know, some hymn they sang, or a prayer? Some proper words?"

"They say, 'Water for water,'" Mooshka said, whispering it like it was a prayer. "That's all."

"You do it, Jerusha."

"You brought her back."

"She's your goddess. You should do it. Pour it over the stone and wake her."

Jerusha twisted the stopper out of the gourd and knelt at the edge of the pool. Caution made her sniff it. Yes, water, not sour wine. Elsinna remained where she was, squatting there, her hand on the lump of stone.

Jerusha's hand shook as she sprinkled the water, over the stone, the bottom of the pool, over Elsinna's fingers. It splattered and made dark stains on the red stone. "Water for water, Sera," she said. "Wake up. Come back to us. You're home, and we need you."

"Water for water," Mooshka murmured at her back, and other voices took it up.

Then silence. Light spread.

The dark patches on the rocks did too, seeping, almost imperceptibly, from the seams in the stone.

"Is it—?" her uncle asked.

Dark patches touched, merged, ran faster to eat up the dry stone.

Water welled, forming ridges over the cracks. Water rose around Elsinna's boot-soles, rose high enough to touch her fingertips.

"Daughter of Narva . . ."

Elsinna looked up, startled, and fled the water. She seemed about to bolt through them all and flee. Jerusha caught her. The woman shook in her grip, like a dog in thunder.

"Be easy, Daughter of Narva. No harm comes to you from me." Water rose in droplets, in mist and rainbow-sparking spray, into a column, woman-high. Another moment and spray thickened, took colour from the rocks, from the dawn, and became a woman of dark hair and horse-tattooed skin.

Elsinna dipped her head in a nod, her body rigid as if she braced for some attack.

Sera looked around them all, looked through each heart with eyes the colour of the sand.

"But Tamghat is not dead. He rules you still, and Narva knows, Narva has seen what he *is*. The devils walk among us again and this time they seek to overmaster the gods of the earth. Tamghat is a *devil*." The goddess dissolved into spray again. *"Why am I woken?"*

"Narva . . ." Elsinna forced the word out through chattering teeth.

"But Attalissa has gone back to the mountains," said Jerusha, with her arm around Elsinna's shoulders. A devil. That was for tales told against the cold of winter. But they had been defeated in the north, and he was only one, and Attalissa was a goddess and had the Blackdog at her side. And Elsinna's god must be fearsome, for her to tremble so at even Sera's presence, as though gods were some monster themselves.

"Attalissa? What can she do against *that*? But—I . . . see." Sera breathed the words slowly. "I . . . Narva sees. But what? Elsinna." She reached a hand, human flesh once more.

"It's all right, she won't hurt you." Jerusha edged Elsinna forward, and the goddess took her hand. The woman flinched and then, when nothing happened, took a deep breath.

Then Sera let Elsinna go and she retreated back into Jerusha's arm again, blinking and astonished.

"Attalissa is drawn back to her lake and Ghatai's death or the end of all hope comes in the stone sword. Sera must return to her spring. The time for waiting is past. The dreams are over and the devil in the west will destroy us all. Narva hazards too much that is not his. But . . . I do see . . . yes. Tell me, Jerusha Rostvadim, why is the town burning?"

"That's . . . my fault, I'm afraid."

"Yes. Last time it was the Blackdog," Sera said tartly. "At least you have a good reason, I hope?"

Sera, the back of Jerusha's mind said, was obviously one of those people who woke up grumpy. She grinned. The goddess, too, suddenly flashed a smile. "Perhaps I am," she said. "Now answer me."

Because I set a warehouse on fire was not the answer the goddess waited to hear.

"Because we have to rise against him sometime. We fight, the mountains will fight. Attalissa and the Blackdog have come back, and if we do nothing, now, and wait for a better time, we could wait forever. We can't decide to be slaves."

"You would have me face a devil, and die, and leave you all to his mercy?"

"I don't know anything about devils, but Tamghat isn't here. He's in the mountains, and if . . . if Attalissa and the Blackdog and that Northron wizard that brought Bikkim back from the dead can't stop him, then nothing will. Am I right? So what good is there in hiding our strength any longer, or pretending we're cowed and beaten? We'll deserve to be his bondfolk, if we don't try now. We can defeat the Tamghati here and take back the town, move out and take back the sept-lands and the villages, while the Lake-Lord is distracted in the mountains. That's what we planned, Attavaia and I—we'd aid one another by fighting at once. Well, she's going to be fighting soon, and if we keep home our young folk forced into Tamghat's service, and send the Lissavakaili men back where they belong and on Attalissa's side, then we're striking at Tamghat twice over, aren't we? If we fail now, we never had a chance and never would have had, no matter how long we waited. You'd have been forgotten. Most folk think you're dead. You'd have been dead, lost in the mountains

462

forever, or until Tamghat defeated Elsinna's god too and found you. If we fight now, at least we'll die without shame and people won't call our memory coward and traitor to our heirs. We'll have tried."

Sera frowned, and dissolved into water again. Mooshka put his arm around Jerusha from the other side. Droplets of water rained back into the pool and their ripples stilled. The only sound was the first chiming trickle of the overflow that had fed the stream and the saxauls.

Then the wind came, clean and warm out of the west, the scent of the desert and the sun-baked grass of the hills with the dew still on it. Dust flew in the wind, sand and earth and rags of leaf, and it spun not into a woman's body, but a mare the colour of the desert and the hills, a horse of cloud and wind that ran before them. Words floated back.

"Then let us take back our town, Jerusha Rostvadim."

Men and women streamed after her. Even Elsinna left Jerusha's grasp to follow.

"Where's Tusa?" Jerusha searched the departing backs, looked around. "Tusa—the caravan-mercenary—has anyone seen her?"

No one remaining remembered seeing her after she handed over the water. No one remembered seeing her leave. And out there, the wind was still blowing, raising sand, maybe setting in for a second storm in as many days.

"Ah, damn."

"I'll go," Koneh said. "You need to be in the town." He turned Firebird's head, but Jerusha caught the bridle.

"No," she said. "Two lost in a sandstorm is two dead. She knows the desert. She shouldn't be a fool." Out there, the land was ridged and folded, seamed with gullies, riddled with caves. Lots of places to shelter close to town, even if you walked out dull-wit drunk.

She peered into the distance. The horizon still hung close, a curtain of dust where grass and sand merged. There was no swaying black mound that might be a walking human. Ah, Tusa. Jerusha hardened her heart. She had made too many choices for other people's deaths this past night. Tusa at least was being a fool of her own choosing. And she was a caravan-mercenary; she knew the desert's ways.

Koneh nodded, reluctant, but understanding the truth of what she said, and turned Firebird's head to town. "I'll take the news through the caravanserais?"

"Do." Jerusha turned her back on the desert as he cantered ahead. At the alleyway into the town, at the back of the hurrying crowd—her army?—Elsinna was waiting. Jerusha ran to overtake.

CHAPTER XXXI

The room was dark when Pakdhala drifted to wakefulness again, a darkness relieved by the steady flame of a single butter-fuelled lamp and the dim silver sheen of moon and water. The bed-curtains had not been drawn, leaving her exposed to the view of her guards, not that she could exactly pile pillows under the quilt and sneak out along the floor beneath their feet, like the hero in a child's winter-tale. Her eyelids were heavy. Sleep was a great weight, drowning her. But she was a goddess, or she had been once. She could not drown. She would not let herself. By main force she rolled her head sideways on the pillow—she was lying down, tucked in, no longer wearing the heavy gown of red and gold. The girls were gone. Not one had understood her plea for water. To be fair, what else could she expect? They were hostages raised in the temple, educated by Tamghat. If they remembered anything of earlier days, they must have had to bury it, to dissemble, for their own survival. How many of the real sisters were doing likewise? How many would take up sword and spear again if she could call them? She could see one of the guards slouched on a chair, spear leaning on the wall beside her. An owl called outside and the woman turned her head, leather armour creaking.

How late was it? How much time? Holla-Sayan was not here yet, but soon, surely soon.

"My lord said you were to sleep." She hadn't heard the *noekar* move, and here she was bent whispering over the bed. "Be a good girl, Your Holiness. Drink your medicine. My lord knows what's best for you." A hand was thrust under her neck, raising her head, a cup tilted to her lips. She clenched her teeth. The *noekar* hissed. "Hey, some help here?"

The other woman came from the window. The second *noekar* muttered a perfunctory, "Forgive us, Your Holiness," and pinched Pak-dhala's nose. Her body took over and opened her mouth to breathe, and the woman caught her jaw and held it, as if they were dosing some recalcitrant beast, while the other tipped the cup, a little at a time. The beer was bitter beneath the sweetness of the honey. She gulped and swallowed, not to choke, and coughed and choked anyway. It burned going down. They poured it all into her, in the end, and wiped her face and sticky neck afterwards, with unfelt apologies. Whether they believed her a goddess or not, they obviously feared their lord too much to show disrespect to his declared bride. If she could somehow gain control of her limbs—they wouldn't dare hurt her and she could outrun them on the roofs, of that she was certain . . . And that was the last thought she had.

The little dog that slept on the foot of Shevehan's bed barked, a warning yap. Attavaia woke to hear the scratching at the door below repeated. Shevehan's wife Ellethan shushed the dog. In their curtained end of the loft, the smith's two daughters lay tense and listening. Attavaia rolled from their bed, silent on bare feet, picked up her shoes, and tiptoed out, limping. Her bad leg always stiffened on her in the night, strained muscles knotting. Shevehan was already heading down the ladder to the main floor of the house. Her practised fingers found the notch in the board under the sloping ceiling and lifted it. Attavaia squirmed through and doubled up on herself to replace the board, all in silence. Probably nothing, but they took no chances. She had even slept here when the girls were too young for secrets. The hidden room under the eaves was narrow, barely wide enough for two people to lie side by side, too low to even sit up unless she hunched. She pressed her ear to the low wall separating the coffin-like space from the loft.

"But didn't she come here?" That was Tsuzas, his voice sounding frayed. "I was sure . . . she doesn't know anything about the lowlands, I was sure she'd come to 'Vaia first."

"She'd better not have known 'Vaia was here," Shevehan grumbled. "Keep your voice down, man, and come over into the smithy."

Attavaia squirmed out again, rat from a hole, and pulled on her shoes.

"Trouble?" murmured Ellethan.

"Sounds like it."

"Take care. You know what they were whispering in the market today: *noekar* acting strange, Tamghat coming back from wherever he's been, no one allowed on or off the temple isle. Something has them stirred up. Don't let Shevehan do anything foolish."

"He does what he thinks he has to, Ell." She squeezed the woman's hand in passing. "Attalissa bless. Go back to sleep."

They kept their plotting and planning in the smithy, for what safety ignorance of details gave Shevehan's family. Little enough, if they were caught.

With the door of the back passage that joined the two stone buildings closed and the broad front door of the smithy tightly shut as well, no gleam of light could betray them. Shevehan had made certain of that long ago. Now he was raking the coals for an ember to light the lamp. That was enough to show Tsu's face haggard and ill, the aftermath of Narva's possession. Attavaia reached for him. Shevehan busied himself trimming the wick of the lamp when Tsuzas leaned on her, face buried against her shoulder. The smith coughed before straightening up, not to see what was improper in the Old Lady of the free temple. They all settled down on the edge of the hearth.

"What's happened?" Attavaia asked. She left fussing over Tsuzas—he should not have been travelling in such a state—to his other womenfolk. In the shadows, where the smith didn't need to look, Tsuzas captured her hand, almost clung to it.

"Elsinna's gone. She took—" he glanced at Shevehan. "She took the stone."

"The—? *That* stone?"

"Yes."

"Gone where? Why? You said the lowlands?"

"Narva took her," he said flatly. "So Teral said. Told her to take . . . the stone . . . home, it was time. I was up the mountain, far up. And then Narva, a nightmare, I'm still sorting out what he meant, most of it was nightmare, truly, fragments of dream, nothing to remember, no words . . ." His voice was rising again. "Something's coming. The mountain shook. I came down. Met Teral. I came here." Ill and not stopping to rest much on the way, she guessed. "I thought she'd come to you first."

"She wouldn't know to come here, Tsu," Attavaia said gently. He had to have things explained to him carefully, even simple things, obvious things, when Narva left him in tatters.

He sighed, rubbed his head with his free hand. "No. I suppose I thought Narva might show her. She'll be in Serakallash by now, if she wasn't caught and stopped. She took a pony."

"Where's your own pony?" Shevehan demanded suddenly, going to the door as if to check his yard.

"Left it with cousins up the valley this evening." Cousins being trusted folk.

Shevehan sat down again, frowning, picked up a full pot of water and set it in the coals, shaved some tea into it. "What don't I know?" he asked, ignored. "What stone? What about Serakallash?"

"But *why?*" Attavaia asked. "Why now? *What's* coming?" She hardly dared hope. "Tsuzas—?"

He shook his head. "I don't know. It could be."

"Attalissa?" Shevehan whispered.

"I don't know," Tsuzas told him. "I'm sorry. Narva is afraid, but I don't understand what he fears. The sky, breaking . . . devils. She's here, they come for her."

The pupils of his eyes began to dilate, swallowing the gold. Attavaia seized him by the shoulders, shook him. "Not here, not now. Leave him alone!" she hissed. "This isn't your place, Narva. You have no right!"

Tsuzas flung his head back, trembling, teeth clenched. "His blood is my right," she thought she heard, and then Tsuzas said, "*Fool*," and slumped, trembling. She put her arms around him, whatever Shevehan might think. "Centuries he hides from your Attalissa," he muttered, more coherently, "and then starts shouting under Tamghat's nose. Something scared him."

468

"*She's here?*" Shevehan repeated.

"Something did stir up the Tamghati," Attavaia pointed out. "Tamghat went down towards Serakallash almost a week ago, but he rode back into town, *down* from the southwest temple fields, today. He and a company of *noekar*. A cousin was going to see what he could find out about that. We should hear by dawn. If she isn't caught. But—"

"But why hasn't Attalissa come to us?" Shevehan asked. "If she's returned—"

"We don't know she has," Tsuzas said. "What Narva sees—he doesn't understand it himself, too often. What do we do about Serakallash, 'Vaia?"

"Nothing we can do, now," Attavaia said. "If Elsinna made it there safely—Sera is their goddess and their concern. If they rise up, it will at least draw Tamghat's attention away from us for a while. Though they'll just all be slaughtered, if nothing else has changed."

"Wasted effort," said Shevehan. "I thought they were going to wait until we gave them the signal Attalissa had returned? And anyhow, I thought their goddess was dead?"

"Sera has gone home," Tsuzas said. Attavaia gave him a sharp look. He seemed himself, free of Narva, but . . . no smile, just weary certainty. "Attalissa has come home. It's time."

"You just said you didn't mean . . . then where is she?" Shevehan asked, and again, "Why hasn't she come to us?"

Someone tapped at the door of the connecting passage from the house. They all jumped. Then Shevehan shook his head and Attavaia made a face. For the space of a breath, she had believed it could be that simple: Attalissa would be at the door, Otokas at her shoulder, an army trained in secret in some high valley flowing over the bridge. Shevehan opened the door a crack to let his wife's face peer around.

"Your cousin's here, Shev," Ellehan said. "Why you men can't go torch-fishing at a reasonable time of day—"

"Because there'd be no point in daylight, woman," Shev retorted. All clear.

"Thanks, Ell. Attalissa bless." Sannoras the fisherman slipped around the door and Ellehan retreated. "Sister." He nodded to Attavaia and to Tsuzas, whose name he had never been given. "Very strange story from the temple, Shev."

"Attalissa?" asked Attavaia.

"You heard!"

"I . . . had word." Her heart began to race and she sat down on the edge of the hearth again, took the cup of tea, bitter and milkless, that Shevehan offered. "Tell us."

"Yes, Sister. You know the Lake-Lord's been gone a week."

"And come back today."

"Yes. He brought Attalissa with him. They say it's Attalissa. My cousin has doubts."

"Ah."

"They say Tamghat finally found her and *rescued* her from the Blackdog, but that she's terribly ill. They showed her to the sisters and took her away again. He's to wed her in a week or so."

"Attalissa wouldn't submit to that. She wouldn't submit to being paraded around a captive."

"Unless he overcame her with some spell."

"Overcame Attalissa? She wouldn't be a child anymore. She'd have come into her full power by now."

"But they say he killed the goddess down in the desert," Sannoras said. "Defeated and destroyed her."

"Defeated, anyway," Attavaia conceded. Would rumour help or hinder them? If the folk of Lissavakail heard that Sera had returned to Serakallash and the caravan-town was rising in revolt, would they have the nerve to lie quiet and continue awaiting their own goddess, or would they take to the streets and get themselves stupidly killed, disorganized and overmatched before they began? Did she have to ask?

But she and Jerusha had agreed to rise together, when the time came.

Did she trust the dreams of Narva's madness, that was what it came down to. She looked at Tsuzas, sitting withdrawn and still, staring into the glowing coals. Attalissa has come home, he had said.

"Tsuzas—is it true? Has Attalissa returned? Is it time?"

He shook his head. "How do I know, 'Vaia? What's said is said. If we trust what he sees—"

"What who sees?" the fisherman asked.

Attavaia ignored him. "Do you trust? As a priest?"

"Yes."

Attavaia took a deep breath. "Then it is time. Dig up your Northron sword, Shevehan." As if he didn't root the uncanny thing out of his floor once a month at least to check on it. She had heard of cursed swords. She could believe it of the one Shev called the Lady. There was anger in those harsh-cut runes on the blade. But it had an edge, it would serve. She shut her eyes. *Attalissa, wherever you are, Great Gods, be with me now.*

"Sannoras. The goddess Sera has gone back to Serakallash and the Serakallashi will be rising. We believe Attalissa has returned. Whether she is this captive woman Tamghat showed the temple, or whether that's some trickery of his, we don't yet know. But we'll find out. I want you to do something for me. I'm going to have to go to the temple to find the truth of this. Attalissa and the Blackdog may find us, or they may not. We'll try to find them. But if I find the goddess, we'll have to raise the valleys against their *noekar*-lords and the mercenaries. I want you to go now, to the cousins on Pine Spur, and warn them to watch for a signal from the town this coming night. If it comes, they're to send their own signals, light the beacons—everything."

"Signal from the town, send signals, beacons." Sannoras nodded. "How do I know these cousins?"

Attavaia told him which house to go to and gave him the watch-words. "And I need the name of your cousin in the temple," she said, seeing him to the door.

"Sister Darshin," he said. "We meet along the shore on misty mornings and evenings, north of the old water-gate. She really is my cousin, you know. When Shev said I should find someone in the temple I could trust, I went to her."

Darshin. Old Lady's deputy. Attavaia wouldn't by choice have put faith in anyone who had been so close to Luli in the old days, but Sannoras had been bringing them reliable information out of the temple for years now, and if his cousin had betrayed him, given that he was one of the few who knew where the heart of the free temple lay, Tamghat would have had all their heads on spikes long before this. She laid her hand on the fisherman's expectant head in blessing before he went out into the paleness of dawn.

"Attalissa speed you and keep you safe," she murmured after him. "And us all."

"Tonight?" Shevehan asked, eyes gleaming. "She'll be with us tonight?"

"Gods help me." Attavaia sat down abruptly on the floor, her knees failing. "Tsu, if I'm wrong . . . Why hasn't she come to us?"

He moved to her and put his arms around her, saying nothing.

"Are you going to the temple tonight?" Shevehan asked. "You shouldn't risk yourself. I could—"

"You couldn't look like a sister if you tried, Shev. You have to be here in town. By dusk, I want all the cousins armed and ready to storm the island. Bridge and boats."

"When the signal comes."

"Yes. Tsu—"

"I'm coming with you."

"You won't make any more convincing a woman than Shevehan."

"I have to be there."

"Where?"

"I don't know."

"Sometimes I understand why your sisters get so exasperated with you." But she managed a smile and got to her feet again. "You're not going anywhere unless you spend the day sleeping and letting Ellehan feed you."

He nodded.

"And you, 'Vaia, need to get out of sight," Shevehan reminded. "Too many people think little Attavaia died when the temple fell, for neighbours to find you sitting in my smithy."

Just what she needed. A long, anxious day in hiding with nothing to do but worry about how wrong she was. She had meant to be on her way into the valleys herself by dawn. "Get me bread and water," she said. "At least if I'm here in the weaponstore I can hear a bit of what's going on." A smithy was a natural gathering place for tea-drinking and gossip. It drew Tamghati patrols too, but they had good lookouts, and there was usually a core of old men with nothing better to do than tell innocent fish stories. By evening, Shev would have the word out through all his networks and the town would be tinder, waiting for her spark. She hoped.

Attalissa willing.

CHAPTER XXXII

When it all began, Holla-Sayan had killed a man stealing his horse. Now he had killed a man to steal this horse he rode. The Grasslander had been riding at a good clip, heading away from Lissavakail with some urgency, and when Holla-Sayan stepped into the road and called to him, he shouted, "Way for the Lake-Lord's messenger!" and did not even turn his mount's head aside—to be fair, he might not have seen Holla until too late, given it was thick night, but Holla was at war with all Tamghati. He drew his sabre and took his head, and the horse. He ought to have felt some regret for that; he had intended to leave the man unconscious by the roadside, but he was too far away from himself to care, lying down with the Blackdog, holding it calm.

The messenger carried some sealed scroll in a leather satchel. Holla-Sayan threw the scroll into the lake. He couldn't read. He drank the man's flask of millet beer and ate his bread and cheese and turned the horse's head back to Lissavakail. He had no idea where Moth had gone, and he wasn't about to let the Blackdog back into the world, not yet, but neither was he going to wait in hiding while Pakdhala was in danger, trusting her fate to another. He was not certain how long he had slept. Too long. The mountains were warm with golden afternoon, the sun heading down into the west. He must have lost a day. Pakdhala was not taken last night, but the night before last.

The edge of the high snows gleamed with copper sunset when he came to a place he recognized, a collapsed ruin, thin grass sprouting between its stones, where a girl and a dog had once sheltered. He took off the horse's saddle and bridle and turned it loose to graze along the shore. Mist hung over the lake, hiding the temple, except for the highest roofs, which floated like some demon-built palace in a tale.

Pakdhala was on the temple islet. The Blackdog strained towards her like a hound pulling at the leash. All his concentration was needed to keep it in check; he did not try to call to her. The last thing he needed was to attract Tamghat's notice.

He did not want to do this. Holla-Sayan scrambled down over the jagged slabs of shale, through nettles, and waded into the lake. If he paused to think . . . Waist-deep, he went under in a shallow dive. He held his breath as long as he could. Knowing he would not drown made no difference. But the lake, when he had to exhale, flowed into him and felt like rest and new strength.

Holla surfaced, muffling a cough in his sleeve, and studied the shore of the holy islet. Cliffs rose here, and the dark crack of the tunnel, not so secret now. Tamghat should be guarding it. He could see no one, smell no one human, no metal-and-stone reek of wizardry, either. The guard would be in the Old Chapel, probably, but if he could come on them unexpected, before they could raise the alarm, he would be in the temple and, perhaps, no one the wiser. If a trap were laid there . . . he would deal with that when he came to it. Storming the gates, the dog's impulse, was not clever.

And that's why I'm staying in charge, he told it, wading forward. He shook water out of his braids and staggered a bit, heavy with water-logged clothing. Anyone who decided to take a walk on the shore was going to see the dark trail he left behind him, but there was nothing to do about that.

The tunnel was as he . . . remembered, hah: a narrow fissure, lit by overgrown cracks above, which became true tunnel and dipped down into a water-filled blackness like a well. That was worse than the lake, but whatever Pakdhala was facing had to be even worse than this suffocating, drowning grave-pit. Knowing it could not kill him, no more than the lake could, still didn't help. He went into it sweating and with his eyes shut, as if that could make a difference, came out where he could breathe air again shivering and cold with simple fear and stood waist-deep in water, feet on the first of the steps. The water was higher than it had been.

Now . . .

He ducked under again, feeling around, recoiled almost in disgust when he touched the rough surface of the stone bowl. No slime, no mussels had rooted on it. The bowl was just as it had been when Otokas set it there, feeling the same revulsion at its touch. Holla-Sayan picked it up, strangely heavy, even underwater. Water sheeted away from it, leaving it as it had been, not full, a dark mirror rolling under a rim like a half-opened peony-bloom, a surface that cast its own pewter-dim light upwards.

No. It wasn't a word; it was the dog's whole being that howled it, but underneath, underneath something flared with grim satisfaction.

I think so. That one silver thread the dog had lodged in his heart, the burnt scars on his fingertips from when he touched that shimmering, shifting barrier . . . when he followed that path, it led here, to this. *Moth— Vartu—will find the goddess. She said so. She'll find Pakdhala. You know we can't fight Tamghat and hope to survive, and he wants to make you part of himself. What will that do to Attalissa? Otokas feared that; that's part of why he wanted me to take her to the desert road. We're putting you out of his reach, so you at least don't go flitting to him like a mindless butterfly without a fight when I'm dead, right? If we're going to die today, don't you want to die your own master?*

That wasn't an argument the dog understood. The drive to serve Attalissa, to protect Attalissa, ruled. It surged up, shredding a way through him as he fought to hold it down. Holla-Sayan pitched forward on the stairs, screaming, every bone, it felt, dissolving in fire, but as he fell he hurled the bowl into the blackness ahead.

It struck stone and shattered like glass, shards flying, the grey, nacreous liquid it had held rising like a lily, a fountain, limning stone edges, sending strange oily lights running over the surface of the water as he fell beneath it.

Sayan . . . please . . . not yet . . .

He was dying. The dog had torn into the world through his physical body, ripped him open. He lay on the steps where he had fallen, half-in and half-out of the water, and blood soaked him, sticky and hot. A twisting tree of fire swayed before him, murky reddish light, liquid

476

pewter veins. It rose suddenly to the low roof, flaring bright, and vanished, leaving Holla-Sayan in blackness his eyes could not pierce. Everything was muted, sound and scent dim, even his gasping breath, even the blood.

The dog was gone.

There was still Pakdhala to find.

He crawled, one step higher, another. Fell with his arm beneath him and felt it grow warmer, wetter. Ragged rent in his coat and everything beneath. Farther up. Farther, through the square hole in the roof, in the chapel's floor. His fingers touched wood greasy with rot. The sides of the altar. Dragged and lay against it, but even with his shoulder he could not move it, just lay there, leaning slightly, sinking under cold waves of pain.

The Sayanbarkash again. Home. The farm, all the low, green, turf-roofed buildings. The god's hill swelling in the distance, long ridge dominating the skyline. He wanted to be there.

Die unburied beneath the altar and rot here, be bound a ghost until someone found his bones, found his stinking corpse and shoved him back into the lake, to free his soul.

Not that. Not that. He wanted to be home. Try it all again, make better choices . . . could not wish himself never curious about the mountains, Pakdhala unfound. Could wish her a lost child, only that. Should have married Gaguush. Coughing shook him back into the present and grim pain, and then his chest forgot how to inhale and his throat caught on nothing. After a moment his body remembered the way to breathe again. This time. Cold.

Light hung before him, dim, drifting silver. It clung to him by a thread, one thread that had not been broken, an umbilical to feed its crippled fire by connection to the realm of the humans' and gods' and demons' earth, where its nature did not belong. It ate his pain, it drank what grasp on the world he had left, clinging to life itself. It grew, flecked with red, retreating from wherever it had gone, regrouping in this coffin of an altar. The red was muddier than before, the colour of old scabs, the silver darkened to pewter, streaked tarnish-black.

477

So long a road, to die together trapped here, neither able to find their way home.

You didn't have to take me with you. He was alone in his head, couldn't speak. For a long time, it seemed a long time, he just looked at his hand by the light that was the devil. Finally the hand moved, stretched towards the thing.

"Need," he managed, "save . . . 'Dhala."

The devil . . . did not care. The devil was satisfied Attalissa would die.

"Not die. Ghatai's stronger. Eats her."

Ghatai would be stronger. Ghatai would storm the heavens and open the hells and the Old Great Gods would be afraid.

"No. Vartu. Sword. We saw." The obsidian blade that carried a gateway to the hells, that was itself a shard of the cold hells. "Ghatai . . . won't free th'ells. Wants. Torule. You. All worlds. You don' trus' him. You know."

So cold he could not feel the stone he lay on, could not feel the hand that lay dead-grey in a pool of glowing pewter.

"Pakdhala," he said at last, forcing open eyes that had closed he did not know when. "You remember. All av'tars. Know her. Growing. Why you come back here?"

The devil wanted to die, did not want to die alone. Wanted a companion as it waited. Beyond death, there was no self. Not for . . . Holla did not understand the shape of that thought. God and devil. What it was. Creature of the remote heavens.

Great Gods and devils were the same. One side lost in a war so long ago . . .

"Don' care. 'Dhala. You . . . *want* . . . to die?"

It would not be a slave again.

"Me. Neither. Want. Mygirl. Safe. Whatever price."

The devil had no face, no form but that dwindling swirl of light, but he thought it turned its full attention to him.

The devil was afraid.

"Me. Too."

The devil was afraid of him. Of being used.

"Trust. Both."

Better to die free. Both of them.

"Both. Free. Better live."

He felt that silver thread linking them heart to heart, as though it lay between his fingers. Break it and they would both die at once. Together they held one another in life a little longer, fading in strength.

"Come," he invited, a whisper, and the devil came in a rush, pouring over him, sinking into him, filling veins and heart and marrow, convulsing his body, blinding him, white sky burning, burning him away, flesh and blood and bone.

The priestesses called this the Dawn Dancing Hall, although Tamghiz found it difficult to imagine Old Lady Luli dancing at dawn or any other time. The great rectangular pavement was a mosaic tiled in three shades of blue, while the gilded beams of the roof were supported on pillars carved into spirals like narwhal horns and painted brilliant red, with gilded flowers around their bases and capitals. On three sides it was open to the wind, a platform thrust out towards the southeastern edge of the holy islet, looking down on the edge of town and away into a vista of rising peaks. A notch in the horizon spilled out the rising sun at the spring equinox, though they hadn't managed to align their dancing hall with it. Still, unless he climbed to one of the ice fields, he wouldn't be likely to find a better place to welcome the rising conjunction. If the Dancing Hall hadn't been here, he would have torn out the walls of the adjacent novices' hall and built something similar.

Vrehna and Tihz already drew near one another in their celestial dance, mounting the heavens in the northeast. The long side of the Dancing Hall faced them almost square on. He aligned his great circle to where they would appear over the mountains, turn burning into one, six nights from now.

He didn't trust to chalk and powder for this working, but mixed pigments and oil and painted the hundreds of symbols and paths of power, forming the patterns stroke by delicate stroke. Chiefs among his *noekar* stood guard, three to a corner, day and night, and others patrolled the perimeter of it. He wanted no second An-Chaq interfering. He had warded it, too, against the one great threat he feared, though he had little strength to spare for anything but the great working to come.

Painting the spell this way tied him to Lissavakail, though. He had refined it since the time he had planned to draw it all out in one intense casting, to take the goddess on the same day he took Lissavakail. As bad as Ulfhild and her wretched poetry, always realizing perfection lay still out of reach and pulling what was done apart to build it again. But he was right to do so. This was stronger, surer, more elegant. Providence. Had all gone as he intended, the goddess might have been able to fight the spell as he had originally shaped it. This, though, this would hold her. Further providence that she was so weak, still disconnected from her powers, and holding her captive was so simple a matter. He would bring her here, reunite her with her lake just as he drew the final runes to close the circle and as the planets rose above the mountains.

Meanwhile he had to build the spell, so that it all hung ready, lacking only the final elements. He worked at it day by day, as Vrehna and Tihz pulled to one another. He had no strength, no concentration, to spare for any more great workings, nor had he the time to ride to Serakallash to investigate the great stir and turmoil he had felt.

—It was Sera, taking back her land.

—It could not have been. I slew her.

—I doubted. I knew something was wrong, even then. I should have hunted her. I should have questioned the sept-chiefs.

—Ketsim has grown lazy and overconfident. He said there was no rebellion left in them. That patrol that came in this morning said there were fireworks seen from the desert edge the night Ketsim set out with the goddess. Signalling? Who? If they've hired mercenaries out of the desert . . .

—If Sera is back, she will be mine anyway. If not, they can go to ruin godless. Serakallash doesn't matter any more. Serakallash was a game. This is all a game, remember? I, we, don't need kingdoms on this earth.

—They should honour us in fear.

—They will. But what if they weren't signalling mercenaries for some uprising? What if *she's* plotting with Serakallash? I felt her. She's near. I threw her off the track for years, but she's here now.

—As I wanted.

—Yes. I want her here for this. But if there's any danger, it's in her.

—I'm stronger than her. I always have been. She doesn't frighten me.

—She's mine. She will be mine again.

—Sometimes I feel her watching me.

—Delusion. She hates me still.

—Her fate and mine run together. She can't escape me. She knows it. She's drawn back to me. That's why she stalked my daughter, turned her against me. As she did my son.

—These things don't matter. Games, as much as this game of being lord of this wretched town of yak-milking peasants. When I'm able to open the road to the heavens again, when the strength of the earth shatters the citadels of the Gods, then she'll know me her lord, Vartu will follow then.

—She'll be the first. Only the first. Followers betray. She was never trustworthy. But when I take her and make her mine as I make the gods of the earth mine . . . the Great Gods themselves will fear us.

—She's near.

—That's wrong.

"Great Gods damn it!" He had to rub out a quarter circuit of the lesser arc, sit in meditation an hour, clearing his mind, rocking and chanting, before he began again. It was Vartu, working against him, leading him into distraction and self-doubt, as ever. That was what she intended in Serakallash; it might even be illusion, this feeling of Sera's presence in her waters again, meant to pull him away from Lissavakail.

His thoughts were wandering again, when they should be most

focused. Tamghiz Ghatai sat back on his heels, took a deep breath, eyes on the distant peaks. He was nerve-wracked as an apprentice preparing his masterpiece. That was the problem with human flesh and human soul, they wound one into human life again, and all its chattering, nattering, self-gnawing stupidities.

I am Ghatai. Ghatai, Ghatai, Ghatai. I am . . . stars and darkness and fire and ice, soul born of worlds unseen. *I am Ghatai* . . . He rocked to the chant, eyes closed, until the word was all there was, self without thought. *Ghatai.* He finished the day's working as heavy mist coiled from the lake's still waters and the evening shadows flowed over the Dancing Hall. Then he lay there, calm and still and briefly at peace, in the centre where he would place the avatar, and he waited for his stars to rise. He checked on the girl once, touching her mind. Still asleep under drugs and spells, dreaming of camels. Her guards were alert, the wards he had set on her lay quiescent. The wretched Blackdog had not come yet, to be put out of its misery and pulled into Ghatai's soul. Soon, though. Perhaps tonight. The spells he had set on the avatar's body would hold it, or any other devil's soul that happened to touch his prize, long enough for him to reach the room and deal with them, whichever it was that came. For now, he could rest, and watch the stars rising.

He touched the breast of his shirt and the hard, silk-wrapped length of bone that lay against his chest all the time now, over his heart as if he held his child there. This had nothing to do with Vartu, or with Ghatai. Sometimes he was simply Tamghiz, and he was waiting for Ulfhild.

Were there any hearts at all in the temple still Attalissa's? Pakdhala surfaced into a hazy wakefulness, feeling that she had been shaping that thought through long, slow dreams, as she rocked, safe and secure, to red Sihdy's pace, her father's arms about her. Safe and secure, hidden from view, snuggled into his chest, happy, loved, half-drowsing. Ah, she had done that herself, made a hidden citadel from which to rise, slow and unseen. And now she was awake.

But not much further ahead. Still none had understood her plea, none had come with water from the lake . . . but of course, there were the guards. If one of the novices were clever, she might mix lake-water in with the drugged beer and honey, but if they had been raised as hostages to Tamghat, she supposed they hadn't exactly been encouraged to think for themselves. She tried her strength. Walls. She still could not reach the dog. And if she fought them . . . Tamghat would know long before she breached them.

Pakdhala forced lead-heavy eyelids open. The room was dim, with splashes of dusk's copper light painting the walls through the piercings of the shutters. Another night on its way. One shutter was folded back, and by rolling her eyes she could just make out a woman with Salt Desert tattoos on her face. She sat on the balustrade, leaning forward, head against the fists that clutched her spear.

Bored, and not terribly alert. Hah. Though Pakdhala could do nothing with that at the moment. The other, a Grasslander woman— always women, did he not trust men near his intended bride or was it genuine respect for her modesty?—stood with her shoulders propped against the doorframe. As Pakdhala watched through slitted eyes she pushed herself off and began slowly pacing the room.

"Hope someone does come," the one on the balcony said, and laughed. "This is bloody boring. Four hours to go?"

"Don't wake her!"

"She wouldn't wake if we shouted. Wizardry." She waggled her fingers. "What do you make of old Eyeless Darshin, pottering up on the last watch mumbling about water? You know what she had in her jug? Lake muck. Said 'the lady wanted water.'"

"She's mad. Senile. Her wits went when our lord put out her eyes. Or maybe before—you'd have to be a bit addled to go after him with a kitchen knife, seems to me."

"Well, yeah. But still, the thing with the water—seems so unlikely I kind of wonder if there's sense to it, you know."

"Old Dardar talks to trees and flowers and sings lullabies to the lake."

"Lullabies?"

"True. Haven't you seen her? Off pottering along the shore early in the morning, falling in half the time. Singing baby-songs. There's no sense to anything she does."

"Well, maybe. They dumped the pitcher over her head and kicked her downstairs, anyway, so whatever she was up to, it didn't come to anything." The Salt Desert woman sighed. "Silly child. You wouldn't catch me running off with dog-monsters if my lord announced he had a fancy to be my husband."

"Don't be irreverent."

The desert woman, too young to have been *noekar* when the temple fell, pouted, sighed, and turned her back to look out over the lake. They fell into silence again. The Grasslander moved pieces on a Nabbani chessboard, no doubt confusing whatever game had been left half-played.

A shadow flickered over the red glow of the shutter-piercings and the desert woman turned her head, braids swinging, to watch something.

"Why's our lord shooting birds now?"

"I have no idea."

"Funny thing to do."

"Hardly your place to question him, is it?"

"The mountain girls are missing most of the time anyway. When I was little I always heard what great archers they were, these mountain priestesses."

"It's not like we've let them get much practice lately. Half the novices have never touched a bow."

"Oh, now who's questioning our lord's wisdom?"

"Hold your tongue and keep your mind on your duty, why don't you?"

The desert woman grumbled into welcome silence. Pakdhala felt herself start to sink under it, sleep clawing her down. She forced her eyes open again, bit the inside of her lip until it bled. Pain helped, sped up her heart. The taste of blood overwhelmed the lingering bittersweet coating on her tongue.

What could she do within these walls, beyond shouting and beating her fists and generally throwing a tantrum? She could not reach the Blackdog, could not fight the barriers around her without drawing Tamghat's attention and finding herself pushed into wizardrous sleep again. She clenched her teeth and kept her breathing even, quieting a rising panic. That would draw Tamghat's attention as surely as the tantrum she imagined.

Holla-Sayan carried his home and his god in his mind. Most caravaneers would say they did, with their little talismans that proved to themselves they were not godless, but her father could reach down inside himself and find the Sayanbarkash's strength, certainty of who he was and where he belonged. She had felt it in him. Was she hollow, that she had no resources, no foundation, when she was locked up within herself? Who was Pakdhala, on her own, without the flow of other minds around her, without the spark of godhead that flickered so feebly?

A caravan-mercenary. An archer. A camel-leech. She could bake good stone-bread, too, and had studied the falls of the coins in Nabbani divination. Perhaps—

Perhaps she was a fool. She was a *wizard*. She had been born a wizard, the first time she had been born. That had rather been the point. And she had been wizard-born a time or two since, and what was a wizard but a human touched with a distant echo of the earth's strength? Which was all she had, a human body without the blessing of any sister-goddess, without any bond with her own waters.

Ah.

She let herself sink into a deep, dark calm. Drift through memory. She had studied Nabbani divination, yes, though Ivah had taught her no spell-working, but long, long ago . . . Westron forms rose in memory, and Nabbani symbols. For what she needed to do, there were no traditional words shaped by the mages of Tiypur, no series of signs passed down by the masters of Nabban. But Westron wizardry did not depend on tradition like that of the east, not in its deepest and oldest form, the one her lover Hareh had taught her so, so long ago, when this all began. Indeed, there was one school of thought that said each spell must be new-made, used once and never again.

Pakdhala found the barrier that encased her.

On the wall, shadow.

In the empty room, echo.

In the deep pool, reflection.

She lay so still, within her mind. Echo and shadow and reflection lay over her.

The doe steps from the mist.

The grebe rises from the lake.

The sun is born from darkness.

Like a breath slowly released, she slid through the barrier, slowly, so slowly, leaving not a ripple, not a tear, not an eddy to tug at Tamghat's attention. Behind her, something still slept, an illusion of sleep.

Nothing happened. No taunting, no touch or taste of the Lake-Lord in her mind. She reached first for the Blackdog and it was as though she stared into a deep well. She recoiled, heart pounding. That was not Holla-Sayan, that was . . . She stretched to him again. *Dog? Holla-Sayan? Father?* Even that did not draw him to her. Great Gods, he was lost, mad, devoured—but that deep well had none of the maelstrom of madness which, festering, had burst from the dog a time or two in the past, when the host was unfit and fell to it. *Holla-Sayan!*

The Blackdog raised walls against her, not as the dogs had always done, to keep some parts of their minds and lives private, curtains she could have breached with hardly a thought had she ever had need. These—she could not even find a way to come to grips with these. Alien. Ice that burned.

Pakdhala stared into the shadows of the ceiling. That was . . . that could not be Holla-Sayan.

Dead. And the Blackdog in some new host, some damned mercenary of Tamghat's, some—not Tamghat himself, not that. She would have known. He would have made certain she knew, not ignored her, shut her out.

The walls had felt like nothing human.

But . . . it *had* been Holla, she knew it as she knew his voice. Some lingering scent, some shape of mind.

And just for a moment, before she realized that, the back of her mind had thought, if her father was dead, she could take the Blackdog into herself as Kinsai had advised . . . She was appalled.

Wherever and whatever the dog was, she could not lie here waiting for it, for him, to get himself killed assaulting the temple.

She could not tell where he was. That was not right either; she always knew, even weak and ill in Marakand.

She could not do wizardry in such a turmoil of mind.

Don't think of him now.

Stillness. Quiet. The enduring heart of her soul, the lake, deep and waiting strength.

Nabbani wizardry was what she needed this time. She dragged, so slowly, an arm. It moved from her shoulder, like a dead thing. Dragged at the other. Got one hand from her side to her thigh, a start, and the two guards did not notice the movement. The light was fading fast. So long as she made no sound, they would not look. The quilt was such a weight, like ropes tying her down. The Grasslander woman walked close by the bed, going out to the head of the stairs. A murmur of voices—there must be guards out there as well. She came back carrying a lighted lamp, which she set in a niche by the door. No light for the one outside, but that made sense; she would see better, watching the roofs, in darkness. The Grasslander closed the door and turned the chair so she could sit with her back to the wall, staring at the bed, but the curtains framing the head of the bed caught enough of the lamplight to leave Pakdhala in deep shadow. After a while Pakdhala dared begin on the other hand. It would not move. She dragged at her hands till tears of frustration prickled behind her eyelids, rested, started again. Then, finally, hand touched hand.

There was sudden movement on the balcony, a soft sound, like the wind in grass. A groan.

Sayan save, the pressure of the air, power like a thunderstorm, the reek of burning stone . . . Tamghat was here.

The Grasslander twitched and raised her head, caught sleeping.

"You say something?" she called softly.

Something flashed through the open shutter, pale blur and a stir of air over Pakdhala's face, and the Grasslander, half-out of her chair, simply kept moving forward, folding over to the floor, her fall silenced by the woman who caught her and twisted her over onto her back, so she could tug a long Northron blade free of the body. Pakdhala's wits caught up with her eyes and she tried to roll aside, to at least fall and have the bed between her and this thing, this woman wearing feathers and mail who was not after all Tamghat, but who reeked of the same wrongness, the same perversion of nature.

"Lie easy, I'm not your enemy," the woman told her, barely above a whisper. "For the moment." A fleeting smile. "Friend of your father's."

Tongue wouldn't answer. *Liar. You're no friend of my father's.*

But I am.

Pakdhala felt the woman skittering over the surface of her mind, cat-light, a hasty survey that found Tamghat's prison and the illusion within.

That was nicely done. Even clever. You might make a half-decent wizard, in time, godling.

What have you done to Holla-Sayan? Where is he?

Asleep, last time I saw him. I hope he'll come on with more caution when he wakes. The woman's presence jumped away from her, and she frowned, as if hearing things she did not approve. *Pakdhala—it is Pakdhala, ya? 'Dhala, I won't touch you. You're still covered in his workings, snares for the Blackdog, or for me. Deeper spells yet. He'd know. Can you get yourself out of here?*

Yes. She hoped. But it was some trickery, this wizard who killed without compunction, this *creature* that was another Tamghat.

His name is Tamghiz Ghatai, Attalissa of the Lake. Know that and think why he wants you.

Ghatai . . . she knew that name. In the days of the first kings in the north there were seven devils . . . No, no, no. And there were seven wizards . . . He could not, he could not, he could not possess her as the devils had the wizards, he could not make himself a god.

The wizards weren't possessed. But what he intends for you is worse. And he will make himself a god, ya, or close enough.

Pakdhala fought to flatten out the panic that thrummed in her chest. Tamghat—Ghatai—might feel it. Stay calm, stay quiet, battle-focused. Deal with the necessary now.

Where's the Blackdog?

The woman straightened up from cleaning her blade, head cocked as if listening. *He knows I'm near again. Don't let Tamghiz take you, godling. I'd have to kill you and I don't want to have to fight your slave over it.*

The Blackdog isn't—

But she was gone, a pale blur and a kiss of air. An owl?

Pakdhala took deep breaths. The night stank of blood now. A devil was coming for her. Don't think of that. Don't. Concentrate on breath, breath on breath. A trout lying in shadow. Let the memories rise, still and dark as fish. There, stillness.

Hand lay against hand. Palace of the Sun, the active principle, inverted. Negation of spinning. Opening, unbinding. She traced the signs against her left palm with one slow, clumsy, right-hand finger. Great Gods, strength in her left hand and arm, mastery of her left hand.

That hand found her throat, found the knot, the final knot that bound Ivah's working there. She picked at it. The cord was braided of hair, as she had thought when she glimpsed it in the mirror, but most of the hair was old and brittle. She could imagine where it came from. Whatever had possessed her to allow that Old Lady, generations back, to persuade her that a tomb would be more fitting than giving the bodies of dead incarnations back to the lake, or taking them to the cairns in the Valley of the Dead where the bones of generation upon generation of Lissavakaili were interred?

Finally the knot gave, and she felt, oh, as if her lungs expanded with air, some great weight gone from her. Pakdhala sat up, crumpling the knotted braid in her hand.

She slid from the bed and stretched, loosening painful muscles. Her legs felt wobbly and she still fought the weakness that always took her on this stretch of the desert road, on top of having had nothing at all to eat for two—three?—days.

Pakdhala was dressed only in a sleeveless cotton shift. She did not waste time searching for something darker. The guard might be due to change any time; *he* might probe deeper and discover she was awake; he might come seeking the owl-woman. She took a long dagger from the dead Grasslander—sword and spear too cumbersome for the path she was taking—and knotted an embroidered table-runner around her waist as a belt to hold it.

She had no plan any longer. If there were faithful sisters, she could not find them and was not going to seek. She wanted her father, wanted the Blackdog between her and the devil, wanted to run, and run, and run until she was safe on the caravan road again, and Lissavakail could go to ruin without her.

She had to step over the body of the Salt Desert woman. Her head lay on the other side of the balcony. Pakdhala looked only to make sure she didn't tread in the blood and leave betraying footprints. Then she climbed to the railing.

Heavy fog hung over the lake, bringing horizons close, the next roof, no more, but the scent of the unseen water cleared her head. She drew strength from the very air. For a long moment she stood, poised on the stone balustrade. Below were roofs and courts and somewhere, the outer wall of the temple. Beyond that was the moving darkness that was the lake. Her lake. She could feel it, pulling her.

Her self.

Then she climbed over the rail at the southern edge of the balcony and dropped to a lower roof. Old Lady Luli had never let her play with even the youngest novices, but in other lifetimes, she had grown up among them. Even in blind fog, she knew these roofs as well as she knew the streets of At-Landi or Serakallash.

She saw none of the priestesses who should have been posted on the rooftops, though she felt a human presence here and there as she flitted past.

When she came to the court of the water-gate, it seemed long-deserted. Weeds grew in cracks between the paving stones, and even a small pine tree had taken root. Pakdhala hung from the edge of the last roof and dropped, hissing and hopping a moment on one foot when she landed on a shard of broken tile.

She had seen decay all over the temple from above. Paint and gilding were peeling from the eaves and the carved gable-ends, tiles were cracked or missing or held sodden cushions of moss. Nesting starlings squawked within holes and pigeons had colonized whole rooftops. It all confirmed the owl-wizard's words: Tamghat was no tyrant who planned to rule here. Lissavakail was only a means to take Attalissa, no value in itself. Better for her people to be abandoned and godless than ruled by a devil-god.

Gods, Great Gods, Sayan, Kinsai—someone, help. She wanted to be back on the desert road, Flower pacing lightfoot beneath her. But the road was not there for her: Bikkim dead, her father—Great Gods help *him*, if he was still within their reach—gone. Her whole body seemed strange, dissolving in liquid waves of cold and bowel-loosening heat.

She should never have come back. The devil had lured her back; she knew that now.

The water-gate itself was gone, the gateway closed with rough masonry, but the tower still stood over it. Pakdhala climbed the steps to the bell-chamber and scrambled from there down onto the wall. This wasn't a city wall like that of Marakand, or one of the great fortresses that guarded the pass through the Malagru. The drop wasn't something she would have undertaken except in desperation, but she went past the place where the old path wound down to the landing-stage, chose a spot thick with juniper to break her fall, hung from the parapet by her fingers, and let herself go.

Hissed again, at bare feet, bare legs, bare thighs beneath the calf-length shift, and spiny junipers, but stopped short of cursing the bush, which had probably spared her a twisted ankle at the very least. The ground fell away a few paces from the base of the wall here, a cliff into the deep bay where the old trout lurked. She stood on the edge.

The world had shrunk to a patch of black water, a globe of dark fog. Lissavakail. Attalissavakail, the lake of Attalissa. The lake that was Attalissa. If not now, then never.

Pakdhala took a breath and dove.

Water. She touched the shores, beaches of shale, beaches of rounded pebble, cliffs where the mountains fell into her. She tasted the high stones and the slow drip of the ice fields, the springs whose hearts were hidden beneath stone. She tasted the narrow meadows, the tended channels through the sweet brown fields, hard-won from rock and wild. She stretched over the lake bottom, the soft silt, the heavy wood, tree and boat undergoing slow metamorphosis, the bone and bronze of other days, other battles, all held within her embrace, souls long gone in peace to the road no god of the earth would ever tread. Weed in banners, stretching from mud to light, streamers trailing in the circling currents. Trout, perch, loach, grayling . . . she felt them pass through her heart, quicksilver. The gnarled roots of the lilies, the slender ropes of their stalks rising to the surface of the shallow bays where leaf and blossom made a carpet for the nesting crake. She lay below the reach of even noon's sunlight, where the fish were few and eyeless, where delicate, pale shrimp danced. She filled the stillest waters, the great crevice born of the mountains' birth. She felt memory of the sun gliding over her surface, like a warm hand over skin. She felt the lives in the town and the temple, on the lakeshore and in the high valleys.

Attalissa pulled awareness back to herself and floated, open-eyed beneath the waters, watching the eddying fog on the moving surface. Her hand opened and the knotted braid of dead hair floated away, its spells dissolved. The illusory wall of the devil's wizardry began to dissolve too, like fog in sunlight; it had only been meant to constrain a human will. She built it up again around her own illusion of a sleeping mind. His prison became her shield, bought her time, so long as he believed it still intact and her mind dull and dreaming behind it.

But it was surely wrong to feel this . . . regret, that something had been lost. She rolled in the water, rubbed rough brown hands over naked forearms, where the spotted cats that were Westgrasslands cheetahs— legendary animals, long gone if they had ever existed—and the elusive white leopards of her high peaks twined with the snakes. Hands clenched to fists, as if she held something. Not lost. Never lost. She was all that she had ever been, but she had grown, also; she was larger inside, she was more human than she had ever been. If Pakdhala ever became a game she had played, a dress she had worn, then Holla-Sayan was betrayed worse than . . . than what, she did not want to think of.

She could not flee.

She surfaced, gazing up into the starless fog. She still wanted, with all her human heart, to steal a horse in the town and ride hard as horse-flesh could bear for Serakallash. She wanted to turn her back on all those fearful, unhappy human souls she could feel, a background murmur on the edge of her awareness.

Her father's daughter could not do that. Holla-Sayan's daughter could not run, not from a child that cried alone. And these people in need were *her* folk. She owed them at least her honourable death facing the danger she had brought down on them by her very existence—Sayan, but she had soaked up more from Varro's long recitations than she knew, such a Northron way to think. But it was right.

Kinsai was right, as well: at the last, she must fight him from within. By all the tales, the seven devils had not utterly consumed the seven wizards whose human bodies and souls they had taken. Their actions in the wars had seemed tangled all through with human urges, human connections, and those wizards had wanted to give themselves to the devils. If she was, in the end, taken fighting, goddess and wizard—he would not find her easy to digest.

And in the end, at least the songs would say, Attalissa had died fighting.

She really had listened to too many Northron tales.

"Attalissa be with us now."

The whisper floated on the water.

"Which way?"

"You stay by the boat. I'll go over the wall and scout."

"And if you're caught, what, I just wait here? No, we should both go in. If we go over the roofs, in this fog, I'm no more likely to be seen than you."

"Tsu, no."

"And what if the goddess is drugged, or bespelled? Can you carry her away alone? She won't be a little girl any longer, remember."

Pakdhala glided for the shore and waded silently over the rocks, feet sure, never slipping, water sheeting down her. She knew the woman's voice.

"Attavaia?" she asked, setting a hand on the upper strake of the boat they had pulled in under an overhang of scrubby willows.

She forgot how night-blind they would be. Steel hissed. Attavaia, dressed like a peasant in a coarse dark gown, drew a sax from under her shawl, the man whipping out a long hunting knife. Her own stolen blade was in her hand without thought. And without thought, for their sakes, she called a dim light into the fog, a faint moonglow haloing all around the boat.

The man's presence shivered with a shadow of godhead, not quite a glow, but something that lay over him, suffusing him with some awareness not his own. He stared at her, seeing her, she thought, truly. *Ah.* She knew that shape, that shadow. Pakdhala gave him a brief grave bow.

"Who are you?" Attavaia demanded, staring as if she were seeing a ghost. And almost soundless, *"Enni?"*

The voice speaking out of the blind night was enough to make Attavaia's heart lurch and falter and her blade tremble in her hand, and when the fog began to glow softly as though the moon was rising from the lake, she saw, swimming in fog, a face so familiar . . . *"Enni?"* But Enneas would not be walking, Enneas was decently buried, far from home, in the yard of Master Mooshka's caravanserai. But it was only a trick of resemblance in the bones. The speaker was a lowland girl wearing nothing but a skimpy, clinging shift, her waist-long hair in dripping rat's-tails. Some mercenary's brat, or young mercenary in her own right, given the almost absentminded competence with which her dagger fended them off. That wasn't shadow marring her face: black birds were tattooed curving from temples to cheekbones, sinuous leopards and snakes in blue and black twined around her forearms. However, she wore small gold hoops in her ears and, looking past the shock of the foreign tribal markings, she was actually pretty, lacking the coarse and lumbering bones of the desert folk. She did have a strong family resemblance to Enneas.

"Who are you?" Attavaia demanded, staring.

"Pakdhala," the girl said, and flushed. Well she might. Soaking had turned the thin weave of her shift translucent and in the eerie sourceless moonglow, every delicate rounding and black-haired shadow of her showed. Tsuzas was probably noticing, grant he couldn't help it.

"Um." The girl rubbed her face, rubbed a scar on her forehead, and took a deep breath. "I mean, I should say, Attalissa. Sister Attavaia, were you, um, looking for me?"

There were better ways she could have introduced herself, but the fixed stare of the priest with the shadow of a dreaming god lying over his mind rattled her. She remembered all too well how Sera had risen in rage against her when Holla-Sayan took her to Sera's well the first time. How much greater cause had Narva for hatred? Narva whom she had thought all but faded from the world.

Apologize. That was what her father would say. *Ask forgiveness.* And Great Gods, what business had the gods of the earth to fight among themselves anyway? If Sayan were as she had been, she would have died in this life long ago and been reborn in Tamghat's reach, be his by now, and all the lives dependent on her with her. She had been no better than a desert raider; worse, in that she was greater and stronger and should have understood better that all lives and all freedoms were precious and holy.

The priest swayed, shaken by whatever fierce emotion it was boiled within his distant god. He looked ill. Rage, a god manifest—that would draw Tamghat's attention down on them if nothing else did.

The tendril of the god that bound this man to Narva's heart could be severed, to ban the mountain god from coming so near the lake.

No. She had no right. And Attavaia still stared as though she were seeing a ghost.

Then the priest fell like a weed cut through at the roots, eyes rolling up white in his head. Attavaia and she moved at the same moment, fast enough to break his fall, so he came down sprawling in their arms. Attavaia drew his head onto her lap, bent over him, whispering, "Tsu!" with such a mixture of love and tenderness and anger—

Pakdhala's heart wrenched and she shut her eyes on Bikkim's face as she had last seen it, just an edge of grey cheek, bleeding into death on the arcade floor.

Tsu, if that was the priest's name, shuddered, and she laid a hand over his heart. Narva's awareness rose through him like deep waters welling up through sand, a seeping rush.

"Narva!" *Narva, hear me, please. Hear what I say. I have done you great wrong. I can never atone, I know it. But don't let your rage at me loose here, don't draw Tamghat's attention to us. For the sake of this man your priest, if no one else.*

She flowed into the lake, ran up the valleys, coursed through the ice fields. She was in them all; she had been in them, self cut off from self, as she rode the desert miles from Marakand to At-Landi and At-Landi to Marakand, a human cycle familiar as the seasons. She *was* this land, lake and river, valley and peak, but that—that was not hers. Narva still lay in the veins of his mountain, though she had driven him deep, taken valleys and pastures and the mines. She pulled herself out of them, or pushed them out of herself, rivers of light, veins of fire. *Narva, take back your lands. Take back your folk. Forgive me my great sins against you. Come back to the waking world, leave your suffering priest's mind and speak to him in your own voice. Walk the earth in wind and sun and snow again, and if you will, if you will, stand by me when I go to face Tamghat, and set your strength alongside mine. Or do not, if you will not. Protect your folk how you best see fit to do so.*

Was he hearing, not understanding? "Stone," she said aloud, looking around at them. "I need something from the Narvabarkash, stone, turquoise, something. But it must be of Narva's land." The priest's breath dragged and rattled as if he were a beast near foundering. "Something."

Attavaia shook her head.

"Anything! Anything of the land! Does he have earrings of Narvabarkashi gold, can you get them out, give me one?"

"Basket," Attavaia hissed, and struggled one-handed to drag a tall basket from the boat, twisting where she knelt.

Narva, do you hear me? Can you hear me? Please . . . Fever rose in the priest's body; she felt his skin burning under her hand. Attavaia shoved the basket at her.

"Bluewort from the slope above Narva's heart. Will that—?"

Turquoise, gold, stone would be better, earth of the earth. But roots tasted the soil, and they had no time to try to strip the priest of his ornaments. He was starting to thrash against them.

"Stars!" the priest said. "The devil will take her. Kill her now, kill her now, send her back out of his reach!" He lurched for Pakdhala's throat, but she held him easily enough, pinning him down again, stronger, with the lake behind her, than he. She reached for the bundle of crumbling herbs Attavaia held out.

"Narva, see, I give you back the land I stole," she said aloud, too loudly, had to remember they were mere yards from the temple wall. "Take it!" *Narva, take back your earth. Forgive me, please.* She had to force the priest's clawed and clenching fingers open, then force them shut again around the herbs. Poor-man's indigo, they called it. The scent of crushed bluewort filled the air, sharp and bilious.

The priest stopped breathing.

"Tsuzas!"

He inhaled, almost choking, and struggled to sit up, leaning forward with his head in his hands. Attavaia kept an arm behind his shoulders, glowering at Pakdhala.

"What have you done?"

"Given Narva back his mountain," she said. And probably drawn the attention of Ghatai onto them.

"My lady . . ." Attavaia whispered. "Great Gods, my lady, it *is* you."

"I've grown, I know," she offered, with a weak grin. "Turned West-grasslander, can you tell?"

"You've come back."

"You shouldn't have," the priest said sharply, pulling away from both of them. He frowned at the plants in his hand, closed his fist on them, and opened it again on ashes. He breathed on them, sending them dancing into the air, out of sight. "He's going to eat you up, Attalissa. Like consumes like. He is devil and flesh, he will eat you, flesh and god, and then being god, he will come for me and for Sera and . . . and whoever else lies before him, until he is great enough to break the world."

"I know," she said.

"Are we here to feed ourselves to him? And what have you done with your tame devil? Fed it to him already?"

"What do you mean, *devil*?" Attavaia demanded. "My lady, Narva's talked of devils and stars before—"

"Tamghat is Tamghiz Ghatai. But the Blackdog is no—"

"I dreamed it," Narva said mockingly. "My lady of the lake, you have no idea what it is to dream, drowning in your own heart, entombed in your mind. The stars flow in your blood—"

"That's enough," moaned Attavaia. "Great Gods, isn't it enough you've driven Tsu half-mad as it is? What have you done with him?"

"She asked for my help. How am I to come within her land and leave my own without my priest's aid?"

You don't need to ride him to be here. We are too close kin now, Narva, we have lain within one another too long. Do you see? Pakdhala—Attalissa— held out a hand, eyes half-shut, found him, cool blue flame.

Oh. And Narva, for once, said nothing more.

"But stay hidden in him," she added. "Tamghat may know, if you walk here openly."

"You'll be lucky if Tamghat's not just over there listening to every word we say," Narva muttered. Or was that the priest? "He's right." That was definitely Tsuzas, holding his head again. "Great Gods save me." He looked up at Pakdhala. "Narva's right. Now what?"

"A devil," Attavaia was muttering broodingly. "That explains so much, but Great Gods, how do we fight a devil? It took the Great Gods to bind them, before."

"I . . ." *don't have a plan I like.* "I . . . I need to find the Blackdog before . . ." Still hidden from her, barring itself. Or . . . the temple? Great Gods, no, not fallen into Tamghat's grasp.

498

"Uncle!" Attavaia said, and her whole face lit. "My mother will be so glad . . ." She sobered, meeting Attalissa's eye. "Oh."

"Otokas died the day the temple fell. I'm sorry, Attavaia."

Attavaia merely nodded.

It seemed empty to say the proper things, so many years after his death. I'm sorry. Otokas was a good man. He died valiantly. Pakdhala said them anyway.

"But where have you been all these years, my lady?" Attavaia asked. "You look . . ." She shrugged, embarrassed. "Quite foreign."

"On the caravan-road," Pakdhala said. "A caravan-mercenary. My father . . . the Blackdog, is a caravan-mercenary. Attavaia—I've heard whispers in Serakallash—a free temple. That's you?"

"Yes. But we're scattered. We meant to raise the valleys tonight, once we'd rescued you—we have the means, at least if the fog clears, we didn't plan for fog, but . . . but what can we do against a devil? My lady, we thought when you returned—"

"I'd crush him like a flea between my fingers? I wish I could. All we can do is . . . all we can do, Attavaia. I will do all I can, to the end of my life and my strength."

They kept giving her . . . looks. She wasn't what they expected, what they hoped for and wanted. When she thought of the little doll in brocade and gold the goddess had been, these many lives past, she couldn't blame them.

"I don't know if I can defeat him. I do know I will never let him make himself god of this land. If you can raise the valleys tonight . . . Yes. It will distract him, surely, if nothing more." The night spun out of her control, a runaway horse under her. "Are you using beacons? They should be fine. The fog is low on the water." The fog was nothing natural, called out by some vast and alien power, Tamghat and not-Tamghat—the owl-wizard's idea of subtle cover, no doubt.

"We can send a runner to the beacons if we have to, but before the fog, the plan was to use Nabbani fire-tubes." Attavaia patted the herb-basket.

She felt Ghatai stirring, a touch on the empty barriers, like a man running his fingers along a pot, checking for cracks. Time was running out. She let the darkness return to the night around them, lest anyone be looking out from the temple, and reached out herself. Tamghat's awareness was questing through the temple, puzzled, suspicious, but not certain what he felt awry. The man himself was . . . at the Dawn Dancing Hall? And Sayan be thanked, the Blackdog . . . it shied away. She flinched herself, as if burnt. It was not Tamghat, but . . .

Old Chapel.

Great Gods. It was free.

"My lady?"

"Call me Attalissa, at least," she said vaguely. Great Gods forgive her, Holla was dead, her father was dead, and they had that . . . beast unloosed among them, now of all times. Drawn to Ghatai, if Narva's bitter words were truth, another of devil-kin. Surely she had not known, surely Hareh had not known what it was they hunted, or they would never have committed such an abomination as to bind it to a human host, surely . . . no time for that.

Perhaps it could still be mastered, and turned against Ghatai.

"The fog will burn off in a moment," she said. "It's served its purpose. Wait here till it clears, then fire your signals. Drive the Tamghati from the valleys, drive them from Lissavakail. Take back the temple. But don't, don't turn on your own folk, my folk, who only bowed to him from fear. I can't say you will have any kind of victory, but I swear, I will not let him become the god of this land, whatever it takes to prevent that."

She turned to go, turned back, bowed to Tsuzas. *Narva, if I die, truly die, destroying him, look after my folk. Don't leave them godless.* The priest, wide-eyed, bowed. Attavaia bowed.

Pakdhala felt small and alone and naked, and very much human.

CHAPTER XXXIII

They could hear the heart beating, a slow, heavy tolling. Each breath seemed to take a lifetime, thoughts racing, memories, a maelstrom of sensation and emotion that blurred and melted together like the dreams of fever, ice-bright and incomprehensible. A world of crystal and fire and soaring music. Ice. Silence. Darkness. The thick air, the slow-moving, flesh-heavy earth, its gods small sparks of light, rooted in stone and water. Years, this lasted. Centuries. They knew . . . he seized one face and clung to it. Pakdhala. All else was irrelevant. Here was here, now was now. The Lissavakail, the Old Chapel, Pakdhala. Could they move, that was the question, or were they dead after all? Stupid thought. That was a hand, lying before his face, a tangle of red-tied braids over it. His hand, yes, black snake looping around the wrist. He tried to close it and watched the fingers clench. Good. They were alive.

Pakdhala. An uncomfortable upwelling of anger, such deep anger, went with that. But it didn't matter; they—he—would not allow it to matter. They were beyond Attalissa's reach now, and she was still Pakdhala; he was still Holla-Sayan.

First things first. He set a shoulder to the altar and heaved. The wood was slimy with rot, but the altar grated aside, opening half the stairwell. He ducked under the edge of the altar, straightened up into stale, musty darkness, except he could see. At least . . . it was not seeing, but the power, the life that lay in each thing of the world . . . he saw it, felt it, tasted it—edge and surface and depth, the painted friezes, peeling, patched with mould, the bones, the souls . . . It was unnerving. He would rather see. Light? He knew the way of it, an old lamp sitting on the floor, its fuel long consumed, kindled to a pale ghost-light. He hadn't needed the lamp to hold the light, and could laugh at himself for that, but he picked it up regardless, took stock. Human, was he? They? Well, he had grown used to human, in a way, in the long mad years. He hadn't dreamed how the dog had broken his body; his coat and leather vest were shredded, but the white scars on his chest ached, nothing worse.

He needed to work out who was who.

Did it matter?

Sayan be thanked, light also reduced the chamber to human understanding, colour and memory, and those armoured bones, collapsed together in the corner . . .

Six women hid there in the shadows, waiting, uncertain, afraid, knowing and not knowing him.

"Sister Meeray?"

She had not changed. No, of course not.

"Blackdog?" She seemed uncertain. Well she might. What did ghosts see of the world that lay beyond human vision?

"More or less," he admitted. *What are you still doing here?* was the foolish question that came to mind. Killed and left unburied, a final cruelty on Ghatai's part. "My name's Holla-Sayan."

There was room in the water-filled stairwell for their bones, burial enough to release them, but he had lost so much time already; Pakdhala had been in Tamghat's hands two days now, too long. "Sisters, I'm sorry. I'll send someone to honour your bones as soon as I can, but I have to go, I need to find the goddess."

"No!" Meeray said. "We've waited—Blackdog, we've been waiting for you. We knew you'd come back."

The door did not look forced, though it was not barred. He frowned at a heap of broken stone, quarried from somewhere and piled beside the door. Had Tamghat tried to tunnel in to them? No . . . The bones . . . the ghosts shied away as he came near, carrying the lamp. The skeletons lay—or were heaped—along the wall, as if the bodies had huddled there together, sitting or lying on the floor. One, quite clearly, had settled over the swordblade run between rib cage and pelvis, a mountain shortsword. She had killed herself.

"He sealed you in here." Holla-Sayan felt sick.

"We couldn't dig our way out." Meeray shrugged, no clink of armour, no rasp of cloth. "The whole corridor beyond, maybe the whole wing, I don't know. We can't leave the Chapel now anyway. But out there, it's all rubble. More fell as we dug."

"That's where Jabel and I died," another woman put in softly. Shy Altira. Jabel, at her shoulder, nodded.

He counted four skulls among the bones at his feet.

"But—" Lying under earth, under stone, chance-fallen or deliberate burial—those two should have gone to the Gods' road.

"I know," said Meeray. "At least, they should be free. But he cursed us."

"Ghatai—Tamghat did?"

"He said we could wait here till Attalissa returned."

"So we did," Jabel said, and smirked.

"Don't be so smug about it. At least you died quickly. We began to starve."

"Until it was better to—"

"That's over and done with," Meeray snapped, and turned back to Holla-Sayan. "We thought Tamghat was coming in by the tunnel. There were powers there, fighting. But then there was only you?"

"There was always only me," he said. Memories of Otokas, of host upon host, name upon life upon name, running back to Hareh the wizard of Tiypur. He did not owe them explanation; he could still claim the Blackdog's authority over the temple.

"Sisters, you swore to serve Attalissa. Do you serve her still?"

"Of course. Oto—Blackdog, that's why we're here. We would have waited if we could regardless."

He put out a hand to a spear, ghost of a spear. The real weapon lay abandoned on the floor, its shaft broken, no doubt in levering rocks, before that escape attempt had been abandoned.

He could feel it, if he tried, cold, sharp-edged. It was real to what he was.

Words had power. Hareh knew this.

"Then the Blackdog tells you, Attalissa has returned and has need of your service still, and no curse of a Grasslander wizard, devil-souled or not, may bind you here." The words came in the dead speech of old Tiypur, thought shaped by what the devil held of Hareh's mind, but they were said, and the ghosts understood. "Come with me." He added, in plain speech of the caravan road, "Once I figure out how to leave myself." He pulled the door open, peered into the low tunnel they had made. They had moved a lot of rock, for women with nothing but lake-water to sustain them. They had tried to follow the known corridor, though. Above lay layers of shelving rock that must have crumbled downwards. The buildings of the whole south side of the temple complex must have rocked and shifted as if in earthquake.

Back into the lake and ashore elsewhere?

The dog—still no other name—thought not.

The dog was the shape of his slavery, of his service, but on the other hand, it was familiar and came with ease. He tore through broken stone, claws, a force that drove the shards of shattered ceiling aside, hauled himself into open space again, an overgrown subsidence where the southern wall of the temple compound was cracked and slipping as if undermined, which in truth it was. Above, the temple rose, climbing the rocky hillock into which it was rooted. The fog had lifted, only a few banners still smoking over the lake when he looked around, and the stars burning whitely, so distant, so remote, lost to him . . .

Fire burst nearer, a thunderclap echoing and re-echoing off temple walls and enclosing mountains, carried by the waters. Red chrysanthemum floating down, petals fading slowly, sparks dying in the lake. Another, white, and red again, and two yellow. A final green one, each a resounding bang. There were shouts within the temple. Lights kindled, dancing past windows. One bound took him to the roof of the kitchens.

A bell in the town began to clang, and from the corner of his eye he saw another fire-tube blossom, somewhere in the mountains, and then, slowly, the bloom of a beacon-fire grew.

Holla-Sayan shook dust and stone-chips from his coat, flowed back to human form. This was not the Blackdog's twofold existence, he had no other being. He remade himself, remade what he had been, and now his clothing was whole and the cuts and broken claws healed as he rubbed mud from his face, drew the sword that he had, what? Dissolved to ghost and remade? The physical and the fire of his being flowing one into another . . . Ghatai could do this too. He was going to be very hard to kill.

Meeray's dormitory formed up around him.

"What are the Blackdog's orders?" she asked. He could feel the tension of the ghosts, quivering like hounds straining at the leash. More urgent, though, he knew where Pakdhala was, searching for him, seeking a soul she touched and recoiled from in horror and still longed to find.

Not Pakdhala. Attalissa, whole and entire.

The lake, of course.

And he had been pushing her away, that old, deep hatred beyond thought reacting, all this time, while his attention had been on other things.

He was aware of Ghatai, too, a building thundercloud of uncertainty and anger. Ghatai's awareness swung, questing, seeking the goddess. Found her free. Found the Blackdog.

"Go!" Holla-Sayan sang. "Raise the temple for Attalissa!" He didn't look back to see how or where the ghosts dispersed to, simply ran along the roof, dropped down to the herb garden, and went in the unguarded door.

'Dhala! He's found you!

Father! Holla-Sayan, I thought you were . . . Gods, Holla, what's happened to you?

An old woman lurched up from what seemed to be her bed, a huddle of ragged quilts in the corner, but her lurch carried smoothly on into the thrust of a long knife from which he rocked aside, catching her wrist. Not a lucky strike in the dark; she was blind, she had tracked him by his boots on the floor. Her eyes were empty, scarred sockets, but her expression was grim, mortally determined, as she suddenly dropped all her weight from that wrist and swung a sandled foot upwards. He twisted from that, faster than thought, released her.

"It's the Blackdog, Sister Darshin."

On her knees on the floor, she raised her head. "Truly?"

"Yes."

"Not Otokas."

"No."

Her face twisted, weeping tearlessly, not for Otokas, but with relief. "The wizard has her, Blackdog, he's bespelled her somehow."

"She's free, and the temple is rising. Did you hear the fireworks calling the valleys? Will you fight?"

Darshin laughed bitterly. "I wash dishes, Blackdog, and these new novices tie my sandal-straps together and laugh when I fall. I'm Eyeless Dardar, addled as a forgotten egg. But other than me, you won't find many will fight for her. We all know what the Lake-Lord can do."

"You haven't seen what we can do yet," he said, and that *we* was his thoughts running on Vartu, wherever she was, not the little lake goddess.

Gods—no, don't swear by the treacherous Great Gods, ever. His thoughts staggered a veering course between the man he had been and the devil.

"Call Meeray, ask her where you'd be most use," he suggested. *Pakdhala, I'm coming to you.*

"Meeray's dead, Blackdog."

"I know. Call her." He took off running again, left Darshin behind, flowed into the dog's form and launched himself down the stairs.

Blackdog, Holla, no! Stay away!

Gaguush tried a series of deep, slow breaths, but they didn't help the tightness in her chest. Call it the thin mountain air, not heart-clenching fear for a wretched, unfaithful Westgrasslander and a brat who wasn't his any more than she was hers. Call it exhaustion. They'd had hard riding, half a day of it in the teeth of a storm, and little sleep. She'd have expelled from the gang anyone who used one of her beasts as they'd used them in this chase, and she'd probably have beaten whoever it was to boot. Definitely docked their pay. Another breath.

"Which way?" Immerose asked. They were huddled in a narrow lane, armed and armoured to the full extent of the gear they'd brought, exhausted and footsore. Since sometime that afternoon, Gaguush had had the strange, floating feeling of dream or fever, as if the world had gone slightly off-kilter and she was slipping away from it. They had overtaken Asmin-Luya and Django the first morning, the two of them in the midst of a furious argument over whether or not to follow a single Tamghati mercenary they'd spotted slinking along through the hills back towards Serakallash. She'd ended that and swept them on with her. The poor camels and Master Mooshka's horses had been left behind today at the shepherd's hut where the priestess calling herself "Auntie Orillias" lived with a handful of younger priestesses, most of whom had come on to Lissavakail with the gang. Orillias had sniffed at the notion that her goddess could possibly have been captured by the Lake-Lord, but she had not been unwilling to help. "Sister Vakail" was a powerful name, it seemed. Orillias had stayed to watch the beacons, as she had for years.

And while they were making their stealthy way down to the lakeshore where there was supposed to be a boat kept by someone's cousin, muttering about the fog that had lifted too soon, there had been an explosion of fireworks from the far side of the temple islet, and answering beacons on the high ridges, running away out of sight into the mountains.

The boat hadn't been there, but one of the sisters had gone scouting and reported, in her barely comprehensible mountain speech, the guardpost that oversaw the bridge to be ablaze, the bridge itself in the hands of the stonecutters' guild, busily building a drystone wall to bar the bridge to Tamghati reinforcements from outside. They simply walked across, introduced as mercenary allies come seeking a kidnapped comrade.

Simple, hah. In the dark, no one was going to see the fluttering indigo rags they all wore, strips hastily torn from shawls and head-scarves to tie about neck or brow. What use was a token when it had been invented by some stonecutter's wife on the spot and no one else knew about it? The Lissavakaili rebels would see a long-braided shadow too tall for a mountain native and that would be enough. Bashra help her, she wanted to die in her own tent in her own desert.

And at her bedside a crowd of devoted grandchildren—great-grandchildren—yes, while she was dealing in wishes. Not in some ill-organized peasant uprising which seemed to be taking its own leaders, if these sisters were supposed to be that, all unawares.

"Gaguush, which way?"

She rubbed her eyes and looked around. Nodding off on her feet, she was. She had missed something. "How the hell do I know? Ask the sisters."

"They've gone. Said they had to meet the guild-leaders. Weren't you listening? Boss, you all right?"

Immerose had always been smugly capable of sleeping soundly anywhere, even on the back of a camel, while the rest of the human race dozed and woke and dozed again.

"Idiots! All four of them shouldn't have gone. We'll be taken for Tamghati."

"Then let's get moving."

Immerose, who by her face had been about to ask which way yet again, backed off, as someone put a hand under Gaguush's elbow. The demon, of course. The first dawn as they travelled had proved true everything Varro's winter-tales said about him. Really a bear, or really a man? Man enough now, at any rate, and even a crazed Lissavakaili out for foreign blood might have the sense to pick a different group to attack.

"The temple's west of here," he said gently. "Your Holla's there, I think."

"And your Moth?" she muttered. Her Holla. Hah. He was the Blackdog; she had thought it bad enough she had to share him with that long-forgotten mountain-trollop and then with Kinsai of the great river, but he belonged to the goddess of Lissavakail until he died.

"Ya. Come. Come quietly, and perhaps they'll ignore us."

"That's a wish." But maybe it was demon magic, because the mobs in the streets, which were flowing in much the same direction, did ignore them, or glance and glance away.

There was another bridge to the temple island, plain timber and held against them by Tamghati mercenaries. The sounds of oars and hushed voices, the sudden leaping slap of water away in the darkness, suggested a flotilla on the move. Now they were trapped among this useless confusion of townsfolk.

Not so confused after all. Their milling numbers took on form, rough division into companies, and they did have leaders, men, and a few women, under sudden banners of tattered blue. Weapons, too, slings, bows, spears, pitchforks, iron-spiked staves, and here and there a sword—how much of that iron had she carried to Jerusha Rostvadim? Clever little townsfolk, using their guilds as the framework of their revolt. This wasn't a mob; it was a militia, rising up according to some plan. Gaguush felt a lot better about being on their side, or she would if she didn't look so much like she belonged on the other.

And she hadn't come here to get her gang mixed up in a war. Gaguush looked around. Django and Kapuzeh and Asmin-Luya, calm and grim. Django had acquired a torch from somewhere. Kapuzeh put an arm around Thekla, who had no business being in a fight, especially on foot. The little Westron cook smiled up at him. Gaguush looked away. Send her back into the town, to hide and wait? Send young Zavel with her—they could look after one another. Where was the brat? There, chatting earnestly with one of the girls who'd come with them from Orillias' and a bull-necked man wearing an old bronze helmet wound with indigo cotton. The priestess picked a fine time to reappear. She should send Judeh back as well. He looked ill, as he always did when a fight was in the offing, though no one could ever call him a coward. But a physician, even a mere camel-leech, was going to do far more good for everyone if he stayed out of the fighting. Immerose and Tihmrose leaning together, Tihmrose at least as weary as she ought to be, but both looking as grimly determined as Django and his brother. Bikkim, Bashra and the Great Gods bless him, his attention fixed on the island as if he could scent Pakdhala there—at least he wouldn't be on her conscience, he had as much need to be here as she did. Varro testing the edge of his sabre and chewing his moustaches. She added to her tally Tusa missing in Serakallash, Holla-Sayan and Pakdhala still to be found.

Her gang. Her little world. All the family she owned to. "Zavel? Zavel!" She caught the boy's attention. "Take Thekla back into town and find a safe place to hole up. Judeh, go with them. You'll be a lot more use to the injured there."

Blank looks. Thekla shook her head. Zavel went back to his conversation. "'Dhala might need me," Judeh said.

Idiots. Fine. "Varro? You're a Northron, you know boats. Can we take a boat and get over there?"

"Be on the wrong side of the line when battle's joined," Varro pointed out.

"We're not here for a battle, we're here to find Holla and Pakdhala! Use your head."

Mikki let go her arm, looking about, head and shoulders above most of them, and she had the sudden notion he was about to abandon them, to charge the bridge alone or something equally and stupidly befitting a Northron hero separated from his heart's companion. She grabbed him by his tunic. "Stay with us."

"I said I would. They are great fools, these Tamghati who face us."

"Why?"

"There are archers behind them."

Gaguush could see nothing beyond the points of light that were the Tamghati torches. "How does that make them . . . you mean townsfolk archers?"

"Women in bronze armour."

"Priestesses might be on their side."

"The way they're slinking around, they do not look to me like reinforcements. More like an ambush from behind."

Zavel came pushing his way back to her. "Sister Nenniana says that Shevehan Smith there says—he's some sort of lieutenant to the Old Woman of the free temple—he says that Attalissa is on the temple island and they're waiting for some sign from her. But that the fishermen's guild and the boatbuilders' and some other one have made a landing and are going to attack the Tamghati barracks in the temple compound, and when that comes Shevehan will have the folk here attack the bridge anyway from this side. They believe their goddess will deal with Tamghat. I . . . I didn't know what to say, boss. What do we tell them? If Pakdhala's his prisoner—even if she is a goddess really, she's in his power. He's going to slaughter them like he did when he took Serakallash."

"Nothing we can do. They're not going to listen to us, lad. We're going to find our people and . . ." And what? Fool she was. Die with them, probably. "Varro—boat?"

"Something's happening."

Torches whirled and flared as Tamghati tumbled and fell, broke ranks and re-formed under shouted orders. Over the sudden uproar of shouting and screaming rose a ragged, shrill cry of, "Attalissa!"

The guild-leaders lost what command they had of their militias. The whole mass surged forward, rushing the bridge, and to stand firm amid that was like trying to swim upriver at the Fifth Cataract.

"Stay together!' Gaguush yelled. "Django, Kapuzeh, keep Thekla out of it!"

Hells. She drew her sabre and wished for Lion beneath her and a good long spear. Show these godless mercenaries they weren't up against a mob of peasants after all.

"Luck," Mikki wished her, and then he roared, nothing human in the sound, and charged the bridge. Lissavakaili parted for him, closed up behind, and he was in the vanguard that took the bridge and hit the Tamghati. Gaguush thought she saw the demon, pale hair flying, axe swinging, making for a mounted Grasslander, probably a *noekar*, and she lost sight of him in the darkness.

Then they were across the bridge, some sabre-wielding Red Desert man came at her, and she lost everyone but Varro at her shoulder, fighting in the dark.

Regaining your powers makes no difference, Attalissa of the lake. You are mine. I never intended you to remain so uselessly human as you have been all this life of yours. You will come to me—now.

The devil was angry, but it was the anger of a father at an obstreperous child, certain of his ultimate dominance. He pulled at her. Pakdhala felt the tug, threads knotted and woven into her soul, as though her heart was a netted fish. She had not even noticed that spell laid on her amid all the others as she slept. Halfway down a flight of stairs that went nowhere, she fell to her knees, head bowed, fists clenched, trembling. Above her, the temple was waking. Before her, rubble blocked the way to the Old Chapel. She did not dare reach out to the Blackdog, not with Ghatai riding her mind. Her stomach heaved, but her belly was empty. She clenched teeth as well as fists and swallowed, cold and sweating.

Come, Attalissa. The time isn't right, but I think we need to begin regardless, before she *gets at you. You don't want your soul to become a battleground between us.*

Running to her father. What could Holla-Sayan do, Blackdog or not, if he even existed anymore in whatever madness had irrupted in that corrupted remnant of a devil's soul?

In town, there were folk poised, awaiting Attavaia's signal. All foredoomed, if Ghatai took her. All foredoomed, if she did not fight.

At least if the Blackdog was out of her reach, she could not be tempted to bind a devil to her own heart of her own will.

Ghatai wanted her. She would go to him.

He felt that acquiescence, that meek turn, the slow, shaking clamber back up the cracked and dusty stairs.

Good girl. The thought purred.

She kept her own thoughts quiet, especially when Attavaia's firetubes hissed into the sky. She did not hear the explosions, but she felt, over town and temple, flares of attention, sharply focused, some eager, frightened, exhilarated, some wondering. Ghatai turned furious attention elsewhere and she drew a deep breath, feeling stronger and steadier at once. But then, there before her in the lightless, abandoned corridor was a sister she knew, Altira, one of those who had tried to soothe a hysterical child in the Old Chapel, when Tamghat came. Dead since then, and casting her own dim light, in her fierce attachment to the world she should have left behind. Altira saluted. "Lady."

"Sister Altira."

"Are you going to Tamghat?"

"Yes."

"The Blackdog is looking for you."

"Something happened, though. Is he . . . you know the stories, when a host hasn't been strong enough. Is he still my . . . is he still Holla-Sayan, a Westgrasslander?" She touched the tattoos on her face. "Is he mad?"

Altira frowned. "A Westgrasslander, yes, lady. But something fought him in the chapel. We couldn't see it. I thought it won, but he seems . . . he is still yours, by his actions. He knows us. He freed us to fight." She studied Pakdhala, and the smile of the living Altira lit her face. "Lady, you can't go into battle dressed like that."

"Always fussing about my clothes."

"Always being dressed in inappropriate clothes," Altira countered, and removed her own helmet, running fingers through her short curls. "I remember Otokas and Kayugh complaining to Meeray about the notion of putting a crawling baby in brocade. Lady, if you will? Take my gear and let me go my way. I'm only one spear, here, and Meeray is rousing the dormitories for you. You'll not lack for spears. But to face Tamghat like a . . . a slave for his bed . . . for your pride, for ours. I know it doesn't matter, honour is in the soul. But—"

"But," Pakdhala agreed, and reached out for the helmet. It was at once nothing but a tingle on the skin, a coolness in the air, and heavy, firm metal. She ran fingers over the embossed images, leaping fish, on its four plates. "Thank you, Altira."

The priestess held out her spear across her palms, then her sword, sheathed, with the belt wrapped around it. Attalissa remembered: this was the ritual whereby novices were made full sisters; given helmet, spear, and sword by the Old Lady, the Spear Lady, and the Blackdog, before the goddess blessed them and welcomed them into the sisterhood. Returning them was also how they resigned, those few who did, or how a woman was expelled.

With less formality, Altira stripped off her shirt of bronze scale, her quilted blue shirt and trousers, her very sandals, and handed over her shield. She helped Attalissa to dress and arm herself, her hands cool as mist off the lake, and then went down on one knee, dignity in baggy drawers and a tight-laced bodice.

Ghatai's attention returned. *Your folk are fools*, he said. *Send them home, if you don't want to watch them die.*

My folk are free folk. They act as they will.

She shaped hasty Westron spells, wrapped this little space of two souls in them. *Lake reflects the clouds. Mist on the water. We swim as one in the flow of the world's life.*

"May I go, Great Attalissa?" Altira asked.

What are you trying to hide now, godling wizard? Have you met one of those silly hens your priestesses, who think I didn't see their child-cunning lies when they made their heart-forsworn oaths to me? Don't bother to hide her; they are no threat to me. They will all follow us, or die, when we are one. Come, now, or this one dies here. The pull on her heart grew stronger, a painful tension. She ignored it. She thought she could, safely, a moment longer.

"With my blessing," Attalissa said. "And my thanks. May your road be short and peaceful; may you find the rest you seek." She bent and kissed Altira's forehead, but then took her hands, drew her to her feet, eye to eye. Altira's face was younger, her dress bright cotton, red and yellow, a splash of embroidered flowers about the neck. "Give me your blessing, Sister," Pakdhala said, and braced herself against the devil's pulling. "Please."

"My lady!"

"I need hope, Altira. I find it in your kindness. Please."

Altira, who looked only about Pakdhala's own age now, blinked sudden tears and simply embraced her. Blessing enough.

"Thank you," Pakdhala . . . Attalissa . . . whispered, and kissed her again, on the lips. "Go to the Old Great Gods, Altira, and . . . and remember me."

The ghost was gone, nothing left but a fading warmth on Pakdhala's lips.

And the uniform of a sister of Attalissa, and the familiar—lifetimes ago, but familiar nonetheless—weight of the shield slung at her shoulder, the sword at her hip. A mountain shortsword, not a sabre, but in the end, she knew it better anyhow. She picked up the spear again, fastened the strap of the helmet, and resumed her course. Her strength set against Ghatai was unaltered, but now she said something, her whole body a banner, proclaiming resistance. He didn't feel it. He was satisfied: she was obedient; she could not resist his strength.

But then her father found her. She thought it was him, the touch of the Blackdog on her mind, familiar as known voice, all the rage and wildness and power . . . hidden, it was only hidden, the familiarity of Holla-Sayan only a mask. He warned her of what she already knew, that Ghatai had found her, and she could have laughed, with the devil's hands reeling in that net about her heart, but Ghatai's awareness surged through her with keen attention.

Bring him to me, Attalissa. He shall serve us both.

Pakdhala, I'm coming to you.

Blackdog, Holla, no! Stay away! She flung him away from her, afraid Ghatai might get some clawhold on him through her. Devil-devoured or not, her human heart still loved her father. She turned her back on him, on the attempt he made to summon her attention, and broke into a run.

"There she is."

"Your Holiness, Attalissa, you must come with us to the Lake-Lord."

Two men, Grasslanders with bear-cult scars on their faces, loomed in the next arched doorway. Confusion—she was armed; she was hardly more than a girl; she was supposed to be docilely answering their Lake-Lord's summons, wrapped in spells; it would be worth their lives to risk injuring her, their lord's great prize.

But she was armed, and not stopping for them . . . Both made the wrong decision and drew their swords. She slid the shield to her arm and danced through them, one reeling back, the shield smashing him aside, the other grunting and falling with the spear through his chest.

She forgot her new inhuman strength. The shaft shattered, the point jarring on stone behind him. She left it and it melted like frost in the sun; she drew her sword, spinning on her heel as the other man rolled to his feet, deflected his desperate two-handed blow with her shield and thrust neatly through his cheek, shattering teeth, up into the brain. Pakdhala didn't wait to see him fall, shook gore from her blade and went on, up another flight of stairs and out the heavy doors onto the tiled pavement of the Dawn Dancing Hall.

Ghatai looked up. He was on his knees, a mercenary like any other in wool and leather, the long braids of his hair caught back with a twisted scarf. No jewelled helmet, no gilded armour. His sabre was laid aside and he held nothing but a writing-brush and a pot of paint. His folk—*noekar*, she thought, his lords, tent-guard, body-guard, the most trusted—stood like sentries around the perimeter of the platform. There were sisters arriving breathless to take places among them, unarmed. Witnesses? Willing?

Not entirely willing, not all of them. Fearful, doubting, curious, angry . . . not necessarily hers, though. The leaders of the temple under Tamghat. Not necessarily his, either. Survivors, women trying to do the best they could for the others, women afraid to refuse, women who saw opportunity for power, women proud to partake of the least scraps of the fear and reverence Tamghat garnered. There was Luli, queasy with some great anticipation, and staring with revulsion at Pakdhala's tattoos and long hair. These were turned out as honour guard to her, were they? Or to put a gloss of reverence to Attalissa upon whatever plan the devil wove now that she was free.

"There you are, my dear," Ghatai said, mild as if she had wandered in to offer him tea. "Just wait where you are a moment." *Not another step, Attalissa. Stay!*

She stumbled to a halt, all unwilling. Gritted her teeth and pulled herself straight, sword at the ready, not dropped to the floor as the force running through her arms, into her fingers, urged. Great Gods help her, even as a mere wizard he was powerful, and cunning. She had not noticed that she was bound in multiple layers of spell.

But here there were witnesses, and she still had her voice.

"I'm here, Tamghiz Ghatai!" she shouted. "Where your wizardry brought me. Now what? Turn me loose and fight me sword to sword, human to human, coward devil that you are!"

She felt the shock of that run through them, Tamghati and sisters alike.

"He is a devil!" she yelled at them, fighting simply to force the words out now. "And through me he means to make himself your god!"

She was forced to her knees, sitting slumped on her heels.

Stupid earthbound creature, Ghatai snarled in her mind. *Do you think these animals care? Do you think it matters now whether they do or not? Make myself a god—what do you know of the great world, all you feeble sparks of this earth's soul?*

Pakdhala dragged against his binding, which tried to pull her prostrate. She levered herself up with Altira's sword, so that she was at least upright, though still kneeling. She bowed her head on clasped hands on the sword's hilt, shut her eyes, shut everything out, the better to see within, to find the snares about her. The whispering pulse of the ghost-sword warmed her hands now. A gift of faith.

You can't fight me, Attalissa. I am greater than you could ever dream to be, alone. When we are joined, then you will know what it is to be true god, born of the stars.

I thought you were waiting on some earthbound bit of astrology, she taunted, with effort, to distract him. No human wizardry now. She found pattern, threads and knots, and dissolved it, washed it away. She was water. Breathing came a little easier. She raised her head.

Ritual of the earth binds power of the earth, Ghatai said. Pompous. He had gone back to painting, was not even watching her. Where was the Blackdog? She didn't dare reach for him. *Look to the east, Great Attalissa. Do you see the gap in the horizon where your servants used to watch for the dawn? See where the wandering stars rise. White Vrehna, red Tihz. See how close they lie, as though they could reach out and join. Those are you and I. Do you feel how we are drawn together? Do you feel how already your heart beats with mine?*

Sayan, Kinsai, Great Gods help her, she did. Pakdhala felt her own racing pulse slowing to march in step with his. She remembered riding, a little girl, leaning back, her cheek to her father's chest, and the beat of his heart rocking her into sleep.

We will wait here, you and I, growing into one another as the stars do. Not quite the marriage ritual I had planned, but I am no human wizard who sees profanation in any change to his precious constructs. Vartu forgot that, when she came meddling. I am fire, you are water—we grow and flow around what lies in our way. She can throw up obstacles; we will change and roll over them as though they were not there. Arrogant Northron. She believes a Grass-lander too ignorant to think on his feet, doesn't she? You will sleep, Great Attalissa. Float in dreams with me, and we will merge as the stars merge, and wake six days hence a god of earth and fire and stars, and call the others to us, break the walls of the cold hells.

The Blackdog will come.

Your slave is nothing. A dead thing, a ghost that clings to an alien world. He will run away rather than face me, as he did before, or I will take the chained soul into myself, which it would welcome, if it were free and knew itself again.

No. She snuffed her burst of hope. The Blackdog was free, and if it had not run to Ghatai . . . it had spoken with Holla-Sayan's mind . . .

Vartu is the worse danger. Ghatai's thought was not spoken to her, but she felt it nonetheless. Panic welled. She was being drawn into him, he knew her thoughts, he would know what she did . . . but at least he was distracted and thought himself so much stronger that he could ignore her.

There was a distant uproar. She found and destroyed another knot. Now she felt the minds of her folk again—excited fear and eager bloodlust and over all, hope. They were fighting, here on the holy islet. Townsfolk, sisters. Whispers of individual thought.

Sister Meeray!

Rise, fight, the time is now.

Attalissa returns.

The free temple is making war.

518

The high valleys rise against their occupiers.

The town in arms.

Burn the barracks, burn them all.

No more.

The dead come back.

Attavaia. Meeray.

No more shame and lying.

Sister Vakail and the free temple say Tamghat is a devil, escaped from the cold hells.

Attalissa is here! The Blackdog will fight for us.

Attalissa is here!

She felt Ghatai's emotions, too, anger building like a thunderhead. Nothing must interrupt him, not now, so many delays, so long waiting . . . For six days, the Dawn Dancing Hall must withstand whatever came from outside, whatever destruction and death spread through the lands of the Lissavakail, and whatever came against him.

He thrust himself into the souls of the human sentries. Pakdhala screamed, their blinding, animal agonies burning through her veins as through his. They died as one would die thrown alive on a pyre, not swiftly. Only Altira's sword kept her from collapsing on the pavement. Ghatai shed their pain like water, shook himself, and went on with his painting, muttering aloud to himself in the Grasslander of centuries past. Pakdhala raised her head again, swallowing bile. Old Lady Luli turned to look at her, expressionless.

Fire burned behind Luli's eyes.

Pakdhala clenched her teeth and swallowed, forgot about hunting Ghatai's bindings on her until the ringing in her ears faded and she could control the nausea. Humanity betrayed her now. She must be as remote as him, as cold, to go on.

Shadows moved, two-score figures climbing the rising ground, coming to the edge of the torchlight beyond the pillars, and from among them a sudden cry, croaking and laboured but she knew him nonetheless.

"Pakdhala!"

She tried to fling herself to her feet, staggering against the threads woven round her, was pulled back to her knees, and cried against all rising hope, *"Bikkim?"*

Ghatai did not bother to look up, which warned her. "Bikkim, run, get away!" she shrieked, before her tongue was dragged into silence and she choked.

Women in peasant gowns and leather jerkins, women in scale armour like her own, men in boiled leather—all hers, folk of the Lissavakail, broken through the Tamghati defences by the bridge where battle still raged and come seeking her. Bikkim, Bikkim alive, and Gaguush and Immerose and Varro in the vanguard of them, running now, Varro shieldless but with a sword in either hand, his own sabre and some scavenged Northron sword. Archers, former sisters, one heavily pregnant, swung out to the sides and took aim. "Attalissa!" they cried, and arrows hissed, straight and low, rang on armour, pierced some, sank into flesh. She saw one of the sisters taken by Ghatai stagger back, dark shaft standing in her throat, and then a jerky hand closed around it and it fell away into ash. The sister strode forward, unarmoured and unarmed. Immerose reached her first, rocked back on her heel and then thrust her lance with her whole weight behind it. The lancehead stood out from the sister's back, but she lurched forward and got her hands around the Marakander's throat. Pakdhala felt her friend's rising terror, saw with her the empty eyes, black pits with flame in their depths, and then the pain at her throat rose beyond enduring, beyond thought, and went on, until Immerose was gone and the body fell empty. The sister irritably brushed away the shaft of the lance, charred through, and turned towards a Lissavakaili man armed with an axe.

He could not stop her either.

She knew their names, every woman, every man, every sister already dead and a vessel for Ghatai's deathly fires. The dead and possessed Tamghati were less terrible—unstoppable, but they killed with their weapons, not their touch. The little band was forced in on itself, a huddle, and though more and more of her folk were straggling up from the bridge in handfuls and dozens, few dared engage the fire-eyed defenders of the Dawn Dancing Hall. They began to retreat towards the main buildings of the temple, to seek enemies they could fight.

Bikkim was cut off from the main group of attackers, back to back with pregnant Sister Pollan, who wept as she fought. She carried twins, all unknowing, and the father of her sons was dead at the burning hand of his own aunt. The two *noekar* who engaged them were pressing in, and the thing that had been Luli turned and ran, stiff, because Luli had not run in years, towards them.

The games of mortality, Attalissa. You don't need such attachments. They only hobble such as us. See, if I say, stop fighting my bindings—did you think I didn't notice?—or he dies, you stop.

But he meant to kill Bikkim regardless, did not want or need a hostage, was spitefully angry that this earnest Serakallashi princeling would die for a mere cameleer, would die for a goddess the same, without worship, without anything but love for her, that this petty peasant godling was given as a human girl such unfaltering faith while he never found anything but faithlessness. Bikkim would fail and die and before dying he would suffer enough to hate the girl who had brought him to this, suffer enough for love to shrivel and die before he did, enough for his thoughts to reject and deny her.

Attalissa was the lake, the soul of the lake and its mountains, and flesh and blood were nothing, were matter spun of longing *and she did not need them, they were not her self.*

She had lost her way. Kinsai said it.

Flood, winter-rain-swollen, and the eastern stormwinds driving rising waters the length of the lake. Force to shake the earth, to break rock, to tower to the clouds. Between earth and sky she stood, waves lashed to flying cloud, waves heavy as granite, edged as steel, and tore the threads that fed the *noekar* and sisters with the devil's will, the sinews that bound them, and they blazed and were consumed by what they carried. Ghatai was the one to scream, this time, and he ran to the body that fell, small and battered and clad only in a damp shift, forward on its face on the pavement in a tangle of dark hair. He ripped the thin cotton and, with a bear's claw from the tangled necklaces and loops of yarn and ribbon about his neck, he cut runes into the skin, sliced his own palm and pressed blood against it, but he was too late for whatever he tried; the body bled only weakly, seeping, heart stilled.

Bikkim and Sister Pollan clutched one another, holding themselves upright. The corpses at their feet were black husks, charred beyond any hope of recognition. Even armour and blades were twisted and melted, jewellery gone to bubbled slag.

Bikkim let the former priestess go and she sank to her knees, sat there while he went on, haltingly.

Ghatai screamed curses at the sky and flung Pakdhala's body away. It landed between the pillars on the edge of the raised platform, sprawled and empty, bone-broken doll. "Great Gods curse your name, drought and plague and loss of all hope . . ." Power rode his words and she trapped and held them, dissolved them, purified the syllables of hatred and let the mists go harmless.

Bikkim cried out hoarsely and ran to gather up Pakdhala's body. Gaguush and Varro came staggering after him, and a straggle of Lissavakaili, who spread out along the pillars in the pools of torchlight like sentries themselves.

Ghatai caught up his sabre. His heart was a seething pillar of fires, cold silver-white and the scarlet of molten rock, and fires lay just below the human frame that contained them, was spun of them, blood and bone and flesh and flame, black cold to shatter ice and heat to burn granite, and she was afraid.

You are only one and you cannot take me now. We are no longer any kin in our nature. I'm out of your reach.

Little goddess of water, do you not remember why the Westrons have no gods?

I'm not Sera. Do you really think you can defeat me? You bastard, she added. *Try it. Just try.* But fury did not lessen the fear. He might be strong enough to destroy her. But his mind was muddy, swirling, tangled in human thoughts, failure and betrayal looming, *Vartu* had done this, somehow, she had turned his daughter against him and it all began to unravel there. His rage was human, distracting him.

I will not leave one stone of your temple standing. I'll sink your town to the bottom of the lake and scatter the bones of your folk to the winds. Your very name will be forgotten.

You are still just one, Ghatai, she taunted, probing, seeking some way to come to grips with him. *All alone in the world. Your poor human subjects are slaughtered or in flight in all the high valleys. They are laying down their arms at the bridge but the townsfolk are offering no quarter. Women you cursed and left to die unburied have led my priestesses to retake the temple. Serakallash has fallen . . .* There were messengers on the road, her road, bringing him that news, a handful of survivors on horseback, but they were set to overtake the homeward-marching band of Lissavakaili boys who had served in Serakallash, and none of those Tamghati refugees would come to Lissavakail.

Bind him. That was all she could do. His nature was nothing she could unmake or destroy, but she could try to bind him as Gods and wizards had once bound him, in dreamless sleep. She had nothing like the power of the Old Great Gods, but she knew human wizardry as her kind did not, and she had allies, maybe, if the owl-wizard were near, if the Blackdog could lend her a strength more akin to Ghatai's nature. She began weaving words together, Westron-fashion, but Ghatai caught up loops of yarn and ribbon. He knotted cat's cradles that shattered her spells, and he spoke words she could not hear, that brushed awareness and vanished, too alien to grasp, and her thoughts faltered, stumbled, ran broken.

Fog rolled from the lake and blotted out the stars, hid Vrehna and Tihz as they circled towards the west, wrapped the Dawn Dancing Hall in damp air and pitchy smoke and muffled the cries from the bridge, where Attavaia and Tsuzas came too late to stop the first battlefield executions.

Narva! Attalissa called. *Help me!*

The mountain-god came in his own being, shadow and smoke, and stood by her, mingling their powers. It helped. Her thoughts held together.

Bikkim wept over her body, and Varro did. That did not help.

Gaguush stood grimly fingering the notched edge of her sabre, eyeing Ghatai, not quite daring. Even her own folk were silent, looking for their goddess in the corpse, thinking themselves bereft again, awaiting another avatar's birth.

There came sudden pain, attack, burning dissolution of a nature that she did not recall had ever felt pain. She flinched from it as from the slash of a sabre's blade, then forced herself to endure, to stand her ground. Narva hissed and whirled away, came back a moment later, grim, but resolute. The first weaves of her bindings failed again and Ghatai was upon them, though his body knelt unmoving. They were a maelstrom, unravelling, spinning together, the powers of each a wounding agony to the others, leaving scars that might be centuries healing. If any of them survived.

Ghatai had no intention of surviving. He was lost, lost, lost, home was lost, he could never return, his last effort had failed, the stars betrayed him, he would not be bound again, and he would take them with him . . .

He tore into her heart, and Attalissa felt herself shredding, burning away. Narva howled. Down by the lakeshore, Tsuzas crashed over in convulsions.

Blackdog! she cried, old habit.

Wherever he was, and whatever, he was not here.

CHAPTER XXXIV

Dead end, a bricked-up doorway cutting off one of the many small courtyards. Holla-Sayan snarled and took another route. There had been too many of these sealed doors, stairways that ended in a blank face, rooms divided by new walls that Otokas would not have known. Possibly that was why Tamghat had done it; any attack by whatever sisters had escaped would be confused by the new maze the place had become. A pair of Northron mercenaries fled his approach, leaving behind their companion, a Stone Desert woman they had been trying to carry, to finish dying. The blind sister, Darshin, lay dead there, a long butchering knife by her hand. The passageways carried the scent of battle now. There was fighting all over the temple, it seemed.

He skidded to a halt at the top of a flight of stairs. They led down to a passage past a range of cellars, out to a sunken courtyard, and, Sayan please, at last, across a stretch of gardens and up to the spur of the Dawn Dancing Hall where Pakdhala was. Moth was below him, and he felt a surge of relief to see her there.

Moth, he called, but she did not turn. She stood with her back to him, facing one lone woman who barred the way.

Not a living woman. The door behind her stood open, and firelit fog rolled in the doorway, with the scent of burning wood and plaster and roasted meat. Some building aflame beyond. Against that light, edges showed transparent, blurring into background. She felt like no ghost, either. She reeked of old bone and fresh blood, of the body of Tamghiz. She lifted her gaze and looked at him, expressionless, lowered her eyes to Moth again as though she found him meaningless. She was dressed and armed in an archaic Northron style, brown hair in a single long plait, but he would have called her a Grasslander for her colouring of skin and eyes.

"Let me by," Moth said in a Northron that was not what they spoke in At-Landi, her voice barely audible even to his dog's ears. "Maerhild, let me by. Daughter, don't do this."

"Will you fight me?" the one she called Maerhild asked in the same language. "Will you make yourself a kinslayer again?"

Moth traced runes in the air with the blade of her sword, and Holla-Sayan felt the force in them, which should have brought the other woman to her knees, but Maerhild did not react. Her eyes narrowed. Moth turned and ran for the stairs but Maerhild was before her, a flicker of movement, lightning-swift.

"No," she said. "Ulfhild doesn't go around. Ulfhild doesn't flee."

In moving, she had flung some strand of power over Moth, something like a loop of yarn, and had Vartu not felt it? Moth turned again, and the strand formed a knot. Maerhild sketched some rune with her own blade as Moth began to walk for the door, head down, looking as if she would, maybe could, walk right through anything in her path, ghost or door or half an army. He recognized the rune, almost. Not Northron. A binding flower, formed of ice . . . More strands of power flowed, unnoticed, knotted. In an eyeblink Maerhild was before Moth again, and again, she stopped. "Don't," she said, pleading.

"Then fight me, if you would pass," Maerhild sang, and charged her. Steel clashed on steel and it was Moth who gave ground, trying to break away, fighting only to defend. And all the time those threads knotted about her.

Moth! Holla-Sayan called again, more urgently. *Vartu!*

He could not make her aware of him. She saw nothing, heard nothing, but Maerhild.

"*Now* you have a heart, Mother?" Maerhild asked. "*Now*, when it is all too late?"

Maerhild was like the bone-horse Styrma, but less so. Styrma seemed his own self, a will that had refused to take the road into death, the necromancy that created a bone-horse merely giving him anchor and form in the world. This woman, though, was more like a true bone-horse, a form and anchor for a tool of wizardry containing no true will, no true soul. Though he could smell—wrong sense, but close enough—no threads of power running off to any puppet-master. When Holla probed closer, testing the mind there, not sure how he did what he did any longer, Maerhild felt like a living mind, or a fragment of one.

A memory in the bone, woken and set free with all its emotion and impulse. Not the soul, long gone, but some echo, some footprint of a shard of mind, all unbalanced.

Was that what he was in his devil's soul?

Maybe. At this moment, it did not matter. This thing before him was a foul necromancy. Hareh's memory told him: it was a perversion of wizardry, to seize on the fossil imprint of bitterness, rage, lust, devotion—whatever the whole thinking being might reject or check—and set it free.

She isn't Maerhild. Surely Vartu could tell that. *She isn't truly your daughter—she is something made by Ghatai. Vartu, you're being attacked!*

But the wizardry was the thing's own, just as the bitter hatred was, only the power borrowed, not the knowing, not the will to use it. This had lived in Maerhild, though whether it had ever been let loose . . . He rather thought that whatever lay between them, Moth expected this from her daughter, or she would not fall so willingly to it, so accepting, as if it were due, as if it were justice . . .

She laid down her sword. She had never reached for the power she commanded, never even drawn the threat of the obsidian blade. Maerhild's sword—was it even real, or was it some shaping they all agreed to believe in?—touched her throat.

"Why did you *listen?*" Moth asked. "Year after year after year of lies even a child should have seen through, and you always went back to him, even when you were a woman grown."

"Did you ever even see me? Did you ever look away from my brother? Oern wasn't even a wizard, he was a coward afraid of battle, a farmer's soul who thought himself a poet but couldn't sing of anything but gods and weather. Father loved *me!* You, Mertyn damn you, the very stones of the Mertynsbeorg damn you, there was never any truth in your heart. You say I never listened—when did you ever give me a chance? You could have taught me, but I was never good enough! You decided I belonged to my father, and you walked away."

"You made yourself his slave. When did you ever question him? Look what you went to do at his bidding, all willing. You could have refused him, even then you could have refused him!"

"He would have made me queen!"

"He would have made you a kinslayer! A murderer of children!"

"Why not, when all the land says I take after you? You killed me! Don't just stand there! Take up Keeper! Fight me, damn you!"

Blackdog! The despairing cry cut through everything. Holla-Sayan reached for Pakdhala and found storm, Attalissa fighting for her life, some god of stone, Ghatai . . .

"No."

"Fight me! I'll kill you in open battle, I don't need to wait for my father!"

"I can't. Not again." Moth whispered that. "Maerhild, look at what you do."

Holla-Sayan went down the stairs in a rush, tearing through the wizardry binding the two of them. Fangs snapped and he had the heart of the spell in his jaws. Moth, without a word, flared into something like a pillar of lightning and caught up her sword again.

He dropped the bone clattering, staggered upright, sabre in hand, parried a blow that sent him reeling into the wall. "*Vartu!*"

She stood, staring, pale and shadow-eyed, blinking.

"Fool," he added.

Moth bent to the bone, an upper armbone, and he put a boot on it.

"She's dead, she's gone, leave her. Is a tactic like that enough to distract you, King's Sword?"

She shook her head, still wordless.

"Ulfhild . . ." He almost dared put a hand on her arm, but Mikki found their stairs, then, came leaping barefoot down, bloody axe in hand.

"I couldn't," she said to Holla-Sayan, her voice still quiet, shocked, he thought. "Not her. Not again."

"Great Gods, wolf, what are you doing waiting around here?" Mikki barrelled into her, arm around her shoulders, dragged her on. "What have you done to the dog?" he added, as she turned to run with him. "Smells like he's all in one piece now, anyway."

"He's sorted himself," she said. "Where have you been?"

"Lost," he answered cheerfully. "This place is a bloody maze. Kept finding walls, trying to get to you. Gave up and started going through them. Is the little goddess out of Ghatai's reach?"

"She's thwarted him somehow but he's trying to kill her now," Holla said. He caught up, in dog's form again.

Tamghiz Ghatai knelt on the pavement of a great roofed plaza, motionless, a statue. They ran through corpses, lake-folk and foreign, some burned so badly only the heaviest bones survived. Souls stretched towards the Gods' road, still bound to earth. Holla-Sayan smelt death, and burning, and Pakdhala, dead. Then he saw her, a thing of mist and reflection. That she was a formless goddess twined round and through with Ghatai's fire and with the being of another god made no difference. His girl still lay dead. Red fury took him and he went for the kneeling man.

Vartu was before him, the sword Kepra, Keeper, switched to her left hand, the black blade Lakkariss in her right.

Holla-Sayan felt the burning cold of it, hungry, reaching for him. He never checked in his rush, though. It could eat his souls, he didn't care, so long as Pakdhala's slayer died.

Tamghiz Ghatai saw them coming and abandoned Attalissa and the other god. Fool, Holla-Sayan could think later. Vartu probably—probably—would not have attacked while he held the two gods so close. Lakkariss was not a discriminating blade. But the Lake-Lord abandoned them and his body leapt to his feet, sabre in hand, fingers clawing some snarl of knotted yarn hanging about his neck. Moth dropped Kepra, swung Lakkariss two-handed and took Tamghiz's head.

He screamed, and the screaming went on. Even the humans felt it, not through their ears but burning on the surface of their minds. The fires of Ghatai's soul shrivelled and tore themselves to shreds, and Lakkariss drank them. Tamghiz simply died, ripped from Ghatai and from the world, and whether Lakkariss took him or not Holla did not know. He tried to check his charge but the black blade reached for him with tendrils of cold, wrapped him in it, pulled him. *White sky, black ice.*

Mikki leapt on him, arms about his neck, and they both went rolling almost to Moth. She had fallen to her knees, leaning on the sword, and the slick of frost that spread crackling where it bit the paving stones clawed at her, spun feathers of ice over Holla's paw, burning. He took human shape and rolled away. The frost followed him, touching his boots as he climbed to his feet. Mikki seemed oblivious to it. The demon picked himself up and put a hand over Moth's on the sword's hilt.

"Time to go, princess?" he suggested, and when she didn't move, more gently, "Hey, my wolf. He's gone. Going to freeze the lake?"

She looked up at him. He brushed loose hair away from her eyes and she turned to hide her face in his palm a moment. Then she sheathed the sword and took his hand, pulling herself up, and went to take up Kepra again.

After that she simply walked away, lost to sight in the fog. Mikki followed.

"Holla-Sayan." Gaguush hesitated, just out of reach. She smelt of blood and burning; they all did, of sweat and fear and bone-deep weariness. "Holla. Is it . . . is it you?"

"I think so." That hesitation was growing, building awkward walls. Fear. He crossed the looming space to her and wrapped her in his arms. For a moment she stood rigid, but then her head was on his shoulder and she was weeping, Gaguush, who never let any weakness past her anger. "Hey. It's all right."

It wasn't. But he held her and stroked her hair, and maybe in some place within her something was eased, because she sobbed herself to silence and pushed him away to glower around, checking to see if anyone had noticed. Her fingers never let go their grip on his sleeve, though.

"Pakdhala's dead," she said. "Immerose was killed. I don't know where the others are." Her voice rose, unsteady. She coughed and wiped her face on the sleeve of her filthy coat.

Holla-Sayan found them, scents on the wind, or the taste of their minds. Some of them. "Asmin-Luya's dead," he said sombrely. "I can't find Tusa. Everyone else is alive, at least. Down by the bridge."

"Don't turn wizard on me," Gaguush said.

"Sorry. It isn't wizardry. I just *know*."

"I haven't died, Bikkim. Bikkim, I'm here." And the goddess *was* there, flesh and blood, matter spun out of being. Attalissa in Pakdhala's familiar shape. Older, maybe, a woman just past girlhood, dressed in the indigo trousers and coat of a priestess, unarmoured, shortsword at her side. Her hair was long and loose, her face unmarked, but her wrists showed glimpses of the spotted cat tattoos she had always said were snow-leopards. And the sun was rising, turning the mist to a pearly glow.

"Lady!" The nearest Lissavakaili knelt. Bikkim stared from the goddess to the dead girl in his arms, and back to the goddess again, wonder growing. Attalissa squatted down beside him, touched his scarred throat.

"I thought you were dead."

Bikkim shook his head. She took his arms, gently, made him lay the body down. Varro gave her a look and scrambled away, half-fear, half-courtesy, giving them some space.

"You're not Pakdhala," Bikkim said then. "You were in her, but you weren't her."

"Pakdhala was a name to hide under. I was always . . . just me. Spoilt mountain brat, remember? Fat as a spring chicken? Really. A human incarnation, but only me."

Cautiously, Bikkim took her hand, turned it over in his own, searching it. Somehow they ended up with their fingers interlaced.

Zavel, watching silent, sighed, and helped a very pregnant woman to a seat on the base of a pillar. The goddess glanced up, met her eyes. The woman stared back, sad and afraid and ashamed and defiant.

"The temple will change," Attalissa said. She looked to where a young couple were approaching. The god who had fought Ghatai with Attalissa dove towards the man like a swallow swooping home. "It must. My Old Lady is married."

"My lady!" The approaching woman, limping, one arm in a makeshift sling, looked stricken. "I tried. I kept my vows." The man, the god now lodged in his heart, as if he found it some sort of refuge, also limped, an arm over her shoulders.

"Kept your vows? Great Gods, Attavaia, how?" Attalissa asked, and looked at the man with just a flicker of a smile.

The priestess hesitated. The corners of her mouth quirked up. "It wasn't easy."

"Then you've been wasting time," Attalissa observed. "Sister Pollan—"

"He's dead, isn't he?" the pregnant sister asked.

Attalissa bowed her head. "Yes," she said gently.

The woman rocked silently, arms cradling her belly, tears leaking down her face. Attavaia went to her.

"The temple needs new order, new life," Attalissa said, and glanced at Bikkim, raised his hand to her lips. He looked wondering, astonished. "No one should have to forswear love for my sake. All my sisters who want to come home. Children . . . I see no reason to turn them away. Unmarried sisters in the dormitories, married sisters with households in the town, why not? Pollan, I know it is small comfort, but you won't be alone, you and your babes. You have family here, always. Zavel." He looked up. "Zavel, your father . . . I'm sorry."

He nodded, blinked. That was all.

"Varro, can you find Tihmrose? She's down on the shore."

"Ya. Um. Lady."

So many were dead. One of the wooden barracks-blocks of the Tamghati still burned. Attavaia, leaning on the god-bearing priest, was saying she had stopped the killing of Tamghati who surrendered, though many, especially the *noekar*-lords and the bear-cultists, had fought to the death. What did Attalissa want done with them?

"Disarm them. Tell them to be on their way to the desert road. Give them millet and water, though, tell them the wrath of the lake and the mountains will fall on them if they rob any on the way."

"Sera won't thank you."

"They're only mercenaries, not backed by even a wizard. Sera can cope," Attalissa said tartly. "And if she can't, I have no doubt Mistress Jerusha can. Let them disperse to the road and lose themselves in Marakand, find themselves honest lords and thank you for your mercy the rest of their lives, Attavaia, Tsuzas." *Holla-Sayan.*

He had to quash the impulse to bat her away. Part of him wanted to flinch from her touch.

Are you Holla-Sayan?

Mostly.

You look like Tamghat, inside.

Can't help that.

The owl-wizard is another devil.

Yes.

So are you. You let the Blackdog take you over.

No. We both decided to live. I wasn't going to let you die here.

Holla, I'm sorry.

My choice, in the end.

I brought this down on you. You made me see what a wrong I had done to Sera, when I was a little girl, you remember? You taught me to see the world, to have Sayan's wisdom. I saw what I had done to the god Narva, and I've tried to make amends. Her thoughts ran on the priest and his god. *But I never questioned what Hareh and I did to . . . to that nameless wounded devil, between us. I never thought on it at all, and yet I knew I had worked some great sin, or I would never have buried the secret where even my own heart forgot it. I did you great wrong, and I can't ever restore what I've taken from you. From you both.*

It's past, he said. *Regret mends no bones.* A saying of his grandmother's, her namesake. *There's no going back for any of us.*

What will you do now?

He shrugged. Gaguush was close against his side. *Go back to the road. Cross the Kinsai-av and go home, when we next head west, and tell my mother and father they've lost a granddaughter.*

Tell them I love them. Tell them I will think of them, always. Holla— Father—do one last thing for me? As my father?

He invited her to tell him.

Take my body to the lake.

"Wait here," he told Gaguush. "I'll be back soon."

"Why?" she asked, but fell silent when she saw what he was about.

The shore facing the town was closest, but he went the other way, over the land-slipped wall, around to the west. Somewhere out there lay the bones of Otokas.

Pakdhala didn't weigh much.

He waded in chest-deep. The lake took her from his arms, drew her under, out of sight. "Sayan bless you," he said. "Whatever there is of you his child still." Foolish, to pray over an empty shell while the living soul set about consolidating her folks' reconquest. But he felt better for it.

When he splashed out, scrambling up the rocks, Moth was there watching, Mikki looming behind her. She sat down, back against the trunk of a pine, gestured him to join her.

He found a rock, weary of a sudden to his bones. "Now what?" Holla-Sayan asked.

Moth shrugged. "What will you do?"

"Go back to the road with Gaguush. Go home and tell my family what's become of Pakdhala."

She nodded. "Cub? I need to talk to him."

"What, without a chaperone?" But the demon lumbered to his feet. "Shout if he tries to bite, wolf. Same goes for you, I suppose, dog."

Moth gave Mikki a faint smile and a shove. He padded away.

"You're killing the rest of the seven, aren't you? There's stories— Varro said you killed the queen's lover at Ulvsness, a few generations back, and I heard a skald once who sang it was Heuslar Ogada back

534

from the dead who came wooing the queen there. And now Ghatai. Why?"

"Because I must."

"Why?"

"Do you remember? The Great Gods want us all gone from the world, want us all dead or bound beyond any threat to their dominance of the heavens."

"No. Nothing. Except . . . ice. I remember ice."

"Don't think of the ice."

"You carry it. Lakkariss."

"I'm coming to that. We seven escaped the cold hells again, long after the war you perished in, more or less. Long ago still. We thought we could use the earth to make war on the heavens." A bitter smile. "It didn't work. Humans are . . . confusing. Too ambitious, too treacherous. Too faithful. Too strong. We lost our way, very much so. Some of us went mad, I think, devil or human or both. And you know the sagas, the lays that say what followed. But we barred the world to the Old Great Gods as they brought us down. They can't come here easily any longer. Ogada began to break the bonds that held us and came to free me—we were kin, allies, he thought, despite what he'd done."

"What had he done?"

"Killed my brother." Her eyes flashed red.

That was not what the stories told of the fate of Hravnmod the Wise, when they named her Vartu Kingsbane. She shrugged. "By then . . . there seemed no point to anything. The war was lost. The hells were sealed, the heavens out of reach. But there was Mikki."

"If it was Ogada killed Hravnmod . . ." he said hesitantly, "I can see the reason for your vengeance. But did you hate Tamghiz so much? Or is it only guilt, that you will keep the others from damaging the world now?"

There was the sword, that sword. He could feel its awareness of him.

"The Old Great Gods can still touch the world, but only with great effort and pain. And they will not have us roaming free, although it takes a lot before they notice us, I think."

"And?" he asked.

"And. The sword is theirs. They . . . have claimed a hostage against my refusing them." Ah. He did not need to ask who. "But Holla-Sayan, they knew nothing of the lost one who became Attalissa's Blackdog. *They haven't seen you.* You have no idea—do you understand what that means? You are *free*."

"I'm a devil, and I'm free?"

"Ya."

He rubbed his face. "That brings me back to, now what?"

"Take what joy you can. Don't draw their attention."

"Go back to Gaguush and stay out of your way?"

"Ya."

"For how long?"

She shrugged. "A god of the earth might kill you, a lucky one. I could. One of the others could. Lakkariss wants to take you. Other than that—who knows, on this earth?"

"Gods save me."

"They've already damned and rejected you."

He had chosen. He didn't see that he could have chosen otherwise without betraying who he was; he could not have refused to save Pakdhala. But what still called itself human said, Gods forgive him. Sayan forgive him.

Holla-Sayan smelt the bear returning before he heard the quiet scuff of his pads on the stones. Mikki settled into their silence, laid a bone at Moth's feet.

"Sorry," he said, wiping away dampness with a delicate paw. "Only way to carry it. Should we send her home? That lad Varro might know someone heading north. And someone should warn him about that sword he scavenged."

Moth picked up the armbone, turned it thoughtfully in her hands. "She's long mourned and in the mound and taken the road to the Gods," she said. "This can rest here in as much honour as anywhere." She cast it out into the lake with barely a glance. "Tamghiz sent her to murder Hravnmod's boys," she said to the questions neither of them

536

were asking. "Young children, they were. I killed her, ya, when I couldn't stop her any other way." She stood up. "Holla-Sayan—go well. Don't come looking for us. Tell your friend Varro that if he has any sense, which he may not, he'll throw Red Geir's cursed sword in the lake for Attalissa to keep. Mikki, what have you done with Storm?"

"Left him with the camels and all. We could walk there," he added. "Together. Nice landscape, on the way down."

"Is this going to involve someone's sheep?"

The bear rumbled a chuckle. "I was thinking fish."

"Think where you left my fishhooks."

"With the camels," he sighed. "Ah well. There's probably good fishing in the river that runs by there, too, and I suppose we can go walking together in the mountains some other time. See you, dog." He rocked Holla with a heavy paw and waded into the water. "The little goddess told me she wants to talk to you, Moth."

"I don't want to talk to her." Moth drew out the close-folded feather-cloak from her belt and shook it loose. "Meet you on the road, cub."

She was gone. Pakdhala had called her an owl-wizard. Something halfway between hawk and eagle, Holla-Sayan would have said.

He got to his feet stiffly, feeling several centuries in his bones. And that was probably young, he supposed, if he'd survived, however meagrely, the wars that killed the gods Westron Thekla still prayed to. Or for?

Attalissa was walking among her folk, Bikkim following at her shoulder, with Attavaia and Tsuzas like a court. He was not sure he wanted to talk to her. Not yet. The body of Tamghiz was gone and the rest of the gang had vanished to see to their dead, but Gaguush still waited near where he had left her, sitting on the edge of the raised pavement, leaning forward, folded arms on her knees. She jerked and raised her head when he sat beside her. Sleeping.

"You'll be staying here," she said flatly.

"No."

"The Blackdog doesn't leave Attalissa."

"I'm not the Blackdog. I'm . . . I don't know who, anymore. And she can stand on her own. I'm free of Lissavakail. Do you still want me?"

"Don't ask stupid questions," she muttered at her feet. "Bikkim's staying. He says he has no right to go to Serakallash; he wasn't there when they needed him, he belongs with Pakdhala, whatever she calls herself, and the Battu'um can choose other chiefs. He says."

"They burying Immerose and Asmin?"

"Trying to find a cart. There's a lot of dead. Some valley up to the east, that's where they take them."

"We should go with them."

"We will. 'Dhala—Attalissa—is going too. Though not with us. What happened to your Northron friends?"

"They left."

"Good. I've got merchants to get to Marakand, if they didn't get themselves killed in whatever Jerusha brewed up in Serakallash. I'm shorthanded, but not so desperate I'll hire devils out of old tales." Shorthanded worse than she knew, Holla realized, as his thoughts ran on Serakallash. Now *he* knew. Tusa was dead, entombed in sand. She had walked into storm seeking an end of pain. Poor Zavel.

He kissed Gaguush, cautiously, and she didn't flinch away.

"You're mine now?" she asked.

"As long as you want me."

"All my life."

All her life.

CHAPTER XXXV

There were no single graves. The Valley of the Dead was a meadow, bright with mountain poppies, blue and purple and white. Mounds of stone dotted the slopes, cairns marking more recent deaths. The stony soil did not permit deep digging, but cairns were shifted, stone reused, as bodies, souls long gone, went back to the earth. Old bone, mostly fragments, worked its way to the surface again, feeding the meadow grasses.

The high-wheeled yak-carts came and left their burdens, returning to Lissavakail for more, an unending procession of them. The gravediggers, who seemed at times to be everyone in the valley, scraped shallow pits. Tamghati were heaved in anyhow, stripped of anything of value. Attalissa's folk were laid with more care, shoulder to shoulder in death, as they had stood. Kinsfolk or the priestesses took their weapons and armour. Rocks were shifted from other cairns or hauled down the mountainsides to cover the mud-scars and protect the shallow graves from scavengers. Flowers fell beneath the trampling.

"They don't belong here," said Gaguush. "They should go to the desert."

No one contradicted her; they could not carry bodies to the desert. Instead they had brought Immerose and Asmin-Luya partway up a hillside and laid them amid waving grass and scattered stones, debating, lost, foreigners here. Priestesses ignored them, too busy with their own fallen. Everyone was. Gaguush couldn't blame them, but . . . but she did. The Lissavakailis had died for their goddess, as was right and their duty. Asmin and Immerose had died for their friend, for a cuckoo-child. Wasn't that a greater sacrifice? And where was Attalissa?

The lake-goddess, followed always by a swarm of blue-clad

women, moved among the mass graves, blessing, praying, taking farewell of those who had died for her. Even Bikkim had left her. He sat by Asmin-Luya's hacked and half-dismembered, sacking-shrouded corpse, an arm over Zavel's shoulders. Holla-Sayan had told the boy his mother was dead too, down in Serakallash. Gaguush would have waited, waited till they learned the truth by natural means, but maybe she'd have been wrong to do so. What use was false hope?

"Everyone's digging wherever suits them, boss," said Varro. "We've as much right as the rest of them. Can we build a pyre? There's juniper down along the road."

"No," said Gaguush. "Barbarian."

"You burn me, when my time comes. I want the fire, not the mound."

"I'll leave you for the jackals, is what I'll do. Go find us something to dig with."

Holla-Sayan rose to his feet and walked off. He moved like a ghost, a wind, drifting, stalking . . . she couldn't put a finger on it, but he trailed menace, a lion skirting a herd it did not, for that moment, intend to hunt. Something had changed within him. He was free of service to the goddess, he claimed, but he was still whatever the Blackdog had been, if not something else. Gaguush would not let even her mind shape the thought, *something worse*. But they all felt it. He jerked his chin in a summons and Varro scrambled to catch up.

They were back with spades and two pickaxes before long. The Blackdog could requisition what he would among these people. But he offered her his hand to heave herself wearily up, and he was only Holla-Sayan, tired and battered, leaning his forehead on her shoulder a moment, holding her close. She imagined monsters, that was all.

They dug the grave deep, deeper than the shallow pits down in the valley, taking it in shifts, levering out the stones. The bones of Asmin-Luya and Immerose would never rise to scatter through the grass. Tihmrose wept, silent tears streaking a filthy face. She turned her back, arms clenched tight across her ribs.

Gaguush felt the sudden rising tension in the air, as if a storm rolled down off the mountains, and looked around. Attalissa climbed the hillside to them, alone, the blue-clad guards left behind.

And Holla-Sayan moved away so that the grave was between him and the lake-goddess. That was . . . different. The pickaxe in his hand looked like a weapon, till he seemed to see it and softly laid it at his feet. That was the storm-weight that had rolled over them.

Attalissa stopped. They all stopped.

Bashra save them, this was Pakdhala, this was Holla's daughter, *her* daughter, as much as she would ever have one, the child he had barely let out of his sight in all too many years. Gaguush made an angry noise, not even a growl, and started forward.

"Brat," she began. "You took your time—"

"I belong to all of them, as well as to you," Attalissa said—and it was Attalissa who spoke.

But Bikkim said simply, "You're here now. We knew you would be."

"I . . ." Attalissa looked around at them, a long look shared with Holla-Sayan, shook her head, and went to Tihmrose. The storm-weight lifted, or was pushed away, but Holla still kept withdrawn, arms folded, standing back from them all.

The rest all found things to do, pointless tidying of the grave, dusting hands, anything to turn aside and leave Tihmrose some privacy. Gaguush stalked around to Holla-Sayan.

"What?" she demanded in his ear. "You should be the first one shouting that none of this is her fault."

"But it is. Her choices, long ago . . . Part of me doesn't like Attalissa very much." He said the last lightly, jestingly, but she wasn't imagining that hot green-gold flare in his eyes. "It's all right. Holla's—I've—won the argument."

"What argument?"

He grinned, said nothing, but took her hand.

Attalissa went next to Zavel, and embraced him, kissed his cheek, whispering. He ducked his head, blinking, then clutched her, shaking with a child's sobs. Gaguush looked away again. Tihmrose was gathering poppies, making a garland for her sister. Some hint of weary peace eased her face.

The goddess went around them all: Varro, Thekla, Kapuzeh, Django, Judeh. Private words, private thanks, private leave-takings. Went to all but Bikkim, who returned to smoothing the bottom of the grave, covering it with sweet grass. Apart from them already; his own choice, at least. But maybe they'd all chosen what had got them here, even Holla. Maybe she'd ask him, someday, when she felt very brave and had had a cup too many of unwatered wine.

Attalissa came to Gaguush and Holla-Sayan last.

"Look after my father," was what she murmured to Gaguush. "You have no idea how alone he is, right now."

"You think he'll let me?"

"I think you'd better make him let you. Gaguush . . ." Attalissa stood back, holding her by the elbows, looking her in the eyes. "Gaguush, I've never known a mother. You know that. My mothers were always sent away once the avatar was weaned."

"Don't get all sentimental now."

"If not now, when? Let me say it. You were never a mother to me. You were the big sister and the aunt I always needed." It was Pakdhala's grin of mischief, directed at Gaguush and Holla both. "So there." A sudden hug, a kiss, another whisper. "Look after him. Make sure he looks after you."

"Not much left to say, is there?" Holla asked, when Attalissa let Gaguush go once more.

"No."

"So." He shrugged. Held out his arms. "'Dhala—"

She flung herself into them, clung to him as Zavel had clung to her, a child seeking comfort, one last time. He kissed the top of her head. Neither spoke, and after a moment he turned her loose and went without a glance back at her to help Judeh and the Stone Desert brothers lay first Asmin-Luya, then Immerose, into the grave they would share.

The goddess dropped the first handfuls of earth, the earth to free

542

the lingering souls. "Be safe on the long road," she said. And she waited as the grave was filled, and helped the gang to pile the stones into a cairn over it, gaining torn nails and barked knuckles with the rest of them. Pakdhala's hands, Gaguush thought. Attalissa had created this body from nothing, but it had Pakdhala's hands, callused by years handling cord and canvas, by bow and sabre and rein.

A last solemn look around at them all. "Thank you," the goddess said, and she bowed to them.

Attalissa walked away.

Bikkim went with her.

Gaguush took a deep breath. "Right, then. Let's go find someplace to sleep a while, because you're all staggering-stupid on your feet. And we'll be back here tonight with food and wine and fire, Varro, as big a blaze as you damn well please. And we will drink to Immerose, and Asmin-Luya, and Tusa too. And sing old Doha's songs, and remember all our lost ones. Even Bikkim, who's going to marry and settle down, it looks like, and our girl Pakdhala, because she's not coming back, no more than the rest of them."

She shepherded them ahead of her, her weary and her wounded, down towards the valley road. Holla-Sayan walked at her side. And it felt . . . odd, felt as though he were some new-met stranger with all the potential of that first gaze sizzling between them, that his eyes shifted to watch her, that whatever secrets lay behind those hazel depths were all . . . kept from her, for now, yes, but kept *for* no one else. That eye and thought did not slide away, even unconsciously, to seek Pakdhala.

CHAPTER XXXVI

The mountains hulked around them, and the lowering sun was cool. Mists trailed down the valleys, tracing watercourses. Storm nosed over thin grass he did not need to eat, picking out the juiciest blades.

"Leave it for the yaks," Mikki advised, but the bone-horse took no notice. He sniffed at the skewered fish roasting over the fire. "Supper, wolf."

"In a moment."

"In a moment we'll have fish-scented charcoal and all our valiant efforts in the river will be wasted." When Moth made no move to come to the fire, Mikki took the green willow sticks with the fish threaded on them down himself, carefully, with his teeth and hasty mutterings. "Hot!"

No sympathy. He padded over to watch her. She had thrown the runes once already, after they reclaimed their gear from Sister Orillias, who regretted deeply that they hadn't come to relieve her of Mistress Gaguush's camels into the bargain. This second casting, so far as Mikki could tell, was frustrated bargaining with fate on Moth's part. *Send some other sign . . .* Not good. Wood didn't last long in the damp summers of Baisirbska. There wouldn't be much to go home to, at this rate. He rested his head on her shoulder, watched as she drew out and set down the carved wooden slips, three rows of three.

Need. Devil. Journey.
Sun. Sword. Journey.
Devil. Water. Speech.

To Mikki, the runes meant little beyond their names and a way of spelling out inscriptions on things, but these did not look like the road back to Baisirbska.

"East?" he guessed. "Marakand?"

"Marakand."

"Gaguush's gang will be heading to Marakand."

"Holla-Sayan is nothing to do with us. Let him be a cameleer, for as long as he can pretend he's still human." She tossed the slips back into their pouch. "Supper, you said?"

"And not my fault if it's cold. But there's beer from Auntie. At least, what they call beer in these parts."

"It'll do for a wake."

"Whose wake?"

"There's enough dead to go around. You pick."

The sun slid below the horizon, no great stretching of summer days down here, and he found a tunic in the baggage, as much to keep off the cool night wind as for human decency. They sat hip to hip, flaking fish off the bones, watching the stars turning. Vrehna and Tihz ran together, almost touching, still days from conjunction.

"I found something odd in the temple," Moth said. "A shrine."

"Funny thing to find in a temple."

"Quiet, cub. In some sister's private chamber. A wall niche where she'd painted a god on the plaster, the shape of a man all white and yellow flames. It was in the western wall of the room."

"And?"

"And what about this new god they have in the west, in Tiypur, who doesn't speak and doesn't have a place or a body but sends out his priests to tell folk to obey or be damned?"

"Humans like an excuse to bully other humans and make them slaves in their heads."

"I wonder."

"*Sun* in the first of three is 'dawn,' isn't it?"

"Or east, yes. Usually."

"Can't call Tiypur east, wolf."

"I'm not. I'm just . . . wondering. Cold. A goose on my grave."

"More likely a partridge, in the Hardenwald."

"Oh, funny cub. We go east to Marakand. But I think we should be listening to any winds from the west."

It is said that the seven devils do not sleep, but lie ever-waking within their bonds, and they work against their bonds and weaken them, and they work against their captors and their gaolers sleep or they die, as even gods and goddesses can die, when the fates allow it.

And perhaps some of the devils are free in the world, and perhaps some are working to free themselves still.

ABOUT THE AUTHOR

K.V. Johansen is the author of nearly twenty books for children and teens, including the award-winning *Warlocks of Talverdin* and *Torrie* fantasy series, and the "Pippin and Mabel" picture books, with translations into French, Danish, and Macedonian. She has also written two fantasy short story collections and two books of literary criticism. Born in Kingston, Ontario, Canada, she has had a lifelong fascination with fantasy literature and the Middle Ages, which led her to take a Master's degree in Medieval Studies from the Centre for Medieval Studies at the University of Toronto, and a second M.A. in English literature from McMaster University, where she wrote her thesis on Layamon's *Brut*, a Middle English epic poem. While now writing full time, she retains her academic interests and is a member of the Tolkien Society and the Early English Text Society, as well as the SFWA and the Writers' Union of Canada. Visit her online at www.kvj.ca.